the

End

of

August

ALSO BY YU MIRI (TRANSLATED BY MORGAN GILES)

Tokyo Ueno Station

the
End
of
August

YU MIRI

Translated by Morgan Giles

RIVERHEAD BOOKS | NEW YORK | 2023

Acknowledgments from Yu Miri:
Thank you to
Morgan Giles, Laura Perciasepe, Glory Plata, Nora Alice Demick,
and everyone at Riverhead and Tilted Axis Press.
Particular thanks go to
Lucia Bernard for her beautiful design.

Acknowledgments from Morgan Giles:
Anton Hur, Hideo Furukawa, Jack Jung, Rachel Park, Soje, David Boyd,
Arthur Reiji Morris, Deborah Smith, and Sean Price

RIVERHEAD BOOKS
An imprint of Penguin Random House LLC
penguinrandomhouse.com

This translation was funded in part by English PEN and Arts Council England.

LIBRARY OF CONGRESS CONTROL NUMBER: 2022061398

ISBN 9780593542668 (hardcover)
ISBN 9780593542682 (ebook)
International edition ISBN: 9780593714683

Printed in the United States of America
1st Printing

BOOK DESIGN BY LUCIA BERNARD
FAMILY TREE BY NERYLSA DIJOL

Destiny and freedom are solemnly promised to one another.
Only the man who makes freedom real to himself meets destiny.

—MARTIN BUBER, *I AND THOU*

| CONTENTS |

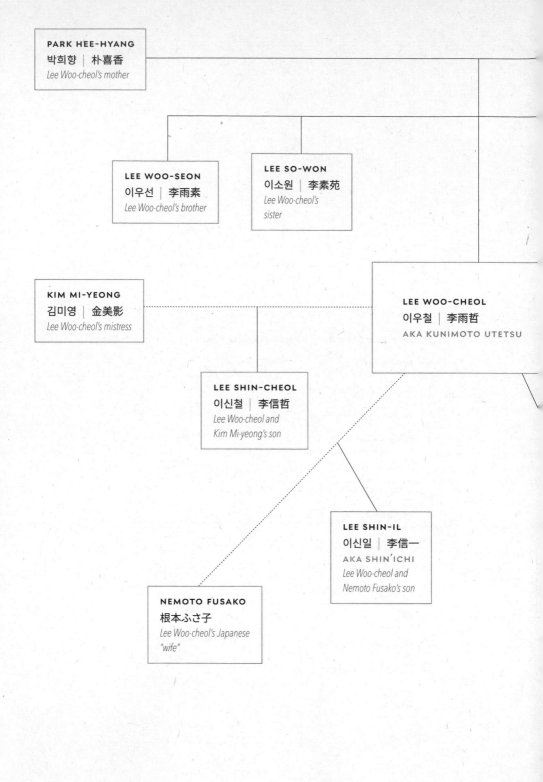

PARK HEE-HYANG
박희향 | 朴喜香
Lee Woo-cheol's mother

LEE WOO-SEON
이우선 | 李雨素
Lee Woo-cheol's brother

LEE SO-WON
이소원 | 李素苑
Lee Woo-cheol's sister

KIM MI-YEONG
김미영 | 金美影
Lee Woo-cheol's mistress

LEE WOO-CHEOL
이우철 | 李雨哲
AKA KUNIMOTO UTETSU

LEE SHIN-CHEOL
이신철 | 李信哲
*Lee Woo-cheol and
Kim Mi-yeong's son*

LEE SHIN-IL
이신일 | 李信一
AKA SHIN'ICHI
*Lee Woo-cheol and
Nemoto Fusako's son*

NEMOTO FUSAKO
根本ふさ子
*Lee Woo-cheol's Japanese
"wife"*

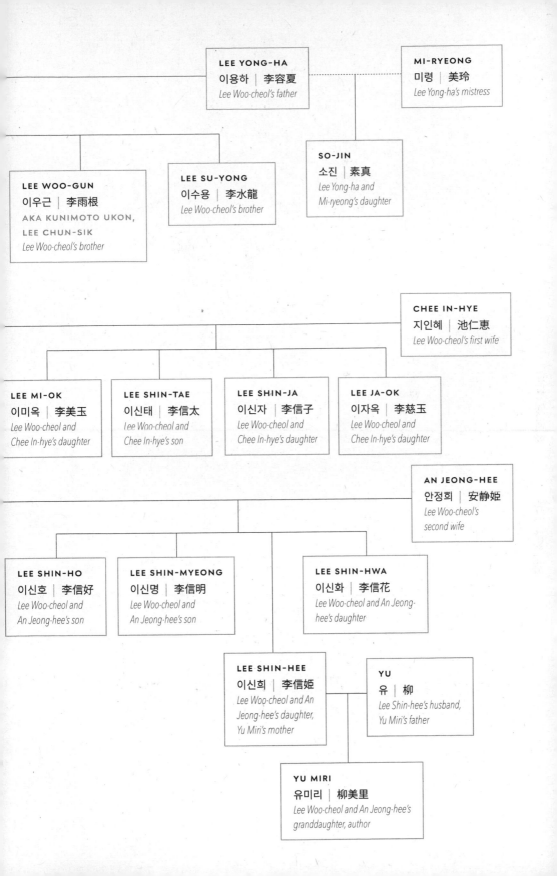

LEE YONG-HA
이용하 | 李容夏
Lee Woo-cheol's father

MI-RYEONG
미령 | 美玲
Lee Yong-ha's mistress

SO-JIN
소진 | 素真
Lee Yong-ha and Mi-ryeong's daughter

LEE WOO-GUN
이우근 | 李雨根
AKA KUNIMOTO UKON, LEE CHUN-SIK
Lee Woo-cheol's brother

LEE SU-YONG
이수용 | 李水龍
Lee Woo-cheol's brother

CHEE IN-HYE
지인혜 | 池仁惠
Lee Woo-cheol's first wife

LEE MI-OK
이미옥 | 李美玉
Lee Woo-cheol and Chee In-hye's daughter

LEE SHIN-TAE
이신태 | 李信太
Lee Woo-cheol and Chee In-hye's son

LEE SHIN-JA
이신자 | 李信子
Lee Woo-cheol and Chee In-hye's daughter

LEE JA-OK
이자옥 | 李慈玉
Lee Woo-cheol and Chee In-hye's daughter

AN JEONG-HEE
안정희 | 安静姫
Lee Woo-cheol's second wife

LEE SHIN-HO
이신호 | 李信好
Lee Woo-cheol and An Jeong-hee's son

LEE SHIN-MYEONG
이신명 | 李信明
Lee Woo-cheol and An Jeong-hee's son

LEE SHIN-HWA
이신화 | 李信花
Lee Woo-cheol and An Jeong-hee's daughter

LEE SHIN-HEE
이신희 | 李信姫
Lee Woo-cheol and An Jeong-hee's daughter, Yu Miri's mother

YU
유 | 柳
Lee Shin-hee's husband, Yu Miri's father

YU MIRI
유미리 | 柳美里
Lee Woo-cheol and An Jeong-hee's granddaughter, author

ONE

Lost Faces and the Sound of Countless Footsteps

│ 잃어버린 얼굴과 무수한 발소리 │ 失われた顔と無数の足音 │

Running the riverside but there's no sound of water   no sound of wind   the water and wind are both pretending they're not there   all I can hear is the sound of my breathing   in-hale ex-hale   in-hale ex-hale   my breath is a whip in my heart a red horse running around inside me   each drop of sweat becomes a shout and is shaken off   I'm shouting no I'm not   I'm singing   **my bones are Korean   my blood is Korean   this blood these bones   will live in Korea   will die in Korea   and be part of Korea**   the song spurs my legs on   faster   faster   there is no pain under my left kneecap   nor from the blister on the fourth toe of my left foot   now! there is only now   pull ahead right now   **if my mother and father are looking for me   tell them I've joined the Kwangbokkun   ari, arirang   suri, surirang   arariyo   Kwangbokkun, sing arirang!**   pull ahead?   from who?   aren't I running along the bank of the Miryang River? isn't this my hometown?   what path am I running instead?   is this a competition?   am I in the lead?   I can't hear the sound of others' breathing   in-hale ex-hale   in-hale ex-hale   that's me breathing   in-hale ex-hale   in-hale ex-hale   no sign of my shadow, my constant companion in-hale ex-hale   nor can I see the rising sun on my chest   it's completely dark no moon no stars no cast shadows   if I turn back maybe I can see something   but I can't turn back   someone might be coming up behind me

holding their breath   run   leave somewhere behind   get closer to somewhere
else   that's the only thing that's clear so   run   hana, dul   hana,
dul   hana, dul   hana, dul   clench your asshole   lift your thighs   let your
hips lead   hana, dul   hana, dul   raise your head   swing your elbows   close
your eyes   like a bird flying straight   **a fierce wind is blowing   a fierce
wind is blowing   a fierce wind is blowing in thirty million hearts   boats
gently bobbing on the sea   have come to take the Kwangbokkun on
board   at Arirang Pass   the drums beat on   in Hanyangdoseong   the
Taegukgi waves**   the song blows through my body   an old song   but one I
don't tire of singing   just like you never get tired of a name   songs and
names alone die out if not said aloud   names   my name   in-hale ex-
hale   in-hale ex-hale   there is only one thing I can tell you   in-hale ex-
hale   in-hale ex-hale   I'm getting short of breath   I take a deep breath   let
it out   another deep breath   let it out   that's better   in-hale ex-hale
in-hale ex-hale   lead with your hips, fire out your voice   Lee Woo-cheol!
in-hale ex-hale   in-hale ex-hale   my father's name is Lee Yong-ha   my
mother's name is Park Hee-hyang   my brother Su-yong died when he was
one   my second brother, Woo-seon, died right after birth   my sister So-won
died at eleven   my third brother, Woo-gun, was killed at twenty-three   the
only one still living is my sister from a different mother, So-jin   in-hale
ex-hale   in-hale ex-hale   oh, Woo-gun   you looked just like me   same
height   same way of running too   I'm the one who taught you how to
run   in-hale ex-hale   in-hale ex-hale   you joined the Korean Democratic
Patriotic Youth League   **the fundamental social cause of illegal activities
violating the norms of communal living is   the exploitation of the
masses   we know   that as we destroy the major causes of their poverty
and destitution   inevitably we shall also eradicate illegal activity**   in-hale
ex-hale   in-hale ex-hale   you were afraid of being tortured and having your
legs broken   you fled from safe house to safe house   but in breaks between
meetings and pamphleteering   you still couldn't stop running   1948, an
August afternoon   you were running on campus   some right-wing student
had informed on you and nearly a dozen police came   you ran away   in-hale
ex-hale   when you tried to jump the wall   in-hale ex-hale   they shot you in
the leg   in-hale ex-hale   limping, bleeding   in-hale ex-hale   you ran

in-hale ex-hale   five hundred meters up a mountain   in-hale ex-hale   you
passed out near a reservoir   **we do not know   at what speed   or in which
order they will be eradicated   however   we do know that we will destroy
them   and with their destruction   we will also destroy the state**   I had
been smuggled out and was hiding in Japan   I learned later that you'd been
shot and dragged in   in-hale ex-hale   when   where   were you killed   we
couldn't even bury you   in-hale ex-hale   Lee Woo-gun   tell me   the names
of the men who killed you   what day you died   where they dumped your
body   in-hale ex-hale   in-hale ex-hale   I was twelve when I held you in
these arms   looking at your baby face   I will protect him   I won't let him
feel any sadness, I vowed, and yet   aigo   neomuhada!   sesange maldo
andwae!   I couldn't even see your face in death   in-hale ex-hale   an August
afternoon   an evening shower cut through the cries of the cicadas like a
knife   in-hale ex-hale   I ran by the riverside after the rain with my
brother   did you hear me, Woo-gun   stay away from the water   in-hale
ex-hale   don't slow down   I can hear the sound of you breathing loud as if
your whole body is a throat   in-hale ex-hale   in-hale ex-hale   the river
runs   I can't see or hear you near me   in-hale ex-hale   but I sense you   I
can smell the rain   in-hale ex-hale   it's rain that muddies the path   it's han
muddying my heart   in-hale ex-hale   the river runs   where does it run
from   in-hale ex-hale   my abeoji was a wandering fortune teller   always
drifting   in-hale ex-hale   after he exchanged vows and cups with my
eomoni   he quit reading faces   in-hale ex-hale   he sold rubber boots at the
foot of Namcheong Bridge   **I was mistaken   I was mistaken   I was
mistaken   I came as a bride in a carriage   I was mistaken**   in-hale
ex-hale   I'm the only one my eomoni gave birth to who remains   do you
know the legend of Arang, who was killed protecting her purity   in-hale
ex-hale   is it due to her curse that   my brothers   and my sister   in-hale
ex-hale   died virgins   in-hale ex-hale   they are dead and   my brothers
wander lost now, bachelor ghosts   **the bird crying in the pine trees   sounds
so sad   does it suffer   the curse of Arang?   the moon that falls on
Yeongnamul   is clear but   the Namcheong River just   flows silently**
in-hale ex-hale   in-hale ex-hale   oh I'm short of breath   hana, dul
hana, dul   oh you dead, not buried in the soil of your hometowns but

cremated   your ashes washed away, you dead with so much han   hana,
dul   hana, dul   you mongdal ghosts   give your grievances to my legs
now   in-hale ex-hale   body and soul may tire but   in-hale ex-hale   han
never tires   in-hale ex-hale   in-hale ex-hale   Su-yong   Woo-seon
So-won   Woo-gun   a person's name is heavy   and heavier than the names
of the living   in-hale ex-hale   are the names of the dead   nothing is heavier
than a name   **As part of the process of integrating Korea within the
empire and in accordance with the wishes of imperial subjects to be such
in deed as in word, the pathway to gaining a family name has been opened
to you.**   in-hale ex-hale   Kunimoto Utetsu?   Say it again!   say what—
Kunimoto Utetsu?   **In particular, as we implement the draft system, the
imperial army will carry out its service as one unit, regardless of origin.
Although there was once an idea of having Kims and Lees mixed into the
imperial army, for the above reasons the merits and demerits of this have
soon become apparent.**   I fled the draft and hid away on a boat to
Japan   in-hale ex-hale   I was found by the military police in
Shimonoseki   I ran   in-hale ex-hale   was that a bird   the MP gasped in
astonishment   in-hale ex-hale   call my name   call my name like you're
driving in a stake   in-hale ex-hale   in-hale ex-hale   I ran   no matter how I
ran   to shake off the name Kunimoto Utetsu and arrive at the name Lee
Woo-cheol   in-hale ex-hale   in-hale ex-hale   where am I running?   Japan?
Korea?   in-hale ex-hale   it's pitch-black, I can't see anything   although any
country must have a sky   I can't see one here   is it the middle of the night?
why am I running and not sleeping?   am I running while I wait for the
dawn?   why?   in-hale ex-hale   I feel like step by step I'm expanding the
night   in-hale ex-hale   what if I'm not getting closer to anywhere   but
instead getting farther from somewhere?   in-hale ex-hale   in-hale ex-
hale   my feet make no sound   like I'm running barefoot   in-hale ex-
hale   grass? soil? gravel? sand?   I can't feel anything on the bottom of
my feet   where am I running?   in-hale ex-hale   I can't feel my legs
either   is it because I'm not in pain?   in-hale ex-hale   the spit wells up in
my mouth   in-hale ex-hale   I gulp it down   in-hale ex-hale   it tastes like
swamp water   in-hale ex-hale   I want to drink cold water and calm
down   my breath is speeding up   Woo-cheol!   Calm down!   breathe

deeply in out and again in out tighten up your shoulders lift
them now relax loosen up yes in-hale ex-hale in-hale ex-hale the
wind the wind is blowing don't slow down lean forward a little clench
your stomach muscles hana, dul hana, dul attack the wind hana,
dul hana, dul let your iron voice ring out carry the smell of blood
oh, you wind that spreads fire! **"Mahabanyabaramildasimgyeong
gwanjajaebosal haengsimbanyabaramilda . . ."** the sound of sutras and a
jing wind their way into my eardrums hana, dul hana, dul **"Grandfather,
when you died none of your family was there such a sorrowful way to
die being beaten to death is not the only sorrowful way to die a death
witnessed by no one is also sorrowful."** it's a woman's voice talking
about me **"Mahabanyabaramilda Lee Woo-cheol, born December 19
in the year of the Black Rat in Gyeongsamnam-do, Miryang, Ne-il-dong,
number 75 aje aje bara aje."** who is calling my name?! **"She has come
from a foreign land thousands of ri away grasping tens of thousands of ri
of rope to ask what did my grandfather's face look like what kind of
person was my grandfather your halbi will be here soon so while we
invoke the teachings of the Buddha we do not need any other ancestors."**
that's my granddaughter there! the oldest daughter of my daughter who
lives in Japan I must go to her **ggeumjadonga eunjadonga uri
baegokdongi!** (a child like gold a child like silver a child like white jade)

Three mudangs and one baksu begin the ssitgimgut to call forth the spirit of
Lee Woo-cheol.

The baksu sounds the buk drum and jing gong while reciting the Heart
Sutra.

The young mudang standing in the doorway lights a piece of white paper
and releases it into the darkness to drive away unwanted spirits.

The altar's candles have been lit, and red, white, black, green, and yellow
slips of paper with the names of the gods of the five directions, the obangsinjanggi, written on them hang from a geumjul.

Yu Miri looks at the colors of the apples, pears, persimmons, watermelons, oranges, bananas, chestnuts, jujubes, and tomatoes arranged on the altar.

BAKSU: Mahabanyabaramildasimgyeong gwanjajaebosal haengsimbanyabaramilda. A long time ago, a long, long time ago, when Lee
Woo-cheol's family lived in Miryang, Lee Woo-cheol worked
hard to make this country's dreams come true, to protect this
land, this sea. Then, his body lost to death; he became a spirit
bearing so much han. Today, why do we call for this ancestor's
spirit, what do we wish to pray for? Wollijeondomongsang
gugyongnyeolban samsejeburuibanyabaramilda.

The sound of the jing intensifies. The arm of the young mudang shaking
the shinte quivers like a rice plant, and she begins to sob.

MUDANG 1: It's your halbi! Your halbi is here!

MUDANG 2: (in the voice of a young child) Halbi! Welcome in!

MUDANG 3: (in a man's voice) Aigo!   Somehow you have come here   all
this distance   indeed you have come   aigo!   I've
missed you

MUDANG 2: (in a child's voice) Halbi is very pleased.

MUDANG 3: My lovely granddaughter who I named   why have you
come to call for your halbi?   Have stories about your halbi
reached your ears?

YU MIRI: I want to talk to you, Halbi . . .

MUDANG 3: Oh, the wind is picking up! It's trying to blow our voices
away   aigo!   this damned wind!

YU MIRI: I can hear you perfectly. Please speak.

MUDANG 3: We'll speak when the wind stops.

It was late, midnight, and although it was mid-March every exhaled breath
was white. The door was open to invite the spirit in. Outside the door a white
cloth had been spread out with a pig's head, fruit, root vegetables, grilled fish,
white rice, bibimbap, dotorimuk, sirutteok, sweets, and makgeolli arranged
on top of it. A ten-thousand-won note lay enclosed between jeogoripaji and
chima collars folded longways and three straw sandals lay at the top of the
blanket to represent a bridge.

MUDANG 3: I am a spirit who can only hear voices   but this wind
blows past my ears interfering   My lovely
granddaughter   run   run and chase off the wind

MUDANG 2: *(tugging on Yu Miri's hand like a spoiled child)* C'mon, run!

Yu Miri lets go of the breath she had been holding, gets to her feet, and starts running in place.

MUDANG 3: Hana, dul   hana, dul   listen while you run   hana,
dul   hana, dul   did you know that I sometimes rest on your
shoulders   aigo   you have tried to die so many times
in-hale ex-hale   unable to live any longer   on the land of
another country   in-hale ex-hale   your eomoni and abeoji
do not know   did you know   the times you slipped away to
your room without anyone noticing, locked the door, and put
the belt around your neck   the times you climbed over the
railings of a tall building   the times you stared into deep
water   that I was the one who stopped you   in-hale
ex-hale   in-hale ex-hale   I'll come along with you   hana,
dul   hana, dul   we'll run together   I'll introduce you to
the past   hana, dul, hana, dul   so let's run   ok gateun nae
sonjuya   my precious grandchild   run run   ask the
wind   in-hale ex-hale   make sure to ask the wind where the
river begins

MUDANG 2: Your halbi was good at singing too. Sing, Halbi.

MUDANG 3: Spring comes to Arirang Pass   sparrows come to Arirang
Pass   it is hard to watch you go   it is dear to see you
come   ari, arirang   Arirang Pass is the pass by which
you come   but no matter how I cry   you alone do
not cross

MUDANG 2: Run! Faster!

YU MIRI: *(waving her arms broadly, lifting her thighs higher)* In-hale
ex-hale, in-hale ex-hale.

MUDANG 3: You're not married yet?

YU MIRI: I have a child but I have no husband.

MUDANG 3: Then how do you have a baby?

Droplets of sweat fall from Yu Miri's head where she runs in place in front of the altar. She wipes her face with the sleeve of her cardigan.

YU MIRI: In-hale ex-hale, in-hale ex-hale, my child's father left, in-hale ex-hale, when I was six months pregnant.

MUDANG 2: Aigu, your halbi is crying.

MUDANG 3: Aigo, bulssanghan geot, you poor thing   you and your eomoni always were drawn to disappointing men

MUDANG 2: This child's mother's head hurts, her stomach hurts. Hey, Halbi, cure her.

MUDANG 3: Shin-hee suffered so much   she worked to the bone   so that you could eat   aigo, Shin-hee   bulssanghan nae ttara, my poor daughter!

MUDANG 2: (acting like a very young child) I'll tell Eomoni she should be careful this year. She's been not so well for three years now, this year she shouldn't go for walks too far.

MUDANG 3: What can I do for your eomoni, aigo!

MUDANG 2: Once Halbi is released from his earthly troubles and reaches nirvana she will recover. Fill a glass for your halbi.

Yu Miri pours makgeolli in the cup on the altar and then bows three times in the Korean style, getting on her knees and bowing until her forehead touches the ground.

MUDANG 3: in-hale ex-hale   your future husband is in front of you   please promise yourself to him next year or the year after

YU MIRI: (nodding) Is he Japanese?

MUDANG 3: Yes, he's an ilbon saram.

MUDANG 2: (in a child's voice) This girl is very strong-willed—she won't become someone's bride so easily.

MUDANG 3: Don't worry   you've already met him   in-hale ex-
hale   what is your son's name?
YU MIRI: Tomoharu.

Yu Miri traces the characters for Tomoharu in the mudang's hand with one of her fingers.

MUDANG 3: Oh, Yo-yan   a nice name   you used one of the characters
from Miryang
YU MIRI: His father, in-hale ex-hale, chose that character.
MUDANG 3: Happy and liked by others   in-hale ex-hale   he brings
cheer to people
YU MIRI: The man I'm seeing says he doesn't want to meet my son, but
will he one day?

Yu Miri tries to read her grandfather's expression on the tanned face of the middle-aged mudang.

MUDANG 3: They cannot meet   in-hale ex-hale   it is better that they
don't   your son will become very attached to   the man
you marry   in-hale ex-hale   he will come to think of him
as his abeoji   in-hale ex-hale   Is your halmoni   in-hale
ex-hale   An Jeong-hee still living in Japan?
YU MIRI: She passed away in February last year.
MUDANG 3: Aigo! Really?
YU MIRI: Really. In a hospital in Tokyo . . .
MUDANG 3: Was she sent off with flowers and fire like an ilbon
saram?
YU MIRI: Yes, she was cremated. Your son Shin-ho took her remains
and buried them in Miryang. Next to you, Halbi.
MUDANG 3: I do not rest in my grave   in-hale ex-hale   I run   in-hale
ex-hale   in-hale ex-hale   in-hale ex-hale   in-hale ex-hale
YU MIRI: Where do you run?
MUDANG 3: On a dark road with no sign of other people   in-hale

ex-hale   I run thousands of ri through the night   millions of
ri through the night   in-hale ex-hale   in-hale ex-hale   the
wind drives away the dawn   in-hale ex-hale   morning is shut
away within a prayer   in-hale ex-hale   is this something
anyone could stand   running through an endless night
in-hale ex-hale   I am full of regret

YU MIRI: What do you regret?

MUDANG 3: What? Everything   *(anger rising with the corners of her
eyes)*   What do you want me to say!

YU MIRI: There's just so much I want to know. Why you stopped
running, why you left your country and your family behind
to go to Japan alone, why you ran a pachinko parlor, why you
started running again at the age of fifty-eight, why you left
everything behind again and returned to Korea alone, why
you had to die alone . . .

MUDANG 3: in-hale ex-hale   the wound opens in the darkness   in-hale
ex-hale   the pain resists its exit yet simultaneously is
voiced   in-hale ex-hale   write down the voices that echo in
the darkness   before they're swallowed by the wind
in-hale ex-hale   write it all down

YU MIRI: Why do I have to write?

MUDANG 3: in-hale ex-hale   why write?   in-hale ex-hale   that's not for
you to decide   you must write

YU MIRI: I do . . .

A night wind blows in through the door; the mudangs sound the buk and
jing with all their strength.

BAKSU: Mahabanyabaramildasimgyeong gwanjajaebosal haengsim-
banyabaramilda.

MUDANG 3: in-hale ex-hale   in-hale ex-hale   Yu Miri   bring your
name back to this land   and then begin on yourself   in-hale
ex-hale   you have not yet begun   in-hale ex-hale   it is
unforgivable that you should end before you begin   in-hale

ex-hale   I give you my talent   all of it to you   *(His voice disappears as if washed away; he is without a doubt staring at Yu Miri's face. Then, suddenly, in a rough voice):* Take off your face!   Listen to the drops of blood falling!

YU MIRI: . . .

MUDANG 3: *(as if his voice is cutting through)*   Put your mouth to the wound!   Sip the blood and pus!

BAKSU: Wollijeondomongsang gugyeongnyeolban samsejeburuiban-yabaramilda.

MUDANG 3: *(the aggression fading from her face and voice)*   in-hale ex-hale   in-hale ex-hale   take care   not to be swallowed by the wound   in-hale ex-hale   I cannot turn you back any longer   in-hale ex-hale   because I am always running beside you   in-hale ex-hale   in-hale ex-hale

MUDANG 2: *(quietly turning her head toward the door)* Halbi, your son is here.

Lee Woo-cheol's third son, Lee Shin-cheol, comes in through the door.

MUDANG 3: Oh, he's here! Shin-cheol-ya!

YU MIRI: *(offering her left hand to Shin-cheol)* Hello, nice to meet you.

LEE SHIN-CHEOL: *(shaking hands with Yu Miri)* I'm sorry I'm late. I'm a Christian, so I wasn't sure whether to come or not . . .

MUDANG 3: I did something truly awful to you   in-hale ex-hale   in-hale ex-hale

MUDANG 1: *(eyes narrowing)* I can see it. This guy and his eomoni wearing all black sitting in the corner of a room. They're doing that because they cannot eat.

MUDANG 3: I'm sorry   I'm so sorry   in-hale ex-hale   I made you a child without a father   aigo!

The mudang embraces Lee Shin-cheol, choking with tears.
The mudang sobs so hard it is as if the walls might fall down. There is

nowhere in this world that her cries will not reach; her voice itself does not swell or raise itself—it has been pushed to the back of her throat.

MUDANG 3: I'm really sorry   in-hale ex-hale   in-hale ex-hale   as a father I gave you nothing but your name   in-hale ex-hale   your mother   in-hale ex-hale   Kim Mi-yeong is she alive?

LEE SHIN-CHEOL: *(setting his gaze between the mudang and Yu Miri)* She is. She's eighty-eight. She's hard of hearing—even if you shout, she can't hear you—and she's not very with it, so she can't even write. But every day without fail, when she opens her eyes in the morning, and before she goes to bed at night, she prays to the Lord. Her prayers are the only thing she says with no mistake.

MUDANG 3: But in the old days   your eomoni   in-hale ex-hale   sprinkled water on the earthenware pots on the jangdokdae and put her hands together in prayer   in-hale ex-hale   in-hale ex-hale

LEE SHIN-CHEOL: She became a Christian after you separated.

MUDANG 3: Whether you're a Christian   or a Buddhist   you still have ancestors   in-hale ex-hale   did you know of your abeoji's death!

LEE SHIN-CHEOL: I was in Libya when I heard you died. I worked for the US Air Force for fifteen years. I was a radar specialist, the only Korean assigned to the communications division, but they let me go because of President Carter's disarmament policy. I went to Switzerland, Sweden, Saudi Arabia, all over the world. I was in Libya for four years from 1976.

MUDANG 3: After your eomoni left me   in-hale ex-hale   how did the two of you live?

LEE SHIN-CHEOL: She became a housemaid on the US base to feed me. When I turned sixteen, I started working as a gardener and went to night school instead.

MUDANG 3: Aigo   how I made you suffer   I'm so sorry   in-hale
 ex-hale   in-hale ex-hale.

LEE SHIN-CHEOL: If I may speak bluntly, I always hated you. I don't
 think that hatred is fully gone even now. My eomoni always
 told me, Shin-cheol, be like a child of God, pray that your
 heart will become as calm as the heart of your heavenly
 father. But however much I pray, the han piled up in my
 heart won't go away.

MUDANG 3: What do you know about me?!

Lee Shin-cheol drops his head, and the mudang grabs his shoulder.

LEE SHIN-CHEOL: I don't know anything about you.

MUDANG 2: Halbi, it's time to go back home now, please. Off on your
 way to nirvana.

MUDANG 3: I can't go like this   how could I leave my son and
 granddaughter

BAKSU: Guan seum bosal, namu amita bul . . .

The sound of the buk and jing shake the March night.

MUDANG 3: in-hale ex-hale   in-hale ex-hale   Shin-cheol   thank you
 for coming   from now on hold your head high in spite of
 the memories that make you lower it   you did nothing
 wrong   (gradually the sound of breathing becomes louder
 than his voice)   take good care of your eomoni   in-hale
 ex-hale   soon I will   in-hale ex-hale   come for her   in-hale
 ex-hale

LEE SHIN-CHEOL: Abeoji . . .

MUDANG 3: in-hale ex-hale   in-hale ex-hale

Now a small kkwaenggwari gong joins the buk and jing, and the wind
blows harder as if the sound of the instruments has spurred it on.

Yu Miri stands up.

The moment the wind blows in through the door, Yu Miri feels her grand-father's breath pass just behind her ear and tug on her back.

MUDANG 2: *(merrily, eyes shining like a child's)* Three of them! That's
right, three halmonis. *(laughing uproariously)* 'Cause Halbi
was quite the man. There's the first halmoni *(pointing at Yu
Miri)*, your halmoni, and the ilbon saram halmoni!

The mudang shakes the kkwaenggwari violently in front of her face.

MUDANG 2: We don't want any fighting, so don't all come in at once!
One at a time, ladies!
MUDANG 3: *(a voice, searching for an exit, wrenches the mudang's lips
apart)* Aigo! aigo!   Thank you for calling me   thank you!
I'm your halmoni *(turning to face Lee Shin-cheol and Yu
Miri)*   But I don't share a drop of blood with you two.
YU MIRI: Are you Halbi's first wife, Chee In-hye?
MUDANG 3: Where are my daughters?

The mudang looks around the room anxiously while making a motion
with her right hand as if fiddling with a ring on her left ring finger, although
she wears no gold ring.

YU MIRI: Mi-ok and Shin-ja aren't coming.
MUDANG 3: Well then   who should I talk to?
YU MIRI: Talk to me.
MUDANG 3: Whose child are you?
YU MIRI: I'm the daughter of Shin-hee, born to Lee Woo-cheol and
An Jeong-hee.
MUDANG 3: An Jeong-hee!   You look nothing like that woman!   The
woman who ended my marriage   and took him for her own!
And you're An Jeong-hee's son too?
LEE SHIN-CHEOL: My eomoni is Kim Mi-yeong.

MUDANG 3: Kim Mi-yeong! I remember her   she was a dancer at the OK
        Café   getting her breasts out and wriggling her hips   she's
        the bitch who tempted my nampyeon!

LEE SHIN-CHEOL: My mother is a little feeble-minded but she's a good
        person. Eomoni didn't tempt anyone; he tempted her.

MUDANG 3: Where he ran women would follow   one after another after
        another after another   not just An Jeong-hee and Kim
        Mi-yeong   he had more women than I could count on both
        hands   I'd beg him to break it off with one   he'd promise to
        do it   but then he'd go see them in secret   when I gave him a
        piece of my mind, he wouldn't come home   he had two sons
        with An Jeong-hee without me knowing   and a son with Kim
        Mi-yeong   which must be you, right?   He removed me from
        his family registry   but I and our two daughters waited   I
        waited and waited and waited, long enough to think that
        hating him was the same thing   for years and years and
        years   but he never even passed by my front door   I left
        home   leaving behind my thirteen- and seven-year-old
        daughters   he left me   I left his daughters   if Shin-tae had
        lived he never would've left me   aigo   my darling son!
        Shin-tae was a boisterous, bright kid   he was always coming
        home covered in bruises from scrapping with other kids in the
        neighborhood   that man loved Shin-tae more than he loved
        life itself   after Shin-tae's seventh birthday   his hair started
        to fall out   the medicines didn't work   so we called a
        mudang   she held an uhwangut ceremony for us   from five
        in the evening until four the next morning we stayed
        awake   the mudang shouted as she exorcised the demons
        from his body with a sword   japgwiya mulleogara, get out!
        once Shin-tae started slipping away we did a fake burial to
        try to trick the gods   we rolled Shin-tae up in a rush mat and
        carried him into the garden   on top of the mat we put a dried
        cod and a sword   aigo   my darling son   Shin-tae was
        covered in dirt   then on three eggs we drew an amulet and

wrote his name   we hit him with them returning him to
life   Shin-tae bore it all   he never cried   the mudang's orders
sent me from pillar to post   pour some alcohol   no not
that kind   go get another kind   go get some water from the
well   no not that well   go to another well   ten pigs'
feet   buy a chicken   strangle the chicken with your own
hands   cook some rice   do it again   all I wanted was to be
by my son's side   but there was no space for me to sit   what
month was it   I can't recall   it wasn't hot or cold   the cherry
blossoms were falling   and the balsam was in bloom   so it
must've been late spring   Mi-ok and Shin-ja colored their
nails red with the balsam flowers   the uhwangut was a
mistake   damn bogus mudang!   we paid her five hundred
yen!   Shin-tae was hospitalized at the Jesaeng Hospital in
Busan   I stayed with him in the hospital for three
months   they feared it was infectious   so my husband and
our daughters could not come to visit   the pain spread to
every corner of his body   it got so bad that holding him
would hurt him   all I could do was pat his hand and talk to
him   Oh, Shin-tae   get better soon and come home with
Omma   I want to go home, Omma   I want to see Appa   I
want to ride on Appa's shoulders while he runs   the morning
of the day he died   Shin-tae's dry, bloodless lips moved   I
want to go home, Omma   his voice was almost nonexistent
but I heard it   he said he wanted to go home   I put my face
close to his and whispered   let's go home   Omma will carry
you   that was the last thing I said to Shin-tae   he couldn't be
buried because his father and I were no longer married   he
was cremated and put in the Miryang River   we cried and
watched the river water flow until the sun set   July 1941   it
was a sunny day   an ilbon saram official came and disinfected
our house   we left the door open for days but   the smell of
the disinfectant never went away   from that day on my
nampyeon did not come home

The branches of the gingko tree blow in the wind as if they feel her pain.

BAKSU: Guanseum bosal, namu amita bul . . .

MUDANG 3: Shin-tae was such a gentle child   he was so sweet that death wanted him for its own   death followed his footsteps and took him   aigo!   do you understand how a mother who lost her only son feels?!   *(a groan escapes from between clenched teeth)*   that man robbed Shin-tae of his name   six of his children born to three other women have Shin in their names   Shin-cheol   Shin-myeong Shin-ho   Shin-hee   Shin-hwa   Shin-il   that man betrayed Shin-tae!   Does he think his son will let that stand?   Shin-tae is a mongdal ghost and he hates you   you will never be happy   however much you struggle!

MUDANG 2: Oh, she's gone! Halmoni has gone!

YU MIRI: *(standing and calling toward the door)* Wait! Please wait!

BAKSU: Namu maha banya baramilta . . .

YU MIRI: Come back, please!

MUDANG 2: *(clasping her hands behind her back and kicking at the floor as if sulking)* Aaah, she's gone, and she's not coming back. But there's another halmoni hidden in the doorway. A Japanese halmoni. Did Halbi have an ilbon saram wife?

YU MIRI: Yes. Nemoto Fusako was her name.

MUDANG 3: *(running out the door)* You horrible woman! My granddaughter called for me, not you! Sseok ilboneuro doraga, go back to Japan!

MUDANG 2: Oh, your halmoni was blown in!

MUDANG 3: *(her joy clear from her face and movements)* Aigo! Uri sonjuya, my grandchild!   Miri, Miri!   Aigo, it's Miri!

The mudang embraces Yu Miri.
Yu Miri feels the mudang's heart beating.
Their shadows merge, each adding depth to the other.

MUDANG 3: *(pressing her lips to Yu Miri's cheek, running her hands through her hair)* Aigo, jokuna, I'm so happy! It's my granddaughter! Uri sonjuya! Aigo, my darling   look how lovely you are my granddaughter, you are a sight for sore eyes   aigo!

Yu Miri's face is slick with the mudang's tears and snot.

Yu Miri puts her strength into controlling her throat and continuing to smile; then, realizing that if she keeps trying to smile she will probably start crying, she brings the mudang closer to her.

MUDANG 3: A long time ago   long, long ago   I lived just down from Yeongnamnu   I had a son and a daughter but your halmoni suffered much   the wife before your halmoni abandoned her two daughters and remarried   his lover ran off and left behind a baby   *(resting her chin on Yu Miri's shoulder and glaring at Lee Shin-cheol)* that baby was you   I married off those two daughters abandoned by their mother   it was ten years before your mother came to collect you, her own son   your halmoni really suffered   why was I able to overcome?   there was affection in your halbi's eyes   strength in his arms   his chest was broad and warm, that's why   the war ended and the ilbon saram left   I thought finally we could live, just me, your halbi, and the children I actually carried   but aigo!   your halbi disappeared   I learned he went to Japan   your halmoni took her four children and got on a night train to Busan   I opened a restaurant at Busan Port   there I heard stories from people who had come back from Japan   but nobody knew Lee Woo-cheol   there was nothing to do except go to Japan myself   your halmoni got together all the money she had or didn't have and got on a boat   when I got to Moji   I grabbed the first Korean I saw and asked   do you know a man by the name Lee Woo-cheol? he's five foot nine   forty years old   slim-faced with small

eyes but not almond-shaped ones like a fox   when he laughs
his eyelids close and he looks gentle   he's very nice   he likes
to talk and he's good at making people laugh   he was a long-
distance runner   he doesn't run now but he hasn't lost his
muscles   he can always run   maybe he is running   there
isn't a person alive whose head wouldn't turn at the sight of
him running   his back muscles moving perfectly   his arms
swinging   like a crane taking flight   once he starts running
no one can catch him   I heard a rumor he was in Sannomiya,
so I went there   I heard a rumor he'd been seen in Ikaino, so
I went to Ikaino   I walked until the balls of my feet were
blistered and bleeding   when I finally found your halbi he
was with a Japanese woman   he had a one-year-old son
named Shin'ichi   aigo   ige museun iriya, I couldn't believe
my eyes!   I left behind the place where I was born and raised
to walk across a foreign land in search of him   and he's been
taken by an ilbon saram!   your halmoni slapped her across
the cheek   then I looked at her reddened face   her round,
swarthy face   her eyes were like a sad baby deer's but   her
lips had a stubbornness to them as she held back from saying
what she wanted to   I was much prettier than her!   I had
given him many more children than her!   that
woman   she'd been hidden over there till now but your
halmoni ran her off   shameless bitch!   stay away from my
granddaughter!   don't ever let me see you again!   my
children and I came to live in that woman's house   aigo!
the first moment that woman and I laid eyes on each
other   han snuck into my heart   spinning its threads like a
spider   weaving its web in my heart and my mind   aigo,
how painful!   my heart aches!   my head hurts!

The mudang grabs at her breasts with both hands, then with those fists
that tore at her hair, she begins to pound her thighs.

BAKSU: Namumahabanyabaramilda . . .

MUDANG 3: How it hurts!   the han did not leave even when I died   but
I'm happy my granddaughter came to see me today, so happy
so happy   have many of my relatives come?

YU MIRI: It's just me. *(restating)* Shin-cheol is here.

MUDANG 3: Aigo, Shin-cheol   I'm sure you think the worst of me   have
you forgotten that I raised you from the age of seven?

SHIN-CHEOL: *(silent)*

BAKSU: *(beating the drum)* Namugwanseeumbosal
namuseokgamonibul . . .

MUDANG 3: I didn't come to hear a bunch of sutras   I came to hear my
granddaughter's voice   is my great-grandson well?

YU MIRI: My mother's taking care of Tomoharu.

MUDANG 3: Aigo, Tomoharu, my darling, I only got to hold you four
times   He was my first great-grandchild

YU MIRI: When he gets a little older I'll bring him to Miryang.

MUDANG 3: You brought him to the crematorium, thank you   his little
hand clasped the chrysanthemum before putting it in my
coffin   *(clasping her palm over her left ear)*   right above
this ear

YU MIRI: I—I guess he did.

MUDANG 3: Miri   Miri   uri sonjuya!   you don't know how happy I am
you summoned me tonight!   *(while singing "Miryang
Arirang," she begins dancing in front of the altar)*   Look
here   Look here   Look at me   Like seeing a flower
blooming midwinter   look at me   ari, arirang   suri,
surirang   arariga nanne   I came over Arirang Pass   Finally
to meet my love   I couldn't even hear his voice   I was just
so embarrassed   I was mistaken   I was mistaken   I was
mistaken   to come here as a bride   I was mistaken

The baksu and aksa play a fast rhythm on the buk, jing, changgo, and
kkwaenggwari, as the three mudangs dance around, their shouts of "Oho
hoi!" "Orussu!" "Chotta!" and "Jalhanda!" bringing life to the room.

MUDANG 1: Hoi! Hoi! Iri oneora, come here! Your halmoni says she has no money!

At the mudang's insistence, Yu Miri takes several ten-thousand-won notes out of her pocketbook and stuffs them into the mouth of the pig's head on the offering table—then into the nose and ears too.

MUDANG 2: *(with an innocent expression and a faltering way of speaking)* Halmoni, have all you want today. Now it's my turn to sing, and you two have to dance too.

Yu Miri gets to her feet and, imitating the mudangs, she raises her hands to shoulder height and begins to do a Korean dance, shuffling her feet.

MUDANG 3: Shin-cheol! You don't want to dance with me because I'm not your blood?   If you dance to please my spirit things will improve for you, you know   and for your eomoni too   so dance!

BAKSU AND MUDANG 2: *(in unison)* **What does it do to get angry   what does it do to fret   life is a dream you have in spring   what is there to do but play?   ninano   nilliri ya   nilliriya   ninano eolssa jota   eolssiguna joa   the bees and butterflies   flutter here and there   stopping by flowers   and flying away**

Yu Miri is dressed by the mudangs in a three-cornered white gokkal and a dark red hongjeonik, the clothing of the seongju, the guardian of the home. She waves an obanggi over her head in time with the dance.

MUDANG 1: Jalhanda! This girl is better than me!
MUDANG 2: If you and your mother had been born in this country, you'd have been mudangs too. It's those who struggle with their minds and hearts who become mudangs. *(tugging at Shin-cheol's arm, pulling him to his feet)* Don't just sit there, dance!

Lee Shin-cheol, shuffling reluctantly in place, follows the movements of his niece and begins to get into the rhythm.

MUDANG 1: *(clapping and grinning)* His last wife's granddaughter and
        his lover's son are dancing!
MUDANG 3: *(cackling)* Aigo, what a world!
MUDANG 2: Halmoni is laughing.
MUDANG 3: Gomapda, gomawo, thank you, thank you.
MUDANG 2: She just danced out the door.

One mudang sways with the beat of her heart.

Another mudang offers out a bamboo pole with red, blue, white, black, and yellow obangsinjanggi attached.

The red has a tiger, the white has three children, the blue has the god of the mountain shrine, the black has two dragons, and on the yellow, there is an old man writing. It is a sinjanggeori, by which one's fortune can be told by which color is pulled.

Yu Miri pulls the red one, which symbolizes attainment, and Lee Shin-cheol pulls the black one, which symbolizes evil.

MUDANG 3: *(standing up roughly and hitting Lee Shin-cheol's back with
        the pole)* Who are you! Why did you pick the black one?!
        No matter how much you value your God, you have no
        relatives! You have not even seen your father or mother!
        You have no son or daughter! You're an octopus at the
        bottom of the sea!
LEE SHIN-CHEOL: I'm very sorry. I will take this to heart from now on.
MUDANG 3: *(as if barking)* What will you take to heart?!
LEE SHIN-CHEOL: I will respect my ancestors.
MUDANG 3: What have you been doing all this time?!
LEE SHIN-CHEOL: I haven't been doing anything. . . .
MUDANG 3: *(with eyes as black as oil)* You haven't been doing anything?
        Have you been to your ancestors' graves?

LEE SHIN-CHEOL: I haven't. . . . But from now on I'll—

MUDANG 3: You'll pay for it!

LEE SHIN-CHEOL: Please forgive me.

MUDANG 2: *(singing while laughing)* You'll lose your money, you'll lose
your love, you'll lose your shoes. . . . Hahahahaha,
hanpuneomneun geondari, hahahahaha . . .

The kkwaenggwari intensifies, fanning the flames of anger, as the mudang
thrusts Lee Shin-cheol backward and looms over him.

The sound of the mudang's palm slapping is like an explosion; Lee Shin-
cheol goes down without resistance.

MUDANG 3: *(straightening up, she begins to stomp on him)* I'll kill you! I'll
trample you!

MUDANG 2: Aigo, how horrible to be trampled! Hahahahaha!

MUDANG 3: Do you understand?! You can believe in God, you can
believe in the Buddha, but that has absolutely nothing to do
with respecting your ancestors!

LEE SHIN-CHEOL: I understand.

MUDANG 3: Jota! Get up.

MUDANG 2: Pour some alcohol for your ancestors. And don't forget to
offer some words to the alcohol.

Lee Shin-cheol pours some into the offering cup and, facing the altar, puts
his hands together.

The mudang pushes Yu Miri from behind toward the offering table, urging her to carry out an oracle ritual by piercing the pig's head with a three-
pronged spear. If the spirits are satisfied by the gut, the pig's head will stand up
to hear and transmit the wishes of those who carried it out.

Yu Miri stands the three-pronged spear up in the mound of salt that is
part of the ceremonial supplies and spears the pig's head on it, but no matter
how many times she does it, every time she takes her hands away, the head
falls.

MUDANG 2: *(perking up her ears)* Rain . . .

MUDANG 3: *(blinking, holding her breath)* It's raining . . . it has been for a while.

Yu Miri turns her eyes to the door, but she sees no sign of rain. Even the wind has stopped.

MUDANG 2: Dragged through the rain . . . blood flowing from his leg . . .

MUDANG 3: Mountains . . . Going into the mountains . . . there's a hole . . . a big hole . . . the rain gathers, turning it to mud . . .

BAKSU: Gwanseeumbosal, namuamitabul . . .

YU MIRI: *(after taking in a breath and pausing)* Halbi's brother Lee Woo-gun went missing when he was twenty-three. He was shot in the leg while he was running around his school's grounds. . . . My grandfather was a long-distance runner, and his brother was a middle-distance runner. His brother also apparently held a time record that made appearing at the Olympics a real possibility. . . . The police pursued him because he was a leftist.

MUDANG 3: He was pushed down . . . into the hole . . . I can see two men in the hole.

MUDANG 2: *(begins singing in a thin, reedy voice)* **You soar with the wings of your cold will over endless solitude your lonely heart yearns and yearns again and dies and is reborn to die once more a poor soul** . . .

MUDANG 3: Shh! His mouth is moving . . . Like a fish only his mouth is moving . . . There's dirt in his mouth . . . He wasn't buried after he died . . . He was buried while he still had breath in him . . . The rain is falling hard . . . Oh, the rain . . . If we don't dig him out, he can't speak or even cry.

YU MIRI: If we could find his remains somehow, we could bury him next to Halbi . . .

MUDANG 3: Your fate is not to find his bones. It is to lift up his spirit.

His spirit, which holds down your family like an anchor.
That is not all. Your halbi, your halbi's brother, your
halbi's first wife, his firstborn son, your halmoni, his
Japanese wife, they all bore a heavy han that weighs
them down. Can you promise that you will lift them up?
If you fulfill your promise it will end, but if you don't,
your promise continues. And it won't end even when
you die.

MUDANG 2: If you're not sure it is better not to make a promise.

Yu Miri finds herself caught up within the word *promise*.

YU MIRI: *(straining to force out her words)* And if things stay as they
are, I will be weighed down with them?

MUDANG 3: You and your son will be too. So which is it, to sink or to lift
them up? This fate was yours from the moment you were
given that name.

YU MIRI: My name?

MUDANG 3: A long, long time ago, even before your halbi's halbi was
born, Miryang was called Miri.

MUDANG 2: The Miri Plains.

MUDANG 3: You bear the name of this land.

MUDANG 2: You cannot run from your name.

MUDANG 3: Will you promise?

YU MIRI: *(hesitating)* Yes.

MUDANG 3: So you do promise?

YU MIRI: I promise.

MUDANG 3: Pray that you will fulfill your promise.

Yu Miri gets down on her knees, hands at her forehead, and prays like a
Korean, then she sits seiza with her hands clasped like a Japanese. She feels the
wind blowing between her palms.

Suddenly, the mudang puts a bright red chima over her head and shakes
her whole body.

MUDANG 2: Who are you?

Sobbing comes from within the chima.

MUDANG 2: What is your name?

The mudang shakes her headdress, the red chima quivering wildly.

MUDANG 2: Where were you born?
MUDANG 3: Miryang.
MUDANG 2: Are you related to the Lee family?

The sound of hair and silk rustling comes from under the skirt.

MUDANG 2: What is someone we haven't summoned doing here? Tell me
    your name.
MUDANG 3: Namiko   Haruko   Aiko   Miyoko   Fumiko   Yoshiko
    whatever name men liked, that's what I was called
MUDANG 2: Are you ilbon saram?
MUDANG 3: I cannot say the name my father gave me   I was often
    called Namiko   but I don't want to be called
    Namiko   don't call me by any name   I am five years
    younger than Lee Woo-gun   my house was near his too   I
    have three brothers   I was the only girl   my father died less
    than one hundred days after I was born, so I don't know his
    face   my mother worked in another family's fields   she
    provided for us   the year I turned twelve my mother
    remarried   my stepfather who had two daughters   we
    hadn't even lived together for a year when his daughters got
    married   I couldn't call my stepfather "abeoji"   it was the
    end of August   I was with some neighborhood friends
    singing a song we learned at school as we stomped in our rain
    boots on the banks of the river   rain, rain   fall,
    fall   Mama   is   coming with an umbrella   pitch, pitch,

chap, chap run, run, run the Lee brothers were running
up on the embankment in Miryang everybody knew Lee
Woo-cheol everybody in town said that if the Tokyo
Olympics three years earlier hadn't been canceled that he
would've made it in-hale ex-hale in-hale ex-hale the
smell of sweat and the sound of breathing went past us in-
hale ex-hale in-hale ex-hale the tall evening sun of the
August sky cast both their shoulders in a red glow in-hale
ex-hale in-hale ex-hale the sound of breathing got farther
away in-hale ex-hale in-hale ex-hale when I get married I
want to marry someone like Woo-gun he wouldn't have
you anyway Woo-gun goes to Choyang Commercial
School in Busan, you know he'll marry someone from a
good family hmm but maybe he'll fall in love at first
sight with who? well, with me, obviously I will awaken
love within him oh, oh that girl is dripping wet she's
crying under the willow tree pitch, pitch, chap,
chap run, run, run when the sun started to set hana
ppajyeotda dul ppajyeotda my friends had all gone
home a man I didn't know approached I had been left all
alone, and he spoke to me in not very good Korean "Won't
you work in a Japanese military clothing factory? you
get lots of money can eat nice food get to wear nice
clothes if you work three years you can go home before
that if you get married you can go home anytime" if I
talked to my mother and brothers about it they would've
said it was unacceptable for an unmarried girl to go off on
her own and stopped me but my stepfather would probably
have been relieved to not have me around I had just turned
thirteen but he wouldn't shut up about how I needed to get
married soon if I worked in Japan that would be three
more years he couldn't marry me off, which would put an
end to it I promised the Japanese man I would meet him
at Samnamjin station at eight, and went home the next

morning   without telling my family, without even a change
of clothes   I boarded the train with him   the train was
called the Continent, headed for Mukden   it was the first
time I'd been on a train and I was so, so happy as we left the
countryside behind   I was exhausted from all the
excitement, you know   I'd been so looking forward to
seeing the Han River but   I fell asleep right before we got
to Yongsan   I had a dream   I was lying down, my hands
folded over my stomach like a dead person   the sun was
coming down on my closed eyelids   I could smell the grass
after a rain and heard the sound of the river   in-hale
ex-hale   in-hale ex-hale   I heard the sound of
breathing   in-hale ex-hale   when I opened my eyes   in-
hale ex-hale   the sun had dried up all the rain   in-hale
ex-hale   and four legs swayed closer to me   in-hale ex-
hale   someone tapped on my shoulder and I awoke   it was
raining outside the window   there was now a girl about my
age sitting in the seat behind me   she must've gotten on at
Gyeongseong   I thought we'd be working in a military
clothing factory together   the next station was
Dalian   Dalian   19:45   arriving at 7:45 p.m.   the
conductor said as he went around   at Dalian we would
stay one night before being put on a boat   but the port I
arrived at was not Shimonoseki but Shanghai   from
Shanghai I went down the Yangtze River   until I arrived at
Wuhan   I was told to change into a simple dress   they gave
me a set of red clothes   I cannot talk about what happened
after this   there is only one person I told my life story
to   that is Lee Woo-cheol

YU MIRI: Where did you meet him?

MUDANG 3: On a fishing boat going from Dalian to Busan.

YU MIRI: My grandfather never told me he went to Dalian . . .

MUDANG 3: One day in August 1945   I stepped outside carrying some
washing   when I saw a straw-paper flyer posted on a nearby

wall THE JAPANESE ARMY SURRENDERS the
soldier on guard duty was not there so I ran the sun was
blazing sparks falling on my head and my shoulders it
burned even into the shadows smoke rising
everywhere the statuesque sunflowers shone their black
eyes at me like Japanese soldiers at the internment camp in
Dalian I waited for a boat home I received a distribution
of wheat flour from the Americans I passed the threadbare
evenings with my threadbare body it was a big fishing
boat just as the boat left the harbor my heart stopped I
was fifteen years old my country had been liberated but I
had lost the face to be able to meet my mother and brothers
and friends again my body trailed behind me like a loose-
skinned dog where and how should I live now? why did I
have to go on living anyway? it was late at night I went up
on the deck, it was raining fine, fine rain the kind where
you can't even tell if it's getting you wet or not somebody
else was on the deck I could not believe my eyes I called
out Lee Woo-cheol, is that you? then I told him my
story I wanted more than anything for someone to listen to
me he got soaked in the rain with me he cried with
me he even told me we should travel back to Miryang
together then he asked me my name but that was the
only thing I could not tell him honestly even after he
returned to his cabin to sleep I stayed up on the
deck with my face turned up toward the rain rain,
rain fall, fall Mama is coming with an umbrella pitch,
pitch, chap, chap run, run, run I sang it over and over
again while I was singing I thought I'd go back to my cabin
when the rain stopped but the rain wet my face a sob
welled up and my song was cut off I said my own name
aloud abeoji! the one thing no one can violate is the name
given to me by my abeoji eomoni! they cannot lay a finger
on the name my eomoni called me it is the name of a

thirteen-year-old virgin   I embraced my name   the rain fell
harder   I jumped into the sea

The mudang, having finished speaking, turns around and around still
wearing the red chima over her head until she faints.

The two other mudangs hurry to pull the chima off her head and lift her
body up, but the mudang lies limp.

MUDANG 1: The night before you came to Miryang, Unni had a dream.
A dream of rain falling on tall trees. It was a message from
the gods that if we did this ceremony, misfortune would
occur, mongdal ghosts would come, the gut would not be
fulfilled. But Unni said that no matter what might happen,
she had to do this gut . . .

The baksu helps her drink some water, and the mudang comes around and
opens her eyes.

MUDANG 3: When the girl jumped into the ocean she called out her own
name. That name now rings in my ears.
MUDANG 2: *(lazily singing "Miryang Arirang")* **Look   look   look at
me   like a flower that blooms in midwinter   look at
me   ari, arirang   suri, surirang   arariga
nanne   Coming over Arirang Pass**

The mudang leans in close to Yu Miri and whispers the name in her ear.

MUDANG 3: Respond to her name with your face; respond to her face
with your name.
YU MIRI:
MUDANG 3: Do you understand?
YU MIRI: Yes.
MUDANG 3: Accept her into your family as a bride.

YU MIRI: What?

MUDANG 3:   Make her Lee Woo-gun's bride. Have a funeral for her and for Lee Woo-gun. You must hold a gut for a posthumous wedding. Once their spirits are married and return to Miryang, they will become protective spirits for the two of you.

MUDANG 2:   *(singing while waving the jing)* **Having finally met him   I could not hear a word he said   I was so shy   Ari, arirang   Suri, surirang   arariga nanne   coming over Arirang Pass**

MUDANG 3:   *(all the energy draining from her voice and eyes)* Please pray.

BAKSU: *(reciting as he hits the buk)* **Namuhaneurisiyeo gucheoksillyeogini   taejeongchingiyeo . . .**

MUDANG 3:   It has been a long ceremony, so please sit at ease.

Yu Miri and Lee Shin-cheol sit next to each other.

The sutra lasts for more than an hour, but the two keep their eyes closed and hands clasped.

Lee Shin-cheol prays fervently, without wiping away the tears streaming down his face.

MUDANG 2:   *(whistles the melody of "Miryang Arirang" like a drunkard walking down a dark road, then starts to sing another song)* **I'm going   I'm going home   Taking my child's hand   to go plant potatoes and millet   in my hometown on the other side of the mountain** *(remembering another song)* **I asked and asked   and I arrived   where you were   a cold night wind blew   I could not see you there**

MUDANG 3:   *(casually)* Aigo, uri sonjuya, wonderful, jalhanda.

MUDANG 2:   *(her voice straining)* **I'll ask that moon   where you are**

MUDANG 3:   Jalhanda, jalhae!

MUDANG 2:   **I cried and cried   no matter how I searched   where did you go**

Lee Shin-cheol sits with his arms wrapped around his knees, sobbing.

MUDANG 2: Uncle Shin-cheol is crying. He has a heart, but he has no money. He wants to treat his niece from Japan to some good food, buy her nice clothes, but he just can't. That's hard; his heart hurts. You wouldn't say it, Uncle, but your life must be quite difficult.

LEE SHIN-CHEOL: (taking a handkerchief from his pocket, wiping away his tears) I'm fine.

MUDANG 2: You may say you're fine, but you have no money.

LEE SHIN-CHEOL: No matter what I do it never goes right . . . I was breeding and selling dogs to be eaten, but they were inedible . . . I sold them all off and (blowing his nose forcefully into his handkerchief) now if I don't find some work . . .

MUDANG 2: Next year things will be fine, but this year is not good; this year you will suffer more and more—this is what your abeoji says.

LEE SHIN-CHEOL: (crying again) My niece has moved me. From now on there are guts that I must do, as his son . . .

MUDANG 2: When you cry, your abeoji cries too. He says he wanted to die holding his sons' and daughters' hands. He really wanted to see you again before he died. (resting her face in both of her hands like a child) He had eight children, but he cooked and ate alone; he drank alone. And he died alone. In a pitch-black house, his stomach ached, he writhed around, with nobody to call out to, and nobody to say his name . . .

MUDANG 3: Please pray.

LEE SHIN-CHEOL: How many times?

MUDANG 3: Three times. To your ancestors, not your God.

As Yu Miri and Lee Shin-cheol stand, raise their hands, sit, and prostrate themselves three times, the baksu hits the changgo.

The three mudangs decorate their shoulders and backs with paper jeogori for the dead, then they repeat laying out a long white cloth in front of their bodies. This is a gopuri ceremony, meant to release the dead from their han and lead them to nirvana.

MUDANG 3: *(singing with the changgo)* Go and be free. We cut a
thousand ties, ten thousand ties, go to paradise. When
the sun goes down have a rest under the tree and go.
Take all your bad luck with you and go.

The mudangs tear apart the "bridge" of the white cloth with their bodies, clearing the path for the dead.

As soon as all the ceremonies of the ssitgimgut are over, all the solemnity disappears from the main mudang's face, and she looks no different from any kindly ajumma selling beansprouts in the market.

MUDANG 3: *(with a hand on Shin-cheol's shoulder, speaking like a middle-aged woman who likes to be helpful)* This man is your
samchon. Your mother's brother. They did not share the
same mother but that doesn't change the fact that they're
both your halbi's children. While they're both still alive,
you should bring him to Japan and introduce him to your
mother. Because they're siblings. Of course they want to
meet. Right? Obviously, it would've been nice if he'd met
your halmoni while she was alive, but you didn't know about
him then, right?

YU MIRI: I knew that he was in Miryang, but then I'm not very close
with my relatives in Japan either, so . . .

MUDANG 2: *(turning as if checking where the sound of a bell was coming
from)* Because your samchon here and there have their
peculiarities. I know, you don't have to say anything, I can
see it in your eyes. *(laughing)* But this uncle is kindhearted.
When you go back to Japan, tell everyone about him so that
he can meet them all. That is what your halbi wants. Because
they're all Halbi's children.

MUDANG 3: *(sounding exhausted, as if she has not slept for many days)* Tell your mother to take care of herself. This year she should not go out on rainy days. Get herbal tonics for her. Traditional medicine—poyak. If she gets through the year safely, she will be fine for a while. Your son is smart. Very smart, so send him to a good school. *(quietly, as if she is powering down)* Take it all outside and burn it.

YU MIRI: *(clasping both the mudang's hands)* Gamsahamnida.

Yu Miri and Lee Shin-cheol follow the mudangs outside to hold a ceremony to send off the spirits of the dead they invited.

MUDANG 1: No turning back.

The mudang pours makgeolli on the ground, then sets fire to all the paper items used for the ssitgimgut.

Lee Shin-cheol and Yu Miri face the fire, their hands clasped in prayer.

They had been told that if the smoke went straight up to heaven their wishes would be heard, but the dawn sky sucks up the smoke, making it difficult to tell where it went.

Thoughts go through Yu Miri's mind about the things in the fire that draw the curtain closed and other things that could pull back the curtain.

Just then, as if it had been waiting to do so, a sheet of rain falls.

The fire is extinguished.

The spirits that had been brought back encircle the two of them, becoming part of the rain, touching their hair, their skin.

Lee Shin-cheol's head drops like a prisoner's; he stares at the paji and jeogori for his father that have survived the fire.

Yu Miri turns her hands up to face the rain. The rain wets her palms. With her finger she writes a name in her palm.

Yu Miri.

The sound of the rain grows, like the applause of an audience asking for a curtain call.

TWO

42.195 km 4:54:22

| 42,195킬로미더 4시간 54분 22조 |
42.195km 4時間54分22秒 |

In-hale ex-hale   in-hale ex-hale   I'm running   in-hale ex-hale   I'm running a full marathon!   in-hale-hale   in-hale-hale   no   in-hale ex-hale is better   in-hale ex-hale has a better rhythm anyway   in-hale ex-hale   in-hale ex-hale   in-hale ex-hale

"What's my minute pace right now?"

"Fast. About five and a half minutes per kilometer. You could drop back a little."

"If I could keep at this pace, what would my finish time be?"

"Hm, around three hours, fifty-two minutes, four seconds."

"I'm going to slow down anyway, so while I can still run, I'm going to run. What's the rule, what minute pace do I have to do not to be disqualified?"

"A seven-minute pace would put you right over the line, I think. For first-timers, the five-hour finishing time limit isn't a hard-and-fast rule anyway. How's your knee?"

"Fine for now. . . . I'm trying not to think about it. . . . I feel like when I think about it, I start running differently to protect it."

"Got it. Forget your knee. Your head's slightly tilted to the right. Good, keep it straight now. One two, one two, one two one two, one two!"

The muscles in my legs and arms respond to the voice of my coach, Satō Chieko   one two   one two   one two one two   one two!   a male runner comes in between me and my coach   one two   one two   my elbow hits him   one two one two   one two!   passed him   now what kind of runner have I just passed   I turn and look back   a crowd   one two   one two   there's a crowd in front and behind me   one two one two   one two! they said there's twelve thousand taking part today   so if I've passed five thousand people I must be somewhere near the middle   in-hale ex-hale   in-hale ex-hale

"Everybody's flying today, but they always slow down in the second half. Just think of the people ahead as people you'll be passing later."

"But I can't keep up a five-thirty pace either. I ran a six-thirty during training, remember?"

In-hale ex-hale   it's not even been four kilometers yet   but I'm running past the top group that looped back at five kilometers   in-hale ex-hale   in-hale ex-hale   in-hale ex-hale   in-hale ex-hale

"Wait, he's not here, is he?"

"Fujita Atsushi? Look, over there, there he is. Second group. Of course if he's here he's hoping to win, but he's holding back in hopes of winning the Berlin Marathon in six months, or so I heard."

In-hale ex-hale   in-hale ex-hale   they're running a three-minute pace   what was my granddad's pace   when Sohn Kee-chung took the gold at the 1936 Berlin Olympics his time was two hours twenty-nine minutes and nineteen seconds   in-hale ex-hale   Sohn had a three-minute pace, so   my granddad must've been close to that   in-hale ex-hale   I can't catch up with that, but   I can get a minute or a second closer   in-hale ex-hale   what did he do it for?   started running again at fifty-eight years old   in-hale ex-hale   started competing to win in big marathons at home and abroad   in-hale ex-hale   left his family and went back to where he was born   in-hale ex-hale   even the morning of the day he died he went running by the riverside   in-hale ex-hale   what was it about running that pulled my granddad in   in-hale ex-hale   I want to know what happens inside a person

while running 42.195 kilometers   but   in-hale ex-hale   what's happening
inside Fujita Atsushi, who goes to major races aiming for victory   and what's
happening inside me, someone who doesn't even know whether she'll finish
the race   must be completely different   in-hale ex-hale   Fujita Atsushi runs
to run   I'm running to write   pace   gender   personality   age   difference
in experience, even   in-hale ex-hale   the unimportant stuff matters more
than the important stuff   in-hale ex-hale   but   if I don't run none of it
matters   it's impossible for me to run at that speed but   I can run that
distance   in-hale ex-hale   I can have that point of contact, that I also ran
42.195 kilometers   in-hale ex-hale   the number of people who haven't run
42.195 kilometers vastly overwhelms   the number of those who have,
so   in-hale ex-hale   42.195 kilometers   can I really do it?   my max in
training was twenty-five   I wanted to do thirty but   I hurt my knee   in-
hale ex-hale   it hurt, it hurt so much   in-hale ex-hale   the iliotibial band on
the outside of my left knee   in-hale ex-hale   because I'm bowlegged and
because of my body weight   in-hale ex-hale   I was born bowlegged, so not
much I can do about that   but   I should get my weight down to fifty
kilos   in-hale ex-hale   my body is heavy   this morning on the scales in the
hotel I was fifty-four kilos   in-hale ex-hale   in-hale ex-hale   but before I
started running I was fifty-one kilos   in-hale ex-hale   my target was to get
down to forty-seven before the race   in-hale ex-hale   but that just put me
under pressure   in-hale ex-hale   so I ate and ate   in-hale ex-hale   sweet
bean jellies   chocolate   cookies   in-hale ex-hale   I ran two hundred
kilometers from mid-February to mid-March   in-hale ex-hale   but I gained
three kilograms   in normal life gaining three kilos is not something I would
notice, but   when I'm running   in-hale ex-hale   the weight's doubled on a
flat road   tripled or quadrupled on a downward slope, so   in-hale
ex-hale   even three kilos   in-hale ex-hale   on a downward slope is like
twelve kilos!   the same as running with a small child in your arms   how
fucking stupid   in-hale ex-hale   it's hurting now I think, my left knee
in-hale ex-hale   if the pain started at the fifteen-kilometer mark   there'd be
27.195 kilometers left now   in-hale ex-hale   what's the best way to do
this   in-hale ex-hale   if I rest a bit and run a bit I won't make the finish line
within the time requirements   in-hale ex-hale   in-hale ex-hale

"Yu, what's wrong?"

"What?"

"You get quiet when you're in pain."

"I'm fine."

"If you're in pain, tell me. Hey, here's the turn-back point."

In-hale ex-hale   in-hale ex-hale   it's odd   was it bad to think about my knee?   it's messing with the way my heel falls   no, that's not it   lead with your heel then grab the ground with your toes   in-hale ex-hale   no, no   looking at the ground rounds your back   in-hale ex-hale   lift your eyes   extend your back   forget your knee   forget your weight   in-hale ex-hale   don't think of anything   in-hale ex-hale   but when I don't think while I run my foot rolls over on the outside   because I'm bowlegged   in-hale ex-hale   now really focus on running straight   straight   in-hale ex-hale   if I stop focusing   my little toe starts rubbing and my big toe floats in the air   a week ago when I ran twenty-five kilometers I got a blister on the second toe of my right foot   in-hale ex-hale   if I had been running correctly I wouldn't have gotten a blister there   in-hale ex-hale   my coach warned me   in-hale ex-hale   neither my father nor my mother are bowlegged   but I must've gotten it from someone   in-hale ex-hale   was my granddad bowlegged   in-hale ex-hale   in-hale ex-hale   in-hale ex-hale   in-hale ex-hale   when I ask anyone who knew him when he was active   they all say   they'd never seen a runner with such beautiful form   in-hale ex-hale   he was five foot nine with long legs   looked good in a suit too   five foot nine was   in-hale ex-hale   very tall for someone born in 1912   my granddad's brother was taller, apparently   they must've stood out   in-hale ex-hale   the two of them running the embankment of the Miryang River every morning   in-hale ex-hale   the local children clapping and cheering them on   in-hale ex-hale   I've liked running since I was a kid too   when I was in the fourth year of primary school   in-hale ex-hale   I won second in the mini-marathon that all the students participated in   in-hale ex-hale   how many kilometers was that?   maybe ten?   we ran out the school gates and ran along the Ōka River   in-hale ex-hale   if there'd been a

track-and-field club at my middle school I might've joined   but there wasn't
in-hale ex-hale   but in my second year of middle school I started skipping
school and then I quit   dropped out of school   indefinitely   in-hale
ex-hale   from age fourteen to age thirty-three   in-hale ex-hale   I had
nothing to do with running   I was a chain-smoker until I got pregnant   in-
hale ex-hale   I smoked seven packs a day   climbing the stairs at the station
would make me wheeze   in-hale ex-hale   generally   running a full
marathon after only two months of training   is bad for your health   in-hale
ex-hale   my body feels too heavy   I started running after fasting to drop
down to forty-seven kilos   in-hale ex-hale   my coach said   don't reduce
your intake, lose weight by running   Yu   in-hale ex-hale   if you had the
muscular strength to support a body weight of fifty-four kilos   your knees
wouldn't hurt   you have no muscles, Yu   in-hale ex-hale   she told me that
weight training was better than dieting   in-hale ex-hale   so   I'm going to
stop doing things for other people's sake   I'm not going to think about my
weight!   no regrets!   my knee's not hurting yet so   in-hale ex-hale   for
now put your legs out straight   in-hale ex-hale   land with your heel   like
you're rolling the sole of your foot forward   no   now I'm too conscious
about lifting the tips of my toes   in-hale ex-hale   I'm running on my
heels   too much impact on them   in-hale ex-hale   I'm not following form
at all   in-hale ex-hale   I can't find my form   all my force is going
somewhere strange   like my left shoulder   in-hale ex-hale   lift your
shoulders   drop them   oh, it's Namdaemun   I should be able to see the
starting point at Gwanghwamun from that curve   in-hale ex-hale   should I
tell myself I've done nine kilometers   or that I've still only done nine   either
way that means I've run one-fifth of it   it's about ten kilometers from my
house to the top of Enoshima, so it's like I'm at the Enoshima Benten
Bridge   in-hale ex-hale   still fine   although every time I turn back from
Enoshima my legs start to hurt around Inamuragasaki   in-hale ex-hale   but
I've never started hurting before ten kilometers   in-hale ex-hale   step   by
step   I'm getting closer to 42.195 kilometers   so   step   step   in-hale
ex-hale   totally sleep-deprived   in-hale ex-hale   the ssitgimgut in Miryang
ended at four   I went back to my hotel by the station   to nap   in-hale

ex-hale   got in a taxi at five forty   got to Busan airport at six
thirty   touched down at Gimpo at eight   checked in at the Lotte City
Hotel at nine fifteen   in-hale ex-hale   quickly got changed and got in a taxi
with my coach   made it to Gwanghwamun just before the start   in-hale
ex-hale   really just in time   they fired the starting cannon while I was
stretching and warming up   in-hale ex-hale   but I've had enough to eat and
drink   in-hale ex-hale   I bought two rice balls at a convenience store before
my nap   two pastries   two bananas   a carton of milk   in-hale ex-hale   on
my way from Miryang to Seoul I ate   two rice balls   two bananas   one
orange   three pieces of cheese   in-hale ex-hale   and drank milk and over a
liter of a sports drink so   in-hale ex-hale   the problem is that I'm sleep-
deprived   deadlines weighing on me   this week if I add it all up I've only
slept about twenty hours   in-hale ex-hale   in-hale ex-hale   in-hale ex-
hale   in-hale ex-hale   in-hale ex-hale

"Someone's listening to a Walkman as he's running."
"Oh, that white guy. Lost in his own world, isn't he."
"Isn't that heavy?"
"I guess he's got it in a waist pouch."
"Wonder what he's listening to. I interviewed the director of Teikyo Uni-
versity's track team a while ago; he said that when he's running and feeling
good, he puts on the theme from *Rocky*."

In-hale ex-hale   I read in a book for beginners   that you should run at a
pace where you can still hum   if you can't hum anymore you're going too
fast   in-hale ex-hale   if your pace is too fast your body can't take in enough
oxygen   you get short of breath and can't hum   in-hale ex-hale   what
should I hum   when my granddad came over   we'd always listen to Korean
records   in-hale ex-hale   in-hale ex-hale   he would bend over   putting the
black record on the player and dropping the needle   **Chikchik   pokpok
chikchik   pokpok   ttwii   tteonanda tagwancheolli angaeseorin eung
beolpaneul   jeongeun deulgo motsalbaen   ah, ibyeori jota   dallyeora
dallyeo   dallyeola dallyeo   haneureun cheonghwangjeoksaeh   jeonyeok**

noeul tteodolgo chachangeneun dambae yeongi seorit seorit seorit
seorit pullinda pullinda it was an old record with the patriotic logo on
it in-hale ex-hale in-hale ex-hale when the song would end he'd move the
needle back chikchik pokpok chikchik pokpok ttwii twenty or
thirty times he'd play it in-hale ex-hale in-hale ex-hale Granddad would
sing along in-hale ex-hale so I learned the Korean lyrics haneureun
cheonghwangjeoksaeh jeonyeok noeul tteodolgo chachangeneun
dambae yeongi seorit seorit seorit seorit pullinda pullinda

"Oh!"
"What's wrong?"
"It hurts!"
"Your left knee?"
"Yes . . . same place as always."
"Still, nine kilometers."
"I can't, the pain . . . can I stretch over there for a little?"

It's my iliotibial band again but it's not a dull pain like I had during
training it's like my bones are piercing my flesh from the inside a kind of
pain I've never felt before I tilt both my feet out toward my little toes do
some stretches for my knee my coach takes the cold spray out from her
waist pouch and sprays it on my left knee

"How'm I doing on time?"
"You're still fine. You've been running at a pretty fast pace."
"I wonder what happened. It's never started hurting at this distance be-
fore. . . ."
"Can you run?"
"I'll slow down and see. . . . It hurts less while I'm running sometimes. . . .
Let's go."

Deep breaths in out narrow your stride in out don't think
about putting your feet out in front of you in out just lightly put your

feet down **Chikchik pokpok chikchik pokpok ttwii tteonan da tagwancheolli angaeseorin eung beolpaneul jeongeun deulgo mot- salbaen** in out step in step out step in step out if it were a gash the pain would go out but this is inside in out my heart is pounding in out in out ouch!

"Something's torn."

"What? No, I don't think it's torn. When you twist and extend your knee too much, the bone and ligament rub."

"Don't ligaments tear?"

"I think it's the inflammation. Because these last few weeks, the pain has come whenever you run, right?"

My knee and the head of my coach applying the cold spray to it look far away   it hasn't been ten kilometers yet, but I've already had to stop twice   I might not be able to finish   but   if   I went to the zoo with my son and a tiger leaped out of its cage   I would grab my son and run   even if my leg was broken   I would throw down my crutches and run   if I was walking with my son and a man with a knife started chasing us

"Why are you smiling?"

"Oh, it's nothing, I was just thinking something stupid."

"Can you run?"

"I'll try."

In   out   in   out   there is no tiger or man with a knife behind me   my mother's taking care of my son   in-hale ex-hale   last month after I went away for three days   he was so angry he didn't speak to me for a whole day   in-hale ex-hale   now I'm away for a week   in-hale ex-hale   in another six months he'll be able to speak properly   Mama, I hate you   don't come home   he might tell me   in-hale ex-hale   in-hale ex-hale   it's no good   it really hurts   I can't lift up the tips of my toes   my muscles are putting the brakes on my legs   how do I lift my foot off the brakes

"Yu, think of something nice! When you finish the race, we can eat some lovely Korean food."

"It's beyond that. If thinking about my son or ideas for a novel could take my mind off the pain that'd be great, but my mind's too full of pain."

In-hale ex-hale   ouch   in-hale ex-hale   ouch   in-hale ex-hale   ow!   I can't run away from the pain, so I have no choice but to turn toward it   in-hale ex-hale   focus on it   in-hale ex-hale   I have to calm my heart, stop it from crying out in surprise at the pain   in-hale ex-hale   ow!   in-hale ex-hale   ow!   in-hale ex-hale   but if I manage to get used to this somehow my pulse will   in   out   deep breaths   in   out   I'm only thinking of the pain   in   out   another step forward, toward not thinking about it   in   out   sticking it out against it   in-hale ex-hale   what is it   this pain   in-hale ex-hale   I could describe it as being like someone's taking a huge mallet to my knee but that wouldn't suffice   in-hale ex-hale   when actually, double my body weight   110 kilos   in-hale ex-hale   is pounding my knee into the asphalt   in-hale ex-hale   my coach told me that some people lose half an inch of height from running a full marathon   in-hale ex-hale   no good, no good   grip your hand into a fist   don't relax your hands   if the pain creeps up to my shoulders I won't be able to pump my arms   in-hale ex-hale   the brakes are on in my legs, so I have to pump my arms and move forward   in-hale ex-hale   in-hale ex-hale   in-hale ex-hale   in-hale ex-hale   in-hale ex-hale   in-hale ex-hale   in-hale ex-hale

"Well, we've passed Tondaemun. Two and a half kilometers to the water station at the ten-kilometer mark."

"Don't tell me how much farther I have to go. Right now, I don't even believe I can run one more. Two and a half is a tremendous distance. I'm just trying to make it to that telephone pole, or that tree. . . ."

"Is the pain that bad?"

"It hurts so much. I can handle this step, but I don't know if I can take the next one."

"Got it. Just go as far as you can. One two, one two, one two one two, one two!"

In-hale ex-hale   whether I'm being cruel   or sad   or angry   in-hale ex-hale   if I'm in pain   as long as it's there   I'm satisfied with just the pain   in-hale ex-hale   I've been saved by pain before   in-hale ex-hale   I've sought out pain   in-hale ex-hale   but   there is no pain that won't go away   pain leaves   in-hale ex-hale   pain is certainly strong but   there are things stronger than pain   in-hale ex-hale   there are people who would never give up their friend's name even under the cruelest torture   in-hale ex-hale   even if they're   beaten   kicked   burned   cut   eyes gouged out   flesh stripped off   in-hale ex-hale   to people who believe there is something more important than their own life, pain is   in-hale ex-hale   in-hale ex-hale   in-hale ex-hale   a man who was involved in left-wing activism in the Korean Democratic Patriotic Youth League with my granddad's brother   told me about how torture was carried out in those days   in-hale ex-hale   in the underground interrogation room at the Busan police station   they'd shove toothpicks underneath your fingernails   hang you upside down   beat you with a square pole   make you drink large amounts of water at night   in-hale ex-hale   in-hale ex-hale   was my granddad's brother buried somewhere right after he was shot   or did he die under torture   in-hale ex-hale   the mudang in Miryang   said he was buried alive in the rain   but   in-hale ex-hale   he was afraid of torture, of having his legs tied up and beaten with a stick   in-hale ex-hale   because he was a runner   in-hale ex-hale   but in the end he got shot in the leg   in-hale ex-hale   with a bullet in his leg he climbed a two-meter wall   he ran through wheat fields to a reservoir on top of a mountain   in-hale ex-hale   there he fell   but he had run that far   in-hale ex-hale   to try to infer his pain from mine   in-hale ex-hale   would be wrong   in-hale ex-hale   understand others' pain, people say   I feel your pain, people say   in-hale ex-hale   but that's nothing more than well-intentioned bullshit   in-hale ex-hale   in-hale ex-hale   you can't feel someone else's pain   in-hale ex-hale   no matter how important that person is to you   no matter how much you wish to take away that pain   in-hale ex-hale   you can

only feel the pain of not being able to feel that pain   in-hale ex-hale   in-hale
ex-hale   in-hale ex-hale   in-hale ex-hale   in-hale ex-hale

"Let's stop and rehydrate."
"What's that?"
"A sports drink. Want a Choco Pie?"
"No, thanks."
"Well, if you do want one, I've got some. Right, let's stretch your legs."

I put my left leg up on the guardrail and put both my hands to the
ground   I bring the ball of my left foot up to touch my buttocks   I lightly
hit my calf   deep breaths   in   out   in   out   I put out my right leg   left
leg   ow!   ow!   ow!   the muscles around my left knee scream in unison for
me to cut it out   ow!   the pain is insistent: think you can still run with
this kind of pain?   in   out   in   out   ow!

"It's . . . Can it get worse when you're standing still? I wasn't standing still. . . ."
"You can rest a little longer, you know."
"No, if I rest anymore, I won't be able to run anymore. I'll walk and let
my body get used to the pain, then I'll gradually pick up speed. I'll start
off slow."

I close my eyes right leg   I take a breath left leg   ow!   the pain insists:
still? still?   in   out   try to dodge the paper cups scattered on the
asphalt   in   but stepping over them or   out   stepping on them
is   in   impossible   out   turning my knee even slightly brings stabbing
pain   in   out   I pull back my left leg and kick the paper cups and
walk   ow!   in   out   the pain is standing in my way   in   out   with my
leg that's steady as a pole   in   out   if I keep walking like this I'll end up
cowering before the pain   I open my eyes and look ahead   stop gritting my
teeth   in   out   in   out   right leg   left leg!   in-hale ex-hale   right
leg   left leg!   in-hale ex-hale   I try to sneak past the pain and walk a little
faster   in-hale ex-hale   first, I square off against it   in-hale ex-hale   chase
the pain away   in-hale ex-hale   run!

"Ow!"

"But, Yu, look. That guy's limping too. And that guy's covered in support tape; you're not the only one."

"If all twelve thousand people in this race were in agony, it still wouldn't make me feel any better."

"Well. Going uphill now. One two, one two, one two one two, one two!"

One two   one two   one two one two   one two!   it must be hard for my coach to keep yelling encouragements at me   she's got a cold and a fever but she's still running beside me   one two   one two   one two one two   one two!   and I just keep shooting her down   one two   one two   one two one two   one two!   halfway up the hill everyone starts walking   everyone is walking and I'm running, but the distance doesn't shrink so   one two   one two   one two one two   one two!   their walking pace and   my running pace are almost no different   if so   one two   one two   one two one two   one two!   maybe it makes no difference if I just walk

"You've been passed! That woman is in front of you now, Yu. Look at her back, one two, one two, one two one two, one two! She passed you! Right, going downhill now."

"I'm going to slow down. My knee can't handle the load going downhill. Ow!"

"If you keep your leg stiff the impact of the landing will be worse."

"It hurts so badly I can't bend my knee."

"No matter how bad it hurts, don't bend your upper body. You'll hurt your back. Raise your arms a little. . . . That's right, don't put your force into it, don't think about trying to go forward. . . . Yes, let your own body weight carry you forward naturally. . . . Good."

"Ow!"

"If you tense your leg, your muscles will put the brakes on."

"Ow! Now it's my right leg!"

"And . . . on the outside of your knee again?"

"The same place."

"You're over the downhill bit now."

"What's that over there?"

"That's the sweeper bus."

"Sweeping up people who can't run, I suppose. It's sticking so close to me it's like it's keeping me company."

"Well, it is almost time for the traffic regulations to end."

"It's like it's begging me to get on board."

"Look, there's lots of people on board. We're getting close to the twenty-kilometer mark, after all; lots of people have started calling it quits."

In-hale ex-hale   in-hale ex-hale   maybe it's impossible   I'm running on one leg   dragging my left leg   in-hale ex-hale   and my right knee   in-hale ex-hale   the pain repeats the pain   in-hale ex-hale   the waves of pain become larger with each step   in-hale ex-hale   why am I doing this   does it have some meaning   in-hale ex-hale   for my writing?   so I have the firsthand experience to depict running?   but top runners don't hurt their iliotibial band   my coach said she'd never hurt hers   in-hale ex-hale   I'm going to stop here this time   strengthen my thigh muscles and then try again   in-hale ex-hale   in-hale ex-hale   running isn't my job   it's not even my hobby   in-hale ex-hale   if I injure my leg   I won't be able to give my son piggyback rides or pick him up   in-hale ex hale   I won't be able to sit at the computer for hours on end writing   in-hale ex-hale   most definitely I should get on that bus   in-hale ex-hale   in-hale ex-hale   I'm not running to experience meaninglessness   in-hale ex-hale   I'm trying to find meaning in running   not give a brutal meaning to a meaningless pain   if I resist this meaningless pain   perhaps it will gain meaning   in-hale ex-hale   I'm not confident, it's just a feeling but   in-hale ex-hale   in-hale ex-hale   in-hale ex-hale   since my mom told me when I was five about my granddad being a marathon runner   in-hale ex-hale   I always wanted to try running 42.195 kilometers, just one time   in-hale ex-hale   I cross the crosswalk   the cars waiting for the end of the traffic restrictions all blow their horns at once   of course they're not cheering me on   in-hale ex-hale   they're thinking, hurry the hell up   when they show a marathon on TV they only show the top runners   in-hale ex-hale   I had no idea that it was this tense for the people close to the cutoff time   when they end the traffic restrictions   I'll have to run on the sidewalk dodging pedestrians   and when the light turns red   in-hale ex-hale   a sponge   in-hale ex-hale   everyone's wiping their foreheads and faces with damp sponges and then tossing them   in-hale ex-hale   it's a few hundred meters of nothing but sponges on the road   in-hale ex-hale oh, I can't lift my leg another centimeter   I can't kick the sponges like I did that paper cup   they're tripping me up   in-hale ex-hale   I seem to stumble every few steps   in-hale ex-hale   ow!   I can see the sponges hazily like Monet's water lilies   in-hale ex-hale   imagine crying over some damn sponges   in-hale ex-hale   in-hale ex-hale

"I can't do this!"
"Battling with the feeling that you can't do it is what a marathon is."

I can't even talk back because of the pain   in-hale ex-hale   the red letters on the distance marker are blurry too   20 km   I'm not even halfway   in-hale ex-hale   I can see a water station   I should probably have something to drink but   it's difficult to drink while running   and if I stop, then the pain is piercing when I start again   in-hale ex-hale   in-hale ex-hale   in-hale ex-hale   in-hale ex-hale   in-hale ex-hale

"Want a drink?"
"It hurts more when I stop."
"I'll get one for you, keep running. Want a sports drink?"
"Anything sweet will make me vomit. Water."

In-hale ex-hale   in-hale ex-hale   the sound of my coach's breathing comes closer   in-hale ex-hale   in-hale ex-hale   I take the paper cup and raise it to my mouth   in-hale ex-hale   drink   ex-hale ex-hale ex-hale ex-hale ex-hale   my breathing's ragged   I have to get it under control   in-hale ex-hale   drink   ex-hale ex-hale ex-hale ex-hale ex-hale   throw the cup onto the ground   in-hale ex-hale   the bridge!   Jamsildaegyo   in-hale ex-hale   the river that is the mother of Korea   the Han River!   in-hale ex-hale   in-hale ex-hale   I usually run with no vision correction but   I wanted to see Seoul   in-hale ex-hale   while I was running so   I put in

contacts this time   this is the seventh time I've been to this country   each
time for business, not pleasure   in-hale ex-hale   I think I've avoided coming
for reasons other than work   I didn't want to see it as a tourist   in-hale
ex-hale   and I didn't want to be seen as a tourist either   in-hale ex-hale   my
nationality is Korean   in-hale ex-hale   I'll never live in this country
though   probably   in-hale ex-hale   I'll never talk to the people of this
country in this country's language   certainly   in-hale ex-hale   I avoided
learning Korean   I didn't want to learn my own country's language like it
was a foreign language   and even if I did become able to speak it   it'd be
nothing more than a language I studied and learned   I don't want to hear
Japanese people or Koreans tell me   in-hale ex-hale   oh, your Korean is very
good   I felt that if I ran a full marathon here   in-hale ex-hale   I could
become one with this country's landscape   in-hale ex-hale   I could touch it
with my bare skin but   in-hale ex-hale   the pain hardens the outline of my
body   in-hale ex-hale   I cannot blend with the landscape   in-hale ex-
hale   I want to grasp the pain, pull it out and throw it away   in-hale
ex-hale   if I run while resisting the next wave   in-hale ex-hale   even the
landscape looks pregnant with the possibility of pain   ow!   ow!   ow!
in-hale ex-hale   in-hale ex-hale   now   I am   running over the Han
River   it's been more than ten minutes since I started crossing this bridge
but   I can't see the other side   in-hale ex-hale   in-hale ex-hale   it's so
broad   in-hale ex-hale   I can see bearing the pain as like stopping the flow
of water   upstream the Han River is divided north and south   the north
Han River's source is Mount Kumgang in North Korea   in-hale ex-
hale   water from the north and south come together as one   in-hale
ex-hale   ow!   since I started crossing this bridge the pain has crept
upward   in-hale ex-hale   from my knees to my thighs   from my thighs to
my buttocks   in-hale ex-hale   from my buttocks to my hips   from my hips
to my back   in-hale ex-hale   eventually it will reach my shoulders   if my
shoulders start hurting I won't be able to move my arms   in-hale ex-hale   if
I go a little farther after crossing the Han there should be a water point at the
twenty-five-kilometer mark   still only twenty-five kilometers!   I have to
run another 17.195 kilometers   in-hale ex-hale   in-hale ex-hale   ow!   ow!
ow!   aigo   jukgetda!   I know this word because my father and mother used

it every day   in-hale ex-hale   always a big sigh   before saying this word   and
after   sigh   aigo   jukgetda   I'm going to die!   sigh

**Seoktan baehtan taneunde   yeongiga   peolpeol naguyo   i nae
gaseum taneunde   yeongido gimdo   an nane   eheya deheya   eoyeora
nanda   dwiyeora   heosong sewol   marara   seoul jangan
taneunde   hangangsuro kkeuryeonman   sacheonan gaseum
taneunde   museun suro kkeuryeona**

someone right behind me   is singing   in-hale ex-hale   in-hale ex-
hale   it's a man's voice, slightly nasal   I don't know what any of it
means   but it's got a nice tempo and it's light   in-hale ex-hale   the singing
is getting closer but   I can't hear any footsteps   my coach told me the best
runners run silently but   in-hale ex-hale   good runners wouldn't be
running at a pace just near the cutoff point   in-hale ex-hale   in-hale
ex-hale   in-hale ex-hale   in-hale ex-hale

**Waenomui jiwonbyeongi jugeumyeon   gaette jugeumi doeguyo
gwangbokguni jugeumyeon   dongnip yeolsaga doenuna   eheya
deheya   eoyeorananda   dwiyeora   heosong sewol   marara**

I've known the word *ilbon* since I was old enough to understand what was
going on   my father and mother said it like they were spitting when they
complained about Japanese people   ilbon saram!   in-hale ex-hale   ilbon
saram!   in-hale ex-hale   but my son is an ilbon saram   in-hale ex-hale   I'm
a hanguk saram   in-hale ex-hale   although I speak Japanese   when I can't
express my feelings I speak Korean   in-hale ex-hale   babo!   monnani!
sikkeureopda!   gaesaekki!   aigo, inomu gasina!   aigo, inoma!   aigo,
inomu jasiga!   in-hale ex-hale   in-hale ex-hale

**Sinaetgaui ppallae sori   ttodurak   ttokttak   naneunde   arong-
arong beodeullipeun   jeongdeun nim   eolgureul garinuna**

"Eheya deheya eoyeorananda dwiyeora heosongsewol marara . . ."
"What are you singing?"
"I don't know."
"Yu, are you all right?"
"The guy behind me is singing too."
"What?"

I turned to look behind me, and my coach's face entered my field of vision but my neck! the base of my neck! in-hale ex-hale the pain has made its way up to my shoulders in-hale ex-hale in-hale ex-hale

"Go, Yu Miri!"

Someone calls out to me from behind in-hale ex-hale a man in a white tennis cap and a blue running shirt is standing on the side it was widely reported in the papers that I was running in this race dozens of hanguk saram in-hale ex-hale Yu Miri fight! in-hale ex-hale was he the one who was singing? in-hale ex-hale in-hale ex-hale in-hale ex-hale in-hale ex-hale

"Gamsahamnida."

I can't speak from the pain, so my coach replies instead of me in-hale ex-hale the man runs to get only about a minute ahead of me in-hale ex-hale I wave my hand and go on ahead in-hale ex-hale in-hale ex-hale in-hale ex-hale in-hale ex-hale in-hale ex-hale

"Yu! You can see the Olympic Stadium now!"
"Who cares."

Oh, I talked back again in-hale ex-hale if now I was at the entrance to the Olympic Stadium I might be happy but I still in-hale ex-hale have to run eighteen kilometers even though my arms and my legs are being driven to the edge by pain in-hale ex-hale in-hale ex-hale August 1996 in-hale ex-hale I went through the gate of the Olympic Stadium I had a conversation with Sohn Kee-chung for a Japanese TV project in-hale ex-hale on the orders of the director I was waiting in one of the spectator seats when in-hale ex-hale Sohn appeared on crutches from a gate diagonally behind me just shy of eighty-four years old in-hale ex-hale we stood side by side looking down at the track in-hale ex-hale was my grandfather really a marathon runner? **we ran**

together   your granddad was on the national team   he was number one
in the   five thousand   and ten thousand meters   in-hale ex-hale   is there
anything that comes to mind when you think about my grandfather?   it's
been sixty years   sixty years   everyone's forgotten   there are a lot of
things it's better to forget   do you mean there are a lot of things you want
to forget?   there is no need to say things that would trouble the ears of
everyone in Japan   have the elderly forgotten that Korea was a Japanese
colony?   do the young even know what a colony is?   in-hale ex-hale   in-
hale ex-hale   I suffered the most of any man in the world to win a gold
medal at a marathon   I've lived long enough now to talk to my friend's
granddaughter   but in that time you're now the second generation in
Japan and you can't speak your own country's language   in-hale ex-
hale   as I asked about my grandfather   in-hale ex-hale   I felt he was asking
me back sharply   why are you visiting this country?   why are you in the
Olympic Stadium?   who and what are you?!   in-hale ex-hale   in-hale
ex-hale   those questions became an ache   asking me over and over
perhaps   in-hale ex-hale   even if it's a pain (question) that you've been given
by someone else   you're the only one who can take responsibility for your
own pain (question)   because you're the owner of that pain (question)
in-hale ex-hale   there is no escape from pain (the question)   step by step
bring back the pain (question)!   because you cannot be confused for
someone else   in-hale ex-hale   because you cannot be confused for an ilbon
saram or a hanguk saram   so hurt (question it)!   do not look for an escape
from the pain (question)!   as long as the pain (question) hurts (questions
you)   you must hurt (question)   through your own hurting (questioning)
you must struggle to conquer that pain (question)   in-hale ex-hale   in-hale
ex-hale   as he said that everyone had forgotten   Sohn Kee-chung talked
about my grandfather   both were robbed of their names   when they ran
with the rising sun on their chests   at a race somewhere, standing on the
track, my grandfather asked Sohn   in-hale ex-hale   in-hale ex-hale   **I'm tall
so when I run I go up and down, what should I do?**   in-hale ex-hale   **try
practicing with lead in the heels of your shoes**   Sohn apparently advised
him   in-hale ex-hale   Sohn must've always been running in my grandfather's
head   but   in-hale ex-hale   in-hale ex-hale   after 1940, when the Tokyo

Olympics were canceled   he ran off in the opposite direction to Sohn
Kee-chung   in-hale ex-hale   my grandfather ran away   from the army   his
country   his family   in-hale ex-hale   he shook off everything and sprinted
away   toward a finish line called loneliness   in-hale ex-hale   in-hale
ex-hale   I ran away too   from home   school   friends   lovers   my body
always tense, ready to run away at any moment   in-hale ex-hale   in-hale
ex-hale   always   in-hale ex-hale   in-hale ex-hale   in-hale ex-hale   in-hale
ex-hale

"We're over the bridge! Right, here comes another one of those downhill
slopes you hate. Loosen up your whole body. . . . Yep, just let your arms
swing. . . . Yes, just like that."

In-hale ex-hale   in-hale ex-hale   to my right I can see a statue of a tanuki
from Lotte World   why a tanuki, I wonder   in-hale ex-hale   Mickey
Mouse is, well, a mouse   so is Pikachu   Hello Kitty's a cat   in-hale ex-
hale   the water point at the twenty-five-kilometer mark   in-hale ex-hale

"Still happy with water, Yu? I'll get it."

I take a paper cup from my coach and drink   ex-hale ex-hale ex-hale
ex-hale ex-hale ex-hale ex-hale ex-hale   at the twenty-five-kilometer water
point   ex-hale ex-hale ex-hale ex-hale   I got my breathing under control
quickly but   ex-hale ex-hale   breathing is difficult   ex-hale ex-hale ex-hale
ex-hale ex-hale ex-hale   it went down the wrong way   ex-hale ex-hale ex-hale
ex-hale ex-hale ex-hale   I might throw up   ex-hale ex-hale ex-hale ex-hale   If
I stop and throw up   ex-hale ex-hale   I won't be able to run   ex-hale ex-hale
ex-hale ex-hale ex-hale ex-hale ex-hale

"You should drink a little more."

"When I drink my breathing rhythm goes off, I feel like I'm going to
throw up."

"But if you don't drink, you won't last to the finish line. Let's stop and have
a nice drink."

"If I stop even for a second it'll be over then and there."

I finish drinking the water while running   ex-hale ex-hale ex-hale ex-hale
ex-hale ex-hale   throw the paper cup to the ground   ex-hale ex-hale ex-hale
ex-hale ex-hale ex-hale   people are crouched down in front of a gas station
waiting for the sweeper bus   ex-hale ex-hale ex-hale   twenty people?
ex-hale ex-hale   maybe thirty people there   ex-hale ex-hale ex-hale ex-
hale   the part of me that wants to stop running and   the part of me that
wants to keep running are shorting out   in-hale ex-hale   fireworks are going
off in my eyes   tweet-tweet   tweet-tweet   the sound of a whistle is coming
up behind me   what is that?   tweet-tweet   tweet-tweet   a man in orange
running gear with a blue balloon attached to him, passed by the large leading
group   tweet-tweet   tweet-tweet   tweet-tweet   tweet-tweet   tweet-
tweet   tweet-tweet   tweet-tweet

"What's that, what's he doing?"
"He's the five-hour pacemaker. If you don't get past those people you won't
be able to make the finish line within five hours."
"So if I run with those people, I can make it to the finish in five hours
exactly."

Tweet-tweet   tweet-tweet   sticking right behind the pacemaker   tweet-
tweet   tweet-tweet   matching my breathing to the rhythm of the
whistle   in-out   in-out   has this guy been running and blowing that whistle
all the way since the starting point   tweet-tweet   in-out   no way   they must
switch out every so often to keep up that pace   a huge shout the moment the
twenty-seven-kilometer distance marker came into view   tweet-tweet
in-out   a guy also raised his arms and gave a cheer   hana, dul   hana,
dul   fifty-some-odd men all shouting together, their feet falling in rhythm
tweet-tweet   in-out   how oppressive to run in a group   in-hale ex-hale   I'm
slightly slipping off to the side   in-hale ex-hale   pick up the pace   my coach
picks up the pace too, she calls out to me   one, two   one, two   I no longer
have any kind of energy   one, two, one, two   one, two!   the only thing
inside of me is pain   one, two   one, two   I tell the muscles in my legs about

the feelings I'd like to pull apart from the pain   one, two, one, two   one, two!   the agony is pushing me on   one, two   one, two   run!

"Yu, you're doing well on the uphill! One two, one two, one two one two, one two!"

"Uphill's fine, but what goes up . . ."

In-hale ex-hale   in-hale ex-hale   I pass one person on the hill   then another   in-hale ex-hale   leaving behind the whistle and the men's shouting   in-hale ex-hale   in-hale ex-hale

"You passed over eighteen people! Downhill now."

In-hale ex-hale   the muscles in my legs can't hold up 110 kilos of body weight anymore   juddering and trembling with each step   in-hale ex-hale   each minor bump and dent in the asphalt reverberates in my knees   in-hale ex-hale   the road isn't even   both sides are tilted   in-hale ex-hale   if I don't run in the middle the balance of my left and right knees will   in-hale ex-hale   ow!   there are some seams in the asphalt   in-hale ex-hale   if I don't pay attention I'll fall   in-hale ex-hale   ow!   another seam   in-hale ex-hale   seams in the asphalt   are something you only more or less notice when you're riding in a speeding taxi but   in-hale ex-hale   in-hale ex-hale   can't hear the pacemaker's whistle anymore   in-hale ex-hale   there's just the road stretching ahead like anger   in-hale ex-hale   in-hale ex-hale   in-hale ex-hale

"You're keeping a good pace."

"I'm running and not slowing my pace, but that doesn't mean the pain's getting weaker. It's awful. It's not just my left leg but my right, too . . . and my hips . . . my back and shoulders are going numb too. . . . I can't move my arms either."

"Want to stop for a stretch?"

"No."

"Shall we walk for a little bit?"

"It hurts when I walk, too. If I start walking even once, I won't be able to run again. I'll have to walk to the finish line, then."

In-hale ex-hale   in-hale ex-hale   the pain is trying to tear me apart root and branch   in-hale ex-hale   you think you can survive being torn apart root and branch, it asks as I'm putting my feet to the ground in-hale ex-hale   the pain pushes my head under, trying to drown me in-hale ex-hale   you think you can survive drowning, as I flap my wings in-hale ex-hale   I can't fly away   in-hale ex-hale   dragging my injured wings   flap flap flap   flap flap flap   flap flap flap   flap flap flap   somehow I feel like I'm writing a book that nobody will ever open in-hale ex-hale   the second I saw the red letters of the twenty-nine-kilometer distance marker   tears fell from both my eyes   in-hale ex-hale   in-hale ex-hale   in-hale ex-hale

"Do you want to get on the sweeper bus?"
"No."
"Yu, if you think you'll never run a marathon again, then you can keep running, but if you're thinking about ever running again, perhaps you ought to stop now. . . . Are you crying because you're disappointed?"
"No, it hurts. . . ."
"Do you want to finish within the time no matter what?"
"I don't care about making it within the time limits anymore. If they lift the traffic restrictions I'll run on the sidewalk."
"Even after they let traffic back on the roads? OK, got it. Let's run."

In-hale ex-hale   my coach applies cold spray to my back and shoulders while running   in-hale ex-hale   my tears and snot are salty   my arms hurt   in-hale ex-hale   I can't get a tissue out of my waist pouch   or wipe my face with my sleeve either   in-hale ex-hale   I wipe my nose with my hand and smear it on my tights   in-hale ex-hale   my tears run like sweat, not now not now   in-hale ex-hale   in-hale ex-hale   in-hale ex-hale   in-hale ex-hale   in-hale ex-hale

Sinaetgaui ppallae sori   ttodurak   ttokttak   naneunde   arong-

arong beodeullipeun   jeongdeun nim   eolgureul garinuna   eheya dehe
yaeoyeorananda   dwiyeora   heosongsewol   marara

that song   someone was singing it as I crossed the Han River   in-hale
ex-hale   so that guy wasn't the one singing it, then?   in-hale ex-hale   in-
hale ex-hale   in-hale ex-hale

**Jeongdeun nima   osiryeomyeon   dangdanghage   oseyo   kkum-
sogeman   orakgarak   gugokganjangeul   taeuneunya   eheya   deheya
eoyeorananda   dwiyeora   heosongsewol   marara**

My shadow!   in-hale ex-hale   my shadow stretching out from my feet is
longer!   in-hale ex-hale   in-hale ex-hale   the singing ripples out   in-hale
ex-hale   what time is it?   started at ten so   if I've been running for four
hours it must be two now   in-hale ex-hale   my shadow shouldn't be this
long   where is the sun?   in-hale ex-hale   how's my coach's shadow?   in-
hale ex-hale   short!   and the guy in front of me   and the men in front of
him too, all short shadows!   in-hale ex-hale

Yu Miri!

Someone is calling my name from behind   in-hale ex-hale   with a voice
like the jing the mudangs were ringing   in-hale ex-hale   in-hale ex-hale
in-hale ex-hale   in-hale ex-hale   in-hale ex-hale

Uri sonjuya!

This time it came from right next to me   in-hale ex-hale   the voice was
right next to my left ear   but there's nobody between me and my coach   in-
hale ex-hale   in-hale ex-hale   she did tell me that after the thirty-kilometer
mark   some people start to hallucinate   in-hale ex-hale   in-hale ex-hale

**Miri!   Uri sonjuya!   have you forgotten your halbi's voice?   in-hale
ex-hale   in-hale ex-hale   in-hale ex-hale   in-hale ex-hale   in-hale
ex-hale   in-hale ex-hale**

Halbi?   in-hale ex-hale   is that my halbi?   in-hale ex-hale   in-hale
ex-hale

**I promised you yesterday, didn't I?   that I would run with you and
introduce you to the past   in-hale ex-hale   why are you crying?   are you
crying because you want to wash something away?   in-hale ex-hale**

It hurts   in-hale ex-hale   it really hurts   in-hale ex-hale   in-hale ex-hale

Crying won't take away the pain   in-hale ex-hale   if it's a pain that

can't be killed   in-hale ex-hale   you must live through it and handle
it   as carefully as you'd hold a fish in the palm of your hand   in-hale
ex-hale   in-hale ex-hale

But how   in-hale ex-hale   there's still ten kilometers   how   in-hale
ex-hale   ouch!

The pain is not your enemy   in-hale ex-hale   the pain is your
companion   in-hale ex-hale   in-hale ex-hale   your name is waiting for
you at the end of the pain   in-hale ex-hale

Will I be able to arrive at my name?   in-hale ex-hale

You have one life but   a name has no end   in-hale ex-hale   as a dove
ends its life in the way of a dove   as a viper does the same   I reached the
end of my life in my own way   in-hale ex-hale   my name slipped away
from me ever so quietly   in-hale ex-hale   and ran away   in-hale ex-
hale   running   in-hale ex-hale   run now   the road is much shorter
than you think   in-hale ex-hale   in-hale ex-hale   in-hale ex-hale   in-
hale ex-hale   in-hale ex-hale

Wind!   a headwind   in-hale ex-hale   my shoulders hurt so much I can't
move my chest   in-hale ex-hale

Shake the wind off your shoulders   in-hale ex-hale   in-hale ex-
hale   in-hale ex-hale

It hurts!   in-hale ex-hale   I can't do this anymore   in-hale ex-hale   in-
hale ex-hale

Your halbi will sing you a song: chikchik   pokpok   chikchik
pokpok   ttwii   tteonanda tagwancheolli angaeseorin eung
beolpaneul   jeongeun deulgo motsalbaen   ah, ibyeori jota   dallyeora
dallyeo   dallyeora dallyeo   in-hale ex-hale   Miri   it's the tunnel!

My grandfather's shadow stretches meters ahead toward the tunnel   in-
hale ex-hale   I'm being pulled along by his shadow and song   in-hale
ex-hale   in-hale ex-hale   run!

haneureun cheonghwangjeoksaek   jeonyeok noeul
tteodolgo   chachangneun dambae yeongi   seorit seorit seorit
seorit   pullinda   pullinda

Halbi!   listen to me   in-hale ex-hale   just for as long as it takes to get
through this tunnel   in-hale ex-hale   ever since I was a child I've often

gotten lost   I have a poor sense of direction   in-hale ex-hale   or my senses
are impaired when it comes to place   in-hale ex-hale   but I've never once
cried because I got lost   in-hale ex-hale   in-hale ex-hale   because I have
been lost since birth   in-hale ex-hale   in-hale ex-hale   there was a long
tunnel behind my father and mother   in-hale ex-hale   both had plastered
over the entrance and exit with silence and lies   in a foreign land   in-hale
ex-hale   but   in-hale ex-hale   they were always standing frozen in front of
the tunnel   in-hale ex-hale   in-hale ex-hale   my father and mother were
lost too   in-hale ex-hale   I always thought if those walls ever came
down   I'd want to push my way through that tunnel   in-hale ex-hale   but
then I had my son   and now those walls have to come down   I want to go
to the other side of the tunnel   and tell him what I see there   in-hale
ex-hale   in-hale ex-hale   Halbi!   can I find what I'm after   like a dog
sniffing the ground for a buried corpse   in-hale ex-hale   can I join
together   those bones ground to dust   in-hale ex-hale   can I hear   the
words of those gagged and killed   in-hale ex-hale   in-hale ex-hale   Halbi!
can I   tell about the war that rumbles through this ground   speak before
I'm spoken to   run through a city set on fire   make the spirits sunk by han
smile like the dawn   in-hale ex-hale   in-hale ex-hale   Halbi!   can I
stumble my way through this tunnel reverberating with your footsteps   in-
hale ex-hale   in-hale ex-hale   Halbi!

**My darling who I named   say your own name now   in-hale ex-
hale   in-hale ex-hale**

Yu Miri

**When you are lost say it again and again   say your name   in-hale
ex-hale   in-hale ex-hale**

Yu Miri

**Start the story unprepared   in-hale ex-hale   like a mistake
right   you're out of the tunnel!   turn your face to the light
hana, dul   hana, dul   hana, dul   hana, dul**

I come out of the tunnel and   my shadow has shrunk   in-hale ex-
hale   same as the shadows of my coach and the other runners   about sixty
centimeters long stretching to the north   in-hale ex-hale   in-hale
ex-hale   Halbi!   where have you gone?   Halbi!

"Yu! It's the Olympic Stadium!"

The waiting crowd of spectators calls out **Yu Miri! Yu Miri!** my name in-hale ex-hale in-hale ex-hale **Yu Miri! Yu Miri! Yu Miri! Yu Miri!** hand after hand waves the Taegukgi one circle divided into bright blue and red, yin and yang balanced in-hale ex-hale in-hale ex-hale the three lines on the upper left represent heaven and spring and the east the four on the lower left the sun and autumn and the south the five on the upper right the moon and winter and the north and the six on the lower right the earth and summer and the west in-hale ex-hale the flag my grandfather could not wear on his chest as he ran in-hale ex-hale in-hale ex-hale the flag lost to me since birth in-hale ex-hale the flag that belongs to a country that is not my son's a sob wells up breathe now breathe I'm about to hyperventilate out in out in breathing deeply I go through the gates of the Olympic Stadium out in out in out in out in out in

"Three-quarters of the way around the track and you're at the finish line! One two, one two, one two one two, one two!"

My grandfather's voice joins my coach's **hana, dul hana, dul hana, dul!** my legs pick up speed in time with their voices one two one two **hana, dul hana, dul!**

"The finish line! Make sure you step on it!"

The second the timing chip attached to my shoelace beeped hah, hah, hah, hah, hah someone who wanted to run more ran out from within me **in-hale ex-hale in-hale ex-hale** his road started at 42.195 kilometers the wind that blew down the road filled his white shirt like a sail **in-hale ex-hale in-hale ex-hale** and a boy of twelve began to run **in-hale ex-hale in-hale ex-hale in-hale ex-hale in-hale ex-hale**

THREE

April 7, 1925

| 1925년 4월 7일 | 1925年4月7日 |

In-hale ex-hale   in-hale ex-hale   my brother   will be born soon   in-hale
ex-hale   Eomoni had a dream where she was eaten by a tiger, so she says it'll
be a boy   and Abeoji had a dream where Eomoni was wearing a silk chima
jeogori, so he says it's definite   in-hale ex-hale   in-hale ex-hale   it's been
tough since Eomoni got pregnant   Halmoni and the ladies nearby keep
going on about how   in-hale ex-hale   if she steps over a fire she'll give the
baby boils   if she steps over a hedge a thief will be born   if she pushes
firewood into the stove with her foot the baby will cry at night   if she eats a
frog the baby will have six fingers and so on   in-hale ex-hale   in-hale
ex-hale   I want a little brother too   definitely not a little sister   if I had a
little brother we could run together   in-hale ex-hale   I'd teach him how to
run   Abeoji gets mad and says all you do is run, what are you going to do,
but   when I was born our country was already gone   in-hale ex-hale
in-hale ex-hale   freedom of   expression   publishing   assembly   association
all are prohibited   in-hale ex-hale   they step on the Korean people, who
have mouths but cannot speak   like a robber in geta trampling the grass
in-hale ex-hale   stabbed   shot   burned   just for yelling Independence for
Korea   in-hale ex-hale   in-hale ex-hale   the waenom continually sowing
seeds of fear in the hearts of each Korean to turn us into loyal subjects
in-hale ex-hale   like hell we'll become loyal subjects!   in-hale ex-hale   I
will not water that seed of fear   not one drop   in-hale ex-hale   I have no
guns or bombs, but I will never submit   I'll run   not even the waenom can

interfere with running   the only time I'm free is when I'm running   it's not
a feeling of freedom like lounging on a heated floor eating a big meal
in-hale ex-hale   this freedom of resisting with my eyes   my ears   my
breath   my heart   my legs   everything within me   pulls me toward it like
a bow   in-hale ex-hale   suddenly the wind   the freedom of suddenly
battling against the wind   in-hale ex-hale   in-hale ex-hale   I'll teach my
little brother this   in-hale ex-hale   in-hale ex-hale   sleepy   so very
sleepy   what time is it now   my shadow is so long   so the sun must be
setting soon   in-hale ex-hale   before the cock even crowed this morning
Eomoni shook me awake   in-hale ex-hale   Woo-cheol   I think your
brother's on his way   go call for your halmoni quick   in-hale ex-hale   in-
hale ex-hale   I ran   faster than a horse   faster even than the dawn   in-hale
ex-hale   I crossed Dongcheon   climbed Mount Chiltan all at once   in-hale
ex-hale   in-hale ex-hale   Halmoni! ireonara! Eomoni needs you!   I
banged on the door of Halmoni's house   she soon came out with a bundle
wrapped in cloth under her arm   I just had a dream   a bright red crescent
moon snuck into your parents' room   aigo   it was melting away like it was
losing blood   I hope the baby's not born under a bad sign   in-hale ex-
hale   Halmoni's back was twisted so   I had to stop so many times   hey!
hurry up!   the baby will be born without you if you don't hurry!   in-hale
ex-hale   in-hale ex-hale   Eomoni was pacing around in pain   Abeoji was
stroking her back but   while Halmoni laid out the waterproof sheet on the
floor   this is the birthing room now   all men must wait outside, she said   in-
hale ex-hale   but I did not move   I'm a man but   how can I just stand there
and listen to my eomoni screaming in pain   in-hale ex-hale   Halmoni
changed Eomoni into a black chima   embracing her body from behind and
shaking her hands   in-hale ex-hale   Hee-hyang! Not much longer, you can
do it!   Himnaera!   in-hale ex-hale   Halmoni faced the altar to the birth
god, where rice, seaweed, water, and a one-yen note were arranged, and she
prayed   sansin halmae   sansin halmae   binaida   geujeo
agiga   musahi   taeeonageman   hae jusoseo   in-hale ex-hale   the
rooster crowed and the dawn broke and still the baby had not been
born   Halmoni mixed a raw egg with sesame oil and fed it to Eomoni
in-hale ex-hale   in-hale ex-hale   she covered her big belly with Abeoji's paji

jeogori and yelled   uri sonjuya!   hurry up now and let your eomoni have
some peace!   show your face to your abeoji quickly!   in-hale ex-
hale   Halmoni asked me   Woo-cheol   there's an ajumma named Bu-san
who gave birth safely to seven children who lives in the house with the big
gingko tree   go run and get her   in-hale ex-hale   in-hale ex-hale   I ran
holding Bu-san ajumma's hand   Bu-san ajumma jumped over Eomoni's
stomach again and again   in-hale ex-hale   but the baby did not come
out   Bu-san ajumma said, wiping the sweat from her brow   in-hale ex-
hale   only the birth of my third daughter took over five hours   that time,
my nampyeon skipped a rock down the river for me   in the Miryang
River   in-hale ex-hale   Halmoni looked at me   Woo-cheol   go skip a rock
down the river for us   and make sure you pray properly when you do
it   in-hale ex-hale   I took a rock from the riverbed and dropped it in the
water   it sunk, not skipping once so   I picked up another and threw
it   in-hale ex-hale   be born soon!   in-hale ex-hale   in-hale ex-
hale   Eomoni lowered her hips from the wall   in-hale ex-hale   I can't, I
have no more energy   ow   help me, someone   in-hale ex-hale   Halmoni
drew water from the well and gave it to Eomoni   in-hale ex-hale   have a
little rest, gather your strength, then give a big push   you're not the only one
in trouble here   the baby can't breathe   the way things are right now is
dangerous for you and the baby   in-hale ex-hale   in-hale ex-hale   Woo-
cheol   go call for the ilbon saram midwife   I don't know where her house is
so go to the station and ask   on your way back take a rickshaw home from
the station   in-hale ex-hale   in the garden my sister So-won was crying,
which   made me angry   babo!   what kind of fool cries now?   your brother
is being born!   uljima!   in-hale ex-hale   in-hale ex-hale   keeping my
balance with both arms   I crossed the baedari, the pontoon bridge,
connected by boats   in-hale ex-hale   in-hale ex-hale   **from Karafuto and
the Kurils   to South Taiwan   the Penghu Isles   and all the Korean
Peninsula   there rules my emperor   and seventy million strong   we fly
the flag of the Rising Sun**   why is *this* song in my head now   in-hale
ex-hale   Woo-cheol, you have such a nice voice   your pronunciation and
volume are both spot-on   just like a Japanese   said Narita-sensei   in-hale
ex-hale   but it's no worse than being taught Japanese words and songs by a

Korean teacher in-hale ex-hale of course Narita-sensei's house must also
be near the station   most of the ilbon saram live near the station   no way
can I ask in the police station   it scares me in there for some reason   in-hale
ex-hale   I can smell miso soup   which reminds me that I haven't eaten
anything since this morning   I swallow the spit that's built up in my mouth
and breathe deeply in-hale ex-hale I open the door of Kameya
and "irasshaimase"   the ilbon saram mistress of the store and the
customers look at me   huff-huff-huff-huff   I read the letters on the scraps of
paper attached to the wall while I get my breathing under control   tamago-
don   oyako-don   niku-don   sashimi   huff-huff-huff-huff   where is the
midwife's house?   huff-huff-huff-huff   the lady came outside and showed
me   "if you go straight down that road there's a photographer's   go down
the alley next to the photographer's and it's the third house down, the
Inamoris' house"   huff-huff   dōmo arigatō gozaimashita   in-hale ex-
hale   in-hale ex-hale   I found the house, checked the nameplate read
INAMORI, then opened the gate   please, we would like your assistance with
my mother's labor   hah-hah-hah-hah   the moment the midwife, much
older than my halmoni, showed her face   the grandfather clock bong
bong   bong   bong   bonged   five o'clock!   I ran for the
rickshaws   carrying the midwife on my back as I ran   in-hale ex-hale   in-
hale ex-hale   in-hale ex-hale   in-hale ex-hale   in-hale ex-hale

The Japanese midwife who Woo-cheol brought put on a white hat first upon
entering the birthing room, then put a white gown like a coverall apron on
over her clothing.

"Please boil some water," the midwife said, rolling her sleeves up to her elbows.

"Mureul kkeuryeojuseyo," Woo-cheol said, translating into Korean for his
grandmother, Kang Bok-yi.

The midwife pulled the black chima up to Hee-hyang's waist and put a
black trumpet-shaped stethoscope to her lower abdomen.

"The baby's heartbeat is . . . weak, but I can hear it all right. The baby's not
breach either."

The midwife took the metal pan of hot water that Bok-yi had brought and added soap to it, applying the mixture carefully from her elbows downward using a brush meant for disinfecting. "Right, relax now, please, don't strain," she said, starting to palpitate, looking at her wristwatch as she measured the intervals between contractions.

"Your cervix is fairly opened, and the contractions are two minutes apart. There's no need to worry. I've heard all the details from the young gentleman here while we were in the rickshaw. The contractions started around three this morning, and it's now two in the afternoon; how many times have you passed water since?"

"Ojum myeot beon nwonna?" Woo-cheol decided to translate only the question and gesture.

Hee-hyang looked at Bok-yi; then, in a small voice, she answered that she hadn't.

"If urine builds up, the baby will find it hard to come down, so when it enters the canal, urine will come out."

The midwife inserted the catheter into her urethra, and soon the metal pan made a sound.

"Aya," Hee-hyang cried, clenching her eyes and gritting her teeth.

"No, no, just relax, please. Take big breaths through your nose and breathe out through your mouth. Yes, breathe . . . breathe . . ."

"In, out, in, out." Woo-cheol showed how to breathe, conveying the midwife's words.

"Just rest until the next contraction comes. How about having a sleep? I'm sure you'll have a dream about holding a darling little baby." The midwife gently caressed Hee-hyang's lower back, moving each strand of hair stuck to her forehead away before mopping up the sweat.

Bok-yi faced the altar and prayed over and over again, prostrating herself, both hands to her head, continually reciting the same words. Sansin halmae, sansin halmae, binaida binaida, geujeo agiga musahi taeeonageman hae ju- soseo.

With the next contractions, the amniotic sac emerged.

"Yes, just like that." The midwife held a piece of gauze to Hee-hyang's anus so that her perineum wouldn't tear. "Don't strain, slowly now, oh, the face has come out on top, I'm going to turn its head," she said, inserting her fingers and turning the head a half turn.

"Slowly, slowly now, yes, now the head's in the right direction," she said, taking the crown of the baby's head in her palm.

"Binaida binaida, sansin halmae, binaida, geujeo agiga musahi taeeonage-man hae jusoseo." Buk-yi's prayers began to build.

"Please prepare the water to wash the baby," the midwife said, interrupting the prayers.

"Tteugeoun mul junbiharanda," Woo-cheol translated.

"The shoulders are stuck. One more big push. Give it your all." The midwife supported the top of the baby's neck with her hand, and the right shoulder came out, left shoulder, arm, chest, back, hips—Hee-hyang lost consciousness.

The baby was motionless in the midwife's hands, like a piece of viscera just extracted. The midwife bent her head, putting her mouth to the baby's, breathing out, in, out, in, and a muffled cry rang out in the birthing room.

"It's a boy."

The midwife waited for the umbilical cord to stop pulsating, then clamped the cord in two places with forceps, tied it off in the middle with a hemp cord, and severed mother from child.

"Please give him a wash," she said, handing the baby to Bok-yi.

Bok-yi washed the baby in warm water drawn in the lid of an earthenware pot, then dressed him in a baenetjeogori made of cotton and laid him down, as the midwife wrapped the placenta pulled from Hee-hyang's body up in straw, tied both ends with string, and put it into the metal washbasin.

"Gamsahamnida," Hee-hyang whispered softly, her tear-filled eyes opening almost imperceptibly.

"It's a healthy boy." The midwife looked at both Hee-hyang's and the baby's faces.

Hee-hyang turned her stiffened neck and beckoned to So-won, who was looking on from the hallway.

"Look, it's your little brother. Where is your abeoji?"

"He's been at Yeongnamnu praying since noon. Woo-cheol, go and fetch your father." Bok-yi turned to the altar and prostrated herself fully in prayer before taking the offerings of rice and seaweed from the altar.

Woo-cheol looked at the faces of his mother and brother lit by the lamp, then left the birthing room filled with the smell of sweat and blood and took a deep breath.

He was hungry. Each breath he took made him feel all the hungrier. Woo-cheol ran, trying to take in as little air as possible, then called out to the dark shadow standing stock-still in front of the gazebo at Yeongnamnu.

"Abeoji!"

The face that turned to meet his was pale and saddened.

"Adeuriseyo! It's a boy!"

The corners of Lee Yong-ha's mouth turned upward, forming a smile.

"Adeuriseyo!" Woo-cheol said it over and over.

"A boy?"

Woo-cheol nodded, on the verge of tears, and turned his back to his father and ran. Was that the face of a father as he prayed for the birth of his child? The face of a father thinking of a name for a child he hadn't yet seen? It wasn't that of a man expecting something to begin but of a man expecting the end of something, a man anticipating going backward, not forward. Perhaps he had been thinking of his two sons buried in the children's burial ground. Woo-cheol remembered nothing from when Su-yong had died at the age of one, but he had been ten when Woo-seon died, and he remembered. He woke up to find that the baby was nowhere to be seen.

He asked Eomoni, who was beating the fulling block, Where's the baby? Eomoni answered without stopping: He's dead, your father went in the night to bury him. Woo-cheol was frightened and began to cry. Where did he bury him? On a little mountain outside of town, the children's burial ground, he only lived three days so they wouldn't give him a funeral or bury him in a grave.

A red crescent moon hung in the sky over the Miryang River. *A bright red crescent moon snuck into your parents' room, aigo; it was melting like it was losing blood.*

Feeling that his grandmother's unlucky dream was starting to come true, Woo-cheol ran down the stone steps two at a time.

At the entrance hung the rope to warn others not to enter the house. As he looked up at the red peppers and charcoal placed in the rope to symbolize the birth of a boy, pride and the throbbing of his heart came rushing up to his face. A little brother! My little brother! My little brother, whose birth I helped with these legs! Woo-cheol pulled one leg behind him, then the other, stretching his calf muscles that had become hard as planks. Smell that seaweed soup, wonder if me and So-won can have some too, no, it's miyeokguk, made from the seaweed used as an offering, so maybe it's only for Eomoni, Woo-cheol thought, gulping down the rather bitter saliva into his empty stomach.

The rickshaw, which the midwife had asked to come back in three hours, was waiting in front of the house.

"She gave birth safely. The midwife will be going home shortly, I think," Woo-cheol told the driver.

But how much would they have to pay him? It might be four yen for the round trip, and then how much would they have to pay the midwife? If they couldn't pay, what would Abeoji do? Woo-cheol rotated his left ankle while he pondered these questions, when Yong-ha appeared.

Woo-cheol and his father passed under the geumjul side by side.

"Hee-hyang, well done."

"Darling, it's a boy."

Yong-ha bowed his head toward the Japanese midwife, who was washing her tools in disinfectant.

"You saved my wife's and son's lives. I will visit at a later date to show my gratitude. Thank you truly."

"I usually stay about two hours to keep an eye on the bleeding, but it is so late now, and her mother is here, so I'll be leaving shortly. If there is much bleeding, or the baby doesn't take to the breast, I'll come right away. Your boy here was such a good big brother."

Woo-cheol quickly cast his eyes downward, rubbing the toes of his left foot with his right foot. "Chulhyeori simhageona agiga jeojeul ppalji aneumyeon baro ogetda," he said, translating only the fact that the midwife would come back if needed.

"Seonghameul ajik mutji motaetseumnida."

"I haven't asked your name yet," Woo-cheol translated.

"I'm Inamori Kiwa."

"Jeoneun I-Yongha-inmida."

"I'm Lee Yong-ha."

"I'll be leaving now. My most sincere congratulations," the midwife said, bowing her head deeply, then leaving the birthing room.

Yong-ha peered down at the baby's face. Nowadays he sold rubber boots, but before he and Hee-hyang married, he had been a traveling face-reader, telling people's fortunes from Mount Paektu to Mount Halla. The bundle Yong-ha had carried on his back when he arrived in Miryang was still on a shelf in the house, and he still flipped through the pages of his books occasionally. He would comment on the people in their neighborhood, making predictions. "People with foreheads that stand high in the middle can expect riches and fame." "Those who walk without swaying will make a fortune and have a long life." "People with dull eyes will quickly head for Hades."

The baby opened his eyes slightly, blinking, almost as if he were trying to look at his father.

The baby isn't crying—this is a child who was revived to give its first cry, but it will not live long. Those with narrow heads die. Unlucky. This child will never grow to be an adult. But if I tell Hee-hyang that, she'll hate me for it. Yong-ha relaxed his face.

"He has very fortunate features. He has the chin of a swallow and the forehead of a tiger."

The baby's shoulders, hands, and feet shook, and it let out a thin, shrill cry.

"Oh, there there, I'm your halmoni, good boy, what a good boy. If your halbi was alive he'd be so overjoyed right now. Once you get past your baegil-janchi I'll take you to visit his grave." Bok-yi pressed her pointer finger into the baby's grip and shook his hand gently.

"Mother, are you going home tonight?"

"I'm going to stay over. You shouldn't touch water after giving birth, so I'll do the housework for Hee-hyang for the next week. And someone's got to feed miyeokguk to Hee-hyang, of course."

"Thank you," Yong-ha said, bowing once before leaving the room.

"Well, I'll go finish up dinner now. There's just the kimchi left to be cut." Bok-yi seemed reluctant as she stroked the baby's palm, then stood up.

"Woo-cheol, want to hold him?" Hee-hyang turned her intoxicated gaze to Woo-cheol.

"May I?"

"Of course, you're his big brother. Take his head in your right hand and support his body with your left. Gently, gently now."

Woo-cheol tensed the muscles of his forearms and picked up the baby. The baby's eyes moved behind his closed lids, and occasionally a smacking sound arose from his lips. How small he was, how light and soft, how warm, how dependent.

If anything happens to Abeoji and Eomoni I'll have to raise him; I'm the only brother he has, Woo-cheol thought, and in that moment the soul he cradled became too heavy for his twelve-year-old arms to bear.

"Rain." Hee-hyang's voice was hoarse, little more than a whisper.

"So it is."

"Woo-cheol, where was your abeoji?"

"Yeongnamnu, why?"

The flame in the oil lamp quavered as if it had been hit by the rain, the shadow jumping over Hee-hyang's face.

"I see. . . . That was a lie, what he said."

"What was?" Woo-cheol swayed the baby, who was fussing.

"About the baby's face."

"Why do you think he was lying?" He looked down at his little brother's face, nestled in his arms.

She paused. "If the rain keeps up, I suppose the river will break its banks again."

"Why do you think he was lying?" Woo-cheol asked once more in precisely the same tone.

"Oh, your eomoni can tell when that man's lying. He always lies to protect his own feelings. Never has he lied to keep from hurting me."

He had never heard his mother call his father "that man" before.

"Woo-cheol . . ."

She wants to tell me something, he thought. Woo-cheol tensed his whole body and gazed at the shadows cast on the wall of himself and his little brother.

"Where was he, really? Where did he go and what was he doing the day when his own son was being born?"

As if in response to Hee-hyang's voice, the rain falling straight down from the sky to the earth kicked at the ground, trampled the fresh new shoots, and ran splashing into the river water.

Has Eomoni gone crazy from the pain, is that why she keeps calling Abeoji a liar? Woo-cheol thought, remembering his father's sad face when he turned around at Yeongnamnu, and how he had looked like a man who would run off toward uncertainty without knowing the way.

The baby cried out, perhaps picking up the beatings of Woo-cheol's heart.

"Shh, shh, Omma's gonna give you some milk, don't cry, don't cry, baby, you're gonna drink plenty of milk and have a nice sleep, now, c'mere, Mama's little sweetie...."

She pulled the string to open her jeogori, and her breasts floated in the light from the oil lamp, almost giving off their own light. The baby fussed at the breast, resisting taking the nipple, but when his mouth was wide open she pushed her nipple into his mouth, and he latched on, forgetting about all else as he began to nurse.

Sleep-a-bye, baby   my precious child
Gift from the angels   way up on high
And when the dog barks   it's far from your room
In your starlike eyes   the little bell of sleep rings

The rain picked up in intensity; the lullaby was sopping wet before it reached the baby's ears.

"The miyeokguk is ready!" Bok-yi entered the room carrying a small table. "There's some for you and your father. Hurry up and eat before it goes cold."

Woo-cheol went down to the store to call his father. Yong-ha was sitting on a stool, his body still as he watched the rain. No, maybe he wasn't looking at anything. From behind it looked like he had been waiting for something, like he was tired of waiting and had grown distracted.

"Abeoji, dinner is ready." Woo-cheol was surprised by how formal his words sounded even to his own ears.

His father always sat at a separate table from everyone else, but tonight he had to eat at the same table. Kkakdugi, white rice, minari namul, but no mi-yeokguk, obviously that was just for Eomoni. April was when preserved foods like kimchi, jang-ajji, and jeotgal would start to run out, but the new crops weren't ready yet; it was the hungriest time of year, Woo-cheol knew, but that night at least he would have liked to eat something hot and go to bed on a full, warm stomach. He arrived at the dinner table with a face bearing a mix of apprehension and dejection.

Yong-ha silently sat down cross-legged and took some kkakdugi with his chopsticks. At the signal of the pickled radish's crunch, Woo-cheol and So-won grabbed their chopsticks. The three did not exchange a single word until the meal was over.

Yong-ha's snoring, the sound of the rain, all noises were dark; even the baby just born that day seemed to be crying in perfect time with the darkness. Ahhhghaaaa, ahhhhghaaaa, ahhhghaaaa. What do I do, I really need to take a shit, I always do it right after I wake up, but today I've been running all over since the crack of dawn and I never had the time. Woo-cheol, struggling with his need for the toilet, got out of his bed and picked up the oil lamp in the corner of the room. When he opened the door, the baby's wailing got louder. Where did I put my umbrella, oh, never mind, I can't hold on much longer. Woo-cheol crammed his feet into the pair of women's rubber shoes sitting on the stone step down from the veranda, covering the hood of the oil lamp that he held in his hand as he crossed the yard. Abeoji said that it was best for the privy to be far from the family home, but Woo-cheol would've preferred it to be closer. He opened the door; the moment he tried to hang the oil lamp on the wall, one of his rubber shoes fell down the hole.

"Jegil!"

Woo-cheol lowered his underwear and carefully placed his feet on the footboard. A drop of water fell on his neck. A leak in the roof. The board and the walls were damp too.

Woo-cheol took four or five pieces of straw from the rope ring, broke them into three, and wiped his ass. Even the straw was wet from the rain. If it's still raining this hard it's gonna keep up till morning, he thought. He would run in drizzle, but in rain this serious he might catch a cold. Maybe I should stop

running. Sleep a lot more than usual, eat more, and go to school. But how long
is Eomoni going to be in bed with the baby? I don't want her to push herself,
but I can't imagine eating that same meal for a week, he thought. As he put
force into his calves to stand up, he thought he heard someone crying right
behind him and turned around. There was nobody there; there couldn't have
been anyone there. Woo-cheol took the oil lamp and pushed the door open
with his bare foot. Suddenly, he had the idea that, though they were buried,
Su-yong and Woo-seon were happy about the birth of their little brother; the
thought made him strain his ears as he went out into the rain. The aejangteo,
the cemetery where children were buried—maybe if he asked Halmoni where
it was she would tell him. The graves of the dead who could never have been
given life, graves that were just little mounds of dirt with no indication of
name, his two brothers who were bundled up in the middle of the night and
carried from this house, their names no longer called by anyone. . . .

Woo-cheol felt that their house had become dark since his brother's birth,
but it hadn't, the darkness already there had increased; no, the darkness itself
hadn't changed, he corrected himself, only the happy event of a birth had
thrown the darkness into relief. Perhaps Abeoji and Eomoni were mourning
the deaths of their two other boys. Su-yong had died seven years ago, but Woo-
seon had died only three years ago, so it was still quite fresh. The forsythia and
dandelions and azaleas had been in bloom; it was spring. When they look at
the baby, maybe they also see the face of their baby who died after only three
days. Eomoni had said that Abeoji's reading of the baby's face was a lie, but if
it was, did that mean the baby had an unlucky appearance? Woo-cheol tried
to remember his brother's face, but he could bring to mind only the image of
his face smeared with blood just after his mother had pushed him out. He felt
that they had to pick a name for the baby soon, or else his brothers would grab
him by the hand and take him away. It was unlucky not to have a name ready
at birth. The rain hit Woo-cheol's body as he walked into it, praying before he
himself realized what he was doing. Su-yong. Woo-seon. Su-yong. Woo-seon.
Chanting these names was his prayer.

FOUR

Arirang

| 아리랑 | アリラン |

The spring sky yawned open wide. The rain had gone away before dawn, leaving puddles here and there on the roads. The river was swollen but had not become muddied. The Miryang River was always so clear that if you looked closely, you could see the backs of sweetfish and salmon. A sandpiper stood on one leg, occasionally dipping its bill into the water or spreading and stretching out its white wings. The cherry trees on the embankment had lost most of their petals in the previous night's rain, but the dandelions, shepherd's purse, and violets along the riverbank were in full bloom, and the azaleas on Mount Yongdu dotted the mountain with splashes of red. With white and yellow butterflies flitting around, women gathered shoots of minari. They casually laughed and traded jokes, but their hands never stopped harvesting. One began singing "Miryang Arirang."

Look   look   look at me
Like a flower that blooms midwinter   look at me

Ari, arirang   suri, surirang   arariga nanne
Coming over the Arirang Pass

Having finally met him
I could not hear a word he said   I was so shy

Ari, arirang   suri, surirang   arariga nanne
Coming over the Arirang Pass

I was mistaken   I was mistaken
I came here as a bride in a carriage   I was mistaken

Ari, arirang   suri, surirang   arariga nanne
Coming over the Arirang Pass

Some women continued all together, singing a parody of "Miryang Arirang."

The bird crying in the pine trees   sounds so sad
Does it suffer   the curse of Arang?

Ari, arirang   suri, surirang   arariga nanne
Coming over the Arirang Pass

The moon that falls on Yeongnamul   is clear but
The Namcheong River just   flows silently

Ari, arirang   suri, surirang   arariga nanne
Coming over the Arirang Pass

In the brightly colored Arang shrine
Arang's spirit dwells

Ari, arirang   suri, surirang   arariga nanne
Coming over the Arirang Pass

A long time ago, when Korea belonged to the Koreans, there was a girl named Arang in Miryang District, an only daughter, admired by many for how she excelled in both talent and virtue. And there was a man by the name of Ju-gi who was in love with Arang. Arang had lost her mother at an early age, and she trusted her nursemaid as a mother, but Ju-gi succeeded in swindling the servant. On the night of April 16, the nursemaid lured Arang out to Yeongnamnu. The full moon shone reflected in the Miryang River, casting its glow on the banks where the violets and twinleafs were in full bloom. When Arang, drinking in the exquisite beauty of the spring evening, turned around, there stood Ju-gi. He confessed his feelings for her, and when Arang attempted to flee, he grabbed her by the shoulders and pushed her to the ground, forcing his body onto hers. Arang resisted violently, and Ju-gi, enraged, stabbed Arang and buried her in a bamboo grove.

Arang's father, having lost his beloved daughter, became most unwell, crying out his daughter's name in agony, until he was sent back to the capital. His successors, one by one, went crazy or died suddenly after taking the post, leaving very few who were willing to serve as magistrate for Miryang District and causing great trouble for the imperial court, until one man, an official named Yi Sang-sa, requested himself to become magistrate.

The very night that Yi Sang-sa took up his post, a ghost with disheveled hair appeared to him. The spirit sobbed, begging him: I am Arang, I'll tell you the name of the man who killed me, please undo the han that binds me here.

The next day, Yi Sang-sa arrested Ju-gi. Arang's corpse was found precisely where indicated, and Ju-gi and the nursemaid were duly beheaded.

Afterward, the Aranggak shrine was built in the very bamboo grove where her corpse had been found, and every year on April 16, a ceremony is now held to comfort the spirit of Arang. The song that the women of Miryang sang in mourning for Arang's death has, according to legend, become "Miryang Arirang."

A white butterfly, emerged from its chrysalis earlier than any other, with its wing split already though it was only April, flitted across the river. The air

smelled of minari. A hint of jebbikot too. Nothing smelled bad, nothing at all.
Even the smell of sweat that rose from the armpits of the women every time
the wind blew was almost obscenely sweet.

"I'm so glad it didn't rain on the Arang Festival this year. Year before last it
rained and they had to hold it inside the shrine, remember?"

"The festival girls this year were all so pretty."

"One of them was Hong-hee, who lives across from me."

"She was the prettiest."

"Oh, I forgot, I saw a geumjul up on the gate at Woo-cheol's house."

"What was in it?"

"Peppers."

"I heard it was a difficult birth and Bu-san ajumma couldn't help, even
though she had seven kids herself. They had to call for that ilbon saram midwife."

"Wonder how much that cost."

"Well, indeed. Must've been pretty expensive."

"Ten yen, do you think?"

"The baby was born, but of course that doesn't mean they're in the clear.
They've had two in a row die on them, two boys."

"Got to be careful till you get to the first birthday."

"I mean, their second son died when he was one. You can't relax until
they're at least five. You know, they really ought to call a mudang."

From among the conversations humming rose, floating in the air more like
a scent than a sound, and again the women began to sing new words to the
melody of "Miryang Arirang."

If my mother and father are looking for me
Tell them I've joined the Kwangbokkun

Ari, arirang   suri, surirang   arariyo
Kwangbokkun, sing arirang!

A fierce wind is blowing   a fierce wind is blowing
A fierce wind is blowing in thirty million hearts

Ari, arirang   suri, surirang   arariyo
Kwangbokkun, sing arirang!

The boats gently bobbing on the sea
Have come to take the Kwangbokkun on board

Ari, arirang   suri, surirang   arariyo
Kwangbokkun, sing arirang!

At Arirang Pass   the drums beat on
In Hanyangdoseong   the Taegukgi waves

Ari, arirang   suri, surirang   arariyo
Kwangbokkun, sing arirang!

One woman covered her mouth with her hand and whispered, "The son of the Baeks who run the rice shop was taken away last night in the rain by a detective. Apparently he was a go-between for the Heroic Corps."

The smiles never dropped from the women's faces; only their hands moved, still picking minari. Planting rice, harvesting rice, wringing chicken necks, plucking the feathers, rocking babies, making kimchi, plowing the fields, sweeping the house, getting water from the common well, doing the washing, boiling and bleaching the washing, soaking it in starch and working it by foot, hitting the washing against the block, getting together kindling, grinding grains, cooking them, weaving, threading the needle, making the children's lunches—no matter how they cried, or gasped in pain, or trembled in fear, their hands never stopped moving.

"The waenom will cripple him. Teacher Kim's son, you know, they broke his legs, his kneecaps came flying right out like peeled potatoes."

"They use soldering irons, rods, electricity, they pour water up your nose, stick tacks under your nails, stuff strips of paper up your you-know-what. . . ."

"Better to be allowed to live even if crippled. Choi Su-bong, the kid who threw a bomb at the Miryang police, was only twenty-one. He made the bomb at home, but all his family said they had no idea. Every night he was sleeping with it under his head like a pillow."

"How long's it been since that happened?"

"Almost five years now."

"That was really something, the way the windows of the police station shattered."

"But not one waenom died. When it happened in Busan, they killed the chief."

"Su-bong had prepared not to run, so he cut his own throat with a knife. But he didn't manage to kill himself."

"He was caught and hanged."

"Aigo, he was the family heir. . . ."

"Kim Byeong-fan got three years in prison. Should be out soon."

"He's already out. Nobody knows, but I'd bet he's gone to Shanghai to work with Kim Won-bong."

"Sure are a lot of Miryang saram in the Heroic Corps."

"A lot? It's at least half."

"Well, thereabouts. Anyway, their leader, Kim Won-bong, is from here, so that's why. Kim Won-bong stood out since he was just a kid. He got expelled for throwing a Japanese flag down the toilet, even."

"How are the boys from that family doing?"

"Lee Gyeong-nyeom only had two kids, Won-bong and Kyung-bong, but her husband's second wife had lots of kids. Nine boys and one girl all together."

"They keep following the family even after release. They order you to let them know if you have any contact or if he comes back. A few days ago, his father, Kim Ju-ik, was fishing in a nearby river when he was dragged in by the police who told him, Hey, you, those are ill-gotten gains, make your son surrender and we'll make sure your job and life are secure."

"Aigo, who would fall for such a lie? Kim Ju-ik's no fool."

A larger woman who had finished gathering enough minari to make into a namul for that night's dinner stood, let down her chima from where she had tied it up, gathered up the minari stems under her arms, and climbed the embankment. Another woman took off her chima in the tall grass and waded into the river in just her underwear, picking up clams in the shallows. White, persimmon, earth-colored chima jeogori strings swam in the spring wind. Each woman's face was hidden beneath a straw hat to keep the sun off, but they could not hide their long, sweaty necks or slender ankles.

From the embankment looking down at the women, the men fishing for sweetfish from the pine grove looked as if they were at complete rest. The scene held only one moving thing. The schoolchildren coming down the stone steps at Yeongnamnu in two lines—

In 1910, when the Japan-Korea Annexation Treaty was signed, a shrine and concrete torii were built at the top of the mountain where Yeongnamnu and the Aranggak shrine stood, looming over both the centers of faith for the people of Miryang for more than five hundred years.

Korean schoolchildren were obliged to visit the shrine at six every morning to clean the grounds; they would then go home briefly for their breakfasts before returning to Yeongnamnu, where they gathered to go to school in groups.

The pudgy little boys, bearing cloth bundles, went down the embankment and crossed the pontoon bridge. Food was lacking in the spring; the children's faces were as pale as invalids'. There were so many boys in hemp hanbok and undershorts, boys in paji and jeogori with buttons, boys in tight-necked jeogori; it was easy to count the girls in chima and jeogori, as there were so few.

The spring breeze snuck in through the gate where the geumjul hung, brushing gently against the branches of the willow tree as if caressing a girl's hair, then left.

Woo-cheol had overslept by an hour. As he cut through the yard, he scattered the roosters that were circling around the hens, in estrus, wings lowered. The second he passed under the geumjul and emerged into the sunlight, a simple joy rose from the soles of his feet up toward his stomach. It's spring! Woo-cheol looked at the new day before his very eyes. This was the first morning of his brother's life. If he could've, he'd have liked to pick him up in his arms and show him. It's spring! Spring! Woo-cheol jumped over a puddle with cherry petals floating on the surface and began to run.

Woo-cheol liked running at sunrise and sunset the best. He liked how his shadow that hadn't been there before when he left the house came out with the sun and followed him, and he liked how the shadow that had tailed him

since he left the house melded into the night with the setting sun. At that moment, the shadow stretching out diagonally to his right was only a head taller
than Woo-cheol. He should've woken up early to run. His abeoji wouldn't
stop with the sermons about how if he had time to run he had time to study,
so Woo-cheol had to get out of the house before his father got up if he wanted
to run. Halmoni had slept late, so no breakfast that day. Would he not get
lunch either and have to wait until evening? Usually nobody had to wake him;
the head rooster's cries would awaken him—but perhaps because he'd gotten
up at a strange time to go to the toilet it hadn't worked. He'd missed the visit
to the shrine for cleaning, but maybe Narita-sensei hadn't noticed he wasn't
there. If he had noticed, Woo-cheol would be in trouble. He'd never been
punished himself, but he wondered which was worse: being forced to stand
with his arms up, or having the soft flesh of his palms or calves struck with the
cane? Both seemed awful. He should've stayed home. Should've said his
mother wasn't well. Well, it wasn't a lie; she really couldn't get out of bed by
herself. Oh, Woo-hong!

"Woo-hong!" he called out, and Woo-hong turned around and stopped on
the pontoon bridge.

"The baby came!"

Woo-cheol ran down the bank, arms swinging, then ran across the pontoon bridge to his friend, keeping his arms out to keep his balance.

"Is it a boy?"

"Yeah."

"Seems kinda boring having a brother twelve years younger than you. You
can't play together."

"No way. I'm gonna teach him everything," Woo-cheol said, putting his
arm around his friend's neck, then poking his sides.

"Pabo! You moron! You're gonna make me fall!" Woo-hong loosened himself from Woo-cheol's arms, then gave a spirited laugh, lightening the air.

A student from Miryang Common Primary School, clad in a tall-collared
uniform, passed right by the two. His eyes slipped from the boys' jeogori to
their paji, stopping for a second above their straw sandals, before veering off to
the river.

Just before Miryang Common School, where Korean students went, was

Miryang Common Primary School, which was for Japanese students. The Japanese kids wore athletic shoes or leather ones; the more fortunate Korean kids wore rubber shoes, while most went to school in straw sandals. More than a few had to walk for hours on gravel roads to get there, blood streaming from their heels and insteps.

Woo-cheol and Woo-hong became conscious that the Japanese were looking at them and ran up the banks of the river, purposefully shoving each other in the head and back as they went.

"What poseurs."

"Those thieves act like they're better than us."

"Waenom never look us in the eye. They don't even want their eyes on the same level as us."

"They look down on us. They call us Korean whores."

"Did Narita-sensei notice I wasn't there earlier?"

"No, I don't think so. He looked next to the offering box like always, but his arms were folded and his eyes were closed. You didn't run this morning?"

"I thought it'd be raining."

"It rained till the morning, sure."

They looked up at the sky. There was no sign of rain. When the river rose, the kids who lived to the north in Seong-an were unable to get to school. The previous year the water rose forty times, detaching one side of the pontoon bridge, and the town was separated by the river for days.

"Nice weather."

"Sure is."

They watched a white cloud drift slowly toward Jaeagsan.

Before they went through the school gate, Woo-cheol sighed deeply. Once he went through that gate, he couldn't speak Korean; the Korean language was forbidden at school. Narita-sensei was extremely zealous. Most of the teachers were of a mind that teaching Koreans to read was pointless, but not Narita-sensei. He had a passion for turning his students into imperial subjects. So he was far more ill-natured than the other teachers, who just messed around.

Two days before, during a fencing match, Hyo-ji had accidentally called out "Himnae!" to cheer one of the other boys on. He was then forced to stand with his arms above his head for the entirety of class. Violations of the prohibition were always punished. Koreans, adult or child, knew they could not speak about anything real. In front of the waenom, they had to be like grass, silent even when trampled or plucked. Gangdo ilbon! The Japanese villains who got into Gyeongbokgung and slayed the empress! Gangdo ilbon! The damn waejeok who turned Korea into a colony and the Korean people into slaves! Gangdo ilbon! The fucking Japanese dogs who took our land, language, and freedom but still sniff around for more, like they haven't had enough! Two years before Woo-cheol was born, the Korean Empire had been erased from the map. But it hadn't been totally erased. In the hearts of the Korean people, in his heart, it existed.

The students, just back from the morning assembly, lined up their notebooks, pen cases, and moral education texts issued by the governor of Korea on their desks, speaking to one another in Korean-accented Japanese as they waited for their homeroom teacher to enter the classroom. There were 215 boys and 35 girls in Woo-cheol's year; the year was divided into five classes of roughly fifty students each. Only one class was coed.

The bell to signal the start of class rang throughout the school; as the sound of the teacher's footsteps got closer, the students stopped talking and got in place. The moment the classroom door swung open, the head boy, Moon Ki-deok, ordered them to attention, and they all straightened their backs.

"Bow!"

"Good morning!" the students said simultaneously as they bowed.

The teacher, wearing a high-collared jacket, put a teacher's edition and a student's edition of the moral education text on the lectern, then looked out at his students' faces.

"Good morning."

Woo-cheol stared at the wood grain of his desk, thinking he was about to be censured for missing the morning shrine visit, but the teacher began to call roll for attendance.

"I wonder what you all made of the principal's speech at assembly this morning. Those who understood, raise your hands."

All forty-eight students raised their right hands.

"Kin," the teacher said, pointing at Kim Jin-bom, who was sitting in the very back. The teachers always used the Japanese pronunciation of the students' names.

"We are beloved by the emperor."

"Anyone else? Boku."

Park Wan-tae and Park Gyeong-jun, who sat side by side, stood at the same time.

"Not you. The Boku on the right!"

Park Gyeong-jun turned bright red and sat down.

"The soldiers who have gone to war are making a tremendous sacrifice. When we grow up, we too must become such admirable soldiers."

"Indeed. Now, turn to page four. Who wants to read?"

"Hai," Lee Woo-cheol said, raising his hand.

"Go ahead, Ri."

"'Part three, filial piety. Ninomiya Kinjiro's household was tremendously poor, so since he was young he had helped his father and mother. When Kinjirō was fourteen his father passed away. His mother struggled to make ends meet and gave her youngest child to relatives, but she worried so for that child that she could not rest well each night.'"

"Wonderful. If the rest of you practice reading aloud in a loud, clear voice like Ri does, you'll all be able to read as well as him."

The teacher did not notice Lee Woo-cheol pursing his lips as he sat down.

"Hai!" The students all raised their hands at once.

"Go ahead, Haku."

"'Kintarō, knowing his mother's feelings, said tchu her, "I will work as hard as possible, so please bring back my little brother." His mother was joyous and went that evening tchu the relative's house and brought home the child she had entrusted tchu them. Mother and child were delighted tchu be reunited. Filial piety is the source of virtue.'"

"Delighted to be reunited."

"Delighted tchu be reunited."

"Not tchu, to! To!"

"Tchu."

"Say ta-chi-tsu-te-toh."

"Ta-chi-tchu-te-toh."

"Enough! Everyone."

Paek Yoo-yong sat back down, his face strained, as the students read aloud from the text together. The teacher wrote the character for *piety* in the center of the blackboard with white chalk, turning back toward the students as he beat the dust from his hands.

"Today's lesson is about filial piety, but what does that mean?"

The students raised their right hands at once.

"Kyo."

"It means treasuring your parents."

"So, Kyo, how do you do that?"

"At harvesttime, the sickle got dull, and my father said go get one. I ran back to the house and got a sickle."

"That must've been tough. What did your father say?"

"He said thank you."

"And how did you feel?"

"I was happy. I thought I will do it again."

"Who else has showed filial piety?"

The teacher pointed at Kim Yeon-soo, sitting in the front row next to the window.

"Kin, tell us what you've done."

"My mother went to the hospital, so I ran the shop. I gave the wrong change. But my mother told me good work."

"Very good. What did your father say?"

"My father died two years ago."

"I imagine even in the next life your father was delighted. Kyou, In, I didn't see your hands up. Don't you have anything to share?"

Yoon Jeong-hak and Kang Jong-oh stood, their eyes downcast. Park Sang-hong, who sat next to Yoon, quickly whispered, "I help harvest the potatoes."

"No helping!" The teacher threw a piece of chalk, which missed its target, hitting Lee Woo-tae square in the forehead instead.

"Boku, come to the front!"

Park Sang-hong stood and went up to the lectern.

"Hands or legs, which will it be?"

He hesitated. "Legs."

The teacher took a rod from the blackboard's ledge. Park stood at attention, eyes screwed up tightly.

The teacher swung the rod down on his calves.

"Now go back to your seat. You two, stand with your arms up until you think of a way you showed piety."

Yoon Jeong-hak and Kang Jong-oh raised their arms on the spot.

"In the back!"

The two boys moved to the back of the classroom, their arms still held high.

"Page eight, learning. Who wants to read?"

"Hai!"

"Go ahead, Sai."

"'Kinjirō was sixteen when he lost his mother. Eventually, the two brothers were taken to their mother's village, and Kinjirō went to the home of their uncle named Manbē and was entrusted to him. Kinjirō followed well his uncle's commands and worked all day. At night he read books, learned characters, and wrote thirty pages of practice. His uncle detested how much oil was used so he stopped Kinjirō's evening studies, therefore Kinjirō raised rape himself and took the seeds to town to trade for oil and studied every night. His uncle again said, "Do housework instead of reading books," so Kinjirō stayed up late doing household chores, then afterward he studied. When Kinjirō was twenty-one he returned to his own home, exerted himself working, and later became an important person.'"

"Sai, what do you make of that?"

"Kinjirō studied hard, so he became an important person."

"Indeed. Ninomiya Kinjirō, through filial piety, was close to his brother, and excelled in study and work. This story tells us what the Imperial Rescript on Education says: 'Ye, Our subjects, be filial to your parents, affectionate to your brothers and sisters . . . pursue learning and cultivate arts, and thereby develop intellectual faculties.' Everyone, do you understand?"

The words *Imperial Rescript on Education* made the students adjust their postures, pulling their chins upward.

"Turn to page twenty-three. Right, Haku. Read loudly for us, and mind how you pronounce your *z*'s, *t*'s, and *b*'s."

Paek Yoo-yong coughed, clearing his throat, then began to read aloud.

"'Part twelve, honoring God. In our country there are shrines everywhere. These shrines celebrate Amaterasu Ōmikami and usually the emperor or people who have done great things for the country. The Chōsen Jingū in Keijō, the capital of this country, is dedicated to Amaterasu Ōmikami and Emperor Meiji. The people of our country have since long before been passionate in their desire to honor God and visit shrines with a pure heart. We must also visit shrines and pay our respects to God.'"

"Right, that's better than before. You can do it if you try. Now, Haku, what are your thoughts on that reading?"

"We go every morning to the shrine on top of the mountain to clean. What we are cleaning is not just the shrine but also our souls."

"Precisely. We clean the shrine for different reasons than we clean our house or school. The emperor is thought to be in shrines, so if we don't clean as reverently as if in prayer, we will get punished. Got it?"

"Hai." Paek Yoo-yong sat down.

"You two, unbend those elbows!"

Yoon Jeong-hak and Kang Jong-oh gritted their teeth and snapped their arms back out.

"Ri, read out the Imperial Rescript on Education."

Lee Woo-cheol stood up as quietly as possible, setting his gaze near the teacher's left ear and taking a deep breath. If he stumbled or stuttered he would get the rod.

"'Know ye, Our subjects: Our Imperial Ancestors have founded Our Empire on a basis broad and everlasting and have deeply and firmly implanted virtue; Our subjects ever united in loyalty and filial piety have from generation to generation illustrated the beauty thereof. This is the glory of the fundamental character of Our Empire, and herein lies the source of Our education. Ye, Our subjects, be filial to your parents, affectionate to your brothers and sisters; as husbands and wives be harmonious; as friends true; bear yourselves in modesty and moderation; extend your benevolence to all; pursue learning and cultivate arts, and thereby develop intellectual faculties and per-fect moral powers; furthermore advance public good and promote common interests; always respect the Constitution and observe the laws; should an emergency arise, offer yourselves courageously to the State; and thus guard and maintain the prosperity of Our Imperial Throne coeval with heaven and earth. So shall ye not only be Our good and faithful subjects, but render illus-trious the best traditions of your forefathers. The Way here set forth is indeed the teaching bequeathed by Our Imperial Ancestors, to be observed alike by Their Descendants and the subjects, infallible for all ages and true in all places. It is Our wish to lay it to heart in all reverence, in common with you, Our subjects, that we may thus attain to the same virtue.'"

"I imagine none of you can understand the Imperial Rescript on Educa-tion now, but when you get into high school you will learn what it means in depth. For now, just repeat it and repeat it. The emperor's words are to be re-spected far above those of your parents. The emperor has affection for us, his subjects. We too must love and respect the emperor. We must offer our lives as subjects for the emperor. The Imperial Rescript on Education says, 'Our sub-jects ever united in loyalty and filial piety have from generation to generation illustrated the beauty thereof. This is the glory of the fundamental character of Our Empire, and herein lies the source of Our education.' Remember this well. Kyou, In, you can go back to your seats now."

The two dropped their arms and returned to their seats, just as the bell rang, as if it had waited for that moment. The head boy, Moon Ki-deok, gave the orders.

"Attention!"

"Bow!"

As the teacher's footsteps got farther away, the students' tension was re-leased but not fully. If they carelessly spoke in Korean and someone tattled, punishment awaited.

Woo-cheol went out into the hallway and into the toilet. Kim Yeon-soo was in the stall next to him, urinating.

"So why don't the Japanese students have to clean the shrine? We clean it every morning. . . . If the emperor is in the shrine, then—"

"Everybody knows why. So what's the point in stating the obvious?" Woo-cheol said, pulling up his trousers and leaving.

When he got back to the classroom, Woo-cheol stuck his head and chest out the window. A spring breeze was blowing, but he could not be swayed like the grass. As he'd read the Imperial Rescript on Education aloud, the words pulsed in his mind like waves of pain. The teacher had praised him. So why did being praised make him feel so miserable? What could he do to stop this miserableness from seeping out of his eyes? The breeze caressed Woo-cheol's cheek, but he felt only pain. He wanted to run. He felt that if he ran, he could outdistance the pain. He wanted to run, run, outpace this pain, until he disappeared into the distance.

"My arms are still asleep."

"My shoulders hurt."

"Look, I've got welts on my calves."

"I think that's just smeared blood."

To get a little farther from his classmates' voices, Woo-cheol stuck his whole upper body out the window. Every time the teacher called on him he didn't know what to do; should he just stutter on purpose or mispronounce words instead? But his voice always escaped from his throat before he'd decided what tack to take. Breathing in this sadness like pollen scattered on the wind, Woo-cheol remembered the face of his brother born just the day before and was surprised at himself for having forgotten about the new arrival. I have a brother! My brother! He wanted to see his brother, to call out his name right away. The baby had been born in the spring, so a name with that character in it would be nice. Chun-jae, Chun-ik, Chun-son, Chun-ho, Chun-gi—how jealous he was that his brother would get to have his birthday in April every year. Everyone would really feel like celebrating; it was spring! Woo-cheol watched a sparrow flying toward Mount Yongdu faster than the passing clouds. No one could restrict him either. In the long run. Which would go first, the waenom or him? The waenom would not go; it was impossible. So that meant he'd have to shed his own blood to shed theirs. This thought stuck in his mind like an arrow, almost knocking Woo-cheol over. To keep his balance, he thought of more names for his baby brother. Chun-il, Chun-bin,

Chun-hen, Chun-soo, Chun-bong, Chun-bo, Chun-gil, Chun-sok, Chun-bom, Chun-yong, Chun-tae, Chun-gu, Chun-yong, Chun-soo, Chun-woo, Chun-hong, Chun-yong, Chun-gun, Chun-un, Chun-sik . . . Planted in spring, a shoot emerges, grows quickly, and becomes a tall tree. Lee Chun-sik. A nice name. When he got home he might just casually tell his abeoji the idea. He heard the sound of the door opening and pulled his body back into the classroom, just as Jeong Woon-cheol and Lee Woo-tae placed the organ they'd just brought from the school office in front of the blackboard. Singing next, then, Woo-cheol told himself, and swallowed a sigh.

The door swung open while the bell was still ringing. The students did not notice the teacher's entrance over their chatter and the sound of the bell.

"Be seated." The singing teacher took his place at the lectern.

"Attention! Bow!"

The students then put their singing texts out on their desks; the teacher sat down at the organ.

"We'll start from page forty today. 'Commander Hirose.'" The teacher stepped down on the organ's pedal and played the intro, then demonstrated the song.

> *Roaring guns, falling shells*
> *Rough waves now wash o'er the deck*
> *The commander's shout pierces the dark*
> *"Where's Sugino? Someone check!"*

"Now, Ri, you sing it."

Woo-cheol, who had kept his head down so as not to get called on, sang along with the organ.

"Do you all generally understand the lyrics? Now, everyone together."

The students sang together.

"Where is this song set? Commander Hirose Takeo is a man who became a military hero during the Russo-Japanese War. The ship Commander Hirose was commanding was sunk by Russian destroyer torpedoes and suicide bomb attacks outside of Port Arthur. 'Roaring guns' means the sound of large guns, a booming sound. Do you know what 'deck' refers to?"

The teacher stood up from the organ and drew a boat on the blackboard, circling the deck area.

"This is the deck. 'Rough waves now wash o'er' means the seawater is coming up over the deck. It is time for everyone to get into boats and escape, but Commander Hirose cannot find his subordinate Sugino. So, with all of this in mind, let's sing it again."

The teacher sat back down at the organ, played the introduction, and the students sang.

"Verse two." The teacher first demonstrated by himself.

Thrice Hirose called 'round the ship
No reply heard nor trace he could tell
Sinking now beneath the waves
And harder yet fall the shells

"It was not a naval ship but a normal boat called the *Fukui-maru*. The ship was sinking beneath the waves, harder yet fell the shells. . . . But still Commander Hirose searched desperately for Sugino. Take it from the top."

The students sang the first and second verses together.

"Verse three."

Hirose had just to board a boat
But vanished in a blasting shell
Deepest regret out of Port Arthur
Know heroic Hirose's name well!

"Sing the third verse, then all the way from start to finish."

When the students finished singing, the teacher placed his hands on the lectern and looked out over their faces.

"The moment he got on the boat, an enemy bomb fell on him, and Commander Hirose fell into the sea, leaving behind only pieces of flesh. We must always be willing to offer our lives, as Commander Hirose did, for the nation, for the emperor. Our lives are entrusted to us by the emperor, so when the moment comes to return them, we must do so happily. You all read the Imperial

Rescript relating to education in your morals class, right? Which emperor gave us the Imperial Rescript on Education? Raise your hand if you know."

"Hai! Hai!" Everyone raised their hands.

"All right, Chou."

"Emperor Meiji, sir."

"That's right. The Imperial Rescript on Education was given to us by Emperor Meiji to show us, his subjects, a very important path that we must never forget, even for a moment. The ancestors of the imperial household, a tremendously long time ago, built the nation of Japan with the highest affection, bestowing a deep blessing upon all subjects, and we subjects follow the way of loyalty and piety, all our hearts as one. This is the truly beautiful wind that has blown continuously in the Empire of Japan, from long ago to the present day. Emperor Meiji's stated wish was not just that his subjects should follow this wind, but that Emperor Meiji himself should do so together with you subjects. And so he gave this imperial rescript to you here in Korea in the forty-fourth year of the Meiji era. You must all be happy to think you have become subjects of the Empire of Japan, which has the honor of having such a grateful emperor. You have been awarded the emperor's favor, so if you just follow his teachings day and night with devotion and continue down the path set for you as loyal subjects, step by step, one day, this beautiful wind will blow too in the land of Korea. Today, join your hearts as one with the soldiers who are giving their lives for the nation in enemy lands and sing 'Battle of the Sea of Japan.'"

The teacher wrote the lyrics on the blackboard; the students' eyes followed the white letters, listening to the sound of the chalk hitting the board.

Enemy ships appear, approach
On this moment hangs the empire's fate
So let all join together to raise
The signal of the flagship
The beautiful sky is clear but the wind is rising
In the sea at Tsushima, the waves too swell

Capital ships, advance
Cruiser ships, fall back

Like shooting rats in a trap
Watch, watch, how the enemy ships disperse
Torpedo squadron destroyers, if you should escape
Then give chase and fire

The teacher spread his chalk-smeared hands over the keyboard and began to sing in a voice so loud that it could be heard in the hall.

"Now, everyone, in big, loud, brave voices! 'Enemy ships appear, approach...'"

The students' voices, given as sacrifices, did not glorify anyone, did not revere anyone; they took refuge in the sound of the bell signifying the end of class.

"Right, we'll stop here, then."

"Attention! Bow!"

The teacher vamped a G, C, and G on the keyboard: ban, ban, ban.

Woo-cheol pulled the words to the song from his throat and vomited.

Ex-hale ex-hale ex-hale, still two hours until lunch break ... ex-hale ex-hale, hard to ... breathe, ex-hale ex-hale ex-hale. **If you continue down the path set for you as loyal subjects, step by step, one day, this beautiful wind will blow too in the land of Korea.** Any wind that blows in Wae blows in Korea too. Carrying the first cries of countless babies, drowning out countless pleas for mercy, conceiving countless nights, birthing countless mornings, that wind had been blowing since before Woo-cheol was born, would blow after his death, that wind that filled his shirt like a sail, always by his side as he ran.

The wind tickled Woo-cheol's nasal cavity with the scent of twinleaf, running its fingers over his sweaty nape; then, as if whirling a leaf up in the air, it blew the melody of "Miryang Arirang" into his ear.

A fierce wind is blowing   a fierce wind is blowing
A fierce wind is blowing in thirty million hearts
Ari, arirang   suri, surirang   arariyo
Kwangbokkun, sing arirang!

Kim In-soo and Park Tong-ming began singing a song mocking Woo-cheol, who had his head stuck out the window during break time as always.

Roaring guns, falling shells
Rough waves now wash o'er the deck
The commander's shout pierces the dark
"Where's Woo-cheol? Someone check!"

He turned, on the verge of shouting at them in Korean, but instead, he said in Japanese, "Guys, shut the hell up" with a glare before rushing out into the hallway. Woo-cheol ran, stepping on his own shadow that stretched out slanted before him. Ah! Ah! His shadow cried out in pain. **Enemy ships appear, approach   the fate of the empire hangs on this moment   so let all join together to raise   the signal of the flagship   the beautiful sky is clear but the wind is rising   in the sea at Tsushima, the waves too swell** Woo-cheol found himself humming not "Miryang Arirang" but "Battle of the Sea of Japan." As he pushed down on the pump of the well in the corner of the schoolyard, he spat out curses in the forbidden Korean language, his voice drowned by the water pumping out.

The bell signaling the end of fourth period was also the bell signaling the start of afternoon break.

The students took their aluminum lunch boxes out of their cloth bundles. Their lunches consisted of barley with a little white rice mixed in, with kimchi, kkakdugi, soybeans stewed in soy sauce, shepherd's purse namul, and the like. In Woo-cheol's class, only nine students had brought lunch, so at the chime of the bell, the majority ran out into the schoolyard.

The yard had only iron bars and a sandbox, but the boys kicked rocks, played with rubber balls, or played train with a straw rope. The girls jumped over a rubber rope, singing songs they learned in their singing class: Hello hello, mister turtle, oh, mister turtle, tell me why, nothing in the world, is as slow as you, oh tell me why, you are so slow . . .

Woo-cheol was all alone in the back part of the yard between the school and the gymnasium. He relaxed, enveloped in the smell of grass, occasionally stretching his hamstrings, with the feeling that he was separated from everyone and everything. He was hungry. When break was over he had two more hours before he could go home. He imagined his eomoni would be asleep in her room with the new baby, and that Halmoni would be busy taking care of them both. Dinner would most likely be the same as the night before, kkak-dugi and minari namul. Woo-cheol remembered what had been in the lunch box of Choi Jeong-cheong in the seat next to him, and his mouth watered. Steamed egg and beef stewed in soy sauce and sweetfish pickled in sake lees. Stop thinking about food, he told himself. Woo-cheol lay faceup on the grass, his arms folded beneath his head. He was thirsty too, but he didn't want to go out where everyone else was. For the next twenty minutes, until the bell rang, he wanted to give his tongue and throat a rest. He wanted to think about his brother's face, but there was a film over his memory, and all that would come to him were two eyes, wet as rain. Feeling that those eyes were gazing deep into his soul, Woo-cheol began to feel slightly uneasy. But the eyes didn't open. I'm so tired. It's only spring, but I'm so tired.

"Oh, so you're sleeping out here, are you? I've been looking for you."

It's Woo-hong, he realized, opening his eyes.

"Are you all right?"

"Gwaenchana. Ah!" The word had slipped out. He covered his mouth with both hands.

"I think we're fine here. Nobody heard."

"You never know who's listening." Woo-cheol sat up, blinking.

"I'm speaking Korean because I don't want any Japanese to hear. Read this."

Woo-hong pulled a clipping from the *Dong-A Ilbo* out of his trouser pocket.

"It's an interview with Comrade Kim Won-bong. My brother said I should read it."

A gust of wind blew through the poplars; Woo-cheol grasped the clipping hard between his thumb and middle finger so that it did not blow away. The gently quivering shadow of the newly sprouted leaves covered Woo-hong's face like black lace.

TWO MOVEMENTS IN UNISON — PART ONE:
KIM WON-BONG SPEAKS FROM SHANGHAI

Woo-cheol read the headline and felt his saliva turn sour with anxiety. He wasn't great at reading Korean, and the article had some words blanked out due to censorship, so he found it difficult to understand without reading aloud.

"'You ask me if there is anything I want to say to my compatriots in Korea, and of course there is much I want to say. But it is impossible, is it not, for me to say what I really want to say in any newspaper. Were I to say what I really want to say it would not be printed, and even if it were to be printed, it would certainly not be my real words.

"'My position on ███████████ has already been declared in my manifesto, and I believe that our actions through to the present have made that position obvious. It seems true to say that our movement is divided into two schools of thought: nationalism and socialism. Recently, I have seen over and over again articles debating the connection between these two tendencies. To state my opinion on this subject plainly, in our position as Koreans, it is not a matter of saying that the nationalists and socialists must cooperate; rather, the national-ist movement must become the socialist movement, and socialists too must become nationalists. On one side, it manifests as a nationalist struggle, and on the other as a class struggle, but when it comes to struggling together for the Korean people's existence, prosperity, freedom, and equality, is there really a difference between these two movements' positions? I have confidence that they can work together.

"'In *The Communist Manifesto*, Marx said that the history of all hitherto existing society is the history of class struggles. However, before class struggle came the national struggle, and we must not forget that the national struggle still continues. It is an indisputable fact that the peoples of ███████████ are ███████████ing the people of Korea and that the proletarian class of ███████████ is ███████████ing the proletarian class of Korea. Members of the proletarian class from ███████████ come to Korea and in two or three years they become the bourgeoisie.'"

Woo-cheol looked at Kim Won-bong's photograph. The caption read, "Kim Won-bong in his schooldays," and in the picture he was a boyish-looking youth, no older than Woo-cheol.

"TWO MOVEMENTS IN UNISON—PART TWO" was even more censored.

"'It is a fact that immigration from ██████████ increases by the day, and that this does not prevent the destruction of the way of life for the peoples of ██████████, and if people from ██████████ were to become more numerous on Korean soil than people from ██████████, even if a ██████████████████ world were realized, it would not be a ██████████████████████ for the ██████████ people.'"

Woo-hong said, "I'll lend those to you. Read them at home, slowly." He then pulled a straw-paper pamphlet out of another pocket.

As he read the words *Declaration of Korean Revolution*, Woo-cheol felt every muscle in his body tense, ready to run at any moment.

"I can't lend you this, so just read the last part."

The spring breeze blew gently past Woo-cheol's ears; he breathed in deeply and tried to make his exhalation meld with the wind.

"'Outside it will become the "sword" of destruction, and inside it will become the "flag" of construction. If one lacks the conviction to destroy and has only the foolish idea to build, the revolution cannot even be dreamed of for five hundred years. Now, knowing that destruction and construction are not separate but are as one, knowing that after a popular destruction must come a popular construction, knowing that the destruction of thieving Japan's power can only come as an injury to it by means of the construction of a new Korea through popular violence, knowing that we are standing on a "log bridge," the Korean people on one side and thieving Japan on the other, and if we don't destroy them we'll be destroyed, all twenty million of us must join as one and go down the path of violence and destruction.

"'The people are the headquarters of our revolution.

"'Violence is the only weapon of our revolution.

"'We will go into the people, we will join hand in hand with the people, and through endless violence, assassinations, destruction, rioting, we will overthrow the reign of thieving Japan, topple all that is unreasonable in our lives, make it impossible for one race to oppress another, make it impossible for one society to plunder another, and create our ideal Joseon.

"'Organization of Righteous Bravery

"'Year 4256 (January 1923).'"

Woo-cheol silently handed the pamphlet back to Woo-hong and put his hand on a branch of knotweed. He heard the snap of the twig breaking.

"I will lay out the targets of this violence—assassination, destruction, rioting. One, the governor of Korea and government officials in Korea. Two, the Japanese emperor and government officials in Japan. Three, spies and traitors. Four, all of the enemy's facilities," Woo-hong said.

Should I ask him now, or should I say nothing? Woo-cheol wondered as he stripped the skin from the twig, exposing the white, bone-like stalk.

"Japanese immigrants are the machinery of Japan's thieving government and the vanguard who threaten the existence of the Korean people; thusly, they must be destroyed by our violence."

The round face of the midwife who had delivered his brother sprang to mind. *I'm Inamori Kiwa*, she had said in a slightly hoarse but soft voice. What kind of violence would destroy Inamori Kiwa? An explosion? Handgun? Knife? Bludgeon? Inamori Kiwa lying faceup in a pool of blood, arms blown off by a bomb, all that remains of her face her gums and gold teeth—Woo-cheol blinked repeatedly, trying to drive away that image, but Inamori Kiwa came closer instead in stark outline.

"I wonder how the Japanese feel about this."

"How would I know? I've never been Japanese," Woo-hong said flatly.

The stems of the knotweed exposed by the wind were splintering, as dry as dead branches. Woo-cheol tossed the twig and wiped the sweat from his brow.

"We have no time to spare," Woo-hong said in Japanese, pronouncing the words precisely as if reading aloud.

"No time to spare?"

"When Comrade Kim Won-bong was our age, he walked around Miryang and collected eighty yen to reopen the school that had been closed by the empire and gave it to the principal. When he was seventeen, he went off traveling with just the clothes on his back; at nineteen he enrolled at the Dehuacheng School in Tianjin; at twenty-two he learned how to build bombs from a Chinese revolutionary and formed the Heroic Corps with thirteen comrades."

Woo-cheol no longer knew whether he should speak in Japanese or Korean.

Korean was, of course, forbidden on school grounds, but if they used Japanese and a teacher overheard them . . . Woo-hong, who kept switching between the two languages, didn't seem to know either.

"Aren't you scared carrying that pamphlet around? If someone finds it . . ."

"I'm not scared of the police. I'm scared of what I might become. In a few years, I'm going to go to Shanghai and join the Heroic Corps. Destroy the waenom, liberate the motherland, defeat the ruling class, redistribute the land."

Woo-cheol breathed in softly so that Woo-hong did not notice, then spoke. "Kim Won-bong's sister is in group five."

"You mean Bok-cham? My eomoni said she's the second wife's kid."

"Oh, so she's his half sister." The voice that came out of Woo-cheol's mouth and entered his ear was thin as a stretched rubber band.

"He has one brother by the same eomoni, seven from the other, and Bok-cham is the only girl. My brother was in the same year as Ik-bong."

"So did Ik-bong give you this pamphlet?"

"Yeah. The police keep such a tight watch on that family that they can't even get a single postcard from Won-bong. They haven't seen him in nearly eight years. My brother—" Woo-hong swallowed his words.

The tall grass rustled. Half a minute passed. The sound of laughter came from the schoolyard. It had been perhaps a minute now. Tired of squatting, Woo-cheol leaned against the wall, stretching his legs out; that action got Woo-hong talking again.

"They say the death toll of the Kantō earthquake a year and a half ago was ninety thousand people, but that doesn't include Koreans. Tell me, Woo-cheol, how many Koreans do you think died crushed under the rubble? They didn't just die in the earthquake; rumors went around that Koreans were poisoning the wells and next thing you know, six thousand of our compatriots had been killed, did you know that? And the killers weren't just the police and soldiers; it was normal Japanese people killing people in their own neighborhoods too. They can't tell who's Korean just by looking, so they got everyone who might be Korean and asked them one by one to say, 'Jū en go jū sen,' ten yen and fifty sen, and if they said it with a Korean accent, like 'Chū en ko chū sen,' they cut them with swords, clubbed them, stabbed them with bamboo spears. And not just men, but also women, children, and babies—they slit their throats and rolled the bodies out of the way like logs. They left no door unknocked. And yet here they are, still eating white rice and taking huge shits like everything's fine. If you killed a dog you'd barely be able to eat after, right? But the waenom eat just fine. So we must be nothing more than mosquitoes or flies to them."

Woo-cheol did not understand why, even though he was listening to Woo-hong and not Narita-sensei, he felt as if he were sitting in his uncomfortable desk chair, hoping the bell would ring soon. He cast his eyes down to where his and Woo-hong's shadows met.

"However many of us the waenom kill, they don't ever count the Korean dead. My brother told me that the number of comrades killed by waenom in the Korean independence movement and the March First Movement was greater than the number of Japanese military deaths in the Sino-Japanese and Russo-Japanese Wars put together. They say that Japan annexed Korea under mutual consent, but we fought to protect our country. It was a war. And the war isn't over yet. Not until there's not a single waenom left in Korea. Tell me, Woo-cheol, the Korean people don't have soldiers or tanks or battleships or fighter planes, so how else should we fight this war?" He turned his straight, pointed gaze on Woo-cheol.

Nothing worthy of being called a wind was blowing now, yet Woo-cheol's head had been wavering for a while. He didn't know what he thought or didn't think, or wanted to think or didn't want to think. He knew that he was being asked something. But at that moment the inside of his head was so noisy that he did not think. If he tried to think now, he felt, he would just stumble on Woo-hong's words—no, not Woo-hong's words, Woo-hong's brother's words, no, no, the words of countless comrades—

"My brother wrote a will and gave it to me. He said, 'If I die give this to Father.'" His voice was clear but trembling.

Woo-cheol moved his lips. No sound came out.

"He's left Miryang."

"It's just you and him, isn't it? And if you join the Heroic Corps, then . . ."

The bell rang out in the silence between them. They stood up without a word and began to walk.

"What class do we have next?" Woo-cheol asked, in his usual voice.

"Arithmetic," Woo-hong said, in his.

"Oh."

"You're in class five next term, right?"

"Yeah, is that bad?"

"Of course it is, I'm in class nine."

"Wow, amazing."

They laughed. Woo-cheol watched Woo-hong laugh and thought about how a person's expression could change just like that. Chikchik pokpok, chikchik pokpok, the first-years were still playing train with the straw rope when Woo-cheol and Woo-hong came into the schoolyard.

"Race you to class," Woo-hong said.

"OK, let's do it," Woo-cheol echoed his friend's tone.

"Go, Lee Woo-cheol!"

"Catch me if you can!"

They ran, elbows jostling against each other.

In-hale ex-hale   in-hale ex-hale   Woo-hong sounds like he's struggling to breathe   in-hale ex-hale   faster   faster   faster!   in-hale ex-hale   his breathing is behind me now   way behind   in-hale ex-hale   in-hale ex-hale   **Tell me, Woo-cheol, the Korean people don't have soldiers or tanks or battleships or fighter planes, so how else should we fight this war?** in-hale ex-hale   me too   in-hale ex-hale   Woo-hong   me too   in-hale ex-hale   I sometimes think I have to shed my blood to shed theirs too   but Woo-hong   in-hale ex-hale   no matter what   in-hale ex-hale   I can't forget **Inamori Kiwa's** name or face or voice   **it's a war**   in-hale ex-hale   that's right   it's a **war**   the waenom see us only as **Koreans**   we have names and faces and voices but   in-hale ex-hale   we're just **Koreans**   but   what I mean is   to **exterminate Inamori Kiwa** as a **Japanese**   in-hale ex-hale   in-hale ex-hale   **exterminate**   in-hale ex-hale   **exterminate**   in-hale ex-hale   but   if   my abeoji   my eomoni   my little sister   my newborn little brother   were **exterminated** just for being Korean, like after the earthquake   in-hale ex-hale   like mosquitoes or flies   in-hale ex-hale   then maybe I could kill **Inamori Kiwa** just for being **Japanese**   in-hale ex-hale   could I **exterminate?**   in-hale ex-hale   exterminate   in-hale ex-hale   exterminate   exterminate   exterminate   exterminate   exterminate   in-hale ex-hale   no   that's not what I'm thinking about   so what are you thinking about, then? Woo-hong would say   in-hale ex-hale   words will not carry my thoughts   words leave thoughts deserted   in-hale ex-hale   and words   are ruined the second they're voiced   in-hale ex-hale   the only time thoughts and words and voice are united is when calling a name   in-hale ex-hale   in-hale ex-hale   I want to keep my thoughts inside   in-hale ex-hale   without changing them into words   in-hale ex-hale   in-hale ex-hale   action   is not when thoughts are turned into words and when words are voiced   in-hale ex-hale   it's when thoughts are suddenly given voice   in-hale ex-hale   in-hale ex-hale   I run   not tripping up on words   wrapped only in my breath   in-hale ex-hale   until the swallow's cry and   the wind that blows through the reeds   become my breath   until the place where the wind and my breath run out   in-hale ex-hale   in-hale ex-hale   in-hale ex-hale   in-hale ex-hale   in-hale ex-hale

FIVE

The Miryang River

| 밀양강 | 密陽川 |

The water of the Miryang River is so clear that you can follow the movements of fish by the shadows cast on the riverbed. In April the river is, as the saying goes, half water, half sweetfish; it is so full of sweetfish going upstream to spawn that the water appears darkened. Delicious even raw, which some attribute to the quality of the water and some to the lichens on the riverbed, it is said that since the earliest days long ago people would come from Hanyang, hundreds of ri away, to eat Miryang sweetfish.

There is a legend about Miryang sweetfish, called "The River Prince."

A long time ago, there was a prince in Silla. Ever since he was old enough, he loved to play in the water, and once he learned to fish there was never a day when he wasn't seen by the bank of the lake. He often snuck away from court to go out with his rod on fishing boats, and the fishermen gave him the nickname the River Prince. The prince's heart flowed broadly from river to river; once, he told his father, the king, "I have no need for land. Give to me the rivers of this country." The king heard the prince's request and gave him the rivers of Silla as his domain. The prince, delighted, left the capital of Silla and traveled continuously from river to river. In the middle of the fifth month, he drifted to a location where a branch of the Dandong River threads itself between two villages. The commoners there who learned to fish from the prince pulled Miryang sweetfish from the river, it is said.

Yeongnamnu, the pavilion looking down on the Miryang River from the mountainside, was built in 1844 as part of a state guesthouse on the grounds where Yeongnamsa Temple once stood, before it burned. One must turn their back to the river to climb the stone stairs; the beauty when one again faces the river upon reaching Yeongnamnu is enough to make one think that Yeongnamnu was built not for the sake of its own beauty but to show off the beauty of the Miryang River and Mount Jongnam. From there, one can look out to the very edge of the plains, which were once called the Miri Plains.

A woman, on her own, leaned her body against the railing of Yeongnamnu. The clusters of poplars looked up at her from the morning mist rising off the river, Mount Jongnam rose up showing its dorsal, blotched red with azaleas, the sun's light polished the surface of the river like a mirror reflecting the green of the trees, but the woman did not look at any of that. She simply surrendered herself to the feeling of his lips and hands still lingering throughout her body.

Her name was Mi-ryeong. Her house and his were both on the banks of the Miryang River. They were so close that even if one dawdled it would not take ten minutes to walk the distance. Each day, he went from his house, located by the pontoon bridge, to her house, next to the cedar trees at the base of Yeongnamnu. Daily without fail.

Leaving home after the evening meal was difficult, so he would come to call after breakfast or lunch. On market days, he was so busy that he had to hire scores of men to help, but still he would slip away from the store, pretending he was going out to buy cigarettes.

"I want to see you every day, I want to see your face every day, just for five minutes even, no matter how busy you are, can't you find five minutes? Just five minutes a day, I ask nothing else of you, oh, darling, promise me."

He kept his promise to her. He had gone to her house the day before, the day before that, and the day before that, while his wife was having contractions.

Remembering what had happened three days prior, the woman touched her upper lip and sighed. Without a word the man had removed his wide-brimmed hat to show his face, then untied the strings of her jeogori with one hand, rolling up her chima with the other. Up, up went their bodies, shaking, and when she no longer knew whether she was shaking or being shaken, he removed his body from hers.

She raised her right hand and spread her fingers on the nape of his neck, asking without speaking: Why won't you look at my face? You haven't once looked me in the eye today, why?

In response the man pushed her hair behind her ears and cast his body to the ground, faceup.

She hung over him, bringing her lips close to his, waiting for words to arise, but he was silent. She licked the sweat pooled in his navel. He shut his eyes. Her mouth moved lower, yet he let out not a sigh.

The woman lay down, her hair spreading over his arm. His wife was due soon, she had heard a while back. Always their gentle silence included the promise of the next day, but the present day's silence irritated and troubled her.

He's afraid of missing the birth; he might not come tomorrow—if he doesn't come tomorrow, he will never come again.

Blood rushed to her face, even to her ears, filling her eyes, turning the man's face red.

Late at night, when the town was sleeping, she went to his house. The moment she saw the chili peppers in the geumjul hanging from the gate, her heart cracked open like an egg. Now, his broad back, his tight shoulders, his smooth chest, his short hands with splintered, flat nails, his lips that seldom smiled would never be hers. It was clear as the river to her that she would never live with him.

The fact that he'd had a son ten years before they'd met was unfortunate but couldn't be changed, but to have a son now, after they'd met—that woman had Sansin halmae on her side, no doubt, while Mi-ryeong must've somehow made an enemy of her.

She had seen that woman's face before. The morning after the first time they had made love, she had gone into his shop to buy some rubber shoes.

"How much?"

"Forty-five sen."

When she took her change, their fingers bumped into each other. She saw the gold ring digging into his wife's plump finger, and in that moment, she felt as if his wife were crushing her heart in her bare hand.

Where the woman stood shifted from shade to sun, but she did not move a muscle. The River Prince who drifted down from the capital must have made love to women on riverbanks throughout the land.

I was drawn to him because he's not from Miryang. Because he drifted here from somewhere else and may drift on to somewhere else again. I cannot stay with him. But if he leaves me, how am I to go on living? I want a baby boy. A boy who looks just like him and I want to raise him by the river.

The woman turned toward Mount Jongnam and put her hands together. *Binaida binaida sansinnimkkae binaida, geu saramui aireul gatge haejusiso amujjorok sanaeareul gatge haejusiso. Please, let us have a child, let us have a baby boy.*

The woman noticed now for the first time how Mount Jongnam was red with azaleas. And it wasn't just the azaleas out; the dandelions and shepherd's purse and violets were in bloom on the riverbanks.

I'm in full bloom too. Not because I hate him, not because I've stopped chasing him.

Since the first time he had embraced her, what she had feared was not hating him but needing him. This fear grew as their trysts became more numerous, each time they met, hating him passionately, needing him passionately.

She slept but the fear did not. It shook her awake and made her walk the riverbank. However much she walked, she could not drown that fear in the flowing waters or wash away her hopes. The previous night she did not go in the direction of the pontoon bridge, but now she wasn't sure, she might go under the geumjul, where she could hear the baby's cries ring out.

What would she do if she passed under that geumjul? He would probably never forgive her for causing hurt to his family. Family. She was not his family. What was she to him?

The previous day she had not gone outside until the afternoon. She had done nothing other than occasionally gaze in the mirror, fixing her hair and makeup. She had kept her hands between her thighs, just waiting for him to come.

When the sun began to set above her skin, the sound of the garden gate groaning rose to her ears.

The man sat down in the garden.

"I only have five minutes today."

"Come inside."

"No time for that."

"You don't get to decide how long five minutes is. The clock doesn't either. When I say it's been five minutes, you can go. If I say you still have time, you still have time."

The man did not take off his shoes. He looked up at the cedar trees.

"I guess the ilbon saram planted these when they built the shrine."

"That was when I was eleven, so maybe fourteen years ago."

The man looked at her face in silence. She was beautiful. She was less than five foot three and slender, but she had smooth, silky skin and breasts that looked ample even under a chima. Her thick, black eyebrows highlighted her almond eyes, making her look, from the eyes at least, like a determined young girl, but the thinly sketched bridge of her nose and her lips, like a cherry blossom in bloom, softened the overall impression of her face.

"Mi-ryeong."

He said her name for the first time.

The woman looked at his face in silence. She knew her own beauty. She wanted him to look at her more. She didn't want to leave his sight. She wanted him not to look at any other woman. She wanted to fill his eyes.

She pulled the strings and let her jeogori slide from her shoulders, opened the collar of her undergarment, and exposed her breasts.

"Yong-ha."

She said his name for the first time.

"Yong-ha, Yong-ha, Yong-ha, Yong-ha."

She whispered, gasped, moaned his name, tears falling from the corners of her eyes. The droplets fell like rain on the valley of her breasts, tinged with the evening sun. Faced with this beauty, he could not even reach out to touch. She was the one who reached out. Their shadows, melted together, called each other's names as they stretched out in the dusk and began gently, gently to move.

The woman realized she was now standing in the sun, but she did not try to move into the shade. Is there anything more terrifying than the light of the sun, that another day has dawned? Today she must wait again. Waiting drained more from her than standing in the sun on a bright day.

Soon, his son would climb those stone stairs up to the shrine to pray and clean. She had never seen his son's face before, but she was certain she would know him when she saw him. Holding in her mind the face of the man she saw every day and that of his wife, who she had seen only once, she waited for their eldest son to walk up those steps.

The spring breeze lifted up the hem of her chima, inflating it. A girl with a ponytail walked up the steps, looking up at her. Then, not more than a few minutes later, the steps were full of boys with short hair, and she spotted their teacher too. Some students greeted her with an "Ohayō gozaimasu"; she grinned at them and said, "Annyeong."

"Don't get in the way, stay in two lines on the left," the teacher shouted, and the students grouped to the left. The teacher began to sing a military song, shaking his fist, and the students proceeded toward the shrine, singing.

Our regimental flags are streaming
The marks are all the Rising Sun!
The more our flags are torn with shots
The more honors we get in the field
You, Japanese soldier,
Don't be behind your flags!
Go on until the very end
Go on until your heroic end
Don't cower behind your flags
What do we have to fear?
What shall threaten us?

She didn't know these words. In order not to step on her chima, fluttering in the wind, she took each step carefully as she started walking down. When their song had passed by Yeongnamnu and cut into the arbor, one boy came running up the stone stairs.

That's him, her heart screamed, jumping in her chest.

The sound of his panting came closer.

"Annyeong," she called to him. You're late!

His chest swung side to side as he ran, taking it two steps at a time. The sound of his panting joined in her mind with the sound of his father's. The wind blew harder. Her chima wrapped itself around her legs, the strings of her jeogori chasing after the boy, *haneul haneul, haneul haneul, haneul haneul.*

When the sun was right above the cedar trees, the man came to her house. She gave him a cup of chunseol tea where he sat in the garden and asked him carefully:

"So what name did you choose?"

He did not let the startle he felt show as he sipped the tea.

"Haven't decided yet."

His face was like a bolted gate, and while she looked at it, words she had not yet thought began to spill out of her mouth.

"You have to pick a name quickly and use it a lot, the baby isn't fully in this world yet, he's between this one and the other, you know, the god of death is calling him the name he had before birth and you should be calling him his new name, it's like tug-of-war."

To shut her up the man stuck his hand inside her blue chima. She relaxed her thighs under her chima, leaned her head against a post, and closed her eyes.

"Open your eyes."

She looked at the face of the man between her legs.

"No." She pushed his face away with both of her hands, but she could not pull her hips away. She put her fingers in his hair, gripping lightly and writhed.

"Aigu, forgive me . . ." The woman clasped her hands over his ears so he wouldn't hear her gasp. The cedar trees sighed, shaking their branches; the two pillows in the bedroom grew tired of waiting.

From under his body, she heard the sound of falling water.

The straw-thatched roof has sucked in the rain, become full and now it is falling, she thought, so how long has it been raining for? When they were in the garden there hadn't been a cloud in the sky. What time is it? Have we really been making love that long? But why is all the water falling in the same place? It always dripped from the edge of the eaves behind the bedroom, drip, drip, drip, drip.

The man wiped the sweat from his eyes with the back of his hand and sped the movements of his hips. She could not hear the water falling anymore. She clung to his body slick with sweat, her back arching with a cry.

The man pressed his lips to her eyelids, then dressed. She heard his footsteps growing farther away and the garden gate closing, yet she stayed as she was. She could no longer hear the water. Perhaps it was just a brief shower. She could smell the rain. She smelled it more now that it had lifted than when it was pouring down. The same as his sweat.

She raised her body up by her elbows and sat naked in front of the mirror. Traces of his fingers remained on her arms and shoulders, and of his lips on her nipples, stinging from being suckled too much.

You are not mine but I am yours, so brand me with your lips and fingers; if not . . .

If not, then what?

A yellow butterfly that had flown into the room hovered above the futon. Do the butterflies know the scent of his sweat too? It must be a female, then. The woman slowly put on her underskirt and hemp jeogori, absentmindedly stood and wrapped her wrinkled blue chima around her body, tied the strings on her chest twice, put her arms through the sleeves of her jeogori and tied it. Then, ignoring the butterfly as it tried to fly into the mirror, she gripped a strip of silk in her mouth and tied her hair back. She carefully traced the contours of her mouth with her lipstick brush, then painted her lips a pale peach color; the butterfly, lost, beat its wings into the mirror, yellow dust falling onto the surface.

Holding the hem of her chima, she climbed the rain-slicked stone steps up to Yeongnamnu. As she leaned her body warmed by the sun against the railing at Yeongnamnu, the sky changed from madder red to purple.

No one was by the river. The women gathering clams and picking minari, the men fishing for sweetfish, the boys wrestling, the girls skipping stones, and the old people sitting on the ground watching the river flow by, all had gone home when the rain began to cross the Miryang River.

The woman was alone. With each groan of the pontoon bridge, the sky brightened and the white full moon surfaced above Mount Jongnam. In the darkness, she could see two old ladies walking toward her from the direction of the bridge. Both of their heads hung down like convicts'; one carried something. A baby? No, not a baby. Their white- and peach-colored chimas fluttered as they neared the stone stairs. It's that woman's eomoni. She had spoken to her once while soaking at the Unha Public Baths, so she was certain. The other woman was Bu-san ajumma, who had helped that woman give birth. What were they carrying? It was wrapped in straw and tied with rope at both ends. Oh, it had been three days since the baby was born, she realized, it's time to wash the placenta.

The two old women passed Yeongnamnu, passed the cedar trees, passed the woman's house, and went down the embankment in front of Arang's tower. The water became deep there; it was known as a place where one could catch many eels. The old women grasped the ends of the bundle, swung it two or three times, giving it momentum, then flung the placenta toward the middle of the river. Then, for a few moments, they each pressed their hands together, before going back the way they had come.

Just as Mi-ryeong started to walk down the steps, she heard a woman screaming for help behind her and turned around. There was nobody there. A tepid wind touched her cheek; her skin bristled.

It's Arang's spirit, she thought. It's nearly the anniversary of her death; her spirit has come back. Why should Arang, never embraced by a man or filled with child, look fondly on placentas being washed before her grave? Of course she's angered.

The woman turned her body to the full moon and went down the embankment.

The straw-wrapped placenta bobbed in the depths. It was just close enough that she could fish it toward her with a branch. Pushed out of that woman's body, proof that she and he had been one, their son's home when he had been inside her—the woman broke a willow branch and grasped it tightly.

I should pull it from the straw and sink it, so that her placenta is pecked at by sweetfish, entwined with eels, cut into shreds by crabs!

The placenta floated slowly, slowly away from the woman, escaping; she ran off chasing it. Her rubber boot plunged into a puddle, splashing muddy water onto the hem of her chima, but she did not stop.

A song drifted from the woman's mouth. It was one she had learned from a traveling man from Jeju when they had slept together.

The water that flows from Mount Halla
Has washed over and ruined a thousand trees
Aayan, oya, ohyo

The water that flows in Byeoldopo
Has ruined the anchors of a thousand ships
Aayan, oya, ohyo

The water that flows from my eyes
Has scorched and ruined a thousand hearts
Aayan, oya, ohyo

The sky and the moon and the moon on the surface of the river brought out the spirit of Arang, leaning her body against the railing at Yeongnamnu. Arang did not look at the woman and the placenta. She simply lingered in the beauty of spring, in spring itself.

SIX

The First Seven Days

| 초익레 | 初七日 |

Samsin halmae, full of mercy, please, please, protect this baby fragile as a water bubble so that he may grow up healthy, we are ignorant and know nothing, can do nothing, Samsin halmoni, please protect him, please let him live long, until the hairs on his head turn white.

Bok-yi and Bu-san prayed repeatedly before the altar laden with seaweed soup, white rice, jujubes, grilled sweetfish, rice cakes, and straw, and each time they prayed, they added on a new wish: May this child never worry about money, please watch over him so that he never encounters illness or accidents, please give him the strength to excel in learning. Please give him a hardworking, faithful wife who will bear him many sons. Bok-yi and Bu-san prayed on their knees, pressing their foreheads to the altar, until the smell of the baby's shit filled their noses.

"Oh, oh, somebody pooped. Don't worry, Omma will clean you right up," Hee-hyang said, opening up the baby's baenetjeogori and lifting his legs gently as if they were flower stems.

"This one, even when he poops, he never cries. Woo-cheol cried immediately, letting us all know. This morning, when the birds awoke me, he wasn't crying, but I could smell it. He'd pooped quite some time before and his butt was just red raw. So, please, little man, cry for Omma."

"Oh, what a fragrant smell. Smells just like Omma's milk, doesn't it? Good

boy, what a good little boy." Bok-yi cut a strip of white cloth about thirty centimeters wide and two meters long with scissors and passed it to Hee-hyang.

"I always put my oldest son in diapers. But you, you've had seven kids one
right after another. No time to change diapers at all, might as well just strap
the baby on and let it all fall down your back," Bok-yi said, bundling up the
dirty diaper and putting it in the basket.

"I wonder what the Japanese do. We've got heated floors covered with oiled
paper, so it hardly matters, but they . . ."

"With those tatami mats they have it'd be no laughing matter. I bet they
keep their kids in diapers until they're three."

The two older women were so fascinated by every little thing about the
newborn's tiny body that they forgot they were in the middle of prayers.

"He's a little small," Bu-san said, her eyes narrowing as if appraising him.

"My milk still hasn't really come in yet."

"I know, my dear, that's why you have to eat. Breakfast, snack, lunch, snack,
dinner, snack; you need five or six meals a day or it won't come in."

"She's never eaten much."

"Aigo, what are you talking about? She's got to eat, eat, eat, like a silk-
worm," Bu-san sputtered.

"Well, I'm making her eat. Usually she eats barley rice, and my grandsons
and granddaughter eat the white rice, but since she got pregnant, I've been
making her eat the white rice."

"Before our third son, my nampyeon used to catch eel and carp for me."

"Her husband doesn't like fishing,"

No, he has other pastimes, Hee-hyang silently corrected, then sighed
deeply.

"You want to feed him?" Bu-san asked, interpreting her inability to produce enough milk as the reason for her sigh.

Hee-hyang, engulfed by her own sigh, looked at the baby, her eyes clinging
to its face.

"Bo-geum over in Sammun-dong gave birth a few days ago, so shall we go
ask her?"

"My breasts are full," she said, exposing one and sticking the nipple in the baby's mouth, but the baby fretted, spitting the nipple out, complaining to its mother that her letdown was bad.

"I think the baby's weak latch may have something to do with it, but feeling panicked about it all probably isn't helping either."

"If you can't produce enough yourself, you should get some from someone else. But, my dear, you know, you cannot leave the house until the thirty-seventh day, no matter what; no matter who dies, you must not go to the funeral. If you walk through the gate of a house that's holding a funeral, the baby will start crying the same way you do at the ceremony. Weddings are out too. You cannot eat the food of another house. Whatever's broke around here you must not use a nail, it'll make a hole in the baby's body. And under no circumstances must you throw out the ashes from the hearth. You'd hate for the baby to throw up your milk, wouldn't you?"

"I told her all that back when Woo-cheol was born. She knows already," Bok-yi said.

Hee-hyang's eyes reflected her heart's scattered emotions, but her lips were arranged into the shape of a smile.

"Do you? I thought you might've forgotten all that."

"Bu-san ajumma, aren't you the one who's forgotten? You got so caught up in talking you've forgotten about Samsin halmae."

"Aigo, and in the middle of prayers and everything!" Bu-san hit her knees with her hands and returned to the altar.

"What's left to ask for?" Hee-hyang laughed, changing the atmosphere in the room.

Bok-yi and Bu-san looked at each other.

"Let's see: longevity, fulfillment, fortune . . ."

"And we already prayed for a good wife . . . Well, then, we might—"

"Hold on. I have one last thing."

Hee-hyang took the baby off her breast and laid him on the bed; then, taking care with her midsection, she slowly raised her hands to her forehead, got to her knees, and prostrated herself.

"What are you praying for?" Bu-san asked.

"I can't say it." Hee-hyang sighed, her voice sinking.

The baby began to cry hoarsely.

"Oh, what an awful lot of tears."

"And such big old drops from those teeny eyes." Bok-yi wiped his tears away with a cotton cloth, cradling him in her arms, and the baby stopped crying.

"About the name," Bu-san began.

Hee-hyang said nothing. She looked at the face of her son in Bok-yi's arms. She felt that if she looked away from him he would fall and scatter like cherry blossoms. My heart has been gouged. So deep that it cannot heal. But somehow we're connecting. When I look at his face, somehow.

Bok-yi also said nothing. Bu-san could only listen to the two women's silence.

"Daddy, hurry up and give me a name," Bok-yi said, gently shaking the baby's right hand clasped around her index finger.

"I think he's just got his mind on other things," Hee-hyang said, as if it did not concern her.

"You've given him a son, what else could his mind be on?" Bok-yi said sharply.

"Where is he, anyway?"

"He was in the shop just a while ago . . ." Bu-san looked at Bok-yi's face, seeming concerned.

Hee-hyang sat down in front of the mirror. "I'll go have a look," she said, speaking to her mother in the reflection as she twisted her hair up with a silver hairpin with a lucky bird decoration.

"I'll make dinner tonight. It's the seventh-day celebration, so I want Woo-cheol and So-won to have lots of good food. Let's buy some sweetfish. I'll serve it sliced raw. You can only eat sweetfish in the spring, so it would be a shame not to eat lots of it now. Then I'll fry onions and garlic chives and, oh, we must get some ssuktteok."

Hee-hyang's vision blurred, dots and blotches of light floating and blending before her. She did not realize she was crying until the tears reached her mouth and she tasted their saltiness. When she picked up the gourd to draw water from the well, she felt a heavy pain pressing down on the muscles of her shoulders and neck. She'd had a difficult birth, without a moment where she wasn't straining every muscle from her forehead down to the tips of her toes; she had gritted and ground her teeth so hard that she had burst blood vessels in her face, and all the while he was—she could not cry, if she cried she would be carried away by sadness, crying, she could not take leave of herself now, not when she had three children to care for. Hee-hyang washed her face with the well water; then, gingerly, as if stepping across a river, she proceeded to the garden.

The older women gazed at the face of the baby, who was beginning to drift off to sleep, his arms raised above his head as if cheering.

"People are starting to talk," Bu-san said, dropping her voice.

"Hope their talk doesn't make it here."

"It's a small town, and it's been going on for nearly two years."

"Oh, Hee-hyang knows. But if Woo-cheol and So-won find out . . ."

"Aigu, they'll find out soon enough. You can't keep mouths under lock and key."

Bok-yi inhaled sharply, held the breath, then exhaled deeply, before taking another sharp breath. The joints of her hands, resting in her persimmon-colored chima, were white from the force with which she clenched them.

When Hee-hyang opened the back door, Yong-ha was sitting on a stool and sewing a black school cap of the sort worn by Japanese children.

"Honey." The voice that came from her mouth was so soft and sweet it surprised even her.

"Are you all right?"

"Yes, from today I can handle water again, and meals can go back to normal too."

"And your mother?"

"Eomoni's going to stay a little while longer. There are still so many things I can't do for the time being, and she's worried about the baby too."

"She's a big help," Yong-ha murmured, turning back to the hat.

"Honey."

"What is it?" Yong-ha stopped his hand holding the needle and coughed slightly as if trying to clear something from his throat.

"Please give the baby a name."

"Yes, I've been thinking about that—how about Woo-gun? Using the characters for *rain* and *root*."

"Woo-gun . . . ," she repeated.

"You don't like it?"

She paused. "No, I think it's a good name."

"I'm going to have to head out for a bit now. I should be back in a little under an hour."

"Oh, I see. . . . Danyeooseyo."

Yong-ha went out into the light-filled street. The spring wind had plastered cherry blossom petals to the glass door, torn them off, then stuck them back again. Soon Bu-san ajumma would come take her place at the store and she would have to go do the shopping, but her hips were strangely heavy as a millstone. Hee-hyang lowered herself onto the stool where Yong-ha had just been sitting and picked up the school cap, needle still stuck in it. Had that man been thinking about a name for his son as he sewed, or had he been thinking of something else, stitch, stitch, stitch?

"Woo-gun." Hee-hyang tried saying her son's name out loud. It sounded nice, but something about it made her feel it was an unlucky name. Innumerable raindrops falling from a pitch-black sky, becoming countless white roots growing in the pitch-black earth—Hee-hyang shuddered, her hand going to her abdomen. Instinctively she tried to protect her stomach, as if she were still pregnant. Her stomach was soft and flabby, like an inflatable ball that had been flattened.

Woo-gun was supposed to have three brothers, not just Woo-cheol. They're gone, but I can't make it so they'd never lived. I carried them in my womb, birthed them with this body, held them in these arms, gave them these breasts to suckle—

For only one day had Woo-seon nursed and cried; the second day of his life, he had just slept and slept, never making a whimper, until he passed away in his sleep on the third day. His white baenetjeogori became his burial clothes.

Su-yong had been a smiley baby. He smiled when their eyes had met; he smiled when that man gave him a ride on his shoulders, when Woo-cheol tickled him, even when he peed. Su-yong in his baby shoes, running and laughing—Mama, rice. No go night-night. Mama, hold! Owside, wawk. Doggy, good, come. Look! Birdy, lots! Mama, look! One year and six months. April 14; the following day was Su-yong's death day.

Su-yong. Woo-seon. Their names are carved on my body. Su-yong. Woo-seon. But not on his. Whatever he loses, whatever he ruins, he himself remains forever untouched. That's why he can do what he does, all the things he does. . . .

Through the gap in the door that Yong-ha hadn't closed properly, one petal snuck in, whirling through the air and falling at Hee-hyang's feet. Hee-hyang looked at the image of herself reflected dimly in the glass door and felt a sadness that she thought might strangle her. A woman neither ugly nor beautiful, neither old nor young, a woman who turned no heads as she walked down the street—rumor had it that the other woman was young and beautiful. Rumor had it that Hee-hyang was pitiful. Each time the rumors reached her ears, she imagined the woman a little more beautiful than before. She had never seen her. In reality, she's probably not that pretty.

Do I want to see? Do I want to go look? Now?

Suddenly, she saw her husband's hand stretching across a woman's stomach, white and flat as paper, and Hee-hyang crushed the flower petal with the toe of her rubber boot. I don't want to see her face! Why should I? If she dared show her face in this very store, I wouldn't look! I want to send that woman and her face off into darkness the same as I'd blow a candle out.

A gust of wind blew in; Hee-hyang looked up. An old woman in a dark-blue-and-white kimono and dark brown obi was standing in front of the store. It was the ilbon saram midwife who had delivered her baby. Hee-hyang lifted her heavy hips and opened the door.

"I was near, so I thought I'd drop by."

Hee-hyang felt her voice squirming on her tongue. Ohayō, kon'nichi wa, arigatō, shitsurei shimasu, sumimasen, o-kanjō, wakarimasen: all the Japanese words she knew added together wouldn't help her talk to an ilbon saram. And Woo-cheol and So-won wouldn't be home until after two.

"O-kagen wa dō desu ka?" *How are you feeling?*

Mistaking *o-kagen* for *okane*, "money," Hee-hyang flushed and looked at the ground.

"Okane, jom gidaryeojuseyo," Hee-hyang said.

"Oh, you can pay anytime."

Hee-hyang hesitated. "How much?"

"Whatever you feel. All I did was help. How is the baby? If you don't mind, I'd like to see him."

Hee-hyang passed through the garden and showed the midwife to the bedroom. When she opened the door, the two old women stopped whispering. Bok-yi stood and bowed, but Bu-san went as pale as a peeled potato and merely smoothed the wrinkles of her chima with her hands.

"Well, he looks very well indeed. Oh, he's opened his eyes." The ilbon saram midwife smiled, the wrinkles on her face multiplying.

Hee-hyang looked at the midwife's face from the side. Her wrinkles were deepest at the corners of her eyes and the sides of her mouth, while her brow was smooth as wax. The face of a happy woman, Hee-hyang thought. If you keep a smile as the years go by, this is how you look.

"Has your milk come in?" the midwife asked.

Hee-hyang tilted her head.

Bok-yi and Bu-san looked at each other silently, ears turned as if listening in on noises in the next room.

"Your milk, has it come in?" The midwife lifted her shriveled breasts in both hands and made a suckling sound with her lips.

Hee-hyang shook her head.

"Open your shirt a little and lie down," the midwife said, using gestures to get her words across.

Hee-hyang opened her mouth and hesitated for a moment; then she undid the tie and opened her undershirt, unbuttoned her underskirt, and lay down on the bedding. Bok-yi and Bu-san began to let go of the breaths they had been holding as they watched the midwife's blotchy, wrinkled hands massage Hee-hyang's breasts, pushing into pressure points.

"Now, sit up and try to feed your boy."

Hee-hyang pressed her left nipple to Woo-gun's lips. He began to make little suckling noises, and from the gap between her breast and his bright red lips, not yet fully latched, white fluid came gushing out.

"Right, now try the other side."

Hee-hyang tried to get him off her left breast, but Woo-gun was now latched on tightly and didn't want to move.

"Woo-gun, time for the other side now," Hee-hyang said to the baby in Korean. "Look, listen to what your mother tells you. In a minute you can drink all you want, so come on now, just let go, please!"

The moment she finally managed to pull him away, her milk shot out, hitting the midwife in the face.

"Aigu!" Bu-san shouted.

"Aigu, mianhamnida," Bok-yi said, and hurried to wipe the midwife's face with a white cloth.

The corners of the midwife's mouth lifted, and a smile slowly spread to Bok-yi's eyes; the two women faced each other and exploded. Bu-san laughed so much her shoulders shook, and Hee-hyang threw her head back, laughing too. The four women's bodies shook and twisted; they held their stomachs and kicked their feet under their chimas; they carried on laughing until Woo-gun began to cry in surprise at the top of his lungs.

"Well, good, I'm glad that's improved." The midwife took a handkerchief from the sleeve of her kimono and dabbed at the tears under her eyes.

"Thank you for your help," Bok-yi said in Korean, still choking with laughter as she bowed her head to the midwife.

"Woo-gun, oh, Woo-gun," Hee-hyang said, grasping the baby to her chest, as if trying to stifle the laughter still rising from it.

"Woo-gun?" Bok-yi said, her laugh now successfully shrunk to a smile. "So his father has given him a name. Woo-gun. Oh, what a nice name. Woo-gun. Woo-gun . . ."

"Is his name Woo-gun, then? What characters have you used?"

Hee-hyang traced the characters for *rain* and *root* in the midwife's palm with her pointer finger.

"That's a lovely name. Rain is a blessing from the heavens, and roots drink in that rain, making trees and grass and flowers grow tall. His father must've chosen the name out of hope that his son will grow up healthy."

Hee-hyang tilted her ear to the midwife's voice. She didn't understand what the woman was saying, but she knew that she was praising her son's name. Just knowing that made her so happy she wanted to cover her face and cry. Since giving birth, she could not keep a lid on her feelings. Her anger would soon boil over; her sadness, too, kept overflowing its brim.

"If I stay too long, I'll keep the baby from eating, so I'd best be on my way now," the midwife said, gathering the hem of her kimono and standing.

Bok-yi saw the midwife out.

"I'm going to go out and do a little shopping," Hee-hyang said to Bu-san ajumma. "Please look after Woo-gun until Mother gets back. I'm sorry, but could you please cover for me in the store?"

"You've just given birth, dear, so take care. Don't catch a cold."

For the first time in ten days, Hee-hyang picked up her purse and bundle and went outside. At the market she bought mugwort rice cakes, at Dongyong she got a little garlic chives and green onions, and by the time she had finished buying some sweetfish from Sang-chong's house on the other side of the river, the sun was half hidden behind Mount Wooryeong.

Hee-hyang stopped on the embankment. The cherry trees along the riverside were just starting to sprout leaves, but the ones the ilbon saram had planted on the temple grounds were in full bloom now, and with each rush of wind they shook off pink petals. They were thin and round, a different species than Korean cherry trees, Hee-hyang thought. She turned her eyes from the cherry trees to Yeongnamnu, then from Yeongnamnu to the cedar trees, and timidly descended. The sun had set, yet the lights were not on. If he hadn't returned to the store yet, then he must still be in there, in the darkness with that woman— Hee-hyang could see the woman's house and her own house at the same time.

This close! The anger blurred her vision; the trunks of the cedars looked like they were heaving. Hee-hyang felt tears welling up. Haneunim, please, crying here would be all too pathetic, please, let these tears stay in my eyes and never reach my cheeks—she looked up at the moon until her eyes dried, when suddenly the bundles in her hands became heavy and Hee-hyang sank to the ground next to the pontoon bridge. The water flowed, it would repeat, she would endure, and the next day, like water flowing, the pain would return, she would endure, it would repeat—maybe he's testing me, to see how much she could take. He's not doing it openly, nor is he hiding it. Because look how close her house is; he's committing adultery somewhere less than ten minutes from home. Hee-hyang flung the tears dripping from the tip of her nose off to the water's surface.

That first night he untied my blouse and I started to take off my chima, I made a vow to my ancestors. I pledged to spend my life with this man, to share my sorrows and joys with him until one of our lives ends; I vowed to be his wife.

Hee-hyang stood up, keeping the other woman's house out of her sight, and crossed the pontoon bridge. The cicadas keened. The wind blew; the hem of her chima fluttered. And suddenly, Hee-hyang felt the lower half of her body become as weightless as the wind. There was a woman in white standing on Yeongnamnu. For a second she thought it was the other woman, but no, it was Arang. Watching her. She did not feel surprised or afraid. Her pulse did not race. The smell of flowers floated in the air, along with sadness. The same smell as when Su-yong died. Hee-hyang breathed in deeply the atmosphere quivering with sadness and began to sing Arirang.

The bird crying in the pine trees   sounds so sad
Does it suffer   the curse of Arang?

Ari, arirang   suri, surirang   arariga nanne
Coming over the Arirang Pass

The moon that falls on Yeongnamul   is clear but
The Namcheong River just   flows silently

Breathing became easier, and all the visible things and all the invisible things started to play their sounds: joljol joljol   maengkkong maengkkong   eummae eummae   jaecheobio jaecheop   eungae eungae. Woo-gun is calling for me, she realized. Hee-hyang's breasts were swollen with milk.

SEVEN

The Third Seven Days

| 삼칠일 | 三七日 |

A white figure could be seen coming out of the house by the cedar trees. It was three in the morning; all the roosters were asleep with their heads tucked under their wings, and all the women who would prepare breakfast still asleep too with their heads on their begae. The figure was a woman in a white jeoksam and sokchima. She stooped next to the well and drew water from it with the gourd, carefully transferring it to an earthenware pot and taking it to the garden. Then she slithered out of her clothes, hanging them on a branch of rose of Sharon, brought her fingers to her hair, and loosened her braid. The waves of black hair that now fell to just below her ass stood in contrast to the paleness of her naked body.

She scooped the water and poured it over her head once, then again. Immediately her pale skin turned as red as if she had been beaten, but the woman continued to pour the water over herself intently, singing something to herself as she went.

Now changed into a dark blue chima jeogori with a sseugaechima covering her head, she arranged the bowls of jeonghwasu, seaweed soup, three bowls of white rice, and the mortuary tablet on the altar built at the northern end of her bedroom, then struck a match and lit the candles.

Ancestors, I pray, I pray, please let me have that man's child, somehow, please, let me have a boy.

The woman shouldered a large bundle and hurried down the road by the riverside. She had to climb Mount Yongdu and find the source of its spring water before the birds and dogs began to cry. The ritual had to be done in a secret place or it wouldn't work, so she had to go and come back without being seen by anyone. It was pitch-dark.

But I can walk there without stumbling. Because my spirit rushes on and on ahead of me, like a lamp lighting the way.

She made no noise. As if she were walking on the bottom of the sea. All the houses and trees and flowers and people had sunk down there too.

And that man and that man's wife and that man's children, all of them, all—but, the truth is, I alone am sinking. My voice cannot be heard by anyone. If I cried for help now it would only float to the surface as bubbles.

She felt that if she had his baby, if she had a baby boy who looked just like him, she would be pulled out of the water. When the baby is pushed out with the amniotic fluid and gives his first cry, my voice will come back to life too. That man leaves silence in his wake.

Of course I'm drowning in it. And he's probably never even wondered how much I'm sinking into that silence. I fall to my knees, hug them to my chest, I spread my knees and receive him, but all the while I am nothing but a fish in a bucket smacking its mouth.

And when he is not here, I see his eyes, I hear his voice, I smell his scent, I feel him. The feel of his canines, sharp as I thought when I touched them with my tongue to check, and of his hot tongue, lapping like a dog's as it drinks water— if the desire passed down in her body, her thighs would melt and she wouldn't be able to walk, so she had to walk as if walking away from him.

Suddenly, a light flickered upstream and floated off. Her heart was beating hard; she opened her eyes wide trying to see through the darkness. What was it? Dokkaebibul, a will-o'-the-wisp? Just the moonlight playing on the river? No, it was brighter than that. She was scared. But it wasn't as frightening as lying still in her bed. When she lay still, the fear caressed her heart as gently as a feather. When she was seized by the fear that he would not come again the next day, wherever she looked frightened her, and she became unable even to open her eyes.

And if he doesn't come tomorrow, I will never be able to have his baby and will eternally be left behind in my inner voice. When the fear becomes so huge that I cannot suppress or forget it, then there is nothing to do but something like this. Even now, the fear was so close to her that she could almost feel it by her side, but it could not be inside her. If it nestled inside her and became one with her, she knew it would surely kill him, his wife, or her.

She would do anything to have his child. If you stole a scrap of the cloth used to clean a coffin at a funeral and wore it you could conceive, aireul ganneunda; if you took the fruit from a branch growing eastward of a mulberry bush from another person's garden and ate them, aireul ganneunda; if you took shavings from the nose of a stone sculpture of the Buddha and boiled them and drank the water, aireul ganneunda; if you turned a tiger's tooth into a decoration and wore it over your chest, aireul ganneunda; if you stole the underwear of a woman who had many children, aireul ganneunda, aireul, aireul, aireul ganneunda, if on the seventh and seventeenth of every month you held a mountain ritual without being seen, aireul ganneunda. That day was neither the seventh nor the seventeenth. But she had wanted, regardless, to start that day. Because it was the day of celebration for the baby's first three weeks of life. Because it was the day the geumjul at his gates would come down.

She gathered the hems of her chima, tied it on both sides, and walked up the mountain path. As she walked the narrow way between the pines and saw-tooth oaks that blocked the moonlight, their shadows melding with the darkness and deepening it, suddenly, she heard a noise that sounded like it had been wrung from the throat of a strangled woman, as something flapped its way over her head. A horned owl. She put her hand to her chest and breathed deeply, trying to tear away the fear that had stuck itself tightly to her; her hands flew to the unkempt hair tucked into her collar, brushing it away.

Calm down, calm down now. Nothing to be frightened of, nothing at all.

Look   look   look at me
Like a flower that blooms midwinter   look at me

Ari, arirang   suri, surirang   arariga nanne
Coming over the Arirang Pass

Having finally met him
I could not hear a word he said   I was so shy

She stumbled over the root of a tree, interrupting her singing. The woman stretched her back and slowed her pace, going onward with her eyes fixed on the path that continued upward. Almost the moment she entered the mountain her legs and lungs were already crying out. The backs of her calves and thighs hurt. She turned her chin up but could not see the crescent moon or the stars through the branches and leaves, right, left, oreunjjok, oenjjok, oreunjjok, oenjjok, as she walked a feeling of sleepiness rose up from her feet. She had not slept since that evening, when she had drifted off in his arms. The night before, too, she had been unable to sleep.

Maybe I should take a break. But if I stop now I'll fall asleep against a tree trunk.

Mi-ryeong!

She turned and looked back over her shoulder. No one there, no reason for anyone to be there, not this deep in the mountains. She rubbed her eyes with the back of her hand, but in her agony, she could see only two things: her left and right feet, chafed by her straw sandals and smeared with blood.

Left, right, oreunjjok, oenjjok, oh, Yong-ha, Yong-ha, Yong-ha, Yong-ha, I don't really know whether I want my wish to have your son fulfilled or if I want to be set free from it. Yesterday, I turned my back on your words when you said, "Ganda," *I'm going.* You put your arms around my body, buried my face in your thighs, and moaned. "Of course I wish we were always together, Mi-ryeong, I don't want to leave you, Mi-ryeong." It was your voice, next to my ear, everywhere. "Mi-ryeong, you're so beautiful. This part of you, and this, and this, all of you belongs to me."

She realized she had stepped in mud and looked around her. Water gushed out from between two big rocks, forming a little spring.

She unwrapped her bundle, taking out the items for the ritual and placing them on top of the rocks from which the spring water gushed; she arranged the white rice, jujubes, rice cakes, and dried pollack roe, then placed the candles in their holders and struck a match.

Without concern for dirtying her chima jeogori, she turned toward Samshindang, folded her knees, put her forehead and both her palms to the ground, and repeated her prayer.

Sansinnimkke, I pray, I pray, please let me have his baby, somehow, please, let me have a boy.

From a straw bundle she grabbed a fish, a galchi, and threw it at an old sawtooth oak tree. Aireul ganneunda! The galchi fell to the ground, not even grazing a branch. *Kphwik.* It hit the rock, making a useless, horrible noise. She had heard that if you threw a fish and hit a tree branch you would conceive, and she'd gone and bought a galchi as long as a snake, and yet! She grasped the fish by the head and swung. *Kphwik.* No matter how many times she threw the galchi, it did not reach the branch. *Kphwik.*

She threw the galchi again, and the moment that it gently bounced off a branch of a pine tree that was not much bigger than she was, rain began to fall. Thinking it was her own sweat, she wiped at her forehead with the sleeve of her jeogori, but she wiped and wiped and yet it still ran down her face. When the rain began to hit harder, rustling all the leaves, she turned her palm skyward for the first time.

Rain, the heavens' answer, my wish will be fulfilled, I will have his baby.

With her whole body draped in rain she descended the mountain smiling. Oreunjjok, oenjjok, oreunjjok, oenjjok.

The rain fell, dissolving the darkness that precedes the dawn, and chose to stop when the woman reached the riverbank. The ashen morning sun peeked through a break in the clouds, and moment by moment the ring of light spread.

She breathed in the smell of morning. Morning had its own smell, quite aside from the smells of doenjangguk and kimchi on the breakfast table. It had been a while since she'd happened to meet a morning.

Since I met him I have painted over all my mornings and afternoons into nights, into darkness. *Kkokkio*, a rooster crowed. I have to get home before the women lift their heads from their pillows, if anyone sees me, it will all have been for nothing. Please don't let me be seen by anyone. *Kkokkio!* Oh, rooster, please don't crow till I'm home, do what you can to help my wish come true.

· · ·

Anger squirmed inside her heart, waking her up. The anger always awoke earlier than the roosters, shaking her until she got up. Hee-hyang turned over, her face stiff with rage. Still asleep. His hair had grown considerably, and his eyebrows, which hadn't been there at birth, were now thick.

He looks like me around the eyes, I suppose, but when he's got them closed like that he looks just like that man.

Yesterday he sought out my body. When he stuck his hand inside my jeoksam and took my breast into his palm, I rolled over, turning my back to him, but he wrapped his arm around me from behind and started to rub my breasts. With the same hands that rub her breasts, touch her down there, open her legs, mess up her hair. The same hands. No matter how I try to let him in, my skin rebels. When he pushed up my jeoksam and took my nipple into his mouth, my boiling rage overflowed from my throat. My legs pried open by his legs, I braced them so that my body would not shake, so as not to call out I paced my breaths with the darkness behind my eyelids—

Mngh, ah, ah. Woo-gun spread his palm, trying to grasp something. *Ah, ah.* His eyes were not yet open. He's peed or pooped and now he's uncomfortable, she guessed. Hee-hyang lifted her head from the pillow and gently pulled back the blanket, bringing her nose close to the lower half of the baby's body. She smelled nothing; maybe he was hungry? How long ago was he fed? He had started crying in the middle of feeding. There was the smell of shit, and then that man had left the room. What time was that? She had wiped Woo-gun up and changed his diaper, then nursed him back to sleep. It had still been dark out, so perhaps it had been somewhere around three in the morning.

Woo-gun, today it's three weeks since you were born. When you open your eyes, Omma will have to get up, so until then show me your precious little sleeping face. Omma's going to be very busy today. In a little bit your halmoni is going to come over to help, and when she gets here, first we're gonna take down the geumjul and burn it by the riverside, and then we'll make breakfast for your abeoji and hyung and noona, and then we have to give you a bath. And that's when the hard part starts; all our relatives and neighbors are coming to see you. Halmoni has made you some new clothes and a wrap, so you're gonna be all dressed up today.

Woo-gun stretched in his sleep; startled by his own movement, his half-closed eyes opened. Hee-hyang got up to her knees, placed her left hand under his neck, fingers splayed, placed her right hand under his buttocks, then slowly, gently, pulled him up close to her own body.

"It's morning, Woo-gun."

Hee-hyang shifted her left hand from supporting his neck and rested his head in the crook of her elbow, bringing her face closer to his as she spoke.

"Jal jani."

Woo-gun raised the corners of his lips, looking happy.

"You smiled! Your first smile! Was it funny when Omma said that to you? Jal jani! Woo-gun, so many people are coming to see you today. They're all happy that you're a healthy, growing boy, and they're going to celebrate with us!"

Woo-gun stretched a hand up toward his mother's face.

"Smile for me again, Woo-gun. Jal jani!"

Woo-gun smiled, and Hee-hyang smiled back at him as if making a promise.

"Jal jani."

The baby yawned so broadly that his face creased between his eyes and nose, sinking back into sleep in his mother's arms. Hee-hyang moved her right hand from supporting his buttocks to his back, gently pulled her left elbow until his neck was supported by the palm of her hand, lowering the baby's body while taking care to keep him level, until she placed his bottom on the bed and slowly laid his upper body down. Gingerly freeing her arm from under his bottom and her hand from his neck, Hee-hyang pressed her lips to Woo-gun's cheek and lay down.

Woo-gun, your omma's not happy, but I've got you and Woo-cheol and So-won, so I'm not unhappy either; you are my life, and if the unthinkable happened, Omma couldn't go on, I'd have no reason to live. Su-yong and Woo-seon, at rest in your graves, please, do what you can for your brother, give him your strength so that he can live long enough and happily enough for the both of you.

As Hee-hyang listened to the faint sounds of Woo-gun sleeping, breathing in the smell of his milk-scented breath, she felt her thoughts melt away against the warmth of the baby's skin. When all the strength in her mind and body felt as if they had gone right out of her, Hee-hyang found herself floating faceup on the surface of the Miryang River, gazing up at the bright blue sky.

Jal jani, she greeted the sky, and it glimmered laughingly.

When the night sky covered the town like a lid, shutting the river and mountains and houses up in darkness, the woman who had been waiting at length in the garden heard the sound of the gate opening and watched the silhouette of the man approaching.

"Today was market day—I've been so busy I didn't even have time to eat. The goods I bought from the wholesaler in Busan came in on the nine o'clock train, so I had to run to the station with my cart, load everything up, and run back...."

"You poor thing..."

Lies, she thought. There are six market days a month, but never before had he not come to her before sunset. Why lie when there was no need to make excuses? Did he really think she didn't know?

"He looks so much like you."

"Eh?"

She laughed.

"Where did you see him?"

"Oh, not the baby, of course, silly. Not while the geumjul's still up and the baby still can't leave the house. Where would I have seen him? I simply passed your oldest at Yeongnamnu. It was bound to happen someday, wasn't it? I live so close, after all. Why are you pulling that face?"

She reached her hand toward his, but the moment their fingers met, he turned his face and sighed deeply. In his silence, her mind raced.

I must keep what I did in the mountains a secret, I've heard some couples pray together, but I am not his wife; she's his wife, Park Hee-hyang. His oldest son's name is Woo-cheol, his youngest is Woo-gun, his daughter is So-won.

No one outside of his family knows the name of the boy who died just after we got together. He was buried in the aejangteo, without even a funeral. I heard he had another son buried there, but that was a few years before we met. That woman bore him four boys and one girl; she's good at producing heirs. . . .

"April, May, June . . . it's almost summer."

"Yes."

"I've never set foot outside of Miryang, you know."

"I assume that's true for most women here."

"If we're still together by the summer, take me to Busan, will you? I want to get out of Miryang, take a train ride, see the sea."

"Right."

"Just once I want us to spend the night together and see the morning with you."

She wrapped her arms around him and pressed her ear to his chest, listening to his heartbeat. What she'd just said, had she really said it aloud? Or had she instead just whispered it in her mind?

Hee-hyang usually only put in one cup **hana** of the rice but now scooped **hana, dul, set** into the bisque pot, then another **hana, dul, set** of well water, submerging the rice; then, she washed the rice with her hand, as if scrubbing the inside of the brimming pot, rustling it; she poured out the cloudy water, then again *rustle, rustle, rustle.* She got the bamboo basket and scooped **hana, dul, set, net, daseot, yeoseot, ilgob** of the wheat she had boiled three days before and dried under the eaves, then added it to the pot on top of the drained rice.

Sister, oh, big sister, how is marriage treating you?
Sister, oh, little sister, please don't ask
A wife leads the life of a dog
Mountain ash in one field, chili peppers in the other
Both will cause you pain
But not as much as being a wife
It is hard to cook rice in a watermelon
It is hard to put chopsticks on a rickety tray

Hee-hyang sang as she gathered pine twigs and needles from where they were dried and stored behind the house and threw them in the range, tossing in a lit match and working the bellows until scarlet flames rose and the smoke from the pine needles snuck into her hair and inside her jeogori. The charcoal in the brazier just wouldn't turn red for her. She crouched down, working the bellows hard again, and the coals reddened before her eyes and the water in the pot began to boil. She plunged the minari she had picked that morning into the water in the washbasin, removing the grit, then sank it in the boiling water with chopsticks; now, time for that ninety sen's worth of beef. Hee-hyang placed it on the chopping board and sliced it thinly, *ttok ttok ttok ttok*, then put sesame oil into a tin pan and in the scant amount of time before it began to sizzle, *jigeul jigeul*, she put the minari in a bamboo sieve and poured cold water over it, then wrung the greens with her hand to remove the moisture, before putting them in a small bowl and seasoning them with salt and soy sauce. One dish done. She stir-fried the beef in the now-sizzling oil, took the seaweed from the pot where it had been soaking and chopped it, *song song*, then added it and the water to the pan with the beef. Now she just had to wait for it to simmer. The sweetfish could wait a while, they lose all flavor when overcooked, but if she did them after the rice and miyeokguk they should be done in time. She arranged the doenjang-pickled garlic on a dish; the maneuljangajji was ready. Hee-hyang rolled up the sleeves of her jeogori and went over to the earthenware pots, opening the lid of the largest one and pulling out some baechu kimchi, stained bright red.

> *I go fifty ri to draw water*
> *Ten ri to pound the rice*
> *Keep fires going under nine kettles*
> *Fold the bedding in twelve rooms*
> *It's tough to walk 'cross a log bridge*
> *But a father-in-law is tougher once crossed*
> *A tree's new leaves are blue-green*
> *But not as much as my mother-in-law's veins*

The seaweed began to *bing bing* around in the hot soup and the beef's brown scum began to rise, *bugeul bugeul*. Hee-hyang removed the scum with a ladle, and just when it began to simmer she added a pinch of salt and tasted the soup. Masitda, so good, beef really did have a richness that chicken couldn't compete with. She put a lid on the nickel silver pot containing the miyeokguk and set it to the side of the stove; when she took the lid off the iron pot, white steam arose, *morak morak*, and engulfed her face.

Almost done cooking, better reduce the heat.

She pushed the pine kindling to each side of the stove with a pole to bring down the flames, then cracked **hana, dul, set, net, daseot** eggs, still warm, and mixed the whites and yolks well, sprinkled on sesame oil, salt, and the green onion she'd finely chopped, *ttok ttok ttok ttok*, then put it all on top of the rice and put the lid back on. In five minutes the steamed egg would be ready; she had to take care not to leave it too long, or it would be no good.

Now for the sweetfish. Hee-hyang put the grill on the brazier, grabbed a live sweetfish from the basin, and pierced it with a bamboo skewer from the mouth, then did the same for the rest: **hana, dul, set, net, daseot**. When she blew into the mouth of the brazier, the mouths of the sweetfish smacked, *ppakkeum ppakkeum*, and the tails flapped, *palttak palttak*; their transparent eyes soon clouded and their scales became blistered from the fire.

My father-in-law is a fierce bird
My mother-in-law is a scolding bird
One sister-in-law is a glaring bird
The other is a pecking bird
My brother-in-law is a moody bird
My husband is a dimwit bird
My child is a crying bird
And I'm the only sulking bird
They'll hear nothing for three years
See nothing for three years
Say nothing for three years
And once you live through all that

Hee-hyang opened the lid of the iron pot and took out the bowl of steamed egg. The egg was just right, and she could smell the delicious scent of egg and sesame oil. All done now, she just needed to dish it up. Hee-hyang set a bowl on the dinner tray and dished up rice with a wooden spoon. White rice for her husband, white rice for Woo-cheol, half rice half barley for So-won, same for her eomoni, and Hee-hyang would have barley. She added the water used to wash the rice back to the pot, which still had rice stuck to the bottom, and put the lid on; with that, she would make Woo-cheol and So-won's favorite, nu-rungbap.

My face was like a pear blossom
Now it's like a pumpkin's yellow bloom
My hair once looked like hemp
Now it's unruly as bush clover
My hands that were like pearls
Now look like a fish's fins
My blue cotton chima is wet with tears
My apron, wet with snot

Hee-hyang let down the rolled-up sleeves of her jeogori, undid her chima from where she'd tied it up above her hips, and wiped the sweat from her face with a hand towel, then picked up Yong-ha's tray and left the kitchen. She didn't hear Woo-gun crying, he must still be sleeping, better feed him while everyone else was eating,

I've been in motion all day, for the fourteen years since I married him, like a spinning top going *baeng baeng baeng*, hitting my own body with a string, going *baeng baeng baeng*, from morning to night *baeng baeng baeng*, until my eyes feel like they're going to fall out of my head, but I can't stop, I'll go on like this till I die, *baeng baeng baeng, baeng baeng baeng*. And even if the ears that once listened to my stories and the heart that once accepted mine are now turned to another woman, *baeng baeng baeng, baeng baeng baeng, baeng baeng baeng*, because my hands are for making those children's meals, my voice is for calling their names, my ears are for hearing their stories, my heart is for accepting theirs, my breasts are for giving him milk.

Only Yong-ha sat cross-legged at a separate tray, while the rest of the family sat around the low dining table. Yong-ha picked up a piece of steamed egg and put it into his mouth, and at that cue, Woo-cheol grabbed a skewer of sweet-fish and So-won took a spoonful of miyeokguk. Talking during dinner was never allowed, but the special food she'd made to celebrate three weeks of Woo-gun's life made the children's eyes glimmer, and without thinking, they shared words of praise.

"Masisseoyo, you know, Miryang sweetfish really do taste different," said Woo-cheol, as he ate.

"They smell slightly of watermelon," Yong-ha said, sounding fatherly.

"Sinnanda, there's beef in this!" So-won's eyes crossed slightly as she stared at the piece of beef in her spoon.

"You really should be thanking Woo-gun. After all, it's his celebration."

"But Woo-gun can't eat any of this. I feel sorry for him." So-won turned her head and looked at her mother, who was leaned up against the wall nursing the baby.

"Woo-gun gets Omma's milk," Hee-hyang said, looking down at his little clam-like palm grasping her nipple. The only times she could breathe a sigh of relief were when she was feeding him or listening to the children speak.

"I hope he gets big soon so he can eat lots of delicious food," So-won said.

"That's a way's off; he hasn't got any teeth yet. First, we'll give him rice porridge one spoon at a time, then little, tiny bits of rice, until he's one, when his teeth should start coming in."

"Early to walk, early to sit, early to speak, early to chew, never to grow," Yong-ha said, as he picked at a scrap of beef stuck between his teeth.

"What does that mean?" So-won asked.

"It's not good for a baby's teeth to come in early or to learn to walk and talk too soon."

"Hmm. How old was I when my teeth came in?"

"You were very young. You had all your teeth before you turned one."

"So am I not good?"

"No, girls are always faster than boys."

Spurred by the feeling in the air that it was fine to speak, Bok-yi set her chopsticks on the table and started to ramble.

"But, you know, so many people came today, your family from over in Michon-ri, and your younger brother from Anbeob-ri, and your uncle from Gagok-dong, and your niece from Ne-il-dong, even Bo-seon came all the way from Daegu, and lots of people from the neighborhood, so about thirty people in all, don't you think? Because we had nowhere near enough galchi for everyone. Oh, and Gyeong-chil brought little Yeong-ok, who's just turned two; he and Woo-gun looked like two peas in a pod. Woo-gun takes after your side a little more, doesn't he?"

"No, Eomoni, he looks just like his father."

Hee-hyang felt that Woo-gun's sleepily sucking lips were directly touching her soul; she closed her eyes in rapture. How good it would feel to just fall asleep like this with the baby in her arms, but she hadn't eaten yet, and she still had so much work to do: cleaning up after dinner, steaming the wheat and making preparations for the next day's meals, mending clothes and socks—there must be something else she was supposed to do too. . . . Bok-yi's disapproving voice echoed in the hollows of her mind, half full of dreams.

"I suppose?"

"Honey, doesn't he look just like you?" Hee-hyang opened her eyes drowsily and looked at her husband's face for the first time that day.

"I'm not sure yet. A child's face can change so much, you know."

"Hey, Eomoni, why did you take him out of his party clothes? He looked so cute." That was So-won.

"It's easier for a baby to be in something simple like this. He still can't stretch his arms, so wearing something that stiff is hard for him. And he wets his diaper a lot."

Hee-hyang put his little chin on her shoulder and started beating his back to try to burp him, but he fell asleep just like that, so she gently laid him down on his bed, then put some kimchi on top of her now-stone-cold barley, brought the spoon up to her mouth, took a bite, swallowed, and began to peel the skin from a peach when everyone else had started to eat the soup she'd made from the rice stuck to the bottom of the pot.

"Abeoji, teach me how to catch sweetfish," Woo-cheol said, reaching for a peach from the plate.

"I haven't gone fishing for years now." Yong-ha stuffed a peach into his mouth too.

"But if you catch the fish yourself it's free."

"I guess that's so."

"If So-won and I fish, then everyone can eat sweetfish."

"But I don't want to go fishing," So-won said.

"You're really starting to have quite the cheek on you."

"You're the one with cheek, Oppa."

"So-won, don't talk back to your oppa like that. You could just gather clams."

Suddenly feeling that someone was missing, Hee-hyang looked around at her family. That man, Woo-cheol, So-won, Eomoni, Woo-gun—everyone was there.

"Hey, Omma, I wanna go for a walk. Let's go up to Yeongnamnu."

This child, who is usually so good and never tries to get her way, now says she wants to go for a walk right after dinner when I'm so busy, calling me Omma even though she's over six years old now—she must be feeling sad because I've been glued to Woo-gun.

Hee-hyang stood up, wiping her hands on her apron. "Sure, let's go. Honey, we're going out for a little bit. Eomoni, I just fed him, so he shouldn't wake for a while, but would you look after Woo-gun for me?"

Soon it would be the end of April, but the wind that hit her cheeks was chilly. Hee-hyang breathed in the fresh air, carrying the smell of water, and took So-won's hand.

Woo-cheol stopped in front of the pontoon bridge.

"I'm going to run around the river once. I'll be back in twenty minutes, so would you two go up to Yeongnamnu? So-won, don't tell Abeoji, whatever you do. He won't shut up about how running's a waste of studying time," Woo-cheol said, then ran off in the direction of Mount Jongnam, lit faintly in the moonlight, disappearing into the darkness before either had the chance to wave him goodbye.

Hee-hyang climbed the stone steps hand in hand with So-won and remembered how two weeks ago she had seen the ghost of Arang. She would not tell So-won that; the child frightened so easily.

So-won went straight to the place where Arang had stood, leaning her body over the railing.

"Eomoni, look! A boat!"

At this late hour a fishing boat's lamps floated on the river, it was to the south, so perhaps it was heading to the station, it must be carrying someone with something urgent to do, a birth? An injury? Illness? The death of a relative?

"Arang's festival is over."

"It is."

When Arang's festival was over, sweetfish became scarce, women washed their hair with sweet flag water, the mountain lilies bloomed, and by the time people made offerings of rice cakes made with the new crop, Woo-gun would probably have started crawling.

"I really wanna be one of the girls at the Arang Festival. When do you get to do it?"

"Once you're old enough to get married, I think."

"How many years until I can get married?"

"Well, some girls get married at sixteen."

"So ten more years."

"Don't get married that young, you'll run off and make your eomoni so lonely."

"But what about Oppa and Woo-gun? You'll have them," So-won said quietly, as if sulking.

Hee-hyang stroked her daughter's soft hair and wondered if one day she too would be trapped inside a house, betrayed by her husband.

"Aigu, So-won, but you're my only precious daughter."

She felt her words had been swallowed up in the silence of the air, like they had been absorbed by somebody's ears—was somebody listening to their conversation? Arang?

"What's wrong, Eomoni?"

Her daughter's eyes looked back at her strangely, lips smiling. What was wrong? It didn't look like So-won's face, Hee-hyang's eyes were just blurry from lack of sleep, that was all, but there was something frightening—Hee-hyang pressed So-won's face to her chest, talking to her, protecting her daughter from the darkness that reached out to touch her.

When she opened her eyes, it was dark. Someone's voice was ringing in her head, not her own, the voice of a woman she'd never heard before, maybe the cries of a woman she'd seen in a dream but didn't know, now tangled up in her ears—

Oh, I'm tired, feel like I could drop right back into the same dream, straight in like a shard of glass.

The woman went against her drowsiness and opened her eyes, propping her upper body up by her elbows.

The moonlight cast the woman's silhouette on the paper doors.

I've turned my back on the shores of reality to the sea, to the sea, being floated only from dream to dream. The moment I left the shore was perhaps that morning. I've been told it was morning when my eomoni died too, but I had just been born so I remember nothing. That morning, when I was sixteen, I got the news that my abeoji, who had left the house saying he'd be back before the sun rose, had drowned; he had gone out on a fishing boat from Yongdu-mok, but they could not find his body. I never saw my abeoji in a dream; he had never come to me in death—I could not even remember his voice. His final words, Hae jigi jeone doraonda, *I'll be back before the sun rises*, I remember only like a deaf-blind person tracing their fingers over words carved in wood over and over. Eomoni. Abeoji. I feel the darkness of this house holds within it the shadows of those who were here and who are not here anymore.

The woman lowered her upper body and reached a hand into the darkness, covering the man's cheek with her palm, touching the stubble of his beard with the pad of her finger, tracing his nose with her fingernail, tickling the tip of his nose. Then she pulled his hand toward her from the darkness. His hand swiftly went down, grabbing her ankle and crawling upward. When his hand lost its way, tempted deep between her legs, a warm fluid began to flow from within her. Her period had started. She went to the kitchen, head shaking from a disappointment that hit her like seasickness, and there she washed off the blood and fastened a few layers of cloth between her legs. If they were in each other's arms they could talk, but if they weren't it was harder; what should they talk about for the next five days? Maybe they had nothing left to say. Did he have lots of things to talk about with *her* every day? Did they talk about their children? The store? She would have liked, if she could, to sneak into his house, hide in the cupboard, and secretly listen to their conversations.

She lay down, folding her hands on her stomach like a corpse. Her eyes were closed; her ears alone were open, turned toward the darkness.

EIGHT

Baegiljanchi

| 백일잔치 | 百日宴 |

"Hey, Eomoni, why did you go stand by the road and hand out rice cakes? Isn't that a waste?"

"It's called 'buying a life.' Today is the hundredth day of Woo-gun's life, you know? If you give cakes made from pounded white rice to one hundred people the baby will grow up to live to one hundred."

"Oh. Then what's that? That rope that Bu-san ajumma put around Woo-gun's neck?"

"That's also to pray for his long life."

"But why rope?"

"Why, why, why, is all you ever say."

"Why? I'm asking Eomoni, not you, Oppa. It's none of your business."

"It's my business because I can hear you."

"Hey, Eomoni, tomorrow, can I take Woo-gun on my back when I go to In-so's house to play?"

"So-won, Woo-gun isn't a doll. You can carry him once around the garden, but he's just learned to hold his head up, so you can't give him a piggyback ride for long. And he's heavy, you know."

"Oh, he's not heavy. I carried him around yesterday."

"If you try to carry him to In-so's house, I promise you'll regret it. He's almost twice as heavy now as he was when he was born."

"Hey, Eomoni, Woo-gun is really funny. Today, he was trying to suck his fingers, right, but he just couldn't get them in his mouth, right, and he stuck his fingers up his nose! Then he laughed at himself!"

"He's started laughing out loud lately. And when he cries, he cries a lot too."

"He's stopped fake crying."

"Are you sure you're not talking about yourself?"

"Oppa, when do I fake cry?"

"'Ahhh, ahhh, Oppa is being meannnnn.'"

"Hey, Eomoni, Woo-gun says 'ah' and 'ooh'—does that mean he's speaking?"

"Yes, he is. When he says 'ah' or 'ooh,' if you look at him and talk back to him, he'll be happy."

"I wish we could take Woo-gun to the baths with us. . . ."

"He had a bath this morning in the washbasin, so he doesn't need another one."

"Would he go on the boys' side?"

"Not yet. When he gets to be about five, he can go on the men's side with his oppa."

"Woo-gun's not crying, is he? Today, when he looked at Halmoni, he started crying."

"He hadn't seen her in a while."

"Aigu, Halmoni looked like she was about to start crying, like maybe he'd forgotten her face."

"She was not about to start crying; that's an exaggeration. You always exaggerate."

"But she really did look like she was gonna cry."

"So-won, don't talk back to your oppa, he's the eldest son."

"Abeoji's at the top, then, Oppa?"

"That's right."

"That's dumb. Why couldn't I have been born a boy?"

"'Why couldn't I have been born a boy?'"

"Quit copying me."

"'Quit copying me.'"

"Stop it!"

"'Stop it!'"

"Woo-cheol, don't antagonize your sister."

"Hey, Eomoni, In-so said she ate some Japanese rice cakes."

"Probably because In-so's abeoji works for Joseon Gas and Electric."

"She said they were reaaally sticky, not like the ones you gave out earlier."

"I've never eaten a Japanese rice cake. What are they like?"

"She said they were good."

"'She said they were good.'"

"I'm just going to ignore Oppa now. Oh yeah, the other day, Ho-seong, who lives in Gyo-dong, you know those trees near Yongdu-mok? The ones with the huuuge trunks?"

"Those are cedars."

"Well, Ho-seong climbed a cedar tree and then jumped and landed in Yongdu-mok! We didn't follow him up so he thought we might have drowned so he jumped. And then my leg got caught and—"

"I've told you, you're six years old now, you must stop going swimming naked with the boys."

"Hey, Eomoni, is it true that mongdal ghosts come out at Yongdu-mok?"

"Well, lots of people have drowned there. . . ."

"Yikes, that's scaaary. Ul-son and Oh-sun both say they've felt their ankles being grabbed while they were swimming."

"Please be careful. River water is cold, you might get a leg cramp and drown."

"If you drown do you sink?"

"Yongdu-mok is full of weeds, so lots of people apparently don't float up, but if you drown in the shallows you'll float. Enough, anyway. Today's supposed to be a happy occasion."

"Hey, Eomoni, what's that flower called?"

"Which one?"

"Look, that red flower near the gate to that house, can you see it?"

"Oh, that's crepe myrtle."

"And that one?"

"That red flower over there?"

"Yeah."

"That's a hollyhock."

"I want it to grow in our garden too. Why do we only have four-o'clock flowers?"

"So-won, I had no idea you liked flowers this much."

"Oh! Look, there! That white bird!"

"Huh? Where?"

"Near the delta! There's a big white bird there!"

"You just never calm down, do you?"

"What do you mean?"

"Look at that flower! Look at that bird! If you don't stop looking around so much when you're walking you'll fall into the river."

"Merong! None of your bus-i-ness! Hey, Eomoni, what's that bird called?"

"That's a stork. It's summer now, I guess. Migratory birds bring the seasons with them: in spring, the swallow; in summer, the stork; in fall, the gray heron; in winter, the swans."

"It's not just birds, is it? Flowers do it too. In spring there's azaleas, in summer there's crepe myrtle, in the fall there's wild chrysanthemums, and in the winter there's . . ."

"In the winter there's?"

"In the winter there's . . ."

"You have no idea, but you talk like you're so big."

"Flowers bloom in the winter too, you know. Christmas camellias. They're your eomoni's favorite flower."

"In the spring we have clover flower jeon and mugwort rice cakes, in summer it's samgyetang and cold noodles, fall is mushrooms and chrysanthemum jeon and hwachae, and winter is jook with red beans and rice cake soup and cinnamon punch and white rice cakes."

"Oh oh oh, well, if we're going to talk about food there's so many it's hard to list."

"Hahahahaha, that's 'cause you're a little pig."

"Why are you laughing? Quit it!"

"Hmh hmh hmh hmh."

"Hahahahaha."

"Sto-op! Hey, Eomoni, I want watermelon."

"Hmh hmh hmh. Let's swing by the market on the way home from the bath."

"'Look at the sky, look at the ground, everyone hold hands, as we dance around, as we swing our hands . . .'"

"Quit singing, you're so tone-deaf!"

"'Look at the sky, look at the ground, everyone hold hands, as we dance around, as we swing our hands . . .' Hey, Eomoni, listen . . . no, just forget it."

"What? You started to say something, tell me what."

"But Oppa is listening."

"Well, don't say it if you don't want your brother to hear."

"But, Eomoni, I . . ."

"Then hurry up and say it. Abeoji is getting farther and farther ahead of us."

"Oppa, go ahead with Abeoji!"

The daughter put her mouth to her mother's ear.

Sseureuram sseureuram sseureuram sseureuram, the cicadas are so loud, but I can't get any closer to hear better. *Sseureuram sseureuram sseureuram sseureuram*. What if she's whispering about me? Does she realize I'm following them?

Thump-thump, sseureuram, thump-thump, the sound of my heartbeat is harsher to my ears than the cicadas' cries. If he turned now, he'd see me in an instant. No, he won't turn around, he won't. Why? Intuition, intuition, and it's never failed me yet. Oh, his son is running up to him, he's saying something to him. *Thump-thump, sseureuram, thump-thump, sseureuram, thump-thump*. Oh, be quiet, joyonghi hae!

". . . I guess I can't, Eomoni?"

"No, you can, but we can't buy it for you right away. Having a baby costs a lot of money. In three years, you'll start school, right? Then we'll buy you crayons and clothes and athletic shoes."

"In three years? But In-so already has all of that."

"Well, you're not In-so, you're So-won. Of course she has things you don't. But you have lots of things In-so doesn't have too, right? It's not right to want what others have."

"But I do want them. Even if In-so didn't have all that stuff, I'd still want it."

"If you hold on for three years, don't you think it'll make you much happier when you finally get it than if you got it right away?"

"But in three years I might not want it anymore."

"If you don't think you'll want it then, you must not want it that badly. When you really want something, it doesn't matter how long it takes."

"But I want it now."

"So-won, you're a big sister now, you need to stop being so selfish."

Whistling? The sound of whistling, coming from his mouth. That song I taught him. He's thirty meters from her, but he's thinking of me.

She adjusted her hold on the metal washbasin with her toiletries in it and sang along with his whistling as accompaniment.

I had a love, one as big as the sky
As big as a mother's love, that's what I had
Days go by, then turn into months
I could die for you, my love
For such a love we had

The whistling coming from his lips and the singing coming from mine— the sound of both can be heard by my ears alone. His wife can only hear her daughter's sulky voice and the sound of the cicadas and the river, and the "Ice cream! Get your ice cream!" calls of the hawker, and the *ding-ding-ding* of the wind chimes hanging from the house.

Oh, he and his son have gone into the baths. The woman pursed her lips tightly, her lipstick painted on so thick that they had cracked like a bright red cork, and sped up her pace, getting near enough that she could now step on the mother's and daughter's shadows.

"Oppa doesn't stay in the bath long, but Abeoji likes to stay in for a while. What does he do?"

"I don't think your oppa just gets out and leaves your father in the bath."

"I can't take it, I have to get out."

"Then you just say the word and go cool down in the dressing room."

"I can't cool down in the dressing room when it's so hot in there. Let's say we're going home early and go buy some ice cream."

"You won't be too full for your dinner if you have ice cream first?"

"I could have five and still eat dinner. We can have an ice cream while we go to the market to get a watermelon."

"Oh, you've got it all worked out already," she chuckled.

The pair took off their rubber boots and opened the wooden door to the women's bath.

"Annyeong haseyo."

"Today was your hundredth-day celebration, wasn't it?"

"It was. Thanks for your kind wishes."

Sitting at the counter was Gyeong-soon, the owner's wife. As Gyeong-soon handed Hee-hyang her change, she saw the face of the next woman opening the door to come in and gasped, knitting her eyebrows.

The Unha Public Bath was where all the rumors of Miryang came together. As wife and daughter and mistress began taking off their clothes, the women sitting on the benches cooling down in just their underwear suddenly fell silent, exchanging glances as they listened carefully.

Every time their curious or hate-filled gazes pierced her face or breasts or stomach the woman was blanketed in exultation, as if she were at a festival, as if she were at the hundredth-day celebration she couldn't have attended.

Mother and daughter put their washbasins near the concrete bathtub to save their place, drew water from the bath with the wooden buckets provided, poured it over themselves from the shoulders down, then stepped into the tub.

"Oh wow, it's hot!"

"Once you're all the way in for a while it won't feel so hot."

"I can't, it's too hot."

"It's really not that bad."

"Eomoni, tell them to cool it down!"

"I can't, some people like it this hot, you know. If you just wait you'll feel a tingling, and then it won't feel so hot anymore."

The woman turned the wooden washbasin over and sat down on it. The mirrors were clouded by the steam. She wiped it away with her palm, but the mirror soon clouded over again, leaving only the red of her lips visible. *Thump-thump thump-thump thump-thump thump-thump.*

"I'm getting out!"

"Not until you count to ten."

"Hana, dul, set, net, daseot, yeoseot, ilgop, it's too hot!"

Mother and daughter got out of the bath. *Thump-thump thump-thump thump-thump thump-thump.* Even in this heat and humidity all the hairs on the woman's arms stood on end. A plump woman turned her head to look at the woman through the clouded mirror. Was it someone she knew? Someone she didn't know? It was as if she had awakened long before but had her eyes still closed, the faces and scenes from her dream dissolving and receding behind her eyelids. What am I actually seeing here?

What do I really want to see here? A glimmering, hot wave pierced through her body, the spray splashing over her face, shoulders, and breasts. *Thump-thump thump-thump*, a red haze came to her eyes. *Thump-thump thump-thump thump-thump thump-thump!* Unable to bear the swell of her heart's beating she stood, forgetting even to cover the front of her body, and entered the bath.

"I thought it was kinda dark in here and look, Eomoni, the light bulb's dead!"

The woman looked up from her place in the bath to where the girl was pointing at the ceiling. A bare light bulb. It looked like she could reach up and change the bulb while still sitting, but when she looked down, she realized that even on her knees she would not be able to reach. *Thump-thump thump-thump thump-thump thump-thump.*

"The bulb's not dead, they're just trying to save money. Electricity's expensive, you know? And it's still only evening, so it doesn't need to be on."

Even without trying to listen, one could hear the conversations in the men's bath. The two sides were separated only by a pine-board wall.

"I heard that old man Hyo-gil talked to Kim Won-bong when he was holed up at Pyochungsa."

"That was when Won-bong was thirteen or fourteen, right?"

"I heard he read Sun Tzu and *The Wuzi* nonstop and when he tired of reading, he would get the children from the village together, split them into two platoons, and make them have a rock-throwing fight."

"Kim Won-bong has always stood out, ever since he was a kid. In the dead of winter he'd go to Gamcheon and cut away the ice over the spring so he could take a cold bath, and he'd climb Yeongnamnu as part of his daily routine. Every morning he'd go up to the top and shout, 'Long live Korean independence!' which panicked us so much that we went up to stop him, so the next time he went to Mount Yongdu and shouted it, then, we went up again, so he went up Mount Sanseong and again: 'Long live Korean independence!'"

"Shhh! You're too loud."

"Aigo, there's no Japanese in here. The ilbon saram wouldn't get in a bath with Koreans, and they all have baths in their houses anyway."

"But there might be an informant."

"Who here could be an informant? That's the Park family, the Kim family, Chae abeoji, Un-nam, Woo-cheol and his abeoji, and that's Shin-tok—all people we know!"

"Long live Korean independence!"

"Quit it, cut it out."

The woman got out of the bath and sat next to the girl. *Thump-thump thump-thump*. The mirror reflecting nothing, pure white, even when she wiped it with her hand. *Thump-thump thump-thump*. Still white as could be; was the steam inside her head as well? No, she just felt a bit dizzy; she would close her eyes for a moment, just for a little bit. *Thump-thump thump-thump thump-thump thump-thump*.

"Eomoni, what about your hair?"

"I'm not going to wash it. If you want to wash your hair here you have to pay five sen to the lady at the counter, you know."

"But she wouldn't know if you washed it anyway."

"She comes around to check sometimes. And then when we leave she'd see my hair was damp and then she'd know."

"In-so's family has this soap they use and it's so white. It's not like brown soap, 'cause it doesn't get all mushy when you get it wet, and it makes a looot of bubbles, and it smells really good."

"Get in the bath one more time and then give yourself a wash."

Hee-hyang and So-won got in the bath together and soon, they started talking to Yong-soon ajumma from Ssangmun-dong.

"Thank you so much for taking one of the white rice cakes from me today. You made his life a year longer."

Yong-soon came over to Hee-hyang, so close that their shoulders were touching, and whispered in her ear.

"She's practically your shadow, isn't she?"

"Hm?"

"You really don't know? That woman over there, she's your husband's . . ."

Yong-soon ajumma's whispering in her ear. But if I stop washing my hair now and look up it would look suspicious. The woman slowly wrung her hair and wrapped it in a cloth, then took a bar of brown soap from her brass wash-basin.

"Eomoni, it's really hot."

"Try and bear up."

"White, black, red, blue, yellow, green, yellow-green, brown, orange, gray, peach, light blue. Those are the twelve colors of crayons that In-so has."

A pause. "Oh."

"There's also one with twenty-four colors too. I wonder what colors that one has in it. I want some so much I'd be happy with six colors. The ones with six colors have black, yellow, green, orange, peach, and light blue. Eomoni, are you listening to me?"

"I'm listening. Red and blue and green, right?"

"That's only three colors. I can't do it! I'm feeling dizzy! I'm getting out!"

Thump-thump thump-thump. Her head shakes, lolling like Woo-gun's head. It's hot, her chest feels heavy, it's hard to breathe, her lungs feel like they're collapsing. Was it a coincidence? Why? *Thump-thump thump-thump*. Why, why would this happen by chance? *Thump-thump thump-thump*. Did the other woman notice? The blood was burbling up from her heart; it was hot! A red mist came over her eyes, red as a marsh, the hot water coming to a rolling boil. Red, white, black, blue, red! Red! Red! Red! Hot! I wish I could stop breathing and drown my face in the hot bathwater right now, but no, they all want a reason to laugh, that woman, and her, to laugh at me—

"Eomoni! How long are you going to stay in there? Come wash me!"

"You're six years old; wash yourself. I'll wash your back for you in a little bit."

I can't get out of the bath now; the other woman would see me naked. I'm looking at her, her naked body. *Thump-thump thump-thump thump-thump thump-thump.* I see her, but all my eye takes in are colors. Black, white, peach, white, peach, black, white, red, red, red!

The woman looked at the palms of her hands, damp with soap bubbles. *Thump-thump thump-thump.* She wanted to wash the girl's back for her. If that woman dies, I'll become her daughter's eomoni, so what would be so strange about me washing her? So-won, your new eomoni will buy you a nice set of crayons. White, black, red, blue, yellow, green, yellow-green, brown, orange, gray, peach, light blue, *thump-thump thump-thump thump-thump thump-thump.*

"I mean, General Won-bong can magic himself anywhere, you know."

"Are you serious?"

"Aigu, have I ever lied to you? When was it, when Won-bong came home, someone informed on him, and the police were frantic and went to his house, but there was no one there, just one fly buzzing around. Since then, the cops gave him their own little nickname: the Fly."

"Hyo-gil halbi, what's General Won-bong's face look like?"

"He has slightly dark skin, manly, graceful features, and he's tall and slender. . . ."

"I guess he can't keep the ladies off him."

"No, he keeps well away from them. General Won-bong drinks, but he doesn't chase girls."

"I guess that's how you get to be twenty-seven without a wife or kids."

"Yong-ha, what do you think about General Won-bong's features?"

"I couldn't really say without actually seeing him in person, but going by the photo of him they printed in the *Dong-A Ilbo*, his eyes are clear and his brow is prominent, so he has wisdom. His gaze is steady, so he has fortitude and righteousness. His face is balanced, so I would say he is an admirable man with tremendous prospects."

"Kim Won-bong, Samyeong Daesa, and Kim Jong-jik—the three greatest men Miryang ever produced. Hey, Woo-cheol, do you know who Samyeong Daesa was?"

"Yes."

"When the Japanese invaded in the 1590s, Samyeong Daesa joined a righteous army and defeated the waejeok, then went to Japan himself to bring home 1,391 of his captured countrymen. And Pyochungsa, where Kim Won-bong was confined when he was younger, is a place where Samyeong Daesa is revered."

"Kim Jong-jik wrote the 'Jouijemun,' a letter of condolence to Emperor Yi of Chu regarding his murder by Xiang Yu, thought by King Sejo to be critical of his murder of King Danjong, and for that reason during the Literati Purges after his death, he was posthumously decapitated."

"So people from Miryang have long had a tendency toward resistance."

"Legend has it that the morning that Kim Jong-jik was born, the water in the Miryang River turned sweet all of a sudden."

"And Choi Su-bong, the guy who threw a bomb into the Miryang police station, cut his own throat with a knife, but, aigo, he didn't die and wound up getting the rope. . . ."

"Choi Su-bong and Kim Won-bong were childhood friends, you know."

"He was expelled from Miryang Common School because he told a wae-nom teacher who said that Dangun was Susano'o-no-mikoto's brother that actually, Susano'o-no-mikoto was our Dangun's great-grandchild."

"Aigo, how stupid can a teacher be! Dangun was around almost forty-two hundred years ago, and Susano'o-no-mikoto lived twenty-seven hundred years ago, at most."

"No one in the Heroic Corps expects to die at a ripe old age. They don't have an 'all together' attitude, they think: let me get killed first. Park Jae-hyuk, the one who posed as a Chinese bookseller to infiltrate the Busan police, then pulled a bomb, not a book, out of his bag and killed the police chief, wound up taking his last breath during interrogation."

"But Kim Ik-sang, the one who got into the Korean government-general offices in the guise of an electric company employee, certainly managed to get away after he threw his bomb."

"Aigo, isn't he the one who tried to stab General Tanaka Giichi, missed, and got dragged off to Ilbon?"

"Yeah, I read about it in the *Dong-A Ilbo*. Apparently, when the presiding judge asked that any evidence beneficial to the defendant be presented, Kim said, there is only one thing that would benefit me, and that is Korean independence."

"He got the death penalty and he's sitting in Kumamoto Prison right now."

"You think he's still alive?"

"If they killed him it'd be in the papers."

"And that Kim Chi-sop, the one who threw the bombs at Nijubashi Bridge by the Imperial Palace, was in the Heroic Corps too. He said he carried bombs to Ilbon to give comfort to the souls of his six thousand countrymen who were massacred by the Japanese after the Great Kantō earthquake year before last."

"Is he still alive?"

"He's still on trial."

"He'll get the death penalty for sure."

"They say Kim Chi-sop made a statement in court. He said, 'Under the governor's administration, we Koreans are lower than dogs or pigs. And the common people of Japan have not been allowed to know this reality. I wanted to let them know. We demand independence for Korea. And until we have it, we will fight to the last man, to the last hour.'"

"Destroy the waenom, liberate the motherland, defeat the ruling class, redistribute the land."

"Oh, Woo-cheol! You're well-versed, aren't you?"

"We're sitting here in the bath while members of the Heroic Corps are getting tortured...."

"Aigo, so what are you going to do, get out of the water and join up now?"

"In-deok, from the Koh family in Nae-il dong, went and joined the Heroic Corps. That family is so rich they got In-deok into Otsuki Keisei School. His abeoji went around bragging for weeks."

"Did he bring a lot of bombs into Miryang, then?"

"Aigo, they arrested him before he even killed one of the Japanese dogs."

"He got three years in prison, but he got parole after a year and six months and came back here for a bit, right?"

"They sold their house and assets and gave the Heroic Corps almost three thousand yen."

"That much! Aigo!"

"Their family had been landowners for generations, you know. Aigo, didn't they have two sons and two daughters?"

"I don't suppose we'll see independence before I'm dead and buried. By then everyone Woo-cheol's age will be grown and have kids of— Hey! The water's too hot!"

"Too hot!"

"It's boiling!"

Hearing the men's voices, Gyeong-soon came down from her counter and opened the wooden door to the women's bath. Mworagoyo! She couldn't believe what she saw: Hee-hyang and her husband's mistress in the bath together! Gyeong-soon suddenly felt as if she were naked too. Her eyes snapped upward. Shameless! Why is no one saying anything? Hee-hyang must have no idea. Gyeong-soon stopped in front of her and dipped her hand in the bath.

"Sorry, just checking. Oh my, that's hot, I do beg your pardon, I'll go tell them to damp down the fire. Excuse me, Yo-jeong! Hello! Do your washing at home!"

"It's just three shirts. What's the harm?"

"Absolutely not. You know the rules!"

"Aigo, don't be so straitlaced. Just give me five more minutes and I'll be done."

"Cham da!"

Gyeong-soon clicked her tongue and returned to her counter.

The water was so hot! But if she got out of the bath first, then she'd have to show her ass to that other woman. *Thump-thump thump-thump.* The other woman had gotten in the bath after her, so she still had a bit more capacity to cope with the heat. She'd just been thinking about getting out, actually, when that other woman had gotten in! Gaegateun nyeon! You get out first, bitch! *Thump-thump. Thump-thump.* My parts are soaking in the same water as hers. And my husband fucks both of us. I can't deal with this! It's too hot! Under the water, Hee-hyang grasped her knees tightly.

"Eomoni! I forgot soap!" Woo-cheol's voice jumped over the wall between the two sides of the bath. "Can you throw me some?"

"I still haven't finished washing, so I'll break the soap and give you half. Oppa, I'm gonna throw it now, hana, dul, set!"

"Aigo! Look where you're throwing things!"

"Eomoni, I'm getting out now. I'm tired of waiting!"

The two women's eyes met.

Thump-thump! Thump-thump!

Thump-thump! Thump-thump!

Don't you dare look away from me. I've done nothing wrong, nothing!

My eyes go to her eyes, and hers to mine. *Thump-thump! Thump-thump!*

Thump-thump! Thump-thump!

Thump-thump! Thump-thump!

Both women looked away at the same time.

We're not the only ones stark naked here, everyone is. *Thump-thump! Thump-thump!*

So why do I feel like I stand out so much, as if all the others were clothed? *Thump-thump! Thump-thump!*

Thump-thump! Thump-thump! All the women seemed to be throwing glances at her.

Thump-thump! Thump-thump! Aigo, how embarrassing, I want to hide my face.

Driven by a hatred that surpassed her shame, Hee-hyang got out of the bath with a splash.

On the men's side, someone's husband started singing.

Descendants of Dangun, my boys
You know our nation's humiliation
Unable to bury our parents
And our sons will still be servants
Heaven and earth is so wide
But wherever we may go
We are treated so coldly
Driven out for no reason
Do not forget, do not forget our enemies
Nor the shame of annexation

To regain freedom and independence
We must dedicate ourselves
My countrymen without a country
I'm ashamed to be alive
We must shed our sweat and blood to
Wash away the shame of the country
Build your bodies strong
To do the same for the land
Our purpose must never be forgotten
So say farewell to your families
All you boys, and go abroad
Whatever enemies we may face
Grit your teeth and battle on
Sharpen your swords on Mount Paektu
Graze your horses at the Tuman
At the cry to advance
Beat your battle drums
Don don, hurray hurray, hurray hurray, hurray hurray!

"Hey! Quit peeking!"

The women grabbed wooden washing buckets and stood up, scooped hot water from the bath, and poured it on the men on the other side of the wall.

"Aigo!"

"What was that for?"

"Chae-ajussi was the one peeping, not poor old Hyo-gil. Now his head's dripping wet!"

Laughs rose at the same time from the men's and women's baths; the bath-house was filled with laughter and steam.

Hee-hyang wrung out her washcloth and covered her breasts with it, then looked at her own face in the mirror. *Thump-thump thump-thump*. That hadn't been that funny, really. Everyone had just wanted to laugh; they'd been holding it in. They'd all wanted to laugh ever since me and that other woman got into the bath, oh, how they must've wanted to laugh. *Thump-thump! Thump-thump!*

"Eomoni, you're bright red."

Hee-hyang's eyes were narrowed with hatred; she could only peer out at the world through small holes. Black, white, black, white, two eyes, whose eyes?

"Eomoni, are you all right?"

When she let the washcloth slip, she saw a milk blister on her nipple, like a globule of pus. How disgusting. Sucked on by children, stretched out like a cow's teat but black as charcoal. Black, black; when she squeezed her nipple, milk shot out at the mirror, white, white, white.

"Eomoni? Are you all right?"

"I'm fine."

"I think Abeoji's getting out of the bath already. Wash my back quick."

The soap is brown, the bubbles are white, her back is white, her arms are white, wash, wash, wash, white, white, white . . .

So-won giggled. "I wonder if Abeoji and Oppa got splashed too."

"It's nothing to laugh about, young lady."

The other woman is standing now. If she turns this way, she'll see me. *Thump-thump thump-thump!* She's coming this way. *Thump-thump! Thump-thump!* Should I say something? *Thump-thump! Thump-thump!* The woman picked up the brass basin that had been next to So-won and carried it away, disappearing from Hee-hyang's sight. That's right, get out of here! Get out of this bathhouse! Get out of Miryang! And don't let me ever see you again! Was her husband still in the men's side of the bath? Just then, she heard the wooden door to the men's bath open. Could it be? Perhaps the two of them were giving each other a sign. After this they'd rendezvous at her house. *Thump-thump! Thump-thump!*

"So-won, could you go tell your abeoji that I need a little more time so not to rush?"

"Abeoji! It's So-won!"

"Yes!"

"We need a little more time, so don't rush!"

"Sure!"

"Oppa! It's So-won!"

"You're embarrassing me, cut it out!"

Ah, dahaengida, he's still in the bath, then. What should I do? Is there anything I can do except get back in the bath? There's no way I could get out of the

bath stark naked in front of that woman once she's clothed. If she's still cooling
down in the changing room in fifteen minutes' time, what do I do? I might just
slap her across the cheek. What do you think you're doing! What do you think
you're doing? I should ask you the same thing, you thieving bitch!

"Come on, Kim, sing us one more song!"

"Since we're all here, let's sing one together. Hyo-gil halbi, your choice."

"Well, then, let's sing a Kwangbokkun song."

"All right! Ba-rump-pa-pa, ba-rump-pa-pa, ba-rump ba-rump, ba-rump-
pa-pa!"

Twenty million countrymen, stand up
Stand and bear your guns and swords
Take back from the hands of the enemy
Our lost motherland and our freedom with your blood
Old or young, man or woman
Even children, all must rise
Even the plants of this country damp with dew
And the spirits lying in their graves too
Soak the fields with hot blood
Dye the rivers of your homeland red
Beat all the enemies of the motherland
Until the bell of freedom rings

Hee-hyang held her breath and opened the wooden door to the changing
room. She's not there, aigo, thank God. Hee-hyang spread her towel on the
bench, and she and So-won sat down, then took a scoop of well water from the
large wooden basin and drank it. Gu-gulp, one scoop, gu-gulp, two, gu-gulp,
three, until finally the stiffness in her tongue and throat was gone.

"Eomoni, I want some too."

"Ah, I'm sorry, here."

"Mm, masitda! I never had water this cold before."

"It must've just come out of the well."

A few women finished dressing and walked past the counter, passing a few
women coming in.

"Thank you, gomapseumnida."

"Welcome, eoseooseyo."

Yeon-hee, who had just walked out with her washbasin under her arm, came back to the counter, her expression changed.

"Aigo, my boots are gone!"

"Do you suppose someone must've mistakenly put them on and left, then?"

"Some mistake that would be—I just bought them yesterday from Mr. Lee's store. They were brand-new white ones too."

"We can't keep watch over your shoes, you know."

"And last year, someone stole my chima from my basket in the changing room. It was a silk one, cost me ten yen!"

"I don't know anything about that."

"You thief!"

"Aigo, who do you think you're talking to?"

Hee-hyang and So-won hunched over as they walked out between Gyeong-soon, who was looking down from the counter, and Yeon-hee, who was looking up, hands on her hips.

As they put on their rubber boots, Hee-hyang looked out at the street in front of the Un-ha Public Bath. He and Woo-cheol were still not there. Nor was the other woman.

"So-won, let's wait for your abeoji and oppa."

"What? But I want ice cream."

"They'll be right out."

"But can't I eat ice cream while I wait for them?"

"No, you can't."

The two held their washbasins and waited for Yong-ha and Woo-cheol to come out. The evening cicadas were buzzing: *sseureuram   sseureuram   sseureuram   sseureuram*. And what bug was that that cried out: *gwitteul gwitteul   gwitteul gwitteul*?

"So-won, what is that bug making that noise?"

"That's a cricket."

Gwitteul gwitteul   gwitteul gwitteul. They're taking their time, I wonder why. Hee-hyang looked at the entrances to the bathhouse. In the middle of each of the wooden doors was a panel of frosted glass, on which the word *men* or *women* was painted in black. The character for *man* looked noble, she thought, but the character for *woman* was tipped forward, as if it were stumbling, and she wondered why the paint had dripped down like that. *Gwitteul gwitteul*, flowing like blood, *gwitteul gwitteul*, like tears, *gwitteul gwitteul gwitteul gwitteul.*

"Abeoji!"

"Honey, what took you so long?"

"You should've just gone on home without us."

Sseureuram sseureuram sseureuram sseureuram, the cicadas were shrieking, but she couldn't tell where they all were hiding— *sseureuram sseureuram*—nor could she tell where her husband's heart was. *Sseureuram sseureuram.* Her head felt like it was about to split. *Sseureuram sseureuram sseureuram sseureuram.* Someone is trying to crack my skull, is it you, honey? That woman?

"The bathhouse is about to close."

"It's summer; everyone just bathes in the river instead."

"But at Chuseok and Seollal it's so busy there's barely a place to sit."

"It costs too much. Twenty sen per person. That's eighty sen for four!"

"Don't be so cheap. Today's Woo-gun's hundredth day, after all."

"Ice cream! Ice cream!" The young man hawking his wares, metal box dangling from a strap slung around his neck, came closer. "Ice cream! Get your ice cream!"

"Hey! That's Jeong-tae!"

Woo-cheol suddenly ran off, and So-won, left behind, ran after him breathlessly. Hee-hyang followed them as if dragging herself there, step by step, step by step.

"I've got you beat this time," the boy selling ice cream said to Woo-cheol.

"You can't beat me."

"Woo-cheol, I feel sorry for you if you're about to haggle with me over four sen."

"Two for two sen, and I'll admit defeat."

"Thank you."

"Well, you're welcome. You better do your best on my homework over the summer break."

"Leave it with me, chief."

"It's two sen, ma'am."

"Oh my, really? Are you sure?"

"Yes, ma'am."

Hee-hyang handed over two sen and peered into the metal box. The long, colorful ice creams were buried in unhusked rice: red, yellow, blue, peach.

"I'll have the one with little red beans in it, please."

"I'll take yellow."

"Right, let's go to the market. Honey, you can go on home ahead of us."

"I'll go with you. It'll pass the time."

Sseureuram   sseureuram   sseureuram   sseureuram. The people passing them on the road, men, women, young, old, were all wearing white hanboks. Once it turned summer everyone started wearing white, like baby clothes, like mourning clothes; summer was at once the season of beginnings and ends, white, white, white.

Melons, peaches, apples, pears, green onions, eggplants, onions, garlic, cucumbers, potatoes, laver, green laver, soybeans, red beans, green beans, soy flour, wheat flour, rice, wheat, millet, mackerel, beltfish, shark, jujubes, chili peppers, squid, kelp, dried pollack roe. Colors, colors, colors, colors, even twenty-four crayons wouldn't be enough.

Since she was a child, Hee-hyang had always loved the time in the dead of summer when the market stalls were just about to shut down. The darkness gathering; the melon-hawking farming families sitting on the bare ground, yawning widely; the bored-looking faces of the ajumma selling millet and the ajumma who always gossips as she steams corn but has now exhausted her supply of rumors, turning toward the few straggling customers and straining her voice to yell, "Best price, I'm losing money here, two sen each, everything must go"; the customers' gazes unable to settle like the moths and other winged insects beating themselves against the bare light bulb in front of the store, not looking down as they passed right by the minari and sangchu, past its best, and the few carps and loaches floating in their containers, with their white bellies showing.

The ajummas swayed as they walked off, rolled straw mat under one arm, wooden samjibak full of unsold apples and pears balanced on their heads—

Hee-hyang called out to a farmer who was loading watermelons into a wooden frame for him to shoulder and carry off.

"How much?"

"I'll take five sen. I've got to go all the way back to Mount Bihak. It's a lot to carry, so I'll give you a big discount."

Hee-hyang paid the five sen, cradling the watermelon in her arms. It weighed less than Woo-gun. She wondered how her baby was; she had to hurry home. *Hurrying home.* These were her favorite words of all. From the Joseon era to now, under Japanese rule, people hurrying home had always felt the same.

Whatever times we live in, we are rushing home down a darkened path, to a home where our kin have lit the lamp and wait for us. I won't go anywhere. The decision that I will die on this land was made for me the moment I was born here. Not like him, the eternal wanderer. And if he were to run off with that woman, I would still hurry home. To my home, where my children wait for me.

Once she left the market the road quickly turned darker; she heard the sound of a wind chime she hadn't been able to hear before, *tling tling tling tling*, and Hee-hyang unconsciously rocked the watermelon, as if it were a baby she was trying to soothe to sleep.

"Hey, Eomoni, can we get a chime and put it on the veranda? Eomoni, did you know that inside those wind chimes, there's a little stick, and there's a little fish hanging from that stick? And when the fish moves it makes a sound. *Tling tling.* Hey, where do they sell wind chimes?"

"I suppose they'd have them at the variety store."

"Do they have other kinds?"

Hee-hyang, tired of looking down, cast a smile in her daughter's direction instead.

"Let's look and see next time."

Tling tling. The family put the sound of the chime behind them and headed outside the light. *Tling tling.* Hee-hyang felt the waves of wind wash into her white chima as she walked. *Tling tling.* The path on the riverbank was nearly pitch-black. The plants had lost their color, killing all trace of themselves, but the insects were more present than ever. *Kitoul gitoul sarura sarura chii chii chii chii.* Hee-hyang breathed in the smell of water blowing from the river. *Joljoljol joljoljol*, the sound of water nestled right up to her.

"I guess it's not long till Baekjung," she heard So-won say, somewhere far away.

"Still a while yet. Once summer's over and autumn is here."

"The dance of the idiots at last year's was really funny."

"What'll we have this year, beef or dog?"

"There's really nothing in that head of yours but food."

"Baekjung's probably the only time when landowners and servants drink and eat and sing and dance together."

"And the waenom?"

"They wouldn't come to a Korean festival."

"Expel the waenom, liberate the motherland, defeat the ruling class, redistribute the land."

"You can't say that kind of thing outside of the baths. The Japanese bastards have ears everywhere."

"I don't care if they do hear. Everyone's thinking it."

"Exactly, everyone's thinking it, but nobody's saying it. You must get that."

"I get it . . . I really do . . . but . . . if . . ."

"If what?"

"Nothing."

Woo-cheol let his arms drop and breathed in the summer night air and its scent of freedom.

"Hey, Eomoni, what happens if it rains on the day of the Baekjung?"

"It rarely rains in the summer."

"But if it did rain, then what?"

As they approached the pontoon bridge, Yong-ha began to whistle. The melody is familiar, but what is the song, oh, it's a love song. It's the one I used to sing as I worked in the kitchen, when we'd just gotten married—Hee-hyang strained to hear her own memories.

Everything about you is my love
Oh, my deepest love
My feelings, I know, are unchanging

I've pledged my love to you
Oh, dungdanggi, my love
Dungdangga dungdangga
Deonggi dungdangga, my love

At the end of a day, washing my hands and feet and face beside the well, taking off my jeogori and chima and socks before lying down next to him, touching each other as we talked about all the little things that had happened that day, softly embracing him when he swelled with desire, waiting until his breathing had slowed to talk about tomorrow and feeling our bodies again seek each other out, slowly, gently loving each other, yes, loving each other, and falling in that placid tranquility until we slept—

"Hey, Eomoni."

"Yes?"

"Are you all right? You were miles away."

"What is it?"

"On the day of Baekjung, right, what happens if it rains?"

"Summer rains fall hard and stop soon, so it would be just fine."

"Oh, is he crying?"

"So he is."

"Woo-gun probably wants milk."

Hee-hyang went through the gate to the house as if leaping into open, outstretched arms. With each step she felt lighter, heavy layers peeling away from her.

"I'm home, Woo-gun, Omma's home."

NINE

Doljabi

| 돌잡이 | トルジャビ |

The soft April wind set the jeogori strings of the women picking minari fluttering in the same direction as the dandelion, shepherd's purse, and violets waved, but it was unable to shake awake the sky, which slept deeply under its cover of thin clouds. Spring women, spring flowers, spring butterflies, spring water, spring fish; all things under the heavens were lost in the sky's sweet and tedious dream.

"I think the girls at this year's Arang Festival are probably going to be Kim from the rice store's daughter Seo-ryeong, the town scribe's eldest girl, and Jeong-sun, don't you?"

"Eh? Jeong-sun? Is she that old already?"

"Girls turn into women before you know it."

"Seems like just yesterday she was running around barefooted and snot-nosed."

"I hear she's quite the beauty now."

"Think she'd marry my boy?"

"Oh no, andwae, andwae, leave the pretty girls alone, they're too stuck-up. He needs a strong, hardworking girl who will give him lots of babies."

"You can't know if a girl will have a lot of children or not."

"Aigu, all you have to do is look. If she's got wide hips and a big ass, well, there you go."

"Well, what about someone like Cho Chee-hyang? If he married her, I'd have to take care of them both."

"Your boy's a sucker for a pretty face."

"Aigo! All men are, but a bride isn't just for the head of the household; she belongs to her in-laws too. Her face is the least of all you should worry about."

Look   look   look at me
Like a flower that blooms midwinter   look at me

Ari, arirang   suri, surirang   arariga nanne
Coming over Arirang Pass

Having finally met him
I could not hear a word he said   I was so shy

Ari, arirang   suri, surirang   arariga nanne
Coming over Arirang Pass

It could have been because the women's voices swelled, or because the wind picked up, or because a man carrying a fishing pole and a corrugated steel container made his way down to the bank—it isn't clear—but a small bird suddenly flew out of a thicket where the white, red, purple, yellow flowers had burst into bloom and white and yellow butterflies danced, then rode on a wave of wind, going up and down with it, until it reached Mount Adong, where the shrine and Aranggak pavilion were, and flew into a gap between the trees.

The women were not so much looking for areas of the embankment with lots of minari as they were moving with the sun like cats, chasing after sunny spots then curling up in them.

"Koh In-deok's wife, Lee Bok-soo, is still crying her life away, I heard. Her little sister married into a family in Ne-il-dong, not far away."

"Oh, it's been about half a year now, right?"

"The trial in Daegu was on the eighteenth of December last year—my husband still reads the clippings out to me sometimes, so I guess I've got it memorized."

"Koh In-deok has been in and out of prison though, hasn't he?"

"Of course, because he was part of the Heroic Corps' leadership. He risked his life to throw those bombs."

"Speak quieter, we'll still hear you."

"Speak like your voice is flowing down the river."

"The families and relatives and friends of the three Heroic Corps men on trial all descended on Daegu District Court and somehow two hundred of them got in, while many had to stand outside. The forty uniformed and plain-clothes police and military police went over them with a fine-toothed comb—all the observers got a full-body search from the roots of their hair down to their toenails."

"The women too?"

"Of course."

"Aigo, how awful."

"Lee Bok-soo brought her thirteen-year-old and three-year-old daughters, Yo-han and Chong-gyu, all the way to Daegu just so they could catch a glimpse of their abeoji, but the court was full and they wouldn't let them in."

"Aigo, someone should've let them take their place."

"He died three days later, right?"

"In prison on December twenty-first. Forty years old. The headline read: 'In a Life Filled with Turbulence, Two Prison Sentences.'"

"Does anyone really believe he died of natural causes?"

"Aigu, how could it have been natural?"

"They said it was a heart attack."

"They tortured him to death."

"Shh, don't talk so loud. Lee Bok-soo buried him and never has said a word about how his body looked."

"His brother Kum-sik went with her to collect his body, and I heard they both collapsed the moment they saw his face and started howling so loud you could've heard it in the afterlife."

"I heard a couple dozen of his friends went too."

"Didn't Koh In-deok sell all his property and donate almost three thousand yen to the Heroic Corps? I wonder how Bok-soo manages with four kids on her hands."

"Kum-sik is taking care of her apparently. And Bok-soo works so hard she barely sleeps."

A fierce wind is blowing   a fierce wind is blowing
A fierce wind is blowing in thirty million hearts

Ari, arirang   suri, surirang   arariyo
Kwangbokkun, sing arirang!

The boats gently bobbing on the sea
Have come to take the Kwangbokkun on board

Ari, arirang   suri, surirang   arariyo
Kwangbokkun, sing arirang!

At Arirang Pass   the drums beat on
In Hanyangdoseong   the Taegukgi waves

Ari, arirang   suri, surirang   arariyo
Kwangbokkun, sing Arirang!

One woman suddenly looked up, cutting off mid word. Five detectives were coming down to the bank. The women's backs stiffened as if they'd been shot by arrows through the neck, their minari-picking hands moving with considerable caution. And even after the cops ran off toward the station and they heard the *squeak squeak squeak* of the pontoon bridge rolling, they did not soon relax. An elderly lady broke the long silence with a sigh.

"It's no laughing matter, is it?"

"There must've been an informer. Mr. So-and-So from such-and-such is a Heroic Corps comrade, or the like."

"Aigo!"

"Lot more jjokbari around lately."

"They're all clustered on the best land around the station and market, like they're building a Little Tokyo."

"Kei'ichi Bank, Miryang Bank, Miryang Clinic, Kanagagawa Ryokan, Tateishi Spinning Mill Miryang Branch, Miryang Post Office, Reinan Automobile Parts, Ebisu Ryokan, Shimomura Variety Shop, Miyamoto Photography Studio, Nanba Lumber, Inoue Books, Toyose Western Home Goods, Kadota Stationery, Miryang Printing Company, Nakano Store, Miryang Brewing Company, Ise-ya, Miryang Shipping Company, Usui Tin Plates, Shimomura's Barbershop, Maruniya Store, Korea Gas and Electric Company, Miyake Brewing, Uehara Ryokan, Aso Clocks, Okamoto Candies, Morita's, Yamato-ya Restaurant, Masumoto Pumps, Fuse Groceries, Fukushima Hardware, Katayama White Rice, Tanabe Bicycles."

"Aigu, you've got quite a memory."

"Well, that's something that Kyong-joo learned from her tutor. He said that if she were a boy she could've passed the civil service exams, maybe even made the top grade."

"Aniya. Don't you remember any of the names of the Korean stores you're always going in and out of? And there's so many stores with no sign. You don't go into the waenoms' stores, do you, now? So when you're passing by you read the words on the signs: *Miyamoto Photography Studio, Nanba Lumber, Inoue Books, Toyose Western Home Goods, Kadota Stationery . . .*"

"None of those stores were there fifteen years ago."

"Aigo, there wasn't even a single jjokbari around before the unification."

"And now there's over a thousand of them, I hear. One in every two thousand is a waenom."

"They're pushing us out."

Silence. "Those detectives before, whose house were they going to?"

"Aigo, they'll be killing someone else's son."

"The waenom all have blood on their hands. Man, woman, child, or elderly . . ."

"They looked like they were heading toward Mount Jongnam. I hope your son's safe, you know?"

Pu-ni pursed her lips and pointed at the young man sitting on the stone in

front of Yongdu-mok. He was asleep, his head bent deeply, with his fishing
rod still in his hands.

"Hey! Man-yong! You'll fall in the river!"

Hearing his mother call his name, he raised his head and waved but soon
dozed off again, kkubeok kkubeok—

"At his doljabi he grabbed the brush, so I always thought he'd become a
professor, but what did I know?"

"Who really cares, dear—as long as he's alive and well. Imagine letting
your precious son join the Heroic Corps! You know I think the boys who are
putting their lives on the line in the struggle are admirable, but admirable or
not, you want your own son to live."

"Today must be the Lee family's new baby's dol."

"I held him once. He's a plump and healthy little boy."

"What did he grab?"

"You can't count on the doljabi, you know. They say if the baby grabs noodles or thread he'll have a long life, but the Moon family's baby died three
months after his dol."

The water eroded the sand of the river delta and piled it up, carrying it up
even to the roots of the minari. The women picking the minari and rinsing it
looked vacantly at their hands. Even cracked hands with hangnails looked
white and soft under the water. Breathing in the smell of spring, blown to them
by the wind, the women's heads swayed as gently as the algae in the water.

Look   look   look at me
Like a flower that blooms in midwinter   look at me

Ari, arirang   suri, surirang   arariga nanne
Coming over Arirang Pass

Having finally met him
I could not hear a word he said   I was so shy

Ari, arirang   suri, surirang   arariga nanne
Coming over Arirang Pass

"And what is that fine husband over there doing, do you think?"

"He must be there every day."

"Aigo, poor Hee-hyang."

"He's a sex maniac. You have to wonder how his business is doing."

"On market days he has four or five people working for him."

"Geugeo, daedanhane!"

"He sells those rubber boots at ten sen per boot, so you know he's making a pretty penny off of them."

"I heard that every time there's a funeral that woman turns up wearing mourning clothes."

"Huh? She must be out of her mind."

"They say she always has her eye on the cloth they use to wipe the coffin!"

"Really?"

"Don't they say that if you wear part of one on you, you'll get pregnant?"

"What? I've heard about wearing a tiger's tooth on your breast, but that one's new on me."

"Is she really trying to get in the family way? But she's his mistress! Aigo, how shameless!"

I was mistaken   I was mistaken
I came as a bride in a carriage   I was mistaken

Ari, arirang   suri, surirang   arariga nanne
Coming over Arirang Pass

The wind brought snatches of "Miryang Arirang" and cherry blossom petals to the rubber boot store at the foot of the pontoon bridge. Hee-hyang, who was looking after the store, put her palm on her kneecap where it rested under her chima and began to softly whisper the words to the song. **I was mistaken   I was mistaken   I came here as a bride in a carriage   I was mistaken.** Oh, this is the chima I was wearing when Woo-gun was born. A dark red one, so even if it got bloody it wouldn't show the stains. The first night Yong-ha and I were together I showed him the bedsheet, just as my mother told me, as proof that I was a virgin, but he never saw the plastic sheet that was under me when I gave birth to Woo-gun; Eomoni and Bu-san ajumma took that to the riverside to burn.

It's been a year. I was in such pain that day that my consciousness felt like it had been blown away from my body, like a cherry petal. When I had Woo-cheol it was the first time I'd given birth, so I was wide-eyed at this pain that I'd never known before, but it wasn't such a bad labor. Su-yon and Woo-seon were both easy births, and with So-won, as soon as I'd realized my water had broken I barely had time to push before she was out.

Woo-gun was born smeared in my own blood and agony. I didn't say this to anyone, nor will I, but as I lay there smelling the blood flowing from my own groin I shuddered with a premonition of unluckiness. My trembling didn't stop when the pain began to leave me. I was so scared and worried; my heart stabbed. I shook my head over and over. But I couldn't shake that feeling from my mind. It was less a premonition and more of an afterimage. A muddy black, slimy afterimage of the future. This child will die in pain, will shed so much blood—

It had been a year. Hee-hyang picked up one after another of the cherry petals falling on her chima and placed them in her palm. Today was Woo-gun's dol. At ten months, he had spread his arms wide and walked—hana, dul, set, net, four steps; now he could totter after her without holding his arms out, totter totter tottering in his little baby shoes. He had learned a few words. Food, omma, appa, water, pee pee. His teeth were starting to come in. Pure white, adorable little baby teeth. He could eat anything now, rice, or boiled eggs, or tofu, or fish, or potatoes. Open wide, chomp chomp, chew it well, and swallow.

He keeps me constantly on my toes, making sure he doesn't get hurt. I'm hiding knives and other sharp objects in my sewing box, trying to keep mosquitoes and bees and horseflies and gnats from biting him, cutting his nails twice a week so he won't hurt himself if he scratches his face. But peace of mind is a forbidden thing. The inside of his body is bathed in bright red blood. The blood that flows heavily through him pounds harder than the river, pounding pounding, with regularity, pounding pounding, no hesitation.

I am the guard of his blood. I must not let my watch down. But if, if I were to lose my life before he grows up, who would take over the watch for me?

Him?

My nampyeon, my only husband, our children's only abeoji, the man who keeps hurting me without shedding a drop of my blood. If I hadn't had Woo-gun, maybe I wouldn't have been able to bear this pain. I protect my baby with my arms; with these arms, I cling to him.

More difficult to bear than the pain itself is the fact that it is being repeated upon me. Little by little, little by little, all sensation aside from pain is being paralyzed; I'm losing the will to grieve or be indignant; I have been taken over by pain. Pain is my master, and I am little more than its shadow. The pain persuades me. I don't know how long I will be under its spell, or how far its influence will go, but if I keep slipping under its power like this, it will wear me down, then further down, until soon I will only be able to hurt, like a corpse—

He and that woman are always lurking in the darkness. And even if that darkness seeps into their hair and backs like cold water, even if they are thrown into light by my hatred, the two of them will not release their interlocked hands; they will stay engrossed in movement, moving slowly, surely, nothing but movement.

I was mistaken   I was mistaken
I came as a bride in a carriage   I was mistaken

Hee-hyang sang "Miryang Arirang," conscious at the same time of the hatred shining like a full moon in one corner of her mind, and turned her face toward the street. A whirlwind of dust and cherry petals had clouded the glass door to the store, making it look dim and dark outside as if the street and its passersby had already disappeared.

It was April, but somehow it was muggy. Woo-gun would be miserable if he was dripping with sweat, and if he wets himself I have no change of clothes for him, but maybe I could get away with putting him in his best clothes, if his grandmother hasn't already? Certainly not, I told her that once everything was ready I'd get him dressed, so it'll be fine. Hee-hyang noticed a big spiderweb hanging between the wire to the bare light bulb and the roof beam. In the fine threads of the horseshoe-shaped web only one, two, three cherry blossom petals were caught, and she couldn't see its inhabitant. As she watched how the web undulated and twisted each time the wind blew in, her eyelids became heavy. Any spider that could spin a web that big must be big itself. Where was it hiding? Was it a long-legged brown spider? A black-and-yellow-striped one? Black and hairy? If it was inside one of the rubber boots, a customer might scream when they picked it up or crush the spider when they tried the boot on. It probably wasn't poisonous, but if it were and it bit a customer's foot, then there'd be trouble. Hee-hyang yawned widely and tears ran to the corners of her eyes. She wiped them away with the back of her hand and let her arm drop, realizing then that her armpits were sticky with sweat.

I'm so sleepy, I'll just have a little nap, really just a little one, she thought, closing her eyes, just as the back door opened.

"Annyeong haseyo."

She opened her eyes. A young man, an employee, was standing there.

"Ah, forgive me, I just dropped off for a second there."

"I'll take over."

"Is it that time already?"

"Yes, ma'am. It's twelve."

"Well, then, I'll leave it to you until this evening."

As Hee-hyang approached, the swallowtail butterflies gathered around the well for a drink of water lightly fluttered off. She rolled up the sleeves of her jeogori, scooped some well water with the drinking gourd, splashed it on her face, then gulped down the rest.

She raised her dampened face and felt her drowsiness clear away. She saw. Saw the red petals peeking out from the buds, just beginning to open, of the poppies that she and So-won had sowed together, saw the red pattern on the underside of the swallowtails' wings. Woo-gun, red is the color of fulfillment, of warding off evil, of celebration. Even the flowers and butterflies are celebrating! Saengil chukhahanda! Saengil chukhahanda! Happy birthday! Happy, happy birthday!

Inamori Kiwa sat Japanese-style and listened to the commotion of the Korean language, her eyes fixed as if she were staring at a faraway sea. If she asked, the boy sitting next to her would likely translate for her, but she could pick up a few words, and if she watched the people's expressions, she could generally understand what they were talking about. When she found herself a guest in a Korean home like this, she once again realized that she was in a foreign land. To these people, Japanese were outsiders. She felt like she wanted to explain that she was an outsider, but perhaps not quite in the way they might think, but she didn't know where to begin.

I was born in Tokyo, in Ikenohata, near Ueno. My mother and father were born and raised in Ikenohata; the man I married when I was twenty was born there too. My husband's family had for three generations run a ceramics store, and until my only son started elementary school I helped out with the family business, but we were just barely managing, so I got a midwifery license and started working. My son had heard that if he moved here he could get land for free, and that rice and resources were abundant, so he took his wife and children and crossed over to the peninsula. The more we heard about their life here from the letters and postcards he sent, the more my husband got the notion to do the same, even selling off our house, the land it sat on, and all our possessions; the day we set sail from Shimonoseki on the *Satsuma-maru* was now more than twenty years ago. My son's eldest daughter was sixteen then so she remembered life in Ikenohata clearly, but their son, who wasn't yet three at the time, remembers nothing. His eldest and second daughters had arranged marriages and have their own families here now; the youngest daughter was married last spring and soon will be in her last month of pregnancy. My great-grandchildren's birthplace is here, Kakokudō, in what they call Miryang but we call Mitsuyō, Keishōnan-do, on the Chōsen Peninsula. And to them, Ikenohata, where I was born and raised, is a foreign land they've never visited.

The woods of Ueno and Shinobazu Pond and Tōshōgū Shrine and Yanaka Cemetery appear to me in my dreams; often I lose my breath and feel my heart tremble. I don't know how many times I have thought that I wanted to go home, but I have never once truly thought I'd do it. The *Satsuma-maru* lifted anchor, and in that second, I refused all thought of a place to return.

My husband died five years ago, and he is entombed in the shrine in

Kakokudō. We Japanese built the railways, the public offices, the police stations, the banks, the schools, and the shrines. Each of the resignations and
resolutions we've made to live and die on this land have piled up one by one,
and we have built our town.

I have worked hard not to eradicate my smile. Neither my husband nor my
son, nor myself, whined or grumbled. To get used to the fact that I will never
fully be able to get used to this place, I left myself not a single moment of spare
time for regret or complaint or resentment. What happened happened; you
can't make it so that it didn't. You can only face things head-on and try to do
what should be done. And if you do what needs doing, then you can be proud.
Pride is what pushes me on.

My son and his wife keep telling me, *Mother, you should retire soon and
have some time to yourself,* but as long as my eyes are still black I shall keep
working. My four grandchildren and fifteen great-grandchildren were all delivered by my hands, and I haven't counted, but I believe that I've delivered
more than two thousand children to strangers. I think that's not a bad life. I
no longer have anything to regret, and when my time comes I will do what
must be done. My husband was a childishly impatient man, so I am certain
that he will soon be getting tired of waiting for me. *Hey, what are you doing,
how long are you going to make me wait, hurry up, get your affairs in order.*

Letting out a mental sigh, Inamori Kiwa gently felt the plaid pattern of the
pongee as she spread her palm against her thigh. If I get the boy to translate
the Korean for me, so much meaning will be lost in translation, and even if he
translates well, I shan't be able to understand, just like I shall never understand
these Koreans who bomb offices. The man who had thrown bombs into the
Miryang police station six years ago and got hanged for it was given a just
punishment, I think, but these people revere him as if he were a hero. However
much they might try to explain it to me, I shall never be able to comprehend
the goals of the Shanghai Heroic Corps who conspire to drive out the Japanese people with their despicable bombs. Those bombs might shed the blood
of my son or my grandchildren or my great-grandchildren. These people are
harboring the Heroic Corps, no, these people's own husbands and sons are in
the Heroic Corps. If one says that the existence of Japanese people on this land
is an injury to the Korean people, I have no choice but to keep my mouth

closed, but the very idea that if we don't understand each other we shall kill each other is, to me, mistaken.

We cannot understand each other. We have our position, just as these people have their own, and neither we nor they can trade places. We cannot become Korean, and these people cannot become Japanese. Perhaps in understanding only that we cannot understand each other, there is nothing for us but to avoid each other's gazes even when we meet. But I cannot not meet the eyes of a woman in labor. In the last few years I have delivered more Korean babies than Japanese. Among Korean women, I have been told, I have achieved fame: for a difficult labor, you must get the ilbon saram midwife, Inamori. This delights me. In Korean households, they appear to have a tradition of inviting the midwife to join the celebration for the baby's first birthday and showing them hospitality; seeing a baby I have delivered with my own hands standing and walking is a joy without compare.

Oh yes, this is what I was wearing when I delivered this child. I tied up my sleeves with a sash and put my white gown on, but she bled so much that the hem must be stained. When someone comes calling for me it is always a race against time, so whether it is dawn or the wee hours, all I can do is grab my bag with all my instruments and leap out the front door. My husband complained that it wasn't very attractive, but ever since I was a young woman I've worn nothing but black kimonos so the stains don't stand out.

This baby's name is Woo-gun, yes, a fine name, so it's stuck with me. With his almond eyes and his mouth stretched wide like that, he looks just like a little samurai doll. I wonder if the baby my granddaughter will have next month will be a boy. Or a girl. Perhaps I should name it after Woo-gun and use the character for rain? Rain falls, and the ground hardens. You cannot break a raindrop. Those soaked with rain should not fear the dew. I want my great-grandchild to grow up gracious and strong. If it's a boy . . . Ujaku, Ujō, Tatsu'u, Haku'u . . . If it's a girl, Miu or Ujō might work? I wonder what this boy's name is?

"What's your name?"

"Me, ma'am?"

"Yes."

"Lee Woo-cheol."

"How do you write that?"

"The characters for *rain* and *philosophy*."

"So you are Woo-cheol, and your brother is Woo-gun; what wonderful names. Your father must be quite well-learned."

Names are like obi sashes. Just as a sash left untied means your kimono will slip off, if not tied down by a proper name, your life will be stolen by the grim reaper. Whether you're Japanese or Korean, a person without a name cannot live.

A long time ago, I was asked by a woman from Aomori to give a name to her boy who had just been born. I was surprised and refused: I cannot name a stranger's child.

"I'm not askin' you to give him a real name, the midwives where I'm from in Sannohe give babies temporary names."

A temporary name?

"If you don't give a baby a temporary name, the baby gets hacked."

Hacked?

"I mean the baby will get all chapped and ugly."

I was only in my twenties then, and so in my confusion I blurted out my brother's name, Junzō. The young mother fed her newborn son, calling him over and over: Junzō, Junzō. Nowadays, I can understand the meaning of that custom. Putting a temporary name onto a baby, floating in the space between life and death with nothing of its own yet, is a ritual to bring it into the fellowship of the living. I have not counted the stillborns, yet so many babies cannot give that first cry. The babies with umbilical cords tangled around their necks, those who suffocated in breech, those born prematurely, those born with no brain—I have had to tell all these to young mothers who have just finished giving birth, with my white apron, hands, and arms still covered in their blood. One cannot lose one's courage then.

Babies who have died without time to be named will not be at rest. They cannot be called by name as are the living, nor as the dead can their names be carved, so they can only float in the space between life and death for all eternity. But more unable to be at rest are the mothers whose children have lost their lives before they were named. If a child at least has a name, it can be called, and with one's voice they can be comforted, held, prayed for.

My grandparents on both my mother's and father's sides suffered and are dead, and I have no memories of their faces, what kind of voices they had, what they liked, what they hated. What I remember is only their names, which I learned from my parents: Ryūkichi, Su'e, Shigesaku, Yone.

When the Buddha will come for me is only known in his heart, but next month I will turn sixty-nine years old. He must be coming for me shortly. It will be difficult for my great-grandchild, due next month, to have a memory of me as a living presence. But I can leave behind the name Inamori Kiwa. Names are precious mementos passed down through the generations.

"Say, Woo-cheol, what is the Korean for *great-grandmother*?" Inamori Kiwa asked, her fingers tracing over her obi fastener, decorated with a pine cone and arrow feathers with gold lacquer detailing. As mementos of her mother went, the little things like this that her mother had loved came just after her name.

"Jeungjohalmeoni."

"Jeungjohalmeoni. And *great-grandchild*?"

"Jeungsonja."

"Jeungsonja." She chuckled. "Oh, it sounds so cute."

Yong-ha looked at the profile of the midwife laughing and talking to his son in ilbon-mal. Since she had come into the house, she had sat with her legs folded under her the whole time. That was no small feat; he couldn't imitate it. And then there was the obi, constraining the stomach, which couldn't be good for you. The hem was very small—what did she do when she needed to go to the privy? Never mind that; from the way they sit to what they wear, these ilbon saram like uncomfortable things. It was the custom to invite the midwife to the doljanchi, so he had brought her here in his trailer. She had eaten the miyeok-guk and white rice and minari with obvious relish, which was nice, but the problem was the present. Usually they would give the midwife socks or under-garments, but no ilbon saram would wear anything they could give her. He had talked it over with Hee-hyang, then bought a pair of zori from a kimono store in Ne-il-dong, but would she like them or not—these ilbon saram don't show their emotions so you never know what they're thinking.

Stupid Woo-cheol, quit saying things I should be saying instead. I want to talk to her, but I can't find anything to talk about. Oh, I know: I'll explain the meaning of all the things on the birthday tray to her. Simplify it so even an ilbon saram can understand.

In Korea, the first birthday is called doljanchi. The dolsan, or birthday tray, holds items that were determined long ago. Each has a meaning and contains a wish. First, there are three varieties of doltteok, or rice cakes for celebrations. The baekseolgi, a steamed rice cake, symbolizes a prayer for holiness and innocence; the susugyeongdan, little sweet dumplings that take their red color from red bean paste, represent a wish to acquire virtue and be protected from misfortune; the songpyeon, crescent-shaped rice cakes with red bean paste or sesame inside, show the wish for the head to become full of knowledge. The doltteok will later be put on a plate and taken around to neighboring houses. In return our neighbors will put bundles of rice or metal or cotton on the plate. Returning the plate that brought the doltteok empty is shameful. And then we sit the baby in front of the dolsan, but instead of sitting on a cushion, we put the baby on a bleached cloth.

But what do I say if she asks why the bleached cloth? There must be some kind of tradition behind it, but I'll be damned if I know what it is. If I hesitate, Bu-san ajumma or my wife's mother will step in to help, but then I can't save face as the head of this household. So skip the talk about the bleached cloth. Yong-ha cleared his throat slightly so the midwife couldn't hear to prepare his voice.

"What are the items lined up on the tray?" Inamori Kiwa asked Woo-cheol, but Yong-ha didn't know because he didn't understand what she asked.

"Soon Woo-gun will grab one of the things on the tray, which will predict his future. If he grabs the thread or noodles, he will have a long life. If he grabs the jujube with its many seeds, his descendants will prosper. If he goes for the rice or money, he will be rich. The brush, inkstone, paper, and practice book mean he will be a scholar and have some fame. The arrow means that he will be a general. It's called doljabi."

At the word *doljabi*, Yong-ha realized what his son had been explaining to the midwife and cleared his throat once more to avoid showing his disappointment.

"And for a little girl?"

Woo-cheol turned to his father and asked, "Abeoji, what do you lay out for a girl?"

"A ruler, an iron, rice, noodles, a chestnut, thread, minari, and a coin."

When he'd judged that Woo-cheol had finished translating that, Yong-ha said in an impressive tone, "In Korea when a boy is born it is said, grasp the mulberry arrow and shoot, in all directions of heaven and earth—this is the wish for boys. Is it the same in Japan?"

Woo-cheol translated: "In Japan are people happier about boys too?"

"Yes, it's the same in Japan. Whether in the city or the country, people are more eager for a boy's birth, and when a boy is born we give out a hooray."

Woo-cheol translated: "It's the same."

Yong-ha asked, "How many children do you have?"

Woo-cheol translated.

"I have one son, but I have one grandson and three granddaughters."

Woo-cheol translated: "Adeureun hanande, sonjaga hanae sonnyeoga se-siranda."

Yong-ha said: "It is fitting that you have only one child, and it is a boy."

Woo-cheol translated: "How fitting."

She chuckled. "What is fitting?"

Yong-ha laughed. "Han gok hasijyo."

"He wants you to sing," Woo-cheol translated without a smile. Going between Korean and Japanese was not his strong suit.

"Very well, I shall sing a song that I often sang as a young girl while tying my obi." Inamori Kiwa arranged her hem and raised her hips.

Mukau yama no naku tori wa
Chūchū tori ka
Midori ka
Genzaburō no miyage
Nanya kanya morota
Kin sashi kanzashi morota
Byōbu no in ga oitaraba
Chūchū nezumi ga hiiteta
Doko kara doko made hiitetta
Kamakura kaidō no man'naka de
Ichi nuke ni nuke san nuke sakura

Yo yo matsuyanagi, yanagi no shita no bōsan ga
Hachi ni me-me sasarete
Itai tomo iezu
Kayui tomo iezu
Tada naku bakari

In the middle of her song Hee-hyang came into the living room wearing a crimson jeogori and a bright orange chima, with a cheery smile on her rouged lips. She lay Woo-gun down on a cloth and put trousers on him, followed by a robe with green, red, yellow, blue, and white sleeves, then a sleeveless robe like the ones worn by officials at formal occasions in the Joseon era. She then tied a doltti, an especially long belt for birthdays, around him before setting the bokgun hat on his head.

Once Woo-gun grabbed the edge of the dolsan and began to walk, the family, relatives, and neighbors started to applaud.

"Jalhanda!"

"Geureokuryeo!"

"Aigo, janghada!"

Inamori Kiwa sat Japanese-style and listened to the hubbub of the Korean language, her eyes fixed as if she were staring at a faraway sea. What kind of future would this boy have? she wondered. And in that moment she felt something hot rise up from her chest to her throat.

Reach for it, reach for your future. Whatever future that might be, well, you must grab it.

The baby stumbled and fell onto the knees of the midwife who had delivered him. She pulled a hand towel from inside her sleeve and wiped away his tears and snot, then lifted him high up in the air until they were eye to eye. The baby's eyes were as dark and clear as the water at the bottom of a well, undisturbed in any way.

"Otanjōbi omedetō gozaimasu," she said. *Happy birthday.*

The baby stuck his hand in her mouth and laughed.

TEN

November 24, 1929

| 1929년 11월 24일 | 1929年11月24日 |

The atmosphere, abandoned by light, drifted through a baseless nostalgia; the trees' shadows hung still over the fallen leaves as if imprinted on them. The cold, dry wind made a whistling sound as it whipped up the dead leaves and moved the shadows, almost blowing the little sparrows searching for something to peck at up like dust bunnies, but the birds puffed out their wings and withstood the wind.

The steel-blue sky, the frozen river, the leaves scattered on the ice that looked like dried fish, sliding across the surface every time the wind blew. The little sparrows, not missing the moment that the wind weakened, nimbly leaped into flight and cast themselves into the dried vegetation on the riverbed.

Chikchik pokpok, chikchik pokpok, chikchik pokpok, chikchik pokpok, the Keijō-bound regular service blew its whistle as it crossed the rail bridge in front of Mount Yongdu, leaving a trail of smoke trailing behind it as it went off into the distance. A dog tied up in someone's yard gave a howl as if it was chasing the train off, and howls rose up throughout the streets of the town.

The *ding ding* of the bell announcing the end of the school day hung in the air, and it seemed as though even the light of the winter afternoon would be swallowed up by the sky along with the sound of the bell; the Korean children with their cloth bundles ran out through the school gates and the area around the river became alive with laughter and joshing, and suddenly the sun peeked his face out from behind a slit in the clouds as if he had just remembered that he'd forgotten something, giving the pale landscape a taste of the sun's light.

The pontoon bridge was fixed in its place in the river by ice, and even when the children jumped up and down, it would not creak. The adult Koreans in their overcoats and cotton scarves, their faces clouded by their breaths, walked as if they were trampling their own shadows into the leaves. Across the pontoon bridge, along the embankment, were stalls selling roasted sweet potatoes and chestnuts, and at every crunching sound of footsteps coming closer, the sellers would start calling out, hawking their wares, but few would stop to buy in the midst of the coldness.

Shortly, boys carrying spinning tops and sleds came out of their houses and gathered at the river. Their sleds were little more than pieces of wood with a wire attached, so they would straddle the board and use the pole attached to the wire with both hands to slide. In less than half an hour, their little hands, chapped and frostbitten from gripping the poles, became damp with sweat, the heat rising from inside their collars.

"My top's the best."

"Spin, spin!"

"Faster!"

The shouts of the boys spinning their tops on the ice mixed with the honking of the swans. Around Yongdu-mok, where the ice was thinning and there were holes here and there, four swans were swimming around in a group. The two parent swans, with white breath coming from their black beaks like a line, were gliding in the icy water, as if guiding the way for their two cygnets, gray and still fuzzy.

Two hours before, the Busan-bound regular service had appeared from the opposite direction, and when its whistle keened, the barking of the dogs had reverberated through the streets, and the parent swans had all spread their big wings as if in concert. Tilting their long necks forward and intensifying the movements of their wings, their bodies lifted up and they glided along the water's edge, so close it was hard to tell if the tips of their wings were hitting the water or not. When one lowered its right wing to turn it was reflected clearly on the water's surface, looking as if the bird's right wing had dropped off its body. With their necks forward at a twenty-degree angle and webfeet stretched out behind them, they slowly gained height. Their shadows were no longer anywhere to be seen. Holding their outstretched wings horizontal, they went higher and higher, with Mount Yongdu and the winter sky as their backdrop, higher and higher, overlapping then stringing out in a line, higher and higher—looking up from the river, the two swans looked darkened as if they were shadows themselves; when they lowered their wings and turned, the outline of their necks and the tips of their wings suddenly were white.

With the two cygnets in the middle of the circle they were describing, the parent swans descended, thrusting their legs out and their webfeet forward before touching down on the water. For a while it seemed that they couldn't keep themselves contained, flapping and splashing water around, zooming ahead and leaving a white trail on the surface of the water, but when the cygnets came over to their sides and crooked their necks or stuck their bills under their wings, the adults stretched their necks toward the sky and: *Honk! Honk! Honk! Honk! Honk! Honk! Ding! Ding! Ding! Ding!* The bell for the end of classes at Miryang Common School interrupted the swans' song.

The Japanese kids wrapped in their dark blue overcoats with fox-fur collars appeared on the other side of the river and crossed the pontoon bridge, but the Korean kids didn't give *them* a glance, nor did the Japanese kids look at *them*. Miryang Common Primary School, where the Japanese went, and Miryang Common School, where the Koreans went, were only ten minutes' apart by foot, and many of the children even lived near one another, but Japanese and Korean children did not play together. The language they were taught in was the same; everything else was different.

The *whoosh* of the north wind rattled the doors of the houses, unconcerned whether they were Korean homes or Japanese homes, and when nobody would let it in it became a draft and snuck in, but before it could permeate everything with its coldness, the wind was already rushing on to the doorway of the next house.

At one house, on a rush mat on the veranda, an old woman who could barely see any longer was tying giant white radishes up with straw rope. She was quick, and the frame for the radishes was hanging from the eaves in no time flat. Next to the old woman was her granddaughter, wearing a red padded jacket, who sometimes snuffled as she played cat's cradle. Mountain, river, field, horse's eye, drum, then back to mountain as the wind whistled in and shook the string in her hands.

At another house, ten or so men and women from the neighborhood were gathered eating steamed potatoes, drinking unrefined rice wine, and singing as they weaved straw sandals, baskets, and bags.

Village of flowers   village of birds   my hometown
Green fields   when the south wind blows
Village of willows dancing on the riverbanks
Oh, I recall how once I played there

The wind that jumped outside whistled again hoarsely along with the song, and the people passing on the street hunched over, shrugging their shoulders up, repeating all these useless gestures, and the dried grasses shook their heads violently as if they were crazy. *Whoosh*, the wind crossed from one road to another, from one house to another, *whoosh, whoosh*ing onward.

At one house, a young husband was twisting straw into rope, and his young wife, facing him, was doing needlework.

At another house, two sisters of nine and ten had their legs stretched into the heated table as they played with beanbags. Inside the beanbags, which their mother had made from old socks, were roasted red beans and three clasps. They had pleaded for bells, but she wouldn't buy them any. The clasps and beans scraping against one another made a sound like a broken bell. *Scrape scrape, o-hitotsu o-hitotsu osaarai, scrape scrape, o-futatsu o-futatsu osaarai, scrape*, the older sister dropped the ball and opened the string holding it closed, taking out the beans from inside and putting them in her mouth.

"That's no faaair."

"It is too fair, the person who dropped the ball gets to eat them."

"Well, then, I'll drop one too." *Scrape scrape scrape, o-hitotsu o-hitotsu osaarai, scrape.*

"That's no faaair, you did it on purpose!"

At another house, although it was still hours till dusk, all the shutters were closed, and a young man was holding a can that resembled a gourd, packing it with gunpowder. At the moment the wind lowered its voice and began its retreat, the bare light bulb overhead that had been casting a gloomy light onto his work died. He straightened his shoulders with a start and looked around, then stood to make sure the shutters were locked before lighting a match. A pinprick of light blossomed, and the man's face was dimly illuminated, but before he could light the lamp, *whoosh* came the wind and blew out the fire.

At another house, a woman was in the midst of labor. Her hair still in daeng-gimeori, the pigtails of the unmarried woman, she had her legs spread wide and was pushing. She had with her only one widowed aunt.

"Sansin halme, sansin halme, geujeo agiga musahi taeeonageman hae ju-soseo," we pray for a safe birth. Her aunt whispered the prayer toward the shrine to sansin, prostrating herself.

Her niece pushed, grunting out the words *pray, healthy, boy.*

"Sansin halme, geujeo geonganghan sanaeai hana ssuk nake haejusoseo," we pray for a healthy baby boy, the aunt said.

"Oh, it's dropped, the baby's coming," the woman yelled, and her aunt rolled up her niece's skirt to have a look. The amniotic sac was coming out.

"Aigu, open your legs wide, push, himnaera! Himnaera! Aaaah!"

She gathered all the strength in her body and put it into one place.

"Here it comes! The head! One more push! Himnaera!"

The wind shook the flame of the candles in the room, then rose, rushing off to be with the father of the child.

He was keeping watch over the store with his four-year-old son. The boy was helping take rubber boots out of the trailer and line them up on the shelves.

"Oh, well done, Abeoji will have to give you a ride on his shoulders later."

"Abeoji, buy me roast chestnuts."

"Oh, well, I might."

"Do they cost a lot?"

"Not so much."

"How much?"

"Maybe five sen."

"They take the chestnuts from a mountain?"

"Well, I guess they must, yes."

"I wanna take chestnuts."

"Well, your abeoji will take you to find them, then!"

"Eeee! Going with Daddy! With Daddy!"

The wind blew at the fire in the brazier trying to notify him of the birth of his child, but it had only the slightest effect on the fire's intensity, so it gave up and meandered on toward the garden.

A woman was standing there alone. Though it was winter, she wore a white cotton jeogori and a black chima, tied around her waist with a hemp cord. Beside the well were a large, flat stone, a knife, and a pot full of boiling water. *Thundundun, thundundun.* She heard the sound of a drum. She didn't know if she was being rung by something or if she was ringing it herself. Only she and the wind heard the sound. In time with the sound of the drum, the wind whistled, and the woman shuffled forward. *Thundundun, thundundun, whoosh whoosh.* Winter's mask was plastered on the woman's face. *Thundundun, thundundun, whoosh whoosh.* The woman lifted up the wings of the hen sitting on its eggs in the corner of the garden. *Bwawk! Bwawk!* Brown feathers scattered themselves. *Bwawk! Bwawk!* The hen thrashed its legs, trying to free itself, but the woman was standing on the bird's legs with her rubber boots, putting pressure on them. With her left hand she grabbed the hen's wings; with her right, she wrung its neck, hana, dul, set, net, daseot, yeoseot, ilgop, the hen opened its beak wide and stuck out its white tongue. *Thundundun, thundundun, thundundun, whoosh, whoosh.* The hen stretched out with a cluck and tried to kick, but the woman dug her thumb into its throat. *Thundundun, thundundun, whoosh, whoosh.* The hen closed its snow-white eyelids and went limp. The woman took the hen by its legs and dunked it headfirst into the boiling water and, slowly, as if she were rubbing the inside of the pot with it, swirled the hen's body around, once, twice, then let go. She used the tip of the knife's blade to put the hen on its side and submerge it. She grabbed its legs and pulled it from the water. She laid it down on top of the flat rock, facing upward. *Thundundun, thundundun.* The woman reached out to the hen, steam rising. First the legs; she peeled off the yellow skin smoothly. Next the feathers, like shucking a corncob. *Thundundun, thundundun.* The woman saw how her hands moved as if they had their own will. *Thundundun,*

thundundun. Some of its intestines were hanging from its anus; probably they had come out when she'd wrung the bird's neck. Bright red, her palm burned, although she couldn't feel the heat. She drew water from the well and stuck her hand in it and instantly felt the intense coolness soak into her skin.

She put the hen in the hot water again. The longer it stayed in the water, the easier it would be to pluck the feathers, but the skin and meat would start to cook if she overdid it, so hana, dul, set, net, daseot, then she pulled it from the water and put it on the flat rock. She could barely see her own hands for the steam rising from the hen. *Whoosh, whoosh,* the wind fanned the steam up. The crest and head and legs and the intestines falling out of its anus were now white. *Thundundun, thundundun.* The woman plucked the feathers, sometimes dunking her hands in cool water. There were few feathers left now, just the pins that stuck out like the spikes of a cactus. Grab, pluck, grab, pluck; it required a fair amount of strength, dunk fingers in cold water, pluck, pluck, pluck, *thundundun, thundundun,* dunk in water, pluck, pluck, pluck, *thundundun, thundundun.* She grabbed the legs with one hand and brought the bird's anus up to eye level. There were still feathers around it. Each time she applied force with her fingers, the head, falling forward, wobbled in the air. Pluck, pluck, wobble wobble. She splashed well water over it, then put the hen in the water in the metal basin and scrubbed hard, as if she were trying to get the dirt off a radish. When she lifted up the wings, now little more than skin and bones, there were still feathers on the undersides. Grab, pluck, grab, pluck, she would not miss a single one, she would strip the hen bare. She grabbed the feathers on its small, hard head, and pluck, pluck, plucked. The woman changed the water in the basin and washed the bird again. She scrubbed, scrubbed like she was washing a baby's diapers. She pulled at its head and rubbed its neck; the contraction of the skin caused its eyes to open halfway. The eyes had been boiled and the membrane was over them, but near the outer corners of the eyes she could see faintly its black eyes. Scrub scrub, her hands moved swiftly, but her pulse beat so slowly it was unnatural, like a snake in hibernation, *thump-thump . . . thump-thump . . . thump-thump . . .*

Ije kkaekkeutaejyeotji, looking nice and clean now. The woman scooped water from the well and washed away the feathers from the stone, then laid the bird on it. *Thundundun, thundundun, whoosh, whoosh.* She grabbed the knife, stooped down, and made a cut at one of the bird's joints. She snapped it, chopped with the knife, right leg! Make a cut, snap, chop, left leg! She threw the legs in the metal basin. *Thundundun, thundundun.* She drew the knife's blade from the breast to the stomach. She pressed the edge of the blade into the flesh. Dark blood came gushing out, turning the hen's white skin red. The blood got under her fingernails, into the cracks on her hands, snap, snap, she put all her strength into snapping the bird's rib cage, as if it were a double-hinged door that wouldn't open.

With her left hand pulling open the rib cage, she put her right hand into the pool of blood and turned the knife upward. *Thundundun, thundundun,* with the tip of the knife she slit the bird's throat, up to just under its beak. *Thundundun, thundundun.* The movement of her hands could not be stopped. She felt she wanted to say something, but like her hands, her voice wasn't up to her expectations. Her vocal cords would not move. She pleaded. Not knowing what she was pleading or what she was pleading to, still she pleaded with her full body and soul. Her breast and back felt as if they were held between two boards, and now more strongly than ever, please, sallyeojuseyo, sallyeojuseyo, sallyeojuseyo!

She stuck her hand inside the hen and tore away the lungs stuck to the rib cage and threw them into the metal basin. Igeon mot meokgetda, we can't eat this. She ripped out the stomach and threw it away too. Igeotdo mot meok-getgo, or this either. She set the heart and liver aside. Igeohago igeoneun meo-geul su itgo, these are fine. The woman gently, lovingly, let her hands slide inside and untangled the intestines, so fresh they might still be pulsing. *Thundundun,* the strange warmth in her hands, *thundundun,* the heat of life itself becoming steam, *thundundun,* she held its viscera in her hand and re-moved it. *Thundundun, thundundun,* inside the hen, now completely stripped of all its internal organs, rattled blood-covered eggs. They were bare egg yolks, unprotected by shell or egg white, hana about the size of one Ping-Pong ball, dul about the size of a chestnut, dul about the size of a jujube, dul the size of ginkgo nuts, net the size of a soybean, aigo, there were hundreds of even smaller ones the size of maggots! She pushed the yolks the size of grains of rice off the top of the stone with all the blood, using her knife. The knife was drip-ping with blood from blade to handle.

Aigu, it looks like I've killed somebody! Who did I kill? Who do I want to kill?

Thundundun, thundundun. Even her bare feet inside her rubber boots were bloody, this lukewarm sticky blood. *Thundundun, thundundun.* She cut the gizzard in half and removed the membrane, then pulled out the gizzard. Once she washed away the blood and sediment with well water, the white organ, which looked gray in some places and yellow in others, looked like a blind sea creature that might still swim around the seafloor. *Thundundun, thundundun.* She found something that looked like a testicle hanging off one part of the ovaries. She opened the membrane carefully with the blade of her knife so as not to damage what was inside; globs of egg white dribbled out, and into her palm dropped a yellow. An egg that would've been laid the next day, that would've had its shell formed that night. She set the yolk with the other small ones that she had already taken out, then unraveled the guts so they stretched out. *Thundundun, thundundun.* She put the tip of her knife inside and opened up the intestines. *Thundundun, thundundun.*

She brought a pinch of coarse salt out from the kitchen, massaged the intestines with it, then washed them. Then, finally, she hit the chicken's legs with the handle of her knife—*thundundun, thundundun*—pulled the bones out, and threw them away.

It had taken rather a long, blood-soaked time. The afternoon light was beginning to fade. A fly that had come out of nowhere was on the gizzard, rubbing its hands together. *Whoosh whoosh*, the wind chased away the fly, and in its place dropped an ivy leaf, dancing near the bird's heart. *Twitch twitch, whoosh whoosh, twitch twitch, whoosh whoosh.*

The woman dug a hole in the corner of the garden and buried the unwanted organs and bones. If they were left unburied an animal might eat them, and neither a dog nor a pig should ever know the taste of chicken, because then they would attack and eat chickens. She returned to the well, drew some water, and threw it on the stone, wiped away the blood and the fragments of the intestines with her hand, then drew more water and cleaned the knife and metal basin. As the blood seeped into the ground, the woman felt the mask that had been stuck to her face slide off.

On the rock the beautiful intestines glimmered, ill-suited to a garden in

November. Heart. Liver. Gizzard. Eggs. She looked inside the hen's empty abdomen, turned her head around slowly, and saw the three eggs that had been left in the corner of the garden. *Whoosh whoosh*, the north wind got fiercer. To get rid of the warmth that still remained in the hen, *whoosh whoosh, thundundun, thundundun,* the wind brought the sound of the drum from the far distance. *Whoosh whoosh, thundundun, thundundun,* getting harder, faster, harder! Harder! *Thundundun! Thundundun!* Pain, almost like she had been speared, ran through her head; she staggered and fell to her knees. *Thundundun!* Light exploded in her head, *thundundun! Thundundun!* Aigo, nunbusyeola! She clung to the rim of the well. *Thundundun! Thundundun!* Blackness. She could not see a thing. But she could feel someone's eyes. Someone is looking at me through the darkness. *Thundundun thundundun whoosh whoosh,* she heard a different sound than the drum. What is that? A light, faint and dim, came, *whoosh whoosh,* the sound of the wind. She became frantic at the depths of her consciousness. She could not let herself be swallowed up by the darkness yawning open before her. She focused only on the sound of the wind and pushed open the ring of light, and the sound of the drum became farther away. *Thundundun thundundun whoosh whoosh,* now she could only hear the sound of the wind. *Whoosh,* she realized that she was leaning into the well and she took two steps back, hana, dul, but her field of vision lurched and she fell, the wall of the well looming over her like a tower. She pushed with both her hands against the side of the well, leaving two red handprints.

Blood? But I just washed it all off. Whose blood?

She brought her palm up to her face. There was nothing on it. *Whoosh, whoosh,* her vision cleared and the pain in her head lessened. She listened to the quiet of the garden. *Whoosh,* under the faded ink-colored sky, the shadows of the tree branches and dead leaves and the clothes airer and the earthenware pots quivered.

My mouth is moving. Like I'm talking to someone. But no sound or word is coming out. My face is twitching too. Maybe I should sleep it off a little. Ten or twenty minutes.

She put her hands on the rim of the well and stood up.

"Eomoni, are you all right?"

Whoosh whoosh. Hee-hyang waited for the sound of the wind to die down before opening her mouth.

"I'm fine."

"You look awfully pale."

"I just got a little dizzy, that's all." Sweat ran down her back, going from her armpits to her sides.

Woo-cheol's eyes fell to the flat stone. The bird had a small crest and there were eggs, too, so it must be the hen. With only three precious hens, why had she killed one? They'd just had Abeoji's birthday; and So-won and he were both born in December, so still some time away; Woo-gun was born in April; and Eomoni's birthday was in May—so what was the celebration? Jung-yangjeol, the ninth day of the ninth lunar month, was over, and nobody had said anything about anyone getting married, and the ceremony for devotees of Confucian scholars was next month.

"Is company coming?" Woo-cheol asked.

Hee-hyang came out of the kitchen with straw and straw rope, placed the organs inside the chicken's abdomen, bundled the hen up in the straw, and tied it at both ends.

"Go take this for me."

"What?"

"Go take this for me," Hee-hyang said in exactly the same tone.

"Where?"

"The house by the cedars."

Woo-cheol was silent.

"Your sibling's been born."

Woo-cheol raised his chin slightly and looked at the straw bundle.

"Go take it for me," she repeated.

He hesitated. "Tomorrow's the big competition, you know."

"It won't take you five minutes if you run, surely? So go take this there for your mother."

He didn't want to continue this conversation, so Woo-cheol took the straw bundle and ran off, turning his back on his mother.

"And look to see if there's chilis in the geumjul!"

Whoosh whoosh, the wind and the woman seemed to rest against each other as they watched her son run off. *Whoosh whoosh*, when she could no longer see her son's back, she smoothed down her chima with the knife.

Whoosh whoosh, the wind entered his cotton jeogori from the neck. Woo-cheol walked not in the direction of the house by the cedars but toward Gyo-dong, going up a narrow, sloping path. At dusk, the path was quiet, with no sign of anyone else, and it went on forever. Every house's gate had a piece of paper with a wish written on it for a happy New Year or for good health and good weather. Good handwriting and bad, thick ink and thin. Woo-cheol's eyes went to the platform in front of an upper-class yangban house's gates. When they'd been out for a walk recently, Woo-gun had asked him, *What's that?*, and he'd answered, *That's for climbing up to ride a horse*; now he felt like mounting a horse and riding off somewhere. He heard the snarling of dogs fighting in the garden of a house. He smelled the aroma of dinner, pork soup and garlic in fermented bean paste, coming from a kitchen somewhere. When was it, he wondered, that having dinner with his family became agony?

In February his halmoni had died, and at the funeral he'd heard from some visitors who'd come to pay their respects a rumor that the woman in the house by the cedars was pregnant. Ever since, his eomoni had gotten stranger all the time. *She's mourning your halmoni's death; they were so close*, his abeoji had told him, but after the ceremony on the thirty-seventh day, and then even after the one on the forty-ninth day, Eomoni's dizzy spells and nausea had only gotten worse. When it was really bad she stayed in bed for three days, unable even to eat or go to the toilet. She had tried traditional medicine and acupuncture, they had even had a mudang do an uhwangut for her, but she didn't get better, and the reason was, undoubtedly, because the belly of the woman in the house by the cedars was getting bigger by the day.

Woo-cheol adjusted his grip on the bundled hen. What should he say when he handed it over? This is from my mother, congratulations? He couldn't say that. He needed to breathe in the cold air for longer, much, much longer. Woo-cheol crossed the river, listening for any sound of water under the ice, and stood in the middle of the delta. *Whoosh whoosh*, the wind blew straight in his face in defiance. Woo-cheol felt his lungs swell with cold air. There were no swans. Usually they swam near Yongdu-mok. *Honk! Honk! Honk!* Woo-cheol looked up at the sky. The swans were flying. Hana, dul, set, net, daseot, yeoseot, ilgop, yeodeol, ahop, nine of them, their wings reddened by the evening sun, but in the shadow of their wings their bodies were tinged with blue.

How beautiful. Standing in the middle of the river like this, it was like there was no war anywhere. Well, no, he thought, but this delta that I'm standing on right now looks like it's frozen in place, but the truth is that the water flowing under the ice is constantly wearing it down, and soon my big feet won't even have a place to stand.

His thumb, with a splinter stuck in it, ached. Woo-cheol bit the flesh of his finger trying to get the splinter out. Where did he get it? Maybe yesterday at the main building of the shrine.

From the gap in the boards, the afternoon light had stretched long to the side. She had reached out to the object of worship and touched it, then taken off her undergarments. Purely because of the location, the previous day's rendezvous had felt ceremonial.

"Let's just not move until one of us can't stand it anymore."

"With me inside you?"

"Yes."

So we'll see who can hold out. We held each other close with no gap between us, feeling only the parts of ourselves that had started to meld into each other, looking into each other's eyes. She was the one who opened her mouth.

"I can't take it anymore."

"Just a little longer, so warm, feels so good. Ah."

"You're moving. Don't move."

"No, you're moving, look, you're shaking again."

They heard the rustling of someone walking on dead leaves getting closer. *Thump-thump*, the sound of his heart, *rustle rustle*. I moved my hips, slowly, *rustle rustle*, even when the sound of footsteps stopped I didn't.

She bit the back of her own hand to stifle herself. The prayer bell rang. I sped up the movement of my hips. *Clap clap*, the sound of someone clapping in prayer reverberated.

I came.

Thump-thump, our hearts beat in time as the sound of footsteps got farther away. *Thump, rustle, thump, rustle.*

Chikchik pokpok, chikchik pokpok, the sound of the train almost brought Woo-cheol back to reality, but when the whistle blew and the train disappeared toward Mount Adong, he once again slipped back into his memories.

My fiancée. Six months ago Abeoji asked me if I wanted to be introduced to some girls.

Chee In-hye, the seventh of eight children. Only the first and eighth are boys, so she has four older sisters, who all dote on her like she's their own daughter. Her family runs a rice store. Oh, you know the one, the big place next to Shimomura's Barbershop near the station. They have the store plus a house and a warehouse, and they have three or four employees. They're pretty successful, so imagine the dowry. And Chee In-hye is learning from her eomoni how to cook and do needlework, all the training to be a bride, but she also went to private classes until she was sixteen, so she can read and write hangul and Chinese characters, and she loves to read classics like *Myeongsim Bogam* and *The Tale of Sim Chong*.

"She's two years older than you. She's no beauty, but you can't choose a bride by her looks. As long as she's kind, cheerful, and lively. Anyway, all the talk about her is that she'll be a good wife, so I think you should meet her. You'll never know if you don't," Abeoji had said.

Woo-cheol had arrived to meet her without much in the way of expectations, and she certainly wasn't ugly; in fact, depending on the angle she sometimes looked beautiful. And more important, she looked him straight in the eye when they spoke, without affectations. He was charmed by her manner of speaking, imagined that he could spend a lifetime talking with this woman, and decided to have her as his wife.

Once they had exchanged napchae and the nappye, the betrothal, was over, they were allowed to meet just the two of them, and once the rainy season had ended, they had started to see each other every day. Listening to her and her listening to him had started to become vital to him. When she was listening intently to him her eyes smiled, as if her pupils were poking fun at him; they glittered with intelligence—one day in August, entranced by her eyes, he had pressed his lips to hers. Once he had kissed her he could not stop, until her lips and tongue were red and swollen; he kissed her until he didn't know if they were kissing while talking or talking while kissing.

It happened on the last day in August. Since morning the rain had jumped about on the ground. After noon, the sun had poked its face out from the grave of rain, and unable to wait for the rain to ease off, he had run to her house.

In-hale ex-hale in-hale ex-hale just as the rain lifted it had become hot, as if a blaze had surged in the sky. In-hale ex-hale if the force of these flames were to burn everything on earth in-hale ex-hale in-hale ex-hale steam rose from the road and my body in-hale ex-hale in-hale ex-hale in-hale ex-hale in-hale ex-hale in-hale ex-hale in-hale ex-hale

She was sitting on a stool in front of her house waiting.

"I thought you might come when the rain stopped."

"If I didn't come what would you have done?"

"I couldn't think about that."

"You're an odd one."

"Oh, how can you say that? After all, you did come."

She laughed, exposing her small, white front teeth.

He wiped the sweat from his face with the sleeve of his hemp jeogori as he walked along the riverside, with her beside him, treading on his shadow. They climbed, passing a path teeming with green foxtails and plantain, hand in hand, looking out for rocks and brush, until they reached a small meadow hidden by the trunks and branches and leaves of sawtooth oaks.

He gazed at her face.

"What?"

"I wanted to see you."

"We just saw each other yesterday."

"As soon as we've said goodbye, I want to see you again."

"Then I guess we'll just have to be together all the time."

"I want to marry you soon."

He kissed her under a sawtooth oak that buzzed with the cries of the cicadas.

He took her tongue into his mouth. His mouth filled with her saliva. His tongue caressed the smooth reverse of her teeth one by one. The tip of her tongue flicked into movement, and she took his tongue into her mouth. He let her. More. More. When their lips parted for breath, the cheeks of her down-turned face were blushing, and her hair, in daenggimeori, shone in the afternoon sun. *Maeaemmaeaemmaeaem   maeaemmaeaemmaeaem maeaemmaeaemmaeaem   chireureureut   chireureureut   chireureureut.*

She closed her eyes and leaned against the oak, becoming as quiet as the bark. She undid her sash and slipped off her jeogori, then opened her undershirt, without saying a word. The light filtering through the leaves of the trees fell on her breasts, creamy white apart from the pale brown mole to the right below her collarbone.

"You're beautiful."

The words slid from his mouth.

"I love you," she said, her eyes still closed.

The wind blew; the circles of light on her breasts shook. He knelt. He gently caressed one of her red nipples with his thumb, and it rose, becoming hard. Perhaps because the rain had stopped, the ground and grass gave off a sweaty, moldering scent. Cradling one nipple in his palm, he brought his face to her other breast and took her nipple into his mouth. It hardened more in his mouth, and as he licked and sucked, his heart beating faster now, to its limits, he could no longer check his desire. He put his hand on her blue chima.

"No, we can't, we can't do that until we're married. Andwaeyo, butagieyo, anything else you want, but not that, please, no."

She smoothed her chima down, but he grabbed her wrist and pulled her chima up and pushed her down onto the grass.

"Andwaeyo! Sireoyo! I told you, we have to wait until we're married."

She flapped like a hen does when someone grabs its body, thrashing and raising hell.

"Sireo!"

The moment he stopped her mouth with his palm, he felt a dark spirit slip down within him. He pinned down her struggling body and yanked down her undergarments, taking off her undershorts and underwear in one. He grabbed her locked kneecaps with both hands and pulled them apart, and he had just forced his legs between her hips when he realized he didn't have a clue where he should put what. He was distracted. All muscles were strained, his and hers. Suddenly he was inside her, inside! But no matter how much he thrust he couldn't go all the way in. He took a deep breath, as he did before starting to run, and thrust again, and a muffled cry of anguish left her throat. Supporting his own weight with his elbows he rammed, harder, faster.

Her nipples, still showing how he'd suckled them, like a bruise; her legs, held open and unmoving; her pale thighs, now scratched; her right hand, grasping the grass; the toes of her left foot, out of its shoe, bent unnaturally— she looked like she were dying. He began to worry and pressed his ear to her chest. *Thud thud thud thud thud thud*, it was moving; he was glad. *Thud thud thud thud thud thud*. He stroked her hair and put his mouth to her ear.

"Are you all right?"

"Sireo."

"Sorry."

"It was so painful."

"Sorry."

"It still hurts. . . ."

She opened her eyes, straightened the collar of her chima, and sat up.

"What if I get pregnant?"

"I'd be happy."

"That was my first time."

"Me too . . . what do we do with your chima?"

"The blood will come out if I wash it in cold water. . . . My mother told me . . . that if I wash myself well, I won't get pregnant. . . . I'll be right back."

With a childish quickness she kicked off the shoe from her right foot and started off walking, so he hurriedly put on his underwear and followed after her.

She splashed into the river with her chima still on until the water was up around her hips, then turned her back to the flow and stood still. Her blue chima floated with the water's movements, swaying as if mourning that it could not flow away with the water—he closed his eyes and saw a few dots of light dancing in the darkness of his eyelids.

"What, are you asleep?"

He opened his eyes and saw her bare feet. Her chima was dripping, clinging perfectly to her body. Her calves, her knees, her thighs, her hips; he breathed in the smell of the chima that he had gotten wet.

"No, I'm awake."

"Oh no, you were, weren't you?"

"I just closed my eyes 'cause it's so bright."

The sun was behind her, making her face look pitch-black. *Ki! Ki! Ki!* A bird, one whose name he didn't know, screeched out like a warning from the top of a tree.

"Did it come out?"

"Yeah."

"The blood is coming out too."

Her face was very serious as she wrung out her chima like a washrag. He could see her calves, knees, hips.

"You should take it off and let it dry for a little while."

She hesitated. "You're right."

He grabbed her cool, damp hand. Then, accompanied by the smell of the water, they went away from the sound of it, walking into the trees where the sunlight fell almost in lines, and returned to the secret place that only the two of them knew.

She took off her chima and hung it on an oak branch, then crouched down, hiding her body as she reached for her undergarments.

"Show me."

"Sireo, I'm embarrassed."

"There's no reason to be. There's nothing to hide anymore. Stand up."

She stood up and let her arms hang limply. He saw the lower half of her body, now exposed to the August light.

Was that a mole? No, it was an ant, crawling up from her ankle to her calf.

"There's an ant on you."

"Kill it!"

He squashed the ant with the pad of his pointer finger, then made that finger crawl up her leg instead. He parted her damp and clinging bush; inside was warm and sticky, and his finger slipped inside, as if the hardness before had been a lie.

"Open up a little more."

She quietly did as she was told. He put his hand on her thigh and brought his face closer. He brought his lips to hers and moved his tongue, and she drew a breath, panting, *ah, ha, ah, ha, ah, ha.*

"I want you again."

"No, it still stings."

"This time I'll be gentle; we'll go slow."

He took her down to the grass in his arms. He covered her body with his, and the smell of his sweat enveloped her completely. He entered her to the sound of cicadas. *Maeaemmaeaemmaeaem maeaemmaeaemmaeaem chireureureut chireureureut.* She was much softer than before, much more wet. With their fingers entwined he spread his legs and moved his hips. *Maeaemmaeaemmaeaem*, like sliding, *maeaemmaeaemmaeaem*, like sinking, *maeaemmaeaemmaeaem*, like melting, *chireureureut chireureureut*, the cicadas cried. She opened her mouth slightly and let out the breath she had been holding. *Ah, ah, ah*, her breath became shorter with each thrust, *ha, ha, ha, ha ah, ah ah*, until their voices merged and her knees began to tremble. He stopped moving.

"Does it hurt?"

"N-no . . ."

He began to move his hips again, watching her face, but when he could not restrain himself anymore he gradually sped up his movements. The moment when he thought he might come, she opened her eyes and looked straight into his. Her eyes were startling, questioning everything, seeking everything.

"Together forever?"

"Forever."

"Until we die?"

"Until we die."

"Don't leave me."

"I won't."

"Promise."

"I promise."

"No one but me."

She wrapped her arms around his back, and he cradled her head in his hands. A blinding golden light, like looking directly into the sun, ran from his spine to the top of his head, and that light became chaotically mixed up with the feeling that he didn't know whether he wanted to laugh or cry, *ah-ah-ah-ah, chireureureut, chireureureut, ah-ah-ah-ah-ah, chireureureut, ah-ah, chireureureut, chireureureut, ah-ah-ah-ah-ah, chireureureut, ah-ah, chireureureut, ah-ah, chireureureut,* he came inside her.

Just back from the river, she let down her daenggimeori and combed her fingers through her hair, which hung down to her waist. The moment he saw her breasts rise when she combed her hair upward with her hands, he felt, for the first time in his life, the deep sense of having someone else as his own.

She calmly tilted her long neck like a horse and started braiding her hair.

"My unni says she must be crazy, walking around wearing daenggimeori when her belly's so big."

"Who?"

"That woman."

"Oh."

"Nobody in this town's on her side."

"Mm."

"Your father hasn't said anything?"

"Not a word."

"Now don't you have any affairs, honey."

She took the red ribbon from her mouth and tied the end of her hair, then looked up at him, but he could not see her face. He felt bashful, both from the fact that he had been called "honey" for the first time in his life, and from the fact that the taste of her still lingered in his mouth, and the feeling that a line had been crossed and now they could not turn back.

Once he'd put his clothes on, his body felt heavy, exactly as if he'd just gotten out of the river after swimming. From here on, he realized, he would have to live entangled with the lives of others, responsible for her life, yes, and the lives of the children she would have—

He walked the riverside as always and did not remember now what they had talked about, but he had made a joke and she had laughed, freer of care than usual, and looked up at his face in profile. Suddenly, her fingers, damp with sweat, grabbed his.

A woman was walking toward them, both hands on her big belly, moving slowly as if she were walking through water—it was the woman from the house by the cedars. Her face was as fragile and beautiful as a white flower, in spite of having the outrageous thing of getting pregnant while committing adultery less than ten minutes away from her lover's wife's home.

That woman is going to have my little brother or sister, and maybe I've gotten this woman pregnant, he thought, and felt something stir inside him. Sleeping with her before marriage had been less about desire than about wanting revenge on his abeoji. He'd known that his abeoji had been sneaking around on his eomoni and going to see his mistress every day, but he couldn't show his anger at home. This anger, not given an outlet, had burned and hardened within him. And he had poured this anger into her, in the hope perhaps that it would dissolve.

Slowly her face came closer; his neck became hot, and he could not breathe properly. The moment they passed each other, the woman from the house by the cedars looked into his eyes and smiled.

"Annyeong, where are you off to?"

On the spur of the moment, he returned her greeting.

His fiancée bit at her fingernails reproachfully, so he walked faster, away from the woman from the house by the cedars.

"Do you know each other?"

"No."

"She knows you though. But how unbelievable! If I were in her position, I wouldn't be able to hold my head up, let alone grin and say hello like that! Despicable! Why did you bow to her?"

"Out of habit. . . ."

"Oh no, no, you've got to give her the cold shoulder. . . ."

Woo-cheol shifted the straw bundle of chicken in his cold-numbed hands. He crossed the river, listening to the flow of water under the ice and the flow of blood under his skin, then dashed up the embankment. The hen's body and his were both freezing.

In-hale   ex-hale   in-hale   ex-hale   events of the past are expelled from my body with my breath   in-hale   ex-hale   in-hale   ex-hale   if I breathe in new events with the air in-hale ex-hale in-hale ex-hale in-hale ex-hale in-hale ex-hale in-out

Woo-cheol took a deep breath before opening the wicker gate. He walked under the tall cedars and had passed by the well when he heard a woman crying inside the house. She was crying like a small child, unable to stop sobbing convulsively by the momentum of her own voice.

"I beg your pardon!" Woo-cheol bellowed.

A paper sliding door opened, and a middle-aged woman he didn't recognize stuck her head out.

"Who may I say is calling?"

"I'm Woo-cheol, Lee Yong-ha's son."

"Ah, thank you . . . I'm Mi-ryeong's aunt, Ok-sun."

"I've brought this from my eomoni." Woo-cheol held out the straw bundle.

"Jeongmallo gomapseumnida, thank you truly. Please, come in. The baby must be your little sister, so please, come take a look at her."

Woo-cheol hesitated.

"Mi-ryeong's been crying like that ever since she found out it isn't a boy; she won't even try to feed her. I intend to leave her to it until she feels better. The baby is asleep in the bedroom, so please, come this way. Welcome."

Woo-cheol took off his rubber boots and entered the house.

So this is where my father comes every day.

With every step he felt the hatred rising within him like bile; he had to control the muscles around his stomach.

The baby was asleep, swaddled in a white cloth. Her face was yellow, like the sole of a foot, and she was so thin that he could see her skeleton. Was she dead? A chilly numbness spread through his body, and his lips stiffened; even blinking his eyes felt clumsy.

"Born a bastard and her own mother won't even look at her; I'd say she's the most unfortunate of the unfortunate."

Ok-sun knelt, placing one hand under the baby's neck and the other under her buttocks; when she tried to bring the baby close to her body, the baby's lips and limbs twitched, and she began to cry.

"You're all right, you're all right, good girl. Your brother's here to see you. Go on, show him your precious little face. Do you want to hold her?"

"I have to get going." He was grateful that his voice dragged some words out along with it.

"Oh, I see. Well, I'll show you out, then." Ok-sun slid her hand from under the baby's head to rest it in the crook of her elbow; using the other to support her buttocks and back, she stood up.

"That's all right. I'll show myself out."

Woo-cheol put on his boots and quickly walked away from the sound of the woman's and the baby's crying. *Whoosh whoosh*, the wind blew into his cheeks, biting into his skin. When he began to run, the wind buffeting his back, Woo-cheol realized just how much he had been straining every part of his body.

Hee-hyang was in the kitchen preparing dinner.

"I took it there."

She turned; her eyes seemed to be frozen.

"Is it a boy?"

"It's a girl."

For only a moment they looked each other in the eye, then turned away at the same time.

Woo-cheol turned his back to his mother and ran   in-hale   ex-hale   in-hale   ex-hale   ran and ran   he wanted to evaporate   in-hale   ex-hale   in-hale   ex-hale   the anger that coursed through every vein in his body like a toxin   in-hale   ex-hale   Woo-cheol ran up the stone steps to Yeongnamnu, taking them two at a time   hana   dul!   Hana   dul!   Swing your arms! Hana   dul!   Hana   dul!   Put your back into it!   Hana   dul!   Up! Hana   dul!   Onward!   haahaahaahaa   his breath turned white and his nose was running   haahaahaahaa   haahaahaahaa   he wiped the snot with his sleeve   now down   hana   dul!   Hana   dul!   Hana   dul!   Hana dul!   haahaahaahaa   breathe deep   in   exhale   out   in   out   now up again   hana   dul!   Hana   dul!   Hana   dul!   Hana   dul!   All right! At the top now!

Time to go down! Hana dul! Hana dul! Someone's walking up the stairs haahaahaahaa

"Woo-cheol, it's me!"

It was Woo-hong. Both were helping out with their family's business so they couldn't spend time together like they had in school, but they had occasionally met and talked since graduation.

"What's wrong? You're making a horrible face."

Woo-hong came up to the middle of the stairs.

"No, you," Woo-cheol panted.

Woo-hong's face was so pale that it couldn't only have been due to the moonlight. Woo-cheol saw in his friend's face that there was something troubling him.

"Your eomoni told me you'd run off; I've been looking for you everywhere."

"Has something happened?" Woo-cheol asked, still breathing heavily.

Woo-hong hesitated. "We need to talk."

Their shadows went into Yeongnamnu, and the wind held its breath, but the moonlight stirred the dried grass and the cedar trees. It was a totally clear, bright night sky. The full moon was so big that Woo-cheol felt if he looked up he would feel his heels float off the ground, so big that it seemed to be standing still in a drawing someone had made.

"When's the competition?"

"Tomorrow." Finally his breathing had calmed. Woo-cheol took a deep breath through his nose.

"How's your form?"

"Not bad."

"How great it'd be if you won."

They sunk into silence. Woo-cheol turned his eyes away from Woo-hong's and hung his body over the railing. He'd told his friend that the napchae was done, but he hadn't yet confided in him that he'd slept with her. I probably won't tell him that I've been to the house of the woman who lives by the cedars and seen my half sister either, he thought. Only a year and a half had passed since they graduated, but what they couldn't talk about had already grown larger than what they could.

Woo-hong seemed to be whittling his thoughts down to one point, bathed in the light of the moon.

"I'm leaving on the seven o'clock express."

"Where are you going?"

"Shanghai," he said, lowering his voice.

"Shanghai?"

"I don't think I'll be coming back." His words were even quieter now.

A big mass of air formed in his chest, one that could neither float nor sink, and stopped there. Woo-cheol had to say something, just to be able to breathe.

"The Heroic Corps?"

The words flowed between them like static electricity. Woo-cheol looked at his own hand on the railing. It looked still. Like it wasn't shaking.

So is it my eyes that are shaking?

"Have you packed already?"

"I can't really take much. It'd be too suspicious. Just one trunk. I've put it in the storeroom so my abeoji won't find it."

"Have you made contact with your brother?"

"I don't know if he's alive or if he's dead." Woo-hong's head hung down so far that his chin nearly touched his chest, but soon he raised his face and looked up at the moon with a piercing gaze.

"*I want to do something worth dying for.*"

For the first time Woo-cheol felt scared of his friend, and that thought was overwhelmingly sad.

"I haven't got much time."

"I'll take you to the station."

"Here's fine. Goodbye, jal itgeora."

"Jal gara."

The sound of Woo-hong's feet disappeared more quietly than the sound of a leaf falling. Woo-cheol moaned for one, two minutes before he realized that he was making any sound at all. It was as if he could hear the moonlight. As if he could smell it. Woo-cheol dove into himself, somewhere deeper than where anger and sadness come from, deeper even than where cold or heat are felt. It was a beautiful night. The most beautiful night in his sixteen years of life. The wind returned and tried to bring things back to how they were before, but it was already too late, all of it. The ice on the river has melted! Now there was no way to stand on it. I'll run! Even if there's nowhere for my legs to stand, all I can do is run, onward, onward, one foot after the other! Woo-cheol filled his chest with all the things that had happened that day and began to run.

In-hale ex-hale in-hale ex-hale in-hale ex-hale in-hale ex-hale

Her fingers moved inside the covers of her bed as if she were searching for someone's hand. We held hands and lay naked on our backs.

"Not coming."

"What isn't?"

"Not coming."

"What?" His hand softly gripped my wrist, and he stopped moving. Having his baby should've brought us closer together, but ever so slowly he let go of my hand. Spring turned into summer, and once my stomach became so big I could no longer hide it from anyone, he stopped laying a finger on my body. Each time we met, I let my fingers slide against his sweat, but his skin refused my touch.

"Do you hate me?"

"What?"

"Do you hate me?"

"How could I hate you?"

"Do you love me?"

"I do . . . but . . ."

"But?"

"We can't be together."

She said nothing.

"I can't leave my wife."

Silence.

"I hope it's a healthy, good baby."

"What do you mean?"

Now it was his turn to be silent.

"You won't see me again?"

"I want to see you . . . but . . ."

"You won't? Why? I don't care if you won't see me again, but please, meet your child. A boy needs his father."

"You've no way of knowing it's a boy."

"But it is."

To think that was the last time we spoke—in a house so quiet it trembled, waiting in that stillness for him, waiting waiting waiting, what the hell does he mean, I live so close but he says he can't see me! No, I can go see him. But if I did, what would happen? Because the fact that he won't come see me means that he doesn't want to see me. I thought there was nothing to do but kill him. To jump in the river, still carrying his child. But if I'd had a baby boy, he would come to—

A gust of wind blew, and the cedars twisted like a woman bound and gagged—*rustlerustlerustlerustlerustle*. Her cheeks stung; her tears drying. I must've slept at least a little. The candles on the sansin altar had burned out, but the room was faintly light. Could the moonlight alone make it this bright?

The woman stood up, as if pulled by the silhouette of the moon in the east-facing window, but her face twisted in pain, and she leaned against the wall. Her hips, legs, neck, shoulders, arms; it was hard to find any part of her body without pain. She walked on, her right hand pushing against the wall. Hana, ow! Hana, ow! Hana, ow!

Hearing the sound of footsteps, her aunt opened the door to the room.

"Woo-cheol came earlier."

"Woo-cheol? Was his father with him?"

"No, he came alone. His mother sent him with a gift."

"What?"

"Look, see that straw bundle there?"

She slowly turned, her shoulder rubbing against the wall, then cautiously put her buttocks to the floor and unwrapped the bundle. A plucked and gutted chicken.

"What is it?"

"A hen, looks like."

"She's trying to hurt me."

"I can't see how that could be; she's killed and trimmed a precious hen for you, to help your milk flow well."

"Have you really not heard that if you eat chicken the baby will have bumpy skin?"

"Aigu, you know just how to twist things!"

"She wants to do me harm!"

"Aigu, come now, calm down, just look at your baby. Want to give her a little milk? Come now, hold her. You've not held her once since she was born, you know, come on now."

"I won't. I won't hold her until he does!"

"Aigo, what a thing to say."

The woman grabbed the hen by the neck and staggered out onto the veranda, then swung her arm and threw it, aiming for the trunks of the cedars. The hen hit the ground, spilling its eggs, heart, liver, and gizzard over the dead leaves. *Rustlerustlerustle*, the branches of the cedars danced crazily above her head, their shadows creeping out of the garden, *rustlerustlerustle   rustlerustlerustle*.

Someone is behind me. In the second that she thought, I cannot speak, I cannot even turn my head, this must be sleep paralysis, she felt herself swept into someone's arms. Honey? Honey, is that you? Those arms transmitted something more certain, more real than memory through her skin. Oh, I know, yes, yes, I know everything. Nodding, she let her strength leave her and sat down on the veranda, and the arms around her instantly lost their strength too. *Whoosh whoosh, whoosh whoosh*, the wind carried away all trace. The woman turned her eyes to her own hands. Bathed in the silver moonlight, they glimmered as if covered in the scales of a cabbage white butterfly.

Rustlerustlerustle, the woman looked up at the cedars being shaken by the wind. The moon was just above the tops of the trees. She stared at the moon, as if she were questioning it, not merely looking.

I knew I was making a mistake from the very start. But I just couldn't hold back my feelings. I can't erase the fact that we met. I can't make it so it never happened. I met him, and I crossed so many lines I never should've crossed.

Hey, honey, can you hear me? I love you. I don't regret meeting you. I'm not ashamed of having loved you. I love you. I love only you. I love you!

The muscles in her thighs twitched and a slight giggle escaped from her mouth.

Am I crazy? No, I'm not. Why am I not crazy? How can I go crazy? This pain, that pain, and that one, they're all traces of being held by you. I imagine there's no trace of me left on your body. But the pain remains in my body so sharply. I want to leave my body and go somewhere, far, far, so far away—

The light of the moon gently slipped its fingers into the jumble of thoughts within her. It untangled and untangled and still they formed; there was nothing for it to do but illuminate in bright, cool light. Her prayer was only, could only be, one name. Unable to voice this hope, she cradled her aching stomach and grit her teeth.

"Yong-ha." His name escaped through a gap in her teeth. She moaned his name as if calling the name of a lost loved one.

"Yong-ha, Yong-ha, Yong-ha, Yong-ha . . ."

ELEVEN

The Enemy in the Wind

| 바람 속의 적 | 風の中の敵 |

In the shadows of the Busan Public Athletic Grounds the ground rose with ice needles; in the sun it was sodden with melted ice. White, feathery breaths rose from the athletes, gathered from all over South Gyeongsang Province and standing in rows separated by school or company, who occasionally stomped in place to endure the cold, but when the chairman of the Korean Athletics Organization in his navy-blue suit began to climb the stairs to the victory stand, they all snapped to attention. The chairman, solemn-faced, turned and looked up at the Rising Sun flag, the fat on his neck wrinkling.

"Turn east, east! Worship the emperor!" the competition committee chairman ordered, and not only the competition officials and the players on the field but also the families of the athletes in the stands and even the kids selling dried squid and peanuts from boxes hung around their necks all faced the flag.

"All together, the national anthem!"

Kimigayo wa
Chiyo ni hachiyo ni
Sazare-ishi no
Iwao to narite
Koke no musu made

Among all the athletes in their white cotton shirts and white shorts, one boy stood out in particular. Woo-cheol, clad in a red running shirt with the number eighty-nine attached to it, looked up at the flag on the top of the pole, the nape of his neck crinkled. The Rising Sun fluttered from left to right.

We'll be running counterclockwise, so it'll be a headwind. He wanted to think of something else to distract him from his nervousness, but because of the cold these thoughts could only be grafted on. That guy's got good legs, the muscles on the back of his thighs stand out like a racehorse's, no doubt he's fast, but maybe a little too skinny. How many of us are there here, three hundred? No, more, five hundred? Whose idea was it to make us stand here wearing next to nothing in this fucking cold and listen to speeches, and the megaphone is awful, I can't hear a word he's saying. Brr! I want to run fast and warm my muscles up, brr! He stepped in place and heard the sound of ice crunching, and in that moment the desire to win rose up in him. I want to run! Now! Let me stand on the starting line! *Thump-thump thump-thump thump-thump thump-thump!* To calm his thudding heart he put both hands near his navel and breathed deeply, in out in out in out in out in out.

I want to win. But I don't run to win. The truth is, my desire not to lose is stronger. Maybe I run to put myself even one step further away from defeat. Stepped on daily, wrung out, beaten down—the Korean people are defeated over and over. You lose! You lose! And again today! But we must not grieve, we must not get fed up, we must not quit. Because the battle's not over yet. I'll take the battle to the enemy in the wind. Hey! Waejeok! You Japanese bastards! Fight me! My heart spits out insults, appealing directly to the heavens. *Thump-thump! Thump-thump! Thump-thump! Thump-thump! Thump-thump!*

"Fight fairly and do your best to the very end."

Woo-cheol snuffled as he moved back to the edge of the running track where he'd left his change of clothes and athletic shoes and blew his nose on his handkerchief. It was *cold*. His toes were starting to lose feeling. Not good.

Got to run to warm my body up.

He sat down on a cloth and tried to retie his shoelaces, but his hands were so numb he could not untie them in the first place. Woo-cheol breathed on his hands over and over again, then undid his laces, straightening the twists in the parts where they crossed.

Shoes, listen, please, get me over that finish line faster than anyone else, somehow, please, my precious shoes.

Until last spring he'd been running in flat-soled tabi boots, but after long runs the soles of his feet began to hurt, so his mother had asked the shoe store across the road from them to make these, special order. His father had been angry. "Why order shoes from our rivals?" But unlike his family's store, which only sold rubber boots, thin tabi shoes, umbrellas, and hats, the Western shoe store made and sold athletic shoes to the ilbon saram.

I made the order in detail before they took my size. I want them black, made from the softest leather you can find. Thick soles, and I want ten iron studs, about seven millimeters big. May I borrow a pen and a piece of paper? Iron claws, like a child's canines. If you run on leather soles you'll slip.

Woo-cheol tied a bow in his shoelaces and stood up. His right foot felt a little tight. Redo it. He put his heel to the ground, toes in the air, and started to loosen the lace a little from the hole closest to him. He stood up. Now his heel was a little too loose. No good, redo! What am I doing? Woo-cheol tutted at himself and sat down again with a thud. No, impatience is not allowed. To make himself calm down, he slowly and deliberately removed the lace and started over again from scratch. Then, to make sure his laces wouldn't come undone while he was running, he double-knotted them, then stood up. All right, that feels better.

When he stepped in place or lifted his thighs he felt no problem, so Woo-cheol went to run around the outside of the spectator stand.

In-hale ex-hale   in-hale ex-hale   soon the first race would begin   dun-dun-dun   dun-dun-dun   the sound of a drum being hit   Jae-sik, igyeora! C'mon, Jae-sik! Si-gyeong, jimyeon andwae! You can do it, Si-gyeong!   I must be the only one   who doesn't have family in the stands   if she were well Eomoni would've brought So-won and Woo-gun to cheer for me

but   in-hale ex-hale   in-hale ex-hale   Eomoni is in bed   and every
time Abeoji so much as looks at me   in-hale ex-hale   hey, Woo-cheol   if
you do nothing but run you'll die   never forget, you're the eldest son of the
Lee family   in-hale ex-hale   I didn't tell her   since the day we first slept
together   in-hale ex-hale   in-hale ex-hale   sleeping with her is all I can
think about   in-hale ex-hale   her face   in-hale ex-hale   her body   in-hale
ex-hale   her voice   in-hale ex-hale   in-hale ex-hale   if she were here there's
no way I'd be able to focus   I'm fine alone   I've never wished there was
someone to cheer me on   I've always run alone   in-hale ex-hale   every day,
since graduation, every day   in-hale ex-hale   in-hale ex-hale   I jump out of
bed at the rooster's first crow, wash my face at the well, and do stretches   in-
hale ex-hale   I run sixty ri from Miryang to Samnamjin and back   in-hale
ex-hale   in-hale ex-hale   selling rubber boots in the afternoon   from four
to six running full force on the Miryang River's levee   in-hale ex-hale   my
studs sending the dirt flying   in-hale ex-hale   in-hale ex-hale   Woo-cheol
passed the notice board   the top six names and records were written in white
chalk   bang!   at every sound of the starting pistol each muscle in his body
reacted with a jump   in-hale ex-hale   in-hale ex-hale   this was the hundred
meters   next was the two hundred meters so   about three minutes or so
left   ought to keep running up to right before it   in-hale ex-hale   in-hale
ex-hale   in-hale ex-hale

"Next is the fifteen hundred meters category. Would all the competitors
please gather at the starting line?"

Their names were called over the loudspeaker and all proceeded to the
white starting line. They stopped. *Thump-thump! Thump-thump! Thump-
thump! Thump-thump!* They stretched. The man with the starting gun put
the blank into the chamber. The runners put their right legs back, left legs
forward in preparation. The muzzle of the gun pointed up toward the sky.
Every muscle in Woo-cheol's body pulled back like a bow; he stared straight
ahead.

"Ready, set."

BANG! Woo-cheol flew like an arrow released from his own body.

I won! *Thump-thump! Thump-thump!* I won the 1500 and 5000. That means I can go to the capital and I'll get to represent South Gyeongsang at the Chōsen Jingū Race. *Thump-thump! Thump-thump!* Just the 10,000 meters left now. If I can get third place in that then I'll get the right to appear, but *thump-thump! Thump-thump!* I'm gonna win. I'm absolutely going to win! I've got to calm my breathing. When I was untying and retying my shoelaces, I felt the eyes of the other athletes and their families on me. *Thump-thump! Thump-thump!* Oh no, my heart is—*thump-thump! Thump-thump! Thump-thump! Thump-thump!*

Woo-cheol lay down on his cloth, stretching his arms and legs out, my breathing, *thump-thump! Thump-thump!* My heart, it's like a steam train running over the bridge over the Miryang River, *chikchik pokpok, chikchik pokpok, wheeow!* That white cloud running out from it, suddenly, words unaccompanied by a voice came into his head.

I want to do something worth dying for.

In an instant those words drowned out the sounds of people's cheers and applause, all the drums and horns; they filled in the silence inside Woo-cheol's mind.

"Hey, Woo-cheol, Korea has its own flag. Did you know that?"

"What?"

"I've never seen it myself, but my brother told me about it. So you know how the Rising Sun flag is a red circle on a white background, right? The Taegukgi has a circle in the middle, too, but it's part red and part blue."

"And it's called the Taegukgi?"

"Yeah, he said that it was based on a pattern that a temple used during the Three Countries period. He also said in the four corners of the flag there are lines, and that the three and four lines on the left side represent infinity, and the five and six lines on the right represent light."

I felt a stab in my heart; I fell silent. Woo-hong also went quiet. Inside the pain itself there was a sweetness, which had shown us into this miracle of a moment. We saw the Taegukgi, fluttering in the wind. I saw it with my own eyes, and I know Woo-hong saw it too. And in the same way as that moment was born, it slowly disappeared.

The clouds are moving faster than they were a little while ago, and my heart isn't beating as fast anymore. Faster, just a little, right now it feels like it might stop, that's how slow it's beating, *thump . . . thump . . . thump. . . .*

When the next race was announced, Woo-cheol got up. He headed toward the starting line with the same rhythm as the beat. He heard the silent words that nobody else could.

I want to do something worth dying for.

TWELVE

Jeonanrye

| 전안례(奠雁禮) | 奠雁礼(チョナンレ) |

In-hye put her arms around her sister from behind as she tied the strings of In-hye's blue chima above her breasts for her.

"Not too tight?"

"It's fine."

"If you don't tie it tight it'll slip and be unseemly. Your breasts have gotten so big."

"What?" In-hye twisted her neck back.

"If you're not feeling well or your belly gets tight don't just ignore it, give me a sign. Now's the most crucial point, you know." She wrapped a red chima around her sister's body and tied it, adjusting as she went so that the blue chima would peek out at the hem slightly. A blue and red chima signified the union of man and woman.

"So you know, then?"

"Well, yes. You never could hide anything; it all shows in your face. But Abeoji and Eomoni and Oppa don't know. Just us."

"Us? Do In-gyeong and In-yeong and In-soon and In-yu all know too?" In-hye arranged the sleeves of her jeogori and tied the strings herself.

"Of course."

In-hye brought over the yellow-green ceremonial wonsam overcoat, with its five-colored cloth and long, hand-hiding sleeves. This, with large peony buttons and colorful embroidered butterflies, was part of the bridal costume.

"And Yeon-gil?" In-hye asked as she tied the wonsam's strings.

"You don't tie this one, it just hangs down like that. Aigu, what would Yeon-gil know? He's just sixteen."

"Oh, he's only a year younger than Woo-cheol, then."

"But we'll do what we can."

Her sister was behind her now, tying up a large bright red belt with a lucky character embroidered on it in gold thread into a butterfly bow.

"So you must've gotten pregnant at the start of the year, I suppose? Then the baby will come in October. If you just say it must've happened on your wedding night, you should be fine. When the baby's actually born it'll be obvious that was a lie, but all's well that ends well. In-hye, you haven't had any dreams about bears, have you?"

"I always forget my dreams as soon as I wake up."

In-hye put the headpiece decorated with pearls, gold, silver, purple agate, rubies, coral, and orpiment over the bun that her sister had tied on her head, stuck a golden hairpin with a turtle on it through her bun, then wrapped the apdaenggi, a long red ribbon with beads on both ends, around the hairpin with the ends hanging over her chest, then she put the dodeurakdaenggi, a long red piece of damask gold tooled with flowers, bats, pomegranates, and designs for long life and happiness, over her bun and arranged how it fell down her back.

Her sister pressed her pointer finger into the rouge, then drew circles on both of her cheeks, filling them in completely to avoid unevenness.

"You know, pregnancy dreams, taemong, aren't just something the mother has; the father often has them too. Ask Woo-cheol if he's had any. If there's a bear in the dream, it's a boy, and if you see a snake, like a pit viper, it's a girl."

"I'll ask him."

In-hye slipped her feet, clad in white socks with the toe separated, into her bridal shoes, and her sister pulled up the cloth from the mirror.

"You look so pretty, take a look . . . but . . . oh, I feel sad."

"You'll have to come over."

"But I won't be able to come over all the time. Husbands don't like it when their in-laws show up constantly."

"Then I'll come over here."

"You won't have the time. You're gonna be an eomoni in October, you know."

"That word . . . it still doesn't feel real."

"How's the morning sickness? Not too bad?"

"It's quite bad, actually."

"Then just pretend to eat, all right?"

"But just looking at food makes me feel queasy. . . ."

The sliding door opened, and her older sisters, the second and third to get married, walked in.

"Your groom is here."

"Aigo."

Her sisters washed the floor, set up the folding screen with peonies on it, set two candles and three cups of water on a tray, then hurriedly left the room.

"I'm going to go give them a hand with everything. You just have a seat and relax."

Once her sister was out of the room, In-hye approached the mirror and took a look at herself.

I look so beautiful. *Thump-thump thump-thump thump-thump thump-thump*, her heart raced, as In-hye gazed in fascination at herself. It's not just because I'm wearing these beautiful bridal clothes. Happiness is giving me beauty. I get to be with him. To share a life with him. He'll be the father of my child, and I'll be a mother. Oh, won't that be something!

In-hye rested her hands on her belly. Lee Woo-cheol, Chee In-hye, these two names will open up to become connected as one now. In-hye spoke to her unnamed, unborn child.

Today's your appa and omma's jeonanrye. Once wild geese mate, they will not part as long as they live. They're migratory birds full of faithfulness, obedience, loyalty, and love. Today, Appa is going to give Omma a wooden goose and pledge his eternal love.

The mother of the bride and her four sisters and female relatives were busy preparing for the chin-young rye, when the groom would meet the bride.

In the south-facing part of the garden the daeryesang offering table had been set up, and behind it another folding screen with peonies stood.

The offering table held many lucky talismans. On the bridegroom's side, to the east, was a vase filled up to the brim with small beans, and on the western end of the table, the bride's side, was one filled up halfway with sesame seeds; each vase had various plants in it: gardenia, spindle tree, bamboo. There were two turtle cakes made from garaetteok, a long, pounded rice cake, each with a peeled chestnut or a jujube for its head, and jujubes drizzled with honey and covered in sesame seeds, bundles of blue and red thread, two candlesticks, and a bowl filled with rice. On the table there were also a pair of chickens wrapped up in a red cloth, *cluck-cluck, cock-a-ooh-cluck-cluck*, sometimes moving their necks, looking around.

Because birds leave their droppings everywhere and because of the legend that a bird's shadow is unlucky, they had set up a canopy over the daeryesang.

Her sister ran to the house two doors down where the groom's party was waiting and told them that the preparations for the chin-young rye were done; the hamjinabi, the groom's attendant, picked up the box of engagement gifts, filled with jewels, silk, and ornaments, and opened the gate to the bride's house.

Chae-sik, the bride's father, came out to meet him and said, with a bow, "Thank you. Indeed, that looks quite hard to carry."

But the hamjinabi replied, "Please, hold for us at least one dance," and would not hand over the box.

Wan-son, the bride's mother, came carrying a tray with rice wine, steamed beef, pears, apples, and dried persimmons on it, at which the hamjinabi finally handed over the box, saying, "Take care of the groom, please," before sitting down at the back of the garden and starting to drink.

Chae-sik put the box on a tray, faced north, and bowed four times, then went into the room where the bride was waiting.

"In-hye, you must be a good bride," Chae-sik said to his youngest daughter.

"I will," she said, bowing.

"Hama!" announced Chong-hu halbi, who was serving in the role of hol-jaebi, the old man who has studied Chinese classics and administers the chin-young rye, reading out the first point in the order of ceremony.

In-hye shut her eyes and imagined Woo-cheol, wearing a samo hat and tanryong robe, his stiff sash tied like a flying crane going through the gate in his black wooden shoes, being showered with millet and ashes by her relatives and the elders to be purified of evil spirits.

"Juinyeongseoumunoe."

In-hye caressed her lower abdomen as she would a baby's back. Right now, my dad and yours are exchanging greetings.

"Sangchiseok."

Your daddy's walking up to the daeryesang now.

"Gwejwa."

He's kneeling now.

"Sijajibanijong."

He's taking the wooden geese wrapped in the red cloth.

"Jeonan."

He's turning the wooden goose's head to the left and passing it to my mother, and my mother is spreading her chima and taking the goose. She's wearing a peach-colored silk chima jeogori. She's forty-four, but she still looks so young and pretty. You'll see, when she holds you.

"Chianuji."

My mother's putting the wooden goose on the daeryesang.

"Bokbogyeopyeongsin."

Your daddy's standing up.

"Sotoejaebae."

He's taking two steps back and bowing twice. Your mama and daddy practiced this over and over again by the riverside. We prayed together so that your daddy wouldn't get it wrong. Now the jeonanrye's over, and it's almost your mama's turn.

"Haengchinyeongnye."

Your daddy's standing at the eastern side of the daeryesang, facing east. Your mama's sisters and parents' friends are teasing him, insulting him, making fun of him, trying to make your daddy laugh. But he can't. If he does laugh, his firstborn will be a girl.

Even though it's a little late for that now. Are you a boy? Or are you a girl? Are you laughing right now in your mama's belly? In-hye was so filled with affection for the child inside her womb that she gasped, breathing hard. She wanted to stroke her baby's cheek. She wanted to breastfeed it, now. A baby's face hazily expanded in her mind, and when its red lips, chafed, began to open, arong arong, the strength in her knees went. Her flower crown fell to the bed where she and Woo-cheol would spend their first night together as a married couple. In-hye leaned over the chamber pot lined with chaff that her sisters had prepared for them and threw up in it. Aigu, himdeureo! The tears over-flowing from her eyes dissolved the rouge on her cheeks.

"Mobongyeochulmun," the holjaebi read aloud from the order of proceedings, but In-hye couldn't hear.

Her bridal gown clung heavily to her as if it were drenched by an evening rain. Is that sweat? Is this the sound of sweat? It's the first time I've ever heard sweat. In-hye threw up again, looking at her brown vomit. All the sesame rice porridge she'd eaten that morning had come right back up.

I'm trying so hard to eat for this baby, but aigo.

The door opened, and in came her sisters, wearing the blue chima outfit of members of her bridal party.

"Are you all right?"

"I just . . ." In-hye panted.

"Oh, you've thrown up. Get her some water. Oh, and tell Chong-hu halbi she needs a minute."

In-gyeong left the room.

"I'm sorry."

"What's there to apologize for? You're not feeling your best."

"What do I do? My face is sopping wet."

"Don't you worry about a thing. We'll get you all fixed up."

In-gyeong came back in with a basin of water. "Here, I've got you some cold water. Now, drink it right down."

In-hye rinsed her mouth out and spit the water into the chamber pot, then took one sip to wet her throat.

"C'mon, drink some more."

"If I drink too much I'll need to go to the toilet in the middle of the cere-mony. I'm pregnant; I have to go all the time."

Her sisters fixed In-hye's face and clothes.

"Gwaenchana?"

"Gwaenchana."

"Don't push yourself. We're with you, so just relax. Right, let's go."

In-hye hid her hands inside her big sleeves and then covered her face with her hands, and her two sisters helped her stand up. Once they were out of the bedroom, the floor of the hallway was covered with a white cotton cloth, and In-hye quietly tread along the cloth in her bridal shoes until she reached the garden where the daeryesang was set up. Sighs and exclamations of "Ah, how beautiful," and "What a lovely couple," escaped from the mouths of the family and neighbors who had been waiting impatiently for the arrival of the bride.

"Seodongbuseo."

The groom was to the east; the bride stood at the western side. They faced each other now, separated by the daeryesang.

"Haenggwanyeollye."

The bridal party brought a small water basin before them.

"Seogwanunam bugwanubuk."

The groom turned southward; the bride turned to the north.

"Gwansusesu."

The groom removed his gloves, touched his fingers to the water, then flicked it off onto the paper underneath. The bride had only to stoop and pretend to wash her hands, while her attendants flicked water for her three times.

"Gakjeongwi."

They turned to face each other again.

"Buseonjaebae."

The bride, her arms supported by her attendants, bowed twice to the groom.

"Seodabilbae."

The groom knelt and bowed gently toward the bride.

"Buuseonjaebae."

The groom stood; the bride prayed twice.

"Seoudapbae."

The groom knelt once again and returned the prayer.

"Gakgwejwa."

Through the action of both kneeling at the same time, the gyobaerye, their joint vow to live out one hundred years together, was completed, and the hap-geullye, the drinking of rice wine from two cups made from the same gourd, now began.

"Jinsang."

The attendants placed the small trays bearing the gourd cups, carafe, fried delicacies, and dried persimmons in front of the couple. The groom's tray had chestnuts, symbolizing his ancestors and origins, while the bride's tray had jujubes, representing wealth, nobility, and bearing many sons.

"Sijachimju."

The attendants poured rice wine into the two cups.

"Chojakjeju."

The groom drank the first cupful down; the attendants brought the cup up to the bride's mouth.

"Jaejakjaejeju."

The attendants, groom, and bride repeated the same actions.

"Uchimju."

They filled the cups for the third time.

"Samjakhwanjak."

The attendants wrapped the bride's cup in blue silk and pretended to make the bride drink from it.

"Seojipjak."

They wrapped the cup that the bride had pretended to drink from in red silk and passed it to the groom, who drank it.

"Geoeum."

They picked up a piece of fried food and pretended to bring it to their lips.

"Yepilcheolsang."

The four attendants cleared away the trays, and the hapgeullye was com-plete.

"Yepilgaebok."

The groom and bride stood where they were while the four attendants took off their ceremonial robes for them. The groom was now in yellow-gold paji and jeogori, and the bride was clad in her red chima and green jeogori.

The master of ceremonies left and the bride and groom exchanged bashful looks, and their friends threw confetti and cheered for them.

The women moved the daeryesang back slightly and rearranged the place of ceremony, then laid the gifts of dressers, sewing boxes, metal basins, picture frames, pots, spoons, and chopsticks from their friends on the table.

Kim Chin-bom, one of Woo-cheol's classmates, unfurled a rolled letter expressing congratulations.

"Woo-cheol, how lucky you are to have a bride so lovely and happy that she lights up this space. You have my never-ending best wishes that you may have many children. But so that no one says you love your bride so much that you've let running fall to the wayside, please keep at it. Chukahamnida!"

He finished reading the letter and placed it on top of the gifts, and all their friends turned toward the couple and bowed, then the groom went to his prescribed seat in the largest room of the house, the groom's special guests entered the sarangbang, the drawing room, and the bride waited in the smaller room for the feast to be over.

The relatives and neighbors flooded back into the garden and the women piled noodles, rice cakes, stir-fried beef, thin-sliced meats, Spanish mackerel, amberjack, and jeon fritters on to trays for the attendees who were stopping by on their way to pay a visit elsewhere. Ki-jeong, the hamjinabi, who had been drinking since the start of the ceremony, started singing loudly, and the boisterous cacophony of voices became a low stir, the jumbled laughter swallowed up by the refrain.

Kwaejina chingching nane
Kwaejina chingching nane
Mister Star shining in the sky
Kwaejina chingching nane
Let's go let's go, all of us, let's go
Kwaejina chingching nane
Across the river out to the white road
Kwaejina chingching nane
Many gravel paths by the river in this town
Kwaejina chingching nane
Many stories in each life
Kwaejina chingching nane

Put the loom up in the sky
Kwaejina chingching nane
Catch you a goldfish and make of it a shuttle
Kwaejina chingching nane
On the fifteenth of December
Kwaejina chingching nane
Chuseok in August is long gone
Kwaejina chingching nane
The date may pass but the feeling remains
Kwaejina chingching nane

The light, filtered from the evening sun, bathed the garden in spellbound colors. The groom's guests had headed home while there was still sun, so all those left in the garden were people who had not been invited. Neither the women who had come over in their normal clothes in the middle of their washing and cleaning, the white-bearded old men arguing over whether the newlyweds would have a boy or a girl first, the flies swarming around the half-nibbled and dried-out pears, nor the small cabbage white butterflies sipping on the nectar of the blossoming dandelions had been invited. The March wind fluttered one, two cherry blossom petals into the midst of the interminable chatter, trying to draw their attention to the fact that the spring sun was setting.

The groom stepped down into the garden and spoke. "Everyone, I would like to thank you very much for coming to celebrate our marriage today—jeongmal gomapseumnida! Are you not feeling chilly? Please, help yourself to something warm to eat," he said.

One man took his eyes off the woman he'd been talking to and said, "Aigu, wish there was a good bride out there for me."

Another, his mouth so full of food his cheeks stuck out, gulped down a dried persimmon and simply nodded; yet another spat out a jujube seed and said, "May you have many exceptional sons," as he got up from his woven mat.

In-hye was sitting in the bedroom she and Woo-cheol were to share that night, near to the stovepipe for the underfloor heating, when Woo-cheol came in.

"Gwaenchana?" He looked at the woman who was now his wife with eyes blurred by alcohol.

"Gwaenchanayo." Her voice was flat, like water flowing in a broad river.

"Are you tired?"

"A bit."

Someone cleared their throat, and the door opened; In-yeong carried in a tray laden with jeon, stew, and the rice wine from earlier. In-hye silently picked up the carafe, and Woo-cheol held the cup in his hand.

In-yeong turned to In-hye, still looking at Woo-cheol out of the corner of her eye.

"Soon they'll come by to peek in, so don't say anything you wouldn't want others hearing. All right? Chun-ho and Yu-won are here, so let my new brother-in-law take off your clothes and then lay down, the both of you."

In-yeong left the room.

"When did you tell her?"

"I didn't tell her anything. She knew."

"Oh. When's your morning sickness going to end?"

"Hmm . . . Well, hopefully it'll end soon? I threw up all the noodles I ate; it's awful, truly awful. I barely want to eat anything at all."

"Please, you need to eat. You're eating for two, you know."

"Shh!" In-hye put her finger to her mouth.

Chun-ho, Chong-hu halbi, and Yu-won put a little spit on their fingers and punched holes in the sliding paper doors, and with that, the tradition of peeking into the newlyweds' bedroom had begun, so Woo-cheol first took off his own jeogori, undid the ties around his ankles, and took off his paji; then he took off In-hye's crown and removed her dodeurakdaenggi and apdaenggi, before undoing the string and taking off her jeogori. In-hye pulled out the golden hairpin with the turtle decoration and let her one long braid fall down; then, in her underwear, she quietly got into the bed. Woo-cheol put out the candles near the bed, and the snickering on the other side of the door retreated with the sound of footsteps sneaking away.

"So she figured it out somehow."

"Yeah. But we still have to go through the rituals of you taking me to your house and you being invited back here."

"I don't want my abeoji and eomoni to find out."

"Your mother might guess though."

"Well, I guess we'll cross that bridge when we get to it. . . . Are you starting to show?"

"A little."

"Let me see."

Woo-cheol pulled down In-hye's sokpaji and placed his palm near her navel.

"The baby's here, right?"

"I think so."

"Can you feel it moving?"

Woo-cheol lay down on his back next to In-hye.

"Not yet; that's still a ways off. The baby's legs are still like this," she said, her pointer and middle fingers walking their way up to Woo-cheol's chest.

"You're making me ticklish." He grabbed the small "legs."

"My, what big hands."

"Yours are just small."

"No, no, your hands are especially big. Look, I can fit two of my hands into one of yours."

Woo-cheol gently cradled his wife's head and traced the line of her parting with his tongue. In-hye tried to tickle him, her hands clambering up his frame, but she felt his hot sigh near the whorl of her hair and stifled her laughter in his shoulder. The perfume of the camellia oil in her hair and the tang of sweat melded into a scent they both breathed in deeply.

She sensed that her husband's slightly tensed body wanted to be inside her, that he wanted her warm, soft body to embrace him. There wasn't the same reckless intensity with which they had sought each other in the summer by the riverbed, but each was seeking the other out; that was certain. They stayed in their embrace, gently shaking.

"I want you."

"Andwaeyo."

His big, swollen-knuckled hand took hers in it and took it down, down; his thick tongue lapped at her teeth and gums and tongue until no other taste remained; moving her tightly grasped hand up and down, he put her head beneath the blankets, down, farther down; he stroked her chin, he cradled her head, like she was in a cradle, like rocking a cradle.

Your hands, my hands, rocking and being rocked, rocking and being rocked, In-hye, aigu, In-hye, and then your voice from somewhere high up, In-hye! Higher than the eaves, higher even than the stars, In-hye, In-hye, In-hye!

In-hale . . . ex-hale . . . in-hale . . . ex-hale . . . She heard his deep, sonorous snoring. After the desire was gone she always felt a sadness, like her song had been cut off. However many breaths she took she couldn't continue the song, and however close she listened she couldn't hear it. It had vanished completely. Just like that. In-hye gingerly squeezed her husband's hand. It was warmer than before. She let go of his hand and pressed hers to her stomach. She might vomit. She felt nauseated. But there was nothing left to throw up. She didn't want to dirty the bed with foul-smelling brown bile. Sleep. If she could just get to sleep, she wouldn't vomit. If she could just go to sleep now . . . in-hale . . . ex-hale . . . in-hale . . . ex-hale . . . she was breathing a little faster than him . . . in-hale . . . ex-hale . . . in-hale . . . ex-hale . . . in-hale . . . ex-hale . . . she was neither fully awake nor asleep . . . she lay on her back in a small boat . . . in-hale . . . ex-hale . . . drifting over a sea of sleepiness and warmth and nausea . . . was this really what your wedding night was supposed to be like? She'd wanted to have a white cloth spread under her, to show as proof of her virginity . . . what would she do if the worst befell them . . . the sin of having sex and getting pregnant before marriage . . . in-hale . . . ex-hale . . . there were legs next to her legs . . . in-hale . . . ex-hale . . . and arms by hers . . . in-hale . . . ex-hale . . . forever . . . in-hale . . . ex-hale . . .

Kkokkio, that's the rooster, I've got to go running, Woo-cheol thought as he opened his eyes, battling against drowsiness that pressed on him like gravity. Wait. Where am I? Oh, right, I'm at In-hye's family's house. His right arm was numb and his wrist was stiff. He was still far too asleep; he hadn't even turned over. That last dream he'd had was a good one, but he couldn't remember it now. He'd known throughout that it was a dream, a little like he was looking onto someone else's dream. The wind sounded loud; was it clear out? I want to run! The wedding rituals would go on for another week, but going a week without running was no joke—once he took In-hye home he could run, and how could Abeoji and Eomoni stop him! Woo-cheol pacified his impatient leg muscles as he listened to the quiet of the house. It was quieter even than at night, so quiet that the throngs of people who had been there yesterday seemed like a lie; everyone must be sleeping it off. Woo-cheol stretched and looked around at the room, now lighter than it had been just a little while ago. It was the first time he'd slept in someone else's house. He turned his head to look next to him and saw In-hye, asleep, with no trace of makeup on her face. How strange it felt, to have a woman sleeping this close to him, and he wasn't stealing glances either, he was staring straight at her, but she showed no signs of waking.

Is the baby inside of her sleeping too? Or is it up already? Is it a boy? Or a girl? Will it look like me or In-hye? In-hye's sisters are all full-figured; will she be, too, soon? She'd gotten thicker around the hips since she got pregnant, and her ass had gotten bigger too. She hadn't been particularly slim when they'd started seeing each other, but her waist had been smaller and her abdomen had been flat as a palm.

But those days were gone. No, the days stayed where they were; we left them behind, hand in hand. And there weren't two of us anymore, no—that's my baby there, inside her. When the autumn comes, my wife and child will see me off as I leave the house. My wife and child will wait for my return. And when I come home they'll come to greet me. From now on, until one of us dies, either me or In-hye. I'll sell rubber boots for fifty sen a pair and I'll have to provide for them until I die. Is that what they call happiness? It must be. What if I can't bear the weight of it? Must I still carry it nonetheless?

In-hye opened her eyes. Then, unconsciously, she smiled. Woo-cheol looked at her smiling mouth from a close distance. She shut her eyes. He gently pressed the pad of his middle finger to her eyelid, and she opened her eyes and smiled again. They moved their faces closer together than they ever seemed to have been before and smiled at each other. In-hye wanted to commit to memory the smiling face of her new husband looking at her, but her face was so close that all she could see were his two eyes. Her eyes were full of his, as if she had drunk them in with her eyes.

It was the first morning they had greeted together. To share in the quiet of the morning together, they both closed their eyelids again and lay down in the silence.

"Oh, I meant to ask, have you had any dreams about bears?"

"What?"

"If you do, then it'll be a boy, or snakes means it'll be a girl, they say."

"Oh, taemong, right. Isn't that only for the mother?"

"My sister said sometimes the father has them too. So you haven't? Any time since we met?"

"Well, maybe I did, but I just can't remember, you know. I asked my dad once, and he said that before a great hero is born, you have a dream about swallowing the sun or a star."

"I read that once too. In the folktale, Jang-hwa and Hong-ryeon's mother dreams that a fairy gives her a flower, and the mother of Yi Seong-gye, the founder of Joseon, apparently dreamed that a turtle came down from the heavens and went into her stomach. What did you dream last night?"

"I can't remember. It was a really good dream, but the rooster woke me up straightaway. . . . Oh, wait, I can kind of remember. . . . Someone was coming. . . ."

"Someone was coming?"

"Hold on a second, I'm trying to remember. . . . I was running in the mountains—not sure where—the sun was shining down through the leaves on the trees and everything looked so soft, and the road was . . . I was breathing so deeply and so freely that it was hardly like I was running at all, and my breaths were, oh, what would you say . . . I felt so happy. . . . The light was coming in between the leaves, they were rustling as if the light itself was shaking . . . this pure, white light. . . ."

"Was it night?"

"I don't know . . . but I don't think it was. The greenery was so dense it must've been bright. Oh, when I try to explain it, it's nothing like it was in the dream. I'll tell you how it was, and you listen . . . dead leaves were falling, but all the leaves on the trees were lush and green, like it was the middle of summer.... But it wasn't hot, or cold ... so, I was there, watching myself running, over here ... the me that was running was over there ... so I knew, I knew that it was a dream."

"You must've dreamed this when you were just about to wake up, when you were slipping out of sleep?"

"Yeah ... Well, I can't remember what happened next, so I'll just skip over that part. I was in the courtyard at school ... and next to me was ... Woo-hong, yeah, that's right, Woo-hong was there! I opened up an aluminum lunch box and we each ate half. My lunch box. As we ate he laughed. And he, kind of, accidentally spat out some rice. I didn't know what he was laughing about, but anyway the two of us were chuckling.... But, and this is strange, the whole time I was breathing like I was running; the dream I told you about earlier, about running in the mountains, this was still part of it, and another 'me' was still running."

"Then what?"

"That's it. Boring, right? Dreams never sound like much when you talk about them, do they? But when I was dreaming, I was so happy that I thought, Please don't let me wake up.... That's the first time I've ever told someone about one of my dreams."

"It's not boring at all. I want to know about your dreams. Promise you'll keep telling me about them."

"Every day?"

"Every day. So this Woo-hong, is he your friend?"

"He's my best friend."

"Did he come yesterday?"

"No. He doesn't live here anymore."

"He moved?"

"Yeah."

"Far away?"

"To Hanseong."

Woo-cheol had now lied to his wife for the first time.

Woo-hong told the truth to me, only me. He ran off to Shanghai without telling even his own abeoji. How are his abeoji and eomoni doing? I wonder.

Their only two sons have both run off to join the Heroic Corps; has their abeoji been questioned by the police? No, I'm sure that I'm the only one who knows that his brother's in the Heroic Corps. I don't want to lie to In-hye, but she might let slip to her eomoni or her sisters, and then they might tell their husbands and friends, and then that might put Woo-hong's and his family's lives on the line.

"Whatcha thinking about?" In-hye leaned her head on her husband's shoulder.

"Nothing . . ." He traced her eyebrow with his finger, then gently touched her temple and her lips. The morning light was falling on the left of her face, making her skin gleam. As he stroked her long neck draped with her loosened hair with his palm, taking her warmth and softness in with his whole body, he felt his desire begin to rise again. Woo-cheol cradled his wife's face in his hands, her lips slightly parted as if she were sleeping, and leaned in toward her.

But the sound of footsteps outside came closer, and In-hye's eyes opened wide. They both got out of bed and put their jeogori on.

"Can I come in?" It was In-yu.

"Sure, come on in," Woo-cheol said.

"Good morning, jal jasseo. Of course, usually your new bride would make this for you, but since she's not at her best, I made it. So get your stories straight." In-yu carried in a breakfast tray laden with rice porridge with pine nuts and sesame seeds, stir-fried noodles with beef and vegetables, and kimchi.

"How are you feeling?" She looked at her sister.

"I slept so deeply; I'm feeling very well today. All this week, the nausea woke me up every morning, but nothing today. I could almost forget I'm pregnant."

"You'll feel worse later if you don't eat something after you wake up, so please, have a little something. You barely ate at all yesterday, right? The baby's making you hungry."

"Thank you, In-yu, jal meogeulgeyo."

"Enjoy," she said, as she carried the tray from last night out of the room.

As Woo-cheol brought the spoon up to his mouth, he thought about Woo-hong.

I'm seventeen and I've taken a wife. Will Woo-hong still be single when he's twenty, thirty even? But no, turning twenty or thirty means nothing to him. The only thing that has meaning for him is getting closer to the life that he decided on; no, wait, he isn't concerned about his own life. He said he wanted *to do something worth dying for*. Will he ever come back? To the way of living that most people call "life," with a wife and kids? *I want to do something worth dying for.* I have the feeling at some point I'll be guided by those words. But when? And to where?

The door opened, and In-yu brought in a metal basin filled with well water. Woo-cheol washed his face and took a cloth from In-yu to dry it.

"Is Father awake?"

"Yes."

"I'll get ready, and then I'll go meet him."

Woo-cheol brought the front panel of his paji up and to the left and tied it at the waist, then wrapped the strings around his ankles and tied them in bows.

"Right, I'll go first." He stepped out of the room.

In-hye sat down in front of the mirror and let down her ponytail. She put two or three drops of camellia oil in her palm and ran it through her hair, then combed it until it was lustrous, before dividing it into three and plaiting it. She tried to wrap it into a bun at the base of her head, but there was too much hair, or the bun was too big, and she couldn't get it to stay together.

Aigu, why?

In-hye took a deep breath and removed the hairpin, then redid the plait. It was fine until the day before, when she could still just have her plait running down her back, but how long would it take her to be able to put her hair up as quickly and beautifully as her sisters? A month? Two?

In-hye twisted her hair into a ring and stuck in the hairpin, then hid the tail of her braid in the rest of her hair.

I don't know how this is staying up, but I can tell, as soon as I start walking, it's all going to come loose.

She walked out of the bedroom and called out to her sister, who was doing laundry near the well.

"In-yu! I can't get my hair to stay!"

"Aigu, I taught you before, didn't I? There's nothing worse than a wife who sleeps in late and can't do her own hair."

In-yu wiped her wet hands on her apron, then sat her sister down in front of the mirror and combed out her hair.

"Ready? So you make a loop at the base of the braid, and then you wrap the braid around it. Are you watching me? First, braid it tightly, then tie off the end of the braid with a black cloth, and you'll have a perfectly sized loop."

As In-hye let her hair be done by her sister, two years older than her, with whom she'd played gonggi, a game like jacks, or kongjumeoni nori, a beanbag-throwing game, she felt a sweet sadness come over her. Tonight, I'll go to sleep and when I wake up, I won't be a part of this family anymore. In ten or twenty years, when my baby's old enough to get married, will I look back on this day fondly? And will I tell my child and make them hear about it? You know, your eomoni, when I got married at nineteen, I couldn't do my own hair the first morning after, and so on.

"The trick is in the size of the loop. If it's too tight you won't be able to get your hairpin into it, and if it's too big, the hairpin won't hold it up. Once you're done wrapping the tail around the loop, you stick the hairpin into the loop, and it'll hold. Aigu, if you sit with your chima like that it'll get wrinkled."

In-hye straightened out her chima and adjusted herself, her eyes following the movements of her unni's hands. A deep forest . . . a mountain path thick with dead leaves . . . bright white light . . . in-hale ex-hale in-hale ex-hale, in-hale ex-hale in-hale ex-hale . . . He'd said that the feeling of his breath as he ran was happiness. I like watching him run. I like seeing his face as he runs up to where we agreed to meet, too, but I like it better when he's running away from me, waving his hand in the air, telling me to take care. We'll never again meet by the riverside or at the shrine; what a shame.

I wonder what this Woo-hong is like. He called him his best friend, and he doesn't have many friends, so they must have been pretty close. In-hye realized she felt something like jealousy toward her husband's friend. Has he ever dreamed of me? Ever since we first made love, I've had the same dream over and over. In it, I'm naked. . . . I don't know if he is or not—my eyes are closed anyway—he whispers my name . . . In-hye, In-hye. . . . His voice soaks into every inch of my skin, even the softest, smallest hairs on my body that I usually wouldn't notice, are standing up, and the core of my body starts tingling. . . . I'm breathing him in, in, out, in, out. . . .

"Oh, your face has gone all red—are you feverish or something?" In-yu touched her hand to her sister's face.

"Hm? No, I'm fine."

"No, you don't feel like you have a fever; pregnancy raises your body temperature, you know. Well, all done. Tomorrow you'll wake up in a new house. No matter how bad your morning sickness is, you absolutely mustn't get up after your mother-in-law. You've got to be up, with your face washed and your hair done, before the rooster's first crow. You understand?"

"I do."

"You're the baby of the family and we spoiled you—I'm worried."

"I'll be fine."

"Last night I had a nightmare."

"What kind?"

"One so bad I can't even tell you about it."

"In-yu, you're such a worrier. . . . Don't worry about me, I'll be happy."

In-yu took her little sister's look in through the mirror; her eyes blurred with tears.

Once they were done with breakfast, the bride's brother and uncles and other men from the neighborhood sat in a circle in the big room; the tradition of bullying the bridegroom had begun. The groom sat in the middle of the circle, his feet tied together with cloth.

"How was your bedtime snack last night?" the bride's big brother, Jun-ho, asked.

"Delicious."

"What did you eat?"

"Stew and jeon, I think?"

"That's not what I meant!" He grabbed a stick and swung it down on the groom's legs.

"Give us the leftovers." The bride's uncle, Sang-jo, stuck out his hand.

"But we ate it all."

"Ya, inoma!" He struck the sole of the groom's foot with the stick.

"What did you do on your wedding night?" asked an old man with a long, white goatee wearing a black gat, his voice cracking.

"What do you mean?" Woo-cheol hesitated.

"What did you do on your wedding night?!" The old man's sunken eyes sharpened, his wrinkled hand, swollen at the knuckles, fanning himself with a folding fan.

"I took off my wife's clothes," Woo-cheol said.

"What did you do on your wedding night?!" The old man threw down the fan and stood up, using the stick as support.

"Jong-soo halbi's a little deaf so you'll have to speak up," the bride's uncle Yuu-won explained.

"I took off her clothes!" Woo-cheol said loudly.

"And then what?!"

"I held her!"

"How did you hold her?!"

"Uh . . . I can't really . . ." Woo-cheol blushed and looked down.

The old man pursed his narrow pale lips again and huffed. Woo-cheol thought he was laughing until the moment the stick swung down on the sole of his foot.

"Aya!"

"Of course it hurts. Like you hurt her, right?" the old man asked, every word precise.

Woo-cheol hesitated. Holding the foot that had just been hit, he looked in a daze at the old man's yellowed teeth. He's showing me his teeth, that must mean he is laughing. He had gap teeth, but he wasn't missing a single one. How old was this guy? Is this In-hye's halbi? No, he must be older than that. Her great-grandfather?

"Answer when you're asked something! You rude man!" The old man flexed the arm holding the stick and hit him again on the same foot.

"Aya! I'm sorry, I'm so sorry!"

"And after you hurt her, did you show her love?!"

"Yes! I gave her love!" Woo-cheol's voice strained.

"How? Show us. In-hye!" the old man called.

In-hye, her ear nervously pressed to the wall in the other room, spread her chima, put her right knee up, and bowed, then entered the room. Keeping her lips tight, she shared a smile through her eyes with her husband.

"Oh, my great-granddaughter, beautiful as a flower, bright as a star."

"We'll know if he treated her right by the sound of her voice. In-hye, sing us a song," Jun-ho ordered his little sister.

In-hye straightened her back, gently placed her hands on her lower abdomen where her child was growing, and took a deep breath. Her rouged lips moved with a gleam.

> *Won't you buy a flower, a flower, won't you buy a flower, a flower*
> *Sarang sarang sarang sarang sarang*
> *A flower of love*
> *I picked up my flower basket   and went out to sell*
> *Red flowers   blue ones   yellow and white ones*
> *Indigo and purple   pink of all kinds*
> *Gleaming flowers   the spotted ones are pretty too*

She was like a rose of Sharon, bending her head backward to take in the sun and the gentle breeze.

In the middle of the song, In-hye's sisters brought out trays with dried beef and noodles on them, and Jun-ho untied Woo-cheol's feet. The old man started dancing, tugging on Woo-cheol's hand, urging him to dance too.

> *Won't you buy a flower, a flower, won't you buy a flower, a flower*
> *Sarang sarang sarang sarang sarang*
> *A flower of love*
> *Tightly tied budding flowers   bunches of flowers   smiling flowers*
> *Flowers in full bloom   ones that sing and bring the bees*
> *Ones the butterflies stopped and danced over*
> *All their perfumes are in the air*

Rosa rugosa   peonies   chrysanthemums   the grass
All the sweet grasses   Chinese peonies   roses

When In-hye's song had ended, everyone applauded profusely, but the old man silently gripped Woo-cheol's hand and shook it. When Woo-cheol freed his hand from the grasp, the old man didn't know what to do with his.

"Great-Granddad," In-hye said, taking his hand in her palm.

"Your Woo-cheol seems to be a fine young man, but he has picked and stolen away the flower of our family. Aigu, how sad I am. In-hye, aigu, my great-granddaughter, the next time you see me may be at my funeral." He pressed her hand to his cheek and cried.

"Oh, Halbi, I'm going to be very happy. And you'll get to see your great-great-grandchild's face. I promise." In-hye wrapped her arms around the old man's shoulders and stroked his back.

In-hye picked up and put down the lid of the iron kettle three times to announce her departure from the house. She stepped outside; the sun was shining on the front of the house. Its rays were warm, but the wind was blowing hard. Woo-cheol narrowed his eyes against the wind and looked up at the sky, not realizing that In-hye had come out of the house. She looked at her husband standing there.

I love this man. Just the thought that from now on we'll be living under the same roof makes my heart pound, that's how much I love him. In-hye lifted her chin to see what her husband saw. A bright blue sky, and clouds so thin they looked transparent, being pushed along by the wind, whoosh-whoosh, whoosh-whoosh.

It was the most auspicious day of the fire tiger month. The groom mounted his horse, the bride climbed into the carriage, and the bride's mother waved dozens of strips of red paper at them.

"When you cross the river and you're past the Seonghwangdang, throw these to the road to chase off any evil spirits. Be filial to your new family and be a good daughter-in-law. Have lots of children and be happy."

Woo-cheol gave the horse's belly a kick, and they trotted off. Lots of people were gathered near the station to witness the bride's procession. Miryang's Little Tokyo was near the station, so there were more women in kimono than in chima and jeogori.

The carriage carrying the bride's father went by, the bride's brother walking with great strides, and her four sisters, serving as her attendants, walked past, their jeogori strings fluttering in the wind. Bringing up the rear were their husbands, pulling carts full of the wedding implements and gifts for the bride's family.

The Japanese women observing the procession talked among themselves about what might be in the wooden box in the cart.

It contained silk jeogori, chima, and paji for the bride's new in-laws, padded socks for the groom's relatives, as well as soybean flour–dusted rice cakes, apples, pears, persimmons, makgeolli, and marinated beef, but the Japanese onlookers could only imagine that it must hold a sewing box, a dresser, and a doll box.

Inamori Kiwa was walking by and paused by the side of the road, clad in a meisen silk kimono cinched with a pongee silk obi. She gave a slight bow when Woo-cheol passed before her, but he kept the reins clenched tight in his hands, nervous from riding a horse he wasn't familiar with, and looked straight ahead. It's that boy . . . the one who asked me to help with his mother's labor, the one who carried me on his back, and now he's married . . . Oh, life goes by so fast. He told me then that he was studying at the common school, so he must've been thirteen or thereabouts. That was one, two, three, four years ago now? He must be about seventeen, then, almost the same age as Shige's son, but much more grown-up.

We think we want to reconcile and be unified with the Koreans, but there've been anti-Japanese demonstrations in Gwangju and unrest in Shanghai and Manchuria too. And this town, Mitsuyō, isn't safe either, half of the Shanghai Heroic Corps are from here, they could be lurking anywhere. . . .

Inamori Kiwa walked on, battling against the wind. She wanted at least to see the newlyweds off from the foot of the bridge.

The carriage holding the bride slowly began to cross Yongdu Bridge. The window of the carriage opened. For a moment Inamori Kiwa thought the bride would stick her hand out, but instead red paper came fluttering out. *Whoosh-whoosh*, the wind blew the talismanic papers back toward the bride's family home, not a strip falling into the river or on the bridge.

Kiwa looked down at the red paper flitting down around her feet. These, she thought, are talismans, no doubt about that, but they looked to her like bloodstains. A trail of blood left behind by the bride . . .

Oh no, one mustn't think things like that.

As Kiwa felt her heart race in a way that she could not explain even to herself, she watched the bridal procession leave until she could no longer see the husbands at the tail of it. *Whoosh-whoosh, whoosh-whoosh.*

THIRTEEN

Mongdal Ghosts

| 몽달귀신 | モンダル鬼神 |

Oh, it moved. In-hye, pounding peeled acorns in a mortar, moved her hand from the pestle to her big belly. Aigu, the pain. The baby was kicking her as if it was marching in place, turning its body around one full rotation. Was it tossing and turning? Or was it getting into position to be born? She was in her last month of pregnancy now, but her mother- and father-in-law still thought she was only seven months gone. You look just like you're about to give birth, it must be a boy, don't work yourself so hard, you know, there's no end of regret over a miscarriage, after all, her mother-in-law would say as she did all the cleaning for her. Since In-hye had made it to the last month, her body felt heavier, and she'd felt her womb contracting and her belly getting harder more often. She couldn't overdo it, but nor could she just rest; making three meals a day was a daughter-in-law's job. In-hye stood up and stretched her hips, then sat back down in front of the mortar and picked up the pestle again.

"You hear me? When you're about to be born, you let me know, all right, you say, Omma, I'm coming. 'Cause if the contractions start all of a sudden, then you and I are in big trouble, all right? You hear me?"

The baby kicked her hard as if in response.

I've started talking to this baby so much lately without even realizing it. But when I talk to it or stroke my belly, it moves so much.

"The day after tomorrow is your omma's twentieth birthday. So you hurry up and come out soon. Show your face to your omma. Hear your omma's voice. Drink your omma's milk."

In-hye closed her mouth, but she didn't stop talking to her baby.

"Your appa loves crab pickled in soy sauce, and hand-pulled noodles and rice porridge with pumpkin in it too. Auntie So-won's favorite food is dried persimmons. Auntie So-won's taken to me like a sister. I have one older brother, five sisters, and one younger brother, but I don't have any younger sisters, so when I said I'd always wanted a younger sister, So-won said, 'Well, I'd always wanted a big sister, and now I have one, In-hye unni!' And then she threw her arms around me. Uncle Woo-gun is five years older than you, so treat him like he's your older brother. They say your in-laws won't listen to you for three years or talk to you for three more, but my mother-in-law and father-in-law dote on me, and I'm so happy. Right, that's the acorns all pounded. Once I put the water in and steam it, it'll be a delicious dotorimuk. Your uncle Woo-gun loves rice cakes.

"In a little bit Auntie So-won will be back from school, and she'll come in the door and say, danycowatseumnida. Then you and I say, welcome home, danyeowasseoyo."

In-hye put the pounded acorns in the pot and added hana, dul, set cups of water from the basin with the gourd scoop, then gave it a stir with the wooden ladle until the acorn paste dissolved.

"Your appa's out running on the riverbank right now, in-hale ex-hale in-hale ex-hale, your appa's a very fast runner. He's giving your uncle Woo-gun a ride on his shoulders. And when you're big enough to hold your head up, you let him give you a ride on his shoulders too. Your appa's so tall that I can see him coming from a mile away."

In-hye remembered what happened the night before. His warm lips kissing her nape, his broad arms wrapping themselves around her, his big hands embracing her belly from behind—*Ah, it moved, a foot, you can see it through my belly, what an energetic little baby, hey, he's running, hana, dul! Hana, dul! This kid's got potential!* She had sunk into sleep, her head full of satisfied thoughts of how there was no space between his body and hers, like they were made for each other, how there was no separation between her and this baby, the three of them together. In-hye stoked the oven with pine branches and leaves, struck a match and threw it in, then worked the bellows to make the fire rise. She was already an old hand at it; no matter how deep in thought she was, her hands moved automatically. This is my house; this is my kitchen. This is the house where I'm going to raise our child. In-hye scraped off the skin of the pumpkin with a spoon, then chopped it roughly in half, hollowed out the insides, cut it into chunks, and let it sink slowly into the boiling water.

Dear neighbors
Dear neighbors
Lay your flower baskets down
And let's go pick something to eat
Up this way the bracken's good
Down that way it's not yet grown
We'll wash it down in that stream
Then rinse it up in that one
The quarter moon in the sky   in a round pot
Rises like the morning star
Season it with ginger and pepper
Prepare twelve trays
Abeoji   Eomoni
Quick, quick, come quick
Take a pee and wash your face
Then dry it on that silk cloth
It's time for breakfast

A sound came from the wicker gate.

"I think your appa's home now, right, time to hurry."

In-hye mashed the pumpkin with a wooden spoon, then added the rice flour and chestnuts a little at a time, mixing it in from the bottom up.

"Oh yes, when Auntie So-won gets home I must make yugwa, I promised her this morning that I'd teach her."

Is it difficult, she wanted to know.

No, not at all; first you take some glutinous rice flour and steam it, then knead it, then you stretch it out on a floured surface and cut it to the right size, then you let it dry. Then you slowly fry it and soak it in syrup, and once you've coated it in roasted rice flour, that's it.

Sounds pretty easy.

It is easy. The trick is keeping the door closed and letting the heat from the underfloor heating dry it out, because once the wind hits them they'll crack.

In-hye flavored the pumpkin rice porridge, which had now reduced and become frothy, with a pinch of salt. Masitda. She took the nickel silver pot off the stove, took the rice cakes out of the water they'd been soaking in, cut them into squares, and arranged them on a plate, then finely chopped the Chinese cabbage kimchi, mixed sesame oil and soy sauce, then poured it over the acorn cake.

Right, that's the dotorimuk done, the pumpkin porridge is done, the kimchi is cut, the rice just needs to steam, and I'll bake the mackerel pike in a little while.

In-hye let down her sleeves and loosened the sides of her chima, tied below her breasts.

"They all just keep talking about how it's going to be a boy, but your omma's not going to be disappointed if you're a girl, I mean, wouldn't that be fun, the two of us cooking together, doing the sewing together?"

The baby kicked her stomach hard. It made her arms and legs flap, as if she were writhing. In-hye was in such pain she could not even moan; she leaned against the pillar, still holding the knife in her hand. Another kick . . .

I think I might wet myself from the pain . . . I can't even keep my eyes open . . . I need to lie down . . . but I, I still have more to do . . .

In-hye relaxed her gritted teeth and kept breathing deeply, her left hand stroking her belly where she thought the baby's head might be. Breathe in, breathe out, in, out, hey, listen, not now, you hear me, if it, starts now, it'll spoil, tonight's supper, in, out, in, out . . . Sweat started to seep from her hairline, falling on her face. Some stopped at her eyebrows, while some dripped down her chin then down her neck and down onto her chest. Breathe in, out, in, out—it stopped, the baby was now quiet. In-hye pushed her hand against the wall as she stood up.

Once she wiped the sweat from her face with a cloth and opened her eyes, she saw smoke rising from the wind furnace. Aigu, that's not good! She rushed to take the mackerel pike out of the oven and put it on a plate.

"Your auntie So-won is late, I wonder if something happened at school today. If the students won't listen to their ilbon saram teacher they'll make them stand until after the bell's already rung, but I can't imagine that happening to So-won. Her report card was all full marks, she has lots of friends, there's no reason to punish her like that. So she must be getting home soon. But I can't see us making yugwa today, and well, the rice gets softer the longer you soak it, so we'll make it tomorrow."

In-hye took off the lid of the iron pot and dished up some rice with a wooden spoon, then added the water used to soak the rice to the scorched rice still clinging to its bottom and replaced the lid.

She set the tray down on the floor and opened the door to the main room to find her mother-in-law and father-in-law sitting cross-legged, having an argument. The headline of the *Dong-A Ilbo* newspaper that her father-in-law had spread out leaped out at In-hye.

JANG MAKES TRIUMPHANT FLIGHT HOME

"Dinner is ready."

"Where's So-won?" Woo-cheol looked puzzled.

"She's very late."

Since In-hye had married into this family So-won had always carried the dinner trays for her. This was, now that she thought about it, the first time she'd done it herself.

"She talks so much but doesn't listen. That's an unmarried daughter for you," Yong-ha said, turning the page.

In-hye went out through the garden and opened the back door of the store.

"Dinner is ready."

Woo-gun, who was playing around with the rubber boots, turned to look.

"How may I help you?"

So In-hye was now a customer. "I'd like one rubber boot, please."

"That'll be fifty sen."

She pretended to put change in his outstretched hand and saw her mother-in-law smiling.

"So-won isn't home yet though."

"Really?"

Mother-in-law and daughter-in-law looked out at the road at the same time. It was already pitch-black.

For a split second, Hee-hyang grimaced as if she were trying desperately to remember something, then she stood, like a puppet being pulled up by its strings.

"I'll go to the school to see if she's there, so you just go ahead and eat without me."

"C'mon, come eat with me," In-hye said to Woo-gun, holding out both her hands, but he grabbed his mother's hand and wouldn't let go.

"I'm going with Omma."

"But your dinner'll go cold."

"Eat with your sister-in-law," Hee-hyang said in a stern tone.

Woo-gun looked down at his feet and kicked the ground with the toe of his boot, then took In-hye's hand.

Dinner was quiet.

In-hye removed the bones from the fish for Woo-gun.

"Hey, where did So-won go?" He looked out of the corner of his eye at her dish, its lid still on.

"She'll be home soon," Yong-ha said. His glum expression didn't budge.

"Hello, has your mouth gone to sleep? How about you chew properly, swallow, and then you can eat some more rice cake. Dotorimuk is your favorite, and I made it just for you."

It was just after they'd drank the sungnyung made from the scorched rice that they heard the wicker gate opening.

"They're back," In-hye said. Her lower abdomen was hard, so she put both of her hands behind her and stood up slowly.

The door to the main room opened, and Hee-hyang came in. Her skinny chest heaved unsteadily, and her hurried breaths, like the puffs of a bellows, echoed in everyone's ears.

"I couldn't find her anywhere. Her homeroom teacher, Yamashita-sensei, said that she left school as usual, and In-so, who she always walks home with, said that they said goodbye at the pontoon bridge and that So-won went off toward Mount Yongdu, saying that she was going to go gather chestnuts, so I went up to the chestnut trees, and I called for her loudly, but she wasn't there; I can't find her anywhere. Shall we go to the police?"

"The police are just there to protect the waenom and spy on us Koreans—who knows if they'd even do anything."

"Well, then, what do you suggest?!"

"Calm down, dear."

"How can I calm down?!"

"I'll go looking for her." Woo-cheol stood up.

"Me too." In-hye followed after her husband.

"You stay here with Woo-gun. You're not up to what you would be."

Woo-cheol, Yong-ha, and Hee-hyang left the room, and the house became even quieter.

"Where did Noona go?"

"She went hunting chestnuts." In-hye tried with all her might to calm the beating of her heart.

"Is she coming back?" Woo-gun's voice was thin, as if he might start crying at any moment.

"Yes, she is." The voice that came out of In-hye's throat was muffled and husky.

"But what if she doesn't?"

"She'll come home." In-hye forced herself to smile as she peeled a persimmon.

Just what could have happened to her? In-hye wondered. She hoped So-won would come home safe, of course, but the only thing certain was that something had happened. So what was it? Maybe she'd sprained her ankle while she was gathering chestnuts and she couldn't walk. The grandfather clock made a clunking sound and then: *ding, one . . . ding, two . . . ding, three . . . ding, four . . . ding, five . . . ding, six . . . ding, seven . . .* Seven o'clock, it's seven! And she's shivering somewhere in a dark forest . . . crying . . . So-won is such a scaredy-cat!

"Let's go find her."

In-hye wiped her palms, sticky with persimmon juice, on her apron and stood up.

Wandering around like this is pointless, In-hye thought as she stopped by the pontoon bridge. The moon and the stars aren't out tonight, it'll be rain tomorrow, if we don't find her before it starts raining, then—

As she stared down at the dark, black river, she wondered if maybe So-won hadn't fallen into the river, and she grabbed Woo-gun's hand tightly.

"Ouch!"

"I'm sorry."

The moment she loosened her grip, she felt a creeping sensation at her nape and shuddered.

"What's wrong?"

"Nothing." A sharp, acrid smell filled her nostrils. This, she thought, this must be the smell of fear.

"Really?"

"It's nothing." Someone was watching them.

She turned around and saw someone on the stone steps . . . two women wearing white chima jeogori . . . holding hands . . . So-won?

"Let's keep looking."

Following the shadows of the pair dressed in white that had gone up toward Yeongnamnu, In-hye climbed up the stairs, pulling Woo-gun after her. With each step the darkness intensified, and though there was no wind, she felt resistance as if the air was pushing against her. At the top of the steps, they walked on toward Yeongnamnu; in the shadow of a pillar a white chima fluttered. In-hye let go of Woo-gun's hand and walked up the steps. Her heart was kicking in her chest like the baby, her mind was flooded with fear, and In-hye could not think at all. The white shadows, still holding hands, turned around. One she didn't recognize, but the other was So-won. In-hye herself didn't know if she had whispered her name or not. The white shadows disappeared.

In-hye felt all sensation drifting out of her.

So-won is dead.... That was a ghost.... And the beautiful woman holding her hand was Arang....

"If heaven and earth is not searched, the blue river in spring will year by year be red with blood shed by my han...."

"Sister-in-law!"

She breathed deeply and tried to reply, but her cry turned into ragged, heavy breathing.

"Sister-in-law!"

In-hye nodded, her back still turned to Woo-gun, unable to move her body.

"I'm scared."

In-hye used all the force in her body to turn her head, and when Woo-gun came running to her she wrapped both her arms around him. Woo-gun's face was damp with tears and snot.

"Where did Noona go?"

She swallowed the lump that welled up in her throat and spat out some quavering words.

"She'll come home."

Looking down at the river from the pavilion, she saw her husband crossing the pontoon bridge.

"There's your brother; now, I can't run, so you go down before me."

She followed after Woo-gun as he ran down the stone steps, counting the steps as she held her belly, one step, another, feeling as if her feet were being swallowed up by the ground, unable to tell if her feet were moving or not. One step, then another; as she walked she turned back to look at Yeongnamnu, but the white shadows were nowhere to be seen. Is the baby scared too? Gwaenchanayo, your omma's here, I'll protect you no matter what happens, so don't worry, there's nothing to be scared of, and if you see something scary, I'll cover your eyes, and if you hear something scary, I'll cover your ears, and if something scary is chasing you, I'll stand in its way.

Before dawn they heard rain.

"It's raining...."

"So it is. . . ."

"Are you awake? It'll make her sick. . . ."

"Drenched in rain . . ."

"Did she fall in the river?"

With those words the slim possibility of going back to sleep that had remained was gone. Her heartbeat sped up, and the baby began to harden like a swelling. Woo-gun is the only one in this house sleeping.

Why did So-won go hunting for chestnuts? Because they're my favorite food, and she wanted to make me happy? The only place around here with chestnut trees is on the north side of Mount Jongnam, and it's a deep plunge off that cliff, so . . . but she's very good at swimming. . . .

In the back of In-hye's mind she recalled the figure of the woman in white. That wasn't So-won, I was just confused and mistook her for So-won, she'll come home soon.

Danyeowatseumnida, I'm home.

Danyeowasseoyo, welcome home.

Come back, please, just come back, God, somehow, please, bring her home safely, I beg you.

There was a flash of lightning, followed by a bang, which surprised her. The lightning dragged its rumbling along after it, laying waste to the wind, and struck its hand down like an ax. *Bang!* The whole house huddled, and the glass in the windows went *rattle-rattle, rattle-rattle . . .*

"I'm going looking for her." Woo-cheol got out of bed.

"Be careful."

In-hye stayed on her back, watching as her husband tied the strings of his jeogori, cinched his paji around his waist, and did up the strings around his ankles.

"Just lie there and try at least to shut your eyes. And don't let Mother go out, the river'll be flooding, and it's dangerous."

Soon after her husband went out of the room, she heard the sound of rain hitting the ground. In-hye was drained by anxiety and fear. If she could've, she would've liked to wrap her arms around her husband's back and go to sleep, with nothing on her mind, but her husband had gone out into the storm. To look for his little sister who was somewhere out there—In-hye put her arms out to her sides and gradually raised herself up, crawling to the dresser on all fours; then, in the darkness, she tied up her bun and stuck in her hairpin.

Get yourself together, your job is to get breakfast ready, so make it a good one.

Woo-cheol opened his umbrella and walked along the path by the river, slouching. The river wound like a big serpent, surging up its banks. A gust of wind blew, pulling his umbrella in toward his body. This is dangerous, he thought. The second that Woo-cheol's grasp loosened, the wind snatched the umbrella from his hand and it blew away. Goddamnit!

Woo-cheol started running. In-hale ex-hale   in-hale ex-hale   the rain is   blowing into   my face   my arms   my legs   *whoosh-whoosh*   it sounds kind of like someone's voice   a shriek?   A wail?   *Whoosh-whoosh*   that's lightning   in-hale ex-hale   BANG!   That one was close   in-hale ex-hale   in-hale ex-hale   the lightning must've hit and broken that tree in-hale ex-hale   in-hale ex-hale   ow!   What is that?   A pine needle   the wind is blowing the needles off the pines   in-hale ex-hale. Woo-cheol went down the mountain path covered with fallen leaves, his right hand held out to shield his face. In-hale ex-hale   in-hale ex-hale   So-won!   Where are you?   Please come back safe   So-won!   So-won!   So-won!   in-hale ex-hale   in-hale ex-hale   the water is running in rivers, gushing   in-hale ex-hale   got to be careful not to slip on the rotting leaves   oh, I'm gonna fall!   in-hale ex-hale   in-hale ex-hale   my body's getting too hot   in-hale ex-hale   even though there's steam rising from my straw raincoat   in-hale ex-hale   in-hale ex-hale   there's mud in my boot   in-hale ex-hale   my socks are soaking wet   in-hale ex-hale   I can't feel my toes anymore   the hem of my paji is cold   in-hale ex-hale   the cold is rising up to my knees   but in-hale ex-hale   So-won must be colder   in-hale ex-hale   in-hale ex-hale if I don't find her soon   she'll catch pneumonia and freeze   in-hale ex-hale   she went looking for chestnuts   the trees above Yongdu-mok are the best   in-hale ex-hale   big chestnuts   in-hale ex-hale   in-hale ex-hale

Woo-cheol's feet sank into the mire of the chestnut grove and he was stuck. Just then, when the sky exploded with lightning, he saw something hanging from a branch of a chestnut tree. He moved closer, one step, then another. It had a pattern he knew. Panting, he took the black book bag from the branch and hooked it over the crook of his arm and continued forward. The reeds at the cliff's edge were down flat. Did she fall? Into Yongdu-mok?

One of the branches of the willow that leaned over the edge of the cliff hung down, bent like a cane. Woo-cheol steadied himself against the trunk of the willow and looked down at Yongdu-mok. The whispering rain was swallowed up by the darkness. His tongue swelled up, filling his mouth and would hardly move.

What should I tell Eomoni? Woo-cheol thought, breathing in the air, which smelled of only rain and wailing. On the other side of the thick curtain of rain the day was dawning, revealing a gray sky of rain clouds hanging heavily. It was a new morning, but neither the roosters nor the sparrows called. As he stood there in the mire, the only cries to be heard were Woo-cheol's.

For breakfast, there was rice with beansprouts, stewed Chinese cabbage roots, cod milt soup, kimchi, and kkakdugi.

Woo-gun brought a spoon of the cod milt soup up to his mouth, then smiled at his mother and said how good it was, but noticing the vacant expression in his mother's eyes, he wiped the smile from his face and looked anxiously at his father.

"It is." Yong-ha nodded, chewing.

"He's back!" Hee-hyang let her spoon drop from her hand.

"Oh? I don't hear anything." In-hye listened closely.

"You hear that? He's back." Hee-hyang stood up, leaving her spoon sunk in her soup.

The sound of footsteps came closer through the din of the rain. Hee-hyang opened the door to find Woo-cheol, drenched, in the entrance. She, Yong-ha, and In-hye had their eyes glued to the book bag hanging from Woo-cheol's arm, but Woo-gun looked at the drops of water trickling down from his brother's coat.

"I found this hanging from a chestnut tree near Yongdu-mok. She fell in the water," he said, forcing the last words out.

Hee-hyang let out a large breath and clasped her hands to her heart.

"There were tracks where she must've fallen off the cliff...."

A wail finally gushed out of Hee-hyang's mouth.

"Aigo!"

As he rushed to hold his mother back from running outside, the book bag came open, spilling chestnuts in their burr, waterlogged ethics and language textbooks, a red cloth pen case, and an aluminum lunch box on the floor.

Hee-hyang froze, her whole body writhing in agony; she grabbed Woo-cheol's hand and held it against her chest.

"Aigo, So-won! Aigo!"

Thump-thump, thump-thump, thump-thump! It was like hot needles were running through his bloodstream, *thump-thump! Thump-thump!* With every beat the unbearable pain spread from his limbs to the very tips of his fingers, and Woo-cheol's breaths became labored.

Don't cry! What will crying do?! If you cry now, you'll never stop, and no tears will bring So-won back! In-hye's gonna have our baby soon, and Woo-gun is only five, don't cry!

"Eomoni, I can't go now because of the storm. When the storm lifts, we'll go look for her."

In-hye stuck a chopstick into one of the potatoes in the pot to check that it was done, then she picked the pot up by the handles with two cloths and drained the water, before quickly peeling the potatoes' skins. They were fluffy and perfectly cooked.

"Appa and Halbi and Halme went off to Yongdu-mok without eating any

breakfast. And who knows if they'll come back for lunch, so I've got to prepare something that'll be fine to eat whenever they get back."

In-hye carried on talking to her baby as she put the potatoes and some
acorns, boiled for three days until the water stopped turning red, into the
pestle and ground them.

"What should I do with this glutinous rice that's been soaking since the
day before yesterday? Should I make patjuk for dinner tonight, baby? Patjuk is
when you make the glutinous rice into paste and make little balls the size of
quail's eggs from it, then you cook them with the red bean porridge, and you
add a little honey; it's good. So, so good. Don't tell Appa, but your omma's
starting to hope that you're a girl."

Without So-won here next to me, like she always was, talking to me and
helping me with the cooking, the kitchen's so quiet—she heard a sniffling
noise and turned around to see Woo-gun standing in the kitchen door.

"When will Omma come back?"

She hesitated. "Well . . ."

"And Noona?"

In-hye closed her eyes for a moment, then shook her head sadly.

"Is Noona dead?"

She knelt next to him and held his head against her chest.

"Did she fall in the river?" He pushed her arms away, pulled his head back,
and looked her right in the eyes.

She could do nothing but look back into his eyes.

"But Noona's so good at swimming."

"Yes . . ."

"Omma and Appa and Hyung went looking for her, right? So they're gonna
find her and bring her home, right? So soon they'll all come home, right?"

"They'll . . ."

"I'm gonna go looking too."

"No. Go play with Yong-il next door. When lunch is ready I'll come calling
for you."

Woo-gun turned, still sniffling, went to the veranda, and put his rubber
shoes on and went out into the garden, trudging his way toward the gate.

It's still too early, if I don't wait to finish lunch until they get back it'll all go cold. Eomoni taught me that the rice should be as warm as spring, the soup as hot as summer, the jeon as refreshing as autumn, and the salmon as cold as winter. The water jug is empty, so I'd better draw some water. I'll be fine, I'll draw the water slowly, so I don't let any of it touch my belly, and I'll carry it back little by little, so I'll be fine, gwaenchanayo. She looked around for her rubber shoes and put them on, when she felt her back become as stiff as a board and a pain ran through her lower abdomen, but In-hye soothed the pain with her palm as she walked.

It was truly painful. Usually the pain would subside quickly, but just as she'd thought it had gone, she'd be hit by it again; just as she thought it was getting less painful it would intensify. She took two or three steps, then stopped, taking deep breaths to try to overcome the pain, then walked again. The sky was pale blue. The air, brisk as in mid-October, filled her nostrils. The puddles of rain here and there in the garden glimmered in the sunlight filtering through the trees. It's like the sky and air and sun are all in time with us as we hold our breath, waiting. Oh, she thought, I'm twenty today. This is the first birthday I've ever had that nobody will celebrate.

A pain stronger than before ran through her body, and In-hye, still standing, contorted her body, breathing, in, out, in, out, then vomited.

"Your omma doesn't care about her twentieth birthday; I had nineteen parties before anyway. But you, I want everyone to celebrate the day you're born. I want everyone to be full of joy. I don't want to give birth to you now, in the midst of all this sadness, this pain, this unhappiness. Haneunim! Binaida, binaida, let So-won come home safely, binaida, binaida—"

Her prayer was cut off by the pain, but she could not stop walking. Cradling her heavy stomach, she tottered past the well.

Haneunim, binaida, binaida, please let this baby be born safely. Aigo, no! In-hye, you fool! Listen to you praying for your baby when everyone's out searching everywhere for So-won! But still, how can I not, when right now I'm the only one praying for this baby? Haneunim, binaida, binaida, please let this baby be born safely. Haneunim, binaida, binaida, let So-won come home safe, binaida, binaida . . .

She turned out of the gate and found the whole street wrapped in a strange silence. All over the road were scattered broken branches and roof tiles and gates blown down by the wind, and as she stepped carefully through the uneven shadows of the houses and trees, In-hye headed toward the pontoon bridge.

The Miryang River, which was usually clear enough to reflect the sky, was muddied, and So-won was somewhere in that muck—In-hye turned her eyes from the river up toward Yongdu-mok. Once summer came, it would be full of kids swimming nude and jumping from the top of the willow tree into Yongdu-mok, but many children drowned there too. The waters were deep, and there was a lot of plant life in the water, so the drowned didn't float up so quickly. . . .

Unni   In-hye unni

Suddenly So-won's voice came to her. She looked up at Yeongnamnu, but all she saw were small children playing hide-and-seek and elderly people basking in the sun. Ready or not! Here I come! Ready or not! Here I come!

Unni

It was So-won's voice again, pestering, impatient, a little nasal.

Unni

In-hye covered her chest with her palms, *thump-thump! Thump-thump!* Her heart was pounding, *thump-thump! Thump-thump!* It was like her heart was filling her entire body, *thump-thump! Thump-thump! Thump-thump! Thump-thump!*

In-hye unni

The sweet, playful voice tickled the nape of her neck, and In-hye turned. So-won! Just where the path along the riverside starts to turn, So-won was standing. Wearing the white jeogori and black chima she'd been wearing when she left the house yesterday morning. She was far away, and her features weren't clear, but her eyes were looking right at In-hye, firmly, darkly, without blinking. In-hye crouched down in pain, holding her belly, but kept her face looking up. The wind whispered through the trees, sending the yellow and red leaves dancing through the air, but So-won's chima didn't even flutter or whirl. It was as if the place where she was standing alone was disconnected from its surroundings. Though her heart pounded with all its might, warning her, In-hye could not tear her mind from the pain, and bit by bit, little by little, as everything retreated from her, only the sound of water was clear, the burble and rush of it, In-hye walked down to the riverbed as if beckoned by the sound, *burble, burble, burble, burble, burble.*

A large tree had fallen into the river. And as she got closer to the tree, she saw something white floating. What, what is that? A blanket? No, a white dog? She stepped into the water with her rubber shoes still on. When she was in up to her knees, she quickly recoiled. It was a person. Only their back and head were floating on the water. She saw a black daenggimeori braid.

Someone, help! Her voice wouldn't come out. Help! Somebody! Help me!

In-hye got up to the riverbank and ran. There was no strength in her body, as if every single bone in it had been ripped out. She slipped out of her shoes and stumbled over them, falling onto a rock, but she ran and ran—run! She dashed into the hardware store at the foot of the pontoon bridge. The owner, Yong-il, looked at her in surprise, but she could not make the words come out. She took him outside and pointed at the river, and in that moment heavy, panting breaths overflowed from her mouth; even when she covered her mouth with her hand, still they came: *ah-ah-ah-ah-ah-ah-ah-ah-ah-ah-ah.*

Before she knew it, there was a throng around her. Through the gaps between people's heads, she saw that Chae, who worked in the subcounty government, and Kim, who owned the rice store, were going into the river. In-hye pushed up with her knees to the side of her belly and stood. Chae had grabbed her underneath her armpits, and Kim had hold of her neck, and they were bringing *it* to the shore. And on a woven straw mat that someone had brought they laid *it* down.

Aigu   she's naked   was she raped and thrown into the river, do you think?

No   the storm, remember, the water undressed her   When they found Yeong-son, and Ki-won, too, they were both naked, you know   it took a week for Yeong-son to surface   the skin came clean off her hands and feet   and her hair came right out

That was the middle of summer, sure   her face was so swelled   covered in red mold like she'd been burned   and she was always such a pretty thing

Aigo   poor girl   I've got chills all over

She must've been so cold

She's got something in her hands

It's algae   she must've struggled

She's covered in cuts

She fell on the rocks   her skin is gouged at the knees, you can almost see the bone, can't you

She's not bleeding though

Must've been washed away in the water

The river's moving so fast

What's happened to her there

Oh   a fish has been nibbling at her   they like to get at the soft parts of the body   it's ripped open her belly

Aigo   her guts are coming out

Are there fish inside her?

In-hye sluggishly pushed her way through the people, who continued talking, and made her way toward *it*. And then, she saw. The white breasts and pale pink nipples. Her private parts, lightly covered with soft hair. She saw. The froth around her nose and mouth, like a well-beaten egg white.

"T-t-that's my sister-in-law, don't look, please don't look! S-she was only eleven. She'd never shown her body to anyone! She was pure, a virgin!"

And then, she saw. Her clouded, white eyes. The moment that those eyes shone, as if a light had been lit, In-hye's water broke.

When she opened her eyes, her mother, Wan-son, was next to her, hanging over her.

"Where's So-won?" In-hye was surprised at the steadiness of her own voice.

"Aigu, she's wrapped in a woven mat. . . ."

"Where is she?"

"They didn't bring her into the house; she was lying in the garden for a while. . . . Your father-in-law and husband put her in a cart. . . ."

"When's the funeral?"

"There'll probably just be a burial. It's unfilial to die before your parents, after all."

"And her grave?"

"Your mother-in-law was crying and crying—she's really gone to pieces, so I couldn't ask many details, but I imagine they'll bury her somewhere near Gyo-dong. And it won't be much of a grave, more like a small hole with a pile of stones. . . ."

"Aigo."

"You just focus on having this baby. How are your contractions?"

"The pain feels like it's kind of faraway."

"But your water broke, so the baby will come soon, you know. Your chima was soaking wet; Chae and Kim carried you home on their shoulders."

Chae and Kim? Those hands that touched her body, carried me? Aigo. In-hye shuddered, imagining the smell of water and decomposition clinging to her whole body.

"Aigu, to take such a shock and have your water break, and at only seven months along . . . I hope the baby will be born all right. . . ."

"Gwaenchanayo, it'll be fine, I'm sure, a healthy baby. Oh, yes, what about lunch? I was in the middle of making it when . . ."

"I don't think anyone's eaten anything."

"Even Woo-gun? Adults can be patient, but I feel sorry for him. All hungry and sad . . . When they get back make him something."

"You should eat something now too, you know—labor can take a whole day sometimes."

"What time is it?"

Wan-son looked at the wall clock that had been given to this house as part of her daughter's dowry.

"Eleven thirty? No, there's no way it's eleven thirty, is there."

In-hye lifted her head and looked at the clock.

"It's stopped."

"You're right, so it is."

"Eomoni, turn the key to wind it up."

"What time is it now, I wonder."

"Eomoni, please, go look at the clock hanging on the wall in the store. I want to remember what time it was when this baby was born."

Wan-son stood up and left the room. The clock, surrounded by the sigh of silence, looked down at In-hye as if looking for assistance. It seemed utterly unreal to her that she was giving birth, that she was lying here in a room that was not in the house she'd been born and raised in, that her mother was here in this house. And that So-won was dead—she recalled her floating corpse, almost nestled up to that big, fallen tree, and In-hye observed the passing of the seconds on the clock's behalf. *Tick tock tick tock*, she usually wound the clock every day before lunch, *tick tock tick tock*, but this morning it was moving, *tick tock tick tock*, I guess it was about eleven thirty exactly, *tick tock tick tock*, when I found So-won, *tick tock tick tock tick tock tick tock*.

"It was two minutes till three, so I'll set it for three."

Wan-son turned the butterfly key and wound the clock, and as the pendulum started to move, it made a cracking noise like the flick of a fingernail, and then *ding ding ding*, the clock assumed calm and began to mark the seconds, *tick tock tick tock tick tock*, as she listened to that sound her head became muddled with drowsiness—*it* opened its eyes slowly. Maggots tumbling from those clouded eyeballs, blood-covered fish leaping from that mouth. Ah! Ah! Ah! Ah! Ah! Ah!

"Aigu, In-hye, what's wrong? In-hye! Pull yourself together!"

"Oh, oh, I had a dream, So-won's, her face, it was, oh, oh, Eomoni, it's coming, the baby, it's coming, now!"

"Spread your knees, brace your legs, and breathe, phew, phew, phew, phew, just like that, and push with all your strength. When the pain recedes, relax. There's no point pushing the whole time. When the pain comes back, breathe in unison with it and give a big push. Here, have some water."

In-hye supported herself with her elbow as she took a sip of water, then started vocalizing her breaths again, *phew, phew, phew*, like a cat.

"Eomoni, where's the Samsin altar?"

"What with everything that's happened and this not being my house, I just can't go pray at it."

"Well, then, who should we pray to?"

"To Haneunim."

Haneunim! I don't want to give birth today. Or tomorrow, or the day after either. If you can, I'd like to do it after So-won's mourning is over, when the tears of my husband and his family have all dried up, after this sadness that's hardening inside of me has dissipated, please. I don't think this baby wants to be born now either, ow!

The contractions had come back. In-hye pulled back the edge of the blanket and arched her back. Aya! She had never in her life felt pain so intense. She had no ability to think of anything beyond the pain. Sweat began to seep from every pore in her body; her hair was soaked. I can't! Help! If this pain goes on ten minutes more it will break me and the baby both. Help me! Help!

"Keep going!" Wan-son rubbed her daughter's hips with her every cry and wiped the sweat from her forehead.

Aya! But I can't run away. I'm not the only one suffering here. I have to withstand the pain! Even if nobody in the world will bless you, even if no one welcomes you, or embraces you, I will bless you! I will welcome and embrace you! In-hye fixated on a point on the ceiling and gritted her teeth.

When the sunlight was about to disappear, the baby gave its first cry.

The Lee family had already returned from So-won's burial, but the baby's grandfather Yong-ha had gone to the store with his five-year-old son, and the grandmother, Hee-hyang, had shut herself away in her room, so the only one there to hear the baby's first cry was its father, Woo-cheol.

Woo-cheol opened the door to the room. The smell of blood and sweat hit his nose. Reflexively he held his breath; his eyes focused on the two heads lying on the bed. How strange. The features of In-hye's face looked distorted, and they flickered as if seen through a campfire, *flicker flicker, flicker flicker . . .*

"Honey?"

"Hi."

"It's a girl."

"Oh . . ."

"Are you disappointed?"

"She's our baby. How could I be disappointed? Where's your mother?"

"She's in the kitchen making miyeokguk for me. How's your mother?"

"Crying."

In-hye looked at her husband's face, her eyes drawn to his sunken cheeks and pupils. It was the first time he'd seen the face of his child, but she saw no spark of light in those eyes. They looked as if they would meld into the evening dusk along with the darkening room. The baby, clad in a white baenetjeogori, squirmed like a potato bug that had been plucked from a leaf, making little cries in her thin voice.

"Ohh, shh, shh, shh, good girl, don't cry, look at your appa, look, that's your appa; Omma and Appa are here. Don't cry, ask your daddy. Appa, hold me."

He had washed his hands. Over and over again. But they were still the same hands with which he had held the straw-covered body of his sister. The hands that had just dug her grave. That had brought her grave stones. His hands had not forgotten those sensations; they were still alive within his bones. His hands had not yet been set free. They were still captive. But he could not say no.

I'm her abeoji, he thought.

He slid one hand under her neck and the other under her back, then brought the baby close to his body.

"Oh, nicely done. You're probably better at it than me."

"I held Woo-gun a lot five years ago, when he was just born . . . but there's something different about baby girls."

"What's that?"

"I'm afraid to hold her . . . I'm worried I might break her."

Woo-cheol breathed in the smell of his newborn daughter's skin. Was there any smell in the world as sweet and painfully evocative as this? But, he thought, *that smell* is still clinging to my nostrils.

I'd heard that once a drowned body was taken from the water it began to decompose almost immediately, but by the time we arrived at the children's burial ground, I could barely stand to breathe through my nose.

Her perfectly smooth baby skin, I'll do everything I can to protect it from any harm. There are dangerous places in this world. Some dangers you can avoid; some you can't. And in order to protect her, I may have to encounter those unavoidable dangers myself. They don't always come at you head-on. From the left, the right, from behind, above, under your feet, even right now, when we're like this, it's creeping closer, looking for an opportunity to get another hit in.

I hope she grows up strong. And smart. I hope she's timid too.

In-hye craned her arm up gracefully to stroke her husband's cheek, then playfully tugged at his hair.

"Honey, have you thought of a name for her?"

"I thought if we had a boy, we could name him Shin-tae, and if we had a girl, Mi-ok."

"Mi-ok. What a pretty name, just right for a girl. Mi-ok, your name is Mi-ok. Mi-ok," she repeated.

Mi-ok began to cry in her father's arms. Looking down at his newborn daughter whose whole body down to her wrists shook with each cry, he remembered a different newborn baby girl. The baby his father and the woman in the house by the cedars had had together, his own blood whose name he didn't even know—his other little sister.

"Do you mind if I shut my eyes for a bit?"

"You should get some sleep."

"Eomoni's making dinner, so go ahead and eat with your family."

"Night night."

"I'm just shutting my eyes . . ." In-hye pressed her lips to her daughter's head, then quietly closed her eyes.

"Thank you . . . for giving me such a beautiful baby. . . ."

She's asleep, he thought, standing up slowly; In-hye's lips began to move.

"I . . . am so happy to be with you."

"Me too."

"Despite everything that's happened . . . I'm happy, to have your baby. . . . I guess I have to think that though."

"No, I'm happy too. Really happy."

In-hye rested her hands on her stomach, a habit from when she was pregnant.

"Oh, she's not there anymore. It's all soft and flabby, I can't let you see my stomach like this. I feel like I'm drunk. But I don't want to sleep. If I sleep, I'll have horrible nightmares."

"The baby's sleeping."

"Right, I've got to be quiet, I'm a mother now, but, but . . . I . . . I love you."

"Don't speak too much, you'll wake the baby."

"Don't call her 'the baby'; call her by the name you gave her."

"Shh, shut your eyes and your mouth," Woo-cheol said, sounding like a parent, and In-hye obeyed.

Huff huff huff huff huff huff . . . I'm glad you're all right . . . I'm glad I'm all right . . . *huff huff huff* everything else is happened outside of us . . . and now . . . there's . . . no one here . . . *huff huff huff huff huff huff* all I can hear is the sound of us sleeping . . . I can't . . . hear anything else . . . listen, baby . . . I'm going to say goodnight quietly . . . until I wake up again . . . good night, jal jara . . . *huff huff huff huff huff huff drip drip drip*

What is that sound? Water? Water falling? Maybe there's a leak somewhere . . . *drip drip drip* . . . where is it . . . I can't see . . . it's pitch-black . . . *drip drip drip drip drip drip* . . . what should I do . . . if I had a wash basin or a bowl here . . . *drip drip drip* . . . oh, this is annoying . . . I won't be able to sleep if the bed is all wet . . . honey? . . . are you there? Open . . . your mouth . . . and let . . . the blood . . . the warm blood . . . fill it . . . *drip drip drip drip drip drip dri dri dri dri dri dri dri dri dri dri dri dri dri dri dri dri dri.*

It was market day. Sammun, the part of the city on the north side of the Mi-ryang River, was bustling from dawn, but as the sun began to set, there were only a few straggling customers, and women carrying wooden boxes of pears and apples on their heads began to hurry past the Lee house.

"She had a girl three days ago."

"Oh? I hadn't heard."

"She was only seven months pregnant, apparently. See, that girl drowned, right, and the shock sent her into labor."

"And they haven't put up a geumjul, I see. I guess because it's meant to keep away defilement and ward off evil spirits. But when the house has already been defiled . . ."

"I heard Hee-hyang just sobs all day."

"Aigo, poor thing."

"I feel bad for her and her daughter-in-law."

Their voices were far too loud for gossiping, reaching even the ears of Woo-gun, who was playing jegichagi in the garden.

A cricket jumped up from the dead leaves he'd crunched with his foot and landed on the toe of his rubber shoe. He tried to catch it, but as he slowly stooped, it bounded and hid itself under some mulch. He poked and moved the leaves around with the toe, but he couldn't see where it had hidden itself. The ground was covered with leaves.

He thought, Noona would rake them up and I would get them with the dustpan, but Noona is dead. Appa's working, and Sister-in-law's got the baby, and Hyung's running, and Omma's probably still asleep?

Woo-gun took off his shoes and went in the house. It was quiet inside. He walked down the hallway, trying not to make a sound, then put his hand to the door to the bedroom. He opened it just halfway and stuck his head in.

"Omma."

"Oh, Woo-gun, it's you."

"I'm hungry."

"I'll get up."

Hee-hyang sat up and combed her fingers through her hair, sticking it up with a hairpin, then stood up, bracing herself against the wall with her hand.

"I'm so very dizzy. . . ."

"Are you all right?"

"Speak quietly, your sister-in-law and the baby are sleeping. Omma's gonna make you some nice sweet potato pancakes."

The pancakes she made him were warm and delicious and made his belly feel all warm too. Ever since his big brother had gotten married, his sister-in-law had made all the food.

I'll never tell In-hye, he thought, but I like Omma's cooking better.

She took pancakes to his father and sister-in-law too.

I'm so happy Omma's back to normal, he thought. She came out of the room his sister-in-law and the baby were in carrying a straw bundle.

"What's that?"

"It's the placenta."

"What's a blacenta?"

"It's the blanket that the baby had when she was inside your sister-in-law's tummy. You had one too, when you were inside me, and you ate everything through your umbilical cord."

"What's an umbical cord?"

"It's the string that attached my stomach to yours. I still have yours, and I treasure it."

"Where?"

"I'll show you another time."

"What do you do with the blacenta?"

"We put it in the river. We pray to our ancestors that the baby will grow up healthy and safe. Do you want to come to the river with Omma?"

Hee-hyang held the bundle in her right arm and slipped her feet into her shoes.

"Is it gonna rain?"

"No, it's not raining."

Hee-hyang strained her eyes and turned her palm upward. She couldn't physically see it, but she felt a slight dampness on her skin. Like sifted flour, a fine, fine rain—

Woo-gun tottered after his mother, who had started to walk off carrying an umbrella. They walked down the poplar-lined path by the river toward Mount Yongdu, going down onto the bank below the Aranggak pavilion.

Hee-hyang dropped the placenta into the river. The straw bundle, which sunk and reemerged with a splash, became one in her mind with So-won's body, still wrapped in the straw mat as they buried her. The idea of putting her granddaughter's placenta in the very river where her daughter had drowned— Hee-hyang forgot to pray for the baby's health and well-being.

The rain began to fall harder.

She opened the black umbrella.

The drops of rain falling from the sky made countless ripples on the surface of the river.

Hee-hyang had lost all coherence; she now thought the sky and the rain and the river were all one, with the same spirit.

Woo-gun picked at a scab on his elbow and peered up at his mother's face, half hidden by the umbrella.

I can't see the blacenta anymore, so why is she still staring? I'm getting wet, so why won't she let me under her umbrella? Her hands are shaking. Like someone else has grabbed her hands and is shaking them. I'm scared. She's scaring me. I need to pee. I've been holding it for a long time, but now I really need to go. But Omma looks so scary right now. She might get mad if I tell her I need to pee, or maybe she'll cry. What do I do if she starts crying?

"Omma, I need to pee," he said, shifting his feet.

Hee-hyang lifted the umbrella and turned. She wasn't crying or angry, so Woo-gun let out his breath.

"Go do it over there. In three years, you'll start school, and then you'll have to do everything yourself."

She held the umbrella out to her son, and Woo-gun went off toward the river and peed, drawing a figure eight.

The sun set with mother and child still on the riverbank. They couldn't see the rain falling now, but the sound of it hitting the umbrella became louder, *thud thud thud thud thud thud*, all on her own, buried in such a desolate place, *thud thud thud*, we should've given her an umbrella instead of a grave stone, *thud thud thud thud thud thud*, she had the umbrella in her right hand and held her son's hand in her left so she couldn't cover her ears, *th-thud th-thud th-thud th-thud th-thud th-thud*, Hee-hyang let go of Woo-gun's hand and covered her left ear, amid the rain's hiss.

Oh rain, please stop falling, please, stop falling for me, just for tonight, please!

Woo-gun forced his hand into a fist. His fingernails, which his mother hadn't cut for ten days now, cut into his palm.

"Omma, are you all right?"

She's covering her ear so maybe she can't hear me? But she's not covering the one on this side. Is it because the rain is too loud?

"Omma!"

Hee-hyang slowly tilted her neck downward and looked at her son.

"Does your ear hurt?"

"No, I'm fine . . . I'm sorry . . . I was thinking about your noona . . . out there in the rain . . ."

Hee-hyang took her son's hand in hers, both numb with cold, and they climbed back up the riverbank.

The cedar trees stopped her in her tracks. She was walking in the opposite direction to her own house. The string on the wicker gate had broken and fallen onto the ground. They walked through the gate and set foot in the garden. After that woman had a daughter, she moved out of the house without even doing the thirty-seventh-day celebrations and moved into the Dong-A Guesthouse her aunt ran. *Th-thud   th-thud*, large drops of rain fell from the sopping wet branches of the cedar trees, landing on her umbrella. Hee-hyang shifted the umbrella toward her back and looked up at the cedars.

Saasaasaa, in this garden even the rain sounds only like silence. *Saasaasaa   saasaasaa*, her living here, him coming here every day to make love to her, her having his daughter, it's all in the past now, but I feel like I'm the only one, the only one who's been left behind in this story that's now finished. A new story should've started the day he ended it with her and came back to be with me, but . . .

The house cowered in darkness, quiet and chill, giving off the filthy stench of mildew from being uninhabited for a long time. Hee-hyang turned her eyes from the house back to the river. A house dies if people leave it, but the river never dies.

I will have to live every day, every day, looking at the river where So-won drowned. So-won's death will live on along with the river. And just as this river will never dry up, so too will my sadness.

As she stared at the river, blacker than the night, Hee-hyang took a few steps in place without realizing.

Why is Omma doing that? Does she need to pee and she's trying to hold it? Or is she cold, too? 'Cause I'm cold. My cheeks are so cold. She'd usually warm them with her hands for me. *Aigo, oh, my poor little Woo-gun's cheeks are freezing*, she'd say. I wanna go home right now. But I can't leave Omma here and go back on my own. She's thinking about Noona. About how she's out there in the rain and must be so cold. At the funeral when Yong-il halbi died, everybody came, and there was so much food, and everybody was eating and drinking and singing, it was like a festival, but they just buried Noona. There was no food, and the only people who saw her get buried were just me, and Omma, and Appa, and Hyung. Is Omma gonna die too? Everybody dies. Me too? Stop asking questions, Hyung told me, but I guess I'll die too, someday. But I don't want to be in the ground with the rain falling on me. When I die, I hope I die on a sunny day.

Woo-gun saw something shining in the dead leaves and picked it up. It was a blue piece of glass. It was dirty, so he wiped it on the hem of his jeogori and put it in his pocket.

"What did you pick up?"

Woo-gun straightened his shoulders with a start.

"Put it down. You can't take anything from here."

"Why?"

"Because I said so."

Softly clicking his tongue in disappointment, Woo-gun threw the piece of glass at the veranda of the abandoned house. It caught some light from somewhere in the darkness and glinted, then smashed. The rain had at some point stopped. As if it had run out of steam, a silence fell upon the garden, and the invisible perfume of rain began to waft through the air, its force almost visible.

FOURTEEN

The River Prince

| 강의 왕자 | 川の王子 |

In-hye drew some well water with the gourd. So cold! Yongdu-mok was frozen, so why not the water in the well? Was this well deeper than Yongdu-mok? She rubbed the soap against the washing, trampled it with her bare feet, washed it with the well water, wrung it, beat it with the washing bat, then wiped her damp, bright red feet with a cloth and put her shoes back on. Panting, she put her palms together, but still, the sensation hadn't returned to her fingers.

There was her husband's paji and jeogori, her father-in-law's sokpaji, her mother-in-law's sokchima, her brother-in-law's paji and jeogori, her own jeogori, but mostly it was the baby's diapers and clothes. As she pegged up the washing in wind so strong she thought it might snatch it all away, she looked up at the sky.

The morning mist was dissipating, and the sky was turning a gentle blue. An endless blue that stretched on forever, and here I am under this sky, and So-won is not, or has she become a spirit drifting around under the same sky? But I only think that way because So-won wasn't my daughter. If she were, if Mi-ok met the same kind of fate, andwae, I couldn't think that way, andwae, even just thinking about it, no.

Two months had passed. They had gotten through the last two months. And in that time, in order not to disturb the silence in the house, even when walking down the hallway, or chopping green onions, or when she comforted the baby when it cried at night, she had had to do it all slowly, quietly, as if forcing back that silence. And, somehow, it had been two months now.

We've overcome the silence that So-won left behind. But my mother-in-law alone still cradles the silence to her like a baby, refusing to let go of it. This morning when I passed by her bedroom, I heard the sound of muffled crying. But surely, when Mi-ok's baegiljanchi comes around she'll give us all a smile. She was born on the fourteenth of October, so her baegiljanchi will be, let's see, on January 21, just before New Year's. The Japanese all celebrate with the new calendar, so for them New Year's is tomorrow. They're selling pine branches and shimenawa, those sacred straw ropes, and kagami mochi, the stacked rice cakes, everywhere in town, and all the boys and girls seem so busy. I suppose everyone's used to it by now, but having New Year's twice in the same month does feel quite strange.

The rooster approached from behind her. Brandishing its comb proudly, it stuck its beak in the metal basin and suddenly looked up, let out a cry, then drank some water.

"Hss, hss, andwaeyo, there's soap in there. Just give me a second. When I'm done, I'll give you all the corn and clamshells you want."

In-hye poured out the soapy water and chased away the rooster, then ran her tongue over her dry, rough lips and sang:

Look   look   look at me
Like a flower that blooms midwinter   look at me

Ari, arirang   suri, surirang   arariga nanne
Coming over Arirang Pass

Having finally met him
I could not hear a word he said   I was so shy

Just when she'd got up the momentum in her hands to keep hanging up the laundry, she heard a *clatter clatter* of footsteps.

"Abeoji! Abeoji's not well! He fell down from his chair!"

In-hye ran to the store, damp baby clothes still in hand.

"What happened?"

She lifted Yong-ha's head and rested it on her thigh. She saw a red rash on his face, neck, and arms. This was no trivial matter, if this were German measles, then she might get it, and then the baby—

"Aigu!" Yong-ha began to gasp, scrunching his eyes, nose, and mouth.

In-hye touched her hand to his forehead.

"He's very hot."

His face glinted with sweat. In-hye wiped the sweat from his brow with her jeogori.

What should I do, he's out running, and Mother's looking after the baby— I'll have to decide.

"Let's call for the doctor. Woo-gun, you go fetch the doctor, and tell him that Abeoji's in a poor state and to come immediately. And hurry!"

Woo-gun ran to fetch the Korean doctor from his offices across the street.

"Father-in-law, hold on just a little longer, the doctor is coming."

In-hale, breathe! In-hale, breathe! In-in-hale, all I can do is breathe. Hee-hyang? In-hale, where is she? In, my voice is lost in my breathing. In, come closer! Your ear! Yong-ha appealed to his daughter-in-law with his eyes. Her eyes were full, full of fear. In, what are you afraid of? What? In-in-hale, that quack doctor! Why's he not here yet! His office is barely further than the end of my nose so what's taking so long! In, a metallic taste's welling up with my spit, in-in-hale, the base of my tongue's going numb, in-in-in-in-hale, his voice broke through the pain. Aya!

The glass door opened, making a tremendous rattle.

Aigu, Woo-gun, what do I always tell you, the glass'll fall out so be careful!

He saw the doctor's leather shoes, white hem, and black leather bag. Yong-ha panted loudly, feeling the cold wind against his damp forehead.

In-hale, he's taking my pulse, in-in-in-hale, he's rolling up my sleeve and looking at my arm, in-in-hale, he's putting the stethoscope to my chest and stomach and back, in-in-in-in-hale, he's checking my legs and ankles, in-in-in-in-hale.

"What's wrong with him?"

He heard his daughter-in-law's shrill voice somewhere above him.

"Looks like erysipelas."

"What's that?"

"It's a skin infection. Has he had an injury anywhere, do you know?"

"No . . . no, I don't think so."

Yong-ha thought back over the last few days. He hadn't been injured, he had no hangnails or scabs, nor any pains anywhere in his body. He was fine the previous night when he went to sleep, and that morning when he woke up too. Erysipelas? Could it really be? The doctor's face and voice were far away and hazy, as if he were looking down at him from a very high place.

"It's not a difficult disease to treat. After this injection, he should feel better within two or three days."

The tip of the needle sunk into the tenderest part of his right inner arm. It didn't hurt. Compared to the pain rampaging all through his body, the sting of the injection was like a mosquito's bite.

Aigo! Goddamnit! You bastard! Yong-ha threw all the curse words he knew at the pain. You rotten bastard! You thug! Fuck your mother! You son of a bitch!

"Ah, may I ask how infectious it is . . . ," In-hye said quietly.

"Don't worry, ma'am. It's not infectious."

So that's what she was afraid of, well, I guess that's normal, she's got a babe in arms to worry about. Yong-ha looked at Woo-gun. His eyes looked blacker than usual; his face looked small and forlorn. I want to tell him: Don't worry, Appa's gonna get better, go play with Yong-il next door.

"Let him rest, feed him some loach stew to get his strength up, and then come by to collect his medicine."

He put the syringe in an aluminum case. Folded the stethoscope. Closed the clasp on his black bag. Picked up his bag and stood up. There was a violent rattling noise again, and through the trembling glass, Yong-ha watched him leave. *Whoosh-whoosh*, the wind blew up from the ground, *whoosh-whoosh*, the swirling grit of the street turned up the doctor's white coat, *whoosh-whoosh*. Suddenly the tiredness that had been weighing on him was pushed aside by the pain, aigo! He wanted to yell, but the words didn't come, *whoosh-whoosh*, the pain, exhaustion, and shivers were battling it out within him, *whoosh-whoosh, whoosh-whoosh*.

"Lying down here will only make things worse. Hold on to my shoulder.

Let's go slowly . . . yes, just like that. . . . Put your arm around my neck, you can put your weight on me, it's fine. All right? Let's stand up now . . . ready, set, there we go . . . let's start walking . . . left, right, left, right, Woo-gun, open the door! Left, right—go tell your mother!"

Yong-ha awoke, needing to urinate. His daughter-in-law was asleep leaning against the wall. His granddaughter, too, was asleep, with a nipple still in her mouth. He wanted to wipe away the white milk overflowing from the corners of her mouth, but he couldn't even pull his hand out from under the blanket. He had slept the better part of a day, and so he had no idea if it was morning, noon, or night now. *Throb-throb*, that was the sound of pain, *throb-throb, throb-throb*, worse than before he'd gone to sleep, he had no strength left to decry the pain, to resist or endure it, only the strength to be in pain. But incontinence alone was beyond the pale for him; if his daughter-in-law had to take off his damp paji and sokpaji for him, he'd prefer death.

Yong-ha looked at In-hye. Her lead-colored eyelids rose with the shape of her eyeballs, but they did not move.

She must be exhausted from taking care of a breastfeeding baby and nursing me. In just three days she had become completely gaunt. Without sufficient nourishment and sleep, her milk would dry up. . . . No . . . I can't . . . go on . . . like this . . . for much longer. . . . Maybe I should just try going back to sleep. . . . Yong-ha closed his eyes and listened to his daughter-in-law's and granddaughter's breathing as they slept. . . . The baby breathes much more quickly . . . *zz-zz-zz* . . . It's kind of nice to listen to someone else sleeping. . . . It'd be better if I weren't in pain. . . . No, I can't hold out, I'm going to have to get up, no, try to hold it for a little longer, think about something else, anything else. . . . Tomorrow's market day, I wonder if Woo-cheol got in touch with Ki-pyeong and Wan-jae, Ki-pyeong's been working for me for a decade now, so he gets forty sen a day, Wan-jae started last fall, and he's still not up to speed, so he gets twenty-five sen, but maybe Hee-hyang already told him all that. . . .

Just then, the smell of cheonggukjang wafted in through the gap in the door, slowly crossing the floor. Gulping down the saliva in his mouth, Yong-ha opened his eyes. He had no appetite, and if he did eat he knew he'd throw up, but he wanted to try; after all it was Hee-hyang's special cheonggukjang. He swallowed and swallowed until his mouth was dry and he desperately wanted a drink of water. Water, please, water! He wanted to gulp down glass after glass until his stomach was heavy with it.

"Water . . ."

In-hye's eyelids did not move.

"Hey!" Yong-ha choked on his own voice and had a coughing fit.

"Are you all right?" In-hye took the baby off her breast and rearranged her collar.

Yong-ha, still coughing violently, raised one finger and beckoned her over.

In-hye gently laid the baby down on its bed, tied the strings of her jeogori, and brought her face close to her father-in-law's.

"Water."

"You want some water?"

Instead of nodding he closed his eyelids.

"I'll bring you some right away."

He tried to grab her chima as she stood, but his fingertips would not reach.

"Before that." Yong-ha started to cough again. Since the previous night this phlegm had stuck in his throat like slugs; he could not spit it up or swallow it either.

"Yes?"

"Bedpan."

"You need to pee?"

"Yeah."

In-hye undid the strings of his paji and pulled them down, then slid his sokpaji down to his knees. Yong-ha wished that the baby would start crying to drown out the sound, as he overcame his embarrassment and pain and opened his legs. In-hye put the bedpan to his groin and turned her face. Yong-ha, still lying on his back, put the end of his genitals in the bedpan.

"Father, you're all sticky with sweat. Shall I wipe you with a hot, damp cloth? It'll feel nice."

"Water."

"Oh, yes, just a second." In-hye took a look at the baby's face as it slept, then stood up.

"And cheonggukjang."

"Yes?"

"I won't . . . be able to eat it. I can look . . . and smell . . ."

Why is In-hye taking care of me and Hee-hyang doing the cooking? She's my wife; a wife should take care of her own husband. . . . She hates me, she won't say it, but she has han for me over what happened, that . . .

The door slid open, and In-hye brought in a tray with an earthenware bowl of cheonggukjang and a teacup. She helped her father-in-law sit up and brought the teacup full of water up to his lips. Yong-ha slurped one mouthful of water as if it were hot soup, then coughed. She rubbed his back and wiped around his damp mouth; Yong-ha now breathed in the stream rising from the bowl.

"Woo-cheol . . . call him . . . I won't . . . make it throu . . ." The phlegm choked him, making him unable to separate words clearly.

"Father, what are you saying? I know you're in a lot of pain right now, but you'll get better. Didn't the doctor say that this wasn't a difficult disease to treat?"

Yong-ha stuck out his finger and shook it.

"Woo-cheol . . ."

Once In-hye had left the room, Yong-ha put his face down to the side and looked at his granddaughter.

Two months old . . . my first grandchild . . . I won't even leave a shadow in her memory. . . . The thought made him just a little sad. I want her to at least be able to think, that's the kind of man my granddad was. But there's no time now. I'll breathe my last soon. Whatever that quack says, I know my body better. So while I still have breath in me . . . my eldest son . . . Woo-cheol, soon to be the head of the Lee family . . .

Woo-cheol came in the room and stooped over his father.

"Abeoji."

The words writhed on his trembling tongue, but right when they were one step from being voiced, they became exhausted in his mouth, withdrawing deep in the back of his throat with his breath.

"Abeoji, are you all right?"

"I . . . I'm . . ." Oh god, a big lump of phlegm is . . .

Woo-cheol helped his father sit up and held his palm out by his mouth.

"Abeoji! Spit! Spit!"

Yong-ha spat the phlegm into his son's hand, then returned to breathing deeply, in, out, in, out; he began to move his lips as if he were summoning the words.

"Don't . . . bury me . . . burn . . . in the river . . ."

"Father, what are you talking about?!" In-hye shrieked.

"Hush . . . I understand, if the worst happens, you'll be cremated. And then we should scatter your bones and ashes in the river?"

"Mm."

"I promise."

Yong-ha sighed heavily and folded his hands on his chest. Smoke. An open fire? *Whoosh-whoosh*, but when the wind's this strong why isn't the smoke dissipating, *whoosh-whoosh*, what is she cooking?

Yong-ha moved his damp tongue and tried to lick the smoke.

Is she smoking pork or beef, maybe? Ani, aniya, the smoke's coming from me. But I'm not hot. Am I dead?

Woo-cheol could not take his eyes from his father's face. He thought he was trying to move his tongue, his father was smiling, showing his purple gums and yellowed teeth.

"I'll watch over Abeoji and the baby for a while, so go finish eating. Tonight we might have to go to the mountain. Tell Eomoni for me."

Once she was done eating, In-hye came back into the room carrying a tray of dongchimi and sanchaenamul.

"Where's Eomoni?"

"Woo-gun is scared, so they're taking a nap in the bedroom. She said to wake her if his condition changes."

"That's a bit cold . . ." Woo-cheol brought the spoon up to his mouth carefully, trying not to make any noise.

"Well, Woo-gun is really frightened. . . . Since what happened to So-won, nobody's been giving him enough attention, you know? And just when it felt like things were going back to normal around here, his father collapses right in front of him. . . . I feel really bad for him."

I feel bad for this baby too, she thought, but kept the words locked inside her, as she looked down at her baby.

"How long is this kid going to sleep? She hasn't peed or pooped since the evening. I'm gonna have to wake her up to feed her soon."

The flow of the river at New Year's
Oh! It freezes and it melts
Born into this world, there is only one me
Ah-oh   dongdongdari
On the fifteenth of February, my Lord
Oh! Hung himself high
His visage lit ten thousand men like a lantern
Ah-oh   dongdongdari
In March, the flowers will have bloomed
Oh! Like the azaleas of late spring

"He's singing. . . ."

"I don't know this song."

"Before he and Eomoni got married he read people's fortunes by looking at their features. He wandered all over, from Mount Paektu to Mount Halla. But it's strange, when he talked before he had a tiny voice like a mosquito."

He started to wheeze, as if he had used all his breath in the song or was trying with his whole face to breathe. Each breath was too short, and he would stop for such a long time that they almost thought he would never exhale again. Then his fingers, folded on top of each other on his chest, began to twitch; he opened his eyes slightly and started to whisper words that they could not hear.

Suddenly, Yong-ha stopped babbling and took a huge breath, like he was about to go underwater.

"Mi-ryeong!"

Almost in response to her grandfather's shout, the baby began to cry.

In-hye moved stiltedly and picked up the baby, but she twisted in her arms, as if trying to wriggle out of someone's hands, and scrunched her outstretched palms into fists. As In-hye looked at the baby's face, eyes still closed, she almost believed that the baby and her grandfather had been connected in sleep; she rocked her.

"Mi-ok, open your eyes. C'mon, open your eyes, it's time to eat. What's wrong? Why won't you stop crying? Shh, shh, Halbi's trying to rest, Mi-ok, please stop crying, good girl, good girl . . ."

A baby's crying. My baby? The son Hee-hyang had? The girl Mi-ryeong had? Hard to tell just by the crying, I'd like to see its face . . . but . . . I don't have the . . . strength to open my eyes . . . Aya! . . . each breath sends this stinging, needlelike pain through my lungs . . . Aya! . . . somebody . . . help me . . . strange . . . my voice won't leave my body . . . it doesn't even resonate inside me . . . somebody . . . help . . .

"Honey, look at this, you could wring the sweat out of her, even her hair's so wet it looks like I poured water over her."

In-hye cradled the baby, who had finally stopped crying and opened her eyes, and stuck a nipple in her mouth.

I can hear it . . . *suggsuggsuggsugg* . . . the sound of a baby eating . . . and the smell of milk . . . I can smell . . . it's cold . . . dark . . . am I in Eoreumgol? . . . closed . . . open . . . whatever I do with my eyes nothing changes . . . in this darkness . . . closed . . . open . . . I can't even tell if they're open or closed . . . do I have eyes or maybe not . . . put on a light please . . . the light. . . .

"I think we should tell her, you know," Woo-cheol said, chomping on a bit of dongchimi.

"I don't think that's necessary." In-hye looked away from the baby and at her husband.

"But she's my half sister; he's the only father she'll ever have . . . and she's never once seen him. . . ."

"Stand in your mother's shoes for a moment. . . . Are there any other relatives who should be told?"

"I asked Eomoni once if I really didn't have any relatives on my abeoji's side. But she has no idea where he was born or what his parents were like."

What are they talking about . . . my hands . . . feet . . . they're dragging them out from where they were . . . trying to chase me out . . . pushing on my back . . . outside . . . oh, I have . . . I have no strength . . . aigu, I'm outside my body, like I was shat out . . . don't push me around . . . don't push me away . . . you don't have to be rough like that, I'll leave . . . stretched out . . . expanded . . . crushed . . . crammed in . . . Aigo, ayaaaaaaaa. . . .

"Did she never ask him?"

"She did, but every time he'd say something slightly different, so she thought he must not want to tell the truth. Eomoni said she didn't want to ask him about anything he didn't want to talk about."

"Well, I wouldn't be able to take it. A couple's supposed to share their past, present, and future, if you ask me. . . . Oh, look, she's fallen asleep again. Hey, you need to eat a little more, open up those little eyes."

In-hye gingerly poked at the baby's cheek, but her mouth fell away from the nipple and she began to breathe like she was asleep, so In-hye brought her little chin up to her shoulder and rubbed the baby's back up and down until she burped.

"There's no way Abeoji's mistress can come in this house. But maybe my half sister could, if we kept it a secret from Eomoni—"

Woo-cheol broke off as the door opened.

Without looking at the two of them, Hee-hyang came in and sat down next to her husband. Then, like a blind woman ascertaining the shape of something, she began tracing the lines of her husband's face with her palm and fingers.

A hand . . . a hand is running up and down over my cheekbones . . . warm . . . whose hand? . . . it's hard to breathe hard to breathe . . . I drank seawater . . . at Hamdeok Beach in Jeju . . . the wave came right over me with a rumbling splash . . . not another . . . as it gently swelled . . . trying to sweep me away . . . got to get up on the wave before it crashes . . . aigu, I can't move my arms or legs . . . oh, here it comes! and this time it's a big one! . . . that rumbling splash, splash . . . darling . . . somebody's calling me . . . darling . . . that's Hee-hyang's voice . . . darling!

Yong-ha opened his eyes and looked at his wife's face. He looked at the faces of his eldest son and daughter-in-law, who had drawn around him. Then he looked at the face of his granddaughter, cradled in his daughter-in-law's arms. He took each of their faces in slowly, then looked back at his wife.

That's right, she'll be thirty-eight this year in May . . . her cheeks are so smooth they don't fit her aged face . . . too bright . . . what is this light . . . someone's reflecting the sun in a mirror or something . . . Hee-hyang's face is getting further and further away . . . can't take my eyes off her . . . if I do she'll disappear . . . I want to touch . . . my wife's face . . . I can't raise my arm . . . it's turned to lead . . . I want so badly to touch her . . . heavy . . . I raised it . . . too far . . . andwae . . . I can't reach . . . Hee-hyang's face . . . blue-blackening of the bridge of the nose means many misfortunes around this age . . . Woo-cheol . . . bright beneath the eyes and cannot help but achieve his dreams, bright color between the eyebrows and no impediment to following his plans . . . In-hye . . . wrinkles beneath her eyes means she will have enmity with those closest to her . . . Mi-ok . . . the sides of her mouth shine brightly, she will have luck in later years and a peaceful life . . . and me, my features are sharp, naturally free from disaster . . . the most inauspicious face is Woo-gun's . . . low nose and low bridge, will either be poor or die prematurely . . . Aigo . . . Mi-ryeong, now . . . her head is before her feet when she walks, she may have luck when young but will be poor in later years . . . I've never seen the face of my daughter who Mi-ryeong had . . . I only learned her name by asking someone . . . So-jin . . . I'd thought that I might try to visit her sometime if she's alive . . . So-jin . . . what does your face look like . . . the one with the luckiest features was So-won . . . aigu, So-won . . . my sweet little girl . . . why did you drown . . . when the water splashed and the surface of the river closed over you . . . it also closed off our life together as abeoji and daughter . . . the bubbles of the breath forced out of your lungs burbled up to the surface . . . then soon disappeared . . . as if nothing had happened at all, aigo . . . her soul . . . the very soul of my beloved daughter . . . aigu, have mercy on her soul . . . every time I hear the sound of falling water . . . or see the bubbles of drops of rain falling in the puddles under the eaves . . . I imagine your last breath . . . oh, So-won . . . can you see your abeoji's tears . . . So-won . . . I cannot undo your death . . . I'm pitiful . . . and so are you, embracing han as you sank . . . you were our only daughter . . . Woo-cheol and Woo-gun's only sister . . . aigo, what the hell . . . the face of her corpse as they brought her out of the water . . . aigu, it's too bright . . . the light has started to race . . . at great speed . . . to cut off So-won's changed face . . . aigu, I can't catch up with what I can see . . . I can't seeeeeeeeeeee . . .

"Darling!" Hee-hyang yelled, as if scolding him.

At that, the baby threw her hands up, startled, and began to wail.

Shapes are turning into lines . . . lines dissolve into colors . . . white . . . black . . . red . . . blue . . . yellow . . . green . . . yellow-green . . . brown . . . orange . . .

gray . . . peach . . . light blue . . . the colors of the crayons we bought So-won for her eleventh birthday . . . wait? What's happened? The light's quickly leaving . . . in-hale . . . ex-hale . . . in-hale . . . ex-hale . . . in-hale . . . ex-hale . . . it's gone . . . someone blew the light out . . . it's black . . . pitch-black.

"I'll go fetch the doctor." Woo-cheol stood up.

"If you go you might miss your father's last breath." The features and expression on Hee-hyang's face were fixed in place.

"But he can't just—"

"It's too late now for anyone to call his spirit back. He's started his journey to the other side already." Her eyes smoldered with anger.

"In-hye, bring a mirror."

She laid the crying baby down on her bed and came back with the mirror that had been part of her dowry. Woo-cheol held the hand mirror up to his father's mouth. It fogged slightly.

"He's still breathing. . . ."

Only a pinprick of light remained in his eyes.

"Abeoji!"

He could hear someone calling, but he didn't know what they were saying; he could hear someone crying, but he didn't know why they were crying; he could hear someone singing, he didn't know who it was, but her voice was very, very dear to him.

In March, the flowers will have bloomed
Oh! Like the clovers of late spring
Such an envy to behold
Ah-oh   dongdongdari
Don't forget April   Ah!   Do come again, nightingale
So why   my noksa love
Have you forgotten who I once was
Ah-oh   dongdongdari

A gust of wind whipped and howled as it blew, wind coming off the river, the river is very close, it howled, and on the ground the Korean rhododendrons, dandelions, and violets, whip and howl, and the reeds, silver grass, and cogon grass by the riverside all shook, and in the sunny spots of the water sometimes a goldfish's mouth would smack open, and the slim shadows of the fish, hana, dul, set, net. . . .

Aigu, there's too many to count, the sweetfish are swimming upstream so it must be spring now, whip and howl, and on the spring grasses, I'm grasping her wrists and she spreads before me, our bodies overlapping, she is clinging to my back, grabbing my wrists so I can't leave, whip and howl, our bodies heaving panting dissolving into spring, dissolving her full, white smile and—

> *On the fifth of May   Ah!   I offer to you*
> *On the morning of the boy's festival*
> *Something to make you live a thousand years*
> *Ah-oh   dongdongdari*
> *On the fifteenth of June   Ah!*
> *My body like a comb cast down by the waterside*
> *Follows after you in its way*
> *Hoping you'll turn around*
> *Ah-oh   dongdongdari*
> *On the fifteenth of July   ah!*
> *I offer up all that I can give*
> *Praying that I can go to the beyond with you*
> *Ah-oh   dongdongdari*
> *On the fifteenth of August   ah!*
> *Though it's mid-autumn*
> *Because we're together   today feels like a festival*
> *Ah-oh   dongdongdari*

The silvery dragonflies skimming along the surface of the water in a beam of sunlight, the water striders gliding through the forest of reeds, the children scrambling buck naked up the old willow trees, jumping off the cliff one after another, the cheers from the bottom of the cliff, and the applause, Yong-ha! Yong-ha! Yong-ha! Yong-ha!

All right, it's my turn now, then a look down at the bottom of the cliff, and

among the cheering children there's So-won's face and—suddenly a loud laugh
wells up, and everything around begins to quiver.

And on the ninth of September   ah!
The chrysanthemum flowers we swallow down
Make the blooms in the garden grow   even when you're not there
Ah-oh   dongdongdari
And in October   ah!
Like a toppled linden
He too is fallen
And none think back on him
Ah-oh   dongdongdari

He knew who was singing. Omma. A song he'd heard while she'd fed him.
Cradled in her soft, white hands lying down on a cushion of water, whip and
howl, the scent of milk clouded around his face, eyelids caressed by the wind
off the river.

And in November
Under one blanket on a dirt floor   how I miss you
I'm all alone having lost you, my dear one
Ah-oh   dongdongdari

The song stopped.
Whip and howl.
How quiet it was.
Yong-ha.
The voice of the first person who ever said his name.
Yong-ha.
The wind stopped.
Everything ceased.
A nameless, faceless, breathless soul floated down the river.

FIFTEEN

Ipchun Daegil

| 입춘 대길 | 立春大吉 |

The posts of the gates to each house bore branches from a peach tree to ward off evil and posters that read IPCHUN DAEGIL, a wish for the New Year to start with great fortune, but our house had neither.

Down by the riverbed, the girls were playing neolttwigi, jumping on the ends of a seesaw in turns, and I suppose our neighbors were all gathered in someone's garden playing yutnori, but none of us were part of it.

Everyone in every other family was busy coming and going, visiting relatives' houses or receiving their relatives at home, but aside from my eldest son, who had gone running, and my youngest son, who had gone next door to play, we went nowhere and had not even one visitor.

Hee-hyang picked up the bokjori, woven rice scoops for luck, that had fallen near the fence. Hana, dul, set, net, daseot, so there were five young people who didn't know what had happened to this family then? If they knew, and they tossed the bokjori over the fence anyway, then it was harassment. They'd be coming by soon to get the bokjori money, but I certainly won't be paying. People say that if you buy one of these and put it in your kitchen you'll have good luck, but I've lost my daughter and my husband in less than three months—what kind of luck will come to me, and whatever happens next, will I really possibly think, Oh, what luck?

"Tonight I don't have to sleep until the rooster crows."

"Because tonight is suse, the all-night vigil to welcome in the New Year."

"And I love suse!"

"Come now, you sound like a child."

"Eomoni, am I a grown-up?"

"Well, some girls do get married at thirteen."

"I'll go light the lamps."

"It's still early, you can do it when the sun sets."

"But why do we have to have all the lamps in the house lit?"

"Because it's the day when our josangsin, our ancestors, come back."

"Then why do we have to hide everyone's shoes?"

"So that the evil spirits don't find them."

"Why do they come on New Year's Eve?"

"Aigu, all this 'why, why' is so childish."

"Why is it bad to ask why?"

"Your eomoni's busy. Don't just stand there talking, peel those potatoes for me."

"Yes, Eomoni. Can I ask you just one more thing?"

"Sure; be careful and don't cut yourself. What is it?"

"Why do we all have to stay up talking until the rooster crows?"

"I've heard it's to keep away the spirits, but I've always wondered how talking is supposed to do that. Have you asked your abeoji?"

"I'll get to ask soooo many questions tonight!"

"All those questions will make your abeoji tired though."

"Will Woo-gun be able to stay up?"

"Babies get to sleep."

"But if you sleep tonight, then your eyebrows turn white, right?"

"But he can't stay up all night."

"I'll tickle him to keep him up."

"Hey, peel more carefully. You're wasting too much."

"Will Oppa go running tomorrow too?"

"Hmm, I imagine he will. He runs whatever the weather, after all."

"He's getting married in the spring, right?"

"That's right."

"What's In-hye like?"

"She's a kind, smart girl."

"Hmm, so then next year In-hye will stay up all night with us too. What should I ask her?"

"Aigu, make plans for next year and the demons laugh."

"But I'm so excited!"

"Now can you pluck the leaves from the radishes, please?"

"Yes, Eomoni . . . is this training for marriage?"

"What are you going on about?"

"Heh heh heh."

The sound of laughter tickled her eardrums; Hee-hyang turned her head. *Heh heh heh, heh heh heh.* Her mouth hung open, her brow bone was digging into her eyeballs. *Heh heh heh.* The bokjori fell from her arms. She pressed her hands to her mouth, covering the exit for her wailing, *heh heh heh, heh heh heh,* opening up her nasal cavity and somehow took a breath. It's just a buzzing in my ears, she thought, just as a moan escaped her throat, sounding like it was produced by someone else far away; no longer knowing if her hands were covering her mouth or her ears, she let them drop. The laughter ceased. Hee-hyang took breath after breath, filling her lungs. When the buzzing was gone and her breathing had stabilized, sadness washed over her, taking the fear's place.

I don't care if it's a hallucination, I just want to hear her laugh.

How great it would be to go crazy and be able to talk to So-won all the time—she leaned her head backward and closed her eyes, and nausea came creeping up her tight throat.

The house was full of their things. And each time Hee-hyang saw something of her husband's or So-won's, well, it wasn't as simple as saying that she remembered their conversations; they were vivid, as if they were happening right there and then— "Omma!" Woo-gun would call out, and she'd realize, more often than she'd like, that she'd been sitting there for over an hour.

One morning, a couple of days ago, she'd thought about selecting a few things as keepsakes and burning the rest. But then the arms that go through the sleeves of this jeogori aren't here, or the feet meant for this pair of rubber boots, or the hands to hold the handle of this bag, or the hair to rake this comb through, or the head to wear this hat—all of which she understood, but part of her still thought, What if I get rid of everything and then the two of them come back? And yet, she somehow set her mind to thinking about the store and buying in stock and proceeds and their employees, as her hands alone moved busily for two whole days, packing their belongings into wicker trunks.

Hee-hyang picked the bokjori back up, then put them one by one on top of the wicker trunks next to the well, but it was not enough to hide fully all the chima jeogori, paji jeogori, magoja, durumagi, socks, arm warmers, rubber shoes, and straw sandals.

She took a matchbox from the sleeve of her jeogori. What is it I'm hoping to do here? Her mind was numb; she was unable to think of anything. It's like I'm in a dream. A dream that I think is reality when I'm in it, and when I awake from it all will return to how it was before. I'll get out of the bed slowly so as not to wake him where he lies next to me snoring, make breakfast and prepare everyone's lunch, and then I'll gently shake her awake. So-won, time to get up, it's morning, if you don't get up soon you'll have to go to school without your breakfast. I simply cannot believe this is reality. It's like I've been shocked by hearing about something terrible that happened to someone else.

I cannot distinguish between yesterday and today, a rainy day and a sunny one, even between day and night. But time goes on slowly but unrelentingly as if it were delayed, dragging me along with it now too. I'd like to be crushed by the heavy, giant wheel of a vehicle, but time has me chained to it as it rolls on.

I'm so tired. It's hard even to stand. But I'm afraid to sleep. When I lie down, I can't bear the pain in my heart; some nights, I toss and turn, rolling around in my bed until the rooster cries.

Waking is worse than sleeping. When I get through to the morning without having slept, I sleep as if I've been bashed over the head, and only while I'm sleeping can I forget their deaths. In my dreams they are alive, moving. In the moment when I wake, I still don't know that it was all a dream, and after I blink a few times and let the morning sun into my eyes, the sadness and fear begin to rise, like sensation returning to cold feet soaking in warm water. And then I must pronounce their deaths: Lee So-won has drowned in the river; Lee Yong-ha has died of blood poisoning. Each time I wake up, their deaths are renewed, never to become something that happened in the past. Sleep makes up for nothing; waking is only agony.

Once I put their belongings in these trunks, it laid bare their absence, and I could no longer stand to be in the house. Yesterday and the day before, I spent the night in the store. In-hye brought me food, and when she saw that I wasn't eating, she took the tray without a word and swapped the food for pine nut porridge and rice milk. I swallowed them down, but I could not eat until I felt full. When I fill my stomach with food, I am remorseful for the two of them, who will never again be able to eat. And yet, dragged along by time, I feel hunger, but unable to forgive myself for eating spoon after spoon of porridge, I returned it to the brazier half-eaten yesterday.

Yong-ha, and So-won too, had died on market day. As if proof that time kept passing, market day came around five days a month. Nine times since he died, twenty-five times since she died—In-hye is busy with the baby and housework, so I run the store. Woo-cheol always says, *Eomoni, if you keep working your fingers to the bone like that, you'll fall apart; In-hye and I'll do it somehow, so please take a break, Eomoni—if you get ill now, I don't know what I'll do.* But I can't sit still. I have to keep moving like a spinning top, going round and round, and when it loses speed and starts to wobble you pull the string, whirl, whirl, whirl, I can't fall over now; if I did die, I'd be free, but I'm Woo-gun's mother, he's still only five, and he's already lost his father and sister; I can't let him lose his mother too. I am forbidden to die.

Each time I go to the store with him to sell shoes, and someone says, *I am so sorry for your loss,* all I can do is nod, and now Woo-gun too has started to nod solemnly in response. Yong-ha collapsed before Woo-gun's very eyes. I heard he'd fallen near the brazier. I had no reason to be in there, so for me the store is the only place where his and her belongings aren't there and I could make it my refuge, but Woo-gun must remember that moment every day. But I cannot burn everything, of course. Because I still have to work in this store and keep living in this house.

So I sit on this stool, like he did, and I warm my hands at the brazier occasionally, looking out at the people who hurry past hunched over, and I sometimes feel like I'm seeing them through his eyes. I have not taken his place; I have not been possessed by him; he is standing behind me staring at me, his eyes piercing into my own from behind, becoming one with my gaze.

When he passed, everyone in the family ran out of the gates, shouting, Aigo, aigo! Woo-cheol took the doors off in the sitting room and put them near the ondol's stovepipe, spread out four sheaves of straw, and laid him down, with his head facing north. I put cotton wool in his ears and nose, then held his chin to close his mouth. Woo-cheol stood in the garden, grasping the sokjeogori his father had been wearing, and shouted, "Abeoji! Come back for your clothes at least!" before tossing the garment up onto the roof, the traditional calling back of the dead.

Woo-cheol stripped his father naked and wiped his body from top to bottom with a cloth dipped in fragrant water steeped with mugwort. Head, neck, chest, stomach, under his arms, shoulders, upper arms, elbows, lower arms, back, hips, buttocks, genitals, anus, thighs, knees, his joints, his shins, at which point he spoke.

"Eomoni, Abeoji wanted to be cremated."

I was so surprised I looked at my husband, but all I could see were his nostrils stuffed with cotton.

"He said that he'd like his bones and ashes to be put in the river."

I was silent as Woo-cheol finished wiping his abeoji's ankles, the tops and soles of his feet, and his toes, dressed him in the traditional white paji, jeoksam, jeogori, and socks; I watched as he added the layers of durumagi and overcoat.

"Cremation is out of the question, it's almost a second death, we won't even be able to visit his grave. . . ."

"It's what he wanted."

"It may be what he wanted, but it's not what he's getting. How could we do that to the head of the family?"

"I promised him."

As he burned in the furnace at the crematorium in Ne-il-dong, I thought long and hard. Cremation is for the ilbon saram, for those who died of cholera or typhus or the like, or for people who don't have the money for a tomb, so why did he say he wanted to be cremated and scattered in the river? Did he make a pact with someone? With *her*? But what would such a pact mean? If they'd gone for a lovers' suicide and asked to be cremated and scattered in the river together, well, that I might understand, but . . . and Woo-cheol says his dad looked him square in the eyes when he asked, so he can't have been addled by the fever and pain . . . so why, darling? Was it something you thought about long and hard? And if so, then why did you never say a word about it to me?

Woo-cheol put on the white gloves and he's picking out his father's bones, aigu, and he's putting them in a stone pestle and grinding them. *Krrn krrn krrn krrn krrn krrn,* and now that he's been turned to dust he is poured into a plain wooden box with cotton cloth under it. Woo-cheol wrapped the box in the white cloth and picked it up.

I'd been told that only the chief mourner could be in the fishing boat, but I wanted to see him off until the very end, so I went on the boat with Woo-cheol. He wore the gulgeon on his head, tied a straw rope around his stomach, and wore a funeral robe missing the left sleeve, but the captain, strangely, wore the same simple persimmon-colored paji jeogori as always.

As the captain pushed against the riverbed with a pole and the boat left the shore, the Confucian scholar Cheong Gyeong-hong sang the leader of the funeral cortege's song.

I've cast off my life thus far like worn-out sandals
Vacated my palace-like dwelling
Left the babies with my wife
I'm headed to paradise.

All the people from the neighborhood gathered on the bank, joined in together.

Ehe ehe-yo, wolyo cho cho, ehe-yo.

Thin ice had formed on the Miryang River, but near the pine trees at Sanmun-dong the water was flowing freely. *Caw caw!* I turned and looked in the direction of the bird's cry and saw a few swans near Yongdu-mok, where So-won drowned, craning their necks toward the sky. *Caw! Caw! Caw!* They beat their wings, hitting the water. I saw my own reflection in the surface of the water, broken by the prow of the boat, and felt the gentle breeze off the river, unusual in midwinter, caress my cheek. *Sol sol, sarang sarang, sol sol, sa-*

rang sarang. I held the anger I felt toward him. Long before he became involved with that woman, every time he seemed downhearted and lost in reverie, I'd been jealous of whoever he was hiding within him. And eventually, he stopped opening up to me, his wife, about anything at all.

The captain loosened his grip on the pole and the boat stopped. Woo-cheol went down on both knees and opened the lid of the box containing his father. His white-gloved hands tipped the box and—*sol sol, sarang sarang, sol sol, sarang sarang*—my husband was carried off by the wind and the water.

Suddenly, my throat felt tight and achy, and the tears that I hadn't shed once since his death overflowed from my eyes. He'd wanted to leave. He had not been born here; he hadn't even meant to come here. To him, Miryang was nothing more than a place he passed through every now and then as he wandered alone. He'd wanted to leave and couldn't. For the first time, I understand the depth and breadth of his promise to me; no, I always knew but pretended I didn't. *Sol sol, sarang sarang, sol sol, sarang sarang*, the breeze from the river rocked the fishing boat.

"Ready to go back?" the captain said, and started to push the pole again.

"Wait, just a moment, just until this breeze stops." I squeezed my eyes shut and put my hands together. Protect us, our lives and fortunes, until the trees turn to iron; take away all that is unlucky and leave it in the Nakdong River; go to paradise and stay for eternity, ascend to the highest level; and take away all of our children's suffering.

Hee-hyang took his yellowed copy of *Mayi's Physiognomy* and his old bindle out of the wicker trunk. When he'd drifted into Miryang, these two things were all he had.

She struck a match. The flame burst into being, then went downward as if someone was blowing on it, burning Hee-hyang's fingers.

Ouch! She dropped the match.

It fell on *Mayi's Physiognomy*, and the flames began to rise; with one lick, the cover blackened and the fire intensified with each page it ran through. The fire that had jumped to the bindle now licked at the wicker trunks; in an instant, the three trunks went up in flames. From out of the smoke the voices of the past arose, dim and dense.

"Where did you come from?"

"I came to see you, Hee-hyang."

"I asked where you came from."

"You're beautiful when you're angry."

"So when I'm not I'm ugly?"

"Let me read your face and tell your fortune."

"Don't look too closely."

"Sure."

"Is it good? Bad?"

"You should watch your posture when you walk."

"So I've got bad posture. Hey, when are you leaving?"

"I couldn't leave if I wanted to, you know, I can't leave you, Hee-hyang."

"But you want to go?"

"I don't."

"You liar. You'll run off and leave me and the baby someday."

"The baby?"

"I'm pregnant."

"You are?"

"Which would be luckier, if the baby looks like you or if it looks like me?"

"Well, if it looks like me, but—"

"Hey, what if we both go off together telling fortunes?"

"If we're gonna have a baby, I'm gonna have to put down roots in Miryang. But your eomoni and abeoji won't want us to get married, you know. They'll say there's no way they'll let their daughter marry some good-for-nothing drifter they don't know."

"If they say no, then we'll just have to elope. Hey, tell me about Mount Kumgang."

"How many times have I already told you?"

"It doesn't matter; I want to hear you tell it."

"It's so beautiful people say the fairies play there. The water is lovely, and there's a clear lake too. And there are rock formations that look like lions and tigers and bears too."

. . .

"As you get closer to the harbor, suddenly the mountain spreads before you like a folding screen being opened; it's so beautiful it takes your breath away. When you see it from afar it's just beautiful, but once you start to climb there are all these cliffs here and there, like teeth on a saw, that block the way, and that makes it steep and difficult. In the Outer Kumgang area there's a temple called Singye-sa. It was built almost fourteen hundred years ago by King Beopheung of Silla, and during the Imjin War it was there that Seosan Daesa commanded a troop of warrior monks."

"How do you get to Mount Kumgang?"

"From Busan you get a boat to Kosong; from the harbor to Onjeongni at the base of the mountain path is twenty minutes by bus or about an hour and a half on foot. But once the Kumgangsan Electric Railway starts running, you'll be able to go from Chorwon to Naegumgang by train."

"How many days does it take?"

"You spend the night on the boat, so two days."

"Oh, how I'd like to go."

"Right . . ."

"I'll go on my own."

"I want us to go together."

"You'd lie to your wife and children?"

Silence.

"Hey, tell me about Mount Seorak."

"Mount Seorak looks dramatically different depending on the season. In spring everything is budding, in summer it's covered in lush greenery, then there's the autumn leaves, and in winter it turns into a white wonderland. I can show you around all the rock formations and waterfalls. Aigu, Mi-ryeong, there's so much I want to show you."

He put his hands between my breasts, and I closed my eyes and let his voice sink into my bare skin. So beautiful the fairies play there, the water is lovely, and there's a clear lake too—even now, his voice comes up on my skin like a rash.

The only thing he gave to So-jin was the paperwork he sent to the local secretary, Cho Yong-taek. But I didn't hate him for it. I sought him, I pined for him; the only thing I never did was hate him. But he passed on without once calling our daughter by the name he gave her. Aigo, ireol suga! Can there be a name so unlucky as one never used by one's father? So-jin! Aigu, So-jin, bulssanghan ttal!

I'd heard the rumor that he was suffering from blood poisoning. But I never thought that he'd die of it. If I'd known it was that serious, I would've gone through the gates of their house, prepared to be turned away; I would've begged, with my forehead to the ground, "Please, let her meet her father."

I wanted So-jin to see her father's face, even if it was just a glimpse. I wanted her to hear his voice, even just a word or two. If they wouldn't let us be present at the end, then I wanted at least for her to see his face in death, but three days after he died that bitch had him cremated. Aigu, the cruelty! How dare she, how dare she, how dare she burn his body!

That day, I held So-jin in my arms and looked down at the Miryang River from the house by the cedar trees where he had visited me every day. The fishing boat slowly moved through the icy river, and all the people who lived nearby, gathered on the riverbank, sang together, "Ehe ehe-yo, wolyo cho cho, ehe-yo." The captain loosened his grip on the pole and the boat stopped. *Caw! Caw! Caw!* The swans stretched their necks and circled. The moment his son tipped that white box into the water, *whisper whisper,* the branches of the cedars began to shake, *whisper whisper, whisper whisper,* and he disappeared into the wind.

They gave me nothing to remember him by. All I had left was a writing brush and one rubber boot. If they'd given me even one piece of his bones, I'd have tied it with string and worn it around my neck, nestled between my breasts. No, to be honest, I wanted to steal his body. To lay him in my bed, unfold his hands from his chest, and lay my head against it, where there was now no heartbeat. To wrap my arms around him, press my lips to his, run my fingers through his hair over and over again; to hold him until he rotted and dissolved. And then, to look into his eyes, like shucked oysters left out for days on end, to my heart's content, and press my lips to his ears and whisper, Oh, darling, finally you're mine and mine alone, oh, my love, my precious, precious love, my one and only, the love of my life, you belong to me, oh, my sweetheart, saranghaeyo, saranghaeyo, jeongmal saranghaeyo.

You lay me facedown, lift my hips and grab my daenggimeori, and with a thrust you enter me. Ah, geogi, right there, geogiyo! As long as we are breathing, we can sink further, down, to the depths of the depths, splashing around like dark fishes at the bottom of the sea where no light reaches, until we lose sight of the boundary between you and me, *splash splash*—

I turn to you and open my legs as always. You grab my hips and slowly bring your face closer. With your lips you part my lower ones, rounding the tip of your tongue as it goes in and out, in and out, and as I'm moaning and panting you reach your hands toward my breasts, caressing, shaking, kneading them, the power in your fingers building with the speed of your tongue's movements, aya! Your tongue and hands stop moving. Don't stop! Eat me! I want you to eat me, don't leave anything, it's all yours, so eat, eat me up! I arch my back, disheveling my hair, gasping, moaning, crying, collapsing inside my own voice. Now it's my turn. With the tang of the sweat from your armpits in my nose, I peck at your nipples, fill your navel with saliva and lap it up, to fill my mouth with your thing, down to the base, aigu, I try and try but I can't get it to the back of my throat, so with my lips and gums and tongue I work you over, sucking, devouring; come! I want to drink it, I want to drink you! I taste the part of you now shooting into my mouth, and I gulp it down. Oh, I'm dripping wet, feel me, you feel how wet I am? You made me this way, you ought to clean it up.

My hair, hairline, forehead, nose, eyebrows, eyelids, eyelashes, eyes, ears, cheeks, lips, teeth, gums, tongue, chin, neck, collarbone, shoulders, breasts, nipples, armpits, upper arms, elbows, forearm, wrist, hand, thumbs, pointers, middle fingers, ring fingers, little fingers, nape, back, ass, anus, navel, hips, pubic hair, my sex, thighs, knees, calves, ankles, feet, big toes, index toes, middle toes, fourth toes, little toes, there was no part of me you didn't love, no part you didn't kiss, each and every day, thousands of times, tens of thousands of times—did you leave my body to me? Very well, my body is what I'll remember you by. I cannot drive you away, nor can I flee from you. Even now I turn to you and open up, and you move inside me. How long must pass before the sensation of you, enduring on my body like a burn, changes into a faint, distant memory? How long will it take before I lose you? Aigu, if I'd known it would end like this, I would've just killed you. Thrust the knife into you, over and over, the way you thrust yourself into me, my heartbeat trembling with your screams, my whole body splattered with your blood—

"Omma, look!" It was So-jin.

Biting the insides of her cheeks, Mi-ryeong turned and saw the face of her daughter, just under two years old.

"Oh, you got up and walked all on your own, what a good girl! Omma didn't see you at all. I just put you down for your nap, but you're awake already? If you don't nap long enough, you'll be so sleepy when it's time to eat. Your omma's gonna put you on her back so let's go back to sleep."

"Nap, no!" So-jin shook her head hard.

"Well, then, stay awake. But you need to make Omma a promise. Promise you'll eat good?"

"Mm-mm."

"Yes, mm-mm, yum yum."

"'Pit out."

"If you spit it out, Omma won't be very happy. Will you eat?"

"Yeah."

"Right, good answer." Mi-ryeong took her daughter's unguarded face into her hands and gently touched her forehead to hers.

"It's New Year's today. And on New Year's, So-jin gets to eat all her favorite foods. All right? So there's tteokguk and buchimgae, of course, and then there's sujeonggwa and sikhye—I wonder which one you'll like?"

"Ride, ride." So-jin stuck her finger to her cheek as she smacked her lips.

"You want a piggyback ride now?"

"Now! Now!"

"Oh, I think that's the first time you've said the word *now*!"

"Now! Now!"

"You're learning so many new words every day; you're so smart, So-jin! In another year's time, you'll be able to say anything. Omma can't wait to talk to you!"

"Now, dink!"

"Right now, the cook is having his nap time, so what should we do instead? You want to go outside with Omma?"

"Out!"

"Then let Omma give you a ride. The stairs are pretty dangerous."

"'Cary."

"That's right, they're scary; if you fall headfirst and you break your neck, you'll die."

Puff puff puff puff puff puff puff puff, hanging from her mother's neck So-jin swung her head left and right, *puff puff puff puff puff,* as she grabbed her around the shoulders and jumped, *puff puff puff puff puff,* Mi-ryeong felt the nape of her neck dampen with her daughter's drool.

"Do you know what *die* means? It means 'goodbye, Omma.'"

"No!"

"Then hang on tight to Omma's shoulders. Yes, like that, ready? Yeongcha! Aigu, you're heavy, when did you get so heavy?"

"Heh heh heh."

"Listen here, I don't mind if you laugh as long as you don't move! It's really dangerous, right, we're almost there, right, left, right, left."

With her right hand supporting her daughter's bottom, Mi-ryeong held the banister in her other as she went down the staircase, step by step.

"Omma, sing."

"Omma's trying to focus here. We'll both be in a lot of trouble if I mix up my left and right feet and we fall."

"Sing!"

"Aigo, I give up, So-jin. Who do you take after . . . ?"

The magpie's New Year ended yesterday
And ours starts today
I'll wear a pretty daenggi
And nice new rubber shoes
Unni's wearing a yellow jeogori
And my little sister's is all colors
Abeoji and Eomoni are all dressed up too
And we're pleased with our New Year's cards

Someone was at the front gate.

"I've come for the bokjori money."

"So-jin, you give the money to the nice young man. Right, what have we got for him?"

With her daughter still on her back, Mi-ryeong grabbed the bokjori off the kitchen wall and showed it to the young man standing near the gate. From her sleeve she produced five one-sen notes and tried to put them in So-jin's hand, but So-jin nervously pushed her head into her mother's back.

"I guess she's feeling shy. Well, then, here you go. Saehae bok mani badeuseyo."

"Saehae bok mani badeusipsio." The boy, surprised at getting five sen, turned bright red up to his ears. He muttered, "Thank you," almost as if he were angry, then turned on his heel and ran.

Mi-ryeong was brought to tears by the fleeting sight of the boy turning his back to her and running off, but she could not explain even to herself why or what had affected her so. When she snapped out of it, she was crouched down by the pond in the garden, still holding the bokjori in her hand.

"Fissie."

She looked into the water and saw a scarlet-and-gold koi swimming. The light was strange. It was either too bright or too dark, she wasn't sure; it was as if the world had suddenly fallen asleep.

"It's a Japanese goldfish, a nishiki koi."

"Nichiki koi."

Cherry trees, quinces, zelkovas, and Japanese beeches, they all look alike when their branches are bare. I wonder why that is? It's like I'm looking through a pane of glass fogged up with someone's breath; no, it doesn't feel like I'm seeing with my own eyes, it's like I'm in someone else's dream . . . someone's dreaming about me . . . aigu, I feel like I'm being pulled back into sleep . . . I'm so drowsy . . . Mi-ryeong turned her head to shake off the cobwebs, then realized that her daughter, sitting next to her, had no shoes on; she picked up So-jin.

"Aigu, you're barefoot! Right, let's put on your shoes and coat and go to the river to watch the girls playing neolttwigi."

An employee appeared in the garden holding a broom and dustpan, bowed to Mi-ryeong, and began to clean.

"How many guests do we have today?" Mi-ryeong asked.

"All seventeen rooms are booked. We're fully occupied. Mr. Kobayashi, the county interior minister, and Mr. Iguchi, the grain inspectorate chief, are both staying."

"Ask the guests what they want for dinner, and make sure we can give them what they want, whether it's Japanese food or Korean. Ask the kitchen staff to make enough so that everyone can have tteokguk, buchimgae, sikhye, and su-jeonggwa, please. I'm going out for a little while. I'll be near Yeongnamnu; if anything urgent comes up please come for me."

"Danyeooseyo."

Mi-ryeong put a bright red outer coat and silk-woven somjeogori on So-jin, combed her fingers through her daughter's tousled hair, then put a hat with earmuffs and a fox fur stole on her and helped her into her rubber shoes.

"Carry! Carry!" So-jin, arms in the air, bumped herself against her mother.

"I can't carry you. You've got to walk a lot and get really hungry, or else you won't eat enough. Here, give me your hand. Omma'll sing for you."

Put the springboard out in the back garden
Take out the trays, peel the pine nuts, and crack the walnuts
Playing neolttwigi with Unni
I love it so, oh how I love it

As she sang, her daughter's hand in hers, they walked past the pediatrician's office, the pharmacy, the variety store, the bedding store, and the haberdashery. The Japanese stores were all open, while the Korean stores were closed. The ilbon saram celebrate New Year's by the new calendar, and we still go by the old calendar. They happened to walk past the rubber shoe store; she stopped singing and walking. She peered in through the gap in the wooden door, but the paper door was drawn inside the glass door, so she couldn't see inside. Gripping her daughter's hand, she turned toward the gate to the house. *Thump-thump thump-thump thump-thump*, her heart felt like it was in her throat.

I swear my throat's twitching like a frog's. What do I do if someone comes out? That woman? Her son? Her son's wife? I'll bow my head and say, I am so sorry for your loss, then I'll say: I want you to say the same to us, tell me you're sorry for our loss.

"Omma."

She looked and saw her daughter, a short distance away, about to pick up a bowl full of water, and her whole body froze instantly. Mi-ryeong picked up her daughter and kissed her cheeks, soft as rice cakes.

Oh my precious girl, my own sweet little girl, aigo, how darling you are, and with her cheek pressed to So-jin's, she walked away from the gate of this house that had lost its head.

At the riverbank, the girls were playing neolttwigi. Jalhanda, oh, how good they are! The girl on the right side jumped at the top, her black chima billowing, higher, higher! The girl on the left jumped, her deep blue chima whirling around her, jalhanda! I can hear laughter and cheers . . . but . . . I don't know what they're saying . . . it just echoes in my ears shrilly . . . empty . . . absent. . . . I can't find me inside myself . . . though I'm still full of feelings for him. . . . Why am I not here . . : and where have I gone?

"Ride."

"I won't be able to give you a ride anymore. When you get to be as big as those girls, I mean." Mi-ryeong held her daughter tightly and rocked her gently, pivoting on her heels.

Caw   caw   caw, one of the swans cried only three times, then shot out from the group, gliding across the icy water, chasing after another bird that had gone before it to bump their breasts together. As the two swans, so near in appearance that they could not be told apart, crossed their yellow beaks tinged with black at the tips, they turned them to the sky and cried out together, *Caw! Caw! Caw! Caw! Caw! Caw!*

"Oh, look, see the swans? What do you think, is that the mama swan, and that's the daddy swan, and are those their babies swimming behind them? They were gray the last time I saw them, but now their feathers have turned white; they're so pretty. Don't they look cold in that icy river? But they're all right; swans like the cold. When it gets warmer in the spring, all the swan families fly off toward Siberia. Siberia is a very, very cold place. Your appa told me about it. He knew a lot about everything; whatever you'd ask him, he had an answer. Swans lay their eggs in Siberia in summer and raise their chicks there, then in winter when there's no food they fly here."

"Omma, appa." So-jin pointed at the swans, and as she stepped on the soil pushed up by the electric pole, she chuckled to herself.

"So-jin, your omma's appa drowned and died in this river. So I see this river as my enemy. But, you know, your appa was buried in this river, so it's also a grave."

Mi-ryeong, her whole body bathing in the shadow of the dead poplar trees, watched curiously as her own hand stroked her daughter's face. Jalhanda! *Caw! Caw!* Higher, higher! *Caw!* From a dreadful silence the voices of all things are born and disappear. Mi-ryeong, jeongmallo ippeuda yeogido yeogido yeogido jeonbu nae geoda, Mi-ryeong, how beautiful you are, this, and this, and this, all of you is mine. *Caw! Caw! Caw!*

"Omma, sing."

Harsh daddies turn gentle
Even crybabies don't wail
You can hear it from all the houses
The sound of yutnori
I, I love New Year's

Sol sol   sarang sarang   sol sol   sarang sarang, the breeze from the river blew her song away, became one with the song and blew onward, to the other side.

SIXTEEN

June 8, 1933

| 1933년 6월 8일 | 1933年6月8日 |

The sound of the school bell rang out. The site foreman in his white open-collared shirt and earthen-colored trousers yelled, "Break!" and the laborers in Korean clothing pulled the rope with a chant of yeogiyeongcha, sangsadiya and lowered the iron lump onto the riverbank. The laborers coming up from the river or across the pontoon bridge from the other side washed their faces and hands in the water and rinsed out their mouths; Kee-ha and Man-sik, both of whom had just graduated that spring, clambered up the embankment and went into Bok-soon's. Inside, Hong-chae pointed at the forty portions of fermented soybean stews, minari namul, cabbage kimchi, and boiled barley mixed with rice, all ready to go at the requested time, and the two boys carried the pots, bowls, and utensils down to the riverbanks in two trips, then dished up the stew and rice to their superiors. When finally they finished serving themselves, they pushed their way into the circle of men—"Excuse me, can I just . . ."—and started to eat, sloshing the rice and stew together and bolting it down, like it was a competition. On the other bank, the Japanese foreman and engineer sat on rush mats, chatting about something as they opened the lids of their bento boxes. What they say on that bank can't be heard here—the thought made the laborers feel more at ease. Kee-ha stared at the wooden posts in the ground parallel to the pontoon bridge as he munched.

"So there's gonna be a bridge."

"What a dumb thing to say. We're the ones building it, aren't we?" Man-sik picked up a bit of namul with his chopsticks and stuck it in his mouth.

"No, I just mean . . ."

"What?"

"We were always so happy whenever it rained a lot and school got called off."

"Oh, right, now that won't happen, will it. Wonder if we'll be done by next spring."

"You think the sweetfish'll be all right?"

"The damming of the river's just temporary."

"It's just—"

"If you don't eat quicker, you won't have time to go to the toilet."

The oldest laborer, Si-won, slurped his stew loudly.

"I heard the Lees had a baby boy this morning."

"Glad to hear it. That family has been through so much, you know."

"This might be the thing that changes it all. Baby boys are supposed to bring luck with them."

"And the mother must be relieved too. After all, back in the Joseon era one of the chilgeo was if she didn't give you a son."

"What's chilgeo?" Man-sik asked, swallowing some kimchi.

"Chilgeojiak. Seven rules for women to follow, which were also reasons you could divorce your wife. One, not obeying one's parents. Two, not bearing a son. Three, adultery. Four, jealousy. Five, carrying a hereditary disease. Six, talking too much. Seven, larceny."

"They're still going today, then. Chang Nan-gyeong had three baby girls and he divorced her, after all."

"Well, I heard that the girl who married into the Lee family has too much education and she's stubborn as a mule. I guess that's just what happens when a woman learns to read and do her sums. As long as a woman has a lot of sons, who cares if she can do anything other than cook, wash, and sew?"

"And look good."

"I don't think you look to your *wife* for that."

"Aigu, what's wrong with you?"

The laborers all laughed.

"As long as she's as filial as Sim-cheong and as honorable as Hee-hyang, then it hardly matters if you have one daughter," said Jae-seung, putting his chopsticks and spoon in his bowl and setting it on a rock. Jae-seung, who rarely joined in the conversation, was always the first to finish eating.

"You have five girls, don't you, Jae-seung?"

"Aigo, what did you do in your past life?"

"I don't mind girls." His mouth twisted uncomfortably, so much so that the laborers were ready for him to stand up to spit, but Jae-seung didn't move; he interlaced his fingers between his legs.

Si-won got back on topic.

"Even so, Lee Woo-cheol is an important man. Nobody in Gyeongsang stands a chance against him."

"Well, I heard he's in the top five runners in Korea."

"I'd like to see a waenom try to beat him."

"He's faster than a bird or a horse."

"But the thing is, he kept running, even before the mourning for his father was done. That's just not right." Jae-seung did not meet the others' eyes.

"No, I'm sure he was just trying to shake off his sadness by running."

Although the sun was only mildly shining even at noon, the laborers, who had now all finished their lunches and were talking, were starting to develop dark, reddish sunburns behind their ears.

Choi Min-tae scraped the barley and rice stuck to the lid of the pot off as he spoke. "His sister was only ten or so when she drowned. And then not three months later, his father dies suddenly of blood poisoning. None of us can know how he feels."

"Now, how big is the Lee family again?"

"There's Woo-cheol, Woo-gun, Hee-hyang eomoni, Woo-cheol's wife, his daughter, and then the baby boy that was born this morning—that makes six."

"Five mouths to feed, aigu, and he's only twenty. He's doing pretty good selling rubber shoes at fifty sen a pair, I'd say."

"How long's it been since Yong-ha passed?"

"Was it winter the year before last?"

"And he was only forty . . . Poor guy."

"Same year as the Mukden Incident, in September."

"Kim in the rice store takes the newspaper and let me read it, but the way it read, 'The ██th Division Headquarters on the ██th at ████ a.m. started toward Mukden from Liaoyang,' I couldn't tell who'd done what. Why censor even the division number and the time?"

"I guess they must be military secrets."

"The Japanese army wants to hide everything it can."

"That's 'cause the waenom are a bunch of cowards."

"Chammallo maeume an deundanikkene!" *God, they make me sick.*

"January last year, when Lee Bong-chang failed to assassinate the emperor, he threw hand grenades at him."

"They printed the speech that the governor-general of Korea, Ugaki, made, didn't they? That this horrifying incident is truly unbearable. And what's more horrific is that the perpetrator is Korean. He said despite the reconciliation of Japan and Korea, the situation is dire on the peninsula."

"He was a railway man from Hanseong."

"He quit his job and went to Ilbon, cut off all correspondence with his wife and children, I heard, so he probably spent years planning and waiting for his chance."

"Wasn't he in some sort of political organization?"

"All the papers said was that he was charged with high treason."

"I guess he must be locked up somewhere now."

"Aigu, they executed him."

"Right, they handed down the death sentence at the end of September and carried it out ten days later."

"They only found, say, two or three scratches about the size of a thumb on the carriage that the imperial household minister was riding in, didn't they? Aigo, bulssanghaera."

Jae-seung covered his mouth with both hands and spoke quietly.

"What's an emperor anyway? He eats and shits just like everyone else."

"I doubt he eats the same slop as us." Wan-ju made a farting noise and belched.

"Maybe he eats better than us, but his shit still stinks!"

"Aigu, keep your voice down. If the waenom hear you, they'll get you for sedition."

"Aren't we all, Korean or Japanese, equally the emperor's children?" said Kee-ha, who had been quietly nodding this whole time, in Japanese; Man-sik looked at his friend in astonishment.

"Not me." Man-sik could not turn his eyes from his friend's Adam's apple, which bobbed up and down as if he were drinking water or something.

"That's true . . . but . . . the thing is . . . I don't mind being the same . . . but the Japanese get treated differently . . ." Kee-ha's impassioned voice trickled out through his barely moving lips.

"Well, then, if you got the same treatment as them, would you want to be one of the emperor's children?"

"I'm not sure that's possible. They look down on us and the Chinese. . . ."

Man-sik took all he could of his friend's stare; when he could take it no longer, he cast his eyes upon the flow of the river.

Bae Si-jung, from Samnamjin, began to sing loudly.

Make the emperor a servant
Make the empress a maid
Don't work them too hard, Seok Woo-ro's pledge
Let us set as our example
The hero An Jung-geun, who
Attacked ol' Itō Hirobumi in Russian territory
With three shots he killed him
Then "Korea forever!" he cried

"Knock it off, knock it off!"

"The jjokbari don't know Korean."

"Let's say they don't. But they do know Itō Hirobumi and An Jung-geun."

Bae Si-jung chuckled and stopped singing, then got his can of tobacco out of his pocket and stood up, walking slowly toward the river as he rolled his cigarette and lit it. The smoke rose over his shoulder and hung in the air behind him.

"That incident in Shanghai happened January last year too." Bae squinted at the sun, smoke trailing from his mouth.

"The Japanese army's running riot in China."

"Wonder what on earth's going to happen next. Hey, give me one too."

Shin Woo-man took a cigarette from Bae and struck a match; he sucked hard on the cigarette, both his cheeks turning concave.

"Two months after the Shanghai incident, they founded Manchukuo."

"'Five Races Under One Union, Paradise Under Royal Rule,' aigu, who'd buy into that?"

"The waenom do, and they keep rushing in."

"You know they left the League of Nations in March."

"Well, since it was forty-two versus one demanding that they leave Manchuria, they would have had to withdraw their troops to stay in the league."

"It's too late now for anyone to stop their rampage."

"Aigu, what are the Shanghai Heroic Corps doing?"

"They can't do anything either."

"No, General Kim Won-bong will save us."

"Well, maybe, but if they catch him, he'll be hanged."

"The waenom barely notice when a Korean dies; if a death were a breeze, they'd hardly register it. *Sol sol sarang sarang, sol sol sarang sarang.*"

"Aigu, our countrymen killed by the waenom have no breath, and we the living have to hold ours. The only ones breathing freely are the robbers; aigo, bireomeogeul!"

"And they take almost all the rice from Korea back to Japan, so we barely have anything left until the wheat ripens."

"And then all we're left with is the threshing machine and the gourds we put the chaff in."

"In February we were staving off starvation with grass and roots and tree bark; every day it was like a miracle that we were still alive."

"The waenom don't have eyes or ears for us Koreans. They only have mouths and hands and feet."

"Oh, you're on to something there. They order us, punch us, kick us."

"Abuse us, tie us down, and stomp on us."

"No, they've got eyes and ears too. I mean, they're always watching us and listening in, aren't they?"

"That Ugaki bastard, what the hell does he mean by 'the harmonizing of Japan and Korea'? And they have the nerve to mock Korea, calling it Chōsen,

Chōsen!" Shin Woo-man spat on a patch of clover, sending the Japanese words out with his saliva.

"The fucking jjokbari! Stealing from us and then swinging their dicks around!" Yoon Jeong-soo spat some phlegm out on the clover too.

"The site foreman, Yamada, he's got some airs too, but that engineer . . . what's his name?"

"I dunno. We always just call him Four Eyes."

"'Four Eyes'—I like that."

"Well, that Four Eyes is always scared witless."

"I've never seen a jjokbari that timid. His own shadow could scare the shit out of him."

Bae Si-jung tossed his cigarette into the river, took a quick look over his shoulder, and then, with a big sigh, mocked pushing up the bridge of a pair of glasses with his thumb and forefinger. The laborers clapped and laughed explosively, spitting out gusts of kimchi-smelling breath.

"Aigo, what I'd give for a drink or two, even just some makgeolli."

"Let's grab a drink this evening on our way home."

The Japanese foreman and engineer, sitting on rush mats on the opposite bank, put the lids back on their bento boxes, and Man-sik and Kee-ha grabbed the empty pots, bowls, and utensils and climbed up the embankment. The engineer in his thick, black-rimmed glasses rinsed out his mouth with a sip of barley tea from his canteen, and the foreman poked between his teeth with a toothpick as he stood up; he put both hands on his hips and stretched his back before stretching tall, arms up to the sky.

"Back to work!" His gruff cry reached the opposite bank.

The Korean laborers, assembled at the meeting point, again chanted yeogi-yeongcha, sangsadiya as they pulled the rope and beat the lump of iron down on the stake that would become a bridge girder.

Some doves, startled by the banging, took off at once from the opposite bank, fluttering down next to the women picking minari and doing their washing.

"You know, the Lees have had nothing but trouble since that girl married into the family. Their daughter drowned, the head of the family died at forty, neither of which you'd ever imagine happening. She must have awful karma."

"Well, didn't you hear? This morning, before it got light, she gave birth to a baby boy."

"A boy!"

"Oh, that's wonderful."

"Now that she's had a boy, things will change for the better." Jong-sil twisted her head, her bun tied perfectly without a strand of hair in disarray, to find the figure of her husband pulling the rope. They had married only the previous month, and she still had the innocent expression of a girl who had not cast off her childhood.

"If I were her mother-in-law, I'd never forgive her. A grandchild is a grandchild; a husband is a husband." Jin-song, who was no older than Jong-sil but bore a face hardened by the struggles of marriage, smelled Jong-sil's hair oil as she washed clothes next to her and stole a glance at her slender, elegant pale neck, untouched by the sun.

"And what exactly wouldn't you forgive?" Jong-sil asked, her hands still doing the washing.

"Aigu, her daughter-in-law called for the doctor and got him to give him an injection without even consulting her! It's just common sense, isn't it? You don't give an injection when someone's got blood poisoning."

"Those two are close though. Hee-hyang even bought some carp in the market for her daughter-in-law to eat in the last month of her pregnancy."

"No, I've heard they don't get along too, and apparently it's true. Hee-hyang sleeps in the store; they don't even eat together."

"If it were me, I'd rather die than allow that." Jin-song plucked some minari violently.

"He collapsed in front of her, so she panicked and called the doctor, didn't she? I think I'd do the same." Hands still underwater, Jong-sil looked up at the sky.

"You know who I feel sorry for? Her daughter. She was born on the same day So-won's body was found, and eighteen days after Yong-ha died was her baek-il janchi; you can imagine, nobody in that family celebrated, aigo, gayeopseora!"

"Well, they all must be celebrating today; after all, it's their firstborn son."

"Hee-hyang went a little funny after So-won died, and excuse me for saying this, but since Yong-ha died she just hasn't been right."

"They weren't a very happy couple after all."

"And everybody knew about it, didn't they? He went every day to the house of the woman who lived by the cedar trees, and even had a daughter with her. . . ."

"She got married, apparently."

"So she's finally put her daenggimeori up at the ripe old age of thirty-four."

"Apparently she was all dressed up like a kisaeng with a kingfisher-blue hairpin and a silver hair ornament and a diamond ring."

"The Dong-A Guesthouse her relative left her in charge of has a few pretty kisaeng girls working there, they say. . . ."

"Aigu, well, we're no match for Jinju, where there's more kisaeng than flies, but Miryang's always been known for its kisaeng. You know Bae Jeong-ja even lived here for a while."

When the sound of the men hitting the posts that would become the bridge girders stopped, the women also snapped into silence. *Sol sol sarang sarang, sol sol sarang sarang*, the June wind full of moisture blew past, shaking the fresh green tendrils of the willow trees along the riverbank like a young girl's hair instead of the hair of the women, which had been carefully slicked with camellia oil and tied into daenggimeori or buns so that even if they jumped for joy their hair would not become disheveled. *Sol sol sarang sarang, sol sol sarang sarang.* The white of the clovers, the peach of the milk vetch, the yellow of the creeping wood sorrel, the dark purple of the blue-eyed grass, the red of the mock strawberry all colored the riverbanks, and the small cabbage white butterflies, pale clouded yellow butterflies, and swallowtail butterflies danced with the wind, but the sparrows declined the wind's invitation, flying low along the ground, before abruptly turning to snap at insects with their beaks. The pair of winter wrens, standing watch over their nest built from zelkova branches, were so alike in size and color that it was impossible to distinguish their sexes. The one on the right turned to its partner and cawed in greeting, then spread its indigo wings, which had a metallic brilliance to them, and flew down to the riverbed.

As the women waited for someone to speak first, they picked minari and did their washing. *Sol sol sarang sarang, sol sol sarang sarang*, taking the wind stopping as her cue, Yong-nyeo broke the silence.

"You know, I heard at the Dong-A Guesthouse there's always five or six employees and two Japanese chefs."

"Aigu, I've never heard of a Korean employing Japanese."

"I heard most of the guests are Japanese too."

"Well, I wouldn't wonder, one night with two meals is four yen. Only the Japanese could afford to stay somewhere that expensive. Apparently, the big-wigs from the Chōsen Railway Bureau go there regularly."

"Aigu, imagine them flirting with the kisaeng—oh, how horrible!"

"I heard the grilled eel and gomtang are good. Jeong in Gyo-dong used to work there, and they'd let her eat whatever the guests couldn't finish. She said that the head of the local government-general branch said it was better than any grilled eel he'd had on the Japanese mainland."

"Gosh, I'd like to try that once, even if it was just someone's leftovers."

"Oh, stop, I wouldn't set one foot in any establishment that woman ran."

"Aigo, what a nasty creature! Stealing another woman's husband and having his child and then getting married to someone else, and all the while she had the nerve to walk around looking as if butter wouldn't melt! Just what kind of man would have her, I'd like to know!"

"I heard he's from Gimhae."

"So he's not from around here. . . ."

"He's got his eye on her money. . . ."

"But she's hardly a beauty. . . ."

"A beauty? Well, she's thirty-four, isn't she? That's nearly seven years older than you all; she's past it now."

"She might have a kid and be way past it, but she can leave the cooking and cleaning to a maid, dress in all that finery, slather her face in skin cream, slap on some Shiseido or Kanebo perfume, and trick a man that way."

"Aaaigu, all you do is talk about her."

"No, but, well, did you hear, her daughter has polio—her limbs are paralyzed."

"Poor thing. She's only four or so."

"Oh, once you start pitying her that throws everything off."

"Throws what off?"

"Her position with us, of course."

"But her child's done nothing wrong."

"Well, she must've done something wrong in her past life."

"Sure, otherwise she wouldn't be the illegitimate daughter of a dead man."

Sol sol sarang sarang, sol sol sarang sarang, the wind joined in the women's conversation, but whether it was voicing its agreement or trying to interrupt, they weren't sure. Jong-sil stood up and looked around near the pontoon bridge, searching for her husband among the workers constructing the bridge. Ja ganda! Ah! Chagapda! In the backwater, where the sun was falling, some stark-naked children played, sticking their arms and legs out like pieces of wood and letting them drift, then jumping up and diving back under the surface, splashing water on the other children as they laughed. It was June; the water was still chilly. The children wouldn't get out even if they were covered in goose bumps, the little hairs on their arms standing on end, but when the temples of their foreheads started to hurt and their lips went purple, they climbed up onto the delta where they had taken off their short-sleeved jeogori and paji or chima and let the sun shine onto their skin, reddened by the cold water. Jong-sil spotted her husband on the other bank; she stood on her tiptoes and waved her arms around widely. He was pouring concrete into a wooden frame, so he didn't seem to notice. She picked up a pebble and tried to throw it at him, but she missed and it fell right in the middle of a group of kingfishers, making them all scatter into flight.

"Aigu, stop acting like a child. What if you get him to look away and he gets injured?"

"But I'm always looking for him, and he knows I'm here and he won't even give me one look. Can't he just give me a glance?"

Jong-sil pursed her lips sulkily and plucked some minari. The oldest of them, Jeong-son, who had seven grandchildren, was washing underwear and diapers as she began to sing, in a hoarse voice, "Miryang Arirang."

Look   look at me
Like a flower that blooms midwinter   look at me

Ari, arirang   suri, surirang   arariga nanne
Coming over Arirang Pass

Having finally met him
I could not hear a word he said   I was so shy

Ari, arirang   suri, surirang   arariga nanne
Coming over Arirang Pass

I was mistaken   I was mistaken
I came here as a bride in a carriage   I was mistaken

"Ice cream! Ice cream!"

"Come get your candy!"

The young man with the large iron box hanging around his neck selling ice cream and the boy selling candy began to compete with her voice, so Jeong-son stopped singing. She could see old men wearing broad-brimmed hats fanning themselves as they climbed up the stone steps to Yeongnamnu. Beyond the dark treetops of the cedars was the pine forest, where the Japanese who had come on excursions from Sanmun-dong and the center of town would be lazing in the afternoon sun. Someone was running toward them from the direction of Yongdu-mok. Their strides were long, and they were running at a rather fast pace, but they were so tall and slender that they looked comedic, less like a horse or a deer and more like a kingfisher flapping its wings as it ran across the surface of the water. The women stopped what they were doing and looked at the runner.

In-hale ex-hale   in-hale ex-hale   in-hale ex-hale   in-hale ex-hale

They listened, napes stiffened, as he ran behind them.

in-hale ex-hale   in-hale ex-hale

Once the man had almost disappeared into the direction of Mubongsa Temple they all let out a tremendous sigh.

"He was going at quite a clip, wasn't he? I thought he was about to outrun that shirt he's wearing."

"I honestly think there's nothing more beautiful in this world than the sight of a man running."

"Aigu, I'd like to hear you try to say that about your own husband."

With as little effort as if she were moving her arm, Jeong-son stood up straight and smoothed her chima, and the other women stood up one by one and started getting ready to leave. One bundled up straw to carry, one drained the water off a strainer full of sweetfish, one put her basket on her head, one held her washing and her carrying cloth in both arms—the wind, gently waving their chimas and jeogoris, imitated the movements of the women's hands as they washed the grit from the minari.

"I reckon he might be the tallest man in Miryang, what do you think?"

"Well, my husband's no slouch in the height department, but there's something dignified in Lee Woo-cheol's face, the way he holds the bridge of his nose up like that, right?"

"That's the face of a man who goes running come rain or shine."

"My husband won't even tend the fields when it's raining; he just sips makgeolli and plays hwatu with all the old geezers in the neighborhood, aigu, what a disgrace."

"Lee Woo-cheol might just be the pride of Miryang."

In-hale ex-hale   in-hale ex-hale   the wind off the river shakes the willow trees harboring swarms of noisy sparrows   let the sunlight filtered through the trees falling at my feet lift up   in-hale ex-hale   in-hale ex-hale   green! in-hale ex-hale   the green this time of year is the most beautiful   soon it'll all be burned by the sun and turn darker   in-hale ex-hale   I don't think anything's greener than the green of June   in-hale ex-hale   Woo-cheol breathed in the smell of the wind blowing across the river   finally   in-hale ex-hale   I'm forgetting that this is the river that stole my sister's life   that washed away my abeoji's remains   in-hale ex-hale   well, no   how could I ever forget that   in-hale ex-hale   but I think, oh, they're trying to catch sweetfish all the kids are swimming   and look how pretty the light reflecting off it is   in-hale ex-hale   and then I can look at it without thinking about them in-hale ex-hale   in-hale ex-hale   and now I'm   in-hale ex-hale   twenty years old   finally   in-hale ex-hale   finally   gasp   gasp   time has

passed   Eomoni is forty   In-hye is twenty-two   Woo-gun is eight   Mi-ok
is almost three   and this morning   in-hale ex-hale   our son was born
in-hale ex-hale   time isn't unbroken like a road   occasionally there're cliffs
and if you don't climb up the ladders you won't make it   in-hale ex-hale   I
don't want to climb up to the days when we lost my sister and father   in-hale
ex-hale   in-hale ex-hale   in-hale ex-hale   in-hale ex-hale   her face with the
white foam coming out of her nose and mouth like a mushroom   his face
looking like he might open his eyes wide and breathe in everything   in-hale
ex-hale   both of their faces puffy   in-hale ex-hale   far too swollen   I can't
get used to the reality that I see with my own eyes   their voices get louder
in-hale ex-hale   too loud   I can't get used to the reality that I hear with my
own ears   *caw   caw!*   Ice cream!   Ice cream!   Candy   Come get your
candy!   shut up!   I'm begging you, please, be quiet!   in-hale ex-hale
in-hale ex-hale   if I run faster   the sounds and shapes and colors all
shake   crumble   fly away   my memories   and grief   and sense of
loss in-hale ex-hale   all shake   crumble   fly away   in-hale ex-hale   the
reality of life flings off behind me   in-hale ex-hale   just the concept of life
hidden on the other side   in-hale ex-hale   in-hale ex-hale   but   however fast
I go   reality is   in-hale ex-hale   always right behind me   in-hale ex-
hale   aigu, sometimes it takes a shortcut   and before I realize it reality's got
me outpaced   you dirty bastard!   in-hale ex-hale   in-hale ex-hale   and
sometimes I want to disconnect from reality   in-hale ex-hale   now   even
now   in-hale ex-hale   in-hale ex-hale   I didn't sleep a wink yesterday   in-
hale ex-hale   the bags under my eyes are twitching   twitch-twitch   I need
sleep   in-hale ex-hale   if I don't get any I'll be no good   my body   my mind,
all no good   in-hale ex-hale   but   when I close my eyes   through the
darkness they come to me   in-hale ex-hale   and behind them, other dead
too   in-hale ex-hale   in-hale ex-hale   Heroic Corps members tortured to
death   and their families   in-hale ex-hale   teeth pulled   noses cut off   eyes
gouged out   eardrums pierced   face after   face after   face   in-hale ex-
hale   the dead reach out to me one after another   with familiarity   in-hale
ex-hale   welcome   Woo-cheol   in-hale ex-hale   I had trouble sleeping when
I was a kid   I always wanted to be awake instead   I wanted to play more,
more   since I started running   in-hale ex-hale   on my back   on my

side   facedown, even   I'd lie down and before I could even count to ten I was
sound asleep   in-hale ex-hale   in-hale ex-hale   hana   dul   set   net   daseot
yeoseot   ilgop   yeodeol   ahop   yeol   the ten seconds before I fell asleep
didn't feel particularly good   in-hale ex-hale   my futon was a treasured
luxury   in-hale ex-hale   sleep was a calm and gentle rest but   in-hale
ex-hale   oh, sleep   where did you go   where on earth   in-hale ex-hale   in-
hale ex-hale   sometimes in dreams I'm up to my neck in the river   I've never
wanted to die but   my legs, of their own accord   in-hale ex-hale   carry my
body into the depths of the river   in-hale ex-hale   in-hale ex-hale   save me,
sallyeojwo!   somebody, please, sallyeojwo!   in-hale ex-hale   in-hale ex-
hale   last night I drank some of Abeoji's liquor   in-hale ex-hale   my head
started wobbling around   like a baby who can't hold its own head up yet   I
couldn't even walk to the toilet   in-hale ex-hale   I went in the chamber pot
but   in-hale ex-hale   sadness sobered me up   in-hale ex-hale   in-hale
ex-hale   Abeoji's bones were washed away in the river   and my sister's body
was buried in the ground but   this sadness   in-hale ex-hale   can't be
buried   or washed away   in-hale ex-hale   in-hale ex-hale   even running like
this   the sadness   grabs at my heels   runs up my throat in an instant   in-
hale ex-hale   in-hale ex-hale   cuts off my breathing   weighs down my
legs   in-hale ex-hale   so I go onward trying not to be caught by the
sadness   onward   in-hale ex-hale   in-hale ex-hale   the future   in-hale
ex-hale   past   in-hale ex-hale   the future is all in the past   someday my
son   will talk about my past, the past of his father   in-hale ex-hale   about
the past of his motherland, the Korean Empire   in-hale ex-hale   in-hale
ex-hale   I heard that a lot of Chinese were killed   in Manchuria and
Shanghai by the Japanese   in-hale ex-hale   each with a name received from
their ancestors   and a name their parents gave them and still   the
waenom   in-hale ex-hale   erased   that name   did not record it   in-hale
ex-hale   in-hale ex-hale   massacred   pillaged   exploited   raped   tortured
in-hale ex-hale   in-hale ex-hale   the thieving bastards put terror in the
heart of every Korean   in-hale ex-hale   and terror is how they rule this
country   in-hale ex-hale   the Korean Empire   my homeland, stolen two
years before I was born by thieving Japan   did they take everything   did they
take almost everything   or are there still some things they haven't stolen

in-hale ex-hale   should I   teach my son what to steal back   or perhaps what
to protect   in-hale ex-hale   in-hale ex-hale   the underhanded criminals who
broke into Gyeongbokgung and slayed the empress   poured oil on her and
burned her body   and threw it into Hyangwonji   in-hale ex-hale   they said
they were from the Japanese legation and army but   the three men they hanged
were Koreans   in-hale ex-hale   and Lee Bong-chang, who threw a hand
grenade at the emperor's carriage and was caught   suddenly got the death
sentence at the Supreme Court   in-hale ex-hale   and he didn't even graze the
damn carriage aigo   in-hale ex-hale   in-hale ex-hale   even now, while I'm
running   the blood of my compatriots is being shed like rain   their pained
moans rise like steam   their names are being painted black   like ink over a
censored article   in-hale ex-hale   in-hale ex-hale   all of Shanghai turned into
a city of death   the Japanese army occupies everywhere they go   in-hale
ex-hale   when I picked up the newspaper that day   my heart skipped as if I'd
been punched   in-hale ex-hale   three and a half years ago   Woo-hong
boarded a night train saying he was going to join the Heroic Corps   in-hale
ex-hale   jal itgeora   jal gara   the last words we said at Yeongnamnu   in-hale
ex-hale   oh, wind   in-hale ex-hale   give first breath to those about to be
born   in-hale ex-hale   you steal the last breath of those about to die   oh,
wind   in-hale ex-hale   can you somehow whisper in my ear   the
whereabouts of my best friend   in-hale ex-hale   in-hale ex-hale   Kang
Woo-hong   have you joined the ranks of the dead too?   in-hale ex-hale   in-
hale ex-hale   however many dozens   hundreds   thousands of men the
waenom kill   in-hale ex-hale   if they're Korean or Chinese   they'll make it
so they weren't killed   but   in-hale ex-hale   even if they can make it so they
weren't killed   they can't make it so they were never born   in-hale ex-hale
they can't obliterate their very names   in-hale ex-hale   Kang Woo-hong
today my first son was born   I decided to name him Shin-tae   in-hale
ex-hale   **Dangun 4266 June 8   Lee Shin-tae   Father: Lee Woo-cheol
Mother: Chee In-hye**   in-hale ex-hale   in-hale ex-hale   in-hale ex-hale

Woo-cheol passed under the geumjul decorated with red chilies and pine
branches. He scooped water from the well and drank some, then undid the
laces of his running shoes and took them off; now barefoot, he gripped the

water gourd and splash, ah, siwonta, splash, he poured ladle after ladle of water over himself, the water streaming down inside his running shirt, falling down his back and chest like a waterfall. Oh, what a feeling! Woo-cheol peeled his damp shirt from his skin, took the hand cloth from around his shoulders, and wrung it out, then wiped down his body and hair, before changing into the paji and jeogori that had been left for him on the veranda.

"Appa!" Mi-ok came running to him.

"Daddy's home!" Woo-cheol said, still drying his hair with the cloth.

"Appa, welcome home!" Mi-ok clung with her whole body to her abeoji.

"How's Omma and the baby?"

"Dunno. And Omma just keeps holding the baby, she won't hold me at all."

"Well, that's how it is. If your omma doesn't hold the baby and give him milk and change his diapers he won't live. But, Mi-ok, you're a big girl who can eat by yourself, change your clothes by yourself, and go to the toilet by yourself, right?"

"Not fair!"

"Mi-ok, listen, for your sweet little brother's sake, just let it go for a bit."

"No! I don't want a little brother anyway!"

"Now don't say that. Not long ago you were jumping up and down like a little chick saying you'll be a big sister soon; and he's so cute."

"But he's not cute at all."

"If you keep raising your voice like that, you know, Appa's going to have to tickle you." Woo-cheol picked up his daughter and tickled her under her armpits.

She squealed and twisted, thrashing her legs. "Stoooop it!"

"Then promise your appa."

Through her laughter, she promised.

"Will you be good to the baby?"

"I promise!" She giggled.

"Aigu, good girl!" Woo-cheol brought her up to his eye level and held her, cheek to cheek.

"Your beard is scratchy."

"It can be scratchier!"

"Ooh-ooh-ooh, ouch!"

With their cheeks nuzzled against each other's, Mi-ok whispered in his ear, as if trying to hide herself in it. "Appa, do you love me?"

"Of course I do. You're my precious little girl!" Woo-cheol put her up on his shoulders and ran around the garden with her once, then walked with her hand in hand toward the store.

When he opened the back door to the store, he saw Hee-hyang sitting on the stool, her head drooping over. He'd told her time and time again that her body didn't get any rest that way, that she should sleep properly, but she never wanted to leave the store, bringing her bedding there, having her meals there, never leaving except to use the toilet, kitchen, or well. Although nobody had asked her to do so, she had decided to rearrange the store in her own way, and she didn't want to step away from the rearrangement, like a soldier who has struck camp. Halme, Mi-ok called out, and Hee-hyang's head came up and her mouth opened wide, as if she were gasping for breath after coming up to the surface; she gave her granddaughter a tired smile. She dragged her body upright and stood, patting the stool as she said sluggishly, "Come sit," but Mi-ok wedged herself between her grandmother's legs.

"I want Halme's lap," she said.

Hee-hyang sat and took her granddaughter up onto her lap, then started combing her fingers through her long hair, which had never once felt the edge of a pair of scissors. Feeling somehow excluded from this scene, Woo-cheol went back out the door.

In the back room of the house, In-hye and the baby were asleep face-to-face, clinging to each other like potatoes. Woo-cheol knelt before the Samsin altar and whispered a prayer. Oh, Samsin halmoni, please, please, look over this baby, who is as fragile as a water bubble, so he can grow up healthy, we are foolish and know nothing, can do nothing, Samsin halmoni, please, look after this child, please let him live long enough for his head to turn white.

Woo-cheol looked at his sleeping son, who almost looked like he was smiling in his white baenetjeogori. Next to the newborn baby, In-hye's face, with a few hairs stuck to her greasy forehead, looked dull and unhappy. Perhaps sensing him there, In-hye opened her eyes.

"Oh, hello."

"Shh." Woo-cheol put his index finger up to his lips. In a voice that was little more than a breath, he whispered his son's name. "Shin-tae."

"Shin-tae . . . Shin-tae . . ."

In-hye looked at her husband's face as if trying to find a foothold in it to keep her from falling back to sleep, but gradually her gaze listed and her eyes shut. She was lying in a warm, sunny bed, having given birth to her okdongja, a baby boy as treasured as a jewel, and yet for some reason she looked as if she were on her deathbed, having suffered a grievous injury.

"I must look awful, don't I?" In-hye asked, her eyes still closed.

"Not at all."

"Bring me the mirror. . . ."

Woo-cheol picked the hand mirror up from the dresser and put it in his wife's hands. When she had brought it up above her face, she opened her eyes, knitting her eyebrows.

"I look horrible. . . . Honey, you know which mirror this is, right? It's the one we held up to your father's mouth when he was dying, to see if he was still breathing or not."

Woo-cheol could not understand why she would say something like that right now.

"There's more and more people in this house, but the traces of those who aren't here will never go away. . . . I've had two children. . . ."

He didn't know what to say; all he could do was wait for the next words to come from her mouth. He realized with shock that his wife's face, silent as a fallen tree, closed off to expression like tree bark, looked exactly like his mother's.

"I'm so tired, I can't . . ." She shut her eyes again. Before the count of ten, her head had already slipped from the pillow, and the sound of light snoring filled the room.

I can't . . .? What was it she was trying to say? I don't know. What was she thinking about? I don't know.

Woo-cheol listened closely to the stillness within himself. **Sleep-a-bye**

baby my precious child gift from the angels way up on high Eomoni used to sing me that lullaby a lot. **And when the dog barks it's far from your room aigu,** I can't remember the next line. Woo-cheol gently stroked his son's palm with the pad of his index finger as the baby slept, his soft chin exposed. Why is it so hard to think that I'm happy? . . . Am I missing something that would let me be happy? . . . I don't know. . . . I'm sleepy . . . maybe a little sleep . . . beside my wife and son . . . just a little . . . When he closed his eyes he felt the rhythm of running revived within his body. **In-hale ex-hale in-hale ex-hale the faces are shaking they're crumbling they're jumping** Woo-cheol said the names of those faces out loud **Lee Yong-ha in-hale ex-hale Lee So-won in-hale ex-hale Lee Shin-tae in-hale ex-hale in-hale ex-hale in-hale ex-hale**

SEVENTEEN

Long Live Sohn Kee-chung!
Long Live Korea!

│ 손기정 만세! 조선 만세! │ 孫基禎万歳!朝鮮万歳! │

"Appa, look, isn't that rock so pretty?"

At the sound of his daughter's voice, Woo-cheol looked up. Had he been asleep? At dawn, he had run the sixty ri round-trip to Samnamjin station and back, fifteen minutes quicker than usual, which was perhaps why he was so sleepy; every time he sat down, he fell asleep. Woo-cheol put the school cap he'd been sewing down and stood up, stretching his arms above his head.

"Appa, look!"

Mi-ok held up a white pebble in her plump palm.

"Where did you find that?"

"Under the bridge. It was in the water."

Mi-ok opened an empty canister of Kintarō powdered milk. Gray, black, and white pebbles, fragments of glass and brick, girls do love gathering pretty little things, and boys . . . And boys? No, I'm too drowsy, I can't keep my eyes open.

"If you see any pretty rocks when you're running, can you bring them home for me?"

"I don't look down when I'm running."

"Oh, I guess you might fall."

"Exactly."

"Where do you look?"

"Hm-mm, maybe I don't really look at anything."

"Do you have your eyes closed?"

"No, my eyes are open, and I can see things, but I'm not really looking. I guess because I'm always thinking about a lot of things."

"Like what?"

He paused. "Like what indeed . . ."

Clunk-clunk . . . the sound of the can being shaken . . . I must've fallen asleep again . . . so tired . . . but tonight from four to six I have to run the embankment . . . last year my best in the 5000 meters was 16 minutes 16.4 seconds. Of course I'm the best in South Gyeongsang Province, but that record made me fourth in Korea and twentieth in Japan. I didn't get sent to Berlin, but I want to compete at the 1940 Tokyo Olympics, and win the gold in the 5000 and 10,000 meters. . . . Since the year before last when Woo-gun started going to the common school I have to pay sixty sen a month in tuition for him, and Mi-ok's almost six now and Shin-tae's three and he's a growing boy, and then there's Ja-ok, just four months old, and in January next year there'll be another mouth to feed . . . with money on my mind it's hard to keep running, but if I don't I won't get my record down . . . in . . . out . . . in . . . out . . . Is that the sound of me sleeping? . . . I see a hand . . . a big hand holding a jangdo, a small knife in a sheath . . . a man.

The man rubbed soap on his chin and neck, then turned his face skyward, still standing. Who is that? Is that me? Am I trying to shave my face? A big white cloud slowly floated by, and the spot where the man was standing went from sun to shade. That's not me. I'm watching the knife slide over his neck. The moment it turned from shade back to sun, the knife glimmered and the tip of it went upward. Suddenly, blood began to run from his throat, and the man looked at me. Abeoji!

"Extra!"

Woo-cheol opened his eyes, just as a young man in a pure white paji and jeogori ran past the store, scattering papers.

"Extra! Extra! Read all about it!"

Was it war? Woo-cheol stepped outside, wincing from the sunlight and the clamor. The fierce rays of sun had tricked his eyes; he got goose bumps. He picked up one of the special editions of the *Dong-A Ilbo* that had fallen in the middle of the road.

LONG-AWAITED OLYMPIC MARATHON   REACHING
THE PINNACLE OF THEIR CRUSADE   THE WORLD IS
WATCHING   SOHN KEE-CHUNG WINS CONFIDENTLY   NAM
IN THIRD

"Appa, is it bad news?" Mi-ok looked up at her father anxiously.

"No, it's great news. Koreans won two medals in the marathon. Gold and bronze. That's a big deal."

Woo-cheol picked his daughter up in his arms. It felt like he was holding a bundle of kindling; the world seemed unreal. Sweat streamed from his forehead, his eyeballs felt as if they were being steamed, aah! He felt like he could pour all the well water he wanted over his head and it still wouldn't calm this burning sensation. Aah!

"Mi-ok, your abeoji's going to go for a little run. Look after the store until your halme gets back from doing her shopping."

"What do I do if a customer comes in?"

"Tell them it's fifty sen, take the money, and give them the shoes."

"If I have to give change what do I do?"

"Get the customer to figure it out."

"What about the hats and umbrellas?"

"If anyone comes in, they'll be after shoes, I'm sure. You'll be fine, your halme will be back soon, and your appa won't be gone too long either."

Woo-cheol ran up the stone steps to Yeongnamnu two at a time. The old men sitting in the observation pavilion, wide-brimmed hats on their heads, waved the newspaper in the air and cheered, so he sped up and ran to the top faster, went through the concrete torii and sat down by the shrine, *hah-hah-hah-hah, maeaemmaeaemmaeaem chireureureut chireureureut maeaem maeaemmaeaem hah-hah-hah-hah, ji-ji-ji,* victory, Woo-cheol hung his head and, looking as if he were praying, he read the paper.

On August 9, at 3:00 p.m. (11:00 p.m. Korean time), in the marathon held in the Olympic Stadium in Berlin, our own Sohn Kee-chung was uplifting! He cleanly swept past the 56 athletes assembled from more than 30 countries to gain a convincing victory.

First place: Sohn Kee-chung (Yangjeong High School), 2h29m19.2s

Third place: Nam Sung-yong (Meiji University), 2h31m42s

Maeaemmaeaemmaeaem chireureureut chireureureut. He felt that the heat outside and the burning inside him might be confusing his head *chireureureut*, he could not read through it properly.

> Sohn Kee-chung's victory also prophesies the future of the youth of Korea. . . . A son of Korea has achieved a victory on the world stage. . . . Crowds of spectators in the rain leaped for joy in wild exultation at the news . . . explosive cheers throughout. . . . Spectators began gathering, umbrellas in hand, from midnight when the broadcast ended, waiting anxiously for the announcement of the results. At two in the morning, the announcement came from a window on the second story of the building, and the hundreds of spectators cheered. . . . The crossroads in front of Gwanghwamun was filled with such energy as if dawn had broken, . . . Long live Sohn Kee-chung! Long live Korea!

So two nights ago, when I was in my bed, the Olympics started. I must've forgotten, no, it must've been in the newspaper. Only this week, I've been so tired, so, so tired I couldn't read a word. If I'd known yesterday was the marathon, I would've gone to Park's store by the station before practice and he would've let me listen on the radio.

Is this . . . joy?

My heart is trembling with joy. Long live Sohn Kee-chung! Long live Korea! My heart's beating so fast I feel like running a big lap around all of Miryang. No, just running around Miryang won't do the trick; I'd need to run to Samnangjin, Gimhae, to Busan, handing out special editions all the way. But what is this trembling in my chest? This feeling pushing aside the joy as it bubbles up within me? *Thump-thump thump-thump thump-thump!* My heart is trying frantically to push out reality, *thump-thump thump-thump thump-thump!*

Am I jealous?

Ani, aniya! Of course not! Woo-cheol immediate rejected the idea and closed his eyes. I'm not jealous! *Thump-thump thump-thump thump-thump!* How could I be jealous, *thump-thump thump-thump!*

It was at the Chōsen Jingū competition in January 1931, the winter my abeoji died. I ran in the 10,000- and 5000-meter races. I came in second in the 10,000 but a dismal fourth in the 5000. Pyeong Yong-hwan from Pyeongannam-do won the 5000. I'd raced against him dozens of times before, but the runner-up was someone whose face I'd never seen before. I looked at this boy in his white cotton shirt and shorts and work shoes with split toes as he walked up onto the platform. He accepted the certificate, eyes downcast, then walked down from the podium and took his place next to Pyeong Yong-hwan. Even though he was the runner-up, his teeth were gritted as if he'd placed much lower.

He was about five foot six, maybe about 115 pounds. His thighs, front and back, left and right, were fortified with muscles like armor, but from his knees downward his legs were thin and shapely; one glance could tell you that he was made for long-distance running. As his pace increased, he tended to hold his hips higher and kick off hard so his vertical motion increased dramatically, but he used the twisting of his hips to lengthen his stride, and he swung his arms so that his upper body didn't shift position. A very powerful but very quiet running style. His arms and legs swung as regularly as a pendulum; his body didn't rise and fall, as if his legs and the ground were drawn to each other by magnets. What kind of practice could he be doing?

"Turn to the east. Bow to the emperor!"

The chairman of the competition gave the command, and all the runners gathered on the track, faced the Japanese flag, and bowed.

"Gentlemen, all of you who have competed today, I heartily congratulate you on behalf of your country for achieving the desired result of this competition by demonstrating how well you have trained and for proclaiming the spirit and power of the Imperial peoples."

The chairman stepped down from the awards platform and a voice echoed through a megaphone: "This concludes the closing ceremony."

I spoke to him as he was wiping away his sweat with a handkerchief.

"Where are you representing?"

"North Pyongan Province."

"I'm from South Gyeongsang."

"Right, I thought your accent was pretty heavy."

"Well, your northern accent's so strong I can barely tell what you're saying. Where in North Pyongan?"

"On the border with Manchuria, near the Amnok River."

"How did you get to Hanseong?"

"Train; it took about ten hours."

"Want some of my rice balls?"

"Are you sure?"

"Of course. How old are you?"

"Nineteen."

"What year were you born?"

"1912."

"Same."

"Where in South Gyeongsang are you from?"

"Miryang."

"My bongwan is from Miryang, the Miryang Sohns."

"Oh, a yangban family. That's right, I never asked your name."

"You're Lee Woo-cheol, right?"

"How did you know?"

"Look over there."

"Oh, the results board . . . and you're . . . Sohn Kee-chung. Do you want another?"

"But then you'll have less to eat."

"It's fine, I'm going out to eat later."

"Thank you, you've really saved me here; I haven't had anything to eat since this morning."

"That's how you run when you haven't eaten?"

"Drinking water makes your stomach feel full."

"Just water?"

"I'm so cold."

"Me too. Is this your first official competition?"

"Oh, yeah, it is. Nice shoes."

"I special ordered them from the Yang Shoe Store. They put all these little metal studs on the soles so I won't slip, look."

"I watched you running in the qualifiers, and I thought, man, I hope I'm not in the lane next to him. All that dirt your studs kick up would fly right into my eyes."

"What kind of training do you do?"

"What do you mean, man? I just run."

"I, look, I'm pretty tall, right? When I go faster I always end up running on my toes, and the upper half of my body starts to stick out. I consciously try to land on my heels, but I just can't. . . ."

"Have you tried running with lead in the heels of your shoes?"

"Lead? How would I get lead in there?"

"If you can't, then maybe you could try tying it around your ankle with some cloth."

"Huh . . ."

"Running with a rock in each hand is pretty effective too. That's how I ran when I was a kid."

"I bet it's pretty cold up north, isn't it?"

"Right now it's down to four below, but in the summer it gets over ninety."

"How can you run in the snow?"

"If I took a break from training just because it's snowing, I wouldn't be able to run for a lot of the year."

"Do you want to grab some food with me somewhere?"

"I can't, I have work tomorrow, so I have to get the night train back."

"Oh, that's too bad."

"I guess we'll see each other again at another competition."

"Yes, see you then."

"Jal meokeotda." Thanks for the rice balls.

A year later, we met again at the Chōsen Jingū competition, but that time he was wearing the reddish-brown shorts of Yangjeong, the "kings of track and field." Yangjeong High School in Hanseong was famous in the track world, having produced Kim Eun-bae, who placed sixth at the Los Angeles Olympics four years earlier, and the winners' podium at every tournament was awash with their school colors; they were so dominant that the whole grounds would be muttering in dismay if they didn't win.

After he became part of the Yangjeong athletics team and turned to running marathons, Sohn Kee-chung's name roared out into the world. Korean newspapers, and Japanese ones too, referred to him as "the meteoric talent of the track world, Sohn Kee-chung!" Or Son Kitei, as the Japanese press called him, using the Japanese pronunciation of his name. "Sohn Sets a New World Record!" "The Korean Peninsula's Own Son Kitei, the New Hope Shaking Up the Stagnated Japanese Track World." "A Stratospheric Flame in Korean Marathons! Sohn Kee-chung Sets a New Record!" They were unanimous in their praise, and with each world record he broke, the extra editions flew off the presses in Japan and Korea. I learned his story through those articles. The extreme poverty, when he could only eat one small bowl of boiled rice with millet, went to school in the afternoons, and peddled melons and sugar cubes in the evenings, knitted shoes out of yarn to sell, or sold chestnuts he'd gathered to pay his school fees; how when he was young he wore women's rubber shoes, secured to his feet with rope, and ran with blood streaming down his ankles, and how his mother had tearfully handed him a pair of Japanese shoes that she had bought with their meager savings and said, "If that's how much you love running, then I want you to give it your all"; how he had gone to Japan to work, making deliveries and washing dishes at an udon place to scrape together the money to have time to train, how at night he had tied a string to his ankle and hung it out the window so that his friend at the barbershop next door could tug on it just before dawn to wake him up; how his family's house was washed away in a flood—

I thought of myself then as blessed to have never had to compete on an empty stomach; I was ashamed of how I had showed off my shoes to him.

But now he was the fortunate one. And he wasn't the only one; the bronze medalist, Nam Sung-yong, had been recruited to Yangjeong High School's athletics team too. I wish I could be with them at Yangjeong and spend all day running in friendly competition with such worthy rivals, but I have mouths to feed. If I were single, I'd move to the capital and knock on the school's door but—oh, what the hell am I even thinking? I married the woman I love, and I have a gem of a son and a beautiful little daughter too—isn't that all I ever wanted?

Jealousy.

My shirt is stuck to my back with sweat. My shirt and my paji and my shoes and my arms and legs and head all feel tight and uncomfortable. I'm jealous. And this filthy jealousy has got me soaked in sweat down to my very soul.

> The former running coach at Sinuiju Common School agreed to speak to us. Once, when he was leading the students on a run around the Sinuiju embankment, he noticed that one of the students was running while carrying large rocks in his hands. When he asked why one would do such a thing, the student responded assuredly that if he didn't do so, he would quickly leave all the others behind. After running with the rocks in his hands until nearly halfway around the embankment, he then dropped the stones and, in a flash, he had indeed pulled ahead of all the others. That student was none other than Sohn Kee-chung.

So it seemed when he told me five years ago at the Chōsen Jingū competition, "Running with a rock in each hand is pretty effective too. That's how I ran when I was a kid," that it was true. I didn't take him seriously then; I thought he was just exaggerating. Woo-cheol shook the cord attached to the prayer bell. *Clang clang*, the bell rang. *Clap clap*, he clapped his hands together twice, but he did not bow his head or make a prayer. *Clang clang clang clang clang clang*, he pulled the cord insistently, as if trying to rouse someone inside, *clang clang clang clang*, this was where he had embraced In-hye after they exchanged engagement gifts. *Clang clang*, we heard the footsteps and claps of the ilbon saram who had come here to pray as we were engrossed in drawing pleasure out of each other's bodies. *Clang clang clang clang*, Sohn Kee-chung and Nam Sung-yong don't give women a second look, they devote themselves to running and nothing else, *clang clang*, they ran to the world's pinnacle with just their two legs, *clang clang! Clang clang!* Woo-cheol picked up some rocks from near his feet and put one in each hand, then dashed down the stone stairs.

In-hale ex-hale   in-hale ex-hale   my heel's lifting too much in these rubber shoes, I can't run right   in-hale ex-hale   my lungs and muscles don't agree with me running   in-hale ex-hale   jealousy   in-hale ex-hale   jealousy   in-hale ex-hale   in-hale ex-hale   jealousy   fucking jealousy!   Get out of me!

Woo-cheol swung his arms to throw the rocks into the river, then put them in the sleeves of his jeogori and sat down cross-legged on the grass.

On Namcheong Bridge copies of the paper were scattered about, and people walking along would pick one up and give out shouts of surprise and joy. Some put the paper in their sleeve to take home, others read it and threw it back to the ground, and another would pick that up, throw it down again; some of the pages had fallen into the river and were now floating away. Once all of the extras were gone, the town and its people were returned to the stillness of a midsummer's afternoon, as if nothing special had happened at all.

Maa, ooh-maa, on the other bank the goats and cows were grazing, bleating and mooing in contrasting high and low voices. Underneath the bridge, the clumps of reeds shook their heads. They were purple now, but by the time the cicadas stopped calling they would brown, and in the autumn, they would turn as white and fluffy as the tops of pampas grass. A stork stood on one leg, pretending to be a reed, as it hunted fish. It's the season for catfish, giant goldfish, eels, and crucian carps, I suppose. The people cooling themselves in the pine trees, the people fishing—all the Koreans are wearing white hanboks, making them easy to spot. Where's Woo-gun playing? I wonder, I can't see him anywhere, so maybe he's at Yongdu-mok? I've told him off so many times for that, stop swimming at Yongdu-mok, have you forgotten that your noona drowned there, but In-hye's told me that he and his friends still jump from the willow trees into the river. He turned eleven on the seventh of April; now he's in middle school, group B, at Miryang Common School. When I was eleven all I cared about was messing around with my friends too. We jumped buck naked into Yongdu-mok, skewered live frogs, grilling and eating them, stole watermelons from the neighbors' fields to eat. Of course we were loud and awful; at some point we all got drawn into one thing or another, for me I guess it was running— Woo-cheol sighed and lay down on the grass. The clouds, long thin ones, stretched across the sky like a rib cage; but like one without a backbone, he thought, and the clouds hanging at the top of Mount Jongnam look like a swan flapping in the sky, opening its beak, tilting it, changing its direction, aigu, no, it's really flying, the wind must be so strong up that high, the clouds are being pushed about by the wind, changing their shapes, look, it looks like it's been attacked and it's losing its feathers. The clouds float farther and farther away, floating and flowing together, bulging together like plump breasts—how many years has it been, I wonder, since I last looked up at the clouds like this?

Since they built the bridge and traffic became heavier, market days have been much more prosperous than before with the pontoon bridge, but nonetheless, I might only sell ten more shoes than before. I wouldn't think of not selling rubber shoes at all, but they're hardly jumping off the shelves. If there's a war and our lives get even harder, people might be so desperate they'd wear worn-out ones with holes in them, and then they'd probably try to make do with homemade straw sandals. Might be getting close to time to change business. And even if I do set records and make it to the Tokyo Olympics in four years' time, Japan's not going to provide for me. I have mouths to feed: Eomoni, my wife, my little brother, my son and daughters, and the baby that's on the way; will it be a boy or a girl? How many years do I have to go back to get to a time when I thought of nothing but running? Ten? Fifteen? Before I went up to middle school, maybe; I feel like back then all I wanted was to run faster. That desire was so strong that it caught my breath, as if I'd been hit hard in the stomach or back, and there were nights when I waited for the rooster's crow with a desire close to agony. I couldn't think about anything when I was running, but when I wasn't, running was all that I could think about.

Woo-cheol had been following the clouds with his eyes half-open, and now he closed them. I'll get sunburned. I've got this cotton shirt on but it's so hot, it feels like the sun's directly touching my skin. The heat made it hard to breathe, and every movement made the sweat pooling on his temples stream downward. *Wheen-wheen   wheen-wheen*, he thought it was a buzzing in his ears cutting into the buzzing of a mosquito, but the earth began to shake violently, and Woo-cheol grabbed fistfuls of grass with both hands.

But I can't open my eyes . . . it's too bright . . . I'm too sleepy . . . as he stared at the sun through the thin membrane of his eyelids and felt that he might be taken dizzy, Woo-cheol let his body be embraced fully by the heat and drowsiness.

I'm trying to see anything, but no shapes or colors even will materialize for me. But I have just the sense that there's something nearby, slowly sneaking up on me. Oh, I know, this is that dream I had that time I nodded off at the store.

Abeoji? No, it's not my abeoji, it's another man. A bright white, thick cloud covered the sun, and the place where the man was standing shifted from light to shadow. This time he's tall and rather old. His hair is almost entirely white, but the sun is reflected off the few black hairs that remain on his head, and the droplets of sweat on his brow one after another run into the soap bubbles. Still standing, he turns his face toward the sky, and with careful hand movements he moves his jangdo. The moment the sun hazily appeared through a gap in the clouds, the veins on the back of his hand gripping the jangdo stood out, and as the knife went up to his wrinkled throat— I've seen this before, so why let it get me all worked up, just breathe, breathe in, breathe out, in, out. He looked at me. Like he was looking through me at something else. The way I'm trying to look through him at something else too. Is it a mirror? Is the old man me? The jangdo slowly sank into his throat. I can't watch anymore. I have to shout, have to wake up. Oh, oh, aigu, I can't speak! *Whoosh whoosh*, the wind moved the clouds, putting the man's face into shadow, but there's still an amused twinkle in his eyes. He's seen my reaction and he's enjoying it; how can he not be in pain when he's just cut his own throat? This dream is dangerous! If he slits my throat, then I know I'll never return to my body lazing by the riverside. Help me, dowajuseyo! Somebody!

Scree! Chikchik pokpok chikchik pokpok chikchik pokpok, the Hanseong-bound train crossed the railway bridge in front of Mount Yongdu. Woo-cheol breathed in the damp smell given off by the soil and the grass; he wiped the sweat from his brow with the back of his fist, still hotly clutching grass.

Mi-ok was sitting on the stool in the store, dangling her legs.

"Any customers?"

"Nope. I was so ready, but nobody came."

Woo-cheol took the rocks from the sleeves of his jeogori and handed them to his daughter.

Mi-ok stared at the two rocks, scrutinizing them; finally, she said dully, "Dad, these are normal rocks."

"Are they?"

"Well, look, they're not even pretty or that interesting. . . . Appa, why did you pick up rocks like this?"

He hesitated. "I'm not sure myself."

"Get prettier rocks next time, okay?"

"Right." He tried to grin at her, but it felt like someone was pulling his cheeks tightly, and he couldn't manage a decent smile.

Woo-gun ate the sujebi, made with ground corn, with obvious relish as he spoke excitedly.

"So today, it was my turn with the water, so I had to carry the bucket from the school well to the training field over and over again, and Miyake-sensei, who's always saying stuff like 'Just a whiff of your garlic-stinking breaths makes my stomach turn—make sure you brush your teeth before you come to school,' or 'Quit bringing that kimchi for lunch,' and if you say anything he'll give you a smack, well, now he was telling me, 'Bring another bucket, please,' it was unbelievable; he was so worked up. He was yelling out like a radio announcer, 'You know, for the last twenty years, Japan has tried to break world records, but we were always defeated at international competitions, and the global athletics world made fun of us, saying marathons must be shorter in Japan. But the day before yesterday, our long-standing grudge was finally dispelled. A twenty-four-year hope! A quarter century of bitter tears! Team Japan! Our first world conquest!' It was kind of really weird. And then when I was leaving, he grabbed my hand and said, 'At the Tokyo Olympics, it's your brother's turn.'"

Woo-gun smeared some gochujang on a lettuce ssam, then wrapped some barley rice in it and stuffed it in his mouth.

"When you wrap something, don't put the lettuce in your palm and fill it up, and if you put that much in, your mouth will be too full; it's impolite," Hee-hyang scolded.

"Today was really tough though. So I spent all morning watering the vegetables in the school field, right? In the afternoon we gathered pine resin. If we didn't get enough the teacher would tell us off, right, so everyone was looking desperately, but all the trees, even as far up as Yeongnamnu, have been stripped clean, so today we went all the way to Mount Yongdu. Yeon-ji, the ironmonger's son, is really good at climbing trees, but, see, all the trees nearby hadn't been stripped of their bark once you got up pretty high, right? Because everyone's too scared to climb that high. But Yeon-ji did it, he climbed all the way to the top. Then he fell and when he went to the Park Hospital in Gagok-dong, it turned out he'd broken his left foot," Woo-gun concluded, biting into a piece of radish kimchi.

"Aigu, how awful. If he'd fallen on his head and there was a rock or something underneath, it could've been much worse than a broken bone." Hee-hyang furrowed her brow.

"Samchon, how do you get pine resin?" Mi-ok served herself some sujebi.

"You peel some tree bark off with a fruit knife, or you break a branch off. You have to wait a little, then this yellowish-brown sap starts to come out, and you wrap it in some oiled paper. It dries out and gets hard quickly."

"Does it taste nice?"

"You can't eat it. They use it for lamp oil, I think?"

"It's for munitions." Woo-cheol slurped a bit of the broth from the sujebi.

"But what do they use it for?" Woo-gun turned his eyes toward his older brother, as if holding his breath.

"Fuel for freight trucks."

"Oh, look, the resin under my fingernails has turned pitch-black. You can't get it off no matter how much you wash. And in the spring when they made us get poplar cotton, that was rough too."

"They use that as padding for military uniforms."

"Miyake-sensei always says, 'Think of the soldiers who are fighting for our country and work hard to support them.'" Woo-gun threw his head back and looked at his brother, his eyes shining.

"The kids at the Japanese schools aren't out there scavenging as homework."

"Oh, he brought home some pine needles and inner bark for us too. I kneaded the bark into the rice flour; don't they have a lovely pine scent? What is it? Oh, shh, shh," In-hye said, rocking Ja-ok in her left arm, as she brought a spoonful of sujebi up to her son's lips with her right arm.

"Make him eat on his own, for goodness' sake, he's three," Hee-hyang muttered into the dish of sujebi, without looking anyone in the eyes.

Woo-gun picked up a songpyeon, the rice cakes filled with sweet beans and sesame seeds made with the pine bark he'd brought home, and looked at it.

"I pressed the pine needles into them to make a pattern." In-hye's face was as pale and puffy as the hands of a woman who has spent all day picking minari.

Woo-gun put a songpyeon in his mouth.

"It's good."

Shin-tae stretched far, trying to bring the plate of rice cakes closer to him.

"It's rude to pull a plate of food over in front of yourself, no matter how much you want it," Hee-hyang said.

Shin-tae pulled his right hand away and looked at his mother, then at his father.

"Your halme didn't mean you couldn't eat it. Here, have some." Hee-hyang relaxed her mouth to show that she was, at heart, generous, but her smile didn't last long.

Shin-tae picked up a songpyeon and put it in his mouth. "It's good," he said, imitating Woo-gun's tone.

Woo-gun and Mi-ok laughed loudly, and Shin-tae, delighted, wiped his mouth with his sleeve.

"There's a saying: if you can make songpyeon well, you'll find a good husband," said Hee-hyang.

"But then again, you usually only learn to make them well after you've already married," In-hye said.

"They also say if you eat a half-cooked songpyeon while you're pregnant you'll have a girl, but well-cooked ones mean you'll have a boy. What's wrong? You haven't eaten a bite."

"Well . . . I'm a little . . ."

"Just try to eat something; you can always put it back. You're not just eating for one, you know."

At almost the same time as an awkward silence fell over the table, Woo-gun picked up that silence.

"Hyung, you might win the 5000 and 10,000 and still not be noticed, you know. The Olympic glory is the marathon."

Woo-cheol paused. "Do you want to start running with me tomorrow?"

"What? Really? I'm the fastest in school. Not even the older kids can beat me." A glow came over Woo-gun's face; he slurped the last of his sungnyung, the soup made from burnt rice.

"If you're going to run with me, you need to do it every day."

"Yes, sir!" Woo-gun got up onto his knees.

"You mustn't get up as soon as you're done eating. Wait until your abeoji has put down his spoon," Hee-hyang said.

"He's not my abeoji." Woo-gun's voice sounded muffled, as if he was covering his mouth.

"He is." Shin-tae held a strawberry in each hand, taking bites from them in turn.

"Yes, it's strawberry time, say ahh, ahhh," In-hye said, putting a spoonful of mashed strawberries to Ja-ok's mouth, but the baby wouldn't open her mouth. In-hye sighed heavily and put the spoon back on her plate, then pressed her right hand to her chest.

"Are you all right?" Woo-cheol asked.

In-hye coughed violently, overwhelmed by nausea; Woo-cheol picked up Ja-ok, and In-hye ran out of the room, hands pressed to her mouth.

"Is Omma sick?" Shin-tae asked.

"She's not sick. She's going to have a baby," Woo-gun said.

"Do you think she looks a bit thin? She's four months and still can't hold her head up." Woo-cheol's palm cradled the shape of the baby's skull.

"Aigu, she got pregnant the month after she gave birth, so her milk dried up. I went today to see Rye-joo in Gagok-dong again to get some milk from her, but the baby just spits it up as soon as she drinks it, and I don't mean just a little bit, I mean she goes 'Blech!' Aigo . . ."

Ding ding ding, the grandfather clock announced in its beautiful tones that it was eight o'clock; Hee-hyang glared at the dial, numerous wrinkles between her eyebrows.

"Shin-tae, you shouldn't eat anything else once you're done with your sungnyung."

Ja-ok started to cry in a thin, hoarse voice, as if she'd been scolded instead, and the whole family listened to her cries.

. . .

Woo-cheol couldn't sleep since he became aware of the taste of kimchi lingering in his mouth. He tried running his tongue over his gums, tried swallowing down his saliva countless times, but the taste clung on; it would not leave. But strangely the sensation felt quite far from him, as if it were not his mouth or his sense of taste, so then:

Why am I so aware of it? I don't really know myself. It's like I've become a clock with no hands. Inside I'm moving, but outside I'm dead, no, maybe the opposite? Outside I'm moving, but inside I'm dead—either way around works, anyway, somewhere I've sustained a serious wound.

Woo-cheol slipped out of the mosquito netting, slipped on only his paji, and sat down on the veranda. The night air was humid, and the darkness was filled with the cries of newly born insects. *Gwitteul gwitteul sseureuram sseureuram kilililili.* Woo-cheol looked up at the moon. It was not waning in the slightest, a perfect circle. It was over the meridian, hanging in the western sky, so he figured it must be about half past two in the morning. Illuminated by the silvery light of the moon, the white flowers in the corner of the garden looked hazy. Flower after flower breathed out from its small mouth its simple fragrance.

Those are the Chinese bellflowers that my sister grew from seedlings, she always loved flowers from a young age—I'm not surprised that I can remember her this painlessly. I feel like So-won and Abeoji are just out of my sight, and one day, all of a sudden, they'll return. Maybe the two of them are giving some sign that they're here, just as the flowers are giving off their fragrance in the darkness, I just can't pick up on it.

Gwitteul gwitteul sseureuram sseureuram kilililili, it's six years since we married, seven years if I count from when we first met. Year by year, month by month, even day by day, our relationship is souring. This year we've barely spoken aside from mealtimes when everyone is together. And even then, she just tries to get through it without saying anything. Back when we were first together, she'd move her arms and legs so carefree, calling my name—I know when something came between us, it was that day, the day So-won didn't come home, and it's been there since that night.

But her unhappiness and my unhappiness are utterly different things, and they're not something we can share. I didn't make dinner that night for everyone with a belly ready to burst while praying for the safety of my sister-in-law, and she didn't go out in the rain only to find the marks in the ground where her little sister slipped and fell. I didn't find my sister-in-law's body floating in the river, and she didn't cover her little sister in earth. There is far more we didn't share. It's not her fault; there's little to be done. . . . And it's not my fault that she got pregnant a month after giving birth either, it would have been awkward if we hadn't done it, I just couldn't put up with the silence before falling asleep. . . . What else could I do, really? I don't know what else I could have done. . . .

Suddenly the image of an Adam's apple taking the full force of a blade came into his mind. That dream. Was it some kind of premonition? If so, it was clearly a bad one. If he has something he wants to tell me, he'll appear in my dreams again. Will he cut off his head next time? What is he trying to tell me? Woo-cheol imagined the man's face burned into his retinas. His eyes, mouth, neck, hands, the jangdo he held in his hand—the jangdo! He hadn't paid attention to it when he was wrapped up in the dream, but its grip had a turtle pattern. Without a doubt, that was the jangdo that his father had used every night. Ever since he could remember, the grip had been yellowed already, so it must've been something his abeoji had carried with him long before he came to Miryang. Abeoji, why do you want a knife? Should I throw it in the Miryang River like your ashes? Woo-cheol listened closely to the words that writhed on his father's tongue at the hour of his death.

Use it.

Where is it?

In the chest of drawers.

Woo-cheol took the oil lamp from the kitchen, struck a match, and lit it. He went into the main bedroom, opened the chest of drawers, and there it was! The jangdo was at the bottom of the drawer, waiting quietly.

Woo-cheol set the lamp down beside the well and swished the jangdo around in the water in the basin. The lamp ran out of oil and the light went out, but his hands knew what to do next. *Shk-shk-shk shk-shk-shk gwitteul gwitteul sseureuram sseureuram kilililili*, I'd hardly think that the space where the sound of the knife being sharpened echoed and where the insects' cries rang out were the same. Even now a part of me is still in that dream, and a part of that man is in this reality. Just as I saw him in that dream, he's seeing me now, sharpening this jangdo. The knife shone, repelling the moonlight, but Woo-cheol could not stop sharpening it, *shk-shk-shk   shk-shk-shk*. . . .

As the rooster crowed, Woo-gun came out into the garden, wearing a cotton shirt and paji. Woo-cheol had promised to leave him if he overslept; it was nineteen days since they had started running together, and that promise was still unbroken. He'd put in an order for the same running shoes as his own at the Yang Shoe Store, but he'd told Woo-gun to try his for a week, so until then Woo-cheol would have to run in tabi boots. The two of them did radio calisthenics quietly, so as not to wake anyone else, then went off through the dawn streets; once they reached the river path, they began to run.

In-hale ex-hale   in-hale ex-hale   up until yesterday we ran once around the sandbank but   today we're going to run to Samnamjin station   all right?   "Yes!"   *huff-huff   huff-huff*   it's sixty ri round trip   the most important thing for a long run is breathing   second is posture   when you breathe, go   in-hale ex-hale   in-hale ex-hale   two inhales, two exhales   give it a try   in-hale ex-hale   in-hale ex-hale   good   you can't really overdo it   try breathing out hard   *huff*   again!   breathe out hard!   *huff   huff*   so how was that   you can breathe well without overdoing it right?   "Yeah!"   if you're having trouble breathing   open your chest up wide like this   in   out   breathe deeply   in   out   fill your lungs with oxygen   in   out   in-hale ex-hale   in-hale ex-hale   I'll drop back to check your posture so keep running   hana, dul   hana, dul   hana, dul   hana, dul! you're looking a little bowlegged   yes   straighten up   like you're running down a straight line   that's it   in-hale ex-hale   land from your heel and roll to the sole of your foot to shift your center of gravity   in-hale ex-hale   in-hale ex-hale   don't try to hold your body forward   put your force in your shoulders   not that much, you'll start to go numb   in-hale ex-hale   loosen up   move your arms and legs like a clock's pendulum   that's it   now

see   your hips have started swinging side to side   I'm sure you can feel that
yourself   how it's gotten easier   in-hale ex-hale   in-hale ex-hale   *huff*
huff huff huff   "Getting harder to breathe"   if you're losing breath that
means you're going too fast   go at a speed where you can talk to me   when
you're running alone run at a pace where you can hum to yourself   in-hale
ex-hale   if you can't talk or hum   it means you're going too fast   so slow
down   more   slower   to run for a long time it's crucial to maintain a speed
that won't make you lose your breath   in-hale ex-hale   in-hale ex-
hale   look   it's dawn   the sun is coming up over Mount Chiltan   and the
moon is setting by Mount Jongnam   isn't it pretty?   I love running at dawn
in August best of all   in-hale ex-hale   in-hale ex-hale   if you raise your chin
like that your upper body will bend and your lower back will strain   hey,
now   that's too low   if you run hunched like that your lungs will be
compressed and it'll be hard to breathe   in-hale ex-hale   lean forward
slightly and look about five meters ahead   in-hale ex-hale   in-hale ex-
hale   "This is hard"   I'm sure it is   the first ten ri are   in-hale ex-
hale   always hard for me too   but you'll build muscle soon and your legs
will be lighter   just be patient   hana, dul   hana, dul   hana, dul   hana,
dul!   uphill now!   swing your arms!   shorten your gait!   in-hale ex-
hale   in-hale ex-hale   don't hit the ground so hard   just tap your
feet   that's it   in-hale ex-hale   if you don't look ahead   you'll keep thinking
there's more to climb so   look a little farther ahead   no matter how
steep the climb it always ends   there's always a downward slope   but   in-
hale ex-hale   downhill is trickier than it seems   you think it's easier than
going uphill, right?   It's a bigger load on your legs   in-hale ex-hale   in-hale
ex-hale   right, we're at the top!   downhill now!   you don't have much
muscle strength yet so you can walk if you want   "in-hale ex-hale   I'm not
gonna walk   I said   in-hale   that I'd run   in-hale ex-hale   that I'd run
with you   in-hale   I wanna go to the Olympics with you"   ex-hale   in-hale
ex-hale   in-hale ex-hale   I'll run in front of you, so watch me   running hard
with a large gait is the worst thing you could do   on the downhill your back
tends to go back and your belly goes forward   if you lower your arms and
lean sliiightly forward   it's like you're letting the slope take care of your body
for you   you'll go downhill smooth like ice   you can't let up on speed

though   if you keep your legs stiff as rods   in-hale ex-hale   your knees will take a huge impact   and they'll start to hurt, you see   in-hale ex-hale   in-hale ex-hale   once we're down this hill the road to Samnamjin station is flat   in-hale ex-hale   himnaera!   *sseureuram sseureuram sseureuram sseureuram   sseureuram sseureuram sseureuram sseureuram*   "in-hale   I thought   ex-hale   that kind of cicada   only cried at night   in-hale ex-hale   but it cries   in-hale   in the morning too   ex-hale   Hyung   I feel like   in-hale ex-hale   my breathing has calmed down a little   oh yeah?" then we'll run at this pace on the way back too   we'll pick it up a little once we can see the Miryang River   in-hale ex-hale   try to keep up with me   don't worry   keep it so you can't talk   where you're starting to pant   in-hale ex-hale   in-hale ex-hale   *sseureuram sseureuram sseureuram sseureuram   sseureuram sseureuram sseureuram sseureuram*   when it gets lighter those cicadas will shut up   but then the large brown cicadas and the ming-mings will come out instead   in-hale ex-hale   "in-hale ex-hale   look, the top of Mount Chiltan is bright red   in-hale ex-hale   is it setting or rising   in-hale ex-hale"   oh, so it is   in-hale ex-hale   like the sky's been beaten until it bleeds   in-hale ex-hale   in-hale ex-hale   in-hale ex-hale   in-hale ex-hale   in-hale ex-hale

Woo-cheol and Woo-gun poured well water over their heads, leaving damp footprints on the veranda as they headed into the house. On the table was barley rice, doenjangguk, giant radish kimchi, and beansprout namul.

"Where's the paper?" Woo-cheol asked his mother, who was bringing in the mul kimchi.

"It never came today." She set the kimchi down in front of him.

"Really? That's odd. That damn Ki-tae must've forgotten to deliver it. Woo-gun, go down to where they sell them in Gagok-dong after lunch."

"Never mind that, listen. In-hye's morning sickness is so bad she can't get up. It gets far worse the more you do nothing, and I told her she ought to move around, but you know how she is."

Woo-cheol looked at his mother's fingers, their joints swollen and nails yellowed.

When I was a child, I thought nobody in the world had fingers as pale, long, and slender as my eomoni, so is my memory wrong, or have they changed?

"Where's Ja-ok?"

"Sleeping next to Omma." Mi-ok took a spoonful of mul kimchi and stuck it in her mouth.

"Aigu, I still have to go to Rye-joo's to get more milk today." Hee-hyang bent her head, fanning her hand near her throat.

Woo-cheol saw Mr. Park from the Yang Shoe Store across the way coming through the garden, athletics shoes dangling from his hands.

"My shoes!" Woo-gun spat out the barley rice that he had just put in his mouth.

"Woo-gun, not in the middle of mealtime!"

"Go try them on," Woo-cheol said, giving him permission to leave the table.

Woo-gun took the shoes from Mr. Park, then sat down on the veranda and put them on.

"Stand on your tiptoes, then tie them. Carefully, so the laces don't get twisted. If you tie them too tight your instep will start to hurt, and if they're too loose you'll come straight out of your shoes, so let your feet tell you how to lace your shoes."

"And when I get to the top?"

"Do a bow, then double-knot it. You'll get injured if you trip on one of your laces and fall down. And no matter how much of a hurry you're in, you shouldn't land on your heel. You'll warp your shoes that way. For athletes, our shoes are our lives."

"They fit perfect." Woo-gun stood up, looking down at his feet.

"Try running in them."

Woo-gun did a loop of the veranda, grinning as he panted for air.

"They're amazing! I feel like I could fly. Hyung, gamsamnida!"

"Your soup'll go cold," Hee-hyang said.

The grandfather clock in the back room rang out seven times. As if perhaps the sound had reminded him of something, Mr. Park, who was sitting on the veranda watching Woo-gun run, twisted his head.

"So they've shut down the *Dong-A Ilbo*."

"What?" Woo-cheol put his spoon down and stopped chewing.

"I got a shipment of hard rubber from the capital the other day—Ha-yong from Hanseong told me. Four days ago, when Sohn Kee-chung won the gold medal, they had a picture of him in the paper, right? I didn't notice when I saw it then, but the Japanese flag wasn't on his chest. Apparently the police rounded up all the journalists from the *Dong-A*. I imagine some of them are still being tortured now, aigo!"

Woo-cheol started riffling through the stack of newspapers on the floor. He found the picture on page two of the August 25 edition. There was Sohn, standing at the top of the medal podium, the world's top runner, and yet his eyes were almost hidden by his laurel wreath, his head hanging like a wilting sunflower. He was wearing the long-sleeved white shirt and long trousers of the Japanese team's uniform, but the red sun that should have been in the center of his chest was not there. Woo-cheol read the picture's caption.

> **Honor goes to our Sohn**
> (Top) Laurel wreath on his head, a potted laurel tree in his hands! Winner of the marathon, "Our Hero, Sohn Kee-chung"
> (Bottom) Sohn Kee-chung, setting off bravely out of the gates (indicated by X)

Silence glared at each of the Lees in turn. Mi-ok looked from face to face; Hee-hyang fiddled with her golden ssanggarakji, a twinned pair of rings, on the ring finger of her left hand, her eyes strangely fixed; Woo-gun, wearing his brand-new running shoes, just stood there, head hanging down, the place where he was biting his lower lip turning white.

Woo-cheol, fist held to his mouth as he looked at the picture, spread his hand, his fingers moving as if he were touching the air as he spoke carefully, putting his fury into each and every word.

"Jegilal, naga dwejeora gaesaekki doreun jjokbari." *Goddamn the dirty fucking bastard Japanese.*

"If you say things like that . . . ," Hee-hyang said.

Mr. Park from the Yang Shoe Store ran his trembling fat hand through his hair, sniffled loudly, then spoke.

"Sohn Kee-chung will probably have to pay for that too, you know."

"It's nothing to do with him!" Woo-gun shouted.

"Shh!" Hee-hyang held her finger up in front of her lips.

"Well, the waenom sure think it's something to do with him. Without a word, Sohn Kee-chung and Nam Sung-yong made the world aware of Korea, when its name had been blotted out by the waejeok. In a way, you know, what they did might be more powerful than all the Heroic Corps' bombs. In Hanseong, at the news of their victory, thousands of Koreans ran outside, even though it was raining and so late at night, just to cheer for them, right? It's a crime to shout 'Long live Korean independence,' so were any of the people who cheered that night charged? But everyone there must have shouted 'Long live Korea' in his heart. Ha-yong brought me a copy of the *Minjok Sinmun* from Hanseong. This is the editorial from August tenth. Woo-gun, read it for us, will you?" Mr. Park pulled a newspaper clipping out from the sleeve of his jeogori and held it out to Woo-gun, who was standing with his fists on his hips.

"'Our Sohn Kee-chung is victorious. Young Sohn sparkled in the world's crowning victory. Let us state for the record, though, that marathon winner Sohn Kee-chung is not only victorious in the world of sports! Although Korea has given Sohn Kee-chung and Nam Sung-yong misfortune and sorrow, they nevertheless have brought victory and laurels to their homeland. Youth of Korea! Do you understand the meaning of these words!'"

Without wiping the sweat from his brow, Mr. Park continued, his voice that of a man enduring pain.

"In the special edition they printed a poem by Sim Hun, right? I couldn't keep myself from crying while I read it; I read it over and over again until I stopped crying and I had it memorized. 'The hand which writes this on the back page of the special edition sharing your good news now trembles with indescribable excitement. The blood that spilled into your hearts under the skies of a foreign land now runs through me, one of twenty-three million. Our eardrums, which have never heard someone proclaim triumph, are bursting now with the sound of the victory bell ringing in the dead of night. The sky of our homeland, forced into a gloomy darkness, lights up at once as if set fire to by the Olympic torch! Oh, I want to cry out! To grab the microphone and appeal to all the people of the world! "After this will you still call us a weak race?"'"

Mr. Park produced a tin of tobacco from his jumeoni pouch and rolled himself a cigarette, but he didn't have any matches in the sleeve of his jeogori. Woo-cheol struck a match and held out the flame; Mr. Park smoked his cigarette with obvious relish, smoke spilling from his mouth as he spoke.

"The moment he broke through the finish line at the Berlin Olympics, Sohn Kee-chung liberated the hearts of twenty-three million of his countrymen. This incident meant a newspaper was forced to close. Maybe Sohn Kee-chung won't be able to run anymore." Mr. Park snuffed out his cigarette with his shoe; with that leg still tensed, he spoke again.

"But no matter how strong the enemy is, the heart alone cannot be held down or snatched away. We will get up. However much they crush us, we will get up again. We are not slaves."

Mr. Park finished what he wanted to say, and Woo-gun shook his shoulders as if he had been pulled out of a scuffle. Mr. Park crossed the Lee family's veranda, all the while nodding his head as if he were a Japanese papier-mâché puppet.

"Now, I've reheated your doenjang. Eat it before it goes cold again." Hee-hyang sounded like a pleading toddler.

Woo-gun took a deep breath, closed his mouth, and put his hand to the bow in the laces of his running shoes. His tears fell one by one from the tip of his nose, wetting the back of his hand and his brand-new shoes.

After finishing his meal, Woo-cheol went out on the veranda. He rubbed the rain-slicked bar of soap on his cheeks and neck, clasping his abeoji's beloved jangdo. *Maeaemmaeaemmaeaem chireureureut chireureureut.* The clouds changed where Woo-cheol stood from light to shade. Suddenly, as if someone was strangling him around the throat, he found it hard to breathe. *Chireureureut chireureureut.* When he looked into the sunlight, he saw, next to the flowers that his sister had grown, the man standing there. He looked shocked, scornful, mournful—a jumble of all those emotions and more. The moment Woo-cheol's and the man's eyes met perfectly, Woo-cheol was dazzled as if he were looking directly at the sun. *Maeaemmaeaemmaeaem.* When he opened his eyes, sweat and blood were running down his neck and down his chest. In the intensity of the heat, he didn't even notice the pain.

Woo-cheol turned skyward and shouted without making a sound.

Long live Sohn Kee-chung!

Long live Korea!

EIGHTEEN

Flickering

| 명멸 | 明滅 |

I open my eyes and **she's there**   in my heart, which once had been as empty
as an abandoned house   slipping through an unlocked door   **she came
inside**   the bodice of her jeogori gently stretched over her breasts   **she
undid the strings of her jeogori**   her trembling white chima   like a
dream   but my breathing is faint   fascinated by the beautiful scenery I
inadvertently stepped onto the mountain path   **she dropped her chima**   it
was steep   if I did not turn back now it would only get steeper   **she looked
up at the moon outside the window**   the new moon in the night
sky   looked like the face of a woman driven mad by jealousy   the chime of
a clock, nothing like the one at home   it was long past time to go   I can't go
home tonight now   I'll have to wait here   for morning   **she came
inside**   how cold her feet were   as if she'd just walked across the river   **she
grabbed out**   I didn't grab for her   her hand stretched out gracefully like a
crane   her cold, cold hands   once they twined themselves around me I
couldn't get away   her grasp tightened   around me as if in a dream   she
begged me   **she kissed me**   her smiling lips   her white, meaningless
smile   we exchanged a glance like moonlight   though perhaps we
exchanged nothing   not a glance   not our lips   our bodies   our hearts   or
our names, nothing   **she embraced me**   I embraced her too   without the
slightest reaction   I know there must be a flower like this   without scent or

color   just   a white flower   but what is it called   **she put her mouth to my
ear**   she had no words to whisper   she had not even a name to whisper   I
felt the moonlight illuminating the night on my skin   I just embraced
her   just to sleep   just embracing   as the moonlight embraces the
water   as the water embraces the moonbeam   I close my eyes and **she
disappears**

SEPTEMBER 6, 1936
LEE JA-OK   DECEASED   SECOND DAUGHTER

Father: Lee Woo-cheol   Mother: Chee In-hye

JANUARY 22, 1937
LEE SHIN-JA   BORN   THIRD DAUGHTER

Father: Lee Woo-cheol   Mother: Chee In-hye

JUNE 2, 1937   **DONG-A ILBO** *RETURNS TO PRINT*

This paper, which was subjected to indefinite suspension by the authority of the governor-general on August 27 of last year, has been
on standby for nine months, or 279 days. Today we have received
notice of the removal of our suspension, and we shall continue operation from today's evening edition.

After their confrontation at Marco Polo Bridge the Japanese and
Chinese armies appear to have started night attacks; from roughly
1:30 a.m. on the 7th, the blasting of rifles, machine guns, mortars,
etc., roared in the darkness without interruption, and the battle continued through the night.

OCTOBER 15–16, 1937
PARTICIPATED IN THE CHŌSEN JINGŪ COMPETITION

Winner of the 5000 meter race   15m28.4s   A new record for
Korea   ranked third in Japan

Placed second in the 10,000 meter race   32m19.2s   ranked fifth
in Japan

JUNE 6, 1937   BATTLE OF POCHONBO

The group of more than two hundred guerrillas who attacked Po-
chon and the police forces pursuing them finally clashed. At roughly
1:00 p.m. on June 5, thirteen kilometers from the opposite bank of
the Amnok River, more than thirty Okawa troops collided with Kim
Il-sung's faction. On the police side, there have been seven fatali-
ties and fourteen casualties, while twenty-five of Kim Il-sung's men
have died and thirty were injured; the fierce battle continues.

She should have been asleep but **she was there**   did she have something
she wanted to say   fumbling, I struck a match and lit the oil lamp   the dim
light cast a red glow on my arms and her face   this woman who was not my
wife   the other woman   she's pregnant   **she looked at my face**   I couldn't
look her in the eyes   a baby?

OCTOBER 2, 1937
"THE OATH OF THE IMPERIAL SUBJECT"

1. We are subjects of the empire   we will devote ourselves to
   emperor and nation with loyalty
2. We, the imperial subjects, will with mutual trust and
   cooperation   strengthen our union
3. We, the imperial subjects, will elevate the imperial way by
   nurturing perseverance and discipline

She gasped   beneath me   she is pinned beneath my body   this woman
who is not my wife   this woman who is not the woman who is
pregnant   **she looked happy each time I visited**   **she reproached me each
time I visited**   **she howled   she laughed   she broke things**   she hid   I
don't know   which woman is which   I don't know   with each blink of the
eye she changes to another woman   **she curled up into a ball   she
stretched out**   inside my chest   like the pontoon bridge that used to
connect one shore of the river to the other   squeaking as the water pushes
against it   squeaking as it's walked over in rubber boots   in geta   I open
my eyes and **she's there**   I close my eyes and **she disappears**

FEBRUARY 22, 1938
NEW LAW ON SPECIAL VOLUNTEER SOLDIERS

The Law on Special Volunteer Soldiers (Imperial Ordinance), which includes the Korean Volunteer System, was promulgated by the Imperial Household News on February 22 and will be implemented at the upcoming Emperor Jimmu Festival on April 3.

There is a woman   not just one   two   I cannot squeeze two women's names into one family name   but on nights like this she intrudes   into the house   into the bedroom   I can't sleep   I don't think my wife can either   we've been in silent battle for over a year now   she asks me nothing   I tell her nothing   no excuses   or evasions   our new daughter breaks the silence with her cries   my wife turns over, using her elbow as a pillow   with her left hand she gently pats our daughter's chest as she hums a lullaby   **sleep-a-bye baby   my precious child   gift from the angels   way up on high   and when the dog barks   it's far from your room   in your starlike eyes   the little bell of sleep rings**   once our daughter started lightly snoring my wife buried her head in her hands   is she in misery because the other woman is about to give birth   or because of the death of our daughter last summer   most likely both   I wrapped our baby girl who had lived only five months up in a straw mat, placed her body on my back in a wooden frame, and carried her to the aejangteo   my wife was four months pregnant and heavy already as we walked   we entered the aejangteo with a jute bag of stones to throw at any spirits that might appear   let's find somewhere with a nice view   my wife said   I laid our daughter down in a place overlooking Mount Jongnam   aigu, she can't breathe   we've got to get her out of that mat   she undid the mat and exposed the tiny little body to the wind   stroked her hair   caressed her cheek   held her hand   "Ja-ok! JA-OK! JA-OK!"   I had to pull their hands apart   and I was the one too who dug the earth and covered our daughter's face   I felt like I was doing the wrong thing   the idea of her becoming part of this mountain was too much   so my wife searched here and there and brought big stones over   you'll hurt the baby   I tried to get her to stop picking up stones but she kept on laying stones on the fresh burial mound she pulled the hairpin from her bun and used it to carve a rock **Jeonju Lee Family Father Lee Woo-cheol Mother Chee In-hye Buried here Lee Ja-ok Dangun year 4369 September 6** oh god the thought of leaving a child so small in a place so lonesome, aigo let's stay a little longer just a little longer, please my wife held her hands to her stomach and looked down at the mound of dirt I thought about how the curve of her stomach pregnant with my child and the curve of the mound where my child was buried were almost the same and I hated myself for thinking that at least my wife wasn't having those same thoughts and if she knew I had thought that she would never forgive me how long was it after that when I started sneaking around **I open my eyes and she's there** I knew that it was wrong it was so easy to commit that crime so, so very easy

JULY 17, 1938
CANCELLATION OF THE TOKYO OLYMPICS OFFICIALLY ANNOUNCED

Welfare Minister Kido announced on July 16 the cancellation of the Tokyo Olympics, and it was officially confirmed in the cabinet meeting the day after.

SEPTEMBER 28, 1938
LEE SHIN-MYEONG   BORN   SECOND SON

Father: Lee Woo-cheol   Mother: An Jeong-hee

NOVEMBER 3, 1938
APPEARED AT THE CHŌSEN JINGŪ COMPETITION

Fifth place in the 5000 meters   15m30.5s
Top ranked in Korea   Fifth ranked in Japan

JULY 8, 1939   NATIONAL CONSCRIPTION ACT

The National Recruitment Ordinance was announced on July 8; it will come into effect on the mainland on July 15, and the portions relating to the colonies of Korea, Formosa, Karafuto, the Kwantung Leased Territory, and the South Seas Mandate will come into effect on October 1.

FEBRUARY 11, 1940
NAME CREATION SYSTEM COMES INTO EFFECT

The law on creation of surnames and changing of given names, which gives the people of the peninsula the freedom to establish a house and change their surnames in order to steadily take advantage of the "internal unity" policy that has been advocated as a fundamental indicator of governance since the appointment of Governor-general Minami, comes into force today.

The women fought   the woman who just had my son   and the woman pregnant with my son or daughter   neither of which is my wife   of course I didn't happen to be present for this   I heard about it from Kanayama, who owns the rice shop   the two women passed each other on Namcheong Bridge   **she took off her rubber shoe and threw it**   there was no doubt which one that was   the woman who had my son   she had the wild temper of a fighting rooster   her shoe hit the other woman right in the stomach   **she crouched down**   **she took off one of her shoes and raised it overhead**   this time it hit her in the back and fell in the river   jugeora   nenyeondo baetsogui aido   da jugeobeoryeo!   go to hell! you   and your damn baby   can go straight to hell!   **She yelled   she moaned   she walked across the bridge in her socks   she pulled herself up by the railing**   I was told she twisted her stiffened nape and vomited   that it was white liquid that came up, perhaps the water used to wash rice   Deog-I across the way helped rub her back   she gagged and when there was nothing more to vomit up she began to cry   well   that's just what I was told, anyway   Kanayama let me know   a woman like that is capable of anything   the night before last   she killed me   "If you don't divorce your wife I'll kill this baby"   she aimed her knife at our son's chest   he was at her breast and from the corner of his mouth came white bubbles, a contented look on his face as he slept   her breasts, unlike my wife's, stuck out so much they got in the way   if you're going to stab someone then stab me   I said **she thrust the knife at my throat** the blade was pointed upward for a second I felt nothing heat radiated from the tip of the knife I opened my eyes but shrouded in a red mist I could see nothing I resisted the pain but I could put up no resistance to death the Tokyo Olympics had been canceled who knew when the next Olympics would be and even if they held another Olympics in four years somewhere in the world Japan might abstain I'm almost thirty-one I'll never run faster than I do right now my dream is being robbed from me my name is being stolen from me all I have left is my life a life of continually being forced into subservience and giving up I let go and closed my eyes I've heard that on the other side of the Samdocheon, the river of forgetfulness, the flowers are in full bloom what kind of flowers are they I feel like it's springtime **Japanese thistle noazami eonggeongkwi chickweed hakobe byeolkkot daisy fleabane himejo'on gaemangcho Asian plantain oobako jilgyeongi green bristlegrass nekojarashi ganga jipul white clover shirotsumekusa tokkipul tufted knotweed akamanma gaeyeokkwi** their names are different in Japan and Korea and I'm sure they call them something different again in China and America and Germany people only have one name a family name they receive from their ancestors and a name given by their parents only one that will be taken to the cemetery it's the shortest and longest story in the world and the most important word in the world the waenom have plucked the names of the Korean people like weeds Lee Woo-cheol **I opened my eyes and she was there** as if to say that what the knife had told her and what she was thinking were different she removed her hand from the knife, finger by finger it fell to the ground she breathed out through clenched teeth before she had finished she let out a sob **I closed my eyes and she disappeared** shall I imagine she's become a flower her shape and color and smell wouldn't change after all **Kunimoto Utetsu Lee Woo-cheol I opened my eyes and she was there** this woman was **An Jeong-hee Yasuda Shizuko she turned herself the other way** as she wept she **pressed my head to her chest** she ruffled my hair she kissed me crazily I thought I would choke on her tongue **she gripped my**

cock suddenly everything became inconsequential lying there next to our son I embraced her **she moaned** the tears sweetened her voice I was stripped naked my bared soul pleading to the heavens I'll give my life so please! I beg you, rid me of this shame!

MARCH 1, 1939
KUNIMOTO UTETSU FILES TO REMOVE CHEE IN-HYE
FROM FAMILY REGISTER

Approved the same day.

SEPTEMBER 3, 1939
BRITAIN DECLARES WAR ON GERMANY

London's diplomatic circles are certain that the British declaration of war is imminent. Parliament will open at 2:45 p.m. on September 2 (9:45 p.m. on the second of Japan time) and is certain to support the declaration of war. The Privy Council of advisers has decided to hold a special meeting soon and will take all possible measures to organize the wartime cabinet.

Carrying my son on my shoulders I ran around the well *hee-hee!*
clip-clop clip-clop clip-clop clip-clop the son my wife gave me my precious, precious eldest son *clip-clop clip-clop* the heir to the Lee family *hee-hee!* He doesn't know *hee-hee! Clip-clop clip-clop* a woman who isn't your omma has given birth to your younger brother the woman who instigated me no forced me into divorcing your omma by threatening to kill your younger brother *clip-clop* divorce *clip-clop* your appa and omma aren't married anymore *clip-clop clip-clop* it was a sneak attack your omma knew nothing because women rarely see the family register it's entirely possible she may never realize it at all *hee-hee! Clip-clop clip-clop hee-hee!* Your appa is low-down *clip-clop* as a man *clip-clop* as a husband *clip-clop* as a father as a person low-down and dirty! *Hee-hee! Hee-hee!* With my son still on my shoulders I ran out the gate *clip-clop clip-clop* in the shadow of the telegraph pole **she was**

standing she was absent-minded, forgetting that she was pregnant and that she was standing in front of her lover's house **she was wearing a bright red chima** the red chima lapped at her legs like a blazing fire I narrowed my eyes I was overwhelmed with anger that she would wear a bright red chima like that, one that would draw everyone's attention I let my son down from my shoulders Appa! But I still want a piggyback! My son stamped his feet just a minute, son I'll put you back up and we'll run up the steps to Yeongnamnu I approached her and asked quietly what's happened **she looked down, avoiding my eyes** it was still spring but tiny droplets of sweat lined her pale, soft brow of course she must be in the final month now I felt sorry for beautiful women even in their final month of pregnancy I imagined that no matter how many children this woman had she would never have a mother's face she was at her most beautiful when she was distracted like this each time I met her I thought how beautiful she was and each time I met her I thought how pitiful she was I must think that because somehow she's lacking because somehow she's flawed because somehow she's broken we meet we embrace and after we've parted I'm not even sure that I even was with her I always feel as if I've lost sight of her in a fog **she was a dancer at the OK Café** one-two-three one-two-three pale soft as if floating one-two-three one-two-three one-two-three one-two-three **she waved the hem of her dress in front of me** I took her hand and followed the steps one-two-three one-two-three one-two-three one-two-three **when I turned my back she was gone** "Who's she?" my son asked oh, nobody I picked him up and put him on my shoulders, holding tight to his thighs right now don't let go of Daddy's head athlete number 962 from the district of Korea Kunimoto Utetsu on your marks get set go! *Clip-clop clip-clop clip-clop clip-clop hee-hee! Hee-hee!*

MAY 2, 1940
KUNIMOTO NOBUTETSU BORN THIRD SON

Father: Kunimoto Utetsu Mother: Kaneda Yoshiko

AUGUST 10, 1940
PUBLICATION OF ALL KOREAN-LANGUAGE
NEWSPAPERS SUSPENDED

This paper will be discontinued with this issue as the final issue in accordance with the newspaper control policy of the governor-general, and Dong-A Ilbo Co., Ltd., was dissolved today by a resolution passed at an extraordinary general meeting of shareholders held in the meeting room of the head office today. We would like to express our gratitude to all our readers for their continued support for this newspaper over the past twenty years, and we pray for their long-term prosperity, happiness, and health.

SEPTEMBER 28, 1940
TRIPARTITE PACT OF JAPAN, GERMANY, AND ITALY

NOW A "HISTORICAL VOW"—WITH A CLINKING OF
GLASSES AND THUNDEROUS CHEERS

"Long live the emperor!" "Long live Führer Hitler!" "Long live the Italian emperor! Long live Mussolini!" "Long live the Japanese Empire!"—Cheers filled with deep emotion were heard echoing at the foreign minister's residence in Sannencho, Kojimachi-ku, on the evening of the September 27, a starry, moonlit night when the dew fell gracefully.

SEPTEMBER 30–OCTOBER 1, 1940
PARTICIPATED IN THE KOREAN QUALIFIERS
FOR THE MEIJI SHRINE GAMES

5000m   Second place   15m5.2s
Second place in Korea   Eleventh place in Japan

10,000m   Winner   33m23.2s
First place in Korea   Thirteenth place in Japan

NOVEMBER 27–DECEMBER 6, 1940
PARTICIPATED IN MIYAZAKI-UNEBI EKIDEN RACE

Korea and Formosa regions win   Six single stage victories

FORMOSA AND KOREA LEAD—AFTER A FURIOUS BATTLE BETWEEN MIYAZAKI AND NOBEOKA

The outstanding talents of the Korean and Formosan forces were Kunimoto (Korea), who overtook five people at once in the second stage to take the lead, Nishizaki (Formosa) in the seventh stage, and the last runner, Oyama (Korea), whose efforts must be praised, though none should be overlooked for commendation. Kanto advanced to the top of the third stage neck and neck with Tanaka, but due to Futami's slump in the second stage the Korean and Formosan forces were given the title. . . . What especially impressed this reporter after the first day of the race is how the middle-distance runners' efforts were more outstanding and speedier than those of the more solid marathon runners.

KOREA-FORMOSA VICTORY ASSURED—2ND PLACE KANTO SIX MINUTES BEHIND

Korea and Formosa were temporarily held back by the Kantō region as it appeared Kanto was closing in on them, but as always, Kunimoto's superhuman efforts shut them out, as Rakenamo, Kaneda, and Kunimoto set the highest stage record; as usual, Kunimoto displayed his tremendous strength, and his performance, alongside that of Sekiguchi from Manchuria, was among the best in this race.

A BATTLE WITH NO STRAGGLERS—MIYAZAKI UNEBI EKIDEN RACE REVIEW

This race was interesting, with participants from age forty to the tender age of seventeen, with the result that those athletes who were in or around thirty gave more remarkable performances than the younger athletes, showing that not only does experience clearly count in a race, but also underscoring how difficult it is to be a long-distance runner and the value of striving for a long time.

I bought souvenirs for the children at the final point of the race in Nara Prefecture   for my fifteen-year-old brother I got a knitted running top   for my seven-year-old son a papier-mâché deer   for my ten-year-old daughter a

heart-shaped folding fan   for my three-year-old daughter a traditional
doll   for my two-years-and-two-months-old son with the woman who was
not my wife, a frog-shaped ceramic bell   and for my seven-month-old son with
the other woman, a drum decorated with flames   it wouldn't all fit in my
knapsack, so I packed it all in a wicker trunk and gave it to the porter   From
Shimonoseki I sailed on the *Satsuma Maru, splash-roll   splash-roll*   at Busan
station I got on the express   *chikchik pokpok   chikchik pokpok*   I didn't buy
anything for my three women   I didn't imagine they wanted makeup or
trinkets   one of them longed to change   another longed never to
change   which would my wife want, not to change?   Or to do so?   She must
long to go back to when none of this had happened   but   that's   not
possible   now that my sister, father, and our daughter were dead, they could
not return to this world   nor could my two sons return to those two women's
wombs   you can't make it so that what's happened never did   you can only
accept it has happened   no matter how hard a thing it is to take in   if you
can't let it inside you   then it will stay outside for you to carry   to
shoulder   to drag after yourself   something to heave   heave-ho until you
die   heave-ho   heave-ho   heave-ho   heave-ho   and me?   What I long
for   is not to end anything   it's to end everything   ending everything and
starting nothing is a kind of change I suppose

    At Miryang Station there weren't any rickshaws waiting   I walked
quickly, head down, past my wife's family's rice shop   I went down from the
concrete path to the riverside and got on a sweetfish-fishing boat   the
captain seemed like a different person than when we'd scattered my father's
remains   the boat floated on the icy December waters of the Miryang
River   slowly Mount Yongdu approached   as slowly Mount Jongnam got
farther away   the captain started to sing, his mouth moving as if he were
chewing on a piece of dried squid   **"Tie a string to the willow tree   but
you'll never tie down the passing spring   the butterflies love the flowers,
dear   but still they fall off every year"**   as I listened to his off-tune song
without really listening my eyelids became heavier   **I closed my eyes and she
was there**   not my wife or either of my mistresses   a woman I had never
been with or shared a glance with   never spoken to or passed by   she stared
at me, crying   neither the woman looking at me   nor I could blink   **a**

**willow is a willow   a butterfly a butterfly   unfaithfulness is the revenge of
a dream   I have feelings for you, my dear   but still you go off on your own**

I went through the gate and my brother came running out   it's Shin-tae
he's sick   he's had a fever for over a week now   his hair's falling out   the
doctor gave him something for it but his fever hasn't gone down at all   I
threw the presents for the children down on the veranda and went inside, my
overcoat still on   my son looked up at me with bleary eyes and his pale,
chapped lips began to move

"Appa   wow   your name was in the Asahi newspaper   Uncle cut it out
for you   you won six stages, that's so good   how many stages did you run?"

"Seven"

"If you put them all together how far is that?"

"Four hundred and fifty ri, I think?   Fast runners have to run as many
stages as we can   Shin-tae   gwaenchana?"

"You must've passed so many ilbon saram"

"Yes   in the second stage I passed five of them"

"I   wish I could have gone to Miyazaki with you to cheer you on   as
always, Kunimoto's superhuman efforts shut them out   superhuman means
you're so fast you're almost not a person   Uncle told me   it's true   even
when you have me on your shoulders you run fast as a bird, Appa   like your
feet aren't even touching the ground   when I'm better I'll take the clipping
to show Jeong-hak at the naengmyeon place   as always, Kunimoto's
superhuman efforts shut them out"

My son babbled on deliriously then let out a huge sigh   he closed his eyes
and immediately began to snore   I gently laid my palm to his heart   his
heart was pounding as fast as it could in his little chest   *thump-thump!*
Thump-thump!   Thump-thump!   Thump-thump!

APRIL 13, 1941
JAPANESE-SOVIET NONAGGRESSION PACT FORMED

The government of the USSR and the government of Japan, in the
interest of ensuring peaceful and friendly relations between the
two countries, solemnly declare that the USSR pledges to respect
the territorial integrity and inviolability of Manchukuo and Japan

pledges to respect the territorial integrity and inviolability of the Mongolian People's Republic.

Japgwiya mulleogara!   the mudang, wearing a red Janggun outfit, purified my son's body over and over with a knife   we rolled him up in a straw mat and carried him to the garden   on top of the straw mat we put some dried cod to ward off evil   I shoveled up some earth and covered him with it   aigu, not my son!   My precious, precious oldest son!   The Lee family heir!   Aigo!   I know she told us that this heojanggeori is to trick the gods into thinking he's already dead so they can't steal his soul but   wrapping him up like a corpse and covering him in dirt is just too much!   The mudang wrote on three eggs with a brush   **Lee Shin-tae June 8, 1933   Daesu daemyeong**   his name   his birthday   our wish for his health and long life   the mudang raised the hand holding the eggs   the shells cracked with a splosh   the yolks slowly ran down my son's body   binaida   binaida   Janggun, we pray to you   please bring this boy back to life   my son, carried out of the straw mat now, simply breathed out fear   breathed in worry   in   out   in   out   this uhwangut that started at five in the evening had still not ended by two in the morning   my son withstood it all without a moan or a single tear   aigu, despite the pain he must have been in   so much unbearable pain   aigo   in the middle of the josanggeori the pounding of the drums suddenly stopped   the mudang channeled my sister, now a cheonyeo ghost   danyeowatseumnida   *aigo, Eomoni   aigo, Abeoji   hello, Woo-gun   aigu, how big you've grown   and this must be my niece, the one who was born the day I drowned   and the girl next to her is my niece too   yes I can tell   yes   yes   even without an introduction everybody knows who you are   it's something in our blood, the smell of it   smells the same as the blood I shed   Oh, Shin-tae   I never met or spoke to you but   I'm your auntie   breathe in the smell of my blood   I'm all alone in a cold and lonesome place and there's no help for it so   I thought I'd close your mouth and your eyelids and take you to the other world with me but   you've done this gut and summoned me here so   I think I can wait a little longer   if they hadn't done this gut, on the next rainy night your guts would've jammed and you would've died   but   now   your auntie has massaged*

them   tomorrow you'll be able to swallow food again   first eat some pumpkin
porridge   one spoonful at a time, slowly   once you can eat that then try acorn
rice cakes   then after that   get your omma to make you some yugwa   hey,
In-hye unni   that day   you promised me that when I got home from school
we'd make yugwa together   the mudang smiled at her   and my wife hid her
face in her hands and shook her head, sobbing   all the flowers in the garden
were in bloom   the weeping forsythia   the azaleas   the dandelions   the
shepherd's purse   the violets   if my sister had been alive she would've sang
as she picked them   and arranged them in old bottles and cups   the house
would've been filled with flowers   the mudang danced, holding the knife
between her teeth   the baksu beat the drum and the jing as he recited the
Heart Sutra   mahabanyabaramildasimgyeong gwanjajaebosal   haengsimba
nyabaramilda   dum-dum-dum   ting-ting-ting!   The just-sprouted leaves of
the willow tree too quivered at the sound of the drum and jing   dum-dum-
dum   ting-ting-ting!

MAY 6, 1941   STALIN BECOMES SOVIET LEADER

The Soviet dictator Joseph Stalin, the "Man of Steel" as his name
implies, has been appointed chairman of the Council of People's
Commissars (the cabinet), replacing Mr. Molotov, who had served as
chairman and commissariat for foreign affairs and will now serve
as vice chairman.

My son's condition worsened visibly by the day   did we fuck up the
heojanggeori and the gods discovered that he's alive   or did the spirit of my
sister grab hold of him and won't let go   either way the uhwangut
failed   even though we borrowed money from all our relatives and spent
over five hundred yen on the gut it did nothing   I carried him to Miryang
Hospital over by the station in my handcart   I just don't think there's
anything we can do for him here   Dr. Shimomura wrote us a referral for the
Jesaeng Hospital in Busan   In-hye, Shin-tae, and I got the train to
Busan   in the examining room we listened to the doctor   it might be a
communicable disease so if I can ask the family to wait outside, please   my
wife trained her eyes on the white walls of the hallway and said   "I will be

staying in the hospital with him   I am his mother   If I leave him here and go home I will go crazy   I will do anything to make sure he lives   I don't care what I have to do in return   If I could change places with him I'd do it right now   aigo!"   My mother took over running the house and store and caring for the children and a month passed   my wife let me know by postcard how our son was doing but   what I'd received two days ago wasn't a postcard but a sealed letter

To Shin-tae's father

Shin-tae is in an extremely serious condition. I am overwhelmed by the inability of medicine to even pin down the cause or name of his illness and my own inability to ease our son's pain. For the last few days, perhaps because of the morphine he's being given for the pain, when he is awake he is muttering deliriously, talking nonsense, far more than he is lucid, and the thought that he may never return to consciousness makes me frightened to be by his side watching over him.

I believe you may have forgotten, but June 8 is Shin-tae's eighth birthday. He wants to go home. He wants to see his father. For a month I have been with him day and night and have not caught his illness, so I believe it may not be communicable. It may be an incurable disease, one that he has had since he was born. During his rounds yesterday the doctor told me that the fact that he is breathing and talking is in itself a miracle, he may fall into a coma at any time, and that if there is anyone who would like to see him they should see him while he is conscious.

This March marked eleven years since we married, and I have rarely asked anything of you. I may not ask anything from you after this. This is my last request. On June 8, for Shin-tae's birthday, will you come visit him? I hate to think about what might be, but if he should succumb to this illness it would be so very awful. Please accept my request.

Shin-tae's mother

The light of that June evening came through the glass window of the communicable disease ward so peacefully   the room was still and silent in the light of the sun   only the sound of my shoes softly padding across the room reverberated   **room 717   Kunimoto Shinta   No Visitors**   I stood outside the door until I felt I was ready   as I reached out for the doorknob   my wife came out and lowered her head   she walked like that off to the waiting room   I suppose she meant that she wanted me to see him alone   raising the corners of my mouth in hopes that it might look like a smile, I approached the bed   the oxygen tubes stuck in his nostrils   his arms reddened with traces of injections   his hollow cheeks   his eyes and ears, which looked bizarrely large   his bald head becoming inflamed by red boils   with all the strength in my face I kept my smile   I felt that if I relaxed it for a moment I would scream and collapse in tears   my son moved his mouth, so I put my face near to his

Abeoji

Shin-tae   happy birthday

How   old am I?

You're eight years old today

I'll start school next year, right?

Yeah

I thought   when I started school I'd run

Oh

I wanted to run with you and Uncle

Oh

But   that won't happen

Why?

Because   I'm dying

What are you talking about?

Appa   I   don't want to die

And you're not going to either

I'm   feeling   a little sleepy

Then get some sleep

If it's dark when I wake up   I wonder if I died and they buried me   and I get so scared

Your omma is always with you

Hey   do you and Omma get along?

Of course we do

Appa   when I come home I want a piggyback ride

Sure   I'll take you wherever you want to go   Athlete number 962
representing Korea   Kunimoto Utetsu   on your marks   get set   go!
Clip-clop   clip-clop-clip-clop   clip-clop   clip-clop   hee-hee!   Hee-hee!

JULY 13, 1941
KUNIMOTO SHINTA   DECEASED   ELDEST SON

Father: Kunimoto Utetsu   Mother: Ikegami Hitoe

Beating the four corners of the coffin with wooden spikes   my brother
and I carried it across the garden on our shoulders   then turned it toward
the front of the house and raised and lowered it three times   we bowed and
went through the gate   Mr. Jeong, the neighborhood unit head for Ne-il-
dong, had told us that the funeral palanquin could not be borrowed for
someone who had died of a communicable disease   so we had to put the
coffin on my handcart and pull it along   at the Miryang Public Crematorium
I set up the place of enshrinement   and on the offering table I put
white rice   tangguk   watermelon   gourds   old-fashioned rice cakes   and
buchimgae   with the obituary had come rumors that he died of typhoid
fever   so no one came to pay their respects   the attendant avoided even
getting near the coffin   so my brother and I were the ones who had to   push
the coffin into the oven   and pour on the oil and light the fire   we watched
as the coffin was engulfed by flames then went outside   my mother, wife,
and daughters were sobbing, grasping at each other's wrists and
shaking   **aigo   aigu, Shin-tae ya   Shin-tae!   Aigo   aigo**   only my
brother and I kept our wits   I opened the oven and shoveled out the ashes   I
put on white gloves and began to pick out my son's bones   wiped them with
silk   ground them in the mortar   put them in a wooden box   as I did so
my brother was in a piece of land to the north of the crematorium building
an altar to the sasin, the god of death, and to sansin, the mountain spirit   I
wrapped the yugolham containing his remains in a white cloth and went to
where my brother was   the women followed me, weeping   **aigo!   aigo!**
the head of our area had asked me to have him cremated in Busan   and

scatter his ashes in Busan Harbor   I told my wife this in the morgue at
Jesaeng Hospital   she did not nod   the morning of the day he died   he
strained his almost nonexistent voice to say   he wanted to go home   I put
my mouth to his ear and told him   let's go home   Omma will carry
you   Shin-tae didn't have a contagious disease   for nine months we
used the same chopsticks   I slept with him in my arms   if it were
communicable I'd have gotten it   before I got on the sweetfish-fishing boat
I asked my wife

Do you want to come with me?   **Shin-tae!   Shin-tae!**   she could only cry
out our son's name   I got on the boat with his remains   the captain was the
same as when I came home from running the ekiden   the captain struck the
riverbed with the pole   and the boat shook itself free of the women's crying
and left the shore   **aigo   aigo   Shin-tae ya   Shin-tae!**   everything was just
as it had been when my father died   the only differences were   that then it
was midwinter   and now it was midsummer   and that there was nobody to
sing the leader of the funeral cortege's song   I whispered it myself   **Oh rosa
rugosa of Myeongsasimri   do not mourn that your flowers will fall   when
spring comes back again   you will bloom once more   but my life once
passed   is like a fallen leaf**   the captain, gripping the pole, began to move his
mouth as if chewing dried squid and joined in   **eoiya   eoheoya   ah   ah
ha   eoheoya   ah**   the boat stopped   I undid the tie of the white cloth   I
poured my son's remains into the water   I did not want to go back to the
shore   **Oh rugosa rose of Myeongsasimri   do not mourn that your flowers
will fall   when spring comes back again   you will bloom once more   but
my life, once passed   is like a fallen leaf**   the captain, perhaps sensing my
feelings   let the boat float at the same speed as the water   **eoiya
eoheoya   ah   ah ha   eoheoya   ah   eoiya   eoheoya   ah   ah
ha   eoheoya   ah**   on each bank of the river there were children playing in
the water stark naked   unconsciously I searched among them for my son
I knew he was dead   and yet   I didn't know   why   I couldn't see him
among them   I didn't know   once we were around the sandbar I could
see the red pavilion on Yeongnamnu   take us around again   this
time very slowly   instead of a response the captain sang again   **eoiya
eoheoya   ah   ah ha   eoheoya   ah**   the boat slowly passed by my

family clad in their jute mourning clothes and straw sandals **eoiya
eoheoya ah ah ha eoheoya ah** on the third loop around the sandbar
when I saw the red-and-white chimney of the wool company the shimmering
of the river vanished and the peak of Mount Jongnam was cast in red I asked
the captain and he took me back to the bank where my family was
waiting my mother, brother, wife, and daughters were all sitting on a rock
staring at the movement of the water as if engrossed all their faces were
burned from spending the day in the sun I got out of the boat and my wife,
jute cloth on her head, said in a caressing voice **if you hadn't come to see
him I had decided to kill you I'm grateful** Mr. Jeong, the neighborhood
unit chief of Ne-il-dong, must have notified someone because the ilbon
saram from the health department barged in to disinfect our house we left
all the windows and doors open all night but we couldn't get rid of the
stench of the disinfectant still in her mourning clothes my wife carried our
son's clothes and bedding out piled it up near the well and burned it and
when it had all turned to ash and none of our son's things were left my wife
pulled the taehang out from the dresser and took his dried, shriveled
umbilical cord in the palm of her hand I'm going to go for a run, I said I
left the house and I never went back again **I open my eyes and she's
there** I started sleeping at her shop a place near the Miryang Theater a
bar with kisaeng girls that sold lots of booze the place was called
Olympic a long-distance runner who couldn't make it to the Olympics,
sleeping in a bar called Olympic and what's worse three doors down was
the Dong-A Guesthouse, run by the woman who had been my abeoji's
mistress ha what a travesty in the theatrical sense I spent all day every
day idling grief took the color from my days it filled in the ups and downs
of life every little thing was unbearable I was surplus to all requirements
"Why did everyone in your family have such terrible fates? your father
died of blood poisoning sister drowned eldest son died of an unknown
disease and I heard your father's mistress has a disease of the womb and is
addicted to opium and that your half sister's mouth and limbs are paralyzed
due to polio aigu a man who poured his father's and eldest son's bones
into the river if you traveled all of Korea you'd struggle to find another as
unlucky I don't know what I'll do if my sons get it too"

"Sons?"

"I just know this one will be another boy"

"How do you know?"

"A woman just knows   call it intuition"

She slid her panties down, jureureuk   she was a woman who never minded getting naked in front of me or in front of her son   her lower stomach was puffed out like a pigeon's breast   I got her pregnant not after my son died   but while he was still alive   while he was struggling for his life in the hospital   I turned away and she clung to me, arms around my neck   **yeobo   a nae sarang**   the swells of her breasts and stomach pressed against my back   our son, three years old next month, clung to my legs   Appa   Appa!   I wanna clip-clop   I freed myself from her body   put our son on my shoulders and ran outside   Athlete number 962 representing Korea   Kunimoto Utetsu   on your mark   get set   go! *Clip-clop-clip-clop-clip-clop-clip-clop   clip-clop   hee-hee!   Hee-hee!*

OCTOBER 26, 1941
PARTICIPATED IN THE CHŌSEN JINGŪ COMPETITION

10,000 meters—victory   34m16.3s
Top ranked in Korea   thirteenth in Japan

Running around the levee for the first time in days   I heard the sound of someone's breathing behind me, getting closer   in-hale ex-hale   in-hale ex-hale   it was my brother   my brother silently ran up beside me   he was about the same height as me now   and though we were running at a four-minute-per-kilometer pace his breathing was not the least bit affected   in-hale ex-hale   in-hale ex-hale   in the short time I hadn't seen him his Adam's apple now stuck out and his facial hair had gotten thicker   he'd turned from a boy to a young man   in-hale ex-hale   in-hale ex-hale   **dondollari dondollari   dondollariyo**

His voice has changed, I realized   in-hale ex-hale

"You told me," he said   in-hale ex-hale   "that when I'm running alone I should run at a speed where I can still hum   **omaksari   chogajibe**

dondollariyo omaksari chogajibe dondollariyo see it matches
the rhythm of running perfectly   but a week ago   when I couldn't sing the
dondollari dondollari dondollariyo part anymore I switched to the
geoseureomi song"   in-hale ex-hale

"The geoseureomi song?"

"It's pretty good   just try singing it"

"**sso sso ssoraisso geoseureomido namdaecheone geoseureomi
banjjakgeorinda** in-hale ex-hale **geoseureomi oneuldo sso sso
ssoraisso geosoreomido namdaecheone geoseureomi banjjakgeolinda**
oh I meant to say   the jangdo   in-hale ex-hale   I've been using it to shave
with   it was Abeoji's, wasn't it"

"In-hale ex-hale   you can have it"

"gomapda   in-hale ex-hale   I'll take good care of it"

In-hale ex-hale   in-hale ex-hale

Things were good when I was running   dealing with drunks at the bar
was fine   what I couldn't handle happened once I went to bed   with
a six-months-pregnant woman and our three-year-old son sleeping next to
me   in the darkness it didn't matter who was there   the darkness rebuked
me   it was waiting for an opportunity to punish me   the darkness
questioned me repeatedly   even if it doesn't censure me and say I'm
unforgivable I'm guilty   crime   punishment   crime   punishment   a
justification? For who?   My son died   and as my son is turned to the
darkness and listening   what justification can I make that would recover
him   it's all too late now   now   I am   nobody   it's   all over   for me
now   I want it to be all over   if I could stifle all my memories when I slept
how much easier it would be   no matter how happy and splendid a
day   remembering any day from my past is agonizing   I can only think
about a day that might happen in the future   tomorrow   even if it's worse
than today   even if it's the worst day   I cannot avoid tomorrow   even times
like this it's slowly creeping up on me   speaking of creeping up   I haven't
had that dream in years now   the one about the man who looks a lot like me
slitting his own throat with the jangdo   my brother looks a lot like me   not
just in terms of stature   but his face and his style of running too   will that
jangdo be aimed at his throat next?

DECEMBER 8, 1941
JAPANESE EMPIRE DECLARES WAR ON THE UNITED
STATES AND THE BRITISH EMPIRE

IMPERIAL RESCRIPT

WE, by the grace of Heaven, Emperor of Japan, seated on the throne occupied by the same dynasty from time immemorial, enjoin upon ye, Our loyal and brave subjects:

We hereby declare War on the United States of America and the British Empire. The men and officers of Our Army and Navy shall do their utmost in prosecuting the war. Our public servants of various departments shall perform faithfully and diligently their respective duties; the entire nation with a united will shall mobilize their total strength so that nothing will miscarry in the attainment of Our war aims. [. . .]

In witness whereof, we have hereunto set Our hand and caused the Grand Seal of the Empire to be affixed at the Imperial Palace, Tokyo, this seventh day of the twelfth month of the fifteenth year of Shōwa, corresponding to the 2,602nd year from the accession to the throne of Emperor Jimmu.

OUR SEA EAGLES BOMB HAWAI'I

SEA BATTLE UNFOLDS IN HONOLULU BAY

US TRANSPORT SHIP TORPEDOED

AIR RAID ON PHILIPPINES, GUAM

ATTACK ON SINGAPORE

SHOCK ATTACK, LANDING ON MALAY PENINSULA

HONG KONG OFFENSIVE BEGINS

FEBRUARY 6, 1942
KUNIMOTO NOBUYOSHI   BORN   FOURTH SON

Father: Kunimoto Utetsu   Mother: Yasuda Shizuko

MAY 8, 1942
KOREAN CONSCRIPTION SYSTEM ANNOUNCED

The hopes of Korean compatriots regarding the enforcement of the conscription system in Korea have been fierce since the China Incident, and since the implementation of the Imperial Edict on Army Special Volunteers in 1938, the results have indeed been truly satisfactory. As the momentum of the unification of Korea and Japan picks up pace, at the cabinet meeting held on May 8, the government submitted a proposal to enforce a conscription system in Korea and proceed with preparations for various ships that could be implemented by 1945. The matter was decided without objection.

OCTOBER 29–NOVEMBER 3, 1942
FINAL MEIJI SHRINE GAMES

Opening remarks

"I would like to offer a few remarks upon the occasion of the opening ceremony of the thirteenth Meiji Shrine Games.

"As this athletics meet is graciously attended by Their Majesties the Emperor and Empress, and has received a gracious decree from the games' director, His Highness Prince Mikasa, we are further honored by the appearance here of representatives of other palaces; the competitors and all involved must feel a tremendous sense of emotion here today. Let us hope that, in honor of the decree by His Imperial Highness the president, we shall all strive further still to train our bodies and minds and do our utmost to support the sacred work of the construction of a Greater East Asia.

"In addition, we hope that those of you from Manchukuo who are participating today will take the opportunity of this tournament to further the promotion of friendship between the peoples of Japan and Manchukuo, representing one hundred million people with one dream, and will find ways to contribute to the end of the Greater East Asia War. With the further participation of people from all over the Greater East Asian Co-prosperity Sphere, from the northern branch, the central-south branch, Mongolia, and the South Seas, we truly cannot hold back our delight at how this competition has been all the more enriched."

NOVEMBER 3, 1942
KUNIMOTO YOSHIKA   DECEASED   MOTHER

Notification received from head of household Kunimoto Utetsu same day

I opened the door of the Olympic Restaurant and she was there "**Darling   your mother is dead**   I didn't know what she'd said to me   it was like my ears had suddenly been pierced through with a stick   she said one night a week ago your brother came in the bar   'Eomoni is about to die,' he said   he asked how to reach you   but I didn't even know   so there was no way to send a telegram   your competition ended on November third   so where have you been and what have you been doing?   aigu, the funeral and burial are already over"

Thump-thump!   Thump-thump!   There was a pounding in my ears, no words would come out   I put my knapsack down in the entrance hall and went to the house   *thump-thump!   Thump-thump!*   My heart hurt   like it had been smashed   can it stand this   I saw the gates   they came closer   I went through them   if my wife came out now   I would stare unblinkingly   at her eyes   instead of my wife my brother came out   his face was wet   rain?   I looked up at the sky   it was raining   in drops so big you could almost count them drop by drop

"Your wife left"

"When?"

"We didn't know where you were   or when you might come back   so she and I went to the government office to submit the death certificate   that's when she saw the family register   and realized that she had been removed from it   she was gone by the next morning"

"And the girls?"

"They're here"

"Aigu   she ran off and left the kids"

"Mi-ok and I went to her parents' house   we asked where she went   but they said they couldn't tell us"

"Not 'We don't know'   but 'We can't tell you'"

"They said she's not in Miryang anymore"

My brother pursed his lips   and looked down at his ends of his shoes like a little boy   not the athletic shoes I gave him   his feet have grown   they look bigger than mine now   my future as a track athlete has come to an end   but my brother is still seventeen   he can aim for the next Olympics   and the one after that too   oh, what am I doing thinking about that right now   I wasn't here for my own mother's death   I have been so utterly unfilial   and at the very end I have done the worst   my mouth tingles as if I'd just been punched   did my brother punch me?   Is it possible to get punched and not realize it?   but   if someone slit my throat with a jangdo right now I might not even notice   that jangdo   I wonder if my brother's still using it   I raised my eyes and chin just a little and looked at my brother's face   he had gotten even taller than me

"Where is she buried"

"In Gyodong"

"Take me"

He handed me an umbrella, which I opened   my two daughters came out   in the short while that I hadn't seen them they'd grown   Mi-ok was twelve   Shin-ja was about five   *hudeudeuk*   the north winds blowing down from Mount Bihak hit the trees and houses making a sound   *hwing-hwing-hwing-hwing*   I picked up my younger daughter and brought them both under the umbrella   with my brother's back as my only guidance I started walking   *hwing-hwing-hwing-hwing*   muddy water sloshed into my rubber shoes   *cheobeok cheobeok   cheobeok cheobeok*   on the slope of the Gyodong Memorial Ridge underneath a large sawtooth oak was my eomoni's grave   it was so fresh that I could still smell the earth   I put my daughter down from my back and faced the grave   for the first time Eomoni's death struck me as reality   I could not even put my hands together or apologize   I squeezed my two daughters' hands and brushed the rain from their bangs, my two girls who had lost their grandmother and mother at the same time   "Can we live with you, Abeoji?"

"Of course you can   you're my precious little girls aren't you"   I took a handkerchief out of the sleeve of my jeogori   I wiped the snot from my own nose then helped my youngest blow her nose   *hnnngh*   more   hard as you can   that's it   other side   *hnnngh*   how many children had I helped blow

their nose   aigu, my first son, washed away in the river   my second daughter
buried in the earth   more of my family is dead than alive, my
god   **aigo   ireolsuga!**

Drip   drip   drip   drip   drip   drip   all through the night I heard
the sound of water falling   it was a long, long night   it was a long, long
morning   the rain fell without a pause   soaking her burial
mound   drenching my eomoni's face and body   **aigo   ireolsuga!**   I
stepped out of the bedroom and smelled doenjang-guk   is Mi-ok
cooking   not my twelve-year-old cooking with a knife   **aigo   ireolsuga!**
What should I do   there's nothing I can do   I have to sell the house and
shop   and take my brother and girls back to the Olympic   what will she say,
I wonder   if it was just my brother she'd happily take him in   but my two
girls?   If I give into her   her condition will be marriage without a
doubt   she wasn't satisfied by me removing In-hye from the family
register   **why won't you add me to your register?   I've given birth to two
of your sons!   do you want your sons   to go to school and get
bullied   because they saw their own eomoni get married?**   my eldest
daughter set the doenjangguk and bellflower namul on the table, looking
down at the ground   I picked up my chopsticks and took a bit of the
namul   it was a little too salty but it wasn't bad

"Abeoji   how is it?"

"It's good"

"Oh   I'm glad"

I looked at my brother, who was silently drinking his doenjangguk

"I think I'm going to have to sell the house and the store"

"And then what?"

"Go to the Olympic . . ."

"I'm going to go live with our uncle in Michon-ri"

"I see . . ."

"Hyung   what about Mi-ok and Shin-ja"

"They're my daughters   I'll make sure nothing bad happens to them"

My brother crunched a piece of the kkakdugi my eldest had prepared   the
girls started crying again   I stood on the veranda and stared out at the

garden   the rain had turned into a light drizzle   I went outside without an
umbrella *buseul buseul   buseul buseul   buseul buseul*   should I go to her
first and beg her to let my daughters come live there   or should I go to my
wife's parents first and ask them where she's gone   but if they did tell me
where she is   what would I do then   I can't bow my head to her and ask
her forgiveness for removing her from the family register   and tell her
I want us to start things over again   I can't tell her that we can't live
together   but that I'm begging her to come back to this house and take care
of my brother and our daughters again   and besides how should I face
my father- and mother-in-law?   My legs moved   left   oenjjok   right
oreunjjok   my body was not pushing through the air   it was like the air was
unfurling the path ahead and accompanying me on it   oreunjjok   oenjjok
oreunjjok   oenjjok   before I realized it   I was through the chestnut grove
and standing on the slope of Mount Yongdu   right where my sister had
slipped   a gust of wind blew   *hwing-hwing-hwing-hwing*   the wind clearly
called out my name   Lee Woo-cheol!   The wind pushed at my back
hwing-hwing-hwing-hwing   no   I can't do it   I'm a father to three little boys
and two little girls   I'm not allowed to die   I pulled my right leg back one
step and spun right on my heel   I leaned into the darkness that my life
awaits   my legs would not move   I admonished them   I have to live   even
if I can never again get back the real feeling of life   I still have to go on
living   I chanted   oreunjjok   oenjjok   dragging my legs, the ones that ran
5000 meters in 15 minutes 28.4 seconds   oreunjjok   oenjjok   oreunjjok
oenjjok   aigu my legs are so heavy   I wish I had a walking stick   that
reminds me, a long time ago   when I was very small   Eomoni told me

"When a mother dies and they're carrying out her coffin you should walk
with a willow walking stick"

"Why willow?"

"You see, mothers   carry a child and until they're grown it worries us   if
our child is even out of our sight for a moment we get so worried, so worried
that our hearts might burst   the next time you break a branch off a willow
tree, take a look   because it's so tightly packed inside   just like a mother's
heart is packed full of worries"

"I won't make you worry, Omma"

"Oh   really?"

"I promise   and anyway you're not gonna die"

"Of course I will   I'll die before you will, Woo-cheol"

"No   if you die, Omma   I'll die too"

"You shouldn't even joke about that   I want you to live for a long   long   looong time"

"I promise"

APRIL 26, 1943
KUNIMOTO UTETSU AND YASUDA SHIZUKO SUBMIT
MARRIAGE CERTIFICATE

Accepted same day

I opened the door of the Olympic and a little boy was standing there   my son, not from my previous wife or from my new wife   for a moment his name didn't come to me   c'mon   I named him   remember!   I gave almost all of them names starting with Shin   oh that's it   I gave him part of my name too

Shin-cheol   what's wrong

"Omma's gone   Omma   Omma is—"

His face crumpled and he hiccupped   I picked up my son   when he was just born I'd gone over often and held him   I knew he was born in the spring of 1940   I counted, bending my fingers on his back   hana   dul   set   three years old   two years younger than Shin-myeong   and two older than Shin-ho   after she got pregnant with Shin-ho that woman's fierce temper got even fiercer   each time I'd see her, her voice turned threatening   **if you go see her, I swear   I'll pour gasoline on myself and light a match   and I'll take Shin-myeong and our unborn child with me**   even though I was living only a five-minute run away from her   I hadn't gone to see her for over two years   but it was strange   how all of them looked so much alike   my two daughters took after their mother but   all my sons looked like Shin-tae reborn

"I can't understand you 'cause you're crying   stop crying and tell me"

"Omma   Omma   Omma walked me   to the bridge   and said go to
your appa's house   Omma's going far, far away   so listen to what your appa
tells you   and be a good boy   Ommaaa   Ommaaa"

She must've heard that I married Jeong-hee   but   why   do they all go
off and leave their children?   Children they carried inside them for nine
months!   She isn't from Miryang   I heard she was born and raised in
Daegu   left home alone at twenty-four   and started dancing in the OK
Café   I don't know what kind of life she had in Daegu   really all I know
about her   is her face, her body, and her names   Kim Mi-yeong   a.k.a.
Kaneda Yoshiko   something must've made her leave Daegu so she won't be
going back there   I'm sure she's in a dance hall near the harbor in
Busan   pale   and soft   shaking her tits and ass   one-two-three   one-two-
three   she's the type of woman who lives off of men's attention   because
she's got a face and body so beautiful it's a shame   tomorrow she'll take
another man's hand   one-two-three   one-two-three   what do I do with
this child?   There's nothing I can do   I'm his father   I have to pick him up
and take him inside with me   I picked him up and went inside   as I did I
saw children everywhere and the stench of piss hit my nose   my wife had
gone out shopping and left them home   my eldest son was playing cars with
some wood   my eldest daughter was folding laundry with the youngest boy
on her back   my youngest daughter was folding laundry with a pillow on her
back   I took a step in and stumbled on someone's foot   This is your little
brother   He's going to be living with us now   Shin-myeong ya   You're
closest in age   And you're a boy too so be nice and play with him   my
daughters with my previous wife and the sons my new wife had given birth
to   looked at the boy who was clinging to me with both arms around my
neck like a monkey   my youngest daughter came over and turned her
smooth chin up toward me

"What're you called?"

The boy buried his face in my chest   so I answered for him

"This is Shin-cheol"   after that I said something that I had not even
thought before   or   perhaps   it was something I had always been thinking

"All right   listen to me   from now on you're going to stop calling each
other Oppa and Unni   and Hyung and Noona   when you go to school you'll

be called by different names and you'll have to respond to them   Kunimoto
Nobuaki   Kunimoto Nobutetsu   Kunimoto Nobuyoshi   Kunimoto
Tamami   Kunimoto Nobuko   so if you don't use your real names at
home   who will call you them   the Lee family name that was passed down
to us by our ancestors has been taken from us by the ilbon saram   all you have
left are the names that I gave you   if you don't say a name it will die out"

All ten eyes of these five children that three women had given birth to
were turned toward me   the feeling of being watched shot through my
body   my heart shuddered   how were they seeing me right now?   having
exposed myself I had to return their stares   but   I   as a father   had
not   in any real sense   done anything for my children   I opened my
parched lips   moved my slightly swollen tongue   and said the names of my
five children who were living   and two who had lost their lives   Shin-tae!
Shin-myeong!   Shin-cheol!   Shin-ho!   Mi-ok!   Ja-ok!   Shin-ja!

MAY 15, 1943   ATTU ISLAND BOMBED

IMPERIAL HEADQUARTERS ANNOUNCEMENT

On May 12 a powerful American military unit made landing on
Attu Island, in the Aleutian Islands; our garrison was attacked and
is at present in the midst of a fierce battle.

MAY 29, 1943   ATTU GARRISON BATTLE TO A FIERCE END

IMPERIAL HEADQUARTERS ANNOUNCEMENT

Since May 12, the Attu Island garrison has been in an extremely
difficult situation, waging a bloody battle against an enemy who
has often gotten the best of them; on the night of May 29, amid
this fierce fight, it was decided to strike a final blow against the
enemy's main force and show the spirit of the imperial army by
making a spectacular attack with all their might. Henceforth, all
communication was cut off and all are deemed to have fought to a
valorous end. Those who were injured or otherwise unable to join
the attack are understood to have ended their own lives prior to it.
Our garrison was comprised of more than two thousand men, com-

manded by Colonel Yamasaki Yasuyo, while the enemy numbered more than twenty thousand bearing special superior equipment; by May 28, damage had been inflicted on fewer than six thousand of their men.

JUNE 5, 1943
STATE FUNERAL FOR MARSHAL ADMIRAL YAMAMOTO

Following the death in battle of Admiral Yamamoto and the garrison's valorous attack and sacrifice of their lives for the nation, the day of Marshal Admiral Yamamoto Isoroku's funeral has arrived. At the funeral site, the row of imperial envoys graciously dispatched from each palace performed an act of worship; the grief and indignation of all, from the high-ranking officials in attendance to the entire nation, was too much to bear and no eye was left dry—even the trees and blades of grass of Hibiya appeared bent over in sorrow. What's more, within that sorrow lurked an undercurrent of fierceness, of bravery; on this day, June 5, the same day when nine years prior Marshal Admiral Tōgō was buried, the tomb of Marshal Admiral Yamamoto Isoroku now towers beside his in a corner of Tama where the wind blowing through the pine trees reminds all of the sound of the South Sea. But what does the guardian deity of the Pacific, who has died and yet is with us, speak of now to Admirals Yamaguchi and Kaku and the heroes of Attu? The weeping that welled up along the funeral procession was an expression of continued loyalty to his departed spirit. The prayer that was offered on the ridge at the designated time of national prayer, before the blast furnace, was itself a silent national declaration. The ceremony before the coffin, the ceremony of the palanquin, the ceremony of the funeral site, the ceremony of the burial place, all were carried out in the ancient style without any particular variation to reflect his battles, but I felt in it nevertheless the new life of the empire, how the minds of one hundred million were bound together by one fierce thought. We resolve not to forget him, nor this state funeral immediately after decisive battle, this determined oath—

I opened my eyes and she was gone   she was a girl, shaking her daenggimeori   probably   my first wife   it had been years since I'd dreamed of her she was gleaming, bathed in the spring sunshine after we'd made passionate love over and over I looked up at the sun and stretched she stood, without any attempt to hide her nakedness I saw her veins standing out on the pale, white skin on the backs of her knees she plucked a dandelion and suddenly turned back and gave me a smile just like spring itself she blew the dandelion, the fluff scattering over my chest and stomach she touched me with the palm of her hand it felt nice and cool against me like silk

She laid her head on my chest slid down slightly pressing her ear to my heart white dandelion down stuck to her cheek and forehead I thought she looked like a child but I said just do what you want to and I'll do what I want too she took a breath, puffing out her throat and just before she began to sing I woke up but a trace of her song remained I strained my ear for the melody, like the scent of a lily magnolia tree, not knowing if it was there or not **buy flowers, flowers buy flowers, flowers sarang sarang sarang sarang sarang sarang, flowers of love** I took up my **flower box and went out to sell flowers red ones blue ones yellow and white ones indigo and burgundy peach-colored and all sorts glorious flowers the speckled ones are pretty too** memories from over a decade ago came to me suddenly as if they had just emerged from underwater she had sung this song at our wedding, when everyone was supposed to tease me she sang it with her hands gently resting on her lower stomach over the baby I took her great-grandfather's hand and danced **sarang sarang sarang sarang sarang sarang, flowers of love** my March bride whose throat is filled with song like a sparrow's and gives wings to love my wife I came into her life and she into mine twelve years we spent together and we had four children yet now I don't even know where she is burned into my eyelids is an image of her consumed from within by sadness her face, lips strained holding back the tears her shoulders as they rose and fell, back rounded

If you saw the exhaust flame of a B-29 or heard the sound of its engine, you had to immediately report it to the Busan Air Defense Observatory by cable but above me was only the moon, dimly shining it looked full, it looked waning too I stared at it through my binoculars andwae the

bottom was obscured by mist, I couldn't see clearly   the July wind brought
with it smells from the pine forest   the rain that had lasted all day had
soaked the trunks and leaves of the pines, luring their scent out   I breathed
in the strong perfume of the pines   in   out   in   out   though I was on the
top of the mountain where Yeongnamnu was the river sounded as if it were
right next to me *kwalkwalkwal   kwalkwalkwal*   at night not just the river
but also the sky felt much nearer   I picked up my binoculars again and
looked up at the sky   over there, the brightest one, that's Vega, the weaving
girl star   and then a little ways away, that's Altair, the cowherd star   so then
above that is Deneb, part of Cygnus   these three together are called the
Summer Triangle   I remember that   because Miyake-sensei wrote it on
the blackboard when I was in school   the Summer Triangle is slightly to
the west of me   so it must be past midnight now   today is July fifteenth
I have this habit, each time I see the date on the newspaper   I search my
memory to see if this is the anniversary of someone's death   in just twelve
years my sister   my father   my daughter   my son   and my mother
died   *deureureong-zzz-deureureong-zzz*   I could hear the snoring from the
hallway   I looked at the clock   it was two   it was time for his shift but I'd
let him sleep a little longer   I was up until past midnight listening to Kim
talk about his prospects for the future   he said he worked at the Iwata
Hospital next to the Olympic but   it was the first time we'd exchanged
anything more than a hello   he didn't have the money to go to college so he
was aiming to take the licensing exam and become a doctor   anyone who
worked on a two-hour rotation once a week from eight in the morning to
eight the next morning at the Air Defense Observatory   would then be
considered to be serving locally and therefore not subject to the draft   as the
chief of Ne-il-dong, Mr. Kim, explained to me   but I couldn't see that they'd
exempt a healthy twenty-year-old   and if he were assigned to, say, the 13th
Division in China   there was a chance he might be fighting against Kim
Won-bong and his anti-Japanese forces   his father is Kim Won-bong's father's
younger brother   and as a cousin of Kim Won-bong the police kept a close
eye on him   even the patriotic corps   don't know what the hell will happen
next month when the conscription system comes into force   one day
without any warning   the postman will come bearing a red slip in my name:

EXTRAORDINARY MOBILIZATION ORDER

Miryang City, Ne-il-dong 7-5   KUNIMOTO UTETSU

By order of the following mobilization notice,
the recipient must arrive at the designated place
and time and notify the mobilization officer in
charge.
Place of arrival: 77th Infantry Regiment
Mobilizing unit: 77th Infantry Regiment

   Government-General of Korea, Miryang Branch

I took down my binoculars and stared with my own eyes at the vaguely outlined moon   even now   while I was doing this the Japanese army was advancing on Hubei   to the southwest they were occupying Burma   to the south in the Philippines they were seizing public sentiment   battling fiercely in New Guinea   repeatedly bombarding Darwin   to the east the allied German army is attacking Leningrad and Gorky   to the southeast they're fighting in the Caucasus   annihilating the partisans in Yugoslavia   in the west firebombing London   in the south they're occupying Italy   while the Italian army is bombing Syria   and battling in Tunisia   and now bombing in Sudan   war courses through the world like the blood pumping through my body *thump-thump! Thump-thump! Thump-thump! Thump-thump! Thump-thump! Thump-thump! Thump-thump! Thump-thump!*

NOTIFICATION OF DEATH

Miryang City, Ne-il-dong 7-5 KUNIMOTO UTETSU

We are writing to notify you that it has been
determined that on ███/███/███████ date, the
above was killed in action at Attu Island.

In addition, we will process the notification
of death in accordance with Family Register Act
Section 119.

I'm tired of living   but I don't want to kill Chinese or Americans **as a
Japanese soldier**   and I don't want to die at the hands of an American or a
Brit **as a Japanese soldier**   and I don't think I'll see the day when the
Japanese army tires of fighting   no   those who want to fight will never tire
of it   **they** are swinging a huge beam called the Greater East Asian Co-
prosperity Sphere around in the darkness, fumbling to build something with
it   and in that same darkness soldiers' limbs are blown off   exposed to the
driving rain, eaten by birds and insects   and on that death's head no candles
will be lit   and even if someone were to light them they would soon be
extinguished   the nameless dead dissolve into the darkness   **they** can see
only darkness   in war the ideal and the real do not compete with each
other   *sol sol sarang sarang*   I took the waves of wind face-on   where does
the anguished soul inside the body go to once the body has disappeared?
Does it disappear with the body?   Is it sucked into the darkness, becoming
one with it?   Or is it carried by the wind, traveling hundreds and thousands
of miles until it reaches home?   *Sol sol sarang sarang   sol sol sarang
sarang*   the wind stopped as if it had read my thoughts   and I stopped
thinking as if shutting my mouth   the rain fell thuddingly   I pressed the
button on my flashlight   it flickered a few times, eventually giving off light,
but in just seconds it went out

JULY 25, 1943   ITALIAN PM MUSSOLINI RESIGNS

ROME—The Stefani news agency reports that His Majesty the
King and Emperor Victor Emmanuel III has proclaimed as follows:
Italians! From today I assume command of all the Armed Forces.
At this solemn hour in which hangs the destiny of the nation, each
must take his own post of duty, faith, and combat: no deviation must
be tolerated, no recriminations can be permitted. Let every Italian
bow before the serious wounds that have torn apart the sacred soil
of their homeland. Italy shall, through the valor of her troops and
the determination of her citizens, find, in the respect of her old institutions that have always supported her rise, the way of recovery.
I have accepted the resignation of His Excellency Benito Mussolini
regarding his obligations as the prime minister of my government
as well as the minister of state, and I have appointed Marshal Pietro

Badoglio as the prime minister of my government as well as the minister of state. Italians! Today, I am more than ever inextricably united with you by our unshakable faith in the immortality of our nation.

AUGUST 1, 1943   DRAFT IMPLEMENTED IN KOREA

Immediately after events began in China seven years ago, the spirit of patriotic devotion of our Korean compatriots has been demonstrated everywhere, showing their sincerity to the point of tears, and the voices of our Korean compatriots, who are willing to have a conscription system for themselves carried out, has taken the form of a petition to the imperial diet, as the concrete expression of the momentum of the unification of Japan and Korea. Therefore, following the outbreak of combat in China, the government implemented the Imperial Japanese Army Special Volunteer Ordinance No. 95, opening the way for volunteers to be incorporated as either active or first-rank reservists, and volunteers who passed screenings were enlisted in army units to engage in military service.

Since the implementation of this system, the number of applicants has increased sharply every year, with numbers rising from about 3,000 in 1938 to 12,000 in 1939, leaping dramatically to approximately 144,000 volunteers in 1941. As soon as the Greater East Asia war broke out, the number of applicants enthusiastic to be on the front lines and wanting to be of aid to the empire increased, and in 1942 an astonishing 250,000 volunteers applied. Moreover, in our battles in China, these volunteers have been well regarded, and while of course some have been recognized for their distinguished service having died in action, others who survived have been rewarded with medals for their bravery, and among them all, regardless of their home front being the peninsula, there has been a general enthusiasm for the completion of the war, resulting in the desire to do something remarkable.

Thus, in May of last year, the decision was made to implement policy creating a conscription system for our Korean compatriots, allowing their conscription from 1944, and once the announcement of this system was made, the overflowing devotion seen among our Korean compatriots, who have in some cases journeyed to Tokyo to

worship at the Imperial Palace or shown their willingness to repay the Emperor's grace with their lives, has shown the sincerity of
our Korean compatriots, which has upsurged to the highest degree,
forming an inspiring wave across the entire peninsula.

Indeed, the implementation of this conscription system is not
only an honor for our compatriots on the peninsula, it is also a
strengthening of the empire's eternal ability to defend itself, and
an intensification of our belief that we shall win the Greater East
Asia war.

I opened my eyes and the darkness was there   with a headache nailed
into my forehead   like a drunk woman I was weighed on by the heavy
darkness and heat   I tossed and turned, unable to find a good position   this
is fear   fear that is passed on to you and fear that you create yourself have
different colors, different smells even   and this one?   It was both   white?
Black?   Red?   Yellow?   I was surrounded by fears   I put my hand on my
wife's thigh   slid it down inside where her hair clustered   slipped my fingers
farther inside   I do not have the courage to wait for what darkness has to
bring   **I closed my eyes and the darkness was there**   I fled   at full speed
into the darkness   **in-hale ex-hale   in-hale ex-hale   in-hale ex-hale
in-hale ex-hale   in-hale ex-hale   in-hale ex-hale   in-hale ex-hale**

NINETEEN

Rain, Rain, Fall, Fall

| 아메 아메 후레 후레 | アメアメ、フレフレ |

Ame, ame   fure, fure
Kaa-san ga
Janome de   omukai
Ureshi na
Pitch, pitch   chap, chap
Run, run, run

Rain, rain   fall, fall
Mama   is
Coming with an umbrella
Pitch, pitch   chap, chap
Run, run, run

By the riverside three girls were jumping rope. The rope was still only as high as Kyōjun's knees. They had their skirts tucked into the elastic of their panties so the hems wouldn't blow up, and their bowl cuts flutter-fluttered in time with the song. Eiko was jumping and messed up the order of her feet, so she traded places with Keiko to hold the rope.

"What happened? How'd you trip when it's this low?" Kyōjun said.

"I have a crush on someone," Eiko said, taking the end of the black rope in her hand.

"Wait, what? What's that got to do with it?" Kyōjun's eyes widened exaggeratedly.

"Huh? Who is it, who?! Te-ll us!" Keiko asked bouncily, hooking the rope over her leg.

"I know, it's Takahide, isn't it? Oh, did I hit the bull's-eye? I knew it, 'cause whenever you walk past him you always look down at the ground," Kyōjun said.

"Kinoshita Takahide? No way! I always look down at the ground 'cause I hate him. No, the boy I like is . . ." Eiko quickly brought her mouth to Keiko's ear and whispered.

"What? But he's a grown-up."

"He's five years older than us, I think it's just right."

"What? Who is it, tell me, tell me."

Giggling, Keiko whispered in Kyōjun's ear.

"Really? Woo-gun?"

"When I get married, I want to marry someone like Woo-gun," Eiko said, the hand holding the jump rope dangling loosely as she turned over a rock with the sole of her rubber boot.

"There's no way he'd have you anyway. You know, he goes to Choyang Commercial School in Busan. He'll marry a girl from a good family, you'll see."

"But maybe he'll fall in love at first sight?"

"With who-oo?"

"Well, me, obviously."

"Ah!" Kyōjun and Keiko exclaimed at the same time.

Eiko turned her eyes toward Mount Jongnam, where the two of them were looking, then brought her fist up to her mouth, still clutching the handle of the jump rope.

"Oh, no, this can't be real, what do I do?"

Two men were running side by side. One was a young man with close-cropped hair, and the other was in his thirties, wearing a red running shirt. Their heights and features were quite similar too, though the boy stared straight ahead, while the man ran slightly hunched over, as if he were carrying his own arms.

"He's here!"

The girls let down their skirts from their panties. Kyōjun set the rope around her ankles and spread her legs apart, while Eiko momentarily put her end of the rope in her pocket and wiped the sweat from her hands on her skirt before grasping the rope again. Keiko, her cheeks flushed, stamped her right foot, then went inside the ring of rope, as Eiko and Kyōjun started singing, high-pitched and excitedly.

Ame, ame   fure, fure
Kaa-san ga
Janome de   omukai
Ureshi na
Pitch, pitch   chap, chap
Run, run, run

Kakemasho   kaban wo
Kaa-san no
Ato kara   yuko yuko
Kane ga naru
Pitch, pitch   chap, chap
Run, run, run

Kyōjun raised the rope up to her knees. Once it was above knee height it was fine to touch the rope as she jumped, but Keiko, worried about the hem of her skirt billowing up each time she jumped, accidentally stepped on the rope.

In-hale ex-hale, they're getting closer, in-hale ex-hale, in-hale ex-hale, the smell of their sweat and the sound of their breath went past, in-hale ex-hale, in-hale ex-hale, they're gone now.

"They're so fast . . ." Watching them run off, Eiko forgot herself.

"My abeoji says that if they hadn't canceled the Tokyo Olympics three years ago, he would've been there." Kyōjun nestled so close up to Eiko that their shoulders were touching.

"He's too old now, but Woo-gun is still young enough to aim for the next Olympics," Keiko said.

"Where are they having the next ones?" Kyōjun took Eiko's arm in hers.

"I think Seno'o-sensei said they're in London."

"But England's our enemy, so he wouldn't be able to go." Eiko stretched toward Mount Yongdu.

"I can't see them anymore."

"They'll be back soon. They're running around the embankment."

The August light gathered around the girls, sparkling off their dark hair and eyes. Their beauty was still untouched. Occasionally, the southern wind would run a rough hand through their bowl cuts, but for now it simply pressed against their eyelids, gently touching their lashes.

"You know, a little bit ago, the whole world could see your panties, Kyōjun. Did you mean for them to?" Keiko said, breaking the seething silence.

"Of course I didn't!" Kyōjun rebounded Keiko's shriek back at her.

"How long will it be before he's back, do you think . . ." She had wanted to say his name, but her throat had tightened, and so she had just called Woo-gun *him*.

I said it just fine before, jokingly, when I said I'd want to marry someone like him. Maybe I am in love, now, or I fell in it a little while ago, the moment I smelled *his* sweat— Eiko's heart pounded inside her chest like a bouncing ball.

"It's rather dull just to look, you know. When they come past again, let's tell them 'annyeong haseyo,'" Kyōjun said.

"Oh? Which of us?"

"Whoever loses at rock, paper, scissors."

"No way, I can't, really."

"Well, then, you'll just have to lose. Right, rock, paper, scissors, shoot!"

Kyōjun and Keiko both chose paper, and Eiko, drawn into it, threw rock. The other girls both nudged her with their elbows, laughing.

"Oh no!"

"Well, it's no use, we both lost, so you'll have to tell him 'annyeong haseyo!'" Keiko scolded her cheerily, her big, sparkling eyes smiling.

"You ought to, you know."

Kyōjun and Keiko started singing mockingly, clapping along.

Oh, oh   that girl
Is dripping wet   she's crying
Under the willow tree
Pitch, pitch   chap, chap
Run, run, run

Mama, Mama   I'll lend her mine
Here's my umbrella   for you to use
Pitch, pitch   chap, chap
Run, run, run

The August days were long with lots of light. Though the sun was setting toward Mount Jongnam, the almost transparent blue of the sky and the suffocating heat were unchanged.

"But, say, who do you think'll be chosen at next year's Arang Festival?"

"Kanayama Kyoko, don't you think? She's the prettiest girl in her class."

"What? Her, the prettiest? If she's a beauty, then Eiko is, you know."

"Maybe we should go for it. I'll nominate myself."

Eiko listened to them talk, adding perfunctory noises in response or laughter, but she was overwhelmed by the summer weighing down on her, drunk on its sounds and colors. *Maeaemmaeaemmaeaem chireureureut chireureureut chireureureut sseuleu-sseuleu*, I had no idea there were that many kinds of cicadas, *hwing hwing*, that's a mosquito, *buzz buzz*, that's the droning of a bee, *fbizz fbizz*, that's a horsefly, *ribbit-ribbit-ribbit*, and over there the boys from the other class are tying frogs' legs with the leaves of reeds, and then they'll roast them over a cowpat while they're still alive to eat them, aigu, bulssangta.

Oh, isn't that Kaneda Sadayasu from the other class? Yes, that is Sadayasu; oh, the sun's about to set but everyone's still swimming naked, that must be nice, but I can't do that anymore, I'm turning fourteen in October this year, and it seems like when you become a grown-up there're more things you can't do than things you can. Aigu, utginda, how funny, the storks are all in a row facing Mount Jongnam, like they're about to bow to the emperor's photograph!

Eiko took in as much of the water's scent as she could, blinking repeatedly.

As she did, suddenly, the path around the embankment that appeared to ripple in the distance, the fishing boats slowly navigating around Namcheong Bridge, the unnamed birds with strange cries in the pine forest, the screech of the Hsinking-bound express train going over the rail bridge, and all the other things beneath the sun were mixed together and sucked into the cloudless blue sky, until Eiko felt that soon she would be able to see nothing, hear nothing, touch nothing; she stopped blinking and watched intently the August light itself. Nunbusida, oh, how bright it was! Her head and face and body were all deowora, so hot. No part of her body was untouched by the heat. As a red foam rose up and like cellophane cut off her view of the world, Eiko saw herself laying her head against *his* chest. Her legs were shaking from desire. Eiko knew for the first time the summer. And she was sad, realizing that she was still a child who knew nothing. Nunbusida . . .

Sol sol sarang sarang   sol sol sarang sarang, the southern winds blowing down from Mount Jongnam ran up the surface of the river gaining force, whooshing and rustling through the reeds like a fire, flowing through Mincheol halbi's beard, long and white like a willow, blowing up the straw hat of the boy selling ice cream and dropping it in the river, twirling the pinwheel in the hand of the little boy toddling along the bank, and just when she thought it had run up to their feet like a puppy wagging its tail, the wind blew up the girls' skirts all at once, *hwing hwing*, before running without catching its breath up to the Air Defense Observatory at the top of Mount Adong, where Aranggak and Yeongnamnu and the shrine were located.

Eiko pulled out the ends of her hair that had blown in her mouth and saw, on the other side of the potato fields in Sanmun-dong, the Kunimoto brothers running toward them again. In-hale ex-hale   in-hale ex-hale, they were still quite far away, but the sound of their breathing came, following them like a steam train, in-hale ex-hale, so fast, faster even than before, in-hale ex-hale   in-hale ex-hale, and Eiko, who had started to breathe in time with them, began to sing loudly so it would carry, while Keiko took the jump rope from under her armpits in one hand and skillfully began to jump.

Rain, rain   fall, fall
Mama   is

Coming with an umbrella
Pitch, pitch   chap, chap
Run, run, run

Here they were! Eiko jumped with her right foot and stuck her left out, then stopped moving and saw his face front on. Closer to awe than nervousness, Eiko's eyes went dark. She didn't know why, but she felt this was a terribly important moment, it was no mere chance, it was fate that she should call out to *him* now, she thought. His face, slightly inclined toward the river, was so composed it looked cold, but his exhaling lips, his wide, sweat-soaked forehead, and his eyes, in which brightness and depth coexisted, shone fierily. He's here! He's here! Eiko felt her chest lift in time with Woo-gun's breathing, and once again she raised her voice and jumped!

Leave your bag   for Mama to find
Ding ding   goes the bell
Pitch, pitch   chap, chap
Run, run, run

The wind that billowed its way through Eiko's hair carried with it their singing, brushing past Woo-gun's earlobes **"Oh, oh   that girl   is dripping wet   she's crying   under the willow tree"** **pitch, pitch   chap, chap   run, run, run,** he muttered in his mind   in-hale ex-hale   their singing was cut off   in-hale ex-hale   "Annyeong haseyo!"   surprised that someone behind him had spoken he turned and   in-hale ex-hale   the girl in the middle, almost standing on tiptoes, raised her right hand to cheer "Himnaeiso!"   gomapda!   I said in thanks, and turned my head back in-hale ex-hale   in-hale ex-hale   cute girl with a bowl cut   she reminds me a little of my big sister   about the same age too   in-hale ex-hale   in-hale ex-hale   but my noona died when she was eleven and she'll always be eleven next April I turn nineteen   when I see her again in death she'll be younger than me, I guess   in-hale ex-hale   how old will I be when I die? I wonder in-hale ex-hale   and where will I die   in-hale ex-hale   on Guadalcanal? The Solomon Islands?   Burma?   New Guinea?   Australia?   in-hale

ex-hale   China?   in-hale ex-hale   in-hale ex-hale   why is my brother so
quiet   is there something he wants to say to me   in-hale ex-hale   in-hale
ex-hale   something he can't bring himself to say   what   I can't stand
this   in-hale ex-hale   I'll ask   in-hale ex-hale   no, better to stay
quiet   and just keep running until he says something   in-hale ex-hale . in-
hale ex-hale   and besides he stinks of booze   someone told me he drinks
every night   I've never had a drink so I don't know but   can you stink of it
down to your sweat   in-hale ex-hale   in-hale ex-hale   maybe we should go a
little faster   if he gets to the point where he can't hold a breath inside his
body then maybe the words will come out   in-hale ex-hale   in-hale ex-
hale   after he tells me what he wants to say I have to go to the kendo club in
Ne-il-dong   before the sun sets   there's no light so I can't practice after
dark   *hwiing hwiing*   the trees on Mount Bihak are undulating   in-hale
ex-hale   like a sea of green   a large chorus of cicadas   a blue sky so big it
seems to have no end or death   nunbusida!   It's summer!   Maybe tonight
I'll run all night   leave my running shoes by the window and   when the
whole house is dead asleep, sneak out   in-hale ex-hale   in-hale ex-
hale   deowora!   It's like the air itself has a fever!   *hwiing hwiing*   a
tailwind!   I'm going to outdistance the wind   ready, let's race!   In-hale
ex-hale   in-hale ex-hale   in-hale ex-hale   in-hale ex-hale   I crossed the
concrete paving and turned around   and my brother in the distance had
become the size of my palm   have I gotten faster   or has he gotten
slower   in-hale ex-hale   in-hale ex-hale   since the war started the Chōsen
Jingū competition and the All Japan Athletics competition   in-hale ex-
hale   both were canceled   so I don't know exactly   how fast I could run a
5000 or 10,000 but   in-hale ex-hale   my brother's confident that he would
win   but I'm faster   in-hale ex-hale   much, much faster!   aigu   deowora!

Woo-gun put his right heel up on the stone wall, waiting for Woo-cheol as
he stretched the backs of his calf and thigh. *Huff-huff-huff-huff*, now the left
leg, aigu, the left is much tighter, if one side's out of balance that's no good is
it, *huff-huff-huff*; a lizard peered up at him through the stone wall, flicking its
dark purple tongue, sweat fell from his forehead absorbed by the ground; *huff-
huff-huff*, look at the ants, forming a line across the top of the stone wall, don't
you get in my running shoes, I spit-shine these every night you know, hah-hah,

if you crawl inside I'll crush you to death, *huff-huff-huff*, death? I wonder if a fortune teller could tell me if I'll be alive in five years' time or not, *maeaem maeaem chileuleuleu chileuleuleu chichichi chiiii sseuleuleuleu sseuleuleu*, the calls of the cicadas and the sound of his breathing entwined and a strange serenity reverberated through his body, *huff-huff-huff*, sadness and a somehow inexpressible longing filled his heart, breathe in   breathe out, I had that dream again this morning, that awful dream, the one about the man slitting his throat with my abeoji's jangdo, breathe in   breathe out, it's always pretty much the same, but each time I have it it's subtly different, this time there were bubbles slowly running down from the dragon-engraved handle, and the moment the man shook the bubbles off his chest, the gleaming jangdo seemed filled with murderous intent, breathe in   breathe out, maybe I should tell my brother, *eorinae gatgin!* Only silly kids, pregnant women, and old people talk about their dreams, but then I can't quite shake off this apprehension, is the dream trying to tell me something? Because the man's face looks just like mine, breathe in   breathe out   in   out   in   out . . .

As if someone had grabbed his chin and jerked his head around, Woo-gun turned his sweat-stinging eyes back to reality, blinking repeatedly.

In-hale ex-hale   in-hale ex-hale, it's my brother, in-hale ex-hale   in-hale ex-hale, he bent over and shook his knees, then coughed and spit up some phlegm   *huff-huff-huff-huff-huff-huff*, bunches of muscles on his thighs and calves peeked out from his shorts, as if his muscles themselves were showing their anger and failure   failure?   but my brother hasn't failed, it wasn't his fault that the Tokyo Olympics had been canceled, just too bad luck has fallen upon him, my brother *has been failed*.

"*Huff-huff-huff-huff-huff-huff*, you're fast, *huff-huff*, you've gotten so fast, you could probably beat Nurumi's 30-minute-6.2-second-world record in the ten thousand, *huff-huff-huff*, but the war, that fucking war, manghal nomui jeonjaeng!"

"I run every night just like you told me."

"*Huff-huff*, even if you run every day you can't do what you can't do, *huff-huff-huff*."

"I want to run marathons . . . when the war is over."

"Who knows when the war will end, *huff-huff*, or if we'll live to see the end of it."

He stopped talking and looked up at the sky. We heard the boom of engines. The shadows had thin wings with rounded tips. Hayabusa. Hana dul set net daseot yeoseot ilgop yeodeol ahop, ten of them, I wonder where they're going. My brother groaned and then panted again, as if he had just remembered to breathe.

"Let's go."

He ran off toward Namcheong Bridge, shaking off the sound of the engine   in-hale ex-hale   in-hale ex-hale   "The baby'll come in March next year   this is my fourth child with her   so of course the other one says she'll have to have four kids too   in-hale ex-hale"   why is he talking about this with me   and just what should I say in response?   in-hale ex-hale   in-hale ex-hale   "She says the next one will be a girl   and she was right about Shin-myeong and Shin-ho   so I guess she must know   she asked me to give the baby a girl's name   so last night   I gave our unborn child the name Shin-hee"   in-hale ex-hale   from his side profile I could see unhappiness filling his face like sewage   in-hale ex-hale   there must be something else he wants to talk about   I readied myself   "Maybe we should run off together" my brother said hoarsely   in-hale ex-hale   in-hale ex-hale   it took a few seconds for me to understand what he'd said   run off?   Where?   in-hale ex-hale   and why?   in-hale ex-hale   in-hale ex-hale   he leaned forward as if he'd been sent flying then came to a sudden stop   *huff-huff-huff-huff-huff-huff huff-huff huff-huff-huff huff-huff*

"Aigu, my left leg's in bad shape, the outside of my knee hurts, *huff-huff-huff*, let's walk to the bridge, wait, no, slower, *huff-huff*, let's just walk slowly and talk, come closer, *huff-huff-huff*, you know two weeks ago they started the draft here, right? Right now they only want male students over twenty, but if the war starts to go worse, then they'll start sending men in their thirties or even teenagers to the front line, *huff-huff-huff*, so why don't we run away to Japan, I've been there a few times for the Meiji Jingu races and the ekiden, so I know the lay of the land, and we can speak Japanese without the slightest accent, *huff-huff*, we could pose as Japanese."

"I'm not going to Japan."

"Why not."

"Unlike you I've never been there . . . I'm not going to go . . . that's just how I feel."

"*Huff-huff-huff*, but why?"

"Could you imagine yourself running on the frozen land of Siberia?"

"No."

"Well, I'm the same. I can't imagine it. You can't do something you can't imagine, can you?"

"Who can't?"

"Well, anyone . . . and the other thing is . . ."

"*Huff-huff*, what?"

"There's something I have to do here, in this country, in Korea."

"What's that, *huff-huff-huff*?"

"I can't tell you just yet."

"Then I'll go."

"Have you talked it over with her?"

"No, she's a loudmouth, I can't trust she won't tell everyone. I warn her not to tell anybody, and the next thing I know she's blabbing about it. You're the only one I've told."

"I won't tell anyone. Noona is dead, Abeoji is dead, Eomoni is dead, you're the only blood relative I have left."

"*Huff-huff*, I'm gonna call it quits at the bridge."

"I'm gonna do another loop."

"Well."

"I guess this might be the last time I see you."

He paused. "Yeah."

"I just want to ask you one thing. You said that when I was born you thought of all kinds of names for me, right?"

"Yeah, you were born in the spring, so I thought of lots of names with the character for spring in them. Chun-jae, Chun-ik, Chun-son, Chun-il, Chun-sik, Chun-un, Chun-hen . . . But in the end they went with the name that Abeoji thought up."

"I wonder if it would be all right with you if I used Chun-sik as a pseudonym."

"A pseudonym? What do you need one of those for?"

"Through this family registration system, we've been enslaved by the waenom and now thanks to them my name is Kunimoto Ukon, but as a way to show that in my heart I don't have allegiance to them, I want to withdraw from the wae's register. I can't use this name, Kunimoto Ukon, which is covered in shame. So to continue my resistance, to oppose them, to be able to fight I need a new name as my fortress. From now on I'll go by Lee Chun-sik. It's just like you said . . . it's a name that expresses the hope that a seedling planted in spring . . . will sprout and grow quickly to become a big tree."

"Yes—it's a great name."

I hesitated. "Should we say goodbye?"

"No, I'll return when the heat is off."

"Well, then."

My brother stood still, holding up his right hand   I started to run, holding up mine   in-hale ex-hale   in-hale ex-hale   I won't turn back   even if I look back it won't bring back   him or anything else   in-hale ex-hale   nothing will return   what will become of Mi-ok and Shin-ja   I heard a rumor that she'd been seen, baby on her back, crying as she walked along the path by the river   in-hale ex-hale   there's nothing I can do   all I can do is pray   for Mi-ok's and Shin-ja's happiness   for his safety   in-hale ex-hale   **Lee Chun-sik**   in-hale ex-hale   only those who have been deprived of their name can understand   the feeling of hunger that comes from not being allowed to use their true name   not being called their true name   in-hale ex-hale   in-hale ex-hale   the Korean people are starving because our rations for rice, wheat, and sugar are so small   but what we are most starved for is names   the Korean people are hungry for our own names   in-hale ex-hale

Mount Shingo goes ooh-roo-roo—that's the sound of the freight train leavin'
Pulling on the heartstrings of a mother whose baby's leaving as a volunteer
Oh-ran, oh-ran, oh-ho-ya

Living off of fried scraps since there's no grain distribution
Mount Shingo goes ooh-roo-roo—that's the sound of the freight train leavin'
And all I hear's the cries of a mother whose daughter's joined the corps
Oh-ran, oh-ran, oh-ho-ya

A mother cow with only grass to eat, hungry and crying now
Mount Shingo goes ooh-roo-roo—that's the sound of the freight train leavin'
With all our gold and iron, anything that wasn't tied down
Oh-ran, oh-ran, oh-ho-ya

In-hale ex-hale   when will I be able to take back my true name   when will we take back our country   in-hale ex-hale   in-hale ex-hale   aigu   deowora!   it's like I'm being roasted   I wish I'd put on a hat   in-hale ex-hale   in-hale ex-hale   the sun is throbbing like a beating heart   in-hale ex-hale   the light off the river is nunbusida!   in-hale ex-hale   the river flows on even as it reflects the sun   how beautiful it is   the Han River or the Amnok River might be more majestic or beautiful but   this is the river I jump in each time it turns summer   and slide around on each time it freezes over in winter   in-hale ex-hale   it's the river my eomoni washed my diapers in   and the one my halme put my eomoni's placenta in   where my noona drowned   and where my abeoji's and nephew's remains were scattered   in-hale ex-hale   just as blood runs through my body   this river runs through my heart   in-hale ex-hale   in-hale ex-hale   everyone is frightened of violence   baseless rumors are being tossed about   in-hale ex-hale   even my brother   in-hale ex-hale   aren't I more likely when I turn nineteen next year   to be conscripted than him, in his thirties   in-hale ex-hale   if I said I wasn't scared I'd be lying   in-hale ex-hale   of course I'm scared   in-hale ex-hale   will I come of age first   or will the war be over first   the light strained from the sun made everything under the sky appear to be smiling, and in that second   *boom boom*   a Hayabusa   hana   dul   set   net   daseot   yeoseot six   freedom!   Woo-gun smiled up at the formation of Hayabusas   freedom is not about letting power and wealth behave as they please   in-hale ex-hale   in-hale ex-hale   however the powerful might threaten me   imprison me   put chains around my waist   shackle and bludgeon me   brand me   even if they hang me upside down and pour water down my nose   in-hale ex-hale   in-hale ex-hale   without giving into their yoke or pain or fear   I will stand, bearing my own soul   in-hale ex-hale   in-hale ex-hale   in-hale ex-hale   as I run under the sunset glow of the sky   for some reason   in-hale ex-hale   until my eomoni died   her hand in mine   looking eye to eye   in-hale ex-hale   in-hale ex-hale   in her mouth, even when her jaw was so weak she could not close it properly   in-hale ex-hale   in-hale ex-hale   "Woo-cheol   take my hand   Woo-cheol   look into your omma's eyes"   she mistook me for my brother   in-hale ex-hale   though my eyes were the last thing reflected in hers in her final moment   she died thinking that he was taking care of her   in-hale ex-hale   in-hale ex-hale   so salty   my sweat has dried and I'm covered in salt   all right   time to get sweaty again   I'm gonna sprint full force to the kendo club   breathe out   if I get out all the air in my lungs   breathe in   then all of a sudden the air will come in through my nose   Woo-gun strained all his muscles and silenced everything outside himself, just as he did when he was standing on the starting line   **Athlete number 229   Representing South Gyeongsang Province   Lee Chun-sik   on your marks   get set   go!**

As the sun was hiding itself behind Mount Maeum, the gentle peaks of Mounts Cheongryong and Baekho, both connected to Mount Jongnam, were colored with its afterglow.

One girl was sitting on a rock by the riverside, singing a song to herself as she swayed in the evening breeze.

Ame, ame   fure, fure
Kaa-san   ga
Janome de   omukai
Ureshi na
Pitch, pitch   chap, chap
Run, run, run

At her feet lay a black jump rope, stretched out like a snake. Her two friends had, with a hana ppajyeotda, dul ppajyeotda, hurried back to their homes when the slopes of the mountain had started to turn madder red, but she had circumstances that made her not want to go home.

Eiko put her head in her left hand. The sun had set, but it was still hot. Could the sun burn your hair? she wondered. If it could, then wow. In Miyake-sensei's science class, he had showed them how you could use a magnifying glass and the sun to set a newspaper on fire, and that had been really scary. What would happen if somebody aimed a magnifying glass at her head? Eiko stuck her pointer finger into the sandy shore and flung the sand into the water, then let her gaze drift into space.

Again last night that man had said something to her like, Eiko, you're always so absentminded, I think you've got a screw loose. But I'm not absent-minded, I'm observing the air, and maybe it's not even such an exaggeration to say that I'm observing it, the way it moves here and there without a purpose, and when I watch it without a purpose, my mind calms down. No, it does have a purpose, when I can't stand being in the same room as him and I feel like I want to cry, if I stare into the air, a few specks float across my eyes, and at first they're always blurry from my tears, but eventually if they get clearer and turn crimson then they're mine. My mind goes empty. And when my mind is empty, then I must not be sad or anything, right? So that's why, when I go to get water from the well, I stare into thin air, when I beat the fulling block, I stare into thin air, and the more I stare, the emptier I become . . .

Before she remarried, Eomoni was always on my side, and now she just does exactly whatever he tells her. To him I'm not just worthless, I'm a little nuisance who he wants to kick out even if he has to pay my dowry, though he never really says that I'm almost fourteen and I should hurry up and get married, I almost wish he'd just flat-out tell me to get out because I'm in the way. . . . If my abeoji were still alive . . . but he died before my baek-il janchi, oh, Abeoji. . . .

When the sunset was gone it suddenly became dark. If I don't go home soon, I'll get told off, she thought as she picked up the jump rope and folded it in half, then half again, then again, and put it in her pocket, but she could not stand up. *Jol-jol-jol-jol ding-ding eummae-eummae*

chileuleuleu-chileuleuleu "ICE CREAM GET YOUR ICE CREAM"
eummae-eummae ttallang-ttallang from all the noises that sounded muffled as if wrapped in silk floss, only Woo-gun's voice came through. "Gomapda!" Just like if you strike a bell hard it will still vibrate for a while even
once the sound disappears, my heart was still quivering from *his* voice. In-hale
ex-hale *thump-thump, his* breathing and heartbeat were vibrating inside me.
His dark, keen eyes; the way his big front teeth peeked out of his mouth when
he smiled; his face, full of anger and joy— I think of *him*, he doesn't think of
me, aigu, what would it be like for someone to think of me. Eiko put her arms
around her small chest, which was just beginning to swell, and sighed. As the
sigh sent ripples through her mind and body, the sound of someone walking
up from behind snuck up on her.

She turned and a white, open-collared shirt and flat cap appeared from the
twilight. Huh? Does he need something from me? He's walking toward me,
so what does he want with me? Maybe he's lost. As soon as Eiko's face met his,
she glanced at the man's softened eyes.

"Ilbonui gunbok gongjangeseo ilhaji ankesseoyo doneul mani
batgo masinneun geotdo meokgo yeppeun oseul ibeoyo sannyeon
ilhamyeon jibe dorawayo geujeone sijipgamyeon eonjedeunji jibe
wayo."

Eiko burst out laughing. His Korean, which was just word after word
jammed together, sounded weird.

"I can speak Japanese. I'm in fifth grade at the normal school." Eiko didn't
even try to hide the dimple on display on her right cheek.

"Fifth grade, does that mean you're fifteen?"

"No, I started when I was nine so I'm thirteen."

"Thirteen years old. You seem mature for your age. . . . Did you understand
what I just said?"

"Your pronunciation was weird but— Oh, I'm sorry, I shouldn't have said
that. . . ." Eiko worriedly pursed her lips. For a few beats, Eiko's eyes were drawn
to a black butterfly that had settled on the clover between her and the man.
Was it a bat? No, definitely not, it's a butterfly after all, but she'd never seen

one so big before. It took flight, and she saw then that it was about the size of her palm twice over. But didn't butterflies stop flying when the sun went down? Moths are the ones that swarm around streetlights and lamps. . . .

He repeated himself in Japanese: "So what do you think about what I said? Do you want to come work in a military uniform factory in Japan? You'll get lots of money, nice things to eat, pretty clothes too. Once you've worked for three years you can come home, and before that, if you're gonna get married, then you can come home anytime. Recruitment is supposed to be over now, but we're going to Busan tomorrow and your Japanese is so good I'm sure it's fine and maybe they'll give you special treatment."

The man caught her out of the corner of his eye; her mouth was still closed. He said nothing to hurry along her response. His silence contained a cunning-ness, but the girl did not notice. He did not miss, after a few minutes of si-lence, how her upper lip bobbed up like a fish caught on a hook.

"Where would I work?"

"In Fukuoka."

"Fukuoka . . . that's so far . . . isn't it?"

"Sure, it's far, but in the morning we'll get on a train at Samnamjin station and before ten we'll be in Busan. From Busan we'll get on the Satsuma-maru and the next morning we'll be in Shimonoseki."

"And from Shimonoseki?"

"We'll get on a train in Shimonoseki and then, sure enough, we'll be there in three hours. Hakata's a place with a lot of nice folks."

Unconsciously, Eiko had begun pulling at the weeds between her legs.

If I let this opportunity pass me by, then I'll be forced to marry someone my stepfather arranges for me, and unless there's something seriously wrong with the match, as the woman I won't be able to refuse it. No! I just won't do it! I'm not like my eomoni! No way in hell I'd do what a man like that tells me!

"What time tomorrow?" Eiko's voice was suddenly husky.

"If you want the job be at Samnamjin at eight."

"To be at Samnamjin station at eight, I should take the seven thirty from here, I suppose."

"You can't be late, y'know. If you come to work, the biggest thing they're strict about is time too." The remains of his smile hid themselves in his dark black mustache.

I'm the only one in my class who got a nine in sewing, so I have confidence in myself. I'm sure I could sew uniforms better than any other factory girl, but I'm, I'm fast with a needle and thread, but what if they use those machines like the one that Seon-hee from the clothing shop has in her house, I've never used one before, and I feel like I might not be good at it, but if I say I've never used a sewing machine before, then I wonder would they take me on? Maybe I shouldn't say anything, no, no, if I lie and go to this factory in Japan and then they tell me to give it a try and I can't do it, then they'll be mad at me for lying, and maybe they'll send me back to Miryang; I should just ask him, just ask, c'mon, Eiko, ask him.

"Um . . . do they use sewing machines to make uniforms?" she said, her dark face, which she knew had been sunburned, turned pale even in the dusk.

"What? Machines?"

"I only know how to sew by hand. I'm very, very good at sewing by hand though. . . ."

"Oh, gwaenchana, don't worry. It's all specialized, some cut the fabric, some use the machines, some add the buttons and lining, so there's no need to worry. And your Japanese is good, and if your hands are dexterous you can learn the work quickly."

"Oh, good. Then I'll come along."

"Y'know, it must be some kind of fate that we met like this on my last night in Korea. If you work as hard as you can for three years, you could dream of saving up about one hundred yen. However much money you can send to your parents, then that's great respect for them. Your parents won't live forever, y'know, my dad died of lung disease when I was sixteen. I had to quit going to school and started mining for coal up in the mountains of Chikuhō, and that was hard, I tell you. I sent it all to my mama just wanting to make her life a little easier, and I did. You know the phrase 'Filial piety and being cautious of fire should both be done before they end in ashes'?"

"No."

"How about 'You can't put a blanket over a gravestone'?"

"No."

"Well, they must've taught you this one in school: 'When you want to show your respect your parents will be dead.'"

"Oh, yes, that one—"

"There's another one, 'Your parents' opinions and cold liquor both only kick in later,' but I don't guess you've ever had a drink, so you won't understand that one, ha, anyway, tell me, what time are we meeting at Samnamjin station?"

"Eight o'clock."

"Good! Then see you tomorrow."

"Thank you, I'll see you then."

Eiko bowed deeply, her head down by her hips, then watched the man go up the embankment. Hooray! I got a job! But though this man seemed very nice, he did like to lecture me a lot, the one flaw of the whole thing. If he keeps up the sermons the whole way to Fukuoka for two days, I'll be sick and tired of it, but that's fine, I'm really good at pretending to sleep, when Eomoni and that man are sneaking around at night, I always make them think I'm asleep. Oh, now it's night for certain, that man's going to yell at me, I can just tell, you know, 'What is an unmarried girl doing out when it's this dark?' and so on. Well, fine, let him say it, because tonight's the last time. At eight o'clock tomorrow, I won't even be in Miryang anymore. I can think about the future as long as I want while I'm working, that one hundred yen he mentioned is a lot of money, if I had one hundred yen I could go wherever I liked, I could do anything, perhaps I could even go to the girls school in Busan, and if Eomoni calls it quits with him, then maybe we could even live together, just me, her, and Oppa, without anyone else bothering us, hooray! Oh, hooray!

She stamped her right foot hard, just like when playing jump rope, then ran up the embankment. August always has a dissolving kind of smell to it; the afternoons were so dazzlingly bright, and the cicadas and babies and ice cream sellers were always so loud that it was hard to sense it, but at night it's quiet so I can feel it. Yes, that smell, when I take it in I feel like I might dissolve myself too. But today the smell of sweat is winning out, my blouse and panties even are drenched. It's really the kind of time when I'd love to go to the public bath and wash my hair with soap, but never mind, I'm sure there's a great bath near the factory in Fukuoka. And it'll be bigger than the one in the Unha Bath. Too bad for the man who has to accompany me, but he'll just have to put up with my smell for two days. The problem is what to wear, I'd like to wear the dark red chima that I wore on New Year's to play neolttwigi by the river, but if I try to get it out of the drawer, then they're sure to be suspicious, so I guess I'll have to go in normal clothes, and then to keep them from suspecting anything I'll just take the jump rope. "Aigu, you're thirteen years old and you're still jumping rope, what about learning to cook or sew?" he'll say, so I'll have to be very quiet. But maybe I should think up an excuse just in case, because he'll give me the third degree about where I've been and with whom. She looked up at the moon, hoping to find a lie to tell. Full moon . . . I'll tell him the moon was so pretty that I went up to Yeongnamnu to look at it better, and anyway the moon is so pretty tonight . . .

The moon that falls on Yeongnamnu   is clear but
The Namcheong River just   flows silently

Ari, arirang   suri, surirang   arari gannat-yo
Going over the Arirang Pass

In the brightly colored Arang shrine
Arang's spirit dwells

Ari, arirang   suri, surirang   arari nanne
Going over the Arirang Pass

The sound of someone singing fell upon her from above, like the moonlight; she looked up at Yeongnamnu. She saw a woman wearing a pure white chima and jeogori standing there, along the railings of the pavilion. The pulse of the wind and the darkness slowed as if it were trying to go to sleep—then suddenly the wind went berserk.

Thump-thump! Thump-thump! Thump-thump! Thump-thump! Was that Arang? No way! Just some woman cooling herself on her way home from the baths, of course, the wind always blows through there.

Oh, I wonder if it was the mistress of the Dong-A Guesthouse, then? Someone did say she's addicted to opium and wanders around here at night.

Sol sol sarang sarang   sol sol sarang sarang, the tepid breeze coming off the river brushed against her cheek, twirling up her hair. The girl quivered, feeling that she was being embraced by a trace of water. *Sol sol sarang sarang,* the full moon slowly hid itself behind the clouds, and the light emitted from it was sucked soundlessly into darkness. Once I turn that corner there aren't any streetlights, oh no, they're going on and off, I don't like this, I'm gonna run, if I run I might miss my turn. Moths of all sizes and kinds were beating themselves wildly against the streetlight, and in the light their white, yellow, and light blue scales danced down. Once inside the circle of light thrown off by the streetlight, in time with the rhythm of its flickering the light cast the girl's shadow out like a whip and pulled it back to dissolve into the darkness. Aigu, the sole of my shoe is coming off, what did I do, it hasn't been that long since I got them. She shuffled out of the light, straining her eyes in the heavy darkness. What am I so afraid of anyway? That wasn't Arang's ghost, 'cause ghosts aren't real! If they were real, then my abeoji would come to see me. But what was it then, that cold wind that broke me out in goose bumps? I, I'm really not sure if I'll be able to go to Ilbon all on my own. Abeoji, Abeoji, please watch over me, I'll work wonderfully hard and come back with a lot of money, so please forgive me for leaving without saying goodbye at your grave, Abeoji, my only abeoji . . .

In-hale ex-hale   in-hale ex-hale   *sseureuram   sseureuram*   the evening cicadas have started singing   they sure do get up early   annyeong!   A new day has begun   more than any other season   in-hale ex-hale   running this path on a midsummer morning   really makes me feel like a new day has begun   in-hale ex-hale   the large, orange flowers of the Chinese trumpet creeper covering the main gate   the mountain of chilies drying on the veranda   that fucking dog   the sun is barely up and he's already hiding in the shadow of the storeroom panting jeongsin chalyeo, pull yourself together!   in-hale ex-hale   green   in-hale ex-hale   all the green   the stems of the peppers   and the burr of the chestnuts   and the jujubes   in-hale ex-hale   I like the green of the jujubes best   I'd always stuff my pockets full of them on my way home   and Abeoji would say   in-hale ex-hale   aigu   stop playing like a girl   in-hale ex-hale   in-hale ex-hale   only the pomegranates are starting to turn the slightest bit red   like the blush of a girl staring down in embarrassment   if you teased Noona she'd turn bright red right away   in-hale ex-hale   in-hale ex-hale   *byuu-byuu   byuu-byuu*   that's a kite   annyeong!   oh   it's turning, inscribing a circle   like it's saying hello back to me   in-hale ex-hale   though the clouds are moving very fast so the winds must be strong up there   there's a momentum in how it's flying   in-hale ex-hale   in summer there's a momentum to everything   the kind of momentum that brings forth shoots just from someone spitting out watermelon seeds   I forget that my body is also pulled down by gravity   in-hale ex-hale   each muscle in my body is a spring   in-hale ex-hale   carrying me on ahead   in-hale ex-hale   steadily pulling me ahead of feelings of loss and grief   **rain, rain   fall, fall   Mama   is   coming with an umbrella** that song works with the rhythm of running too   **pitch, pitch   chap, chap   run, run, run**   I forget the second verse   I must've learned it in school but   that was three years ago already   in-hale ex-hale   in-hale ex-hale   I wonder if my brother will quit running   in-hale ex-hale   all I wanted when I was eleven and started running   in-hale ex-hale   was to catch up with my brother   to be able to pass him   in-hale ex-hale   in-hale ex-hale   I've got to stop thinking about him   when I turn back at Samnamjin station I'll pick up the pace and then just jump right in at Yongdu-mok   and stay in the water until the cold has seeped into my muscles   in-hale ex-hale   summer vacation is almost over   I've gotta do my homework but   in the summer I don't have time to let the blood run to my head   after a swim I'll go up to Yeongnamnu   in-hale ex-hale   and then while I fan my face with a folding fan and listen to the old people talking and the calls of the cicadas   in-hale ex-hale   I'll sleep   the blueness of the sky has gotten darker   it's gonna be hotter today than yesterday   *sol sol sarang sarang   sol sol sarang sarang   sol sol sarang sarang*

Sol sol sarang sarang   sol sol sarang sarang, the breeze from the river picked up the scent of the camellia oil in the girl's hair, messing up the parting in her bowl cut, which she had combed over and over again, blowing Arang's words into her ear: gaji marara, gaji marala, *do not go, do not go*. A sound like a lock clinking shut resonated in her head, but she straightened her hair with her hands, pretending she hadn't noticed. The breeze sighed and changed its direction, rushing off to Aranggak to let Arang know what the girl was doing.

Deowora! Thirty ri is a lot farther than I thought. Last night when I casually asked Oppa he told me that there were only two trains a day from Miryang to Busan, the 5:54 and the 8:03. The first would've gotten me there too early and the last would be too late, so I decided to walk, but the soles of my feet hurt so, so bad, and I think I'm getting blisters. These rubber shoes are no good, but I didn't have time to get new ones, so I tied the sole back on with straw, but they still clip-clop, and the gravel is getting in, oh not again, ai tto, jeongmal!

She took off her shoe and put her right foot on the instep of her left foot as she got the pebble out. Suddenly, she felt something like suffocation and looked up at the August sky, so heavy with blueness that it seemed it could not bear the weight and might fall. It usually looked like it carried on forever, but today she felt like it was enclosed in a blue chima. *Is there something wrong with the sky or something wrong with my eyes, the sky is blue! Too blue!* She wiped the sweat from her brow with the back of her hand.

Thud-thud-thud-thud, she heard someone running up behind her, *oh, what to do, what if it's Oppa running after me*—she sped up and turned her head.

"Oh!" Eiko cried. *It's him!*

Thud-thud-thud-thud   thud-thud-thud-thud, he's getting closer, it's just like a dream, *thud-thud-thud-thud*. Eiko could not move, as if her feet had grown roots.

"Annyeong!" Woo-gun stopped too.

"Annyeong hasingyo." *He is standing in front of me; he spoke to me*—Eiko put her hands together like a clam and brought them up to her chin.

Their eyes met, neither one looking away.

"It's hot, huh." Sweat trickled down from Woo-gun's hair.

"It certainly is." Eiko put her hand in her pocket and gripped the jump rope.

"Where are you going?"

"To Samnamjin station."

"Are you traveling somewhere?" Woo-gun asked, stretching.

"Yes."

"On your own?" He raised his eyebrows.

"Yes."

"Today's going to be another hot one."

"I believe you're right."

"See you around." Woo-gun waved his right hand as he started to jog in place.

"Annyeong higaseyo." Eiko bowed her head slightly.

In-hale ex-hale in-hale ex-hale, she walked, following the sound of his breathing. Sinnanda, I can't believe that I spoke to him, **sinnanda sinnanda!** Eiko almost floated as she walked. If we stopped and spoke like that every day, then we might become close, he might start to like me. Eomeo, what am I thinking? But it's sort of too bad I never got to see *him* in uniform, when I was so excited for the new school year to start in September. Kyōjun said she'd seen *him*, wearing a white shirt and gray trousers with a black cap. And what's worse I didn't get to show *him* what I'd look like all dressed up for the Arang Festival . . . in a purple-and-jade-green jeogori with an indigo-and-scarlet chima. . . . I guess they'll choose Kanayama Kyoko after all. . . . Ever since I was a little girl I dreamed of being onstage at the Arang Festival . . . and *he* might get married in the next three years, he's already eighteen now. . . . All kinds of emotions hung over her like a dark cloud, bringing her down; a voice erupted from that dim shadow, reverberating in her head: you're too rash, if you leave home all on your own like this you know things won't go well, but Eiko shook her head as if she were waving away a mosquito, clapping as she started to sing.

Rain, rain fall, fall
Mama is
Coming with an umbrella
Pitch, pitch chap, chap
Run, run, run

Eiko opened the door to the waiting room at Samnamjin station. The room was filled with vagrants and seasonal workers, and the air was murky, like the hold of a smuggler's ship after a night spent there. She held her breath and went in. She tried to find the man from the day before and realized that she couldn't really remember his face from the darkness last night.

"Hey!"

Someone called out to her from behind. She remembered his flat cap. He was sitting there on that keodaran gabang, a big bag, smoking a cigarette.

"Hello."

"Good morning."

"You passed right by me, I thought you were just going to keep on going."

"I'm sorry."

"You didn't have much time to think it over, I wasn't sure you'd come."

"But I did."

"Good, so your parents let you go, then."

She hesitated. "My father died soon after I was born, so it's just my mother but . . . I didn't tell her. . . . If I'd told her she would've said no. . . . Is that terrible?"

"No, your mother will be happy if you work hard and come home with lots of money."

"Once I'm settled in I'll send her a letter."

"That's a nice idea. Did you have any breakfast?"

"No."

"It's crowded in here, but once we're on the platform I'll buy you an eel bento. Samnamjin's famous for its eel."

"Sir, I have no money whatsoever. I swear, I'll pay you back for the ticket and the bento once the uniform factory pays me."

"Oh, don't worry about that. Finding an excellent worker like you is reward enough, and I can supply your fare and meals, and even once you're over there, you'll eat for free. Your clothes and shoes are all provided for you too."

"I can't believe you'd do so much for me. . . . I promise, I'll work hard."

"Eel! Eel bento!" squeaked a boy, wearing a navy-blue work coat, whose voice had just started to change.

"Peaches! Get your peaches!" said a boy, holding a bamboo basket of peaches; he had a straw hat pulled down low over his eyes.

Eiko looked at the sunburned arms of the young men and remembered that it was summer break. Two mornings from now, Kobayashi-sensei would be standing at the lectern of her class, calling roll. Ito Yoko? Hai! Kanagawa Yoshimi? Hai! Kanemoto Eiko? And the third seat from the back by the window would be empty. After school, Kyōjun and Keiko would come around to her house. What will Eomoni and Oppa say? I wonder. No, by tonight they'll report it to the area chief of Sanmun-dong and tomorrow morning they'll report me missing to the police.... Then it'll be a serious matter.... If I'm going to turn back, I have to do it now.

"Want a peach?"

"Oh, ah ... No, thank you. I'll be full enough from the bento."

"It's a long journey, miss, might as well buy two or three, you know."

He bought two eel bentos and peaches, sat down on a bench, and took out his pocket watch.

"What time is it?"

"About ten more minutes."

She looked up at the mountains surrounding the platform, Mount Muheul, Mount Maneo, and Mount Cheontae. How strange, everything looks like it's standing still, the trees and the clouds and the air—she heard the loud, shrill pop of a train whistle, *choo-choo, chugga-chugga-chugga-chugga*, and a steam train emerged from the Cheontae tunnel, *chugga-chugga-chugga-chugga*, along the Nakdong River a trail of smoke, like a rain cloud, lingered in the air as the train slid into the platform, *chugga-chugga, chugga-chugga-chugga-chugga, chug...chug...chug.*

"We're in second class, toward the back. Oh no, we'd better run, I think, the train only stops here for a minute."

"I just want to go look at the front of it."

"There's no time!"

"I want to see, just for a second!"

"Listen to me: when the bell rings, you'd better jump on!"

"Sure!"

As she ran, she etched in her mind everything that she saw, like a child lost somewhere she didn't know. The long, tubular locomotive glowed darkly like a gun, the black plate on the front reading in white letters Pacific Second 582. *Pacific, pacific, pacific!* She heard the clanging of the departure bell and spun around, running as hard as she could, not caring that her skirt might blow up. *Choo! Choo! Choo-choo!* The dark green passenger cars began to move slowly through the thick cloud of smoke, and she could no longer see the hawker boys and the station staff with their red flags, all enveloped in the dark fog. She hurriedly turned on her heel and ran to a door, grabbing the handle of it as she stepped up onto the plate and tumbled into the train vestibule. With her eyes obscured by the smoke and her hair, she thought she saw a white jeogori flutter around her, but she blinked twice and the woman was gone. *Chugga-chugga-chugga-chugga*, as the sound of the steam locomotive became crisper and the platform disappeared from view, she closed the door with both hands and pulled on the door to third class.

It won't open, maybe if I try this? No, maybe this? She moved it to the side and the mechanical door slid open; she staggered under the weight of her excess force. The men in the third-class carriage all looked at her. She wiped the sweat pooling on her forehead away with the back of her hand and bit her lower lip.

"Excuse me, coming through, please."

"Aigo, ajig a aiga, honja eode gano—you're just a child, where are you going on your own?" a man lying in the overhead luggage rack asked her.

"Honja aimnida, jeojjogeseo abeojiga gidarigo itseumnida," she said. *I'm not alone, my father's waiting for me once I get there.* She felt it was the first time she'd spoken Korean in a very long time.

She stood up tall so as to look even a little older, and with her arms held stiff, she marched forward.

I wonder if I'll be able to get through? she thought. That man must be worrying about me, if I don't go fast he'll think I didn't manage to get on board, and then maybe he'll get off at the next stop, the next stop is Wondong, isn't it, so when we get to Wondong, I'll go out on the platform and run down to the second-class car, oh no, if I wait until Wondong I'll be soaked in sweat, and I don't even have a change of clothes, so I've got to get through somehow, she thought, as she squeezed herself past the men's chests and backs and arms and knapsacks.

With a sense of achievement, she arrived at the end of the carriage; taking care of how hard she pulled this time, she opened the door. The vestibule between carriages was full of people and baggage too. The man leaning against the door to the toilet was the spitting image of her stepfather and instinctively she looked him in the eyes. He looked tremendously sleepy, and he seemed weary as he chewed on some dried squid; he scratched his cheeks, sprouting salt-and-pepper stubble, with the same hand in which he held the squid. If he looks that much like him, then his voice must be the same too, I want to hear him speak, but no, no, any voice like his can go to hell, she thought as she stepped over a leather trunk and opened the door to the second-class carriage.

She was surprised by the difference between third and second class. The seats in third class were wood, but in second class, they were covered with white cloth, and in the second-class carriage no one was standing. Sitting in the carriage she saw men in their forties and fifties, all wearing the bluish-brown kokuminfuku that immediately told her they were Japanese.

"I guess you're going to rush right past me again. You oughta look around more," a voice called out to her from behind. She turned and bowed.

"Pardon me."

"I thought maybe you missed the train. You're the kinda girl who makes people feel anxious." A tinge of relief flashed across the man's face.

"I'm sorry."

"Well, don't just stand there, have a seat. Take the window seat so you can watch the scenery."

As she sat down next to him, the train gave off a screeching long whistle, *chugga-chugga-chugga-chugga, thu-thunk-thu-thunk-thu-thunk-thu-thunk*, as it began to cross a railway bridge. She did not realize that the river they were going over was the same Miryang River she had played jump rope by every day. If she had looked up, she would have seen Yeongnamnu, but her eyes had fallen to the water, where she stared at the shadow of the train. Even once they were over the bridge, the lamenting echo of the train's whistle still trailed after it.

She breathed in, taking in the man's body odor mingled with the smell of cigarettes.

"Do I . . . smell bad?"

"Bad? Well, we both smell of sweat. It's hot." He lifted the latches on both sides of the window, opening it, and the train's smoke came into the carriage.

"My face will get sooty. . . ."

The door opened, and in came the porter, wearing a blue uniform with gold buttons, accompanied by a guard wearing a white stand-up collar and blue trousers; they removed their hats and bowed.

"I am your porter for this journey. I will be traveling with you until we reach Keijō. Should you need anything, please don't hesitate to let me know. Please have your tickets ready for inspection."

At each passenger, the porter bowed and punched their tickets, with the guard assisting by taking the tickets as they passed down the aisle. The man took their tickets out of his pocket and handed them to the guard. She read the words written on the tickets: *Samnamjin to Mukden, must be used within one month of purchase, 2nd class, 18.8.30.*

"Mukden?"

"Yes, Mukden."

"But isn't that in the wrong direction?"

"You're not the only girl I've got to pick up, so things have changed and now we'll go from Dalian by boat."

"Dalian . . ."

"You'll only be four days later getting to the factory." Ignoring her agitation, he turned to the conductor. "What time do we arrive at Daegu?"

"Nine thirty-two, sir."

"And at Daejeon?"

"We should arrive at twelve forty-six, sir."

"Then I'll buy food in Daejeon. How long does the train stop?"

"Six minutes, sir."

"That's about all it ever is. I suppose we'll wash our faces when we get to Antung tomorrow."

"Yes, sir. At Antung, the train changes from Chōsen Railways to Manchurian Rail, so you'll have a half hour stop there."

The train went into a tunnel. The sound of its whistle reverberated in her skull; she could not follow her train of thought. Mukden? Mukden? In geography class, Kobayashi-sensei had showed them a map. How many centimeters above Miryang was Mukden? From what she'd seen of the map, she felt it was a long way away from Shimonoseki. Busan, well, even her oppa had been there lots, and Kobayashi-sensei had talked about Shimonoseki in class, but Mukden—*choo choo, chugga-chugga-chugga-chugga-chugga*, the steam train emerged from the tunnel, but she felt like she'd gone into a long, long tunnel. In the pitch-black inside of her mind, loneliness and the faces of her family and friends appeared. Eomoni, Oppa, Kyōjun, Keiko, my auntie in Kyo-dong, my uncle in Gagok-dong, cousins Jee-hee and Yong-i, Yong-jin ajumma at the herbal apothecary, Mr. Kim at the rice store, oh, and Woo-gun, oh, I'm leaving my hometown and diving into a strange land among strangers. Maybe this is something there's no coming back from. If I said I was getting off in Daegu, would this man be angry? Oh, of course he would; what should I do?

"Hey, have a peach or something," he said, as if he had seen through her anxiety.

"Thank you."

She peeled the peach with her fingers and took a bite. The juice ran down her chin, dripping onto her skirt, but who cares about a skirt; she just wanted to be absorbed in something, in eating. She ate her peach completely before he had even finished half of his, sucked on the pulp surrounding the pit, and spit it out into the palm of her hand.

"You're a girl who puts her belly before her appearance."

"Have you heard of Kunimoto Utetsu?"

"Who? That was a quick change of subject."

"Kobayashi-sensei said he was the fastest in Korea in the five thousand and ten thousand meters."

"A track runner, huh; Korea's good in the track events. Son Kitei and Nan Shoryu are the pride of Japan. When they stood on that podium and I heard the Japanese national anthem play twice, I thought I'd cry."

"Kunimoto Utetsu is famous too. He was even in the *Asahi Shimbun*. Kobayashi-sensei said he was the pride of Miryang Common School; he stuck the clipping from the paper on the blackboard and read it to us over and over.

'Korea and Formosa were temporarily held back by the Kantō region as it appeared Kantō was closing in on them, but as always, Kunimoto's superhuman efforts shut them out.'"

"Must've been the ekiden, then."

"He overtook five people. If the Tokyo Olympics hadn't been canceled due to the war he would have made the team. But his brother's more likely to make it to the London Olympics."

"But the thing about the London Olympics is," he said. He took a pack of Minori out of his pocket, struck a match, and lit a cigarette.

"That Britain is an enemy country, right?"

"Very good." With the cigarette in his mouth, he rubbed the fabric of the seat trying to smooth out the wrinkles, making new wrinkles that he then smoothed as he looked toward her thighs, where her small hands were arranged, then lifted his gaze to her chest, neck, and face.

"But even if he can't go to London, then he'll certainly make it to the next Olympics. Mr. Kunimoto Ukon is faster than his brother; he's very promising."

"It's great you're so enthusiastic." The man's face, his cheeks sucked in as he inhaled the smoke, looked as if he was contemplating something else entirely.

"Once I save up some money, I'm going to buy a radio, so I can listen to the Olympics broadcasts. About how much does a radio cost?"

"The cheapest you can get is about eight yen, I think. It's great to have some kind of goal, it gives you a reason to work." The man puff-puff-puffed out smoke like a steam train, forming a ring, then gave her a crooked smile.

"Really, I'd like to see it with my own eyes. I'd like to stand by the route and cheer him on. But it costs a lot to go overseas."

She realized she was being more talkative than usual, but if she stopped talking her unease would balloon, so she latched on to whatever came to mind, her family, school, Miryang, and said it as quickly as she could.

They arrived in Daejeon at 12:46 as scheduled. He stuck his arm out the window, brandishing a one-yen note and bought two bentos, some pumpkin seeds, boiled eggs, and fizzy lemonade from the hawker boy in the black stand-up collar who ran up under the window.

"Bentos are better in Manchuria, by a long shot. Tomorrow for dinner we'll buy sushi rolls from Hsiung-yueh-cheng. The bentos in Liaoyang are pretty good too, but we might be there a little too early. From Andong we'll be on Manchurian Rail, and along with the bentos they sell Chinese tea in little clay bottles. The cap is like a little cup, so you just turn it over like this and pour it in to drink it—it's pretty good."

She stared and stared at the disposable wooden chopsticks, something she'd rarely seen, and ate her bento, snacking on the pumpkin seeds as she drank her lemonade, tap-tapping her boiled egg against the windowpane and peeling it carefully from the cracks. Oh, I'm so full, it's been such a long time since I ate until I was full like this, I couldn't eat another thing, I'm feeling sleepy, last night I was so nervous I barely slept a wink, so sleepy, she thought, biting down on the boiled egg with a yawn. *Chugga-chugga-chugga-chugga*, the steam train knocked down some bush clover, trundling on as it brushed through some willow leaves. After Yongsan was Keijō, Hanseong, the capital of Korea, where Namdaemun is, and Changdeokgung Palace and Chang-gyeongwon Zoo, but that's still two hours away, gently sloping mountains, gently flowing river, farmers lined up shoulder to shoulder, prairies, paddy fields, bean fields, cornfields, pepper fields, and green everywhere, green, green, green, like passing by the same place over and over, *choo-choo, choo, choo-chooooo*, if she listened closely she could hear how each of the train's noises were different, *chugga-chugga-chugga-chugga*.

Oh, so sleepy, I can't, *chugga-chugga-chugga-chugga-chugga-chugga-chugga*.... In-hale ex-hale, in-hale ex-hale, I folded my hands over my stomach like a corpse, the August sun pouring intently on my closed eyes. The smell of grass after the rain, the sound of the river, in-hale ex-hale, in-hale ex-hale, the sound of his breathing coming closer, in-hale ex-hale, I open my eyes and, in-hale ex-hale, the sun evaporating the rain, in-hale ex-hale, his legs swaying as he comes closer, in-hale ex-hale, I wake up and get up on my knees in the grass to make sure it's his face, in-hale ex-hale, my hair grows and spreads like wings, reaching all the way up to Yeongnamnu, I think, then I turn my head and it flutter-flutters down like lint, flutter-flutter-flutter-flutter, down, down, the smell of rain, no, it's the river, it's the smell of the rain gathered in the river, I look down and right in front of me is its surface, my face penetrates the surface of the river, but I can't smell the water, there's no splash, no ripples, just complete engulfment, in the water, of my whole body, as if I'm swaddled and being gently rocked. **sleep-a-bye baby my precious child gift from the angels way up on high and when the dog barks it's far from your room in your starlike eyes the little bell of sleep rings** I can't breathe anymore, but I can hear, his breathing as he runs along the riverside, inhale ex-hale in-hale ex-hale, I run with the river, following after him, in-hale ex-hale in-hale ex-hale . . . choo-chooooooooo.

She opened her eyes, thinking she'd nodded off during class. Huh? This isn't school, where am I? A man in kokuminfuku and a flat cap, *choo-chooooo choo choo*, right, I'm on my way to Dalian, to work in a clothing factory in Fukuoka.

"You screamed out, I guess you were having a nightmare."

"A nightmare . . ."

"They say the luckiest things to see in a dream are Mount Fuji, an eagle, and an eggplant, in that order."

"In Korea we say that if you have a dream about playing with a pig, you'll become wealthy, or if you have a dream about falling into a toilet you'll become rich . . . but the dream I just had was about falling into the river. What does that mean? My halme would've known. . . ." Her hair was damp with sweat and her mouth was dry; she had been leaning against the window frame awkwardly, so her shoulder and neck hurt.

Who is this now sitting next to me? Eiko cast a sideways glance at the face of the woman, who was wearing a white chima and jeogori. Her eyebrows were thin, her chin jutted out rather far, and her lower lip was plump, thick, and red. Her skin was as pale as an eggshell, and her daenggimeori, tied with red cloth, were the longest and glossiest that Eiko had ever seen. She was about the same age as Jin-seo unni in Ulsan. But she was much prettier than Jin-seo unni, if a woman like this had lived in Miryang she would've been picked at the Arang Festival beyond a doubt, she really is very pretty, she's got me mesmerized and I'm a girl . . .

"I thought I'd show you the Han River, but you were so fast asleep I couldn't wake you."

"What? Are we in Keijō already?"

"Oh, we're past Keijō now and heading to Shinmaku. We stopped for ten minutes in Keijō, enough time to wash your face . . . Keijō Station is a Western building with a Byzantine-style cupola, built at great expense when Saitō Makoto was Governor of Korea. On the way from Shinmaku to Heijō you can see the Taedong River and the stone-built Heijō Palace, but it's getting dark so we probably won't be able to see them. I'll buy us dinner in Shinmaku. Oh, I should've introduced you. She'll be working with you."

"Nice to meet you."

She responded in Korean. "You too. I can't speak Japanese. I didn't go to school, only lessons at seodang. How old are you?" Her expression could have been either friendly or suspicious.

"I'm thirteen."

"The same age as my little sister. Aigu, leaving your parents to go work in Japan at that kind of age, aigu, poor thing. Well, we'll be working in the same factory for the next three years, so just think of me as your big sister and if you need anything, you come to me. And I'll think of you as my little sister back in Anseong."

The woman's accent was so strong that in places Eiko couldn't understand, but somehow she grasped her meaning. She wanted to ask her about Anseong, and to talk about Miryang too, but she held back, not wanting to exclude the man by speaking in Korean. As if the woman understood how Eiko felt, she stopped talking and looked out the window.

"Rain?"

"Yeah. A journey in the rain is a romantic thing, isn't it?" The man put his hands on both sides of the window and forced it closed.

"Rain?" Eiko pressed her face to the glass.

It was raining. The sky was a dingy, muddy color, and the light outside lost itself in the rain. She cast her eyes on the gray lines that fell one after another. *Chugga-chugga-chugga*, the steam locomotive panted as it ran over the wet tracks. Pulling along its eight cars, the mail carriage, third-class carriage, third-class carriage, third-class sleeping carriage, dining carriage, second-class carriage, second-class sleeping, first-class sleeping and observation carriage, even the *thu-thunk-thu-thunk-thu-thunk-thu-thunk* sound of the train crossing a railway bridge sounded heavy with water. She looked around the carriage and realized that where the seats had once been filled with men in kokumin-fuku, they were all now taken by women with daenggimeori in chimas and jeogoris. The men must've gotten off in Keijō, and these women took their place, she thought. Sky-blue chimas, scarlet-red chimas, light green chimas . . . it's like a bunch of different-colored umbrellas opened up and laid out on the ground.

And I'm the only one who looks like this, she thought, remembering the peach juice on her skirt and looking down in embarrassment. Oh, I do wish I could've worn that jujube-colored chima . . . ah-ah . . . **pitch, pitch chap, chap run, run, run . . .**

"Pardon?"

"'Ame, ame fure, fure.'"

"Oh, the one that goes 'Rain, rain fall, fall Mama's coming with an umbrella,' right?"

"What time is it?"

"It's five twenty. We'll be in Shinmaku in an hour."

"It's evening already."

"Soon enough it'll be night. The days are getting shorter."

"Do you mind having the window open?"

"Go right ahead."

The train started going downhill and the locomotive and the engineers too must have taken a breather, because there was very little smoke. She washed her face with the fresh, humid air and took a deep breath. In Mukden they would change on to the Dove and get off in Dalian, spend the night there and then get a boat—still quite a way to Shimonoseki . . . so much farther to go. . . . She stuck her face out into the rain and looked at the peaks of the faraway, purple-tinged mountains.

Looks like the rain's letting up over there, this is the first sunset I've ever seen in the rain, some parts of it are a deep, grape-purple and others are more like wisteria, some are reddish as if tinged with blood, it's more creepy than pretty, like I'm heading toward the end of the world.

The door opened; the porter appeared, taking off his hat.

"In ten minutes, we'll be arriving at the next station, Shinmaku. If you're disembarking there, please be ready. Take care not to leave anything behind."

"Right, how many bentos should I buy?" The man stood and began counting women wearing chimas and jeogoris. "Hmm, hana, dul, set, net . . . daseot . . ."

"But . . . I'm still full from lunch. . . ."

"My dear, you're a growing girl; once it's in front of you you'll feel hungry. You interrupted me and now I've lost my count. Hana, dul, set, net, daseot, what's after daseot?"

"Yeoseot."

"Very good, I had no idea. One, two, three, four, five, six, seven, eight, nine, ten, eleven."

He touched his flat cap and stood again, calling out to the boy in round glasses sitting two seats ahead of them.

"Hey, in ten minutes we'll be in Shinmaku."

The boy raised his head with a startle and looked around.

"What's with you? You look like you woke up in a trench. Buy enough for thirteen, will you? The train only stops for one minute. If you don't get them in Shinmaku, we'll all have to hold out until we get to Heijō."

Once they were past Heijō, the other passengers' heads started to loll to the front or the side, and once they were past Teishū and about to arrive at Shingishū station, not even the clanging of the bell stopped their snores and teeth-grinding.

"In five minutes, we'll be arriving at the next station, Andong. If you're disembarking there, please be ready. Take care not to leave anything behind."

After Andong we're in Manchuria, she thought, we might've crossed over from Korea already, where is the border? I wonder.

She recalled the map of the Greater Asian Co-prosperity Sphere that had been stuck on the blackboard in her geography class as she stared out the window into the darkness. The squeal of the train's whistle and the rumbling vibrations of its movement roused the woman next to Eiko, who was leaning against her shoulder, but her head fell back again to the rhythm of the train's clattering, this time onto her baggage with her own outstretched arm as her pillow. Each time the train shook, the handle of the umbrella she had tied to her trunk hit her forehead.

I bet when she wakes up her arm is going to be dead, Eiko thought, but then reconsidered: she's sleeping so soundly, I'll just let her sleep. *Thu-thunk-thu-thunk-thu-thunk*, we're going over a bridge again, I guess we must be crossing the Amnok now, we're near where Sohn Kee-chung, who won the gold at the Berlin Olympics, was born and raised, where he went around selling melons and sugar cubes as he ran the embankment of the Amnok River with women's rubber shoes tied to his feet with straw, if only it were light out so I could see the banks of the river, but it's dark, just like it was when we were by the Taedong, so famous for sailing, and the Pyongyang Castle where King Yangwon of Goguryeo lived, and I couldn't see any of it. Maybe in three years when I come home, I'll be able to see it all. Andwae, I'll be coming back by boat from Shimonoseki, and then I'll get a train from Busan, so I won't go through Sinuiju. I might be the one who's traveled farthest of everyone at Miryang Common School, even including Kobayashi-sensei and Terao-sensei, I'm definitely on top, after all I've gone from one end of the Korean peninsula to the other, crossed over to Dalian, and then from Manchuria I'll cross to Japan!

This might be the first and last time I'll take such a long journey, once I get married and have children, I'll barely be able to leave the house, I mean, Eomoni hardly sets foot out of the house except to work in the field or go shopping, and to her Yeongnamnu seems pretty far, and that's not even two ri away. Aigo, what must she be thinking right about now? Maybe she thinks I've drowned at Yongdu-mok and she and Oppa are out looking for me with torches, heading for the darkened river and mountains, calling my name. Aigu, Eomoni! Aigu, Oppa! Oh, I should've told them everything and gotten their permission before leaving home. But then I wouldn't have made the train, it would've been impossible to persuade them in just one night, but, but, but I should have at least left them a letter. What a way to betray my eomoni, who raised me all on her own. Eomoni, Oppa, please forgive me, I'll earn so much money at the factory and I'll repay you, when I get to the factory, I'll write you a letter right away, she thought. In her mind she put the letter she would write in an envelope, then remembered that she really needed to pee; she walked gingerly down the aisle so as not to wake anyone and went out into the vestibule.

She pulled open the metal door, closed it behind her, and checked to make sure she'd locked it before pulling down her panties and squatting over the toilet. It wasn't much of a toilet, only a hole in a plank; the *thu-thunk-thu-thunk-thu-thunk-thu-thunk* sound vibrated up from her groin, and she could see right below her the paving stones of the tracks. I'm gonna be dizzy, an-dwae, don't look down, I'm shaking so much, oh no, if I fall, I'll die, she thought, gripping the handrail as she peed, then straining all the muscles in her body, she stepped down from the platform one foot at a time.

Andong had a big station with four tracks, and the electric lights, under their glass covers, cast a gentle, milky white light over each platform; on platform two, thirty minutes before departure, the Pacific Second 541, having taken on water and coal in preparation, and the trainmen with their red flags waited impatiently for the Continent.

The Continent arrived at Andong at fifty-two minutes past midnight. The Pacific Second 582 was uncoupled from the passenger cars that it had pulled from Busan to Andong, and the trainmen started coupling them to the new engine with brisk movements.

She slapped some water onto her face, dried it on the hem of her blouse, and walked down the platform. The trainmen in their bluish-brown caps and uniforms were connecting the electrical lines and water pipes, waving red and green flags to send some kind of signal to the engineer. The Chōsen Railways porter handed the passenger seating list to the Manchurian Rail porter, who was taking over, and the sooty-faced Chōsen Rail engineer, conductor, and his assistants who got off the Continent dragged themselves along the platform with weary expressions, utterly unlike those they had worn when working, walking past the engineer, conductor, and assistants in Manchurian Rail uniforms without even saying hello.

She sat on a bench looking up at the night sky. Star . . . star . . . star . . . It had rained so hard all the way until Pyongyang and yet . . . this must be what they mean when they say "a starry sky" . . . They're twinkling . . . it's like I can almost hear it . . . the music the stars play . . . The innumerable lights shining in her eyes illuminated the inside of her head; unable to bear the brightness anymore, she closed her eyes. As she did, she felt something like two large palms insert themselves behind her head and underneath her buttocks, and before she could exclaim, her body had floated up horizontally. In that instant, somewhere in the darkness of her soul a memory from when she was just born that had been folded up small unfurled soundlessly like the bud of a water lily, and a strange sense of familiarity spread throughout the reaches of her body. She sensed him, her abeoji, whose face and voice she had no memory of. She thought, so this is how my abeoji held me. Jebikkot gateun uri cheotttal, my first daughter, like a violet—she felt his nervousness and excitement through his warm, thick palms. Is this the past? Or a dream? Abeoji, are you there? Are you holding me? Tears seeped out from the seams of her eyelids. She felt that if she only opened her eyes, her abeoji's face would be right there, but, nunbusida, but—the moment she just slightly opened her eyes, she felt them covered by a cool palm. A woman's hand, but whose now? It absorbed the white light, returning the inside of her head to its previous darkness.

She opened her eyes and saw a large puff of smoke vomiting out with a whistle, white steam mixed in with the black smoke streaming from the engine's smokestack.

It's leaving; I've got to get back to my seat. The *chugga-chugga* of white steam coming from under the cylinder engulfed the train; she broke through the smoke and went into the vestibule of the train. There were a few men in there, knapsacks for pillows, cradling their baggage, lying down on top of newspapers. Were they Japanese? Korean? Manchurian? Chinese? She read the headline on a piece of newspaper sticking out under a man's back.

WANHSIEN ROCKED BY EXPLOSIONS, WHARF IN FLAMES: TEN PLANES SHOT DOWN IN WUHAN, AIR FORCE TAKES DOWN THREE SHIPS

It was the *Asahi Shimbun*, so this man was Japanese, most likely. The clanging sound of the bell rang from the platform, enshrouded in steam, and the train set off with a shudder, *chug . . . chug . . . chug . . . chug . . .* but what did it mean? The dream she had that afternoon about falling into the river . . . and

the one just then where she floated into the night sky . . . falling . . . floating . . .
I wish a fortune teller would tell me what it all means, it must be some kind of
sign, I mean, I don't usually dream at all . . . how strange . . . in both dreams I
was wrapped up and held . . . She fumbled through her memories from her
dreams, trying to cling to the big palm that had supported the back of her
head, where her neck wasn't yet strong enough; the interval between the
chug chug chug chugging sounds of the train got shorter, and as the lights
on the platforms at Andong Station got farther away, her fleeting dream grew
even more fleeting, dissolving into the darkness of her soul like the moon into
the dawn sky, *chugga-chugga-chugga-chugga-chugga-chugga* . . .

Back at her seat, a man wearing a white hemp shirt who stank of alcohol
was sitting next to the man in the flat cap; he grinned, showing his tar-
yellowed teeth, and held out a bag of peanuts. She was full, but she knew that
if she refused, then she'd have to say something, and then this man would almost certainly say something, and drunks always talk loud, and once they
start they don't stop, so he'd be annoying and draw everyone's attention, so
fine, she'd have some, she decided and stuck out her right hand. He turned the
bag up on its end dumping the whole thing, so she hurriedly put her left hand
out too, but not in time; most of the peanuts fell on the floor. She gathered
them up and put them on the lap of her skirt, conscious of the man's gaze as
she broke one's shell and put the nuts in her mouth. In lieu of saying thanks,
she bowed; the man suddenly broke out in loud song.

Shout for the joining of East and West
Rising Manchuria, her wide-open lands!
The corn grows tall on stalks e'er blessed
Rustling, we hear, from its ears so grand
The promise of a prosperous future—
The richness of her earth is never-ending!

Raise up the flag of ethnic harmony
Rising Manchuria, full of power!
Gleaming with hope so fervently
Toward the Sun now she cowers

Following the light of the Imperial Way—
Her people's prosperity is never-ending!

"Shut up! Can't you see people're sleeping? If you sing again, I'll push you offa the train." The man in the flat cap's voice was harsh, like a different person's.

He munched peanuts as he grumbled to himself, but somehow, blessedly, he seemed to fall asleep. His jaw slacked and his mouth opened, and the peanuts, mixed into a paste with his saliva, stuck to his disgusting-looking tongue; in the back of his mouth, she could see a few big gold teeth. She took the peanuts from her lap and put them in her pocket, then stuck one of her elbows up on the windowsill, the way she would've propped up her chin in her dreaded arithmetic class. The air had a completely different smell to it, the rich perfume of soil with decades and centuries of accumulated fallen leaves and rotten wood and the remains of small birds and insects, with the smell of water mingled in it too; the wind must be carrying with it the smell of a rushing river nearby, but wait, there's no wind—it's the smell of the air itself.

It's more the smell of marshes, and I can smell ever so slightly a bonfire. Warm and damp and strong and heavy, when I breathe in through my mouth the air leaves an aftertaste on my tongue like I've just licked brass—she sensed not with her mind but with her nose that she was in a foreign country.

Night fell. She stretched her neck and looked at the wristwatch on the arm of the man who had given her the peanuts. Five minutes past five—Eomoni and Oppa won't have slept a wink either. No! I can't think about them, not until I get to the factory! Don't start with a head full of worries; neither regret nor spear-carriers can come first.

The sky lightened from black to deep indigo, briefly losing its blue and turning gray, but with the rising of the sun the blue revived itself; a deep blue spread across the sky and through the minds of all looking upward. She felt an expansive loneliness, and for the first time in her life she thought about the word *freedom*.

In Japanese class, I raised my hand and asked, "What does freedom mean?" and Kobayashi-sensei told me, "It means acting according to your own will, just as you feel, following your heart," but freedom is such a lonesome thing. A morning all alone is far, far lonelier than a night all alone, because a morning is freer—

The door opened, and in came the porter in his drab uniform with its three golden buttons, accompanied by a young guard.

"Good morning. My name is Yamada, and I'm your porter. It's my pleasure to be traveling with you today. Should you need anything, please don't hesitate to let me know. My apologies for waking you all; please have your tickets ready for inspection."

"Morning." The man in the flat-brimmed cap opened his eyes and stretched, yawning.

"Good morning!"

At the sound of her voice, the woman next to her in the white chima and jeogori woke up.

"Oh, I'm sorry. I shouldn't have spoken so loudly."

"Aniya, museoun kkumeul kkugo isseonneunde. . . . Kkaewojwoseo gomawo . . . ," she said: *Oh, I just had the most terrifying dream. . . . Thank you for waking me.* She looked as if the dream had just been thrown into relief.

"Ohayō gozaimasu," she said, saying good morning in Japanese, dampening down her tousled hair with spit and pushing it behind her ears, though she still seemed half-asleep.

The man who had boarded at Andong was still sleeping in the same position he'd fallen to sleep. His mouth was hanging open, but the peanuts on his tongue were gone: had he swallowed them in his sleep or spat them out?

"May I ask you something?"

"Go right ahead. I'll answer if I know."

"Why are there so many trees cut down around the tracks?"

"Oh, right, that's to improve visibility because they're afraid of attacks by armed bandits and anti-Japanese guerrillas."

"Oh . . . this must be quite a dangerous place."

"That's right; you're not on the peninsula anymore. The peninsula's been part of the Japanese Empire for thirty-three years, but here in Manchuria it's only been about twelve years, so there's still a lot of room between the ideal and the reality."

"That field over there, that's wheat, and over there's soybeans, but what's that? Look, it's over there and there too—it's all the same, some kind of tall grass?"

"It's kaoliang, a kind of sorghum. They grind it into a fine flour and make crackers from it, or they knead it and fry it as dumplings. And they make liquor from it too—Maotai's fifty-five percent; just the smell of it gets you drunk."

"I have another question."

He stuck a Minori in his mouth and lit it with something he held in his palm.

"Go on." The tip of his cigarette bobbed; the smoke took a detour past the sleeping man's face before making its way up to the low ceiling.

"It's about the locomotive."

"You'd better ask one of the engineers, then."

"Pardon me for waking you, sir, but . . ."

The man's eyes fluttered two or three times as if he was trying to go back to sleep; his head jerked forward and he ground his teeth.

"We'll come back to him later," whispered the porter to the guard.

"Excuse me, may I ask you a question, please? Sometimes the smoke that comes out of the locomotive's stack is white like a big fluffy cloud, and sometimes it's as black as a rain cloud, you know? Why is that?"

After bravely asking her question she felt the blood rush to her head slightly and lost her balance; she wrung her hands.

"When coal is added and it starts to burn, the smoke is black. Once it's been going for a while it turns white. When the train is starting off or going uphill we add coal, so that's why it's often black."

"Thank you, sir."

She bowed her head, and the porter bowed too, then moved on to the next carriage.

"You're a curious one, aren't you?" The man in the flat-brimmed cap blew white smoke out of his nostrils like two tusks.

"My grades were always second best to the boy who joined my class in fourth grade, but nobody puts their hand up in class more than me. I think, when I've saved up a lot of money, I want to go to Busan Girls School. If my stepfather will let me, that is."

"Well, I don't see why he wouldn't let you. You'll have saved up the money all by yourself, after all." He tapped the ashes from his cigarette on the floor. Below his seat was a mess of cigarette butts, peach skin and seeds, an empty bento box, disposable chopsticks, and peanut shells.

"Nan yeohakgyoe gago sipeoyo. Sijipgaseo aereul nanneun geotdo jochiman, geujeone na jasineul mandeulgo sipeoyo." *I want to go to a girls' school. I want to get married and have a family too, but first I want to make something of myself.*

For the first time she looked straight on at the face of the woman sitting next to her straight on.

The woman in the white chima and jeogori nodded with a glint of a smile in her eyes. "Kkog gal su isseul geoya." *I'm sure you'll be able to do just that.*

The sound of her voice was much gentler than her gaze and much, much further away. The girl took her gaze and the sound of her voice to heart and wished that she could talk to her more in Korean. I always wanted an unni; I've always been jealous of Kyōjun and Keiko, who have tons of big sisters. But would she do all the things an unni would, like comb my hair and braid it, do my hair ribbons and pins for me, let me confide in her about things that would make Eomoni lose her mind if she knew? I'd be so, so happy if she would. Once we get to the factory I want to talk to her so much; I'm assuming private conversations are forbidden during work hours, but there's got to be lots of other time to talk, like over dinner, or when we're washing up at night, or before we go to sleep.

We're slowing down, she thought, and looked outside to see the train already gliding into a platform at Qiaotou station. The clouds of smoke around it meant she couldn't see clearly, but as far as she could tell not a soul got off the train. They were at the station for only one minute, so, without time to catch its breath, the train set off again soon with a *chugga-chugga-chugga chugga-chugga-chuggaa chugga-chugga-chugga.*

Across this background of blue and green, which could not have been more intense, the Continent drew a black line of smoke, and as she stuck her head out the window, her bowl cut fluttered in the same direction as the trail of smoke. The pale sun, its color lost to the heat, was climbing higher in the sky little by little. She strained to look at what she could see through breaks in the smoke. Where, in this quivering but largely unmoving sea of green, were the cows and goats and people? The wind rushing down from the mountains rippled through the green as if it were water, rustle-rustle-rustling its way toward her, but it was no match for the tornado of wind caused by the train, which forced it back.

The sun looks like it's painted on to the bright blue sky, but maybe that's just my imagination. It was so hot that the sweat was rolling down her face, but she felt cool air coming up from near her feet.

To me there's nothing tranquil and pretty about what I see outside. It's barren and desolate, and I feel it's glaring at me as if to say, quit looking at me.... But why? Why is that? Is it 'cause of what he said about them cutting down the trees because of attacks from armed bandits and anti-Japanese guerrillas?

"The next station is Mukden. Passengers wishing to transfer to the Renkyō Line should change here, please. The train toward Tashihchiao is a local train departing at eleven thirty-five; from Tashihchiao the train to Dalian is an express service departing at thirteen forty-seven. I wish you a pleasant onward journey."

Choo-choo! Choo! The whistle drowned out his voice. *Chugga-chugga-chugga-chugga-chugga-chugga-chugga-chugga-chugga-chugga-chugga-chugga*, preparing to go uphill, the locomotive picked up speed, running right up the steep incline. As she watched how the eruption of smoke turned from white to gray to dark gray to inky black, she imagined the soot-black faces of the engineers shoveling coal ceaselessly into the blazing furnace. *He said when the train is starting off or going uphill they add coal, didn't he, I'm glad I asked, I always need a bit of courage to ask anything, but in exchange I get as much knowledge.* The smoke had turned even darker and she could hear a loud rumbling, like the sound of an earthquake; the clack-clack sound of the passenger cars was trivial, as if it were happening elsewhere entirely. *Up at the front of the train they're struggling with all their might, there must be sparks coming out of the smokestack too, I wonder if there's any danger of one of those sparks falling on dead grass and starting a fire in the dead of winter? How many kilometers an hour are we going right now? Oh, if only there were a guard here, I'd ask him so many questions. Poor Pacific Second 582, you must be out of breath from pulling eight cars, I bet you'd rather be light and* sleek with just one car, but right now I bet if you ran against Woo-gun you'd lose. In the puff-puff-puff-puff of the steam engine she heard the sound of Woo-gun's breathing, *puff-puff-puff-puff in-hale ex-hale puff-puff-puff-puff in-hale ex-hale* . . .

The Continent, having climbed the hill, found itself engulfed in its own smoke and steam as it now ran downhill at a speed appropriate for an express train. Andwae! You can't go that fast! Woo-gun won't be able to keep up! He's falling farther and farther behind the observation car at the end . . . his white running shirt like a handkerchief waving farewell . . . But still he runs, chasing after the smell of the smoke and the clack-clack of the cars, running, running, running! In-hale ex-hale   in-hale ex-hale   *puff-puff-puff-puff* . . . Oh, look at me, letting my imagination run wild again. . . . Maybe my lack of grasp on reality is because I'm always traveling in a cloud of smoke. Where will I land in reality? And what kind of reality will it be? Soon we'll be in Mukden, and I'll have to leave this train too.

The steam whistle squeaked like a little pocket whistle, and for a second she thought she could see, just before the crossing, someone standing there with a horse cart, but with a *clatter-clatter-clatter* they disappeared down the tracks behind her. Mukden must be huge; I always thought Miryang was a big city, especially around the station, but how wrong I was, this is ten times bigger, I reckon, I gotta take it all in and write Kyōjun and Keiko a letter.

The porter and guard again came through for ticket inspection.

"Sir, I'm very sorry to wake you. May I see your tickets, please?"

The man opened his eyes. His broad, relatively flat face had no trace of the displeasure of a hangover; indeed, he had an open and peaceful expression. He took his tickets out from his breast pocket and as he handed them to the guard, he asked, "How much longer till Mukden?"

"Forty minutes, sir."

"Oh? Can it really be that late already?"

He hurriedly looked at his wristwatch.

"Well, I'll be damned, it's already six thirty-five. We left Antung at one twenty-two, so . . . I really was out like a light."

"We wish you a pleasant onward journey." The porter and guard returned to their compartment.

"What station did you get on at?"

"Miryang, sir."

"Where's Miryang?"

"It's about an hour from Busan by regular train."

"You're from the mainland, I can tell. Where are you from?"

"I . . . I'm not Japanese."

"Oh, you're Korean, got that wrong, didn't I?"

He moved his lips like an inchworm, she thought, as he pulled a wrinkled handkerchief out from his hemp shirt and mopped the sweat from his neck, then looked at her face.

"I can tell with about ninety-nine percent accuracy if someone's Japanese, Korean, Manchurian, or Chinese, but you, you look just like a Japanese. Now, look, she's the perfect example of a Korean; see how her chin and cheekbones stick out like that?" he said, gesturing with his chin toward the woman in the chima and jeogori. "You can always tell by the little, narrow eyes, like a fox's." He pulled up the corners of his eyes with his fingers.

"Do you go to school?" he asked.

"Sure."

"So where are you going?" He started rummaging around for something, patting the pockets of his shirt and trousers, lifting up his hips and twisting around.

"I'm going to work in a uniform factory in Fukuoka."

"Boy, you Koreans really do love the mainland. And you must be her chaperone?"

"Yeah," the man in the flat cap responded in a low, cold tone, snuffing out his lit cigarette butt with his shoe.

"I hope you don't have to work too hard. I'm taking up a teaching position at the Nihonbashi Higher Elementary School in Dalian. . . . Oh, blast, did I leave them in the library in Antung? Sir, I'm quite sorry, but could I ask you for a cigarette?"

"Here you go." He tapped the box, decorated with ears of rice, and one cigarette popped out.

The teacher straightened his back and breathed the smoke in deeply, then blew it out his nose little by little as if he were reluctant to let it go.

"You know, cigarettes made in Japan really are the best. I always smoke Bijotai, but they're really hit-and-miss, you know; sometimes they're great and sometimes they're terrible. I'd say seventy-four percent are awful."

"Manchurian cigarettes are famous for how awful they are. Bijotai, Furusato, Kamome, Kyokkō . . ." The man in the flat cap lit a Minori and flicked the match out of the window.

The teacher gazed at his wristwatch and took another puff; he chuckled, disturbing the shape of the smoke. He was now at peace enough to enjoy the movements of the smoke rising up past his face as it quivered in the air.

"Thirty more minutes. When I'm teaching, I put my wristwatch on the lectern and check it all the time while I'm speaking, so I'll end my story at the precise moment we get to Mukden, just you wait and see.

"This is a story so well-known it's even in the South Manchurian Educators Association's supplementary textbooks. The Japanese government gathered young men from across the nation and sent them over here, aiming to cultivate a group of settlers. First, thirty thousand men in 1938, ten thousand in 1940, and thirteen thousand in 1942, and they keep sending them. Some were dispatched to big cities like Hsinking, but some got sent to places like Harbin and Heiho that were under Russian control, and some were even sent to the great plains of northern Manchuria where as far as you may roam nothing, and I mean nothing, obstructs your view. When you're just passing through like this on a train it looks like it's nothing more than a prairie, but once you take a hoe and a spade to it, well, the experts were just astonished. With such moist, lustrous black soil, you know, you can grow crops even without using fertilizer for two or three years, that's how fertile the land is. The burdock root and carrots and pumpkins and corn grown here are shockingly big and taste good too. Once you taste these continental vegetables, you won't want a thing to do with produce from the peninsula or the mainland; I'm serious, just give 'em a try and see.

"These young men who settled the continent were rosy-cheeked sixteen- and seventeen-year-old boys. With their bare hands they took these empty plains and built roads, houses, warehouses, and fields. It must've been very hard for them, you know, being apart from their families, and there must've been a lot of times they wished they could go home. So how did they bear it?

Because something much, much stronger than hardship or loneliness was burning in their hearts. Following through on the lofty goal of settling Manchuria for the sake of their country—with that sense of purpose they dug up the earth with their hoes and spades. If they hadn't overcome their hardships and loneliness, we wouldn't have the pride of being the leading force in the East or see ourselves as having built a new country with our own hands.

"Japan, once an island nation, has been reborn as a continental one. To realize our goal of Five Races Under One Union, the Japanese people continue to cross the sea, borne forth by the fervor of our devoted patriotism, and as we control and instruct the Koreans and the Chinese, we must also dedicate ourselves to development and administration and the elimination of national problems. That means it can't just be like it has been, focused on the cities, where all the politicians and industrialists get together; we need Japanese farmers to take root deep and wide or else it won't work. Even if we build racial unity in cities like Dalian and Mukden, if the five races can't be reconciled in the regions that form their power base, then it's obvious that Japan's management of the continent will end in failure. But it's undeniable that those of us who were born and raised in Japan, the island nation, have some flaws as continental settlers. Now, to overcome that, the government's thinking is that it would be ideal if all of its citizens were educated on the continent for a certain period of time, and I'm in complete agreement with that idea.

"The Youth Volunteer Fighting Corps have been dispatched as part of that ideal; as the vanguard of the Japanese people, their battlefield is to settle this land so as to instill the spirit of the founding of the nation on this continent. I've heard tell that they get up before the sun rises, line up, worship in the direction of the imperial capital, sing the national anthem, raise the flags of both Japan and Manchuria, recite the imperial rescripts, and then they turn toward the rising sun and give three cheers for the emperor. The Japanese blood flowing throughout their bodies is passed through into the sky and water and soil of this continent.

"Well, then, how to share the spirit of Japan with other races who don't have Japanese blood running through their veins—now that is quite the problem. On the peninsula it took thirty-three years for the governing ideal of the unification of Japan and Korea, without prejudice, to permeate and to be realized, but the continent is vaster and has a larger population, does it not? The Korean people have a gentle manner that makes them happy to become tenant farmers for someone from the motherland; they have little arrogance and can't oppose those from the motherland—but on the continent, every coolie, even the women and girls, give you a glare filled with defiance, or even outright hostility. But the thing is, on the surface we're just pretending at indifference, like a cicada perched on a tree trunk, you see, but we're the ones willing to forgo sleep and food to build railroads, roads, and bridges, maintain the sewers and electricity, right, cultivate the farmland and research what crops are suitable and how to improve, and then we give jobs to these people who were living like beggars, and they don't even thank or trust us.

"The main thing is language—the Japanese language is the only thing for it. Only by speaking Japanese will these people develop a Japanese mentality; it's only through the bedrock of the Japanese language that patriotic spirit can enlighten them. The Koreans implemented the Korean Education Act requiring Japanese-medium education in 1911 and in 1940 the name change policy started; you see how much things changed there? That's what we've got to do on the continent too. We must be both educators and rulers. It may take fifty, sixty... maybe one hundred years for Five Races Under One Union to be realized, in its truest sense. . . ."

The teacher rolled the words around in his mouth as if he were savoring them and dropped his cigarette, the fire now having reached the end of the cigarette. With a slight bow, he took one of the cigarettes that the man in the flat cap proffered, then turned to the girl, who had a troubled look on her face.

"My dear, have you ever seen the Manchurian flag?"

"N-no . . ."

"It has in the upper left four stripes of red, blue, white, and black, surrounded by a field of yellow. Red for the south, blue for the east, white for the west, black for the north, and yellow to represent the center; this is to symbolize both that the center controls the four directions and to show the spirit of Five Races Under One Union, meaning that a person of any race who lives in Manchuria will be treated equally. Do you know what the five races are?"

"The Japanese, Manchus, Han, Mongols, and Koreans."

"Very good, excellent. Just remember, the capital is Hsinking and the emperor is Emperor Kangde."

The teacher held the unlit Minori between his fingers and as he pondered, all the while the train ran on toward Mukden, shuddering at curves, houses occasionally flashing past, blowing its whistle five times and slowing down with a judder.

He looked at his wristwatch.

"Five more minutes—well, that's just enough time to sing the Manchurian anthem. The Western brutes may try to attack, but the Eighth Route Army or the New Fourth Army, either one, won't let the Yanks and the Brits lay a finger on this paradise. Long live the Japanese Empire! Long live the Greater East Asian Co-prosperity Sphere!"

Tiān dì nèi, yǒu liǎo xīn mǎnzhōu
Xīn mǎnzhōu, biàn shì xīn tiān dì
Dǐng tiān lì dì, wú kǔ wú yōu, zào chéng wǒ guójiā
Zhǐ yǒu qīn'ài bìng wú yuànchóu

Screeching its brakes, the Continent slid into the platform at Mukden station, and before the train had come to a complete stop the teacher had tucked his leather bag under his arm and disembarked.

The woman in the chima and jeogori put her wicker trunk on her back; the girl stood up, holding only a drawstring purse.

"Eomeo, jimeun?" *Oh, where's your bag?*

"Nan igeosbakke eopseoyo. . . . Sikgudeul mollae nawatgeodeunyo." *This is all I have. . . . I hid it from my family that I was coming.*

"Aigo, jigeumjjeum geogjeonghago gyesigetda." *Aigo, they must be worried about you by now.*

"Hakadae dochakamyeon pyeonji sseul geoeyo." *I'll write them a letter when we get to Fukuoka.*

The moment she stepped down onto the platform, the smell of garlic tickled her nostrils and she felt her mouth start to water. The hawkers were waiting in front of the first- and second-class vestibules. To a man they were all silent, simply showing their wares: whole roasted ducks and chickens in bamboo baskets; shanzhazi yi skewered on bamboo sticks like dumplings; watermelon seeds and pumpkin seeds and salt-roasted sunflower seeds; dried jujubes; apricots preserved in sugar; mahua and shaobing and yuebing and youtiao wrapped up in old cloth; fruits like apples, pears, apricots; bottles of Chinese tea, kaoliang and baijiu and more.

"It looks good, but we have a lot of time so let's go to a restaurant near the station."

She followed the man in the flat cap toward the ticket gate, hearing the hawkers calling out all around her. "Chīfànle ma?" "Guāzǐ!" "Shuǐguǒ!" But the droves of girls with bowl cuts and boys with shaved heads were heading not toward the men selling fruit and seeds but toward the platform where the next train would arrive, carrying steaming lánzi full of mantou and Tianjin baozi.

Once she was through the gate, she cast her eyes greedily all around her at the streets of Mukden, the gigantic buildings, the broad streets radiating out in three directions. She heard a clatter-clatter and turned to her left to see a two-horse carriage coming; the coachman cracked the whip and the carriage passed right by her. *Whap-whap-whap-whap-whap-whap-whap-whap-whap*, she turned around. Pigeons! A hundred? No, two hundred or more, she thought. A flock of gray pigeons went across the sky, gradually narrowing their circles until they landed on top of the redbrick station. She whispered to herself unconsciously: Manchuria, paradise of the Asian people . . .

The group of two Japanese men and eleven Korean women killed their time having lunch at a Western restaurant near the station, peering in at souvenir stores, and wandering around record stores, before returning to the platform twenty minutes before departure.

"How was the omurice?" the man in the flat cap asked, letting out a belch that stank of beer.

"It was very good. It's the first omelet rice I've ever eaten. The red rice under the eggs, tell me, what is it flavored with?"

"It's ketchup. Rice, sugar, sake, cigarettes—there ain't nothing you can't get as long as you're willing to slip a Manchu some money. It's like the long ration lines back on the mainland and the peninsula aren't even real."

"Which one's the Dove?"

"That one over there."

"I'm going to go take a look."

"To make sure we're not stuck with that teacher all the way to Dalian I changed our seats. Welcome to first class."

The gleaming black locomotive, polished carefully, was done taking on water; the coal car had been loaded with coal and the fire grate checked; and checks to the undercarriage had finished—all that was left to do was wait, puffing steam, for the ring of the departure bell. If you looked closely it wasn't black at all, it was a dark blue so close to black, like the color of a night with a full moon, and it was shaped a little differently than the Continent; the front of the locomotive was a smooth semicircle, while the passenger cars were a deep green, like the leaves of a zelkova; Pacific Seventh 12, one two, hana, dul, remember that, hana, dul! Hana, dul!

The Dove left Mukden station at 13:47 as scheduled. As she watched the scenery outside the window, she could not suppress her yawns, and once they were past Sujiatun District, she closed her eyes; before they were at Liaoyang she had slumped over against the windowsill.

When she opened her eyes, the sun was a reddish gold. The shadow of the train undulated across the kaoliang fields, and the smoke was tinged with the setting sun, leaving a crimson trail. A black cloth umbrella was the only part visible of a Chinese farmer in his field, hidden from the neck down by the leaves, and the umbrella, like a stepping stone among the crops, appeared then disappeared, disappeared then reappeared. I was dreaming, I can't remember what it was about, or if it was sad or happy. . . . She stuck her head out the window and felt the air dry the sweat of sleep from her brow, like a cotton cloth hung out all day in the sun.

"Where are we now?"

"We're almost at Hsiung-yueh-cheng."

"Really? What stations have we passed?"

"Liao-yang, An-shan, Tang-gang-tzu, Hai'cheng, Tashihchiao."

"How many more to go?"

"Hsiung-yueh-cheng, Fu'-hsien, P'u-lan-tien, Chin-hsien, Sha-hou-k'ou, then Dalian."

"Just six more stations, then."

"You were so sound asleep I didn't want to wake you. But then you ate a lot this morning and couldn't finish all your lunch. Tonight, we'll have sushi, maybe; they're famous for it in Hsiung-yueh-cheng. Cucumber rolls and inari sushi."

"What time do we get to Dalian?"

"Nineteen forty-five."

"You know the timetable about as well as the guards."

"Well, I've done this trip six times this year."

"All to the uniform factory in Fukuoka?"

"No, no . . . sometimes to a food plant in Osaka, or a machinery plant in Shimane, in which case I take a different way."

"Where will you be recruiting for next?"

"I don't know. We just get the orders from the top, you know. . . . Oh, I just remembered about the dining car."

"Yes?"

"Bet you've never eaten in one."

The man in the flat cap stood up and called to the young man who had joined them at Keijō leading all the other women.

"Hey, I'm going to the dining car."

"Really?"

"For a change of pace."

"Ja sikdangcharo jeonyeok meogeureo gaja." *Hey, let's all go get dinner in the dining car*, he said, and the women picked up the hems of their chimas and stood up.

"Sikdangchaneun ohochanikka josimhaeseo gara, heundeullinikka mariya, hahahaha." *The dining car's car number five, so be careful, 'cause it shakes, hahahaha.*

He had such beautiful pronunciation that anyone would believe he was Korean if told so. Maybe he really is Korean, she thought, looking at his fair, angular face. Should I ask him? For a second, her eyes met with his, small and framed by his round glasses; she looked down, trying to appear nonchalant. The only ones who can ask where you're from are the Japanese; we're the ones who always answer. But somehow, she sensed something brutal in his eyes;

even as a smile filled his face his eyes alone pierced through his face like the lead of a pencil. . . .

The train shook with a clunk, and the women tensed the napes of their necks sticking out of their jeogori collars, slowly shuffling down the aisle.

The tables for four were all full, so she sat at a table for two across from the man in the flat cap. A white tablecloth was spread and in the porcelain vase there was a large, yellow peony, with only the tips of the petals red. The car was lit with a row of eight bare light bulbs with milky white shades. A steward clad in a black, three-buttoned uniform with a black bow tie approached, bowed to the man, and handed them a brown leather-bound menu.

"Welcome."

The man grunted.

The steward returned to the galley, and a waitress wearing a green outfit with a white apron appeared, carrying a silver tray in one hand.

"Welcome. What may I get for you?"

The man read from the menu.

"Soup, steak, cooked vegetables, rice, crème caramel, fruit, coffee—that's the Western set meal, are you fine with that?"

"That sounds fine, sir."

"Two Western meals."

"And to drink?"

"What beer do you have?"

"We have Kirin and Tsingtao."

"I'll have a Tsingtao."

"One Tsingtao?"

"Yep."

She heard something hitting lightly against the dark window and looked to see large drops of rain running down the outside of the glass; the smell of the rain came in through the open windows. The steward and waitress hurried to close the windows.

"The rainy season here hits in July and August. And it's not like in Japan, where it's drizzly and muggy; it really falls hard."

She followed his actions and cut a piece off her thick steak with the knife and put the bite into her mouth.

"How much does this cost?"

The man in the flat cap picked up his frothy beer, brought the foam close to his nose, and smiled delightedly, then drank down the beer in one gulp.

"Mm-ah, one yen and twenty sen."

"What?" She set her fork and knife down on the plate. One yen and twenty sen—the naengmyeon at Hyangchon is ten sen, so this is twelve times more; I'd rather not eat it and just have the money. . . .

"Our apologies for interrupting your meal. The next station is Hsiung-yueh-cheng; we will shortly be arriving at Hsiung-yueh-cheng. Any passengers who are disembarking are kindly asked to make sure they have all their belongings."

The guard and steward bowed and went through the dining car, now filled, thanks to the closed windows, with the smell of beef stew and coffee and brandy.

The man in the flat cap stuck a leg out into the aisle, stopping the steward.

"Think you could swing by first class and shine my shoes? All this traveling's got them looking rough."

"Of course, sir." The steward bowed.

"Hey, miss, some baijiu."

The waitress brought over a glass of baijiu; he brought it up to his mouth and took a taste, then put his lips to the glass again and gulped.

"There's nothing to do on trains and boats but get drunk, but I prefer trains by a long shot. On boats you sway around even if you don't drink, and if you do, then all that swaying just makes you sick."

Just during the one-minute stop in Hsiung-yueh-cheng the rain grew harder, pinging off the sparsely populated platform and the train like oil popping. The signal turned green and the train set off again, the rails sending lonely echoes of *chugga-chugga clatter-clatter* farther and farther on ahead.

The man in the flat cap looked out the window at the Manchu hawkers walking down the platform without umbrellas, carrying boxed meals, mantou and fruits in their arms; wiggling his spoon through his crème caramel, he said, "I'm glad we ate in the dining car. Who wants to eat some dripping-wet sushi? And look at those sheets of rain. The person who thought of comparing rain to the ropes used to hold down sails must've been thinking of rain like this; just look, it's thicker than a chopstick. After a heavy rain like this, then you get a long, intense drought that goes on and on. It's a completely different climate here to the mainland or the peninsula, y'know. At the beginning of this year, I took the Asia Express from the start in Dalian all the way to Harbin, and y'know, up there, half the year the temperature's below freezing, so even within Manchuria it can be totally different.

"The Asia Express—that's the pride and joy of Manchurian Railways; they launched it about ten years ago, and even when the doors are closed it's not hot at all and none of the smoke gets in. I heard even if they had dozens of engineers shoveling in the coal that they'd never keep on schedule, so it's done automatically. From Dalian to Hsinking and then on to Harbin, it goes 120 kilometers an hour with seven carriages behind it; isn't that something? The West might have us beat when it comes to airplanes, but they're no match for us when it comes to trains."

She stared into the black liquid giving off steam in her white cup, then entwined her fingers around its handle and gingerly took a sip.

"It's so bitter. . . ."

"Add some sugar, that'll sweeten things up."

She scooped some sugar from the pot, hana, dul, and stirred it into her coffee, then tried it again: still bitter. She added two more spoons, set, net, and now the coffee was sickly sweet and made the inside of her mouth feel sticky, but in front of him she felt she had to drink it with enthusiasm.

"I'm trying to keep myself awake. One cup of this and you won't nod off all the way from here to Dalian." He stuck a Minori in his mouth and lit it; holding the cigarette in his mouth, he stood up and went to the counter to pay.

They walked through second class back to first class; she looked around the carriage anew. In second class the seats were in groups of four facing one another, but in first class all the seats were in sets of two, all facing in the direction of travel, with generous space before the seats in front.

Somewhat abruptly, the whistle blew, sounding reluctant, and immediately after, the door opened and a young steward walked in carrying a wooden box.

"I'm here to clean your shoes, sir."

"Well, hurry up. And don't be sloppy."

"Yes, sir." The sharp-looking steward got down on his knees, took the bottle of polish and cloth out of the box, and began to polish the man's shoes.

"Are you Manchu?"

The boy hesitated. "Yes, sir."

"Got it in one."

The man dropped a twenty-sen tip into the steward's hand.

"Thank you, sir." The steward returned to the staff compartment, his eyes still cast downward.

They arrived in Dalian at 19:45. She turned to look over her shoulder and looked at the pale, gleaming rails. It was the second night since she had left home and already catching the Continent from Samnamjin station felt like something that had happened years ago; Miryang was far behind her now.

And the next time I'll see Miryang ahead of me is three years from now . . . no, I'm sure I'll get so homesick before then that I won't be able to stand it, and whether I'm asleep or awake I'll be dreaming of Miryang. . . .

"They based this station on Ueno Station in Tokyo, but I think it's prettier than Ueno."

"I've never seen Ueno Station. . . ."

"Oh, of course, hahaha!"

The man couldn't seem to stop laughing. What was so funny? He must be drunk, I mean, he had two glasses of beer and five glasses of baijiu, but he's still walking just fine. I wonder what he's like when he's drunk. . . .

"You take everyone to where we're staying. This gal and I are going to take a little trip around in a carriage," the man in the flat cap ordered the boy with the round glasses, then walked off toward where the horse-drawn carriages waited in front of the station.

So I was right, he is drunk, but I'd like a ride in a carriage, and I want to see the streets of Dalian; after all, tomorrow we'll have to wake up early and go straight to the port, so I won't have any time to walk around. She looked at the broad, rain-pounded paved roads. The Western buildings made of stone; the city buses; brick walls; the fine wrought-iron gates; the August wind blowing, scattering the rain through the leaves of the acacia trees planted along the roadside, suddenly reminded her that it was raining.

It stinks of manure, but there's no fields anywhere near, so how can that be? She took a sniff and looked around. It's horse dung, there's some here and over there, aigu, it's everywhere; in Miryang it's mostly rickshaws, with just one carriage waiting outside the station, so the worst on the side of the roads is dog crap, though in the dry riverbed there's some cow and goat dung. . . . She walked carefully, avoiding the dung, following behind the man, who had suddenly turned untalkative.

He waved his hand and a carriage came.

"First, take us to the main plaza." He climbed up the steps and sat down in the back seat.

"Yes, sir, the main plaza."

The driver swung the whip and the horse took off, the flames of the two lanterns attached to the driver's seat bending quiveringly.

In truth, she would rather have walked so she could take in everything at her own pace, but she knew she wasn't here to be a tourist, this is just a city she was passing through, and perhaps she'd never be here again. . . .

"Yeppeuda . . . ," she said in Korean unconsciously, then said it again in Japanese. "How beautiful it is."

The streetlights lined both sides of the street like trees, casting their hazy light through the rain. There were fifty, no, a hundred.

"It's a purplish white . . . I've never seen light that color."

"Have you ever seen acacia flowers before?"

"No, sir."

"Well, those are acacia trees there next to all the streetlights. In May, they're all covered in white flowers, and when you're walking down this street, you're surrounded by their sweet smell."

"What's the acacia flower like?"

"Imagine a white wisteria flower, in clusters, and when each bud opens up it looks like a butterfly, and then you can see its yellowish pistils—it's really very charming. One time, when I was bringing some girls I recruited over, it was May, and they were all oohing and aahing. Too bad it's not May right now. In the fall, there's things that look like long green beans hanging from the branches, and when they're mature they burst and black seeds spill out. It makes nectar too. It has sharp thorns, though, you've got to be careful, but if you pluck a clump of flowers and chew on it, it's a little sweet. You can make tempura with the flowers too, hahaha, I always turn any conversation back to food. I guess that's just how I am." The man in the flat cap patted his stomach and laughed.

"Oh, yes, you were asking about the streetlights. They used to be gaslights, but a few years ago they electrified them, and I guess they racked their brains trying to figure out how to make them look more like gaslights."

"The plaza's round."

"How can I explain this best to a young lady brimming with curiosity? Hey, take a loop around the main plaza."

The carriage slowly went around the road that formed a double circle around the plaza. She thought about how she wanted to walk along the asphalt path, meandering like a brook, through the dense, lush greenery, and stand in the very middle of the round plaza.

"We'll do another loop; look this time. See how the plaza is the center circle with ten roads radiating out? Well, that's why there's nine buildings surrounding the plaza. Look right, there's the Yamato Hotel, Dalian City Hall, the Oriental Development Company building, the Bank of China, Yokohama Specie Bank, Kwantung Bureau of Communications, the Bank of Korea, Dalian Police Station, the British Consulate General, all standing in a circle.

"The Yamato Hotel is owned by South Manchuria Railway; they have them in Mukden, Hsinking, Harbin . . . I forget where else, but they have sixteen hotels, one in all the major cities of Manchuria. And the inside's just as spectacular as the outside. They ordered all the furniture from Europe.

"South Manchuria Railway isn't your average rail company. They've got their fingers in harbors, mining, iron manufacturing, even in administering the land along the rails, education, and military authority, even; they keep opening up primary and secondary schools all over Manchuria. The employees of the railway are the elite of the elite. They get paid better than at any top company on the mainland, so the top graduates of the universities dream of working there. New employees are recruited on the mainland. The south side of the city is where all the railway's staff housing is; all the streets are filled with brightly colored Western-style houses, like they've been colored in with crayons: green, blue, brown, yellow, red, pink, peach, all the colors of the rainbow. They're all furnished with big rooms with wooden floors, hot water, and steam-powered heating; the nickname 'civilized houses' has even spread back to the mainland."

The man yawned widely, before narrowing his eyes as if he were looking at something in the depths of the darkness.

"I'm sobering up, and I'm starting to get sleepy. Hey, take us to the Tōgō Ryokan in Shinano-chō. It's tricky to get just drunk enough, but I think I'm gonna sleep real well tonight. If I don't have enough to drink, then my mind races and I can't sleep, so I drink until I'm calmer, and then the next morning... Look, the closer we get to the station, the rougher it gets; the area around the station is where most of the Japanese live, broken up into little sections, Wakasa-chō, Mikawa-chō, Naniwa-chō, Ise-chō. Take a step into an alley and there's red lanterns everywhere, all the customers and places are Japanese; it's easy to forget where you are—Fukuoka? Osaka? Maybe Tokyo . . . ?" He trailed off. "Look, look, over there, isn't it just like a Japanese city?".

She was nonplussed. She'd always thought that wherever people gathered, cities sprung up naturally, and the more people there were, then the bigger it got, but Dalian was a city dreamed up in the minds of some Japanese higher-ups and created just as it had been planned. But it wasn't only Dalian, it was Mukden and Hsinking too; the Japanese were, in their minds, revising the entire continent from start to finish . . . One Land Under the emperor . . . **colony** . . . the Greater East Asian Co-prosperity Sphere . . . **invasion of China** . . . Five Races Under One Union . . . **anti-Japanese patriots** . . . settling Manchuria and Mongolia . . . **scorched-earth policy** . . .

This's your room, he said, putting his hand on the door to the room assigned to her, opening it slowly so that the hinges didn't creak; at her feet the laid-out futons swelled in mounds the shape of people. As she thought to herself that it was like the aejangteo in Gyo-dong back home, someone rolled over in their sleep and a mountain moved; she tiptoed through, careful not to step on any of the mounds, and lay down on a vacant futon.

She was sleepy, that was true, but she had seen and heard so much, her head was so full of shapes and colors and sounds and voices that she didn't know what she should think about first. Her body was telling her to rest, not think, but her mind was racing, racing, trying to catch the tail of a word or an image.

The rain was still falling noisily. She hugged her pillow and tried to listen to the sound of the rain. The reverberation of an organ somewhere snuck in between the raindrops.

Blow softly, blow, spring wind
Blow, spring wind, blow, through the willow threads
Blow, blow, spring wind
Oh, spring wind, blow
Gently blow . . .

She sang along in her mind, thinking: whoever's playing isn't very good, it sounds like they're playing while they're trying to figure out where the next note is on the keyboard . . .

but don't blow here, in this garden . . . see, they stopped again . . . **wind, don't blow, wind . . . through the cherry trees . . . don't blow, wind, in this garden** . . . are they playing without a score? It must be a girl about my age . . . **no, don't blow, wind   don't blow   wind** . . . her playing is so disjointed I forgot how the next line goes . . . **a long time ago, when Korea belonged to the Koreans, there was a girl named Arang in Miryang District, an only daughter** . . . speaking as if flinging the words into the air . . . it's Halme's voice . . . **Arang had lost her mother at an early age, and she trusted her nursemaid as a mother** . . . **And there was a man by the name of Ju-gi who was in love with Arang and tricked her nursemaid; the nursemaid lured Arang out to Yeongnamnu** . . . **The full moon shone reflected in the Miryang River, casting its glow on the banks where the violets and twinleaves were in full bloom** . . . on nights when I couldn't sleep my halme would always pat me on my chest and tell me old stories . . . **When Arang, drinking in the exquisite beauty of the spring evening, turned around, there stood a man . . . It was Ju-gi. He confessed his feelings for her, and**

when Arang attempted to flee, he pushed her down, loosening the strings of her jeogori and putting his hand in her chima . . . Arang resisted violently, and Ju-gi, enraged, took out his blade and stabbed her in the throat . . . Halme, dead now for seven years . . . my beloved halme . . . Arang's father, having lost his beloved daughter, went crazy . . . a ghost with disheveled hair at the railing of Yeongnamnu . . . I am Arang. I'll tell you the name of the man who killed me, please undo the han that binds me here . . . once Halme finished her story she would always rub my chest and stomach and watch over me as I fell asleep . . . and I'd doze off feeling her eyes on me . . . sometimes I'd open my eyes slightly . . . see her wrinkled, sun-browned neck . . . oh, what a nice breeze . . . Halme's fanning me with a paper fan . . . She took a breath in, slowly exhaled, and fell gently to sleep. The organ was still playing, somewhere far off, in fits and starts . . . I'm in the sunny backwater of a river, swimming naked, the water up to my neck.

The rays of sun reflect off the surface of the water glittering, *banjjak banjjak*, and my limbs sway, pale in the sunlight, but the water is cold as melted ice. Maybe the sunlight is cooling it, she thought idly, laying her head back on the water and looking up at the sky. It was August, of course. Everything was so green, so lush that it almost looked black. The wind rose; the greenery moved, moved, moved. The wind wasn't coming down from the sky; it was rising up from the river. But there's no sound, she thought. Not from the wind or the river; even my own body is silent. A dead silence. High, high above the tops of the trees, the kites were inscribing circles within circles in the sky, but she couldn't hear them calling to one another. On the banks of the river the reeds were swirling around as if they were fluid, but there was no rustling. She tried putting her head underwater. Bubbles spouted from her nose, but they didn't burble at all. She opened her eyes, moved her limbs, and tried to swim against the current, heading upstream. As she did, every inch of her skin felt a sliminess.

The sweetfish are swimming past me. I'm swimming upstream with the sweetfish, but with the coldness of the water and how hard it is to breathe, I can't do it, she thought, sticking her head above the surface with a gasp.

Was I dreaming? Did I wake up? Instead of taking a breath? She tried moving her right arm in front of her eyes and saw that her skin was bristling with goose bumps. She turned her head and saw a thin belt of sunshine coming in through the gap in the curtains. Halme isn't here, even though when I couldn't sleep, she told me the story of Arang . . . No, I'm not at home . . . I took the Continent, and then the Dove . . . Dalian, I'm in Dalian . . . oh no! Everyone else is already up! But I want to lie here a little longer, my body's chilled through from the water, eueu, chuwo, what time is it? *Guh-guh-guh-guh-guh-guh-guh*, a cooing dove cried faintly; she listened with one ear still pressed to her pillow and heard the *chi-chi-chi-chi-cheep* of a sparrow; *ka-ka-ka-ka-ka kaw-kaaaaw keel-keel-keel*, all the calls of birds she had never heard before mixed together, but the cooing dove she had first heard did not call out again.

She went downstairs and found the two men and ten women sitting at two dining tables, starting to eat. She sat down in an empty chair and looked at the steaming food. White rice congee, green bean congee, mantou, guo-tie, jian-bing, baozi, wontons, yuebing, pidan tofu, pickles, Chinese tea in a ceramic pot with a dragon design—she lifted her arm, heavy with the exhaustion of swimming, and grabbed her spoon.

The pale blue sky had ripples of clouds as far as the eye could see. Oh, I've discovered a cloud formation that looks like tiger stripes! There's clouds with little holes all over like a beehive, it's like the wind is drawing with clouds, see that cloud over there, doesn't it look just like it was just scribbled down? That one's tangled basting thread, and that one's a thimble, and nearby there's a pile of waste thread and cloth scraps, so I think I'd call this the "sewing box."

"Haha, this little lady really is full of curiosity. She's even got her eyes on the sky." The man took off his cap and stretched, letting the sun wash over his whole face.

"But the sky and clouds are so pretty. . . ."

"Oh, see, when the clouds are that high up, summer's almost over."

"What day is it today?"

"The first of September."

"Already?"

"Yep."

It's the start of the second semester, better get serious. She read the words on the sign at the streetcar stop with the same expression as if she were looking up at the class schedule on the noticeboard at school: *Shinanomachi—next stop Nihonbashi.*

Above the streetcar stop, an acacia tree, its bark torn vertically, crossed branches stiffly with the poplar next to it; every time the wind blew, their glossy, rain-washed leaves rubbed against one another, and as they spoke, rain-drops scattered from them and fell, like drops of mercury, making impact around the whorl of her bob. The poplar's branches stretch straight into the sky, no matter what country it's planted in, just like the poplars along the banks of the Miryang River, the ones that cheer *him* on as he runs down the embankment morning and night . . . he should be running right about now . . . in-hale ex-hale. She spread her arms like wings and took a deep breath.

"That big building over there is the Kikuya department store. If you go down the lane just before it, there's a row of restaurants behind it; at night you walk under lots of strings of electric lights. There's a street that intersects Shinanomachi vertically stretching to the east, and Naniwa-cho is on either side of that street. I guess nothing's open right now, but there's a music store, a candy store, a café, a dance hall, an oden place, a soba place, an eel place, a kimono store, a Western clothes store, a shoe shop, a watchmaker, a hardware store, an antiques shop. . . ."

"Just about anything you could want."

"There's nothing you can't find on this continent. Dalian has its own Nihonbashi, even a Ginza; about the only thing it's missing is an imperial palace—hahaha!"

I can't fit everything I've seen in my head. She focused with all her might on looking at the flowers of the silk tree hanging over into the road from the garden of someone's house. As she reached out for one of its brush-like, pale crimson flowers, a green streetcar arrived at the stop with a screech.

It ran right down the middle of Kanbu Street. On either side of the road were horse-drawn carriages, rickshaws, and public buses. Boys in black high-collared uniforms and caps who hadn't seen one another over summer vacation and girls in sailor-style uniforms chatted, laughing, but the workers in their brown or yellowed shirts said nothing, wearing expressions of pure endurance.

"In spring, the coolies come down from Shandong on junks to work. In Dalian there's a lot of work in oil extraction and stevedoring. I can't believe this—even though there's special streetcars for them, here they are swaggering around, not knowing their place. But hey, these Chinks, they don't speak Japanese, they can't understand a word I'm saying. Hey, you stink! The smell of garlic and green onions is unbearable!" The man in the flat cap pulled a handkerchief out of his pocket and covered his nose with it, jabbing one of the day laborers in the side with his elbow.

She heard the Chinese man yelp and exchanged glances with him. Her heart pounded violently. He knows that I'm a Korean, that I'm a Korean who speaks Japanese like a Japanese—she clamped her arms to her sides, pressing against her heart, which felt like it might jump out of her rib cage.

The Chinese man ended the glance as if shutting a door, turning his eyes toward the beautiful streets bashful in the illumination of the morning sun. Ominagi Street, which led to the harbor, brimmed with such an abundance of tranquility that it was almost hard to believe there was a war going on.

The sea! Over that wave there's another wave, and then another, and another, and another, and another, and another! It's so big, it's like there's no end. It's like a big, blue animal, swelling like it's breathing in deep and then flattening back out. The sea! She wanted to scream, but her throat wouldn't let her voice out. She faced the sea, her hands outstretched and fingers tensed. Each time a white wave broke, its shining light entered her, slowing the intervals between her heartbeats little by little, and the fear, surprise, unease, and sadness that ebbed and flowed in the hesitations of her heart were bundled with the light and thrown onto the waves. She felt something strangely hot and dazzling gush-gush-gush through her entire body. Aya, nunbusyeo! But I won't close my eyes, it feels so good! I want more, more light! She shook her head hard, slowly raised her chin, and stared out at the line between the sky and the sea. That white line's called the horizon. As far as she could see, the sea was just as blue as the sky, but white waves bashed into the quay, clustered with mounds of barnacles, where the corpse of a jellyfish floating in an oil slick came and went, pulled in and out by the waves. The wind fluttered her hair, shirt, and skirt, striking against the beads of sweat from her brow and smoothing them out like pebbles on a riverbed.

As she gazed out at the sea she bent, stretching her right hand to her calf. In her sleep she had torn at her mosquito bites and left them bleeding; now she scratched at them with her outstretched, blackened nails. Then she took off her rubber shoes, the soles of which had come loose and were clop-clopping with each step, and barefoot, she put her right foot in one of the rusted rings that connected the mooring ropes, which gave a little bounce, and pretending that she was playing jump rope, she began to sing.

Ame ame   fure fure
Kaa-san ga
Janome de   omukai
Ureshii na
Pitch, pitch   chap, chap
Run, run, run

She remembered that her jump rope was in her jumeoni. As she pulled the pouch out of her pocket, peanuts scattered at her feet. I forgot, that teacher gave them to me, and I put them away without eating them. She cracked a peanut with her teeth and removed the shell, then threw it at a seagull, which had its white wings spread and was crying like a baby. The bird plunged down almost touching her hair, catching the peanuts in midair, but once it realized it couldn't eat them, it let them drop from its beak, hovering on the waves at the base of the lighthouse to rest its wings and voice. She skipped down to the jetty where the lighthouse was and sat on the wall of the breakwater, dangling her legs as she whistled with her fingers to call the seagull.

The man in the flat cap looked with disgust at his match, which wouldn't light in the wind, and raised his head, unlit cigarette in his mouth, to squint at the girl as if he were severely shortsighted.

"C'mere! I got something to tell you!" he shouted suddenly, waving his hand.

The girl leaped up and ran, swinging her limbs wildly as if she were running across a road.

"You can't just run around barefoot like that. What if there's rusty nails or glass around?" He paused. "Say, how old are you?"

"I'm thirteen."

"Thirteen..." He had hurt his voice from smoking too much; even his sigh was hoarse.

"This is the first time I've seen the sea. It takes an hour and a half by train to reach Busan, but most women in Miryang never leave there once in their lives. My grandmother didn't, and probably my mother won't either... Where are we? Where's this sea?" She squinted out at the sea. The sun and the wind shone on the crest of each wave.

"It's the north of the Yellow Sea, at the tip of the Liaodong Peninsula, between Liaodong Bay and West Korea Bay."

"So you mean... whichever way you look you can't turn away from the sea?"

He was silent for a moment. "My duty was to bring you to Dalian Port."

"What?"

The man turned his back to the sun and wind and lit his cigarette, tasting his own resin-stinking saliva.

"I wish you the best." As he exhaled, the smoke was scattered on the wind and disappeared.

Gratitude blossomed in her heart like a flower; she swallowed and choked back tears. For some reason, the man's face looked strained to her. The wind stopped as if it were holding its breath, and a ship approached, dragging behind it a dazzling, snow-white wake. At the prow of the ship fluttered the Japanese flag.

TWENTY

To Paradise

| 낙원으로 | 楽園へ |

Countless stars shimmered in the perfectly clear night sky, and the silver moon, which looked like it had been made of bent wire, shone its light into the vast darkness. She was on the deck, trying to control her nausea, and retracing the path that had brought her here. All the other women had apparently gone south, except for the unni who had been sitting next to her on the train, who was the only one who had gotten on the *Mukden-maru* with her at Dalian Port. That night, Mr. Yoshida, the leader, explained that the ship's destination was not Fukuoka but Shanghai, that the military uniform factory in Fukuoka had enough workers now so they would instead go up the Yangtze River from the port of Shanghai to work in a military boot factory in Wuhan.

I've never even heard of Wuhan, I don't want to work there, I don't know how to sew boots, I bet the food and clothes they give me there will be worse than in Fukuoka, and the dormitory's probably small and dirty too, and in China I might not be understood if worse comes to worst.

I don't know the language, she thought, but then reconsidered: I can't turn back now, I'm going to save up money and go to Busan Girls School, I just need to be patient for three years.

She did not complain or protest. It had taken two days to get to Shanghai, where they had changed to the Daikichi-maru for another two days, and the next morning they would arrive in Wuhan. . . .

Wuhan . . . what kind of place is it? I wonder. . . . There's a big difference between having a little sliver of moon like that and no moon at all; I can't see very far, but everything around the ship is bright but dim. It was cloudy yesterday and the day before that too, so it was pitch-black in all directions, and even when I went on deck, I felt suffocated, trapped. Being on a ship, sireo, all I do is vomit again and again, I feel awful and can't eat a thing. Trains just rattle and shake from side to side, so I was fine with that, and I liked watching the scenery outside, but this is just sireo! It'll be over tomorrow, so somehow, I'll get through it. But if they told me it'd be another day—jeongmal sireo! She could barely stand from the constant nausea and a headache that had her firmly in its grasp; she got down on her hands and knees on the deck and vomited. Bleechhhhhhhh. . . . himdeureo, eomma, sallyeojwo, this is horrible, Omma, save me . . . bleeeechhh . . . the hem of a white chima . . . Unni.

"Don't look down, it'll just make you feel worse. Turn on your side a little. Let's look at the moon together."

My head's on her lap . . . soft . . . her thighs are as soft as rice cakes . . . her cool hand touching my cheek, gently wiping away the tears from my eyes.

The half-moon in the noon sky   so white a moon
Maybe it's a gourd the sun used and threw away
Wish I could   hang it from the   strings of my chima

The half-moon in the noon sky   so white a moon
Maybe it's a shoe the sun used and threw away
Wish I could   hobble around with it   on one of my feet
Wish I could   put it on   one of my baby's feet
When he's just learning to walk

The half-moon in the noon sky   so white a moon
Maybe it's a comb the sun used and threw away
Wish I could   smooth my hair down with it
When I take a break from my milling

She spotted two gold rings shining on the pale fingers combing through her bangs. On the ring finger of her left hand . . .

"How old are you?" she asked.

"I'm seventeen."

"So you're married?"

"What makes you think that?"

"Your rings . . ."

"Oh . . . Yes . . . I'm married." The woman turned her head up to look at the sky.

The girl looked up at her long, white neck and her chin, upturned and thin like the tip of the crescent moon, waiting for her next words, but *splish-splish-splish splish-splish-splish* . . . all she could hear was the sound of water . . . Unable to stand the silence she spoke.

"The moon's so pretty, isn't it, and look at all the stars . . ."

"Wherever you are you're under the same sky . . . In Anseong . . . or Miryang . . . or where we're going, in Wuhan . . ."

"Your nampyeon is . . ."

"My nampyeon is . . . gone . . . the autumn when I was fourteen I tied up my hair . . . by winter last year he was gone . . ."

They were both silent. "Is he dead?"

"No, he's alive . . . most likely . . . I believe he's alive anyway . . . I'd given birth to our son at the end of August; it was the day after his baegiljanchi . . . We'd just finished dinner and I was feeding the baby when he told me, 'We need to talk . . . I'm leaving you after New Year's,' he said, just like that. . . . The baby still had my nipple in his mouth; I laid him down to sleep in the other room and sat back down in front of my nampyeon. 'Leave me—what do you mean?' He started to talk. I just listened. It took all I had in me to listen; I couldn't even think.

"'If we both work with comrades to prepare for the war of liberation, then you and our child's lives will be at risk,' he said. His voice was full of passion, but it wasn't delirious, like he'd get when he was drunk, and his gaze held mine firmly. So I looked back at him desperately and said, 'Well, this is a disaster for me.'

"He said, 'What the waenom are doing is wrong, so what is the right thing to do—that's the question I've been asking myself for a long time, for years even before we met. I met this fellow and spoke with him, and I knew at once that there was righteousness in what he said; we talked over and over again, and I was convinced of that righteousness. I didn't tell you this either, but for the last three years I've been helping some comrades who share the same philosophy as him. I can't reveal his name to even you, my wife. In fact, it's because you're my wife that I can't reveal it to you, and it's not because I don't trust you, but because of the harm that might befall you. When you told me last October that you were pregnant, I had some doubts. Say, that as a father I should stay away from danger. But I deny those doubts: as a father, I shouldn't live in shame. Just doing nothing and waiting for others to take action when there's something that I think is right—I wouldn't be able to live under the same sky, walk on the same ground as them from the shame of it. What could such a man show to his son? I'm leaving at the start of the New Year. I can't tell you where I'm going. And when I leave this house I want you to send me off with the chant for the dead, oh-hon oh-hon, oho-ya oh-hon. There will be no revolution unless the will to dye these mountains and rivers red with one's own blood, not somebody else's, spreads like wildfire. The nation has fallen, but the people have not, and the proof of that is the blood of the Korean people that flows in me is seething with righteous indignation against the heavens. From the New Year, my only home will be the Korean Empire, the one that was destroyed by the waejeok thirty-two years ago. My only loyalty will lie with this country's three thousand ri of land and my twenty million compatriots. . . .'

"Even after my nampyeon finished speaking, I couldn't say a thing . . . that night and the night after that too. . . . There wasn't something I wanted to say but couldn't . . . and it wasn't that I agreed with what he'd said . . . I couldn't find the words to contradict his righteousness.

"On New Year's Eve, I hid our shoes so they wouldn't be found by the devils, but I didn't keep an overnight vigil. When people all over Anseong were going around their houses lighting lamps, we put out all the lamps and lay down with our son in our pitch-black room . . . the final night . . . I held my breath, waiting for my nampyeon to say something, and he lay there still, waiting for me to say something . . . but . . . nothing . . . not a word . . . I held my tongue until the rooster crowed.

"That morning, I gently picked up our baby, changed his diaper, fed him, then put him on my back and stewed rice cakes and beef to make tteok-guk, and I boiled ginger and cinnamon with dried persimmons to prepare sujeonggwa. My nampyeon stuck a branch from a peach tree on the gatepost of the house to cleanse the evil spirits from it, and on a piece of paper made from mulberry bark he wrote 'Ipchun Daegil' and stuck it on the gate. It was our third Seollal together. Bok mani badeuseyo. Bok mani batge. We exchanged New Year's greetings and drank some dosoju herbal liquor; my nampyeon ate jeon pancakes made with cod with obvious enjoyment, then set his chopsticks down. At that moment, our baby, who had been sleeping peacefully, started crying so hard I thought he might pass out. Before I could get up my nampyeon reached out to him. He picked him up with both his hands under the baby's arms, bringing the baby's face up to the same height as his, and said, Yong-hak, the name he had given the baby himself. Our son stuck his hand into his appa's mouth and started cooing, aah-ooh-aaaah. My nampyeon's hands trembled as he held our son. . . . He clung to the baby as if trying to lock him tight within his heart. . . . 'When this country's been taken back from the waejeok, if I'm still alive . . . the three of us . . . I want us to live, roots and branches entwined, like grasses after a storm,' he said. . . ."

The girl leaned against the wall and looked up at the moon. Her nausea and headache had dissipated somewhere; she felt as if the moonlight was slowly making her heart softer and whiter.

"And then he was gone. . . . I went out to work with our son strapped to my back, I was a seamstress, and a maid as well. But there were few jobs available, and if I only relied on rations I'd starve to death; it's good my milk kept up for as long as it did, but then it stopped too. . . . There's a plant called gaebijanamu, plum-yew; if you boil it up with rice it tastes a bit like chicken, or I'd take sake lees from one of those ilbon saram breweries, boil it, and mix in a little sugar and have him eat that, oh, and I'd take the acorns I'd gathered the last year and ground them in my mortar and then mash them together with potatoes to make them like rice cakes, or I would dig up the shoots of miscanthus reeds and boil them and have him eat that, but his face started to get jaundiced, and when I showed him to an acupuncturist, he said he was malnourished. . . . When I went to my head of neighborhood crying, asking if he knew of any jobs, he told me about the military uniform factory. He said, 'They'll only take unmarried women under twenty, but you should be able to get away with it.' It was so hard to leave my baby; I thought I might die, but if I can send money home monthly while saving, and if I can save up about a hundred yen, I can go back home and manage to scrape by....

"Three days after my son's first birthday, I left home. It was a happy occasion, but I couldn't stop crying. My son's malnourished, but he looks like my nampyeon and he's big, about this high. He has two tiny, little white teeth, and though he's faster at crawling still, he can even walk if he has his hand to the wall, and he can stand on his own for a few seconds with his hands out in front of him, hana, dul, set, net, daseot, about that long ... and he calls out, 'Omma, Omma.' Two weeks ago, he started to say simple baby words like *mul-mul* for 'water' or *meong-meong* for 'dog.' ... It's been six days since I left home so maybe he can say some new words now.... And if I'm out of his sight even for a moment, he'll crawl around the house looking for me at top speed. So when I go to the privy I have to tell him, geumbang ol geonikka gidarigo isseurago, Omma'll be right back, just wait."

The woman craned her neck toward the moon to keep herself from getting choked up; she seemed as if she might make it to the moon if she kept going.

"The night before I left, I talked with him. I'm sure you're thinking there's no point in talking to a one-year-old, right? But if I went away without telling him anything, then I just know he'd go around looking for me, crying, 'Omma, Omma...' I said, 'Yong-hak, you listen to me. Omma's going away to work. If she doesn't, you'll get thin and get sick. And if you get sick and you die, you'll never see Omma again, that means "goodbye." Omma doesn't want to be away from you. I want to be with you *all* the time. That's why I'm going off to work. When I go away and work, I won't be able to come home for three years. But I promise. I'll be back in three years. Until Omma comes back, you listen to your halmoni and your auntie, and you behave yourself. Yong-hak, Omma is going to come home. Pinkie promise, and if it's a lie, I'll burn moxa on my finger, I promise....'

"He's at my parents' house. Well, I say 'my parents' house,' but my abeoji died ten years ago, so it's just my eomoni and my little sister now; my little sister, who's about the same age as you, is the one looking after Yong-hak now."

"Yong-hak, what a nice name."

"My husband said he chose it because of the characters, dragon and crane, with the hope that he would grow up to have the determination of a dragon and the nobility of a crane. . . . You know, we lived under the same roof, slept in the same bed, and had a son together, but . . . I never had the slightest idea that my nampyeon was pondering things so deeply he'd resolved to give his life. . . ."

The half-moon in the noon sky   so white a moon
Maybe it's a shoe the sun used and threw away
Wish I could   hobble around with it   on one of my feet
Wish I could   put it on   one of my baby's feet
When he's just learning to walk

"Yong-hak loves that song. I'm sure he'll soon forget about me, but I asked my little sister to sing him that song at bedtime for me, so I know he won't forget the song at least. The next time I see him he'll be five . . . Five years old . . ."

"I don't think he'll forget you. My abeoji died right after I was born, so of course I don't have any real memories of him . . . but . . . the feeling of his hands when he first held me and the sound of his voice the first time he said my name, that's inside me somewhere, deep inside my body like the rumbling of the earth. Of course Yong-hak won't forget you. How could he possibly? You're the only omma he has in this world, and your nampyeon's his only appa."

"Well, he's probably in China, so I might run into him somewhere. But China's twenty times bigger than Korea. . . ."

"I wonder what Wuhan's like. . . ."

"Are you worried?"

"Yes."

"It's a lot different from what they told us first. So? How're you feeling?"

"A lot better, thanks. But I think if I go back below I'll start to feel rotten again. . . . Feel free to have a rest in the room if you like."

"I think I'll spend the night here too. After all, it's the last night of the trip."

She hesitated. "Do you think things are gonna be all right?"

"I'm not sure. Maybe not everything will be all right, but our sights aren't set too high, are they? So even if we prayed, 'Hanunim, please, make all our wishes come true,' I don't think he'd think we were being too greedy. Look, it's the sunrise."

At first, a white light like the light off an oil lamp traced a line between the sky and the water, surrounded by such overwhelming darkness it seemed like it couldn't possibly win, but still, it played for time until seoseohi, seoseohi, little by little, the light soaked into the darkness and at the moment the golden disk of the sun emerged from the water, the positions of the light and darkness were reversed. Thousands, tens of thousands, hundreds of millions of rays of light tickled thousands, tens of thousands, hundreds of millions of lidless eyes, signaling the arrival of morning to the fishes. The first seagull flew out from the harbor to scout the golden road widening across the sea by the second; it screamed as if calling something in the water, *kkireuk kkireuk kkireuk kkireuk*!

The two of them listened to the sound of the water as they shook their upper bodies like waves. The old day had been folded and put away; a new one had been unfurled before them. The sun shone a fresh light on the faces of the two women, but the man with the round glasses stepped in front of the sun, throwing their faces into shade.

"I was surprised you weren't in your cabin; I've been looking for you. I thought you might've killed yourselves. . . ."

"Why would we do that?"

"Well . . . you know . . . if you weren't on the ship, then what else could it be?"

"Sorry to worry you. I was so nauseous I couldn't sleep so I was taking the night air on the deck, and before I knew it, it was dawn. . . . When do we arrive?"

"Look, you see that harbor over there? I reckon it'll be about another hour, don't you?"

"The seagulls have come to meet us! I had no clue there were seagulls by the river too! Look, hana, dul, set! I'd like to throw them something, but I haven't got anything."

The man with the round glasses took a pack of Hōyoku out of his pocket and lit a cigarette, the smoke spilling from his mouth as his eyes followed the seagulls flying alongside as if they were accompanying the ship.

"Wuhan's as far as I go. From Wuhan to the factory you'll ride in an army truck."

"An army truck? Why?"

"It's a military boot factory; it's under the army's administration."

She took this in. "Of course . . . that all makes sense . . ."

Having been on the boat for days, she felt like the ground was shaking as she walked down the pier. The stevedores who had been awaiting the *Daikichi-maru* went into the hold and came back out, large items of baggage on their shoulders and heads. Their faces were the color of burnt sweet potatoes, and every part of them—their legs, arms, necks, faces—was so dripping with sweat it looked like they were rain-drenched.

A khaki-colored truck with a dusty yellow canopy was parked at the end of the pier; two soldiers with bayonets stood next to it. They were wearing khaki uniforms without rank insignia. The man with the round glasses handed a piece of paper to one of the soldiers. "Nice work," the soldier said, folding the paper, and the man left, heading toward the main street without a word to the two women.

The girl looked at the soldiers' boots. Leather. You can't sew those with a sewing machine; are they hand-sewn? Can you even get a needle through such thick leather?

"What are you looking at?!"

"Your shoes . . ."

"Why?"

"I was wondering how they're made."

"It's a miracle you Koreans can even think—sleeping on heated floors has obviously cooked your brains!" He guffawed.

As soon as the two women got in the bed of the truck, it departed. At first they rode down paved roads, but before long they were rattling and jumping around. The soldiers silently offered them a bundle of rice balls and a flask of water, so they quietly ate the rice balls and drank the water.

"Excuse me!" she shouted, ready to be scolded.

"What?!"

"I need to pee."

The soldier knocked on the partition window to tell the soldier in the driver's seat, and the truck came to a stop.

As far as the eye could see was plains. The plains far in the distance looked as if they had been bleached, like a white sea. The girl went into a field of kaoliang plants about as tall as she was. She crouched and peed, then tried to find her way out of the field, but she couldn't tell which direction she had come from, so she ran, pushing her way through the grass with both hands, *rustle-rustle-rustle-rustle*.

Eotteokhaji, gireul moreugenne, what do I do, I don't know how to get back—she looked up at the sky, her chest heaving with each breath. The sun was above her head, at high noon. She heard a rustling noise and turned; a soldier had the muzzle of his gun pointed at her.

"You trying to run away?"

"No . . ."

"If you run we'll kill you."

She rolled up the canopy and climbed back into the bed of the truck, meeting eyes with the woman. A little light leaking through the canopy illuminated the profile of her face, and she could see that the woman's eyes were upturned with anxiety. The truck started to move; all she could hear was the sound of her own teeth chattering. Oh no . . . it's all going wrong . . . I wonder if this is what it's like to drink poison . . . oh dear . . . what can I do? Her sense of time was numbed by being continuously shaken around in the gloom of the canopy-covered truck bed; she couldn't figure out how much time had passed. Rain hit the canopy in heavy plops, growing stronger until it pummeled. **Ame ame, fure fure, kaa-san ga**, she muttered to herself, sticking her hand in her pocket and grasping the jump rope.

"We're here," someone said, shaking her arm; she woke with a start, ears pricked. The truck had stopped, and the canopy at the back of the truck bed was open.

"You yeobos, get out here!"

The girl hurriedly leaped down to the ground, her feet sinking up to the ankles in the red soil softened by the rain.

"I took off my shoes and . . ."

"Leave it! Walk barefoot; I'll give you boots later. No dawdling!"

In the impassive sunset, she moved her legs, stiff as canes, and walked toward the one-story building she could see ahead of her.

She read the letters inked on the sign.

PARADISE

The entrance door opened, and a bald man wearing khaki mining trousers came out.

"You, how old are you?" he drawled.

"Thirteen."

"Thirteen? Goddamn . . . why are they sending us thirteen-year-old kids?" He paused. "Listen here. If anyone asks, you're fourteen."

"Sure."

"And you gotta have a name so, let's see, Aiko—no, wait, Aiko threw herself in the lake, so that's unlucky. You know the myth of Takeo and Namiko?" His pronunciation was unclear, perhaps because his tongue was so long or he was missing too many teeth, and with each word he spoke, spittle flew everywhere.

"No, sir . . ."

"Well, from now on you're Namiko, and you're Kohana. Namiko, you're in room seven, Kohana, room two. Go in there and get changed. When you're done, put on some boots and go to the hygiene room for inspection. Oh, one last thing, everyone here calls me Oyaji, so call me that too."

Oyaji handed each of them one simple dress, two cotton kimonos and an obi, two sets of underwear, and a pair of rubber boots; they walked down the narrow, dark hallway lit by just one bare light bulb hanging from the ceiling. There were eight rooms on either side of the hall, each with a number and name written on a wooden plate on the doorway. Setsuko . . . Fumiko . . . Kinue's plate is red . . . Masako . . . Emiko's is red too . . . Room six, Shizue, read, "No Entry for a Week" . . . She opened the wooden door to room seven and went inside. The room, such as it was, was only separated from the others by plywood; it was open at the top, and the floor was covered with something that resembled straw mats tacked down with bamboo nails. There was a mirror stand, a futon, two pillows, tissues, a metal washbasin; the window, close to the ceiling, had been fitted with iron bars, and the wooden door that led outside had been covered with a blanket instead of a curtain. On either side, she heard the rustling-rasping sound of cloth and paper and the smacking of someone eating something; cigarette smoke and someone's hoarse singing drifted in. **I wanna go home   I wanna go home   All the fun's been and gone   So pair off, partner up   And let's go home . . .**

She tried to take off her blouse, but her fingers were shaking so badly she couldn't get the button through the hole. Unni came in wearing a purple dress with the chest wide open, and silently helped her unbutton.

The two followed Oyaji through the rain and went into a warehouse-like building.

"This is number two, Kohana, and number seven, Namiko."

"I'll start with the oldest." A man in military uniform with two stars on his shoulders washed his hands in a basin.

"How old are you?" a young man in uniform with no stars asked.

"Naineun?" the girl translated.

"Yeorilgobimnida," the woman said.

"Seventeen," the girl translated.

"Take off everything from your waist down," the man with two stars said quickly, barely moving his lips.

"I—" She looked at the two men's faces.

"I know you heard what the doctor said! It's an examination. Take off everything from the waist down and get up on the table."

"Geomsahanikka, araetdoli jeonbu beotgo panja wie ollagaraeyo," she summarized, and gulped, wide-eyed.

Unni took off her drawers and got up on the table.

The assistant soldier rolled up the hem of her skirt to above her navel, took her kneecaps in his hands, and opened her legs; the doctor brought over something that looked like the bill of a duck.

"Aya!"

A mist of horror shrouded the girl's eyes. What are they doing? I'm watching this happen right before my eyes, but I don't know what I'm seeing, all I know is that beyond this haze those two men are leaning in toward Unni's you-know-what. . . .

"Take a look at this. The uterine fundus is raised and the entrance to the womb is pinkish. She's given birth. And if she's not lying when she says she's seventeen, then the baby must be pretty young. . . ." said the doctor, peering into her vagina, which was held open by the speculum.

"You, you got a baby?"

The girl said nothing. If they find out she has a baby, then . . .

"Translate!"

She was silent.

"This little yeobo thinks she can get smart with me!" The soldier-assistant slapped her across the cheek.

"Don't bother; whether she's had a baby or not it makes no difference to her work."

"All right, you're up!"

Her cheek and face were still stinging numb; a sound, like someone scribbling wildly with white chalk on a blackboard, rang in her ears. She took off her panties and got up on the table. Her shaking knees were pulled apart—

"Not a hair on her. How old are you?"

"I'm . . . four . . . teen. Ow!"

Her hips jerked from the pain. She was hurt, scared, embarrassed; her face was hot as if it were burning.

"Don't move!"

"When was your first period?"

"I haven't . . ."

"You really are still a child. . . . All done."

"Get down."

She got off the table and stuck herself next to Unni, shoulder to her arm, who stood as if she were glued to the wall.

"They both passed."

"Go back to your rooms, get changed into your nemaki, and wait there! D'you hear me? Answer!"

She wanted to respond, but her voice wouldn't come out, like there was a hole in her throat. She closed her eyes tightly, thinking she'd be beaten.

"Let her be, she's just a kid," the doctor said.

They walked down a small path between the corn and sugarcane fields. She could not complain, regret, or feel indignant. But what will happen next—the fear rang in her ears, buzzing through her body and mind like electricity running through her. They passed by a few traditional houses belonging to Chinese people, but none of them had a light on, and when she looked closer their doors were gone or the windows were broken; they had been abandoned for quite some time. If only someone was there so she could ask for help . . . nobody . . . nobody . . . nobody but soldiers . . . *Gwitteul gwitteul maeaemmae-aemmaeaem chireureureut chireureureut*, the insects' cries swelled and receded like a wave, then swelled again, and hidden somewhere in the dense trees an owl called out *hoot-hoot, hoot-hoot* as if trying to get her attention.

Oyaji, walking behind them, started to talk.

"Better not get any ideas. You couldn't run away if you tried. I know a woman who was dragged back, had her breasts run through with a bayonet, then she got a gunshot to her you-know-where. She was still alive, so they burned her in front of all the others. They put her on a table and built a fire under her, but then it started to rain and the fire died down, and then when they poked her corpse with sticks, oil started to run out, just gushing everywhere. I still can't eat grilled meat without thinking about it."

She went into room seven and changed into the nemaki robe, but she didn't know how to do up the obi so she arranged the front as best as she could and sat with her knees to her forehead. From the rooms on either side she heard men's and women's voices. *Ah-ahh hahhh ahhhh oohhh* . . . That's the sound of *it*, just like the noises my eomoni and that man made every night when they were doing *it*. . . . Is everyone else here married? Or are they . . . what? What are they doing?

She heard a creak and the door from outside opened; a head poked through the blanket, belonging to the doctor from before. His forehead and brow were deeply furrowed; he looked very cross.

"Lie down."

She followed the doctor's orders and lay down on top of the blanket, faceup. What did he want to check now? Down there again? Or maybe my breasts? My stomach? She closed her eyes tightly. . . . He unfolded her hands from over her chest and laid them to her sides . . . opened her robe . . . ran his hands over her chest and stomach lightly as if sprinkling flour over her . . .

pulled her panties down to her knees . . . then down over her ankles and off . . . she heard the sound of fabric rustling . . . Wondering what the noise was, she opened her eyes to see the doctor taking off his trousers and loosening his fundoshi.

She jumped up. He pushed her by the shoulder and grabbed her by the hair, but she bit the doctor's arm and ran outside, stark naked. That was no checkup! He was trying to do *it*, *it*! No! Sireo! Eomoni and Halme said that if I ever did *it* before I got married I'd have to kill myself, sireo! Sireo! She squatted in a thick lilac bush, huddling as if she were trying to protect the soft parts of her own body with her back.

"Yeobos and dogs, man, you have to beat 'em to make 'em listen."

The moment she realized he'd found her, Oyaji beat her, kicked her, dragged her, stomped on her; she fainted, and he poured water on her, bringing her back to consciousness.

"Don't waste my fucking time! Not even I'd want to sleep with a little brat like you."

Feeling breath on her face, she opened her eyes and saw a big hand . . . bigger than both of her hands put together, crumpling up tissue paper and wiping the blood away from her nose and mouth, fingers spreading across her cheek gently, the other set of fingers between her legs . . . the fingers up above were so soft, and yet the ones below were so stiffly bony it felt like she was being clawed at by a tree branch.

Aya! Eomoni! Help me! Aya! Her ears heard her own cries echoing back at her throughout the whole building; her eyes watched the man moving his hips like he was pounding in a stake.

"They say it hurts the first time, but you get used to it quick. New girls only fuck the commissioned officers, so you'll have it easy for a little while. In the meantime, try to eat up and put a little meat on your bones—damn near thought I'd belly flopped on a wooden raft. This is your chance to repay a kindness, so act grateful when you're serving these soldiers who are fighting for our country."

The door squeaked loudly as it shut. Her soul was looking down at her body from the ceiling. Her lips, which looked less half-opened than torn . . . the purple and blue bruises dotted here and there on her skin . . . her legs, open in an unnatural position . . . her blood-smeared thighs . . . Her soul turned away from the sight of its own body.

She watched the little brown moths beating themselves against the light bulb.

I'm scared to close my eyes. 'Cause if I do, and everything I see now hasn't gone away when I open them again, then that'll mean it really happened. Belatedly, she jerked her tongue back into her mouth and licked the blood. I want to cover my body, but I don't want anything to touch me, every inch of my skin has that man's fingerprints on it.

Another squeak, this time from the wooden door from the corridor into her room. It's Oyaji, she thought, but she barely had the strength to slowly lift her heels and close her legs. It was Unni, who leaned over and put her nemaki back on her. Eiko clung to Unni's body with every part of hers. She breathed over and over again into her shoulder, but she could not cry. When she cried out, aigo, Unni shushed her, putting her fingers to the girl's mouth. Her eyes were filled with tears, but her face was still. Aigo! Unni gripped the girl's arms and pulled their bodies apart, this time putting her pointer and middle fingers up to her own lips.

"If you cry they'll beat you again. Just lie down . . ."

The two of them lay down holding each other. Unni put the girl's head on one of her arms; with the other she rubbed her back with her palm.

"Hurry up!"

"Get out here!"

They heard the sound of the neighboring wall being run through with a bayonet.

Ah hah ooooh ah-ah-aahhh . . .

The sound of a man and woman moaning, grunting . . .

"Close your eyes." Unni wiped the tears pooled in the hollow of her arm away with the sleeve of her robe.

"Aigo . . ."

"Go to sleep, you've got to go to sleep." She closed the girl's eyes with her lips.

"Aigo . . ."

"What can you see?"

"Nothing."

"Well, I can see it . . . look . . ."

"Oh . . . I can too . . ."

In the darkness behind her eyelids the light reflected diffusely, *chugga-chugga-chugga-chugga clatter-clatter-clatter-clatter choo-chooooooo*, the train slid into the blackness of the tunnel without hesitation. Black smoke streaming in through the window, I've gotta close it, the girl pushed down on the hold of the window with her thumbs, shaking up and down . . . it's like I've turned into a moron . . . she gave up and sat back down in her seat and saw her own face reflected in the window, which should've still been open . . . why do I look so sad? . . . once we're through this tunnel we're back in Miryang . . . *choo-choooooooooo!* We're out, nawassda! *Chugga-chugga-chugga-chugga thunk-thunk thunk-thunk thunk-thunk-thunk-thunk*, the train started across the railway bridge over the Miryang River, and she leaned out of the window of the train, waving at her friends playing jump rope by the river. *Chugga-chugga-chugga-chugga thunk-thunk thunk-thunk chugga-chugga-chugga-chugga-chugga-chugga*, another tunnel now, have we passed the station at Miryang? Did I oversleep? The pitch-black hole became bigger and bigger, *choo-choooooo!* As if a totally black bag had been put over her head the girl entered the darkness; after a thunk-squeal, finally, all sound ceased. Maybe I'm dead, she idly thought, just as *chugga-chugga-chugga-chugga, thunk thunk thunk-thunk*, the noise and vibrations came back, choo-choooooooo! That's the whistle saying we're out of the tunnel, she thought, as, *pah-pa-pa! Pah-pa-pah pah-pa-ra-pa-pah pah-pa-ra-pa pah-pa-ra-pa pah-pa-ra-pa-pah*, the trumpet call for wake-up time reverberated.

She opened her eyes. *Thunk-thunk thunk-thunk thunk-thunk-thunk-thunk*, she was still shaking, *chugga-chugga-chugga*, the smoke still clung to her hair, the train's whistle was still in her eardrum, but—*knock knock knock*, there was the sound of rapping on the wooden door, and she clung to Unni, who lay next to her.

"Namiko, Kohana, get up. If you're not out in the yard immediately, they'll beat you." A woman's voice.

Namiko? Kohana? *You know the myth of Takeo and Namiko? Well, from now on you're Namiko, and you're Kohana.* Oyaji's voice rang in her ears, and Namiko turned her back to Kohana, slipping the panties crumpled at her feet up over her body.

The military doctor who had come into her room the night before now opened the door, and the women, wearing simple A-line dresses in different colors, lined up in two rows; before them stood Oyaji and a soldier carrying a bayonet. Yellow dresses, pink, green, yellow, orange, blue, light blue, red just like Namiko's, purple like Kohana's. Hana, dul, set, net, daseot . . . yeol-yeodeol, yeol-ahop, seumul, twenty all in all . . . Namiko, who couldn't put her legs together from the pain, toddled after Kohana like a puppy and took her place at the back.

"Turn to the east. Revere the emperor!" At the soldier's command, the women turned to the rising sun and bowed, then recited the oath of the Imperial Subject.

"One: We are subjects of the empire   we will devote ourselves to emperor and nation with loyalty.

"Two: We, the imperial subjects, will with mutual trust and cooperation   strengthen our union.

"Three: We, the imperial subjects, will elevate the imperial way by nurturing perseverance and discipline."

The doctor from the night before appeared.

"Attention! Bow!" The soldier with the bayonet issued the command and the women bowed.

"They can relax," the doctor said.

"At ease!" the soldier ordered.

The doctor folded his hands behind him and looked around at the women's faces.

"One year and nine months after the war began, the situation has finally reached the decisive moment. To win this war, our army is calling up a vast number of men and sending them to the front lines. These are young men, the same age as you, who are leaving their parents and wives behind on the mainland to fulfill their life-and-death duty. Truly we're depending on your hard work, and while the army may not be able to fully reward you for it, only you ladies can comfort these young men on behalf of the wives they left behind on the mainland. So I want you to treat these soldiers who come to you looking for a moment of peace as kindly as you can. Your kindness will be deeply etched on the heart of a soldier who may not know tomorrow, becoming a beautiful memory for him, and even if he himself is on the front line he will be praying for your happiness. A soldier's prayer always reaches the heavens, and one day that happiness will certainly come to you. The heavens know all about the righteousness of our battle. We have the heavens on our side. The Japanese Empire's victory is assured. And when we win, everlasting peace will come to the lands of the Orient, and all your hard work too will be rewarded. Now is the time for patience. Never forget that you too have taken on an important duty, so I urge you to share the same spirit as the soldiers fighting on the front lines and give your all again today for the nation. Thank you."

"Attention! Bow!" The soldier gave the order, and the women straightened up and bowed.

Oyaji began to sing an army march, and the women stood rigidly and sang along.

Our empire lit by the rising sun
Has an eternal light of glory
Any clouds come heavy and hoary
Will be swept clear by my gun

In countless great wars
We've won famous victories
Wherever our imperial army goes
There's always grace and providence

Our nation, not once has it swayed,
Has a golden governing state
All scoundrels now, like weeds, prostrate
At the tremble of my blade

In countless great wars
We've won famous victories
Wherever our imperial army goes
There's always grace and providence

Should bandits come against
We'll have no fearful cries
With wings to fly the skies
The ground shudders at my fist

In countless great wars
We've won famous victories
Wherever our imperial army goes
There's always grace and providence

The soldier in charge of cooking carried out large vats. Inside, there was rice, potatoes, miso soup with radish, pickled radishes, and dried sardines. The women carried the pots to the dining room of Paradise, dished the food up, and began to eat, but Namiko just stared down at her steaming bowl of miso soup, not picking up her chopsticks.

"Aigo, she's barely more than a child."

"Must've been tricked."

"My mama got tricked too. They told her we're sending your girl to the volunteer corps. When she said no, they threatened her and said if you don't have a son, then you have to send your daughter for the sake of the nation, and if you refuse, that makes you a traitor and we can't have those here."

"Same with me. It's the war, you know, the soldiers are busy fighting, they don't have time to cook, no time to do their laundry either, it's bad; there's work doing cooking and washing, and it pays, so do you want the job, they said. Same with you too, right?"

Namiko stared down at the miso in her soup, now separated and sunk below the meager scraps of radish.

"Where are you from?"

"Jogeumirado meogeoyaji . . . ," Kohana said, urging Namiko to eat a little as she rubbed her fist against the girl's leg.

"They'll beat you if you speak Korean. They'll say you were talking about how to escape."

"No Korean songs either; they'll think you're defiant. If you gonna sing, better learn Japanese songs."

"You just look at the moon, and they hit you; what were you thinking about; you talk to yourself, and they hit you, you were complaining."

"You mess up Japanese pronunciation and they hit you. There's no reason but the soldier is drunk and he's in a bad mood, so he hits you. Aigu, they hit me so much I can't hear out of my right ear, and it buzzes all the time like there's a fly stuck in there, aigo!"

"They hit my back with a big leather belt, look, you can see, left a big scar."

With the tail of a dried sardine still sticking out of her mouth, the woman rolled up the hem of her green dress and showed the scar; Namiko did not turn her face or eyes to see.

"If you don't eat up, you'll get weak and die. That's how Emiko and Oto-maru and Miyako died. Imagine dying in a place like this. You just have to accept that you were ill-fated from birth and keep on living. If you die here, your mama and daddy will be so sad. Even when it's hard, live through it, just live, so you can go back to Korea. Just take a sip of your soup for me, baby."

"You've got to sleep too. Weekdays it's just ten men usually, but Saturdays and Sundays, sometimes I've had thirty or forty. They just take down their trousers and do their business, leave while they're still doing them up, and be-fore I've had time to wash up, the next one's come in. I just spread my legs like a frog, it hurts, it hurts, and then when it's night I close them again."

"Times like that, all you can do is doze off with a man on top of you. If you don't sleep, you're a goner."

"When the soldiers come back from a punitive expedition, we're told to give them special attention, but I just can't bear to do it with scratchy-faced, red-eyed soldiers who took the lives of loads of Chinese. All those soldiers, bragging, 'Baby, I painted ink on my face and dragged a gūniang out from hid-ing under the floorboards, and I did it to her in front of her mother, then did her mother, then her grandma, merrily fucking my way through three generations,' my god. All this, 'Why do I have to pay for a Korean whore when a virgin gūniang is free, and I have to use a fucking condom too.' And they're on you like a tick. If you make a sour face just for a second, it's: 'Yeobo whore, you fucking yeobo!'"

"Winter's the worst though. A man who's just come indoors, cold as an icicle, holding you, and when you think you've finally gotten warm, then there's another cold body wrapped around you . . . And you still only have two blankets even in the winter."

"The scariest is they ask you to die with them. One of them said I can't bear to love you this much, I'll kill you and then myself, and then he stabbed me here. Blood spurted out, aigo!"

"The guys who are going to the front are the nicest. They tell you, I might not make it back this time, and what am I going to do with money on the front line anyway, so I give all my money to you. Normally I say, go die a wonderful death, but I don't say that, I comfort them and say please come back fine. That's the kind of guy I want to be here to see the day he comes back alive."

"The soldiers are scared too. They all want to go back to Nagoya."

"Oyaji said the units here are all from Nagoya."

"Aigu, it's all for the sake of the nation, they say, but all of them are only here because they got drafted. One of them, while he was banging me, was saying, 'They don't even put us soldiers in coffins, I'll never see my mother's face again, God I wish I was a commissioned officer.'"

"Shh."

"Aigu, I want to go home. But I changed trains and boats so many times, I don't know how. If I had wings I'd fly. Ah, I wish I was a gureum, a beautiful cloud, aigo!"

"We're same as the soldiers, can't get out of here alive. When they poured oil on Emiko and Otomaru and Miyako and burned them I took a piece of each of their skulls and I hid them in my bag, but I don't know their real names, so I can't send them back to their mamas and papas. Emiko was from Daejeon, Otomaru was from Yeongcheon, and Miyako was from Gangjin, so I want to live, and when I go back to Korea, I'll bury them on our own soil."

"If I live, I can never see my mama and papa again. I can't get married with a body like this. And what would they do with a daughter who can't get married, you know? Got nowhere to go back to anymore, aigo ya!"

"Emiko and Otomaru and Miyako suffered as they died, but it's less suffering the shorter your life is."

"Shh, it's Oyaji."

Footsteps approached, and Oyaji came into the dining room.

"You can't dawdle in here eating forever, so when you're done, go boil the water and get in the bath. Today's inspection day, so make sure to wash your tools well. If you get gonorrhea in your eyes you'll go blind, so don't wash your face with the same water you wash yourself with. Hey, Namiko, you haven't eaten a thing. I got a lot to teach you and Kohana, so eat up quick. And, Namiko, you're so skinny, eating's part of the job. Eat up! If you're stubborn and don't wanna eat I'll make you pay for that."

Kohana picked up the chopsticks and stuck them in Namiko's right hand; hollow-faced, Namiko picked up a little white rice with the wooden chopsticks and brought it up to her mouth, swallowing it without hardly chewing. Then suddenly tears erupted from her eyes and she clamped both hands to her mouth, running over to the window to vomit. Aigo, bulssanghaera, bulssanghaeseo eojjeoji, Kohana wept, rubbing the girl's back; like a baby choking on milk Namiko sobbed and spat the food up, vomited and sobbed, still bent over and gagging though she had nothing left in her stomach to throw up.

"You're not broken in yet, I get it, but once a woman's body's been had by three men, she naturally gives up, so cry your heart out until then. But you better listen to what I've got to say over your sobs. Namiko, listen and tell Kohana. If she doesn't know what I said later, I'll knock your ass to the ground.

"When the soldiers come to your room, you say: 'Irrashaimase, soko ni okake kudasai.' When they're leaving, you say: 'Arigatō gozaimashita, mata kite kudasai.' Namiko, you teach Kohana Japanese. A month from now, if she can't say the basics, *ichi, ni, san, shi, rice, sake, cigarette, needle, thread*, I'll punish you.

"Three times a month the army doctor does inspections. Today's one of those days, but he already saw you both yesterday so you're exempt. To prevent pregnancy, gonorrhea, and syphilis, you've got two lines of defense: washing, and using a sheath, a so-called iron helmet. But a sheath isn't made of iron, so it can get holes in it or leak. Later I'll give you each a bottle of disinfectant. It's called Chameleon because when you put a few drops of it in the basin it turns the water a pretty purple color. So each time you finish with someone, you wash your tools thoroughly. There was a woman called Tamaki who tried to kill herself by drinking straight Chameleon, God did she suffer, but she didn't die. As punishment, they made her go with a unit. Going with a unit means you're sent with them to the front lines. Putting on a real helmet, gaiters over your trousers and canvas shoes, and with the enemy's planes thick in the sky over you, fucking right on the ground. Some get shot and die, some get abandoned because they can't walk. And if you live and come back you won't last long. In the end, about six months after she tried to kill herself, Tamaki died here, of malaria. I'm telling you, don't get any stupid ideas about imitating her.

"Also, a comfort woman should be a wife to all, partial to none. If you get into a special relationship with any one of them, I'll punish you by starvation. Keep in mind that what you're doing is your duty," Oyaji said, smoking a Qiánmén cigarette.

"They'll all come with a ticket: for enlisted men it's printed in black; for noncommissioned officers, blue; and for officers it's in red. Each man's meant to write on it his unit name and his own name, and the way it works is, I'll collect these tickets from you and hand them to the Kempeitai, the military police. Any man who sees the same comfort woman twice in a month will attract the Kempeitai's attention. This is to keep them from getting too attached and leaking military secrets. The soldiers who have left a wife back on the mainland aren't a concern, but the innocent soldiers who've never known the touch of a woman before, well, sometimes they don't know how to handle themselves, you know, and when transfer day comes, they pull the pin on a hand grenade while they're with a comfort woman and you'll both die in a heap, and you know, some women get ordered by a man they like to not use the sheath or wash themselves and they get pregnant, and they hide the fact that they're pregnant until it's too late for an abortion. But, look, I'll say it now and I'll say it clear. This is a battlefield. If you have a baby, you won't raise it. You'll have to hand it over to a Chinese, with some money too. The Chinese have hard lives too, so that child's destined to be abandoned, starved to death, or, if it's a girl and they do raise her, sold to a brothel.

"There's tickets and there's also discount cards with a black border, and they come in a three-item set with a 'First Assault' condom. Soldiers were bringing First Assaults until last year, but due to the rubber shortage there aren't many new ones. Once it's used the first time it can be washed and disinfected and then it can be reused. After three uses, replace it with a new sheath. The girls do this in the yard every day after bathing and washing, so watch what the others do today and try to remember it.

"When it's your time of the month, put a piece of red paper on your door. But some soldiers don't care, and if there are dozens of men lined up for other girls, then you'll have to pitch in too. Wash yourself well and then take some gauze and roll it up like this and stick it way up into your equipment so no blood comes out and then go to it. If you're running out of gauze I can get you more, so just say. When it's that time, you need to drink salt. You can't just lick at it; you've got to drink it. Guzzle it down, a handful or a plateful, and then your menses will stop. You know, if you put your mind to it, you'll only bleed once every three months or less, they say. Fumiko and Shizue haven't had one for a year. They say it's easier if you don't have bleeding and then you don't have to worry about getting pregnant, either.

"You'll get paid in military scrip. Soldiers are one yen fifty sen; noncom officers, two yen; captains, lieutenants, and ensigns are two yen fifty sen; and colonels, lieutenant colonels, and majors are three yen. The arrangement is for one hour at a time, but when they're lined up, do it quicker. You can hurry them by saying there's men waiting, but most of them are in and out in fifteen minutes. Officers don't have a time limit, and they can stay overnight too.

"Your share is half. Since you're treated as civilian employees, this'll be deposited in the Military Post Office Bank, headquartered in Shimonoseki. Some soldiers will generously give you pocket money, and that money's all yours. You can give it to me to deposit for you, you can send it back home, or you can sew it into your clothes so you don't lose it; it's up to you. When the war is over, your duty is over too, so you can take your bankbook and go home. You'll have a fortune, enough to build a big house and eat off it for the rest of your life if you don't get too extravagant. Until then, it's all about selfless devotion, dedicating yourself to our righteous cause, and just keeping your eyes closed and your teeth clenched for a few years so you can live comfortably for the rest of your life; I mean, you can dedicate yourself to the nation and earn money at the same time, it's serving two ends, two birds with one stone, having your cake and eating it too. For the nation, you hear me, for the nation!

"Breakfast is always at this time, lunch and dinner you take while you're working. Bath time is between nine and ten. After bath time, do your laundry and sheath cleaning and replenishment. Once that's over, around noon the soldiers will start to come, so get ready quickly. You're living in the same place as the imperial army, so try not to interfere with army discipline. The rules are written down in the Army Entertainment Center Regulations, which are posted at the reception. Number one, even if a soldier offers you food or alcohol, you cannot have it. Number two, no eating or drinking in the rooms.

"Also, oh, yeah, don't catch cold. Don't just stay in your room all the time, and when you have time between customers, get some fresh air, spread your arms wide, and take deep breaths. Two times a week after the Oath of the Imperial Subject, everyone does radio calisthenics, so try to remember the routines. But do not go farther than ten meters from the dormitory; I'll know if you do, and if you don't come back, I'll shoot you.

"When there aren't any troops passing through and you have time on your hands, you'll be sent to Wuhan University, where there's an army hospital, to visit the injured. At that time only will you wear a white blouse and trousers with an apron and you'll wear a sash for the Greater Japan National Defense Women's Association, to make you into blossoms of Japanese womanhood, and you'll do the laundry for the soldiers who have been gloriously wounded, wipe their bodies, and speak with them. So if Kohana doesn't hurry up and learn some Japanese there'll be hell to pay.

"As I'm sure you know, since the Pacific War broke out on December 8, 1941, the eighth day of every month was declared Declaration Observance Day. They made a cabinet announcement that every government office and school should hold a ceremony where the declaration of war is read aloud, and that homes should raise the national flag, and shrines, temples, and churches should hold ceremonies of prayer for our certain victory, and here, too, we take time from our work to hold a ceremony on the eighth of every month. After holding a minute of silence for the spirits of the war dead, there's an award ceremony for you ladies. They'll read out, 'Let us honor the achievements of so-and-so, who was the highest seller for August 1943, serving as a model for all comfort women, and has made tremendous efforts to provide comfort to the imperial army,' and then they give out little prizes. Only first, second, and third place get commendation. But even if you don't win a prize, you'll still get treats and recognition for your service, so buckle down with the other ladies.

"If your panties and dress get dirty I'll provide you with new ones, but you're in your nemaki all day long, so they rarely get dirty. If you have time to put on your panties, you sure won't be getting a prize. If you need more laundry soap, face soap, toothbrushes, toothpaste, gauze, cotton, lipstick, face powder, candy, cigarettes, whatever, just tell me. I'll buy it for you and add it to your balance. Kohana's debt is three hundred yen and Namiko, yours is three hundred and fifty. Goes without saying, of course, but you don't get paid until you've paid back your debt."

"Debt?" Kohana turned to look at Oyaji, her hand still rubbing Namiko's back.

"Do you even know how much money it cost to bring you two here?"

"Bit gateun geo eopseoyo! Sambaek enirani, geureoke keundon bon jeokdo eopdaguyo!" she shouted: *I'm not in debt! What three hundred yen? I've never even seen that much money!*

Oyaji flung his lit cigarette at Kohana's face.

"Ah, tteugeo," she screamed, holding her cheek.

"You fucking bitch! You damn Koreans always think you can get cute. Just try using your empty fucking ondol-cooked head. Our army had to pay the middleman who brought you here. Train fares, ship fares, lodging, food expenses, don't tell me you numbskulls thought that was free! Don't fucking try me. Hey, Namiko, how long are you going to stand there whimpering? I'll knock your lights out! Get in the bath and get ready!"

Oyaji kicked over a chair, which struck Kohana's back; Kohana walked out without a whimper, her arm around Namiko.

In a dirt-floored room that was used as a kitchen when Paradise belonged to the Chinese, there were two large earthenware pots. Unlike the hangari used in Korea, these were shiny, brown water jugs. Namiko tilted one and discarded the remaining water, boiled some water in a wok, transferred the boiled water to the pot, and added cool water, mixing it with her palm until it was just the right temperature. Ja, kkaekkeutage ssitja. *C'mon, time to get clean*, Kohana said, and Namiko put her right foot, then left foot into the container and sank into the hot water until it was up to her lip. Kohana, noticing that Namiko's eyes were open, staring unblinkingly like knots on a tree trunk, got out of her bath, moistened the girl's hair with a gourd-ladle, smeared soap on her head, and rubbed it in until she worked up a lather. Aigo, bulssanghaera, aigo, haneunim, geujeo i aireul sallyeoman juseyo, haneunim. *Oh, you poor thing, oh, God, please take care of this child, dear God.*

Namiko and Kohana, their hair dripping, walked past the soldiers armed with bayonets who were on guard, and went out into the backyard, where the other women were gathering. The women plucked used sheaths out of empty cans that had once held pineapples and mandarins, washed them with water in a metal basin, then threw them into a barrel. The barrel contained water mixed with cresol; it was the color of the Yangtze River and had a strong, horrible smell of chemicals.

"Dul da ilbon mal motae?" *Can't either of you speak Japanese?*

"Aniyo, i aineun hal jul aneunde neomu keun chunggyeogeul badaseo." *No, she speaks Japanese, but she's had such a shock. . . .*

"You two, don't you ever do it without a condom. Don't think you could bear getting sick so far away from Mama and Daddy."

"When you get goner-ria, you get red welts that smell awful. Every step it hurts down there, can't take another step."

"That's when they shoot you up with 606."

"It's a glowing red injection. When they put it in, you vomit, it stings in your nose and mouth, your arms hurt, and you can't put your hands in water for a week."

"They didn't give me 606. They stuffed something that looked like a dumpling into my uterus and stopped it up with cotton, let me sleep for a while, and then took another look at it. They put me under a month's quarantine so I didn't get warm food, just cold rice and pickled radish for a whole month, but it was nice to have a long break."

"Condoms can slide off, so it's better to put ointment in there before they start fucking you."

"Still at first I was so swollen I couldn't have gotten a needle in there, so the doctor put a sheath on his finger and put ointment in there for me, but then the next day it was another ten, twenty men. Aigo, eojjeodaga, aigo, nae pal-jaya." *God, what is this, is this really my fate?*

"If you put a little work into it, you'll be better off. If you kind of turn your hips like this and thrust up, the young soldiers won't last five minutes."

"But then it still hurts if they play around with you before they fuck you."

"Well, you have to lie on your left side, then. Put your right hand under the pillow and stick your left hand under your armpit like this."

"Hey, you're smart."

"Look, you're the only one who's gonna take care of you. Are we almost done?"

"I guess so, it's been thirty minutes."

One of the women stood up and picked out one of the sheaths floating like dead jellyfish in the cresol water.

"Looks good."

The women formed a chain, some washing them out inside and out with soapy water, some rinsing them, and some shaking off the water and fastening them to a string under the eaves with clothespins.

"Windy today, isn't it? They'll dry soon."

"Make sure they don't blow away."

"When it's really too much you just gotta take a chopstick and make it bleed and tell them that you're on your period to get a break."

"But even when you put a red tag on your door in the hallway and a sign on the outside door saying you're 'on break,' the soldiers still come in. And if you get blood on them they'll hit you, so you gotta push the cotton up in there, but then after you've done ten or twenty of 'em, the cotton can get into your uterus. And when that happens, there's nothing you can do yourself anymore, you gotta get the doctor to remove it. But it hurts so bad it feels like he's gonna take your uterus out too."

"You're new, so for the first week you'll only do officers, but be careful, be-cause a lot of new girls get pregnant in the first week. The officers know that you're new and clean so they want to do it without a condom. And the girls like you are so naive they don't even know how to put a condom on a man. That's how they get knocked up. I got pregnant the first week too."

"Me too."

"The doctor gave me an injection and this big blood clot came out. I got pregnant seven times in two years, so they operated and took my uterus out. Look, there's the scar. Aigu, damned to be born a woman and have my uterus removed without even wearing a veil once, jegiral!"

"If you're less than three months gone, you can get rid of it by fasting and chewing and swallowing buchu roots for two days."

"I hadn't had my period for ages, so I thought I wouldn't get pregnant, but my stomach got heavy, and when it was time for inspection they told me I was pregnant and it was already too late. But I still had to take customers. One day, I had thirty men and my stomach hurt so bad, I lost the baby. Seems like it had died a long time before, its head and eyes and bones were all mushy like a sea cucumber. But the only thing that was perfect was the penis. See over there, where the red balsam is, I dug a hole there and buried him. . . . They're probably half-dry now."

The woman turned the sheaths, swaying in the wind, one by one, fixed them in place with a clothespin again, and sat back down.

"Oh yes, let me give you Sayuri's clothes. I was the closest to her, so I got them as a keepsake, but Sayuri was so small that I can't wear any of it. But they might fit you just right. I'll bring them to your room later. There's a black crepe chima and a white silk jeogori. Take care of them and wear them when you go back to Korea."

"Sayuri hid that she was pregnant for a long time."

"The doctor we have now is really on top of things, but the old one was always drinking laojiu out of a water bottle so he was easy to fool. By the time he realized she was almost in her last month, Sayuri had a dream about Sergeant Major Shimizu, so she said it was his baby, and we all laughed like, don't be stupid, it could be anyone's, but when the baby was born, it looked just like Shimizu around the eyes and mouth. And Sergeant Major Shimizu also started coming around, rolling up his sleeves and cleaning real hard, and buying her eggs from the Chinese and making her drink them, but the army noticed and he got transferred to the front line. When he left he promised her, when the war is over I want to be with you, but nobody knows if he's alive or dead. Sergeant Major Shimizu gave him the name Yamato, so I guess his name is Shimizu Yamato. Less than a month after he was born, the baby was given to a Chinese couple who had no kids and not a pot to piss in, but then they came back in the middle of the night saying the baby wouldn't even eat gruel, right? Sayuri breastfed him for them, but one day they stopped coming, and when one of the Chinese who cleans for us went to check on the baby, there was nobody home."

"She just sobbed whenever she looked at the picture of Yamato that Sergeant Major Shimizu took. She didn't recover well after labor, and she was yellow and festering from down there up to her navel, and her face went yellow too. She couldn't stand the pain, so she bought some opium from a Chinese. But the skin on her arms was so hard we couldn't even get the needle in."

"I don't know if it was the opium, or if she went crazy, but she'd go out, not even bothering to tie up her nemaki with her tits hanging out, in the middle of the night to stare at the moon and shout, Yamato, Yamato."

"She put on the uniform of an officer who stayed overnight and wandered off toward the swamp until I thought the soldiers on guard would shoot her, then she sat on top of the firewood and screamed, 'Ppalli baereul daeran mariya, Yamatohago gachi joseone deureogal geoya!'" *Fetch me a ship, me and Yamato are going back to Korea together!*

"Oyaji shouted, 'Inoma, you fucking yeobo, I'll make you sane again,' and he started torturing her with electric shocks. And he told us all to watch, so we had to just stand there. Oyaji grabbed Sayuri's hair and pulled it, pulled out the electric cable, stretched out her wrists and ankles, and shouted, 'This'll wake you up, bitch,' as he turned the dial. Aigu, there were flames coming out of her eyes, her whole body was shaking shaking shaking."

"Sayuri passed out, so he threw her outside and threw water on her. Aigu, and it was midwinter. . . ."

"And when we tried to pick her up and bring her inside, he said, 'She's useless now, don't lay a finger on her till she's dead, and if you do, I'll do the same thing to you too,' so . . . what could we . . ."

"In the morning . . . she was lying dead here."

"He's a really awful guy, Oyaji."

The women stood up, their hips stiff with pain, took the clothespins off the sheaths that were now completely dry on the line, and put them in a bamboo basket; a few of them took these and, mouthing and lighting a Furusato cigarette, the wrapper of which read, "Salute, soldier! Enjoy," they took a puff and blew the smoke into each sheath. The woman in charge of sprinkling wheat flour on the undamaged sheaths that didn't leak smoke, rolling them up and putting them in paper pouches provided by the army labeled "First Strike," started to sing.

I know when my favorite's coming
I can hear his boots three ri away
I know when the one I hate's coming
Got a headache the past three days

Someone started singing a Korean song under it. Namiko and Kohana didn't know who was singing—they were singing quietly, so very quietly, barely moving their lips or throat.

Don't forget me
Even if we're apart
Do you remember
When the wild violets were in bloom in the mountains
That wheat field
Where you and I once met

Outside of Paradise, the sun had already set, but the birds trilled and though the leaves had not yet fallen, the wind made a dry sound, as if it were rolling its way through dead leaves.

Inside Paradise, the voices of men and women melded and ended, melded and ended. *Oooh, aah, ahhhhh, ahhhhhhh*, Namiko in her nemaki put her hands over her ears and looked up at the jeogori hanging on the wall that once belonged to another comfort woman, now dead.

She died with the name Sayuri. Nobody knows her true name. She was tricked into this work and could not say her true name. Abeoji, Eomoni,

Oppa, Kyōjun, Keiko, Woo-gun, Kobayashi-sensei, I cannot say any of their names. I am Namiko. Like Sayuri, I have no choice but to die with the name Namiko . . . Ah, I remember now, when Woo-gun's unni So-won drowned in the Miryang River, Halme told me: A dream where you fall into water is an omen of coming disaster, a dream where you're washed away is telling you of death, that poor girl must've had a premonition too, aigu, why didn't she know better . . . ? When I was on the train I dreamed of water over and over again. . . . If I'd known it would be like this, I should've thrown myself off the Continent. I should've jumped from the *Mukden-maru* into the sea, I should've jumped off the *Daikichi-maru* into the Yangtze River. . . . Was Arang still a virgin when she was murdered . . . or did he do it to her first? . . . In the legend she was killed trying to protect her honor, but how much resistance could she really put up against a man with a sword? *Drinking in the exquisite beauty of the spring night, Arang heard footsteps sneaking up behind her. She turned and saw not her nanny but a man standing there. When Ju-gi tried to carry out his plan, he pulled down the fleeing Arang, undid the strings of her jeogori, and put his hand on her chima. As Arang violently resisted, Ju-gi flew into a rage and pulled out his sword and stabbed her in the neck. Only the moon saw Arang, buried in the bamboo grove.* Oyaji threatened that if I tried to kill myself he'd have me assigned to a unit to go to the front lines, but if I strangle myself surely I'll die. That iron grille over there, I'll hang some kind of rope or string that won't break . . . but I'm too short to reach, I'll get one of the chairs from the dining room and bring it in before dawn. . . . Oh, that obi would work. . . .

The sound of a bayonet and boots rubbing against each other approached, and the door opened. The moment the blanket curtain rose, the words slipped out of Namiko's mouth.

"Irrashaimase, soko ni okake kudasai."

TWENTY-ONE

March 3, 1944

| 1944년 3월 3일 | 1944年3月3日 |

The sun emerged from behind Mount Chiltan. The dust, flying insects, and pollen swirling in the atmosphere began to tremble; the dandelion, shepherd's purse, and violet buds on the riverbank slowly opened in unison with the sun; and the white and yellow butterflies that had kept their all-night vigil behind the leaves began to flutter and dance, *hwol hwol, hwol hwol*. Annyeong! Annyeong! The cheerful voices leaped off the stone steps up to Yeongnamnu, and the boys with close-cropped hair dashed hana dul set net daseot—when first the boys who had gone up the stairs taking only every other step had passed Yeongnamnu and were about to reach the gazebo, they raised their chins as if staring up at the torii gate of the shrine and panted, *hah hah hah hah*.

The students from Miryang Common School who were gathered in the grounds looked on at attention as Kobayashi-sensei passed by the hall of worship and prayed, then bowed themselves before they began to clean the grounds with the brooms, dustpans, and rags they held in each of their hands. After cleaning, they would go home briefly for breakfast, then gather again at Yeongnamnu to go to school together.

It seemed that the cleaning was over. The students appeared, led by Kobayashi-sensei, coming down the stone steps and singing a military song.

The battle's over now and we trample
The grass of the battlefield as we march home

Oh, at my feet I find
My friend's bloodstained field cap
Without a thought I pick it up
And hold it firmly in my hands
I won't let you die alone
Tomorrow I'll join you
My flowing tears burn with blood
Counting on my fingers the bullet casings
One, two, three, four—six, seven
See for yourself, Commander

Sol sol sarang sarang   sol sol sarang sarang, Korean women with basins and bamboo baskets in their arms swept down the riverbank with the spring breeze, but none of them were wearing chima jeogoris. Each was wearing navy blue, brown, or black Japanese-style women's work trousers. The wind, which had been looking forward to blowing up their chimas and making the strings of their jeogoris dance, made a desultory whine and blew on toward Yongdu-mok.

If I should return home
I'll go to your sister and your mother
And when I talk about this battle
I'll praise you with joyful tears
Oh, fallen comrade, rest well
Though your body's buried here
This is the true spirit of Japanese boys
A bloodstained field cap!

When the students reached the end of the stairs, they stopped singing and ran off to their homes. A sandpiper, surprised by the sound of shoes echoing across the Namcheong Bridge, spread its white wings and stood on its tiptoes, flying off to Yongdu-mok as if chasing the spring wind, but then it beat its wings and returned to the delta, standing in the water on one leg, its beak pointed at the surface of the river.

The sunlight lay on the mountains and river and houses and roads as if no such thing as night existed, but the water flowing in the Miryang River still held its nightly chill. Just as the palms of the women picking minari turned red and they lost all feeling in their hands, men with fishing rods, bags woven from rope, came down the bank. The men did not wear paji jeogoris, either; they were wearing white or gray shirts with black or brown short jackets. The men and women alike wore straw sun hats with such deep brims that only husbands and wives could tell just who was who.

"This morning, Jeong-hee at the kisaeng place gave birth to a daughter. Yeon-sun halme helped deliver her; she sighed and told me she'd never seen a prettier baby. She said the baby was fair with a pin-straight nose and such long eyelashes."

"Aigu, and her father's not here. . . ."

"Where is Lee Woo-cheol these days? Does Jeong-hee even know where he is?"

"No, she's got no idea. She even came over to mine to ask me if I knew. See, my uncle works at the coal mines in Chikuho."

"I guess he's in Japan, then."

"He stowed away to Shimonoseki and when he got off, the military police spotted him and said, 'Who goes there, stop,' but of course he didn't stop, because, I mean, he's Lee Woo-cheol. So he ran away on those beautiful legs of his and before they realized, he was gone. Apparently the military policeman said, 'Was that a bird? It was no man.'"

"Aigu, I've heard a hundred versions of that already."

"Well, who saw it happen?"

"Must've been someone, because all Miryang's heard about it now."

"But why did he run away? The draft's only for men who'll turn twenty between December last year and November this year."

"But nobody knew that until just recently. Not long ago there were rumors going around that anyone under forty would be dragged off to serve."

"Gi-woon at the Chinese herbal pharmacy just got notice for a physical exam."

"He got a draft notice?"

"No, not one of those red draft notices, a white paper. Gi-woon's eomoni showed it to me herself. One morning, a soldier-type from the county government came in and when Gi-woon wrote his name down, the soldier cut out the ticket stub on the spot and took it with him."

"My eldest son'll be twenty in May, wonder if there's any way to fudge his age in the records."

"Aigu, the county government has all the records, what trick could you pull?"

"I hope he fails the physical exam. What if he drinks tons of castor oil?"

"Aigu, that'll sure ruin his body."

"Sure, but he'll recover. There's no cure for coming home as a bag of bones. If he's just a little sick, the doctor'll know better, so he's got to make himself really sick."

"But didn't the team leader say those who are by chance seriously ill on the exam day should be on stretchers, and those who find it hard to walk should be prepared to go to the exam site even if they have to claw their way there?"

"What's there to do but hide him?"

"Where would you hide him? The police come every day."

"Hide him in your house, and then when the police come, hide him in a hangari."

"Then the Kempeitai will take his abeoji away and torture him. You heard about what happened to Jong-hwi, the barber. He got drunk at a bar and started singing 'Arirang,' and the next morning the Kempeitai came and tortured him because they said he had dangerous thoughts."

"Si-hyeong's little brother is in the Heroic Corps, so they've been following him for a long time already."

"I heard they stuck bamboo needles under his nails and held a glowing red trowel against his shoulders and neck, and he fainted from the smell of his own burning flesh. They'll call all your family and relatives unpatriotic and untrustworthy, they'll all be tailed by police, and you won't even receive rations."

"But if you inform you get extra rations. Lotta rats around these days."

"Can't trust anybody anymore."

"Not even the baby in your own stomach, I swear."

In-hale ex-hale   in-hale ex-hale, a young man in a white running shirt ran across the bridge. It's Lee Woo-gun. In-hale ex-hale in-hale ex-hale, the youngest of the women caught sight from under the brim of her hat of Woo-gun as he approached; unconsciously she stretched her neck so that her nape would look more beautiful, and with damp hands she pushed the hairs that had come loose from her jjokjinmeori behind her ears.

"Him and his brother, both such handsome men."

"Did I hear right that he's going to Choyang Commercial School in Busan?"

"His abeoji and eomoni are dead, his brother's missing, and I suppose he can't exactly stay at his brother's mistress's house."

"She's not his mistress anymore. I heard he actually married her."

"Aigu, secretly taking In-hye off his family record like that . . ."

"She treats In-hye's two girls like they're her maids, while she's out all day gallivanting around."

"Yesterday evening, I ran into Shin-ja on the steps at Yeongnamnu; she was crying and tugging on a little boy's hand."

"That boy's not Jeong-hee's son, you know, he belongs to that dancer at the OK Café, what was her name?"

"Kim Mi-yeong."

"That's right, he's Kim Mi-yeong's boy."

"Aigu, they've all got different mothers, but the boys all look so much alike you can't hardly tell them apart. They're close in age too, right? Imagine sowing your wild oats all over the place in times like this."

"With a son like yours I wouldn't talk like that."

"Aigu, my Man-jae's only got eyes for his wife."

"But In-hye and Mi-yeong both ran off and left the babies they carried for nine long months. They must've known they'd be bullied by a stepmother, and besides, the stepmother in question is Jeong-hee, I mean. . . ."

"I don't know, personally I'd take them with me whatever happened. It's not normal, is it, for mothers to run off and leave their children."

"Didn't I hear she got remarried?"

"Yes and gave birth to a boy."

"Aigu, bulssangta. Mi-ok's thirteen and Shin-ja must be seven. Jeong-hee's going around looking for someone to marry Mi-ok off to."

"But you know, I feel sorry for Jeong-hee's kids too; I mean, their parents weren't married when they were born and their abeoji didn't bless them either. The whole Lee family's got bad luck. Woo-cheol's abeoji died of an infection, his younger sister drowned, and his half sister has polio."

"Oh, by the way, that woman at the Dong-A Guesthouse, after she got remarried and had a boy, she came down with some kind of uterine illness and now she's hooked on opium."

"Aigu, that stuff'll kill you."

"I heard she can't stand anymore; she just spends all day lying down."

"Woo-cheol's eomoni, Hyang-hee, was from the Park family, who were prosperous here for generations, so it must've been that man Yong-ha, their father, who brought disaster to their descendants."

"I mean, he was a traveling face-reader after all."

"But Woo-cheol's younger brother, Woo-gun, is a handsome fellow, he's a fast runner, and he's a smart kid who's going to Choyang Commercial School. And unlike Woo-cheol, he's innocent; he doesn't seem to have a roving eye for women."

"Aigu, Woo-cheol got engaged to In-hye when he was sixteen."

"I'll have Woo-gun for my son-in-law if no one else minds."

"Get in line, you're not the only eomoni with her eye on him."

"But isn't he turning twenty next year? They'll draft him."

"You think the war will still be going then?"

"It's moving under its own steam now, I think. Yesterday at the patriotic team meeting, Team Leader Yasuda said they've wiped out most of the British Indian Army's Seventh Division."

"But can they beat Britain and America?"

They paused.

"How can we lose?"

"I shall not want, until victory comes."

"Luxury is the enemy."

"If Japan wins, you think they'll increase our rations a little?"

"My youngest daughter joined the volunteer corps and she's serving at Mitsubishi Heavy Industries Aircraft Manufacturing Company in Nagoya; but since they only give her enough in her pay packet for her train fare, I send her money every month. Her pay envelope says, 'We live by the grace of His Majesty the emperor, we work by the grace of His Majesty the emperor, and we die by the grace of His Majesty the emperor.' Even if Japan wins, the lives of Koreans won't get any better. The emperor and all the waenom just get to have it good, God I wish a B-29 would—"

Suddenly she gasped, and someone started humming "Miryang Arirang." In time with the melody of *ari, arirang, suri, surirang*, a mountain turtledove chirped, giving momentum to the women's hands as they picked minari.

One of the women smiled, as if in encouragement to her own hands.

"If Japan wins, we'll have white rice to eat."

One of them stood with effort, wiping her wet hands on the waist of her trousers; it was the woman whose daughter had been taken by the volunteer corps. She put the minari she had plucked in her basin and put that on her head, then muttered very deep under her breath, "Meonjeo gallanda." *I'm going.*

"Geurae aesseotda." *All right, good work.*

"Salpyeogaraei." *Take care.*

Sol sol sarang sarang sol sol sarang sarang, the March breeze bent the heads of the tall, straight-stemmed yellow dandelions, *sol sol sarang sarang*, it slipped into a blouse missing two buttons, revealing its wearer's smooth, firm breasts. *Sol sol sarang sarang sol sol sarang sarang*, she crumpled her chin and looked down at her nipples, like two fallen chestnuts, wondering with feigned innocence whether the wind was so strong it would soon strip her naked as she climbed up the bank of the river.

"Heard they had a girl at Hong-woo's house too."

"Yes, today must be the thirty-seventh-day celebrations."

"That family's had its own disaster. I guess it's been about six months since her daughter ran off."

"Her eomoni was frantically searching; she went everywhere looking for her."

"Well, you would for a thirteen-year-old unmarried girl. And she hasn't heard a word from her, so she doesn't even know if she's alive or dead. If she was alive, she'd at least send a postcard, surely."

"But I bet the man of the house was happy to see her gone."

"He's not her real father, that's why. And it's probably why the girl ran away, because she didn't get along with him."

"He asked me if my son might marry her."

"No! But your son's in his thirties, isn't he?"

"His wife died of tuberculosis while she was pregnant with their third child, and now he's got two kids on his hands."

"Imagine wanting to send a thirteen-year-old girl into that kind of situation. He was obviously just trying to get rid of her."

"What do you think you mean, 'that kind of situation'?"

"Aigu, dwaetda dwaesseo. That girl, what was her name . . . she was such a pretty, clever girl; if she hadn't run away I'm sure she'd have been one of the girls at this year's Arang Festival."

Quickly the smile slipped from Arang's face, invisible as she was to the women. *Whoosh*, the wind yelled in anticipation of being interrupted by the women's chatter, and Arang filled her lungs with breath like a newborn baby, then let loose her voice, but all the women's ears could hear was a whirlwind trying to awaken the spring.

The bird crying in the pine trees   sounds so sad
Does it suffer   the curse of Arang?

Ari, arirang   suri, surirang   arariga nanne
Coming over Arirang Pass

The moon that falls on Yeongnamul   is clear but
The Namcheong River just   flows silently

Ari, arirang   suri, surirang   arariga nanne
Coming over Arirang Pass

Whoosh, whoosh, in return for the song, the spring wind blew the light up into the air, *banjjak banjjak*, and then climbed up into the sky. Jeo cheongnyeon jom jabajwoyo, jeogi jeogi dallyeoganeun cheongnyeoneul. Catch that boy for me, that boy running over there. *Whoosh*, the wind raced across the surface of the river to get its momentum up, *whoosh whoosh*, took a shortcut through the pine trees, *whoosh whoosh*, chasing after the young man running on the embankment of the Miryang River, *whoosh whoosh*, in-hale ex-hale in-hale ex-hale, sumsoriga deullyeo, ije geumbangiya, I can hear him breathing, just a little further, Arang reached out toward the boy's shirt, *whoosh whoosh*, in-hale ex-hale, *whoosh whoosh*, the wind overtook him, reached out both its arms and blocked his way, *whoosh whoosh, whoosh whoosh*.

In-hale ex-hale in-hale ex-hale, himdeulda, damn this headwind the spring wind does just what it will in-hale ex-hale feels like it's aiming itself right at me jegil jil geot gatda it must be trying to help me this is good training for my muscles in-hale ex-hale in-hale ex-hale whoosh whoosh it sounds like when I tried to whistle like my abeoji when I was little whoosh whoosh I can whistle better now **ame, ame fure, fure kaa-san ga janome de omukai ureshii na** haven't seen that girl around since that day wonder what happened to her is she off volunteering somewhere? or did she get married? in-hale ex-hale sometimes I think about her probably because she looked so much like So-won in-hale ex-hale in-hale ex-hale in-hale ex-hale in-hale ex-hale

Woo-gun ran down the embankment, put his face directly to the water, and drank.

I slept so little I can barely run. I stayed up copying from the book that Shin-woong lent me and before I knew it, it was time for the rooster to crow. **The world picture is a picture of how matter moves and of how "matter thinks."** Woo-gun took off his running shirt; it slumped on top of the soft, newly sprouted grass in the shape of a capital *T*. I'd like to sleep a little right here, but my head is so full of words that I don't think I could. Unlike when I read something, anything I write down comes to my mind just as it is. **The world, the all in one, was not created by any god or any man, but was, is, and ever will be a living flame, systematically flaring up and systematically dying down.** Woo-gun opened his eyes. Sky. Blue. A blue so pale it would be washed away by the slightest shower. The green of the grass and the blue of the sky, both still pale. But soon we'll drag into summer and it'll turn darker. *Whoosh whoosh*, the wind shook the tender new leaves on the trees. But no matter how hard it blew, the young leaves did not scatter like they would in autumn. Spring is soft and young. And more stubborn than any other season. Chun-sik. Maybe it's because the name my brother gave me has *spring* in it, but when spring comes around, I feel like all the windows of the world have been thrown wide open and I can see everything. **The dialectical method considers invincible only that which is arising and developing.** Woo-gun sat up and raised his hands high as if trying to reach the sky. **The dialectical method therefore holds that the process of development should be understood not as movement in a circle, not as a simple repetition of what has already occurred, but as an onward and upward movement, as a transition from an old qualitative state to a new qualitative state, as a development from the simple to the complex, from the lower to the higher.** Woo-gun stared at the Miryang River, reflecting the morning sun and shining like a silver coin, and the gravel road, which snaked unerringly along the river. **Rich and poor, exploiters and exploited, people with full rights and people with no rights.** It's clear what I'm lacking. Preparation. No, pressure's what I need. With more pressure than I can bear on my shoulders, a sense of purpose would fill me, down to my fingertips. **Only the October Revolution set itself the goal of abolishing all exploitation and eliminating each and every exploiter and oppressor.** Woo-gun shuddered and the invisible shackles on his neck and ankles clanked; he started doing high knees, hana, dul, set, net, daseot, yeoseot, ilgop, yeodeol, ahop, and when he was done with that, he did two hundred push-ups and sit-ups each, up, inhale, down, exhale. Taking another deep breath, he looked up at the cloudless spring sky again. **Development is the "struggle" of opposites.**

Only Arang watched on as the shirtless youth bunny-hopped up and down the stone steps of Yeongnamnu, then up again. The still-drowsy spring wind ran its listless hand through Arang's dark hair, and the scent of plums and peaches filled her white chima. The young man clasped his hands to his hip as if he were holding a baby, as he bounced past Arang, *kkangchung kkangchung*. The string of her jeogori brushed against his cheek and the hem of her chima grazed his shoulder. Arang tried to call his name, thinking for only a moment whether to call him by his birth name or his new one before hailing him: Lee Chun-sik. The young man did not turn. He could not hear her over the sound of his own heart and breathing.

Gasp-gasp-gasp-gasp, aigo, sumchara! Feels like my heart's in every corner of my body. *Gasp-gasp-gasp-gasp*, I'm a ball of heat, and if it gets any hotter, *gasp-gasp-gasp-gasp-gasp*, brother, where are you? If he were here, *gasp-gasp*, no, the only one who can really drive me and encourage me is me alone, *gasp-gasp-gasp*, 'cause only my own ears can hear my voice, and only I can put that pressure on my heart, *gasp-gasp*, just me. **If the proletariat during its contest with the bourgeoisie is compelled, by the force of circumstances, to organize itself as a class . . . by means of a revolution, it makes itself the ruling class, and, as such, sweeps away by force the old conditions of production . . .** Woo-gun sat down on the stairs at Yeongnamnu, his arms propped up behind him to support his upper body. *Gasp-gasp-gasp-gasp-gasp-gasp-gasp-gasp*, I can't just keep panting, I've got to breathe in, in-hale *gasp-gasp*, deeper, in-out, like that, regularly, in-out, slow now, in out, now my heart's behaving itself, in out in, another minute and I'll start running again, if I don't get back home and change I'll miss the train, **true freedom, and the full enhancement of individual talents and abilities, is only possible under Communism,** in-hale ex-hale in-hale ex-hale in-hale ex-hale in-hale ex-hale in-hale ex-hale.

The smell rising from the young man's body drifted past Arang's face. She cast her eyes around. Droplets of sweat were splattered on the ground, but this wasn't the smell of sweat. Blood. His right leg was wet with bright red blood. Aigo, ireolsuga! Arang bent her neck like a wilting flower and with her own eyes, immobilized by grief, she saw the bullet hole. I can't stop it, I can't stop anything, not that girl being taken by the ilbon saram, not the blood flowing from this boy's body, I can't stop it, aigo, all I can do is grieve, i jeongdobakke an doedani, it's no use!

The sky drifted into slumber, clouds still scattered everywhere; *whoosh whoosh whoosh whoosh*, a flock of milky-white clouds crept along with the snores of the wind, and the sun climbed to the utmost height of the blue sky, little by little, jogeumssik jogeumssik, without stopping to take a breath. From beyond the light-filled blue sky came the shrill wail of a steam whistle. Black smoke billowed from the foot of Mount Chiltan, and when the black locomotive pulling the passenger cars appeared along with the sound of steam, *chuff-chuff-chuff,* the tracks at Miryang Station began to rattle, *clatter clatter clatter clatter clatter clatter chuff-chuff-chuff-chuff-chuff-chuff-chuff-chuff* . . .

Each passenger car was full of faces, hands, legs, knapsacks, and trunks, and the stairs from the vestibules and the roofs of the coal cars and passenger cars too were overflowing with Korean men. Passengers scrambled up to the roofs using the windows as a foothold, sitting with their bags between their legs. *Clang clang,* the departure bell rang and the platform guard raised his red flag, and *chuff-ff . . . chuff-ff . . . ka-chunk . . .* enveloped in smoke the locomotive began to move. Just then, a young man in a white shirt and gray trousers ran up, his feet beating hard against the platform, and jumped on the window ledge, but as he handed his schoolbag to a man on the roof, his right leg was frozen. In the dense steam Arang clung to his bloodstained leg. *Chug . . . chug . . . chug . . .* Gaji ma gamyeon andwae! Don't go! You can't go! *Chugga-chugga-chugga-chugga-chugga-chug.*

"Get up here quick! You'll fall!"

"My leg's stuck. . . ."

With the strength of three men on the roof, they pulled him up, as the platform at Miryang Station trailed into the distance behind the train. Left alone on the platform, Arang lingered, her eyes following after the billows of smoke, indistinguishable from the clouds. If he looked back now he might see me, but I know he'll never turn. He'll just keep looking forward, not even knowing what lies in wait ahead of him, aigo.

Woo-gun bent his head and stared at a point in the darkness of the tunnel. That point wasn't light but rather darkness condensed in the darkness. **The chains of imperialism must be severed**—to those words Woo-gun yielded all the space within himself as the whistle blew its shrill warning.

TWENTY-TWO

In Paradise

| 낙원에서 | 楽園にて |

It's a long tunnel . . . though I went in it a long while back . . . I can't see the light at the end . . . the darkness is so oppressive I can't breathe . . . why's the electricity off, *chug-chug-chug-chug, ka-chunk-ka-chunk*, it's rattling so much, my whole body is shaking, *choo-chooooooooooooo!* A shot of pain runs up between my legs, and when I finally exhale, we've made it through the tunnel . . .

Oh, I fell asleep, since Lieutenant Sakano stayed over and I didn't sleep a wink all night . . . I wonder if this guy's almost done . . . Namiko opened her eyes and saw the man moving. I've got a fever . . . yesterday when he was on top of me Lieutenant Sakano looked so far away, like he was four or five meters away from me . . . My stomach hurts, like I'm hungry . . . I've been taking the medicine that the army doctor gave me, but I'm not getting any better . . . I want to go outside and get some fresh air . . . but I can't until the line's cleared, 'cause the next one will just come in right after . . . he's still not done yet . . . I feel like I'm half-buried . . . if I thrust my hips up it'll end soon but . . . my hips are too stiff . . . I'm sinking, *jeom jeom* . . . The man pressed his chest against hers, pushing her head down with both his hands as he sped up the movement of his hips . . . Aya! Aya!

While he was tightening his fundoshi, Namiko crawled on her stomach, dragging herself to the corner of the room where her washbasin was, crouching over the metal basin and washing her crotch with Chameleon; she tried to undo the knot in the sheath and wash out the inside with cresol but . . . it was dark and she could barely see . . . Namiko reached out both hands toward the iron bars, the setting sun behind them like a hole punched in the grille, and with shaking fingers she tried to untie the sheath and put it in the pineapple can, but the high fever had confused her sense of perspective, and she dropped it on top of the red plain dress she had taken off earlier, spilling semen all over the chest. Ah, eotteoke haji, what do I do? Just as she reached for the blue dress hanging on the wall, the blanket over the door pulled back and the next man entered.

"Irrashaimase, soko ni okake kudasai."

Naked, she turned to greet him, and though she heard her own voice rising and falling, she herself had no idea what she had said. The man took off his trousers and undid his fundoshi, and Namiko knelt down in front of him and put a sheath on him. She guessed he was a volunteer, not even twenty years old; he grasped Namiko's breast and entered her with one thrust.

"What's your name?"

"Whatever name you like."

"Then I'll call you Midori."

"Who's Midori?"

"My fiancée back home."

Midori, Midoriiiii . . . The man sped up the movement of his hips, finishing not long after.

Namiko couldn't get up anymore. The pain throbbed, the setting sun shining through the iron bars became as pale as smoke, until only the pain remained. The wooden door squeaked, and she turned her head to see what looked like white tissue paper showering down around her bed like hibiscus flowers.

The next man who entered was Sergeant Katō. Despite the fact that any man who visited the same woman twice in a month would get a warning from the Kempeitai, Sergeant Katō always came to see her once a week, and when he snuck to visit her at dawn, he'd bring her a care package with a toothbrush and soap and a wrinkled five-yen military scrip.

"Nami-chan, how're you feeling?"

"My fever's still high . . . and my stomach hurts . . ."

Sergeant Katō stepped out the door into the hallway.

My sweat is going cold, maybe because it's not my own, she thought, sticking the soles of her feet against the hot-water bottle she got when she was awarded for being the top seller at last month's Declaration Observance Day.

Returning with a metal basin, Sergeant Katō dipped a cloth in the cool water, wrung it out, and placed it on Namiko's forehead.

"Can you give me a cigarette?"

Sergeant Katō put his hand in his breast pocket and pulled out a pack of Golden Bat; he put one in his mouth and lit it, then put it between Namiko's lips. She inhaled as deeply as she could, holding the smoke in her lungs as long as she could, then exhaled with a moan. I can't taste anything, something's wrong with my tongue, it's like smoking incense, the incense when Shizue unni stabbed herself in the neck with scissors and killed herself . . . Aigu, andwae, I don't want to remember what her face looked like when she was dead, not now, silta . . .

"Nami-chan, when the war is over, I want us to live together."

He's sitting in that chair right next to me, but his face, just his face, is blacked out, like a censored newspaper, and his whole body looks like a shadow—this man, he might not have long . . .

"When you go home you'll have the pick of Japanese women . . . you're just saying that now because I'm . . ."

"But you look like a Japanese woman. You haven't even got an accent; I can just tell my parents you're a Japanese girl born on the peninsula."

"But . . . what would you want with someone . . ." Choking on cigarette smoke, Namiko coughed violently.

HURRY UP!

THERE'S MEN WAITING!

They're yelling all at once in front of every room, I can barely hear what I'm saying.

"How's the war?" Namiko asked, her voice cracking.

"We did what we aimed to do with Operation Ichi-gō, but we couldn't destroy the US Air Force's B-29 base or crush the Chongqing Army, so we're wary of enemy attacks with nothing to do about them, there's hardly one section of functioning rail line, and the derailed locomotives were bright red with rust and turned over on their sides . . . We marched so far . . . Maybe two hundred and fifty ri, that's about the same as from Tokyo to Shimonoseki, you know.

"The morning of the first day, we started off singing in time with the steps of our boots, but it was a rough track covered in stones and weeds, so by the afternoon, my feet hurt from the soles up to the ankles, and I felt like I was walking on a pile of needles. After a short break, all that equipment felt so heavy, no one could stand up without someone else pulling them up by the hand. Hunched over, I finally managed to get to my feet, but my unit's inexperienced and there were a lot of reservists with no body strength, so with each step the gap between us and the unit ahead widened until we could hardly see them, so we had to march incredibly fast to catch up with them, and the horses fought it, they dropped their loads, they kicked at us, one of the reservists got cheeky and hung off the side of a Transportation Corps vehicle until he got mowed down, and before we knew it, the unit behind us was passing us. The reservist guys are no good, they don't want to be promoted, they just want the war to be over as soon as possible so they can go home. Most of the time you can tell just from how a guy looks if he's an active-duty soldier. I tried to be careful, but at some point I slung my black hand cloth over the top of my field cap and tied it to keep the sun off, and then I used my field cap to take the hot lid off my mess tin, so I was always black with soot.

"When you're at the end of the marching order, it doesn't matter if the sun's gone down or the sky is white or the sun's right overhead, you have to march, no time for food or breaks. When we finally caught up with the rest of the units and took a break on top of a hill, there they were, the head of the column, marching off like ants through the grassy plains on the other side.

"And marching in the rain is even more miserable. I was up to my knees in mud, couldn't even move my legs—I fell over, and my gun and my glasses and everything were all muddy. There was mud up over the wheels of the transport vehicles, so we had to take everything it was carrying and walk it up to the hill on the other side. Everywhere you looked it was mud, mud, mud . . . No trees or stumps, even, so I had to tie my horse to the saddle I'd just taken off of it. We wrapped ourselves up in blankets and leaned against our packs, and usually we'd tell stories from back home about digging holes in rice paddies with a spoon or hiding in a pile of straw, but no one had the energy to speak. It's cold at night on the continent, even if you're indoors, but maybe because it was raining, I was so cold I couldn't keep my teeth together, and I kept waking up all the time needing to pee. It was hard to stand up, so I just rolled over on my side and pulled it out, but it was so shrunken from the cold that nothing even came out. I squeezed it tight and it made this pathetic *squish squish squish squish* sound. And my blanket had absorbed the rain and gotten heavier so once I was awake it was hard to get back to sleep. But what else could I do except lie there in the rain opening and closing my eyes? The night watch's bayonets shone in the rain, the horses neighed quietly, and someone somewhere moaned in their sleep. I lay there not knowing if I was asleep or not until I did fall asleep, and I dreamed about swimming in a stream in my hometown. The water was cold, my lips were blue, and I was shivering as I swam; I wanted to at least be warm and cozy in my dreams, but when it's cold I tend to have dreams about being cold, I wonder why that is . . .

"And mealtime's difficult too, because we have to procure food for one hundred and twenty people wherever we are. I started off with hardtack, canned food, and rice in my pack, but for three days I'd been out of all of that. So we search houses for rice, miso, and cooking supplies, chase around chickens, pigs, and water buffalo, pick radishes and leaves from the fields, and share it between a few of us. There's never enough rice. These damn Chinese only cook rice for parties or festivals, some kind of celebration; usually they eat steamed buns. I took the lid off a large, shallow pot and saw buns, so I shouted out, 'Bread! Bread!' and we ate them right on the spot, didn't even take them back to the rest of the unit. We're supposed to requisition stuff, but the Chinks had all ran away, and a lot of times we don't find anything of use whatsoever. While we were eating the buns, everyone else was walking through the fields, and someone said they'd found pumpkins, so we went looking for pumpkins, and we were trying to carry as many pumpkins as we could, but there was no rope or anything, so I kept my mouth shut.

"Then sometimes we'd come across a rice field, and we'd hit the plants with stones or wood and fill our socks with the rice to take back with us. But it's almost all chaff, and when you chomp down on it it hurts and it's hard to eat. At first I tried to squeeze the rice out of the hull with my teeth and spit it out, but eventually I got tired of that and just started swallowing it whole. But

despite all that, even on the nights when we'd marched all day without breakfast or lunch, everyone ate up without a single complaint.

"Sometimes we'd requisition a pig, torch the house, and roast the pig. The
company commander just issued the order—this is an anti-Japanese house so
burn it down—and when I went inside to examine it, there was writing on the
white walls: resistance until death, overthrow the Japanese emperor, Oriental
demons, you know. Beautiful handwriting, the kind that makes you admire
the author's courage. It was the first time I'd ever set a house on fire, so I was
nervous, but we all got to warm up while the pig was roasting—that was the
best day we had. We sat in a circle and ate while the fire was still smoldering
and warm, and the pig was great, and the cigarette I had after eating was tremendous too.

"That's the kind of night when the Chinese would attack. When you've
eaten your fill and you're sleeping soundly, then, *bang, bang,* bullets start flying over your head, and you hear splashing coming from the swamps. Some of
the men got shot and screamed out, so then it's, Arms at the ready! Three
o'clock! Take individual fire! And then *boom!* Grenades started drowning out
the platoon leader's orders. The other side, they make grenades out of bamboo, and that's how they trap you, oh, look, bamboo, *bang bang bang!* Shrap-
nel everywhere. And then the B-29s join in, and the bombs start falling like
rain. We don't have grenades, just short swords and a gun for one out of five of
us. And the baby-faced boy soldiers with no battle experience start shaking
in their boots, hugging each other and crying, "Mother, Mother," or "Long
live the emperor!" The next morning, the young ones all get a big scolding
from the squad leader, a big beating, though if they're going easy on them the
platoon leader won't beat them, they just have everyone else beat the guy hard
until they say that's enough.

"So we caught the young Chinks who tried to escape, and Ensign Yamada,
who studied Chinese in college, questioned them, then the commander ordered us to kill everyone we'd captured. We're short on bullets, use your
swords, he said. When you're in battle it's easy to get wrapped up in it and kill,
but it's hard to stab someone just standing there right in front of you. Then,
this Chink, he looked me right in the face and started walking away like he
was kicking the hem of his robe until he got a few meters away where it'd be

easier for me to stab him. My commander started yelling, 'What the fuck, Katō! You're gonna let him fuck with you?' I stared into this guy's eyes and at the moment I grabbed my bayonet, he shouted, 'Long live the Republic of China!'

"Some of the Chinese, my commander just wanted us to test our swords on. Every last one of them, they all have this look like, I'll die for the sake of a new China, my own life doesn't matter; honestly, it made me terrified of how tough the Chongqing Army was. The commander must've felt the same way, because he shouted, 'Don't do it from the back, run him through from the front, and take a good look!' He made me grab the guy by his pigtail and I slashed his throat with my sword, but I couldn't get a good cut, and I was just thinking how much that had to hurt, but the little Chink just looked up at the blue sky, his eyes shining. An older guy, who was drafted and used to slaughter cows, couldn't just stand there watching, so he slit the guy's throat with his short knife, and a plume of blood shot up like a fountain, and I was covered in blood head to toe. His neck was so heavy in my hands. On the commander's orders, we strung him up with a rope and hung him from a branch of a cedar tree. He couldn't have still been alive, but those eyes were still shining, in the middle of his bloody face . . . just gleaming . . . every night when I was trying to go to sleep, I'd see those eyes . . ."

The soldiers lined up outside enduring the cold started singing the bandit suppression march.

How much more mud must we trudge through
Three days and two nights with no food
Rain splashing into our helmets
And the shouts and roars are endless too
I took the mane of my fallen horse
And now we'll never part
The autumn flowers growing wild
Where her hooves left their mark fall
The bugs start to hum in the dusk sky
I'm already out of smokes
And the match I asked for is soaked through

Is this the cold of another hungry night?
Well, if that's how it is, then I
A warrior from the land of the Rising Sun
I'll meet my grassy grave with no regrets
Oh, the Eastern horizon stretches wide
And our allies' airplanes rattle the skies
Our glorious warriors determined
To wipe out our foes
And watch as they burn in flames
The sound of cannons echoing in the hills
The slightest echo of a voice
We'll stain the fields red
And kill all their horses dead
And let flames rise high from mountain huts
In the glory of the broad daylight

An irate soldier ran the wall through with his bayonet, interrupting the song.

THERE'S MEN WAITING!

HURRY UP!

"If you stay too long Oyaji'll turn you in to the Kempeitai. . . ."

"Don't worry, this is meant to be an hour-long reservation. Just pretend like you can't hear those guys, can't hear them at all. I wanted to give you a chance to rest a little, Nami-chan. Besides, I won't be able to sleep unless I tell someone everything . . . And I don't know when's the next time I'll get to talk to you . . ."

"Are you going somewhere?"

"I'm being sent to Binyang to secure it."

I'M WAITING!

ARE YOU FUCKING IMPOTENT?

I'M GONNA CHARGE!

A soldier started kicking the wooden door, but Sergeant Katō dipped the towel in water, wrung it, and put it back on Namiko's forehead, then took the pack of Golden Bat from his chest pocket.

"Oh, down to my last one. . . . You ought to have this one instead."

"I'm fine, really."

"Close your eyes, Nami-chan. Get some sleep."

She could see, through her thin eyelids, the flame of the match, and she heard Sergeant Katō's low voice close to her right ear.

"The commander ordered us to kill anyone who was suspicious and burn down any house that we had doubts about. But it's hard to know, you know, soldiers dress up as farmers and pull guns out of piles of straw in the back of wagons and attack, and young girls hide grenades in their robes and throw them at us, so you can't tell the difference between soldiers and good citizens. And if you get it wrong, it's your life that'll be lost. So we set fire to a house and shoot and kill all the Chinese who run out. The whole road was covered with them so you couldn't walk without stepping on a body. And when you take one step, they start moaning, and they might try to attack, so you gotta stab them in the neck with your bayonet and move on.

"There was this redbrick house, and I don't know how much blood there was, but it was slippery to the touch. You try to cook rice with water from a river full of corpses and the rice turns red. . . . Still, you couldn't say it was dirty exactly, and we were hungry and we had to eat something.

"Everyone got around the bonfire to eat, and then all of a sudden, Sergeant Tsukamoto stood up and pointed into the forest and started shouting, 'A train! Look how it's blowing out red-hot fire as it rolls! I'm getting on and I'm going home! He-ey! Stop! I said stop!' Food was falling out of his mouth all over everything. We all wrestled him down and wrapped him up in a blanket and tried to get him to go to sleep, but he just kept his eyes wide open, not sleeping a wink. I tried to hold my hand over his eyes, but he stared out between my fingers, just muttering away. 'Hey, Katō, it's a hitodama . . . a soul in the form of a fireball . . . look, there's one there too . . . one, two, three, four . . . can't count 'em all . . . so pretty how the blue flames float like that . . . maybe it's a fox's wedding . . . And he carried on like that until dawn . . .

"The next morning, the commander shouted, 'I'll beat some sense back into you!' and slapped him across the face repeatedly with his leather belt, but the man snapped the heels of his boots together, brought his fingers together, and saluted, then reported, 'Sir, last night I delivered words of congratulations to my hometown.' The commander had no choice but to stop and have a medic take him to the military hospital, but I wonder how he's doing now . . . He was a nice guy, knew as much about flowers as any woman, so he wasn't very suited to battle . . . Poor guy . . .

"Sorry for talking so much. I can't talk to the guys in my squad about this stuff, it'll affect morale, and even when I get back to Japan I can't tell anyone what I've seen and done here . . . You're the only one I have, Nami-chan."

Namiko opened her eyes and looked up at Sergeant Katō's face.

"Please take care and come back soon."

"I have something to ask of you."

"Go on."

"Will you give me a little of your hair from down there? As a good-luck charm?"

Namiko stood up with the help of Sergeant Katō, snipped off a little of her pubic hair, wrapped it in a piece of tissue, and handed it to him.

"Thank you. I'll keep it with me, so I won't get shot. In return, I'd like to give you this."

Sergeant Katō placed a photograph of himself and a red amulet with gold embroidery from Atsuta Shrine in front of Namiko.

"I'm fighting for our country and for my own life. Peace won't come to the Orient unless each of us kills as many as we can and leads the Japanese Empire to victory. And I can't die, so I have to kill and stay alive to return to the mainland. When I get back home, I'll forget everything. And you, Nami-chan, you'll forget about everything that happened here and start over with me, right? Before I enlisted, I'd never even hit someone, or taken a punch either, for that matter. I'm an only son, so my father and mother took good care of me; I want to get back home as soon as possible and show them my appreciation, I want them to give them a grandchild to hold right away . . ."

Sergeant Katō wrung out the towel again and put it back on Namiko's forehead, then he stood, as if forcing himself up by pressing his palm down.

"Nami-chan, come back to the mainland with me and give me lots of children."

"Arigatō gozaimashita, mata kite kudasai."

"Oh, don't be like that."

"Sorry."

"You don't have to apologize. I'll scope things out and if it looks like I can get away, I'll come back tonight and bring you something. Thanks for the good-luck charm, I'll keep it with me always."

She saw Sergeant Katō smile and look back and a chill ran down her spine. The shadow of death. In the year and three months since she'd been brought to Paradise, she'd seen off many soldiers who all had that same look about them. None of them had returned alive. Namiko grabbed the red amulet and looked up at the black chima and white silk jeogori hanging on her wall. Fumiko unni, who gave me these mementos of a girl called Sayuri, had the same look about her when she was sitting across the dining table from me. Not a week later she'd hanged herself with her obi. She gave me these clothes to wear when I go back to Korea, but when the war ends, I won't be me anymore, I'll have to become someone else, another me to go on living, in China, or Manchuria, or Japan . . . I wonder if I'll be able to see my own shadow of death. . . . One morning I'll look in the mirror and . . .

Thud—a man opened the door roughly and came in; his uniform had two bars and two stars on it, a first lieutenant.

"Irrashaimase, soko ni okake kudasai." Her voice echoed limply in her own ears.

He took off his trousers and long johns and untied his fundoshi, then stuck himself right in front of Namiko's face. She started to take a sheath out of its wrapper.

"I don't need an Iron Helmet."

"That's the rule."

"That's the rule if you put it in down there. You Korean whores all have gonorrhea, so I won't."

The man took out a pack of Chinese cigarettes called Ruby Queen and lit one.

"I get enough of that anyway. I can fuck as many gūniangs as I want when we're out requisitioning. It's dark and gloomy in here."

Namiko put a little rapeseed oil and a wick on a plate and struck a match, glancing up at the man's face. His eyes look strange. Is he drunk? But he doesn't smell like booze . . . opium? The ones who are on opium are usually the ones who start slashing with their swords or demanding strange things. . . . But if he was on opium his eyes would be sunken into a deep swamp, she thought, but no, his eyes were dancing around like dried sardines in a boiling pot, it's something more restless than that . . . aniya . . . there's something murderous in his eyes.

The man pulled off the buttons on her dress, revealing her breasts, then grabbed Namiko by the chin and turned her face upward.

"You've got beautiful tits and a pretty face. You're a young one."

Namiko gave in and put the man's thing in her mouth.

My red dress is covered in semen, and now the buttons are gone from my blue one . . . what am I going to do? . . . Tomorrow morning, if my fever's broken, then I can do laundry and put the buttons back on, but . . . aigo, jeongmal undo eopji . . .

The man grabbed Namiko's head, as if covering her ears, and began to move his hips.

His hand was much colder than the washcloth that Sergeant Katō had put on her forehead.

"Those gūniangs, they all black up their faces with ink and make cuts to their own heads, but if you shout, 'Sīle! Tuōle!' at them and mimic rolling up your shirt, they'll take it off on their own and show you their tits. You can tell from the tits how old they are. So then you've got a choice of a few young ones, so you say, 'Bī, kàn kàn.' Usually they just take off their kùzi without a word and lie down. So then five or six men will play rock, paper, scissors to decide the order. Hey! Can't you use your tongue better?!

"The fifteen- or sixteen-year-old virgins, their parents'll get down on the ground and beg, 'Jiùmìng, jiùmìng!' Begging for her life. If they're too fucking noisy, they get a bayonet through 'em. They reach out toward their daughter, blood just pouring out everywhere, calling her name, and these girls, the strongest-willed ones, even when they see their parents dying in front of them, they bite and kick and won't let you put it inside. So then you just have to beat her, like, I'll do the same to you, and rape her, but then you're fucked if someone tells on you to the Kempeitai after, so you just say she was in one of those women's detachments, the Niángzǐjūn, and bang!"

The man poked his index finger into Namiko's forehead and laughed.

"Our company commander just tells us not to cause any trouble, so fuck it, méi guānxì. Everyone wants to fuck, even if you've marched for three days and nights without food or water, as soon as you see a young girl you get hard—it's like proof you're still alive. A dead man can't get it up even if he's got a girl's mouth on his dick, am I right? Think you could get a dead man hard?

"One time we took this girl we thought was a virgin and all of us fucked her then killed her, and then all of a sudden from the other room we hear this crying. This guy called Okada was pissing on a baby, aiming right at its mouth with the same dick he'd used to rape its mother, and this was a little baby, still too young to hold its head up, so it was drowning in piss with its arms and legs flailing, and man, I felt awful, like if it hadn't cried then none of that would've happened, but then I thought, my buddies are my buddies, and even if they don't do shit the enemy is still the enemy, and if Japan loses then the same thing's gonna happen to my kid too, so méi guānxì. I bet you think I'm lying, don't you? Well, it's all true. And I got stories that are more interesting than that too, if you wanna hear."

Namiko shook her head, tears in her eyes.

"Oh, that's good, keep shaking your head, and don't use your teeth, if I feel your fucking teeth I'll smash every last one of them, it's a piece of cake to break teeth, just bash, bash, bash with your bare hand, and hey, if you were toothless, you know, it might be good for business, ahahahaha.

"I was walking along singing, 'Even when I'm whorin',' it's all for ol' Nippon,' when these little Chink twin brats tried to walk past me, I hit 'em so hard they flew about a yard, and then I made them march along with us to cook. Made 'em march for four or five days and then I let 'em play, y'know, as entertainment for us. I tied their pigtails together, then tied their hands to each other's, real tight. 'Go wherever you want, guys!' And I gave them a shove and aimed my gun at the legs of one of them, who'd started running, and *Bang! Bang!* Now just try to run with one good leg, dragging the other one along, in the rain. It was so fucking funny watching them trying to get away. 'You lazy bastards! You want a bullet in your other leg? Hurry up and get the fuck out of here!' Everyone was clapping and laughing, ahahahaha, oh, I'm coming, here it comes, here it comes! Better drink every last drop. If you spit it out I'll shoot you in the leg too! *Bang, bang, bang!*"

The man finished and removed himself from Namiko's mouth.

"Arigatō gozaimashita, mata kite kudasai."

She held it back until the man left the room, then vomited in the metal basin full of Chameleon.

She knew that the next man had already come in, but Namiko could not turn to greet him or hold closed the chest of her dress now missing its buttons.

The man undid his fundoshi and asked her quietly, "Are you Japanese?"

She could not speak or shake her head.

"I don't know if it's what they eat, but I can always tell—Korean whores smell like garlic and Chinese whores smell like green onions. But you smell like a Japanese woman."

Namiko took a hit of his awful breath to her face.

"The women of Japan give you their love too. I'm being transferred to Laos. It's not like Wuhan in the south, it's the kind of place where you don't know if you'll be dead by tomorrow . . . All-out suicidal battles in Saipan and Guam . . . I guess that's what awaits me too."

Namiko closed her eyes. The man grabbed her breasts with both hands and entered her. Though he was inside her he did not move, still holding her breasts so tightly that they were shaking. My head hurts, my eyes hurt so much I can barely see, aigo, nunbusyeo! Aya! Aigu, haneunim, please let me go to sleep . . . deeper than the roots of the cedars that grow straight down into the earth . . . a sleep bigger than the wings of the falcons that fly high over the top of Mount Hwaak . . . as soft as the fluff of the dandelions going to seed along the banks of the Miryang River . . . please, I'm begging you . . . please . . . keep my body and mind away from reality . . . a deep sleep . . . you can have every last breath in my body if only you give me that sleep . . . aigu, aya . . . aya . . . aya . . . This man's not moving at all . . . like someone clinging to the wreckage of a sinking ship waiting for rescue . . . yes, my body is my wreckage . . . but it's the last place for salvation for these men . . . their final place of life . . . so then what should I cling to? To life? Death?

She opened her eyes and saw a louse crawling on the man's nape. She stretched out her hand to crush the louse, then slid her hand down to his back, moving his hips like waves and shaking his body. The moonlight shone through a gap in the clouds. It must be because my fever's so high, I can't tell if

I'm hot or cold . . . My whole body's numb, like the time I held the ice . . . Maybe this is what all the unnis were talking about, how to make a man come faster . . .

The man pulled up his trousers and gave her a salute, with an expression that she couldn't tell whether he was being silly or serious.

"Take care of yourself and be well."

"Arigatō gozaimashita, mata kite kudasai."

The look of death. Namiko looked away from the man's face, down at her own breasts, which had ten fingerprints clear as day on them. He might leave this world, but the traces of his fingers might never disappear . . .

No one came in next. Is it over? Today they started coming around noon, hana, dul, set, net . . . I can only remember ten of their faces, but then I was asleep for a while after that . . . maybe more than twenty . . . Anyway, today I'll just go to sleep like this . . . if I wake up tomorrow and my fever's gone down, then I'll take a bath first thing . . . it's been ten days since I last washed . . . I wonder how many lice there are on me right now . . . and there's male and female lice too, so I guess they're mating all over me . . . I comb and I comb but my roots are still covered in eggs . . . when I got that brown cardigan that belonged to Fumiko unni, it was so damp that I held it over the fire to dry it out. All the lice that had been living inside it started crawling out of the loops of the yarn . . . I plucked them off and threw them in the fire . . . pluck pluck pluck pluck . . . this summer there were so many aphids that I was afraid to sleep. I'd turn over my blanket in the morning and a few would jump out, and sometimes they dived into my hair . . . but I got used to it . . . to the aphids and the lice and the mice and the men, I got used to all of it . . . is there anything else lying in wait for me somewhere? Ready to tear me apart with its claws and fangs . . . Gwaenchana, there can't be anything worse left . . . no matter what happens next, there's nothing that can be freshly damaged . . . my life ended when I reached **Paradise** . . . so then why don't I stab myself in the neck like Shizue unni? Or hang myself with my obi like Fumiko unni? Might I still have some hope left in me after all?

She stretched out her toes, but the hot-water bottle had gone completely cold. She wrapped her only two blankets around herself and hugged the pillow that thousands of men had lain on, but the cold still went straight through her skin, down into her bones and blood. Usually if she just stayed still for a little while, a membrane of warmth from her body would form, but ah, *chuwo wae ireoke chuun geoji*, it's cold, oh, why is it so cold. In this chill that gripped her throat, killed all feeling in her lips, and even hindered the movements of her eyes, and in the midst of her unstoppable trembling, Namiko was engulfed in white smoke, breathing the smell of it deep into her body. *Chugga-chugga-chugga-chugga ka-chunk-ka-chunk-ka-chunk-ka-chunk choooooooooooooooooo!* As the train left the tunnel, her beloved Miryang River leaped into sight. *Jebal jom cheoncheonhi dallyeo, jebal!* Please, go slower, please! *Chugga-chugga-chugga-chugga ka-thunk-ka-thunk-ka-thunk-ka-thunk*, oh, it's Kyōjun, and Keiko's there too! And that's Takahide, jumping into the river from a willow, *kersplash!* Oh, oh, and Tetsu'ichi and Norio are stark naked too, *egu-meoni, changbihaera*, oh gosh, how embarassing! Miryang! Summertime! I'm home, back in Miryang! Isn't that Woo-gun there running on the embankment? It is—Woo-gun! Aigu, my heart's pounding, *chugga-chugga-chugga-chugga ka-thunk-ka-thunk-ka-thunk-ka-thunk*, but why is it so cold? The sky's so blue and the river's shining, but, *scre-eech*, suddenly without a sound the whole train slowly started to tilt, and Namiko screamed, putting her hands to the wall, ahhhhhhh!

She fearfully opened her clenched eyelids and saw the morning sun shining in through the iron bars. Traces of a smile still remained on her face, a smile full of joy. . . . She felt if she stayed lying down she would scream and cry, so gingerly she sat up. My fever is . . . a bit lower . . . but I simply can't take a bath or put those buttons back on or do my laundry. . . . Namiko took off the blue dress missing its buttons and slipped the red, semen-stained one over her head.

She opened the inner wooden door and found some hardtack and two cans of oranges. Sergeant Katō must've left these for me before he left, I guess he gave me part of what he could've put in his own pack, I sure hope he doesn't get hungry while he's marching.

Namiko found the can opener under her futon, then walked down the hallway with the opener in her left hand and a can of oranges in her right. Everyone's still asleep, even the officers staying the night, so I mustn't make a sound . . . Namiko gently opened the door to room two, with the ON BREAK tag hanging from it.

Kohana was lying down; her eyes were slightly open.

Namiko sat down next to her pillow.

"Unni, gwaenchana?"

Namiko took Kohana's hand in both her numbed hands, sliding the two gold rings that were about to fall off her ring finger back down to the base.

Unni's baby didn't come out even after she drank tea made from buchu roots. It had happened one morning a week ago. I'd opened the wooden door to find Unni there, nemaki already drenched in blood, up on her knees like a cat trying to lick itself as she was pulling the baby's legs out. It was a breech birth. When I said I'd go call the doctor, Unni said not to. Unni didn't let out a single cry. The baby's butt came out, followed by his shoulders and arms held up as if in celebration, and then finally its head, purple as a grape; with one glance I could tell that it was dead. I pulled out his umbilical cord, careful not to break it as I did, gently, gently . . . then Unni fainted.

Dr. Ito disinfected his hands with cresol and stuck one into her vagina and removed the placenta, then with obvious annoyance he packed her vagina with gauze and sighed. When I asked him why the baby was born dead, he said, "It's the syphilis," then walked out the door still complaining: "I'm a surgeon, you know, I'm only doing this because it was my turn."

"Unni, want to eat a little mandarin?"

Kohana turned her long eyes, just like crevices in rocks on the riverbed as they had been when the two of them had first met, toward the mirror and stretched out a hand to draw a small circle.

On the mirror's stand was a rice ball that had turned blue with mold and some white powder, scattered about. Unable to bear the agony when her belly had swollen, she had bought some opium from the Chinese couple who came there to clean.

Namiko pushed the opium onto her hand mirror, pressed the pad of her finger into the powder, and placed it on Kohana's purpled tongue.

"At least have a little of the juice. You'll waste away if you don't eat something."

Namiko opened the lid of the can, scooped up a little juice with a spoon, and put it in Kohana's mouth. Another spoonful—she tried to bring it to Kohana's lips, but Kohana shook her head slightly, quietly weeping and contorting her body. Namiko gently stroked her shriveled knees protruding from the blanket; in a low voice she whispered the lullaby that Kohana had taught her.

> *The half-moon in the noon sky   so white a moon*
> *Maybe it's a gourd the sun used and threw away*
> *Wish my crook-necked halme could*
> *Hang it from the   strings of her chima*
> *When she's gathering water*

> *The half-moon in the noon sky   so white a moon*
> *Maybe it's a shoe the sun used and threw away*
> *Wish I could   put it on   one of my baby's feet*
> *When he's just learning to walk*

Kohana's face turned gentle again, and her lips moved as if she were trying to speak. Namiko leaned down to listen. "Aigu, Yong-hak ah . . . you've gotten so big . . . my goodness, you can walk now . . . but you look the same . . . doesn't matter how much you've grown, Omma knew it was you . . . you got your eyes from me, and your nose and mouth from your appa, and the shape of your face . . . you look just like your omma, baby . . . Yong-hak ah, aigu, Yong-hak ah, my god, how much you've grown . . . don't just sit there, say, 'Omma,' for me . . . Yong-hak ah . . ." Kohana distorted her face in pain, thrashing her feet under the blanket as she moaned, "Aya, aya . . ."

Namiko grabbed a little opium, rubbed her thumb and pointer finger together, and dropped it in Kohana's mouth for her. Before long, all the intensity that filled her face began to slowly fall away. Her breathing slowed. *Huff . . . huff . . .* like blowing on a baby's rice porridge to cool it down . . . *huff . . . huffffff . . . sssss . . .* Just as she took a big breath in, a gust of wind blew open the wooden door with a clatter, and the woolen blanket lifted up in the flurry. When she looked back at Kohana again, her face looked odd. Namiko pressed her ear to the other woman's chest. Nothing. She held a hand mirror to her mouth. Nothing.

"Aigu, not here, you can't die here, andwae . . . ireol sun eopseo . . . aigu, aigu ya . . ."

Lose the face powder, lose the lipstick . . . Namiko faced herself in the mirror. Her hair, which had been in a short bob when she came to Paradise, was now halfway down her back, by the spring it would probably be down to her hips, and by the time the willow shoots start turning into saplings . . . Namiko combed out her hair, pulled it over her chest, and braided it tightly. She put her hair up into daenggimeori, then put on the chima and jeogori that were hanging on the wall.

The wooden tags on the door that read KOHANA ON BREAK had been turned over. When she opened the door, the other comfort women, wearing chima and jeogori, were gathered around Kohana's body, now clad in a white chima and jeogori and lying on the bed.

On the dresser was the half-eaten can of mandarins, along with the cans of beef, tofu skin, and apples that the women had brought, and someone had put a few sprigs of wintersweet in Kohana's teacup.

As the flames of the candles shimmered, the incense smoke rose, and the women paid their respects one by one, the wooden door opened roughly and Oyaji came in.

"Bed, now. You'll interfere with tomorrow's work."

"But this is her wake." Namiko felt her voice trembling with anger.

"Don't get smart with me, you little yeobo."

"When Fumiko unni died, we couldn't cremate her because there wasn't enough firewood and oil. Please. Please take Kohana unni to the crematorium. Sergeant Katō told me that for the soldiers who die in battle or from sickness, there's a memorial service on the first of every month, and then they put them on a steamship down the Hankou and send their bodies back to the mainland. Can't you at least send her bones back to her hometown, Anseong? She's got a two-year-old boy waiting for his omma to come home. Please, I'm begging you." Namiko crafted her words from pure anger.

Oyaji shrunk back at this unhesitating speech from Namiko, who usually had few words; he stuck a Qiánmén in the space where his pulled front tooth should've been and lit it.

"They put two bodies in one coffin and cremate them, but now they're short on wood and oil, so they don't put them in a coffin at all, they lay them on top of each other, head to foot, and burn them like that. You can't cremate a soldier with a Korean whore, and it'd be a waste of good wood to cremate her alone. You'll have to bury her."

"The clay soil's so hard you can't dig." Namiko looked him straight in the eye for the first time.

"Then make a mound," Oyaji spat, his eyes moving left and right as if he were looking for someone.

"Then when it rains the soil will wash away and she'll be picked at by wild dogs."

"All right, then put her in one of the earthenware vats and bury that. She'll start to smell if we bury her near here, so you can take her out to the swamp on the cart. Whole lot of fuss over nothing—the Japanese Empire won't collapse over one or two broken public toilets." The candle's flame flickered menacingly in his eyes.

Namiko looked down at Kohana's face and bit her lip.

"I gotta say, you all look like sweet little girls right now. Whadda ya say, maybe you should work in your Korean clothes on the anniversary of your country's annexation?" Oyaji laughed as he left the room.

Huddling close enough that their shoulders touched, the comfort women passed around a bottle of kaoliang; one would sigh, "Aigo," and then they would all wail, "Aigo! Aigo!" as if the dam had been broken.

The sky was clear, only a few thin clouds trailed across it like fog. The sun cast a breathless light on the comfort women in their chimas and jeogoris, making their faces, rarely exposed to outdoor light, look all the paler.

A new day had begun, without Unni . . . Namiko gently stroked Kohana's hair inside the vat where her body lay, knees up to her chest. The comfort women began to walk, pulling the cart along, as a noncommissioned officer, carrying a bayonet, followed along to observe.

Setsuko, who had been in Paradise for five years, spoke first.

"You are gone. You are gone and have left behind your poor little son. You have gone, though you still prayed for your missing husband to come home to be with your son."

Eheyo eowayeongcha, the comfort women chanted together in a whisper as they walked on in their rubber boots.

Namiko had heard it was close, but this was the first time she'd seen the swamp. She gazed at the dark green, moss-like surface of the water as she listened to the cries of the birds hiding in the grove and the sound of them crossing from dead tree to dead tree. What could come back out of there . . . The soldier's leaned up against the trunk of that pine tree and he's yawning . . . maybe in a little while he'll fall asleep . . . and then I'll get in the swamp . . . the dark heavy water clinging my chima to my legs . . . surrounding my body . . . then slowly, so I don't slip and fall in the shallows . . . slowly . . . my chest . . . neck . . . head . . . Namiko imagined herself slipping into the swamp without looking back or hesitating, but even that reverie felt so very removed from her, as if she were looking in on someone else's daydream.

The comfort women took the shovels in both hands and dug up the clay-rich red dirt. "Yeongcha!" they shouted in unison as they lifted the vat, then bent at the hips and lowered it into the depression.

Namiko took the scissors from her pouch and cut her daenggimeori off at the base.

One by one, the comfort women cut their hair off, their disheveled heads bending over as they grabbed the red soil and buried Kohana in the pot with their hair and dirt.

Namiko realized a warm liquid was running down her thighs; she rolled up her chima and touched it. Blood?

"Your period's started. Now you have to take care not to get pregnant. Or you'll end up like Kohana." Setsuko's voice was weary with sadness, her eyes hurt by seeing.

Namiko remembered how Unni had washed her hair and body in this pot the morning after the doctor had robbed her of her virginity.

Ja, kkaekkeutage mom ssitja. *C'mon, time to get clean.*

Aigo, bulssanghaera, aigo, haneunim, amujjorok i aireul salpyeojuseyo, haneunim. *Oh, you poor thing, oh, God, please take care of this child, dear God.*

Unni's voice echoed in her head; the ground under her feet fluttered. Namiko hung her head, heavy with sorrow, and sang as if sinking the remains of her life into the swamp.

The sunset is the end of the day
The bell of the mountain temple rings
We all go home hand in hand
Together with the crows

TWENTY-THREE

August 15, 1945

| 1945년 8월 15일 | 1945年8月15日 |

Three hours' walk or forty minutes by horse cart to the east from Yeong-namnu, there's a temple called Pyochungsa at the base of Mount Jaeyak. It is an ancient temple, built in the Silla era, which is said to have trained over a thousand monks during the Goryeo era, and within it are housed relics thought to have belonged to Samyeongdang, including a robe, cheongsam, iron bell, sword, and teachings bestowed on him by King Seonjo of Joseon.

Samyeongdang—born in Muan, Miryang, in 1544, the thirty-ninth year of Jungjong's rule. His birth name was Im Eung-gyu; his bon-gwan is from Pungcheon; his mother was a Seo; his courtesy name was Ihwan; and he had two other pen names in addition to Samyeongdang: Songun and Jongbong. At age forty-nine, when the first Japanese invasion of Imjin broke out, he led roughly one thousand priests into battle against the Japanese, three times facing down Katō Kiyomasa, the lord of Kumamoto Castle, though this would end unsuccessfully; only two years later, the second invasion began. Katō Kiyomasa demanded Samyeongdang for Joseon's surrender, but he spurned this, instead leading his monk warriors into fierce battle again. In 1598, the Japanese army withdrew due to the death of Toyotomi Hideyoshi. At age sixty-one, Samyeongdang was sent to Japan as envoy and spent his days exchanging poetry with high priests at the Honpo-ji Temple in Kyōto and meeting with Tokugawa Ieyasu at Fushimi Castle; he succeeded in bringing back 1,391 prisoners, earning him renown in both countries.

At noon in mid-August, people removed their hats to pay their respects at the monument to Samyeongdang. It is said that roughly a century after his death, the Yulima group of Confucian scholars chose this spot near his birthplace to build this monument. Above the people's heads stretched a sky so deep blue that it felt lower than usual. Instead of exposing the people to its light, the sun scorched and shrunk their shadows, igeurigeul, the blue almost ominous, the heat nearly painful . . .

The people looked around wide-eyed as if they had just awoken from a dream and it was not yet clear whether they were actually awake, not a cough or sigh to be heard; it seemed as though they might all fall asleep standing.

One man shook his head to fend off the drowsiness, then opened his bearded jaw in astonishment.

"Is it sweat?"

No one said a thing, so the man too succumbed to unease; he looked over his shoulder at his wife, but his wife, forgetting that both her hands were holding her children's hands, twitched her sweating nose like a rabbit's.

"Tears?" He turned to look at his wife's face.

"Do you see any eyes on it? Tears come from your eyes, you know?"

The wife kept her eyes fixed on the monument to Samyeongdang.

"It must be sweat. . . . Look how it's coming out everywhere." Like the monument, the man too was covered in sweat all over.

"Sweating at the most crucial moment for the nation." The oldest of the elderly men in the crowd twisted his white beard like a string, nodding his head toward the monument to Samyeongdang.

"I saw it, you know, when Japan annexed Korea, and during the March First Movement too . . ."

"But is this really the most crucial . . ."

"Of course, the Soviet Union has declared war on Japan. And that neighborhood leader Yasuda said that they dropped some new kind of bomb on Hiroshima and Nagasaki."

"A new kind of bomb?"

"You don't know what kind?"

"No idea. Even the papers have only occasionally been getting through since April, you know."

"Why didn't they hit Tokyo? I wonder."

"Hmm . . ."

"They say there's going to be an imperial broadcast, so some folks are getting together at Yasuda's to listen."

"Does that mean the emperor will . . ."

"Apparently he'll be speaking personally."

"The most important moment . . . he must mean it's time for 'ichioku gyokusai,' for all citizens of the empire to smash ourselves like jewels."

"But Samyeongdang wouldn't sweat over a crisis for the mainland, would he?"

"But I saw it, I saw it . . ."

"I wonder if they'll drop the new bomb on Korea . . ."

"No, I don't think even the Allied Forces would do that."

"Well . . ."

They looked up at the monument again. Tracks of sweat ran down it, one after another, as if the monument was being melted by the heat of the sun, but no one moved to wipe it.

The old man put his hands together over his squinting eyes, his mouth pursed.

"This is the most I've ever seen it sweat. . . . What on earth will become of Korea, aigo, bulgilta?" The old man poked the ground between his legs with his cane.

The younger man turned toward his wife once again. His neck was so twisted it looked painful, but he could not turn his back on the monument to Samyeongdang. The couple's two sons who had been right there until not that long ago had gone off to play jachigi, a game involving sticks, in the yard of the school; his wife had her arms, now free, firmly crossed, each hand holding on to the other arm.

"Dangsin, gwaenchana? You've gone pale."

"Gwaenchanseumnida, but you're one to speak . . ." She felt that her husband's presence was fading like a shadow; out of fear she turned and looked behind her. Rows of people had formed behind her without her realizing.

"It's not raining, right?"

"No, it's not . . . In fact, it's been sunny, not a cloud in the sky, for the last few days."

"At least a week ago, no, maybe longer than that, was the last time it rained."

"Someone must be pouring water on it . . ."

"Aigu, who would?"

"Aigo, museopda, museun iri isseullakko . . . ?" *It's so scary, what's going to happen . . . ?*

"Didn't the police try to bury this monument on orders from the government-general? The weather was fine the day they came to do it, but the moment a waenom laid a hand on it, lightning flashed in the sky, beonjjeok beonjjeok, the thunder rumbled, *ureureung ureuureung*, and then bang!"

"And then not even a week later the police chief who spearheaded the whole thing died, didn't he?"

"Yeah, wasn't he found floating in the Miryang River?"

"No, I heard he was struck by lightning and they found his charred body."

"What are you all talking about? He hanged himself."

The man, confused, could no longer tell which voice belonged to whom; he squinted at the Chinese text engraved on the monument.

"The waenom had a bad feeling that it was cursed, so they stopped."

"Aigu, museowola . . ."

"Something terrible's going to happen." His wife's voice bounced off of his eardrum; the man wiped the sweat from his brow with the back of his hand.

Hooray! Manse! Hearing shouts, the crowd turned all at once. **Manse! Manse! The war is over! Japan lost! Long live Korean independence!** The faces of the crowd were distorted with surprise, but as they surrounded the youths, out of breath from running, to hear what they had to say, surprise gave way to joy. **Long live Korean independence! Long live Korean independence! Daehandongnimmanse!** People threw their hands in the air in undulating waves. None turned to look at Samyeongdang. The monument, left behind, continued on its own to sweat.

TWENTY-FOUR

Hollowed Season

| 잃어버린 계절 | 抉られた季節 |

Carrying her washing, she opened the door to the outside and saw sheets of straw paper scattered everywhere. Namiko picked one up from by her feet and read it. **THE JAPANESE ARMY SURRENDERS.** Why on earth, why would someone put flyers like this out—Namiko looked around fearfully. The soldiers on guard were not in their places. Could it—could it be true? Is the war really over? And Japan lost? Gripping the piece of paper, she went back into her room and read it again, sliding her finger over each word. **THE— JAPANESE—ARMY—SURRENDERS.** For the last three days there hadn't been a single customer. Oyaji had been nowhere to be seen either. It's over! The war is over! A tremor came out from the core of her bones; her hand holding the flyer shook, budeul budeul. Namiko stuck her hand under her futon, then shoved the red good-luck charm Sergeant Katō had given her, the silver wristwatch she'd gotten from Ensign Mizuno, and the military scrip she'd been saving up in an empty can into her jumeoni; next, she changed into the black chima and white silk jeogori she'd worn at Kohana unni's funeral.

Namiko went out into the hall and knocked on each of the numbered doors from one end of the hall to the other. The nemaki-clad women who poked their heads out of the doors all looked dulled by tiredness and drowsiness.

"The Japanese army surrendered! Japan lost the war. Remember how no soldiers came yesterday or the day before? No one's on guard—let's make a run for it. If we stay here dressed like this, they might take us for Japanese and kill us. Let's get out of here!"

I don't feel good. I haven't walked anywhere in years, my feet are too weak, I'd never get far. If they catch us just imagine what they'll do. Stupid to think about running away. You're young and sparky, you go for it. The doors closed one by one soundlessly; the women shut themselves back in their numbered rooms.

Door number three had not opened. Namiko went in and shook Emiko's knees; Emiko lay there like a wilted rose of Sharon.

"Emiko eonni, jeonjaengi kkeunnasseoyo. Ilboni jyeosseoyo. Gachi domanggayo." *The war is over. Japan lost. Let's run away together.*

It had been two years since she'd spoken in Korean; the reply came back in Japanese.

"They took out my uterus, my ovaries, my fallopian tubes. And Andō was killed in battle. You know, when he took off his uniform he had a tattoo of a peony on his back. But he was always so nice. . . ."

Emiko lifted the hem of her nemaki and showed the tattoo on her own thigh. *Yasuo*, it said.

"Before Yasuo-san went to Laos, he said, 'I know you can't read or write Japanese, but carry my name on your skin'; then he wrote his name here in ink, stuck the needle in, put vinegar on it once the blood was flowing, then put ink in the holes. It hurt, but I was so happy, and his face looked so serious as he tattooed his name on my body . . . I realized that I was important to him . . . I cried. He got a tattoo of my name too. He's the first one, the only one I ever told my real name, the name my abeoji gave me . . . it's right here, above his heart. . . . He said, 'I want your name right next to what keeps me alive.' But he got shot and died. And my name died too, right above his heart."

Her taut face became even more distorted; she waved her hands in the air.

"Run away? To where though? Without a name, where is there to go home to? I'm fine here, my life's a remnant anyway. . . . I'm sorry, before you go could just give me a dose. . . . I'm so sad I feel like my heart might break."

Namiko filled the pipe with opium and lit it. Emiko took a drag, then said, in a voice like a starling crying in the depths of the forest:

"Arigatō gozaimashita, mata kite kudasai."

. . .

Namiko hadn't run in two years; her legs felt as if they had no bones or muscles in them. But she went on, forward, forward, one more step forward, falling and sprawling over the ground like a cloth, getting to her knees, picking herself up, getting back to her feet, running, falling again—she fell and her spirit alone kept running on ahead, though when she tumbled to the ground, the heat and brightness made her lose her way, looking all around her. She panted, *huff-huff-huff.*

When I was leaving **Paradise** I was afraid of leaving it, *huff-huff,* but now I'm just afraid of going back, *huff,* where am I going now, I can't think at all, *huff-huff,* the main thing is I don't want to go back to **Paradise.**

Namiko looked down at the ground, then ran off in the direction where she didn't see her own footprints.

I feel like my heart's going to burst, but even if it does I have to keep running. No matter how far she ran the sunflower fields were uninterrupted. The sunflowers all stood tall and upright, like lines of soldiers. Some had their faces turned toward the sun, some drooped, and some cast a gleaming watchful eye on her. *Huff-huff-huff,* wae boneunde, *why are they looking at me?*

Like the soldiers armed with bayonets that always stood in front of **Paradise**! Like the soldiers who always looked me up and down! Boji ma! Boji mallan mariya! *Quit looking! Don't look at me!*

She fell again and when she looked up, one sunflower looked like the Chinese boy she'd seen shot dead with his arms tied behind his back. **Hey, you wanna see something, get out here, everyone, we got a Chink spy.** It was a boy with a pigtail, not too far in age from Namiko, hanging his head, his back stiff as a board from fear of death. Company Commander Arakawa pulled out his sword. The boy clasped his bound hands tightly. A gush of blood surged out. His back stayed straight. The company commander kicked his back and the boy fell into a puddle left from last night's rain, his head rolling at Namiko's feet. The sunflower next to it, withered, stalk broken, like Fumiko unni as her thin limbs moved in the flames as if she were struggling—Namiko had screamed. Sara isseo! She's alive! Unni! Mul! Ppalli mul! Water! Throw some water on her! Kohana unni had pressed Namiko's face to her chest and stroked her hair as she said, **She's dead . . . she's dead, but it's the burning that's making her move . . . don't look** . . . She felt that someone was caressing her and put her hand to her head to find that her hair had gotten hot. **The August sun's strong on the continent, a sparrow landing on a tree would get burned and fall off, ha ha ha ha,** Sergeant Katō's laughter came to her now, and when she looked up at the large sunflowers, she saw in every bloom of every flower the living and the dead, their faces mixed together. . . . Namiko heard a whirring noise and tilted her chin even farther up. It was a B-29 flying low. I know they won't bomb anymore because the war is over, but museopda, I'm still scared. Namiko hid herself in the sunflower field. **Those who can stand have a month to live, those who can sit upright three weeks, the bedridden have a week, those who urinate in their sleep have three days, those who cannot speak two days, and those who can't blink will die tomorrow** . . . Who said that to me, who? Molla . . . moreugesseo! It's one of the men who slept with me . . . I don't know which . . . Namiko covered her ears and ran. She ran and ran, but the sunflowers never stopped, like endless life, like endless death, and Namiko didn't know which she was running from.

Inamori Kiwa carried the urn of her husband's ashes, which she had collected from the temple the day before, out on to the veranda and sat, her legs folded beneath her, to listen to the chorus of cicadas. *Ming-ming-ming-ming-ming-ming . . . Manse! Manse! Manse!* It's been five days since the war ended, and still whenever Koreans meet each other, they shout, "Manse! Manse!"

Honey, you wouldn't believe what's happened. On the fifteenth of August, Japan surrendered to America unconditionally. The Koreans burned down the shrine where your ashes were. Mr. Satō, you know, the one who works at town hall, he was chased down by Koreans, so now everyone says it's better to be surrounded by other Japanese, so Tatsuji and Akiyuki and the others are at Kameya Ryōkan. All the Japanese are huddled up at home like cats.

I'm staying here. Tomorrow, after noon, I'll call for a car and they'll carry my belongings into the mountains, but until then I'm staying here. This was our house, after all. Kiwa took a long, deep sigh as she shot a look at the four trunks lined up on the veranda. This is all I can take, dear, they said I had to leave all the things from my bridal trousseau, the paulownia chest of drawers, my ceremonial kimono, the dressing table, all of it . . . Tatsuji told me that on the Busan-Shimonoseki ferry you can only take hand luggage, so for now, I'll bide my time at an inn in the mountains and wait for a private boat. I don't know how I'll make it through a rough voyage at my age . . . I've lived too long, darling. . . . If I'd known Japan was going to lose, I'd have hanged myself from the lintel. I suppose being taken home with your bones by my side is much easier . . . How old do you think I am now, my dear? In March I had my eighty-eighth birthday . . . eighty-eight years old . . . When you and I boarded the *Satsuma-maru* at Shimonoseki, you were fifty-nine and I was fifty-seven; that's thirty-one years ago now. And you died without ever going back to Ikenohata. . . . I'd wanted to be buried here too. . . . I never thought it would end up like this.

Until August 15, I led a happy life. Blessed with one son, four grandchildren, and eighteen great-grandchildren, and these hands helped to birth the babies of three thousand strangers . . . I've delivered far more babies here than I did on the mainland. Fortunately, despite my age I can get around on my own two legs without a cane, and I can see and hear clearly. So even last month I went in a rickshaw across town to deliver twins, a boy and a girl, at a Korean house. More Japanese these days are giving birth in the hospital; the last few years I've only been to Korean homes. For difficult births call the ilbon saram midwife Inamori—that's the reputation I've earned, and it delights me; it's my pride.

Honey . . . I never wanted to worry you so I kept it quiet, but I can't keep it to myself forever, so I'll tell you now . . . It's about Tatsu'u. He's Shige's third daughter's eldest, I don't think you ever held him, did you? No, of course not, you passed before he was born. . . . But then you don't know Shoutarō and Chiyoko either, do you, well, no, I'm sure you do know them, you didn't hold them or give them piggyback rides or walk hand in hand with them, but I know you're smiling and looking down on them. . . . Tatsu'u is . . . Tatsu'u is going to stay in Miryang, he says. Seiji kept at him for days, "You know, you're talking nonsense, you're going back to the mainland, you have to, this is their country now, it's no place for us Japanese anymore," but Tatsu'u was stubborn, he said: "And I'm supposed to believe there's a place for me in a country I've never been to; I was born here in Miryang, I grew up here, this is my home, my family name's Kanesugi, so if you take the 'sugi' off, then it's the same character as the name Kim, so from now on I'll just go by Kim Dal-woo, I'll marry a Korean woman and pass myself off as Korean." Seiji hit him and split his lip, but still he said, "I've made my mind up." I washed his mouth out with salt water and put Mentholatum on it; I didn't say a thing, but in my heart, I was telling him, "Tatsu'u, you're not wrong, this is your home, of course, but imagine what dark times you'll have, because even if you change your name to Kim Dal-woo it's still ilbon saram blood running through your veins . . . You say you'll marry a Korean woman, but will her parents even let you? And even if they do, hypothetically, Tatsu'u, then they'll always be talking behind your children's backs about how they're ilbon saram, ilbon saram. But, Tatsu'u, you're not wrong. Your great-grandmother's going back to Japan, a land she hasn't set foot in for many years, but my heart will come back here to Mitsuyō, to Miryang, and I'll watch over you. . . ."

Darling, there's someone I must meet again. A boy I delivered, his name is Lee Woo-gun—that's right, I borrowed part of his name when I named Tatsu'u. There's only a year's difference between them. If there's anyone I can ask to look after Tatsu'u, it's Woo-gun and no one else. Seiji says I shouldn't leave the house, not even for a second, but, well, darling, you know . . . I'll never walk these streets again as long as I live . . . I never even considered leaving here and now, to be chased out with just the clothes on my back, well . . . so I thought I'd get a rickshaw from outside the station and take a loop around out to the sandbar. I want to say farewell, you know, to the city. So, my love, you'll have to wait here for about an hour. And don't worry, nobody'll lay a finger on an old lady like me. The Koreans aren't as awful as we might think. Going to so many of their houses as a midwife only reinforced that belief for me. They value the teachings of Confucius and my goodness do they respect their elders and betters. In Korean homes, there's a tradition of inviting the midwife to the baby's first birthday party and giving her the seat of honor; I was invited countless times. I was treated like family and given gifts, like socks, sandals, fabric, even obi. That's why I haven't had to buy a pair of socks or sandals for the last twenty years.

Whenever I told you, *I'm going out now*, you just said, *sure*, and nodded.

When I told you I wanted to get my midwifery license, you simply said, *Do as you like, I'm sure you've already made your mind up.* You always believed in me. And I believed in you too. When you told me you wanted to come here, I followed you without saying a word, didn't I? Believing in each other's decisions and doing what should be done according to what we believed . . . That's how we lived for the forty-four years we were together.

So, darling, I'm going out now.

Kiwa gently placed the urn on her altar and put her hands together in prayer.

Slipping on a pair of sandals given to her by a Korean family, she straightened her gauze-patterned hem and opened the door with a clatter; the August sun dazzled her old eyes. Kiwa took a white parasol from the umbrella stand in the entryway and opened it. The main road was full of men heading to the station with their futons and bags on handcarts or horse carts, followed on foot by the elderly and women with knapsacks leading small children by the hand; on the street corner, there were men with household items lined up on straw mats, calling out to Korean passersby. Some were pleading: "If you see anything you like, take it, all I ask is that you help me carry my things to the mountains."

Inamori Kiwa looked down at the city from her place up on the rickshaw. No bombs have fallen here, we weren't killing each other—all felt still as death in the fierce midsummer sun. The camellia sasanqua hedge that goes all the way up to Mrs. Koga's house . . . Whenever I walked past here, holding Chiyoko's hand, we always sang that song: **sasanka, sasanka saita michi, takibi da, takibi da, ochibataki** . . . The crepe myrtle in Mr. Tagawa's garden, filtering the light between its leaves . . . He planted it in celebration when, after six girls, his wife finally gave birth to a long-awaited boy, Tsuneo; I heard Tsuneo became a father himself this spring. . . . I feel so sorry for the families who must make the journey back with a baby; just imagine if they catch something going around on board the ship. . . . The apple trees in the Uenos' orchard, its branches and leaves growing slowly in their ignorance; their apples were always small but they had just the right balance of tartness and sweetness, and I could hardly wait for it to turn cold. . . . Nakano Tofu Shop, where I went to buy tofu every day; Okamoto Confectionery, where the castella cakes were superb; Uomasa, where they came around every morning to take fish orders; the primary and secondary schools that Shōtarō and his friends went to; Ayako and Kazue's favorite, Higuchi-ya, where you could get imagawayaki, thick pancakes with bean jam filling, two for one sen—all of it still exists right here, in a place where I could just reach out and touch it, but soon it'll all be gone. Kiwa never felt compelled to drink personally, but when her cup was filled at a celebration she would not refuse. Her head spun as if she had drunk down cupful after cupful while the sun was still high in the sky. The rickshaw driver, clad in a dark blue happi coat, out of breath, panted: hard to believe what's happened, once Little Tokyo's deserted, we'll have to close up shop and leave too, I was born here, so I've only heard stories about Yamaguchi, where my dad's from, guess I'll have to rely on my relatives, really can't believe what's become of things. Kiwa was so overwhelmed with emotion she could not even make noises of agreement.

She had him wait at the base of Yeongnamnu, then climbed the stone steps and looked back down from the highest point. The children swimming naked in the river were shouting happily. She couldn't tell if they were speaking Korean or Japanese; no, there can't be a Japanese child among them, this river where Shōtarō, Kazue, and Yasuke used to swim now belongs completely to the Koreans.

Kiwa, nearly drowning in a deep emptiness, turned her eyes toward the top of the mountain. The shrine's gone . . . so it wasn't just the shrine in Gagokdong they set on fire. . . . Wait, the cherry trees are gone . . . what on earth . . . they felled them . . . Those trees did nothing wrong. Then who do I think has done something wrong? We Japanese? Me? And what have we done wrong? Kiwa felt sorrow and resentment clarifying her mind. When he died, I felt the warmth leave him while I was still holding his hand; when that coldness spread through my whole palm . . . that's how it feels now.

She turned her eyes again and looked at the Miryang River; there was a pair of storks in the delta. She was too far away to see them clearly, but she could tell from their movements what they were doing. Sticking its beak under its big wings . . . it's grooming itself. . . . I almost feel like I've never seen a stork before . . . I see them all the time, but I never really look at them. But today, every little thing catches my eye. It's less that I'm trying to see things than that they're jumping into my sight . . . Yes . . . that's it . . . everything's saying good-bye to me . . . I can hear it . . . sayōnara . . . sayōnara . . . Kiwa took her right hand off the handle of the parasol and waved to the river. Just then, a young man in a white running shirt and shorts came running up from the stone steps. Kiwa exclaimed slightly, clutching the parasol close over her shoulder.

"Lee Woo-gun, isn't it?"

The young man stopped.

"My name is Inamori Kiwa. I'm the midwife who delivered you."

"Oh . . . My mother told me about you. My brother too." Woo-gun brought his breathing under control, pulling the sweat rag from his neck to wipe the sweat off his face.

"I have a little something to ask you."

He paused. "How about we talk in the gazebo?"

"Wonderful, let's."

Kiwa closed her parasol to better see the face of the young man walking by her side.

"When you were a baby your little face looked just like a samurai doll, but now you look more like one of the Buddha's guardians," she chuckled.

"Let's sit down here," Woo-gun said, wiping at his face with the cloth again in embarrassment.

"I'd like to tell you some memories I have of you."

"Sure."

Kiwa looked at Woo-gun's face, searching it for traces of the past.

"It was early April when you were born. Your older brother ran to fetch me, I got my things together quickly, and then we ran off, with me on his back. How old was your brother then?"

"He would've been turning thirteen."

"It was a difficult birth. Your grandmother prayed the whole time your mother was in labor, you know, I delivered you myself. You weren't breathing. I put my mouth to yours and breathed in and out, in, out, in, out, until you started to cry. You know, as I talk it's all coming back to me.

"I came back to visit out of worry. It was only seven days after she'd given birth, but your mother was already going out to do the shopping and work. She was in agony because her milk hadn't come in, so I gave her a massage. I told her to try putting you on each breast for a little bit, and your mother picked you up and then you started sucking so hard you were making little clucking noises. When I told her to try you on the right, she couldn't get you off her left breast, oh, you were so hungry. Your mother pulled you off the breast and her milk hit me right in the face, oh-oh-oh, how we all laughed— we laughed so much you got surprised and started crying," she chuckled.

"I'm sure you don't remember, but they invited me to your first birthday party. They gave me seaweed soup and rice and some dressed greens; it was all so delicious.

"It was while I was sitting there that I thought of borrowing a character from your name to give to my granddaughter's child. After all, Woo-gun is such a lovely name. It shows so clearly your father's hopes that you would grow up blessed and healthy, like the trees and grass and flowers that grow quickly sucking up the rain, the long-awaited rain through their roots. That's right, I took the character for rain from your name. I gave it to my great-grandson, who was born the same day a month later. Tatsu'u. *Tatsu* means 'to convey, to communicate,' so the name means I want him to grow up to be a man who gives the blessings of heaven to others."

"Tatsu'u . . . what a nice name." Finally released from his embarrassment, Woo-gun looked the Japanese midwife who had delivered him directly in her eyes.

"You know, Tatsu'u is going to stay in Miryang. I have one son, four grand-children, and eighteen great-grandchildren, and they're all going now. It's only natural, we Japanese must return to Japan, after all . . . But if anything should happen to Tatsu'u . . . would you please let me know?"

"I'll do whatever I can."

"I don't even know how to thank you for saying so. . . . You're the only one I could ask."

"You brought me into the world with your own hands; of course . . ."

She thought for a second. "At a baby's first birthday here, you line up a brush, thread, bow and arrow, jujubes, rice, and money on a tray and whatever the baby grabs tells you their future—is that right?"

"Yes, it's called doljabi."

"You were dressed in an adorable little traditional costume; you grabbed the edge of the table and started to walk, and your father and mother and all your relatives started to clap. . . . I was so moved, seeing a baby I delivered start walking right before my very eyes. Do you know what happened next? Have you heard this before?"

"No."

"You didn't grab anything—you stumbled over my lap and fell. So you started crying and when I picked you up, you stuck your hand in my mouth and laughed. Oh, it's so strange, I went to so many Korean homes I can't count, and I had lots of invitations to first birthday parties, but that day's the only one I remember so vividly. Your mother wore a dark red jeogori and an orange chima. . . . How is your mother, by the way?"

"She passed away."

"And your father?"

"He passed, too."

"Oh, I see. . . . How is your brother? He was so fast; I saw in the paper that he represented Korea in the road relay and took home a single stage prize. Oh, that's right, he married a girl from that family who ran the rice shop by the station, didn't he? I saw him on his wedding day, on the back of a horse, and his wife in her palanquin. It looked like it was quite the wedding. . . ."

"They've divorced. We don't know where my brother is. . . . All the people in your memories are gone now."

The world around showed traces of tranquility, as if it had been left behind from all light and darkness, from both liberation and defeat, but suddenly, it felt as if the two of them were wrapped in an absence vaster than the August sky. Woo-gun was aghast at the immensity of all he had lost; Kiwa was nearly suffocated by the immensity of what she was on the verge of losing. *Ming-ming-ming-ming-ming, ji ji ji ji, sseuku sseukuho sseuku sseukuho . . .*

"Oh yes . . . I sang a song at your first birthday. Your father urged me to, you know. . . . I don't imagine I'll see you ever again in my life, so I'll sing it to mark our parting. . . ."

Mukau yama no naku tori wa
Chūchū tori ka
Midori ka

Genzaburō no miyage
Nanya kanya morota
Kin sashi kanzashi morota
Byōbu no in ga oitaraba
Chūchū nezumi ga hiiteta
Doko kara doko made hiitetta
Kamakura kaidō no man'naka de
Ichi nuke ni nuke san nuke sakura
Yo yo matsuyanagi, yanagi no shita no bōsan ga
Hachi ni me-me sasarete
Itai tomo iezu
Kayui tomo iezu
Tada naku bakari

Kiwa covered her wrinkled, spotted face with both her hands, like a little girl who has dropped her ball into a drainage ditch, and began to cry; Woo-gun embraced her.

How long have I been holding her? I think her shoulders have stopped trembling—Woo-gun looked up at the sky, his arms still around the midwife. It had been clear before, but now clouds that looked like a bird's wings cut into pieces floating in the air hung in the blue of the sky.

Kiwa pulled her face away from Woo-gun, smelling the tang of sweat coming from his shirt, her eyes narrowing as she gave a teary smile.

The pair walked slowly down the stone steps. The wind blew; clean, white sorrow bearing no impurities escaped from their bodies and went to drift in the endless blue with the clouds.

Once they reached the end of the stone steps, they turned to face each other.

"Sayōnara."

"Sayōnara."

I can vaguely remember getting on a fishing boat down the Yangtze and getting to Shanghai, but I don't even remember how many days it took from Shanghai to Dalian. When I got on a freight train full of Japanese who were repatriating, the Chinese were shouting, "Guǐchù! Guǐchù!"—Devils! Devils!—and throwing stones at us; one hit me and even now my back aches. Where was it, what stations were we between where the track had been destroyed and I got off the train? From there on I rode in US Army jeeps or on the back of farmers' wagons—I hid in shadows to relieve myself, but I had nothing to wipe with, and menstrual blood was dripping down my legs. When the sun set, I searched for somewhere I wouldn't be spotted right away, and since I'd be in danger if someone realized I was a woman, I put a blanket or cloth over my head to sleep. Anyway, I made it back to Dalian. Dalian, the place I came to two years ago on the Continent and the Dove after being tricked by that man in the flat cap . . . where the rain splattered on the pavement, and the streetlights in their hundreds gave off light that looked like smoke in the rain . . . it was beautiful . . . the first sea I ever saw! The waves rolling off into the distance, wave after wave after wave . . . I took off my rubber shoes and scampered like a puppy down the pier. . . . The sea was glimmering, *banjjak banjjak*, like it was giving a blessing for my new life, *banjjak banjjak*. . . .

When she woke up, someone was next to her, peering at her face. It was an old woman wearing a shiny black jiá ǎo and trousers, with her white bangs arranged sharply across her forehead.

"Yǒu qì ér? Gāi shì huó rén ba?" *Hello? Are you alive?*

She hesitated. "Huó rén."

"Rìběn rén?" *Are you Japanese?*

"Cháoxiǎn rén." *I'm Korean.*

"Zhàng dǎ wánliǎo. Rìběn rén dōu cóng Cháoxiǎn zǒule. Fàngxīn huíqù ba. Huí jiā qù a." *The war is over. The Japanese have left Korea. It's all right now. You can go home.*

The old woman rubbed Namiko's cheeks, black with soot and dirt, with her hands and a smile came across her fair, wrinkled face; she left, walking off in the characteristic way of a woman whose feet had been bound, her arms slightly held out and her hips shaking like a bow.

Namiko covered her head with the cloth and lay back down. A short while later, the cloth lifted from her head and she was handed a steaming pork bun and a drinking gourd.

"Lái wǒ lái kāi." *Take this.* The old woman unplugged the gourd and put it in Namiko's hand. "Hē ba." *Drink.*

As Namiko gulped down the tea and devoured the bun, she sobbed.

The ship is moving. We'll be at Busan by tomorrow morning. We might be in Korean waters already. The ship is definitely headed for Korea. But where am I headed? Where am I going to? In Dalian, I was housed in a US Army tent, where they cut my hair short and sprayed me with DDT to keep the lice off, and then I waited for the ship home in a separate waiting room for women. At first there were about eighty of us, but day by day the crowd grew; there must be hundreds still waiting for the next ship. Some of the women, I could tell at a glance, were also comfort women, but even when our eyes met, I just looked away, unable to speak. I told a Korean wearing a US military uniform: I can't go back to Korea, should I stay in Manchuria, I want to go to Japan— but he told me Koreans have to go back to Korea, so I boarded this ship, little more than a small fishing boat, with more than a hundred other repatriates.

The ship and the shore, separated by the sea—I became afraid of returning to Korea. No matter how far from **Paradise** I am, my body still follows me. I can't push it away and tell it to leave me alone. But do I really just mean my body? No matter how many years pass, I don't think what happened in **Paradise** will ever disappear. . . . No matter how kind the people I meet are . . . I can't smile like nothing happened.

Namiko stood at the end of the deck, clasping the railing. Darkness to my left, right, above, and below . . . Only the repatriation ship cutting through the dark sea, pushing out a white spray as it advances . . . The darkness is skin and the white waves are scars. It looks a little like a river in the sea. A white river that is born from the darkness one second and disappears back into the darkness the next. . . . Manse! Manse! Manse! A cry of joy arose from the cabins again, and a big chorus of "Aegukga" echoed.

Until the East Sea's waters dry and Mount Paektu's worn away
May God watch over our land, our Korea manse!
Roses of Sharon, three thousand ri of ridges and rivers running through
The Korean people to our land will always be true!

As the pines atop Namsan stand, no wind or frost to change them
Let our spirits stand firm whate'er befalls our land
Roses of Sharon, three thousand ri of ridges and rivers running through
The Korean people to our land will always be true!

In autumn's high arching skies, clear and cloudless blue
Our spirits like the shining moon, undivided and true
Roses of Sharon, three thousand ri of ridges and rivers running through
The Korean people to our land will always be true!

Our spirit and our will, come grief or joy
O, beloved land, we are loyal always to thee
Roses of Sharon, three thousand ri of ridges and rivers running through
The Korean people to our land will always be true!

As she listened to "Aegukga," Namiko dragged her body and mind, heavy as lead, as she walked around the deck. No one will come up on deck, no matter how stuffy the air is in the cabins from the number of people crammed in there, because they want to share their joy with others. The sea breeze teased Namiko's roughly cropped hair and licked against her chima like flames—though it was the end of August, it was cold at sea, and the cold numbed her face. Like when he punched me . . . **Yeobos and dogs, man, you have to beat 'em to make 'em listen! This little yeobo thinks she can get smart with me!** Oyaji beat me so much, more days than not. I can hear the whooshing of the wind in my right ear, but my left is silent. That first night in **Paradise**, when I bit the doctor and ran outside, Oyaji beat me so hard I thought I was going to pass out. My ear hasn't been right since then. I'm sure my cardrum burst. **You damn Koreans always think you can get cute! Fucking yeobos! Yeobo! Yeobo! Yeobo!**

In the morning, I'm sure everyone will come up on deck to see Busan Harbor . . . And then they'll sing the song again in the morning light . . . Our spirit and our will, come grief or joy   o, beloved land, we are loyal always to thee   Roses of Sharon, three thousand ri of ridges and rivers running through   the Korean people to our land will always be true. . . . Will I join them? Can I sing that song? Why am I alive? Do I want to live? What will I do with my life? Namiko listened to the sea. What she heard back was her own voice. Irrashaimase   soko ni okake kudasai   arigatō gozaimashita   mata kite kudasai. She covered her ear with her palm and still the voice did not go away. Irrashaimase   soko ni okake kudasai   arigatō gozaimashita   mata kite kudasai.

She made a loop around the deck and returned to the end; a man was standing where she had been before. Like her, he grasped the railing and stared at the white waves in the darkness. He's tall . . . maybe five foot nine . . .

The man turned, sensing her there.

Namiko looked at his face.

She put her hand to her mouth and took one step, then another forward.

"Kunimoto Utetsu . . . Lee Woo-cheol—that's who you are, isn't it?"

"That's me."

"Oh . . . oh . . ." Namiko clung to her own body with both her arms.

"Have we had the pleasure of meeting before?" Woo-cheol brushed his hair from his bloodshot eyes and blinked.

"I'm from Miryang too. I always saw you and your brother Woo-gun . . . Aigu, it's really you . . . of all the people to run into in a place like this. . . . Aigo . . ."

In Namiko's head, the scene on that August day began to play, along with the sound of her own singing. **Ame, ame   fure, fure, kaa-san ga janome   de omukae, ureshii na** . . . I was playing jump rope . . . I had my skirt tucked into my panties . . . **pitch, pitch   chap, chap, run, run, run** . . . my bobbed hair fluttered in the air . . . and Woo-cheol in his red running shirt and Woo-gun, his head shaved and wearing a white shirt, in-hale ex-hale   in-hale ex-hale   in-hale ex-hale   in-hale ex-hale.

"Gwaenchana?"

"Gwaenchanseumnida . . . Just feeling nostalgic . . ."

The voice she heard in her ears was so weak she could hardly believe it was her own. She didn't know when she had started crying; she opened her mouth and breathed, tears rolling down her face endlessly. It's much harder to remember the old days in Miryang than to remember my time in **Paradise**. I can bear the total darkness but not . . . the light shining in like this . . . Aigo, nae sokiya . . .

"How old are you?" Woo-cheol asked.

"I'm fifteen."

"The same as my daughter . . . You went to Manchuria on your own?"

"I was in Wuhan."

"When did you go there?"

"August, two years ago."

"That would mean when you were thirteen?"

"That's right . . . I was thirteen . . ."

"All on your own at thirteen . . . were you in the Women's Volunteer Corps?"

"No . . . I was tricked."

Namiko wiped her tears with the sleeve of her jeogori and grabbed the cold iron handrail. The railing was wet, so she looked up at the night sky; a fine, fine rain was falling.

"Rain," she said.

"It's been falling for a while." Woo-cheol looked down at her, standing in profile.

"I didn't notice at all."

She touched the shoulder of her jeogori; it was damp but not exactly wet. How can a rain be this fine? Finer than a spider's thread . . . it's not making ripples on the sea; it just falls from the darkness of the sky and is swallowed by the darkness of the sea . . .

"Would you . . ."

"Yes?"

"Would you listen to my story?"

"If you're fine with me hearing it . . ."

She hesitated. "I'll never forget it, August twenty-ninth, two years ago."

The two of them looked out at the white waves inscribed by the ship. In the clamor of the waves and the wind and the ship's engine, she began her life story; the rain and Woo-cheol listened without interjection.

"It was a sunny, hot day. I was jumping rope with two of my friends. We were singing a song we learned at school, 'Ame, Ame, Fure, Fure' . . . I could see the two of you running our way. We all had crushes on Woo-gun. For me, it was more like first love than a crush. My friends and I did rock, paper, scissors; the loser had to say something to him. I went for rock, and my friends both went for paper. The two of you ran around the embankment every day, lap after lap . . . You'd go past and then twenty minutes later you'd run past us again, that's how fast you were. We jumped rope while we waited, and then we saw the two of you. My apologies, but the truth is I only saw Woo-gun. I felt like this was a terribly important moment, that it was fate that I should call out to him then, not merely chance. I shouted, 'Annyeonghaseyo!' and Woo-gun was startled and turned to look. I raised my right hand and yelled, 'Himnaeiso!' 'Gomapda!' Woo-gun said, and ran off. My friends elbowed me and teased me for blushing so much, but I thought my heart would pound right out of my chest; I stood there with my hands pressed to my mouth for a while.

"When the sun was over Mount Maeum, Kyōjun and Keiko went home, singing, 'Hana ppajyeotda, dul ppajyeotda.' I . . . I didn't want to go home. My abeoji died before my baegiljanchi. My eomoni raised four children on her own and got remarried when I was twelve. He was a forty-five-year-old man who had lost his wife to consumption and had two daughters, older than me, who he brought with him. They were old enough to marry, so I only lived with them less than a year before they got married.

"I never called my stepfather 'Abeoji.' My only abeoji is the man who gave me my name and died. My stepfather hated that about me; whenever I opened my mouth, he would say, 'Any woman who studies turns into a devil, you'll be fourteen soon so hurry up and get married.' I was in the way. No matter what my stepfather said, my eomoni just kept quiet and went on with her needle-work. She was always on my side until she got remarried, but then she turned into my stepfather's servant.

"I wanted to study. I couldn't think of anything worse than being like my eomoni, getting married to a man I didn't like and being used like a maid and seamstress. My dream was to go to Busan Girls School after I graduated sec-ondary school, but I didn't tell my eomoni or my oppas that, because all three of my older brothers only went to secondary school. If my stepfather'd heard me even mutter it in my sleep, he'd have never let it go. I just know he'd have shouted, 'Going to a girls' school—now I know you've lost it!' and burned all my textbooks.

"Even when the sun had completely set and it had gone dark, I couldn't make myself move. I'd have rather slept outside than go back to that house where my stepfather was. I felt so down that I decided to try to think of something nice, and the first thing that came to mind was the two of you running straight down the embankment at dusk. And the moment that I remembered the sound of your breathing coming closer to me, in-hale ex-hale in-hale ex-hale, and Woo-gun's voice saying, 'Gomapda!' I heard footsteps behind me. . . . When I turned around, a man wearing a flat cap was standing there.

"He said, 'Ilbonui gunbok gongjangeseo ilhaji anhgesseoyo doneul mani batgo masinneun   geotdo meokgo yeppeun oseul ibeoyo sannyeon ilhamyeon jibe dorawayo geujeone sijipgamyeon eonjedeunji jibe wayo.'

"And I . . . I . . . got taken in by his story about going to work in a military factory in Fukuoka. I promised to meet him at Samnamjin station at eight the next morning, and I went home. If I'd talked to my eomoni and oppa about it, I know they'd have said an unmarried girl can't go off somewhere else on her own, and I'd never have spoken to my stepfather about it. So I left home without telling anyone, with nothing but the clothes on my back. There are only two trains from Miryang toward Busan, one just before six and the other just after eight, so I walked to Samnamjin. I wore a white blouse and a skirt with suspenders, like always, and the toe of my rubber shoe was busted so I tied it together with straw rope, but I remember that it still flapped and I had to stop and pull gravel out of my shoe again and again.

"It was a clear morning. I felt like only good things were waiting for me at the end of the road ahead of me. I was very anxious, but I told myself as I walked that this was the path from unhappiness to happiness. I heard the sound of footsteps behind me. I hurried up, thinking that one of my brothers was chasing after me. Well, who do you think it was? Your brother, Woo-gun. I yelled, 'Oh!' Woo-gun smiled and shouted, 'Annyeong!' to me. And then he stopped and caught his breath and looked at me. We both looked up. 'It's hot.'

'It certainly is.' 'Where are you going?' 'To Samnamjin station.' 'Are you going somewhere?' 'Yes.' 'On your own?' 'Yes.' 'Looks like it'll be another hot day.' 'I think you're quite right.' 'Jal gara!' 'Annyeonghigaseyo.' That's all we said, nothing more . . . but it shines for me . . . it's dazzling . . . so much that I think my eyes might burst . . . because what happened next was so tragic . . .

"From Samnamjin I got on the Continent, and on the way I noticed that we were going in the wrong direction, but I believed the man when he told me that we weren't going from Busan, we were going to get on a ship from Dalian. On the boat from Dalian, he explained to me that the factory in Fukuoka had all the workers they needed, so I'd be going to Shanghai up the Yangtze to a military boot factory in Wuhan. . . . Of course, that'd make you think something strange was going on, wouldn't it? But I . . . I didn't challenge him or complain, because I wanted to save up money to go to high school, and I could put up with it for three years. . . . I was stupid. . . . Oh, how stupid I was! It wasn't until I arrived in **Paradise** that I realized where I'd been taken and why."

The rain began to fall so hard that even in the darkness its streams were visible, but neither Namiko nor Woo-cheol noticed.

"The wooden sign said in black ink, **Paradise**. The door opened and a bald man walked out. He asked me how old I was; I told him I was thirteen, and he told me, if anyone asks you tell them you're fourteen. Then he gave me the name Namiko and assigned me room number seven. He handed me a red dress, two yukatas, an obi, two pairs of panties, and a pair of rubber boots. On both sides of the small hallway there were small rooms, each with a wooden sign with a name written on it. Setsuko, Fumiko, Kinue, Masako, Emiko, Shizue . . . I'm sure you already understand. **Paradise** was a comfort station . . . I wasn't taken to a military boot factory but to the Japanese Army's Third Division's regimental base."

The ringing of Namiko's words did not disappear immediately; it hung in the darkness for a while. The sound was not one that would shake eardrums; instead, it sunk into the skin like a chill, paralyzing the senses, and while the two of them endured that sound, they focused their eyes and ears on the darkness, rising in twists and turns.

Suddenly, the sound of the waves and the engine returned, and Namiko spoke again.

"The rest of the story is quite sordid."

"If you want to tell it . . . I'll listen."

"You can't tell anyone. It's a secret that I thought I would take to my grave . . . but . . . the truth is, I want someone to hear it . . . to open up to someone. . . . I want someone to tell me, you may be sullied and damaged beyond repair, but it's not your fault, you were stupid, but it's not your fault in the slightest . . . Otherwise . . . it doesn't matter . . . whether I live or . . ."

"Tell me."

She said nothing.

"Trust me."

Silence.

"I'll never forget what you've told me . . . But I won't tell anyone."

Silence.

"I believe you. That you're as pure as the snow, as innocent as a baby. . . . Please tell me everything."

"Everything . . ."

"I'll listen to it all."

"I . . . believe you."

The rain fell from the darkness of heaven, punching countless little holes in the black depths of the sea. Namiko descended into her first night at **Paradise**. From the pitch-black waves, men's bodies rose up and fell upon her, rising and falling again, panting, moaning, crying, screaming, and all the voices of the people of her past were entwined with the sound of the waves and the rain, more painful, more bitter, sadder, harder even than the past, and Namiko's words, too, pierced countless little holes in Woo-cheol's heart.

Namiko no longer knew whether she had her mouth open and was speaking or whether she was swallowing her own words, mouth shut. Chinese men with clubs roaming the main road, robbing, beating, humiliating the Japanese. A Japanese man who was pulled off a rickshaw and dragged behind it, a Chinese who was betrayed by his comrades, surrounded by them and kicked like a ball. . . .

"I turned to look back the way I'd escaped, and I saw smoke everywhere, sparks were falling, on my head, on my shoulders, even on my shadow . . . I knew I'd go blind if one fell in my eye," she said, covering her face, and in that moment, she felt herself embraced by big arms.

"You're crying . . . for someone like me . . . I . . ." Namiko gently touched Woo-cheol's arm.

He hesitated. "Even if there's no undoing it . . . even if you can't forget it . . . I want . . . I want you to live with all that. It's thirty-five years since the Japanese took over Korea; you and I don't remember a time when Korea was run by Koreans. From the time we were born, we were handcuffed, shackled, choked, and gagged. So they say, hey, you're free now, but they forbade us to walk and now our legs can only stagger, our eyes, unaccustomed to the light, are dazzled; the unbearable pain with each step is . . . But if we keep walking with the pain, I think we'll eventually reach a Korea that belongs to Koreans. No, that's not what I meant to say. I can't say anything . . . anything at all . . . I can only cry . . . but please believe this at least. None of this was your fault. You don't have to be ashamed, because you've done nothing wrong. You can go home with your head held high. Come back to Miryang with me."

She was silent.

"What's your name?"

"I can't tell you . . . mianhaeyo."

"I won't tell anyone what you've told me."

"My Japanese name is Kanemoto Eiko. In **Paradise** they called me Namiko. I can't tell you my true name, the one I inherited from my ancestors or the one given to me by my late father. I mean to keep that locked inside me."

Woo-cheol let go of her body, his hand still on her head, and looked down at Namiko's face, wet with rain and tears.

"But you don't mean . . ."

"I'm not going back to Miryang."

He hesitated. "It's almost morning. We'll be at Busan Harbor before noon. The wharf will be full of people banging drums to greet the ship and celebrate our return. . . . Come back to Miryang with me."

She was silent.

"Let's get some rest, shall we? We'll go to sleep, and when we wake up, we'll be in Busan. We'll get off the ship and get some breakfast at a restaurant in the harbor. Gejang, minari namul, bugeo, miyeokguk—we'll stuff ourselves with all the Korean food we've longed for all these years, and when we're full, we'll sit down and look at the sea and we'll talk. We've got all the time in the world. Let's talk it over."

"I'm . . . going to stay up and watch the sun rise, then I'll sleep."

"Gwaenchan kenna?" *Are you all right?*

"Gwaenchansseumnida." *I'm fine.* Namiko gave him a smile.

"Geureom, jal jageoraei." *Well, then, goodnight.*

"Ye, ajeossido jal jumusiso." *Goodnight to you too.*

Namiko bowed to Woo-cheol's back as he walked down the deck.

"Gamsahamnida."

She couldn't see the sunrise. Hidden by the swirling, lashing rain, the sun turned its surroundings gray and drew a white line on the border between the sky and the sea. Namiko let go of the rain-slicked handrail. I told him my life story. My life is ruined. My life is decided. My life is over. Namiko turned her face to the sky. The rain hit her face. She began to sing.

Ame, ame   fure, fure
Kaa-san ga
Janome de   omukai
Ureshii na
Pitch, pitch   chap, chap
Run, run, run

Kakemasho   kaban wo
Kaa-san no
Ato kara   yuko yuko
Kane ga naru
Pitch, pitch   chap, chap
Run, run, run

Ara ara, ano ko wa
Zubunureda

Yanagi no nekata de
Naiteiru
Pitch, pitch   chap, chap
Run, run, run

Kaa-san boku no wo
Kashimasho ka
Kimi kimi, kono kasa sashitamae
Pitch, pitch   chap, chap
Run, run, run

Boku nara ii'n da
Kaa-san no
Ooki na janome ni
Haitteku
Pitch, pitch   chap, chap
Run, run, run

She sang the song again and again so as to endure the feelings she could not quite reach. She was afraid to stop singing. When the rain stops I'll go sleep in the cabin, she thought; the rain poured into her mouth and a sob overflowed from it, cutting off her song. **Kim Yeong-hee!** She screamed her own name. Abeoji! Only the name my abeoji gave me has not been violated by anyone. Eomoni! No one has laid a finger on the name my eomoni called me. **Kim Yeong-hee!** The name of a thirteen-year-old virgin. She embraced her name, **Kim Yeong-hee. Kim Yeong-hee!** She jumped into the sea.

Nobody saw her. Nobody heard. The wind blew, the clouds broke, and light shone on the place where she had stood. The rain stopped. In the far distance the outline of an island was visible. The sun showed its face, and the light pushed its staff between the clouds, forcing them apart. People came up onto the deck. They gathered not at the stern where Namiko had been, but at the bow, squinting into the sea breeze, pointing at the approaching green island, exchanging smiles and words of joy, and a few who were overcome with emotion raised their arms at the same time. Manse! Manse! Long live Korean independence! Long live Korean independence!

Until the East Sea's waters dry and Mount Paektu's worn away
May God watch over our land, our Korea manse!
Roses of Sharon, three thousand ri of ridges and rivers running through
The Korean people to our land will always be true!

TWENTY-FIVE

Homecoming

| 귀향 | 帰郷 |

Jageunharaboji is coming home! Tomorrow! At last my grand-uncle is coming home! We've been waiting for this day ever since he was released on August 15 last year. The ten of us have been on tenterhooks for so long. For the last six months, Miryang has been in full festivity, and every time people meet they say, like a password, Commander Kim Won-bong is coming back! Yoon Se-joo is coming back! They shake hands and slap each other on the shoulders and shout, Long live Kim Won-bong! Long live Yoon Se-joo! Every day at school my friends and teachers asked me: When is he coming home, have you had any word? Sometimes it embarrassed me, but my pride always won out.

Yoon Se-joo is my grand-uncle, my jageunharaboji. He was one of the leaders of the independence for Korea protest in Miryang twenty-seven years ago; after an arrest warrant was issued for him, he fled to Manchuria. But he didn't only go there to escape arrest: he went to rendezvous with Kim Won-bong, who was setting up an anti-Japanese movement in Manchuria. The two were childhood friends. They lived directly across a narrow road from each other. They were best friends—they played together, learned together, felt the tragedy of the loss of their country together, put the Japanese flag in the school toilet together, and got expelled from school together—they were blood brothers, destined from birth to be comrades.

My halbi told me over and over, how Yoon Se-joo spoke since he was fourteen. He'd say, the struggle against Japan cannot be put aside for even a day. Unless we take back the land that was stolen from us and restore our lost sovereignty, we Koreans will always be embarrassed, we will always be miserable. I give as much thought to dying as to the ends of my hair. I don't care when, where, or how I may lose my life as long as it is in service of the grand project of national liberation.

You can see this spirit in the ten pledges of the Heroic Corps, formed in 1919 by thirteen comrades.

1. We will aggressively pursue all acts of righteousness.
2. We will sacrifice our lives for Korean independence and social equality.
3. We will only accept members bearing a strong spirit of loyalty and sacrifice.
4. The will of the members shall take priority to the will of the corps.
5. We will select a leader of righteous character to represent the corps.
6. We will submit a monthly report, wherever we might be at the time.
7. We will assemble upon request, wherever we might be at the time.
8. We will fulfill the objectives of the corps, though it may cost us our lives.
9. We are devoted all for one and one for all.
10. Those who violate the objectives of the corps will be executed.

Our family couldn't escape our connection with Jageunharaboji, not even for a moment. The newspapers reported that the bombing of the Busan police station, Miryang police station, the office of the governor-general of Korea, the attempted assassination of General Tanaka Giichi in Shanghai, the attempted bombing of the Nijubashi Bridge at the Imperial Palace in Tokyo, the assassination of suspected Japanese spy Park Yong-man in Peking, the Gyeong-buk Heroic Corps Incident, and the bombings of the Joseon Siksan Bank and the Oriental Development Company were all the work of the Heroic Corps. And my jageunharaboji, Yoon Se-joo, was known as Kim Won-bong's right hand, second in command of the Heroic Corps.

In June 1920, when I was still in my eomoni's stomach, Yoon Se-joo was arrested as the mastermind of the plot to bomb the office of the governor-general of Korea. He was imprisoned for seven years and came home, but then he formed an underground organization, the Singanhoe, with Hwang Sang-gyu, a relative of Kim Won-bong's with whom he had been imprisoned, so I have no memory of my jageunharaboji's face.

In 1931, when Hwang Sang-gyu died, Yoon Se-joo went to China again and reunited with Kim Won-bong in Nanking. They founded the Shin Heung Military Academy, then three years after that he became a leader of the Korean National Revolutionary Party; then in 1938 he moved to a place called Wuhan to organize the Korean Heroic Army. The leader was, of course, Kim Won-bong. Wuhan fell after Nanking, so they moved to Kuei-lin, and then to Chungking. That's where we last heard rumors of his whereabouts.

Oh, what pain those of us left behind in Miryang felt. . . . Yoon Se-joo is the youngest of four siblings. My halbi is his oldest brother, but all three brothers were forbidden to hold professions. They couldn't work. They were considered persons of interest, always followed; the police would kick down the door daily, trampling inside with their boots on while we were eating, ransacking the house and then leaving. We had to fend off starvation. All we could do was dry out radish leaves and mix them into our jook for our daily meals. Generous people would secretly give us aid sometimes, and we'd manage to keep body and soul together for one more day. Tomorrow is another day, but we survived today—it is so painful to live day to day.

But never did I hear my halbi or jageunharabojis or my abeoji or eomoni say a bad word about Yoon Se-joo. We rarely said his name, not knowing who was watching or listening, but when the waenom spat out his name, I knew my whole family's eyes would turn to flames. I think I did the same too.

Each time the waenom kicked over our family's humble dining table and the jook and fermented fish paste we'd been eating were splashed on my hair and face, I bit my lip and held back my tears. I will not be humiliated, I'm proud. I was proud of my jageunharaboji for risking his life to fight for liberation. All the blood flowing through my body surged and shouted. Yoon Se-joo! Yoon Se-joo! Yoon Se-joo! Yoon Se-joo!

When the *Dong-A Ilbo* went back into print in December last year, I felt nothing but pride.

My abeoji read the article to us before breakfast.

"'The God of heaven and earth is not ruthless, he has given this nation good omens of liberation; the divine will of our blessed ancestors is immortal, it has again brought the vitality of freedom to our divine people, for they have gladly seen the blessings of the martyrs who have risked their lives for the nation, and they have thought holy the deeds of the crusaders that shone throughout Asia. An inevitable aspect of this world historical crisis though this may be, how incredibly moving it is, how joyous it is!

"'Though the invader Japanese administration used this journal's reporting on the Olympic victory of Sohn Kee-chung as its excuse to issue the ultimate punishment of a publishing ban, today the *Dong-A Ilbo* announces that it has the honor of being resurrected, and by proclaiming the outline of our intentions again today, we strive to form a bond of mutual concern and joy with you, our thirty million brothers.

"'In the nearly twenty years since our first issue, we have been punished with seizure or censoring over one thousand times, suspended from publication four times, and our staff has been beaten and bloodied; the *Dong-A Ilbo*, conceived of as an organ of expression for the people, may have suffered scores of humiliations and persecutions, but this has only resulted in our ultimate struggle to preserve the dignity of our people.

"'We have already taken up our pen. And if this pen should break, our very blood itself pulsates through it; the arrow has already been fired. There is no time for skepticism; there is no end in sight. Our work is derived from none but humanity and justice; we pledge ourselves that our thoughts will become the very sword of the learned.

"'Comrades around the world! Brothers and sisters! We know that our desires are just and our sincerity is worth believing in; we shall not cease our tremendous cheers, and through the completion of the heroic achievement of the liberation of our nation, we shall attempt to forge a brilliant people here forevermore.

"'Today, December 1, Dangun 4278, all of us at the *Dong-A Ilbo*, by drafting these few sentences, offer our tribute to every glorious soul in heaven who shed their precious blood on the front lines of liberation, and at the same time, we appeal to the sentiments of our thirty million compatriots.'"

The wicker gate creaked, and Woo-ja raised her head from her sewing.

"It looks like they're rolling out the red carpet," her abeoji boomed as he took off his overcoat.

"Red carpet?" Her eomoni hung the coat on a hanger.

"They're coming in from Muan, they say. They're welcoming him by rolling out a red carpet."

"Oh, he's finally coming home."

"Yes, not much longer."

Woo-ja was sewing a hanbok for her jageunharaboji. She thought perhaps that after twenty years of fighting in China, he might come back wearing Chinese clothes. He might come in, like Abeoji just did, and take off his overcoat in the entrance—oh, my heart is pounding, what should I say when he comes in? Aigo, eoseo oiso? Aigo, gosaenghasyeotseumnida? Everyone will be so overwhelmed we won't be able to say a word, I imagine. As soon as one of us opens our mouths, we'll all start to cry at once, Halbi and my other jageunharaboji and abeoji and me and my sister and brother . . . Aigo, I can barely see the end of the needle for the tears in my eyes. I'd like him to change into this hanbok as soon as he gets home. I should be able to get it done by tomorrow morning, but if he comes home today—aigu, I have to hurry.

"Muan's got nothing on Miryang. I mean, Kim Won-bong and Yoon Se-joo were both born here, after all. Practically all the Heroic Corps men are from Miryang!" Eomoni set a bottle of unfiltered rice wine down in front of the men.

"Kim Won-bong's a local hero, right up there with Samyeongdang." Abeoji sat down near the door cross-legged.

"That reminds me, you think Samyeongdang's stopped sweating yet?" interjected Halbi, who had been silently smoking his pipe.

"Hmm, with all the celebrating going on, nobody would notice even if he was sweating." The middle brother, thirteen years younger than Halbi and eight years older than Yoon Se-joo, took a sip of makgeolli.

"Reckon he's coming back alive?" Halbi took a puff from his pipe and tapped out the ashes.

"Don't say that, it's bad luck." The middle brother gulped, taking a swig of makgeolli.

"I had a dream the other day. Se-joo had turned into a bird and was flying off somewhere."

"Abeoji, Se-joo is coming home. He's already made it back to Muan. If you're so worried, I'll go to Muan myself right now."

"The moment that day that the area leader told us that we'd been liberated, Un-gyo ran out on the veranda and shouted, 'Yoon Se-joo manse! Long live Yoon Se-joo!' until he went hoarse." The middle brother finished his makgeolli with a grimace.

"I still don't understand why he had to die. Aigu, I thought he'd go to bed with bronchitis and he'd feel better with a few days' rest. . . ." Halbi put his pipe in the ashtray and sipped his makgeolli.

"I thought maybe he'd drink something, so I made some saenggangtang and sat down next to his bed. He looked like he was having a nice dream, so thinking that his fever must've gone down, I put my hand to his forehead, and it was cold as a sheet of ice. . . . Aigu, in another six months they could've been reunited." Eomoni poured more makgeolli into the men's empty bowls.

"Aigu, what a pity. To die without seeing your wife or your child's face, aigo, and he's the only one of us who got married before Se-joo joined the movement, the rest of us are all on our own. No work, no wives, ai-igo, no children even . . . for twenty-seven years, just waiting . . . for the day Se-joo would come home as a hero . . . Aigo, aigo . . ." He downed the makgeolli that had just been poured for him.

Creak. The wicker gate opened.

Abeoji, who was sitting cross-legged, got to his knees and turned his head.

Footsteps approached.

He's alone.

He's come back.

The person who appeared in the entrance was not Yoon Se-joo. He was a stranger in his mid-thirties. He was wearing a drab-colored Chinese suit and a cap.

"Is this the home of Comrade Yoon Se-joo?"

"Yes," Abeoji said, getting to his feet.

"My name is Kang Woo-hong. I fought with Yoon Se-joo in the battle for liberation."

"Where's Jageunharaboji?"

"It pains me to have to tell you this. . . ." The man's eyes dropped to the floor.

Woo-ja clasped her hands together, forgetting she was holding a needle, and stabbed the needle into her left palm. A drop of blood fell onto the purple silk cloth and she shouted, "Egumeonina, ireul eojjae." But nobody was watching her.

"Comrade Yoon Se-joo died four years ago, in the early summer."

Woo-ja didn't look at her palm or the bloodstained cloth. She stared only at the mouth of the man who had come to notify them of her jageunharaboji's death.

"I would like to tell you more. . . ." The man who said his name was Kang Woo-hong took off his round cap.

"Thank you for coming all this way to tell us. Please, come inside." Eomoni gently put her hand on Abeoji's back; Abeoji was standing stick straight staring out at the well in the garden. "Darling . . ."

The man sat down in the doorway, and Eomoni placed a bowl of makgeolli in front of him.

"My brother died in the same battle. I will tell you the story, but it's a long one. . . ." The man took a drink and held his mouth open as if waiting for the makgeolli to go down his throat and settle in his stomach.

"In October 1938 we put together the Korean Heroic Army in Wuhan. Of course, Comrade Kim Won-bong and Comrade Yoon Se-joo were central to this. Together with the Eighth Route Army and the New Fourth Army, we started a guerrilla war against the waejeok, but after Nanking and Wuhan both fell, we had to withdraw to Chungking. There were many Koreans on the continent fighting against Japan, but we were scattered all over. So it was decided to come together in North China under the banner of anti-Japanese action. As a result of these discussions, Comrade Kim Won-bong stayed at the headquarters in Chungking with a fifth of the Heroic Army forces, while Comrade Yoon Se-joo led the rest to North China. They were all independent patriots who had trained to win an armed struggle with the waejeok. My brother was among them. I stayed in Chungking. That's where fate divided us.

"On January 1, 1941, the Korean Heroic Army was divided into first, second, and third corps and headed to North China by ship. It wasn't until July that they all made it to Shàngwǔcūn. My brother was in the First Corps; Comrade Yoon Se-joo was in the Third.

"Then, on May 25 the next year, battle broke out in a place called Tàixíngshān. There were about sixty thousand Japanese troops and four thousand men from the Korean Heroic Army and the Eighth Route Army; in an attempt to make up for the overwhelming gap in force, our men made Tàixíngshān a fortress. After liberation I went there looking for my brother's body, but the area is steep and it was not easy to walk. Tàixíngshān's a mountainous area, nothing but rocks and a few trees; you could call it a natural fortress. The enemy was so large in number that they decided to break up in groups of ten; Comrades Yoon Se-joo, Choi Cheol-ho, and Jin Kwang-hwa led ten men to hide in the mountains. Suddenly, a hundred enemy fighters appeared. Comrade Yoon Se-joo said, 'We'll all be annihilated if we stay here, so let's act as decoy and let the others escape,' and the three of them jumped out in front of the Japanese army. Choi Cheol-ho ran straight up, Yoon Se-joo ran out horizontally, and Jin Kwang-hwa, whose body was weakened by pleurisy, ran down the mountain.

"Choi Cheol-ho heard gunshots behind him as he scrambled up. He hid himself in a cave full of wild goats and waited for the sound of gunshots to stop. After a while, he descended the mountain, concealing himself behind rocks; the men's bodies were scattered all over. He was walking around confirming whether each man was alive or dead when he discovered Comrade Yoon Se-joo underneath a young man. He had been shot at the base of his leg and was losing a lot of blood, but he was still breathing and perfectly conscious. Comrade Yoon Se-joo said, 'I heard Jin Kwang-hwa calling out. He might still be alive. I'm fine; go help Jin.' He found Jin Kwang-hwa at the foot of a cliff. He'd been shot in the shoulder and had apparently jumped to his death. He knew that if he'd been taken alive, they would've tortured him by hanging him upside down, given him the water cure, pulled out his nails, and then executed him.

"Comrade Choi Cheol-ho carried Comrade Yoon Se-joo on his back and climbed back up the mountain, then hid him in the cave while he went off in search of others. He found Comrade Ha Jin-dong and they discussed outside the cave what might be done to save his life, but there was no hospital in the village at the foot of the mountain, nor a pharmacy, and the risk of being informed on to the enemy was too high, so they could not even chance knocking on the door of a house.... Even though he couldn't have heard their conversation, Comrade Yoon Se-joo said, 'Don't sacrifice yourselves for me, you must run, run, regain your composure, and fight.' The two of them disguised the entrance to the cave with brush and rocks, going off in the afternoon to search for other men and returning at night to care for Comrade Yoon Se-joo.

"After a few days, all he would say was, water, water. They went down to the village and searched desperately, but there was no river or even wells. When they returned to the cave, Comrade Yoon Se-joo had apparently put his own urine in a cup and was drinking it. Now, if you keep on doing that you'll get a fever. And sure enough, after a few days of having a high temperature, it was June . . . June second . . . five days after he had been shot. When Comrade Choi Cheol-ho returned to the cave, the brush and rocks around the entrance had been removed, and Comrade Yoon Se-joo was not there. Comrade Choi Cheol-ho quickly searched as he went down the mountain, but he was nowhere to be seen. I'm told before you get down to where the houses are there are terraced millet fields, and that's where Comrade Yoon Se-joo had collapsed. It looked like he had been dead for hours; his eyes were wide open and his mouth, open in desperation for water, was black with flies. The two men gave him a temporary burial on the mountain. The next time I'm there, I plan to make a new grave for him.

"Comrade Yoon Se-joo had one son. His wife, Comrade Ha So-ok, stayed in Chungking with Kim Won-bong to care for their child while treating and caring for injured soldiers and learning how to hold a child in one arm and a horse's reins in the other. I don't know how long they stayed in Chungking, because a fierce battle broke out in the border region.

"We stopped her because it was dangerous, but Ha So-ok said, 'I had a dream that my husband fell off the hill. I just know something awful has happened to him.' She put trousers on over her tunic and dressed their son in the Chinese style with a ponytail so they could pretend to be a Chinese mother and child, and they headed to North China by boat.

"A month later, Comrade Ha So-ok brought back news of Yoon Se-joo's death to Chungking. She is a very strong woman who never betrays an ounce of weakness whatever the circumstances may be; she was like a mother to all of us, always encouraging us with her gentle smile, but that day, her voice quivered as she spoke.

"If you took the time the two of them spent with each other and put it all together, it would come to less than a year, I'd say. The longest time they had was in the spring of 1937, when she was summoned by Comrade Yoon Se-joo, who was hiding out in Nanking, and she went to see him with their son, who was seven at the time. . . . And that was only for two months.

"The day the men left, Ha So-ok took their son to Chungking Harbor to see Yoon Se-joo off. As they were parting, Yoon Se-joo said to her, 'Next time I'll see you in Miryang.' Those were his final words to her."

Tears spilled from Woo-ja's eyes, falling on the hanbok that now would never be worn by the man it was made for. Jageunharaboji would not be coming home. He had died in pain and anguish, without even having enough water to drink. Buried on a mountain in a foreign country without a wake or incense or his loved ones' tears, he was all alone, being eaten by maggots and ants and turning into bone. . . . Aigo, sesange . . . Woo-ja jerked her head down with such force that her chin dug into her neck. Her tears fell, on her hands, the needle, her jageunharaboji's hanbok . . . Aigo, aigo.

"What is their son's name?" Eomoni asked, sniffling.

Eomoni's crying too, Woo-ja thought; knowing that if she saw her mother crying, she would start sobbing, Woo-ja did not look up.

"Nam-seon."

"How old is he?"

"He's fifteen. He looks quite like Comrade Yoon Se-joo."

"We've never met his son or wife. Can we see them?"

"Comrade Ha So-ok said this: 'I will stay and act with the men. I can't leave them behind to go home. I believe that's what my husband would've wanted. He was a man who, even after he got shot as a decoy to save his subordinates' lives, told his comrades that he was fine, asked them to check on his subordinate, and ordered them to run away and continue to fight. My husband and I have been pulled apart between this world and the next, but as long as I follow his dying wish and continue to fight, we are connected. His long-cherished dream of seeing the destruction of the waenom and the liberation of the motherland has been fulfilled, but the path to defeating the ruling class and redistributing the land is a steep one. The yangban are still the elites, the sangmin are still the commoners, and below them are the baekjeong, the untouchable underclass. Though we are liberated from the thieving Japanese, the Korean people have not been liberated. Until the privileged class has been destroyed and the economic pillaging system that exploits the people to line the pockets of the privileged class has been smashed, and all inequality, inhumanity, and absurdity have disappeared from our homeland, I will continue to fight.'

"Comrade Ha So-ok's face was gaunt and exhausted, but her eyes were not clouded by sorrow. To be honest with you, that was the first time I ever thought that a woman was beautiful. Her hair was clumped with sweat and dust, and her face, which did not have the slightest tint of red to it, was tanned and dark, but her beauty shook my soul.

"Then she said, 'It's as my husband always said: Construction and destruction are only distinguished formally; in our spirit destruction is construction, the people are our main headquarters, and violence is the only weapon of our revolution. If I should die in battle, our son shall fight and carry out the will of his abeoji and eomoni.' Then Nam-seon opened his sharp, gleaming eyes, just like those of his father, stiffened his mouth, and nodded."

Kang Woo-hong finished his makgeolli, retraced the path of his story to see if he had told them all, and noticed that he had left one thing out.

"I found out after liberation that the enemy regimental commander was a Korean named Hong Sa-ik. There were, it seems, quite a few Korean volunteers in that unit. While the waenom were testing their loyalty, they probably did set out to kill their fellow Koreans. Hong Sa-ik was executed as a war criminal."

Having finished his duty, Woo-hong picked up his cap from the floor to tell everyone that he was done speaking.

"So nobody's coming home." Halbi turned his pipe, which had gone out, upside down and tapped out the ashes.

"No bones or hair even. . . . How do we have a memorial for him . . . if we have nothing at all?" The middle brother picked up his bowl to find not a drop of makgeolli left.

"Moon Jeong-il, a second-year student at the Shin Heung Military Academy that Comrades Kim Won-bong and Yoon Se-juu were instrumental in setting up, received a fountain pen from him, I'm told, but in all those battles he lost it, and he expressed his regret to you, his bereaved family. On behalf of Moon Jeong-il, I apologize."

"No . . . don't, you told us so much . . . if you hadn't come . . . we would've gone out into the street and searched for him in the crowds of those of you who have returned triumphantly, and then we would've had to face this overwhelming blow in front of so many people. Thank you for your thoughtfulness. Gomapseumnida." Eomoni, crying, staggered to her feet, then clasped Woo-hong's right hand with both of hers.

Kang Woo-hong put on his cap, sat down on the entrance step, tied the laces of his military boots, and stood.

"I'd like to ask you one question, if I may. Does Lee Woo-cheol still live in the same house he used to?"

"Lee Woo-cheol . . . Oh, the marathon runner . . ." Eomoni wiped her nose with the sleeve of her jeogori.

"We were classmates at school; he was my best friend."

"When you say 'used to,' how long ago do you mean?"

"When I left Miryang I was seventeen. I'm turning thirty-four this year."

"Oh, that long ago . . . He runs a tearoom and cold noodle shop near Yeongnamnu these days."

"A noodle shop? So the rubber boot shop closed. How are his mother and father?"

"They've both passed on," Halbi said, lighting his pipe.

"Aigu . . . how is Woo-cheol? I guess he's married with children now."

"Yes . . . but . . . well, you'll have to go see him and talk in person."

"Oh, sillyehaetseumnida, please forgive me. It was inconsiderate of me to ask you all those questions. I want to see Lee Woo-cheol more than my own parents, and I got carried away."

"It's been seventeen years, after all. . . ."

"Well, now . . . I'll take my leave." Woo-hong bowed and began to walk away.

The sound of footsteps went away, but no one was listening. All five of them were left alone with their separate, inner voices.

"What do we do about his grave?" The middle brother sat his empty bowl down between his legs.

"There's nothing we can do," Halbi muttered, exhaling smoke.

"Woon-cheol, write this down. Yoon Se-joo, son of Yoon Hee-gyu and Kim Gyeong-I, died June second, Dangun 4275. Even if there is no grave, we still have to do all the rituals on the anniversary of his death . . . Oh, what a sorry end." The middle brother ran his fingers over the empty bowl tenderly.

Abeoji took out a piece of paper and a brush and inkstone from the writing box and placed them on the floor, groaning as he rubbed the ink on the inkstone.

"He was born on June twenty-fourth, Dangun 4234, which means he was forty."

The moment he dipped his brush into the ink, a joyful roar came from the streets: "Long live Kim Won-bong! Long live Yoon Se-joo!"

Abeoji's right hand began to tremble; tears and ink dripped onto the paper.

Dragging her leg, So-jin made her way through the crowd one step at a time. "Long live Kim Won-bong! Long live Kim Won-bong!"

Someone passed me, then another; a hundred, no, a thousand people must've passed me. Ever since I can remember I'm used to people walking past me, but this is the first time so many people have.

The summer when I was four, I caught polio; at first, I couldn't move my arms or legs at all, but thanks to Eomoni massaging and rubbing them, by the time I went to school my left hand and leg weren't paralyzed anymore, and eventually I learned to walk without needing to hold my eomoni's hand. As I became able to do all sorts of little things, Eomoni's face would bloom into a smile; she'd applaud me, hug me, and rub my cheeks; so wanting to please her and to be praised by her, I'd try something new, like crawling my left hand across the silver tray toward the white porcelain plate of baramtteok, rice cakes filled with bean paste. . . .

But when I went to school, I realized there were only a few things I could do and far more things I couldn't. I can't hold a pencil or crayon well. I can't thread a needle. In phys ed, I always just watched, but if the ball accidentally came at me, I couldn't move away or put my hands up to my face, so I would get nosebleeds. On those rainy days in the middle of winter, I wanted to curse the heavens. It was hard for me to hold up an umbrella with just my left hand, and avoiding puddles was difficult, so I'd get muddy water in my boots. Even when I'd finally make it to the classroom, it took time to unwrap the bundle that Eomoni had tied to my back for me, so sometimes, even when the teacher was standing at the podium and ordering us all to stand, I'd still have the bundle on my back. All the little things that everyone else could do unconsciously were a series of penances for me. Even if I summoned all my mind and energy painstakingly achieving things, nobody was happy for me, nobody gave me praise, nobody even saw.

By the time I got home, all the muscles in my body were screaming; I would immediately lie down on my futon. Even my paralyzed right arm was throbbing with pain—it was intolerable. I didn't want to see anything I saw, hear anything I heard; in honesty, I didn't want to live. I would lie still on my bed like a corpse, and Eomoni would come over and gently comb her fingers through my hair as she sang to me, her voice sweet and slightly nasal.

Blue chima, long chima, wrapped around her waist
With a deep sorrow, it rains
Alideongdeokung seulideongdeokung
What can she do
If her blue chima gets wet, what can she do

With my eyes half-opened I looked at Eomoni's face and soon closed my eyes. Her gaze was always distant as if she were dreaming, but sometimes it would turn dark and heavy, which was very scary. She would mutter wearily . . . Yong-ha . . . Yong-ha . . . Yong-ha . . . the name of my abeoji, who died when I was one. He's my father, but his real wife and legitimate children had nothing to do with me, and he never even held me—all I got from him was my name, So-jin.

After Eomoni remarried and gave birth to my little brother, she came down with a uterine illness; she took expensive traditional medicines, saw dozens of reputable doctors, and even got the famous mudang Kim from Daegu to do a gut to cure her, but she started screaming, "Aigo, gaseumiya, my guts are squirming like a snake, aigo, jungneunda!" and crawled out of her bed in tears, so my stepfather talked to a doctor and she started smoking opium.

It was the time of year when the new leaves are as pale as cherry blossoms. I put a jug of water on a tray and went into her bedroom, and Eomoni's rouged lips began to move and in a faint voice she spoke.

"I've never seen the sea . . . but I've heard about it . . . your abeoji was a traveling fortune teller, before he wound up in Miryang he would walk from Mount Paektu to Mount Halla; he knew all the mountains and rivers of the country. I liked hearing his stories about the sea, so I pestered him over and over, lying there with my head on his arm . . . so I've never seen it myself but . . . I know about it . . . yes . . . I do . . . I know everything about the sea . . . as you get closer to the water the sand is wet and you leave footprints all over clomping through it, cheobeok cheobeok . . . left, right, oenjjok, oreunjjok, breathing in the scent of the tide that the waves give off . . . the white foam wetting your calves, oenjjok, oreunjjok . . . feeling the sand moving with the soles of your feet, oenjjok, oreunjjok . . . stopping when you're in up to your waist . . . waiting for the sun to set over the horizon . . . waiting under cover of the darkness of the sea for him to come . . . embraced by the arms of the waves that turned rough as soon as the sun set . . . pushed away . . . aigu, geurae dangsin maeumdaero haera nan dangsin geonikka, do what you want with me, I'm all yours . . . as my body shakes with joy a black wave rises . . . I'm swallowed by the waves and carried out to sea . . . I relax and entrust my body to the sea . . . jostled by its movements . . . and all I can hear is his voice . . . Mi-ryeong, jeongmal ippeuda yeogido, yeogido, yeogido, jeonbu nae geoda, Mi-ryeong, you're so beautiful, all of you, here, and here, and here, all of you is mine. . . . For fifteen years after he died I waited like the fragments of shells washed up on the beach for the waves to come, waiting, waiting . . . finally . . . listen . . . I know you can hear it too . . . the waves lapping . . . cheolsseok . . . cheolsseok . . . oh, So-jin ah, aigu, gwiyeoun nae saekki, geu saramui gwiyeoun ttal, my sweet baby, *his* precious daughter, aigu, aigu, I can't reach your face . . . please come closer . . . closer . . . closer . . . that's it, put your cheek to mine . . . saranghae, I love you, saranghae, jeongmal saranghaeyo . . . when I die, I want you to cremate me . . . put my bones and ashes in the river . . . the riverbed is where he and I will exchange our vows . . . and my abeoji, who drowned, will be our guest at Yeongdomok . . . So-jin ah, aigu, So-jin, I know he never said your name while he was alive, but try listening to the babbling of the river . . . he's always, always calling for you . . . and when your eomoni is dead, we'll call for you together . . . oh, So-jin ah . . . my So-jin . . ."

Omma . . . my sweet omma . . . who always treated me like a little kid and took care of everything for me . . . who let me eat as many sweets as I wanted every day . . . castella cake from Okamoto's, dried bananas, imagawayaki from Higuchiya, and dried squid, not just as it came, but cooked up with soy sauce and sugar to make it sweeter just for me . . . and beef grilled over charcoal, fed to me piece by piece, aigu, gwiyeoun nae saekki, oh, my sweet baby. At both the Dong-A Guesthouse and the Dong-A Hotel, the director of the Miryang branch of the prefectural government, the chief of the Miryang police, and the Miryang district defense chief were all regulars; until the fifteenth of August last year, we were the most prosperous in Miryang, so even at the height of the war we only ate beef and pure white rice. The other kids always brought barley rice with kimchi and pickled vegetables to school for their lunch, but I'd have white rice, beef stewed in soy sauce, and salted salmon; even Morita-sensei's mouth started watering when he walked past my desk. I hated vegetables, so I'd never even have kimchi on my tray. Every now and then, the chef would make Japanese food for us. Unadon, oyako-don, ise shrimp tempura, sukiyaki, omelet rice . . . mm, masitda . . . masisseo, Omma . . .

The other kids wore straw sandals and rubber boots, the kids from families that had a little money to spend wore athletic shoes, but I wore custom-made leather shoes to school. One pair was brown and the other was black with a round toe. When I was sixteen, I went to the beauty salon with Eomoni and got my bob permed. Eomoni showed the hairdresser a copy of *Eiga no Tomo*, a Japanese movie magazine, and told her, "Make her look just like Mieko Taka-mine." When I looked in the mirror, I didn't look a thing like that movie star, but Eomoni put Amon Papaya Cream and rouge from Kiss Me on my face and then painted my lips bright red, then, roughly tousling my hair and raining kisses on my forehead and cheeks, she said, "Ippeora gwiyeoun uri saekki," telling me how much I looked just like her. "Saranghae, saranghae, jeongmal saranghaeyo . . ." Those were the days when slogans like "Do your own hair at home," "Perms are a luxury," "Luxury is the enemy," and so on were all around, but the school principal was a family friend, so whatever we did, he looked the other way.

I went to a girls' school for only the first year, until Eomoni's pain got worse, and I had to help her smoke opium constantly. I'd stick the soft brown ball onto a sewing needle, hold it over the oil lamp, put it in the pipe, carefully light it, and hold it in Eomoni's mouth for her. She would inhale and I'd have her hold her breath while I counted, hana, dul, set, net. Then I'd gently put a record on the gramophone's turntable, turn the crank, and drop the needle, and she'd absentmindedly sing along until she fell asleep; when she awoke she'd smoke again, singing along as she started to nod off again . . . Eomoni didn't care whether they were Japanese songs or Korean ones; as long as they were sad songs, she loved them all.

> *Though we know not where the flower*
> *Floating on the flowing water will be tomorrow*
> *Our reflections on the surface now*
> *Will never, ever disappear . . .*

My eomoni died two months ago. She was forty-eight years old. My abeoji, who died when he was forty, died on January third, so if she had managed to cling on for another ten days, they would have died on the same day . . . That day, Eomoni woke up covered in sweat, lifted her arms with some effort, and mimed choking herself around the neck. . . . I gave her some opium. . . . Soon her eyelids closed and her breathing became labored, like a bellows. . . . Yes . . . that's right . . . I killed her . . . my own mother who made all my wishes come true . . . no matter how selfish . . . anything I wanted . . . that's why I made her own wish come true. . . . No one has ever spoiled me as much as Eomoni, and I don't suppose anyone ever will . . . saranghae, saranghae, jeongmal sarang-haeyo. . . .

But did she only love me so much because I was his? Though my little brother, ten years younger than me, who she and my stepfather had together, is the heir, she never would even embrace him . . . No, there's only one person in this world that my eomoni loved . . . the man who loved and left her . . . sa-ranghae, saranghae, jeongmal saranghaeyo. . . .

When Eomoni learned that her illness was incurable, she instructed her lawyer, Mr. Murakami, who had been in charge of the accounting, to divide her property between us, the guesthouse and hotel going to her husband and son, and the house by the cedar trees going to me, but then the war ended; the Japanese went home with little more than the clothes on their backs; and Mr. Murakami left without even handing over the books and her will to my stepfather.

My stepfather ignored her wishes. Though Eomoni had pleaded repeat-edly, and he had nodded along, he broke the promise to cremate her and scat-ter her ashes in the Miryang River; instead he buried her in the cemetery on the slope of the mountain, and though he said he would give only her gold jeweled hairpin to my brother's wife and the rest of her jewelry and clothes to me, he kicked me out of the house without even a single thing to remember her by, and I had no choice but to move into the house of my half brother, the son of my father's wife, who hated my eomoni so much she wanted to kill her.

My half brother has his six children, from his first wife, second wife, and his mistress, all living there, so I always seem to have little choice but to sit on the entrance steps or stand in the kitchen, and his second wife pulls horrible faces at me openly, so I found a twenty-eight-year-old man who lives in Sam-namjin. He's an engineer on the Busan Railway, and though I hardly know what to talk about with a man as uneducated and gruff as he is, he's never had anything to do with women, drinking, or gambling, and I figured any house was better than my half brother's, so last month we promised to marry. I have no eomoni to sew me a new mattress and no abeoji to pass the cup to my groom, so I'll have to go on my own, in the back of the palanquin, from one stranger's house to another's. . . .

So-jin lifted her paralyzed right leg and wrenched her right arm, moving forward, step by step. Everyone had left the riverside. She couldn't even hear their cheers. Maybe General Kim Won-bong's already started speaking. For the past six months since liberation, Kim Won-bong had been the talk of all Miryang.

An eighteen-year-old boy leaves his hometown for the cause of the independence of his people and returns home a forty-eight-year-old man. I just know he'll leave as much of a mark on Korean history as Xiang Yu, the military commander who destroyed the Qin and became the king of Chu. They say he once ate four gallons of food at a farmhouse in Daegu. They say he can magic himself anywhere and that in one night he made it to Pyongyang to meet Kim Il-sung and back. After all, he wasn't caught by the waenom even when they offered a sixty-five-won reward because he can transform into a fly; the police called him the Fly and everything. I heard that when General Kim Won-bong arrived at Jedae-ri, he got out of the black sedan, saying he couldn't drive through where his abeoji was; he shook hands with the people in the crowd shouting and waving the Taegukgi as he walked, and the crowd, overwhelmed and brought to tears, followed after him like a school of fish. Last year, with Kim Gu as a go-between, he married a daughter of one of the leaders of the People's Revolutionary Party, and they had their first son, who they decided to name after Ahn Jung-geun, the man who killed Ito Hirobumi.

I'd heard what the people in town were saying, but what with caring for my eomoni and then her death, it wasn't the time for it, and now neither, really—so then why, I wonder, am I going to listen to General Kim Won-bong speak?

At the gate of Miryang First National School, there were young men wearing sashes that said HEROIC CORPS, holding clubs and keeping a lookout. She managed to squeeze herself in to the crowd and get inside the gates, just as the thousands, maybe ten thousands, there all raised their hands and cheered, "Long live Kim Won-bong! Long live Kim Won-bong!"

So-jin climbed up on the planter of azaleas next to the gate, avoiding the waves of people pushing their way in. The people who were nearest to the po-

dium wiped their tears with their sleeves as the people behind them surrounded them, listening to Kim Won-bong's words.

"Mount Jongnam hasn't changed. Nor has the Namcheong River. But so
many comrades have died, and the young men who risked their lives for independence are now gray-headed. What hasn't changed is the masses of people
wearing rags, walking barefoot, hungry and exploited."

Oh, there's Woo-cheol! So-jin half hid her face behind the trunk of a
cherry tree.

"Woo-cheol! I knew it was you, because you're about three heads taller
than everyone."

"Woo-hong?"

"Yeah, it's me."

"Aigu, haneuri musimchi anatda! Woo-hong! You're alive! Aigo!"

My half brother grabbed the arm of the man in the drab uniform and cap
and embraced him; the two slapped each other's backs, evidently delighted to
be reunited.

"I want you to meet Comrade Kim Won-bong. I told him about you over
and over and over. They're calling him a hometown hero. It'll be the meeting
of two heroes!"

I followed my half brother as he walked off, arm around the shoulder of
the man from the Heroic Corps. The two climbed the stone steps up to
Yeongnamnu. They went into a house where the ilbon saram had lived until
liberation, which for the last three months had been home to General Kim
Won-bong's family.

I saw it with my own eyes.

TWENTY-SIX

The Witness

| 목격자 | 目擊者 |

I saw it with my own eyes.

Sure, I'll start from the beginning.

From when I first met Chun-sik, or Lee Woo-gun.

As you know, we're both from Miryang, South Gyeongsang Province. My house was a farmhouse at the foot of Mount Yongdu, and he lived in the rubber boot store not far from the foot of Yeongnamnu, about forty minutes apart walking and fifteen minutes running, so you could hardly say we lived in the same neighborhood. But when we were kids, there were still sweetfish-fishing boats you could pay five sen to take you from Yeongnamnu to the station. The city of Miryang is connected by water. The river twists and there's a sandbar. . . . Could you give me a piece of paper? The river's like this; it flows clockwise. My house was here, Chun-sik's was here, and the school we went to was here. It was close to Chun-sik's house, but it was about eight ri from my house, and school started at eight, so I had to leave at seven to make it on time. There's a shortcut over the embankment. There are rows of cherry and poplar trees all along it, so I was always excited to go to school in April. They say the Miryang River's half water and half sweetfish, and it's true: the river's full of sweetfish. The water's so clear that you can see the fishes' shadows on the bottom. Have you heard this before? Eaten raw, this fish tastes like watermelon, and it's been famous since before the Joseon dynasty: if you eat sweetfish from Miryang, you won't want it from anywhere else. Aigu, mianhamnida, once I start talking about Miryang I just can't stop. Back to Chun-sik . . . whenever I walked over the embankment in the morning, I'd always run into Chun-sik's brother, Lee Woo-cheol. The embankment surrounds the sandbar. He'd be there, running laps at a tremendous speed, and by the time I made it to school he'd lap me three times. The top of the embankment is narrow, and the force of the wind rushing up it makes you feel like you're about to fall into the river, so I would always stop near the edge and cheer him on, yelling, "Himnaera! Jalhanda!"

Lee Woo-cheol is a famous long-distance runner. If the 1940 Olympics hadn't been canceled because of the war, he would've run the marathon and maybe become the second Sohn Kee-chung. His brother Chun-sik was fast too. By the time he went to high school, he was always overtaking his brother. And when he was in high school, he set new records in the 800 and 1500 meters at the South Gyeongsang District Conference. Given the times we were living in, the national tournament wasn't held, but if it had been, it's likely the both of them would've made it to the Olympics, Woo-cheol in the long-distance and Chun-sik in the middle-distance events.

I was with Chun-sik for six years at Miryang Primary School and two years at secondary school, so eight years all together. They didn't mix up the classes, so the kids you were with at the beginning were with you all the way until graduation. We started school at eight years old, but most of the kids were older, ten, eleven, or twelve, even. But Chun-sik was the same age as me, and not only that, but—and I've forgotten how it happened—we hit it off, you might say; anyway, we got along well.

There was an ilbon saram teacher called Hanazaki-sensei. He would always hit us. We both went through growth spurts right at the height of the wartime food shortages, so we were always so hungry we could barely stand it. The school had a field, where students would sow seeds, grow radishes and red carrots, and learn about farming. So me and Chun-sik snuck into the field before the roosters crowed, pulled a few carrots about this big, wiped the mud off them like this, and then ate them. Maybe it was the morning dew, but they were delicious, so sweet. No, see, that's not theft, because actually, when they're all crowded together, it's better to pull every other one out so the others grow better; it's called "thinning out"—it's a standard agricultural practice.

One morning, Hanazaki-sensei got up at the podium and before he did attendance he said, "Hey, which one of you ate the carrots? And be honest." Usually, if you owned up to something, he'd say, "I admire your honesty," and then he'd make you swear in front of everyone that you'd never do it again, and then he'd let you off, so Chun-sik and I stuck our hands right up.

"So it was you two, Nishihara and Kunimoto?"

"Yes, sir."

"You little brats! Idiots, the both of you!"

Well, he hit us so much that I couldn't feel my face for a while.

After that, they put a wire fence around the outer wall of the school, but then you had to take a detour to go in through the gate, so everyone just took a shortcut and climbed under the wire fence. The problem was, you had to go past Hanazaki-sensei's lodging. One day when I was ducking under the wire fence, I heard someone say, "Nishihara, what do you think you're doing?" and when I turned around, it was, of course, Hanazaki-sensei. So he says, "Nishihara, get over here," and I thought it was curtains for me, so I clenched my teeth and closed my eyes, and then he says: you have Korean pickles at home, I'm sure, would you bring me some kimchi tomorrow?

Well, he asked me for it, so I asked my eomoni to let me take him a little. You know how you have two kinds of kimchi: the one your abeoji eats, with the top-quality salted fish and pine nuts, and then the one everyone else eats, with all the scraps and the green parts of the cabbage? Well, my eomoni put some of the good stuff in a little jar and wrapped it up for me. . . . Yes, it is relevant, it's why Chun-sik and I became friends; I want to talk you through it step by step, so just a little patience, please.

So I took the kimchi to Hanazaki-sensei, but I couldn't honestly believe that an ilbon saram could really eat such spicy food. At lunch, the teachers went back to their lodgings to eat. I snuck under the wire fence and looked through a hole in the wooden fence around the dormitory. You know what I mean, right, a knot in the board? I pressed my eye to a hole about the size of a five-sen coin, and then I saw Hanazaki-sensei pouring some hot water into a teacup, washing the kimchi, and then eating it. I knew he wouldn't be able to handle the spicy stuff! I managed to hold my laughter in, but then a week later, when he passed me in the hallway, Hanazaki-sensei said, "Hey, Nishihara, I'm out of kimchi, bring me some tomorrow." So then I went home and talked to Eomoni, and she said, "A little kimchi's a small price to pay for you not getting hit," so I started taking it to Hanazaki-sensei every Monday. So each time I went to peep through the fence at lunch, and sure enough he was washing the kimchi. But then, the third week, he quit; he just put the kimchi in his mouth and ate it. Well, I was impressed. That was the first time I respected the man. . . . Yes, I'm almost done, Chun-sik's about to appear.

This was during the war, so there'd be food substitution days, if you remember those. Due to all the shortages, in order to save white rice, we'd have flour or bread or potatoes for lunch instead. On substitution days, the teachers would eat in the classroom with us too. Hanazaki-sensei's wife was called Kazue. So Kazue-san would sneak up before lunch and put his lunch on the windowsill at the very back of the classroom. And nobody saw her. We'd always sneak looks at the back during class, but unfortunately, there were never any witnesses. Hanazaki-sensei's substitute meals were mostly sweet pastries. And I know they were, because Kazue-san would always leave one wrapped up for me too. All the other kids were jealous, but thanks to the kimchi, nobody said a word about it. This is when Chun-sik, known at the time as Kunimoto Ukon, comes in. I told him, "Hey, this is good. You want half?" . . . Yes, I always ate it in the classroom, because if I tried to eke it out it would go bad. . . . I mean, it was given to me, so it was up to me, you know, I could eat it all myself or I could split it with my best friend. . . . I said, "best friend" . . . Yes, in those days, we were best friends. I'm sure he would've said the same.

Neither of us were good at studying . . . we weren't at the bottom of the class, but somewhere in the middle. So what did we do? Sports. Chun-sik spent all his time outside of school running on the embankment of the Miryang River or going to the boxing gym in Ne-il-dong, and I did anything you could call exercise. Soccer, baseball, swimming, judo, kendo, sumo; in those days, sports wouldn't get you anything, so my parents didn't encourage me to do them, and in fact, when they found out I was so passionate about sports, they desperately tried to stop me. So we both kind of stood out.

I don't mean to brag, but even though Miryang is a very small city, it has four boxing gyms. Miryangers always rank high in every event at the South Gyeongsang Tournament. Miryang's not just sweetfish, Yeongnamnu,

Samyeongdang, Arang, and Miryang Arirang; it's also known for sports and fighting. And, of course, the Kunimoto brothers were at the very forefront of that. One time, I was asked to box someone . . . it was Chun-sik who asked . . . this was seven years ago, when we were fifteen or sixteen. He met me on the riverbank and taught me the basic stance and how to throw a few punches. Two months later, he told me, "All right, you've improved a lot, so come to the boxing club and let's fight," so we ran there side by side, to the boxing gym in Ne-il-dong. It was the first time I put on gloves, so then suddenly I'm up in the ring and we're facing each other, and then *bang*, he punched me hard. And he's saying, I've stopped, I've stopped, look, I stopped. He'd hit me in the nose and tears were just streaming down my face. I remember thinking that boxing is inhuman. But Chun-sik wouldn't let me leave the ring early. You know how when you're running and dodging around, your legs go out, right? Well, he said, look, if you do that you'll lose. I took off my gloves and ran away from the gym.

Now, I'm confident when it comes to fighting. You don't need any skill. Boxing, judo, kendo, whatever it is, they all have a certain form you've got to follow, don't they? But fights don't. Head! Hand! Foot! Teeth! If you're not an all-rounder, you can't win a fight. But the thing is, Chun-sik was absurdly good at both boxing and fighting. He was tall, about five shaku and nine sun, around five foot nine, and he had muscles all over like armor, and he was famous not just in Miryang but here in Busan too. As a track athlete first, second for fighting, and the final thing he was famous for, I'll tell you about now.

It happened when we were twenty-one. Chun-sik transferred from Cho-yang Commercial High School to what's now known as Gyeongnam First Commercial High School, and I went to Miryang Agricultural School. So I hadn't seen him since we were seventeen when we graduated from Miryang Secondary School. His sister, dad, and mom had all died, and his brother was now the head of the household, but you know, he was quite the philanderer, and his wife left him, leaving their two daughters behind, and the woman who had been his mistress moved in, so with all of that, Chun-sik moved in with some of their relatives on their mother's side, but then, probably because he couldn't handle the mess of living off someone else, I heard that he'd moved into the dormitories at his school.

I saw him on a sports field in Busan for the first time in four years. It was a friendly match between my school and his . . . But a fight broke out. It was during the final for the 800-meter relay. You know how they shout, on your marks, get set, go? One of the guys from my school, his elbow hit one of the guys from Gyeongnam and the guy stumbled. Their pep group rushed over and got in the face of our guy, shouting, "I saekki! Deombyeobwa!" and trying to hit him.

At my school I was always the one most confident in a fight, so I turned to them and said, "Hey, what are you doing, it's the middle of the match, aren't you guys ashamed, aren't you embarrassed?" My school only had our team there, about twenty people, but those guys were locals, and they had hundreds of kids there cheering for them, maybe a thousand . . . They were screeching at us like a flock of crows.

Then who do I see running full tilt from the other side of the field but Chun-sik? "Ya, geuman hae! Geu nyeoseok nae chinguya!" *Hey, stop it! That's my friend!* They all swarmed back to their spectator seats. If he'd said jump, they would've said how high. "Hey, Cho," he said, "Busan's not Miryang, if you do shit like that in Busan they'll jump you and kill you. . . ." Chun-sik kept talking, but the drum and flute corps were beating their drums right next to us . . . Ratatata dum dum ratatata dum dum ratatata . . . I don't know how to put it, but at that time I felt something quite different from nostalgia. Chun-sik is extraordinarily tall, right, and I'm shorter than average, so I had to look up at him. My neck was craned and my throat was twitching like a lizard's. . . . I could barely see . . . the sun was behind Chun-sik, right . . . his face looked dark . . . all the tension had dissipated at once, I felt light-headed and stumbled. . . . He caught my arm. . . . I shook him off . . . and turned my back to the sun.

Then five months later, I think it was, I moved from Miryang Agricultural School to Busan Second Commercial High . . . Why? Because of soccer—I was good at soccer and they recruited me . . . That's right . . . Then, as you all know, I joined the Korean Youth Organization. I was known for my fighting, so one of the older guys, Park, who was the group leader, came to me and bowed and said that they needed me, and that I would be his right-hand man. Park was in the grade above me at Miryang Agricultural School, I couldn't say no ... That's right ... the chief inspector ... his job was to train young people who would work for the sake of our liberated homeland. Park told me that Chun-sik was a leader of a local branch of the Democratic Patriotic Youth League. I was totally ignorant about politics, but I was aware of the Workers' Party of South Korea. They're a communist organization, all reds, ppalgaengi, commies, you know. So, the chair of the Youth League was Go Chan-bo, the head of the Workers' Party of South Korea's youth division. ... That's right ... they're all tied together ... they say there's 780,000 members nationwide. ... The moment I heard that Chun-sik was the leader of the local Youth League, my blood boiled. Park showed me one of their flyers ... Yes ... yes ... that's the one ...

1. We will unite all democratic, patriotic youths and join forces to build democratic independence.
2. We will dedicate ourselves to purge all remnants of Japanese imperialism and feudalism in Korea.
3. We will devote ourselves to the political, cultural, and economic interests of the youth.
4. We will actively participate in the reconstruction of Korea by adhering to the declaration of the Moscow Conference.
5. We will work closely with young people across the globe to establish permanent peace.
6. We will especially strive to refine our minds and bodies, discover the truth, revive national culture, disseminate and encourage scientific knowledge, and eradicate illiteracy.

That's right ... this is all pie-in-the-sky stuff, or most of it, the ppalgaengi treat the laws of the Communist Party and the Soviet Union as absolute, they won't allow any kind of criticism or dissent, and anyone who disobeys is purged immediately, right? They're worse than the Spanish inquisition. Or I guess you might say, they want to shackle all the people of the world under one way of thinking, so in a sense they're no different than the Japanese imperialists that colonized Korea and China ... That's right ... I'll get back to the story now . . . Since Busan Commercial High and Gyeongnam High are on opposite sides of the city, I didn't run into Chun-sik again.

The next time I saw him was this year. Near Busan station . . . in Yongdu-dong . . . There's an alley, you know . . . do you know the one I'm talking about? . . . I guess you're right, there are a lot of alleys . . . Hmm, well, it's about ten meters long and it goes out on the main street . . . Well, I called it an alley, but it's fairly wide, enough for cars to pass . . . if you need, I can show you later.

It was raining, and Chun-sik was surrounded by five or six students. Probably from the National Student Federation. At the time . . . I thought I'd go back him up, I didn't really think much . . . No, I'm not a sympathizer . . . I think the ppalgaengi should be crushed until there's none left . . . but . . . Yes, that's right, he's my childhood friend, the pal I shared my snacks with . . . I put down my umbrella and gripped it like a bat and I rushed over in the rain. Meomchwo, geu nyeoseok, nae chinguya! Stop, you bastards, that's my friend! I ran to help Chun-sik. But as soon as I got next to him, I got pushed away. . . . No, not at all, I'm not saying he hates me, absolutely not, Chun-sik's not the kind of man who hates people . . . if he ever considers you his friend, then even if you betray him, he won't lose faith in you . . . He's a man among men . . . The moment our eyes met, I knew what was in his heart . . . It's too dangerous, don't get involved! It's my fight, nothing to do with you, god forbid if the National Student Federation guys remember your face! Domangchyeora! Ppalli! So I ran away . . . I hid behind a telephone pole . . . If I told you I hid there because I was worried, it'd be a lie . . . I wanted to watch . . . to see how he fought against five men . . . if he really was as strong as an ox, like people said. I wanted to see it with my own eyes . . . What a fight it was. He had his back up against the wall like this, you know, I'm sure he must've done taekwondo too, his footwork was wonderful . . . So then the number one runner in all of South Gyeongsang ran away . . . It was a real downpour, but he was faster than the rain . . . His dad sure gave him the right name, Woo-gun, rain and roots, hahaha, hahaha, oh, how I laughed . . . But it's kind of pathetic, isn't it . . . standing there behind a telephone pole getting soaked like a dishrag . . . I stood there laughing and getting wetter, grappling with the defeat that I felt knowing that I'd never be able to beat him as long as I lived.

I know Lee Woo-gun's reputation precedes him; he's already a legend, or a hero. A lot of guys are good at fighting, a lot of guys are fast runners, and there's even a lot of leaders in the Democratic Patriotic Youth League. But you could search the whole country, from Mount Paektu to Mount Halla, for another man who's all three and never find another Lee Woo-gun. Besides, he's tall, and he's handsome enough to turn the head of passersby, even the men. He's kind, and upstanding, and trustworthy. But he doesn't chase women; I've never even heard a rumor about him sleeping around . . . Can you believe it? That that kind of man actually exists? . . . yes . . . it's true . . . And he's my best friend . . . Can you understand what that's like? The pain of having a man like that as your best friend?

Oh, yeah, I should tell you where the name Chun-sik comes from. It's not just a pseudonym. See, his brother Lee Woo-cheol thought up the name Chun-sik before he was born. They decided to use the name his abeoji came up with, Woo-gun, instead, but then the waenom made us all take Japanese names, right, so they changed Lee to Kunimoto and . . . Yeah, and so on. He wanted to break away from the Japanese family registry system, so he started going by the name Lee Chun-sik instead of Kunimoto Ukon. In the spring seeds are sown, sprout, shoot up, and eventually become big trees—Chun-sik once told me, it's a name that embodies the hope that through a communist revolution, once the ruling classes have been defeated and the people have been freed from all exploitation, oppression, and class discrimination, and the class struggle is over and we gain true peace, we can all meet again under that tree. . . . Yes, I'm sure he said the words *communist revolution* . . . He's been a communist since he was eighteen, when he started calling himself Chun-sik . . . Me? Jeoldae anida! No way! Can I have another glass of water, please? . . . gamsahamnida . . . aigu, my throat's so dry . . . another . . . ah, siwonhada . . . the ppalgaengi are ants . . . they should all be crushed . . . No, he's not my best friend anymore . . . he's my enemy . . . Lee Woo-gun is my enemy.

I saw it with my own eyes. Lee Woo-gun had gathered students from Gyeongnam High in a vacant lot in Seodaesin-dong and he was getting them all riled up. He shouted, in a clear and unwavering voice: **Oppose the UN Commission on Korea for implementing their plan to divide and invade Korea! Defeat the pro-Japanese reactionaries and minions of international** imperialism, Rhee Syngman and Kim Seong-gu! Oppose the establishment of a united South Korean government! Hand over administration to the People's Committees! The students chanted: Long live the Democratic People's Republic of Korea! One student ran up and said, gyeongchari onda, domangchyeo, run, the police are coming, and Chun-sik spread his arms like a swan and jumped off the platform . . . He started running . . . One of the students started clapping, and all of a sudden they all applauded . . . It was quite the run . . . He was running away from the police, but he looked as confident as if he were the one chasing them . . . He seemed to glow . . . All the applauding students must've thought they would all bring about a communist revolution with him. Chun-sik is their light. He's got more influence over the students in Busan than Lee Seung-yuop and Kim Sang-ryong, the guys who organized the February first general strike . . . Yes . . . I suppose you're right, arresting him wouldn't be enough . . . He should be killed.

My name is Kim Yeon-tae, a.k.a. Gyeong-am, born June 12, 1927; my official residence is Gyo-dong, Miryang. . . . Yes, I'm the eldest son. . . . That's incorrect . . . No, that's wrong, I'm not an activist for the Democratic Patriotic Youth League. . . . No, I just picked up some flyers from the ground . . . Animnida, I put them in my pocket thinking that I'd notify the police, a whole bundle of them had fallen so I picked them all up, wouldn't it have been awful if the wind had scattered them? I've never handed out a leaflet in my life . . . If someone really saw me handing out leaflets, then bring him here. Let him take a good look at me; he'll know in an instant that he's got the wrong man.

I'm on the Gyeongnam Commercial High track-and-field team. From dawn to dusk I do sit-ups, push-ups, squat jumps; I sleep, eat, even bathe for as little time as I can. I put all my energy into studying and sports. If I had the time to get involved with politics, I'd use it to do sit-ups . . . Lying? How am I lying? Ever since I can remember, my abeoji and halbi and jeungjohalbac always told me that if I ever lied, I'd be in awful trouble, because any man who starts off as a liar soon turns into a thief. And even if I might lie, my legs don't. Hold on a second, let me take off my socks and show you . . . No, no, this is important, so I want all of you to see ... May I put my legs up on the desk so everyone can see? ... Kamsa hamnida ... Sorry, would you ... There, take a look, now aren't these the legs of a genuine high jumper? I'm aiming for the Helsinki Olympics in four years' time. I was the clear winner at the Gyeong-nam qualifying tournament in Busan, and I'm proud of my record of 1m 88cm; you know, it's unrivaled nationwide. My dream is to defeat those bastards who stand on the Olympic podium with the Japanese flag on their chest, make the Taegukgi fly above them all, and let people all over the world know that the Republic of Korea exists ... Of course I don't neglect my studies, though. My other dream is to become a bank manager and revive our nation's economy. Let me show you my hands, see that callus? That's where my pen rests. You can hardly call that a callus, right, it's more like a barnacle, like on the bottom of a ship! ... What? Who said that? Ha, don't make me laugh! Me, on the organiz-ing committee of the Democratic Patriotic Youth League? Hahaha! Ahh! Ahhhhhhhhh! Aigu, aya, aiguuuuu, ayaaaa, ah, hah, hah, hah, I'll talk, I'll talk, just stop, not my legs ... Not my legs, anything else ... I'm begging ... Who told you that? ... No! Ahh, stop! I told you I'll talk! Ahhhhhh! Aigu, aigu. ... Ayaaaa. ... No, no ... I ... I was elected to the committee ... a week ago ... I only know five of the leaders so ... there must be a spy in the leader-ship, aigu, geunyang duna bwara!

Kim Won-bong? Of course I know who he is. He's a hero to everyone from Miryang, no, to all Koreans, isn't he? He fought the Japanese empire for thirty years, from age eighteen to forty-eight, fighting for our independence without concern for the danger his own life was in. Even Kim Gu, the president of the Provisional Government of the Republic of Korea, acknowledged that, and in 1942 he was appointed deputy commander of the Korean Liberation Army; he was on the list of cabinet members of the People's Republic of Korea, de-clared as established in 1945, right there with President Rhee Syngman, Vice President Lyuh Woon-hyung, Prime Minister Ho Hon, Director of Home Affairs Kim Gu, and Director of Foreign Affairs Kim Kyu-sik, as director of military affairs and state, wasn't he?

1. We intend to build a state that is completely politically and economically independent.

2. We are committed to destroying all remnants of Japanese imperialism and feudalism and building a genuine democracy that can fulfill the basic political, economic, and social needs of the entire nation.
3. We will work for the rapid improvement of the lives of workers, farmers, and the rest of the masses.
4. As one of the world's democratic countries, we aim to secure world peace through mutual cooperation with our fellows.

Had the People's Republic of Korea been founded, none of this would've happened . . . Lyuh Woon-hyung being assassinated, Kim Won-bong being arrested on suspicion of leading a strike, the attacks on his family's home in Miryang and the Busan branch of the People's Republic Party . . . Of course I know, everyone in the Democratic Patriotic Youth League knows . . . that in April this year . . . Kim Won-bong went to Pyongyang with Kim Gu and Kim Kyu-sik as representatives of the Korean People's Republic Party for the North-South unification talk, he chaired the meeting, and then he stayed in the north . . .

"Little Moscow" . . . I know that some people call Miryang that . . . after all, the Heroic Corps were full of people from Miryang . . . on February 27, two years ago, when General Kim Won-bong returned triumphantly to Miryang, people from all across the city gathered at Miryang First National School to hear him speak; they all cried. I was eighteen at the time. There were so many people there I couldn't get into the school grounds. I climbed one of the cherry trees near the school gates, and when I saw Kim Won-bong, just a speck from where I was, I was so emotional that I started to shake. When he finished his speech, the crowd, tens of thousands strong, threw their arms in the air and chanted: Long live Kim Won-bong! Long live Kim Won-bong! The next morning at school, Mr. Park wrote the speech out on the blackboard; even now I can recite it . . . "Mount Jongnam hasn't changed. Nor has the Namcheong River. But so many comrades have died, and the young men who risked their lives for independence now have gray hair. What hasn't changed is the masses of people wearing rags, walking barefoot, hungry and exploited. . . ."

Are 70 percent of people from Miryang ppalgaengi? You think so? If you say it's 70 percent, then excluding newborn babies and old folks on their deathbeds, it'd be 100 percent, right? Have you gone around asking people one by one? Or do people just inform on each other? That's what I thought. Nobody says it out loud now because if they do, they'll end up here like me, but in their heart of hearts any born and bred Miryanger is constantly shouting: "Long live Kim Won-bong!"

"The Little Kremlin" . . . hahaha, I'm from Little Moscow, I went to school at the Little Kremlin, so if I wasn't a little bit red you'd have to wonder what went wrong, you know? But the only people who call Gyeongnam High "the Little Kremlin" are you inspector guys and your lapdogs in the National Student Federation. Be our lapdog and take the money, and then you can get a job in the police or at a bank, so be a good little doggy and forget about having any ideas or pride or will of your own! Oh! Ohhhh, ohhhh, aigo, oh! Wh-wh—, aigu, aigo, please! But that's . . . surely. . . . something you'd know more about . . . than me . . . the principal got taken in for questioning dozens of times . . . and a few of the teachers too . . . aigu, aya! Aiguuuuu . . . I don't know about the lower grades, but if you put the three upper grades together there's probably a hundred people . . . Names? I don't know . . . It's true . . . We never all get together . . . because if someone informed, then we'd all be arrested at once . . . It's the same for you guys, the only people you're in contact with are your leaders, whose names and faces you know well . . .

Books I've read? . . . Oh, you mean books that have had an ideological influence on me . . . *The Manifesto of the Communist Party, Das Kapital* . . . oh, and Feuerbach's *Spiritualism and Materialism*, for instance . . . All in Japanese, I'm much faster at reading in Japanese, and I haven't seen anything translated into Korean . . . no, I bought them . . . a guy who had been an exchange student at the University of Tokyo and came home after liberation sold me all his books . . . Where? Behind the US Army Market in Nampo-dong . . . I just happened to pass by, so I don't know . . . it just looked like a normal house . . . Well, I'd say about three hundred, no, four hundred volumes . . . Sure, I can show you where it was, but it's not there anymore . . . I swear! Ugh. . . . oh, ohh-hhh, you don't have to hit me, I'll talk . . . Aigu, aya, I'll talk, I'll talk, I'll tell you anything you want, just . . . But I swear, it's not there . . . Maybe two months ago? Someone told me, so I don't know whether it's true or not, but the rumor is the whole family moved to Japan . . . Their names? When you guys buy books do you go around asking everyone their names? . . . What did we talk about? . . . That sounds about right . . . It cost, oh, twelve yen, or thereabouts . . . Agent provocateur? A bookshop for agent provocateurs? . . . It wasn't a safe house . . . But if I did start lying now what would happen . . . you pull out my nails, break my fingers, my arms, but I doubt you'd let it end there . . . I'm resigned to what's next . . . I don't have the books anymore . . . Feel free to go and search . . . there's no locks in our dormitory. Anyone can come in and take whatever books they want to read . . . Hahaha, because it's the Little Kremlin, of course . . . Any words I memorized? . . . Why would I need to do that? . . . Ahhhhhhhhhhh . . . I'll talk, ah, ah-ah, gah, gahhh, gahhhhhh . . . words . . . words . . . **In proportion as the exploitation of one individual by another will also be put an end to, the exploitation of one nation by another will also be put an end to. In proportion as the antagonism between classes within the nation vanishes, the hostility of one nation to another will come to an end. . . . The workingmen have no country. We cannot take from them what they have not got. . . . If the proletariat during its contest with the bourgeoisie is compelled, by the force of circumstances, to organize itself as a class, if, by means of a revolution, it makes itself the ruling class, and, as such, sweeps away by force the old conditions of production, then it will, along with these conditions, have swept away the conditions for the existence of class antagonisms and of classes generally, and will thereby have abolished its own supremacy as a class. . . .**

My copy of *The Manifesto of the Communist Party* has a two-color cover . . . red . . . and blue . . . wait, maybe it was green . . . ah, aigu, jollyeo . . . I haven't slept a wink since yesterday morning . . . could I please sleep just a little? . . . Chaga! Ah, ahhhh, aiguuuuuu . . . Ahhhh, aigo! . . . Lee Woo-gun? . . . Right . . . Yes . . . you want to know about Lee Chun-sik . . . yes, that's the same person . . . He's from Miryang, on the track-and-field team at Gyeongsam High. . . . I'm in room 205 on the second floor, and Lee Chun-sik is in 102 on the first floor . . . No, there's no rent exactly. You just have to bring some rice from home instead . . . about sixty pounds . . . But Lee Chun-sik's the only one with a special exemption . . . of course it's down to the discretion of the principal, Kim Jae-geun; his family's in the polished rice business, after all, as I'm sure you must know? It's in Gupo, you know, the big . . . Well, that's because he's Lee Chun-sik! He's the only one in the dorms who's exempt from the rice thing . . . Obviously it's because he's a great runner! No doubt he'll make it to the Olympics in the 800- and 1500-meter races. And his mind's quick too. He says he barely studies, but he's always at the top of all his classes. Dongguk University and Kangnung College of Education both invited him to go there when he graduates, or so I heard. He's the pride of Gyeongsam High, or maybe hero is more like it . . . guys like me, we're so afraid we can't hardly speak to him . . . Yes, that's right! It's not just that he's strong, it's that there's nobody in Busan who can beat him. His finishing move is the flying dropkick. That's why he always stands with his back to the wall. Even if you're facing down a big crowd, if you have your back to the wall, then nobody can come at you from behind or the side, right? When they get close, he plants his right foot, and while he's kicking with his left he jumps with his right, and while he's in the air he hits you with his left, bam! Then, while he brings back his left foot, he hits you with his right with the force of the jump, bam! Then, when he's scattered his opponents, he runs away on those quick legs of his! To make a long story shorter, nobody's a match for him, so nobody steps up against him. . . . Enemies? What do you . . . Sure, I have a lot . . . If I had to give an example? The bastards from the National Student Federation.

I'm two years younger than Lee Chun-sik. I passed by him every day on my way to Miryang Middle School. Every time I saw him he was running. Have you ever seen him running? He makes it look so good that even a man like me has to blush. To be honest with you, I admired him so much I started running by the Miryang River too, and I joined the Gyeongnam High track team because I wanted to run with him. . . . Yes, I joined the Democratic Patriotic Youth because of him, too. . . . I heard him speak at a vacant lot in Seodaesin-dong. . . . Suddenly I realized we all were shouting together.

Long live the Democratic People's Republic of Korea!

I had chills. I really saw then that this was what devotion meant. That very day I joined the Korean Patriotic Youth Alliance. Then I borrowed a mimeograph of *The Manifesto of the Communist Party* and I read it that night in bed . . . five times . . . by the fifth time I could say it without missing a word. **The Communists disdain to conceal their views and aims. They openly** declare that their ends can be attained only by the forcible overthrow of all existing social conditions. Let the ruling classes tremble at a Communistic revolution. The proletarians have nothing to lose but their chains. They have a world to win. Workers of the World, Unite! I laid the last page on top of my pillow and stood up. I got changed into my track uniform. . . . It's a red running shirt with white horizontal stripes and black shorts with white vertical stripes. . . . I ran around the dorm. There were still a few stars in the sky here and there. I jumped at the wall and jumped over it. . . . It's about two meters tall. . . . Right, so here's the school gate, and then there's Gudeok Athletics Ground and then the school building's there, right? There's a wall here, and our dorm is on the other side of that wall. Originally you'd have to go out and then go around like this, but it's such a detour that everyone just started jumping the wall . . . A map? You must know what I'm talking about, right? . . . Sure, I'll draw you one . . . Aya! Aigu, my fingers . . . I can't hold the pen . . . Sure, I'll try using my left hand . . . So once you're over the wall, on your right is the baseball field, and on your left is the pool. If you go through the wheat field, there's a mountain—well, "mountain" is a slight exaggeration, it's a hill— anyway, there's a hill, and at the top of the hill there's a reservoir . . . this is my wrong hand so my lines are shaky and I can't draw too well . . . Does that help you understand? . . . Now, where was I? . . . Oh, yeah, I'd just stayed up all night reading *The Manifesto of the Communist Party* and then I jumped over the wall. . . . I started running. . . . The sun hadn't come up yet, but I could see the white lines for the 200 meter perfectly. I sprinted as hard as I could. One loop, then another . . . I quit counting after the tenth one. I just intently recited the last three lines. **The proletarians have nothing to lose but their chains. They have a world to win.** I shook off my own chains and reached the finish line. The dawn had come. My eyes were now open. I was one of the proletariat.

Workers of the World, Unite!

About Lee Chun-sik, you mean? . . . But I've only seen him twice this year . . . the first was in spring . . . I can't recall the date, but the forsythias were in bloom so I think it must've been the end of March . . . I was at the track, running, when I heard someone shout, "Hey, Gyeong-am!" I looked over and saw Chun-sik there. With his peculiar smile. . . . It's a bashful smile, with his lips slightly twisted. . . . He was running pretty fast, but he had a knapsack on his right shoulder, and he was kind of slouching like this and humming as he ran alongside me. . . . It was that song, the one girls sing while they're jumping rope . . . You know . . . Oh, I can't remember what it's called . . . **ame, ame fure, fure, kaa-san ga, janome de omukai, ureshii na, pitch, pitch, chap, chap, run, run, run . . .**

Yes, that's right, neither Chun-sik or Gyeong-am are our real names. Obviously, the idea is that if we carelessly use each other's real names, we're giving away information to the enemy, but more important, the idea is also to embody the concept that while in a bourgeois society the past rules the present, in a communist society the present rules the past, so first we must leave the family system of the past to be reborn as part of the proletariat.

The second time? Oh, the second was . . . a month, no, two weeks ago . . . it's behind Bupyeong-dong Market, I think, there's a store selling American stuff that they get from the US Army . . . I was just about to go in to buy some cheese, when I ran into him. . . . He looked pretty shabby that day. . . . He needed a haircut and a shave bad, and he didn't have a cent on him. . . . What was he wearing? He had on a white exercise shirt and black school uniform trousers. . . . That's the only time I've ever seen him look like that. . . . His cheeks were so hollow I asked him, "What are you eating?" He smiled vacantly and said, "Whatever I can get my hands on." I told him to wait for me and went into the store; I bought a can of butter and a can of cheese. "Want one? This one is butter, and this one is cheese," I told him, and he picked the butter. . . . No, it was really nothing. The shop owner lent him a can opener and he ate it with his fingers. . . . Maldo andwae! You wouldn't say that if you knew Lee Chun-sik! He's not the kind to beg for food. . . . But he's the type of man that everyone wants to do something for . . . if only to see that embarrassed-looking smile . . . We sat down on a bench and ate butter and cheese. . . . The sun was setting. . . . The sound of cicadas was coming from somewhere above us . . . *sseureuram sseureuram sseureuram sseureuram* . . . There was nothing in front of us but a road, which was getting darker, but somehow, I felt like we were sitting on a rock looking out at the Miryang River. . . . I knew it would make us both homesick, so I didn't say that. . . . Neither of us have been back home for years. . . . The station's crawling with cops and if they spotted him and arrested him on a train, then not even Lee Chun-sik would be able to get away. . . . He'd never go home by train. . . . It'd be quicker to run back. . . . Miryang's about ninety ri from Busan, right? . . . What we talked about that night? "It's very nutritious." "Masitda." That was about it. . . . I said it was very nutritious, and he said it tasted good. . . . A code? Hahahaha, what else could "nutritious" mean? Ha, no, I meant exactly what I said. . . . We were hungry. Because we're agent provocateurs, right? . . . He's not in the dorm right now . . . until last year he moved from dorm to dorm, sleeping in a new room every night, but the police are keeping a close eye on the dorms, so it's too dangerous for him to sleep there . . . you never know where and when Lee Chun-sik's going to appear . . . I can't contact him. . . . Me, his go-between? Who told you that? My legs! No! Not my legs! Aagggghaaaaaa! Aigu, ooh-waaaaa! . . . Oh, oh . . . oooohhh . . . I'm his go-between . . . Next Saturday afternoon . . . the dining room in the dorm . . . ooohhh. . . . Thirty, forty people . . . Lee Chun-sik too . . . before that we were going to run . . . oooohhh . . . In the morning . . . At the track . . . Aigu, aigu, naega museun jiseul! I deoreoun palja!

I don't want to live anymore. I've sold him out; I can't go on living. Please, kill me. I can't show my face to the world any longer. Do it now—kill me right here and now. But . . . I have one final request. Please don't hurt my family back in Miryang. My little brother and sister . . . they don't even know the first thing about Marx. . . . I don't want them to know that I'm dead either . . . oh, I spit on my own name, ooooh, aiguuuuuu . . . Don't tell anyone my name . . . Please . . . Kamsa hamnida . . . Please, kill me quick. I can't forgive myself . . . I'd kill myself with my bare hands if I could . . . I don't want to live a second longer . . . please . . . please . . . oooooooh . . . Aigoooooooooo . . .

TWENTY-SEVEN

Rain, Rain, Fall, Fall

| 아메 아메 후레 후레 | アメアメ、フレフレ |

The young shooter quickly undid the snap on his shoulder holster and took out his Smith & Wesson Military & Police before his body trembled with excitement. He cocked the hammer and heard the clink of the cylinder rotating. Gripping the revolver, he extended his arm, locked eyes on the target, then lined his gaze up with the front and rear sights. He's running . . . and fast too . . . nothing I can do but take aim when he comes this way . . . he's coming, coming, coming . . . watda! . . . he's fast! Aigu, he got past me! . . . Jegiral! . . . Hey, quit shaking . . . he's just one little commie . . . heart, slow down! Gwaenchana, gwaenchanayo . . . **Yea, though I walk through the valley of the shadow of death, I will fear no evil: for thou art with me** . . . breathe deep . . . in . . . out . . . commie bastard. . . . In . . . Commie bastard . . . commie bastard . . . commie bastard . . . in . . . out . . . my arm's stopped shaking . . . I can't hear my heartbeat anymore. The young shooter, his arm and gun as one, set his sights on the target. If he comes this way, he's still fifty meters away. Aim fifty centimeters above his head, no, I can't risk hitting his heart. The commander's orders were to take him alive. Aim for his face and hit him in the legs. Dwaetda! The young shooter put his finger on the trigger. Bang! A bullet and flash flew out of the muzzle. The muzzle recoiled from the impact as if a hard ball had been thrown at it; the young shooter relaxed his wrist and absorbed the impact.

Missed!

The target turned around.

The young shooter breathed in the stench of the white smoke, tightened his grasp on the hot barrel, set his sights on the target's face, and pulled the revolver's trigger.

Bang!

He's running!

Aigu, I missed again!

"It's the cops! Run!"

The hundred or so students exercising all started to scatter; the four-man police squad grabbed their revolvers and chased their target.

"Don't lose him!"

The target got smaller before his eyes; the young shooter gasped for air. Hah-hah, fucking reds! Hah-hah-hah-hah, you goddamn commies! Aigu, he's getting away, hah-hah, aigo, jegiral! Ahead of where the target was running there was a wall, about two meters high. Got you now! You're trapped! The target took a spectacular leap and planted both hands on the wall. Now! The shooter cocked the hammer and extended his arm horizontally. He looked. The leg. He shot. Bang!

The young shooter and his fellow police officers ran toward the wall. Blood was splattered across the surface. I got him! Majasseo! It was me! I took him down! Hey, look! They turned around to see the entirety of Gudeok Athletics Ground now empty. Just a few moments before, a hundred-some-odd students had been there, running and jumping, and now they were all gone without a trace. An officer wearing the same white shirt and khaki trousers as the young shooter tried to scale the bloodstained wall but couldn't. "Ei, jegiral!" the others jeered, and ran off toward the school gates. The young shooter put his M&P back in his leather holster carefully so as not to get burned by the barrel, then retreated, his eyes still on the bloodstain on the wall, until he was about ten meters back; he started a run-up and when he reached the place where the target had jumped, he jumped too. He grabbed the wall with both hands, like he was doing a pull-up, got his right foot, then his left foot up, and looked over the other side of the wall.

Eopseo!

Domangchyeonna? *Did he get away?*

Seolma!

The young shooter jumped down. The summer grasses at the base of the wall were crushed in the shape of a person, and the commie's filthy red blood clung to the deep green of the cocklebur and white flowers of the Chinese peonies. The young man, trampling the blood with his military boots, suddenly felt a rumbling in his stomach as if he had just drank makgeolli on an empty stomach, along with nausea and chills, and for a few seconds all he could do was stare at his own two trembling hands. The weight of the August light burned his neck and baked the inside of his skull. **Yea, though I walk through the valley of the shadow of death, I will fear no evil: for thou art with me.** A grasshopper jumped out of the bloodied cocklebur, *chirurururup chirurururup*, and the young man, realizing that he had an erection, lifted his heavy head. Where is he? Where'd he go? He couldn't have run away that fast. Into the dorm? No, no, the blood, the trail of blood is heading toward the pool. He blew his whistle twice and heard the sound of hooves clattering toward him. He's mine. Nobody else touch him, I took him down, I'm going to finish the job. The young shooter took his M&P out of its holster and slid the cylinder out to see how many bullets were left. He knew he'd only taken three shots, but all six chambers were empty. He turned the revolver slightly upward and pushed the center of the cylinder with a stick; the shell casings fell onto the grass. He slid out the cylinder and pushed in hana, dul, set, net, daseot, yeoseot, six new bullets with his thumb. Frowning in the path of the sun, which seemed to have spilled all its light on him, he shoved his sweat-dampened police cap down the back of his trousers and looked at the water in the pool on the other side of the green fence. On a hot day like today it'd sure feel a lot better to swim in the pool than shoot somebody . . . Swimming . . . Songdo Beach is only about forty minutes' walk from here, with its beautiful pine trees, but I don't have that kind of time, and I don't really feel like it either. And anyway, swimming in a pool is for these good-for-nothings at Gyeongsam High, the kind of guys who'll still be living off their parents when they're in their twenties, ha, just what you'd expect from the distinguished gentlemen from the Little Kremlin.

The young shooter raced through the wheat field. A flicker ran through his mind, like a mirage, and his head and upper body began to waver. Where the hell did he go? Did it not hit him? Just grazed him? Seolma? He lost too much blood for it to have just grazed him, I hit him, I know I did. So where the fuck is he! I'm five meters from the wall over there now. Where did I get him? The hip? The butt? Leg? Wherever I hit him, he shouldn't be able to run this far. Maybe he's holed up in a house somewhere?

At the strategy meeting the day before, they showed us a map that said if he climbed the hill on the other side of the wheat field there was a reservoir, but this is no reservoir, it's a damn swamp. In the huge shadow of a cedar tree, he saw a black-and-white and flesh-colored mass tumbling. The heat and nervousness blurred the colors and shapes, and for a moment he had no idea what he was approaching, but then: a red running shirt with white horizontal stripes and black trousers with white vertical stripes . . . the uniform of Gyeongsam High's track team . . . one step away from the swamp . . . maybe he was going to jump in and kill himself . . . The young shooter's legs folded beneath him. He put his ear to the man's heart as if he were going to rest his head on his chest and heard: *thu-thump . . . thu-thump . . . thu-thump . . . thu-thump . . .* **Yea, though I walk through the valley of the shadow of death, I will fear no evil: for thou art with me . . .** The shooter brought his face up and looked at the target's. The target's face was not distorted with pain, but his lips grimaced as if waiting for pain's cue, as proof that he had not yet been released from its promise. The shooter felt his body embraced by the heat of the August sun; he could feel the beating of his own heart more strongly and loudly than the target's.

The shooter shouted the target's name.

Lee Woo-gun!

The beautiful light of mid-August illuminated without hesitation the trees and houses and roads. The sun hung a little farther west in the sky than at high noon, the blue of the sky was just a little clouded, and the heat too felt somewhat subdued. A cattle truck crossed the road and suddenly came to a stop; there was a boy wearing a broad-brimmed straw hat with a large, iron box hanging from his neck passing quite close by the side of the truck, yelling, "Ice cream! Get your ice cream!" and from the other side of the narrow lane came a boy, about three years old, pedaling on a rusty tricycle. Just as we heard the creak-creaking noise, a cow went across the road. The impact of the sudden movement collided our bodies together, and moans escaped from all thirty of our gagged mouths. All of us were in some kind of pain. Eyelids swollen and purpled from too many beatings, mouths whose teeth had been pulled and were full of blood, ears that had been amputated and now were just holes, arms and legs warped in unnatural shapes, fingers with nails pulled from them—if we could, we would've waved to the people passing by, shouted, tried to arouse some sympathy from whatever part of them you might call the heart, leave some impression on them, tell somebody where we were dragged away from and what month, day, time it was. The words we hear always come from a mouth, from mouth to ear, mouth to ear—maybe the news that we were alive on such-and-such date at such-and-such time would reach the ears of our fathers, mothers, brothers, sisters, wives, children, friends, comrades, and though it was perhaps unlikely, they might then be able to find our bodies and return them to the soil of our hometowns. There's wire digging into our thumbs and the base of our thumbs, and our mouths were gagged with rope, but we're not blindfolded. A young man whose ears had been sliced off gave a look to a young man whose teeth had been broken, as if to say, we've got eyes, you know; a smile showing that he understood slowly spread across his toothless face.

Next, the tall, lanky kkeokdari of an officer whose turn it had been to drive apparently felt the call of nature, so he jumped out of the driver's seat and ran into a tearoom. There was no wind, so the stink of the piss and shit we were all letting out in the back of the truck hovered above us; we could not plug our noses or breathe with our mouths, so we had no choice but to breathe in the smell of our own stench. An old woman with her back hunched like a camel cricket and a large fabric bundle on her back appeared on the other side of the road; she did not exactly walk with a stick so much as claw herself across the ground one step at a time as she approached, and sixty pupils in unison fixed themselves on her clod-like face.

The old woman stopped beside the truck and looked up into the back; without looking into any of our eyes, she shook her trembling hand, still gripping her cane.

Ppalgaengi!

The officer did up the zip of his trousers and jumped back into the driver's seat, the truck shuddered and let out a belch of exhaust fumes, and we drove off in a cloud of reddish dust.

Sasan Inc. . . . Gupo Drugs . . . Deokcheon Store . . . Lee Woo-gun read the words on the signs.

Maybe we're in Geumjeong-ju. But. Look. Remember. Do something. Tell. Someone.

Woo-gun looked up at the sky. He could see ten or so black kites spreading their big wings, splitting off one by one and swirling in the sky like paper kites.

It was night when we left the warehouse where they'd been keeping us. Night to morning, morning to night, night to morning . . . I don't know where they're heading, but I know once the truck gets onto mountain roads and it stops, that's where our graves will be. No, I'm sure they'll make us walk . . . deep into the mountains where nobody will hear the gunshots . . . that lanky kkeokdari has the big build, but Shorty's the one without a sign of weakness . . . I bet he does taekwondo . . . if they hadn't fucked up my legs I bet I could take him on . . . they shot me in my right thigh, and kicked and stomped on my left heel with their military boots over and over . . . even when they covered my face with a cloth and poured water on me, even when they hanged me from the ceiling and beat me, even when they tied my legs together and tortured me with sticks, I didn't give up anyone's name, and I didn't give them any information . . . but . . . aigo, more than having my life taken, it's having my legs destroyed, aigu, cheonbeoreul badanna! If I'm going to be killed anyway then it's all or nothing, so I'll take off the wire with the expectation that my thumb is going to be torn to shreds . . . six bullets loaded in each revolver, twelve shots between the two of them . . . teullyeosseo da, teullyeosseo, pointless, pointless even to think about it . . . why didn't I run north that day instead of toward the wall . . . even though to the north there are lots of houses, all of them owned by people on our side, and whenever we were being chased by the police they would hide us under the floor . . . aigu, geureon saenggak haebwatja! I thought the same thing hundreds and thousands of times, in the hospital in Toseong-dong, in the torture room at Busan Prison, and in the grain warehouse at Busan Harbor, and hundreds and thousands of times I drowned out the thought, because thinking it would do nothing for me now . . . I want to bite off my tongue and kill myself. . . . Woo-gun tried to push his tongue out between his teeth and the rope, but he couldn't free his tongue from the gag.

Even when the sun began to set, I still felt that the afternoon sun was beating down on my head. Even just sitting the pain of torture smoldered, and with each big rattle of the truck it ignited everywhere in my body. In the mountains, shabby bark-covered houses sat in clumps like trash blown together; the smoke from dinner being prepared fluttered from each chimney. The warm breeze blowing down from the top of the mountains caressed my face, dulled by pain, fatigue, sorrow, worry, anger, and fear, and I heard someone's muffled humming. We all quickly knew what the song was; exchanging looks with each other to confirm that there's no way they'd be able to hear us in the driver's seat, we started humming "The People's Battle Song" without using our tongues or throats, with just our noses.

> Don't mourn the deaths of comrades
> Who fell in battle with the enemy
> Wrap their bodies in the red flag
> The flag we swore to our death or victory
> The voices of our comrades
> Now reborn inside our hearts
> Farewell, friends, on the path of enmity
> Our blood shall seek revenge on your part
> The bayonet of a comrade fallen in the White Terror
> Sways in search of its villain
> Let us destroy now and for all
> The foes who sold off the freedom of our homeland
> The people's battle song

The humming didn't last for long. Thrown by the rhythm of the tires going around, unable to even sigh or clear their throats, everyone drifted off into their own thoughts. The boy next to me started nodding off, leaning on my shoulder, and I looked at him. He had a little peach fuzz on his top lip; his face looked young still, no more than fifteen or sixteen . . . he might only be in middle school . . . He's sleeping on my shoulder and yet I don't know who he is or where he's from . . . I don't even know his name, but we're going to be killed at the same place at the same time . . . Aigu, sesange . . . A few of them seem to know who I am. When they put us on the truck, a few guys gave me a nod. But they don't know my real name. Lee Chun-sik is famous, but about the only students in Busan who know I'm Lee Woo-gun are Park Woon-gyu from Choyang High and Kim Yeon-tae, the guy who just got elected to the Democratic Patriotic Youth leadership . . . Actually, I haven't seen him lately . . . Did he quit? . . . *ka-fwump, bounce, ka-fwump, bounce* . . . He's snoring right into my ear . . . Aigu, it's driving me crazy . . . I wonder what his name is . . . it's the only thing I can't imagine . . . learn the names of all twenty-nine of us at least and then . . . kill us . . . are we going to be killed . . . of course they're going to kill us . . . but how . . . they'll shoot us . . . what else . . . would they do . . . shot to death . . . at point-blank range in the head, *bang, bang, bang, bang, bang, bang* . . . six shots and then they'll reload . . . *bang, bang, bang, bang, bang, bang,* then there'll still be another six men left . . . *bang, bang, bang, bang, bang, bang* . . . if I'm going to be killed let me be first . . . no, wait, if it's that lanky bastard he might lose his concentration by the third shot and miss . . . then I'd play dead and wait for them to leave . . . Aigu, aniya! What's the fucking point, ijen da teullyeosseo . . . before night falls probably, the kid next to me won't be breathing, and me neither . . . Woo-gun looked up at the sky . . . stars . . . I've never seen so many stars before . . . the Big Dipper, Scorpio, Leo . . . I wonder if that bright white, shining star has a name too . . . Woo-gun lost sight of the star as the truck rattled its way up the mountain road, more covered in rubble and potholes the farther up they got, spotted it again, then lost it with another jolt . . . He was so sleepy that his eyes were failing, but when he thought that in a few short hours he would have to leave this world, he regretted every blink . . . Above all he didn't want to be beaten awake from sleep and then immediately shot dead . . . *ka-fwump, bounce, ka-fwump, bounce* . . . I'll wake him up before the truck stops . . . or should I just let him sleep . . . maybe he's dreaming of someone he wishes he could see . . . in the story of Janghwa and Hongryeon her big sister comes to her in a dream and tells her the name of the woman who killed her . . . my brother . . . I want to see my brother . . . though in the hospital and jail and warehouse, even in the back of this truck, I didn't allow myself to think about the old days in Miryang. . . . As tears and mucus ran into his mouth, Woo-gun turned his face up to the night sky . . . now that I think about it, that morning . . . the morning I was shot at the track . . . I'd had that dream again . . . my abeoji's jangdo, the one I kept as a memento . . . usually I woke up as I watched the man grip the handle with its dragon carving and slowly, slowly cut his own throat, but that one time . . . the jangdo was in my hand . . . I was shaving and I went to flick the foam off the blade and . . . the foam was red . . . my head fell to my feet . . . but there was no pain in my neck . . . only in my leg . . . in my right leg, the one the police shot me in . . . Abeoji . . . I never understood what that dream I had over and over meant . . . but now I understand . . . you were trying to warn me about the danger I was in . . . Aigu, Abeoji . . . you died when I was five, Abeoji . . . and in the summer you'd bring back a big watermelon every day . . . Abeoji, how you carried me on your back up the steps to Yeongnamnu . . . Aigu, Yeongnamnu . . . Aigo . . . Aigu, the Miryang River . . . Aaaigo . . . *ka-fwump, bounce, ka-fwump, bounce . . .*

His eyelids grew heavier listening to the snores of the boy sleeping on his shoulder . . . Teardrops ran over the bridge of his nose . . . *ka-fwump, bounce, ka-fwump, bounce . . .*

Woo-gun was awakened by his own snoring and raised his head. The truck was slowing down as it climbed a narrow, winding mountain road covered by trees on both sides. Looking up at the sky between the leaves and the branches, he saw that the light of the stars had dimmed, *ssokdok ssokdok ttakttakttak ttak- ttakttak ssokdok ssokdok jjikjjik jjaekjjaek ssokdok ssokdok*, and the birds hiding in the trees were exchanging their morning greetings with their own singing.

They went around the next curve, and the truck suddenly stopped. The young man, awake now from the jolt of his head dropping, looked around, frightened, and the two inspectors who got out of the truck's cabin stood there, in the glow of the headlights, discussing something with cigarettes hanging out of their mouths.

"Naeryeo!" *Get out.*

They let down the tailgate of the truck; the men were carrying pickaxes and shovels.

The headlights turned off; we followed in the moonless darkness, becoming squirming shadows. This isn't a road . . . it's a mountain . . . a steep one . . . from the ground near my feet crowded with tree roots and granite and gravel, striped mosquitoes rose like smoke . . . oreunjjok, oenjjok, oreunjjok, oenjjok . . . no time to rest, oreunjjok, oenjjok, step, step, the bones of my shot right leg cried out, "Aya! Aya!" and my left foot, with its crushed heel, pleaded, "No more" . . . Oreunjjok oenjjok oreunjjok! Oenjjok! For what! Oreunjjok! Oenjjok! To be killed! Oreunjjok! Oenjjok!

Commodity—Money—Commodity, C—M—C Oreunjjok! Oenjjok! **The result of the whole process is, so far as concerns the objects themselves, C—C, the exchange of one commodity for another, the circulation of materialized social labor. When this result is attained, the process is at an end.** Oreunjjok! Oenjjok! Oreunjjok! Oenjjok! **The slave owner buys his laborer as he buys his horse.** Oreunjjok! Oenjjok! **The most effective economy is that which takes out of the human chattel in the shortest space of time the utmost amount of exertion it is capable of putting forth.** Oreunjjok! Oenjjok! Oreunjjok! Oenjjok! Oreunjjok! Oenjjok! **Work is the active expression of the laborer's own life. And this life activity he sells to another person in order to secure the necessary means of life. His life activity, therefore, is but a means of securing his own existence. He works that he may keep alive.** Oreunjjok! Oenjjok! Oreunjjok! Oenjjok! **Wages therefore is only a special name for the price of labor-power, and it is usually called the price of labor; it is the special name for the price of this peculiar commodity, which has no other repository than human flesh and blood.** Oreunjjok! Oenjjok! Oreunjjok! Oenjjok! Anger made him breathless, his legs pumping like bellows, push, pull, push, pull, push, pull . . . It's the gag in my mouth, aigu, sum-eul mos swigessda, I can't breathe . . . my head's numb, I'm about to pass out . . . He leaned against the body of a young man with a branding-iron mark on his forehead but . . . Oreunjjok! Oenjjok! **There will be no lack of fresh exploitable blood and muscle for the Messrs. Capitalists—the dead may bury their dead.** Oreunjjok! Oenjjok! Oreunjjok!

When they reached the top of the mountain, it was fully morning. The light of the sun was gray and the tops of the mountains in the distance were smoky with fog. As they walked along the ridge, a gentle slope of blossoming thistle and yellow-flowering sedum spread out before them, and a cloud that had crossed several ridges passed through our bodies like water lapping against our legs. Woo-gun saw a dull yellow circle hiding behind the clouds . . . the sun is about to die too . . . I've got a fever . . . I can't stop shaking from the chills. . . .

The two inspectors took out bamboo lunch boxes and canteens from their rucksacks and started eating white rice and jangajji, vegetables pickled in soy sauce. Occasionally they talked about something, but whatever they were talking about didn't reach his ears or mind. As Woo-gun watched Beanpole's mouth munching away and Shorty's throat gulping, he was surprised to feel saliva seeping from the mucus membranes of his gagged mouth. Even though every pore on my body is sweating, and my eyes are dried out with anger, aigo, cham giga maghineun noleus-ida . . .

While Beanpole was squatting behind a pine tree taking a shit, Shorty stuck his shovel in the ground and looked around at their faces.

"Eodi boja, neohago . . . neo." *Right, you and you.* He rolled the words around in his mouth as if trying them out, then wearily lifted his pointer finger.

The boy who had been sleeping on Woo-gun's shoulder and the young man with the brand on his forehead who had held Woo-gun up.

"Son naemireo!" *Put your hands out!*

Shorty cut the rope of their gags with a knife, then severed the wire between their thumbs with a sharp stone.

"Yeogida gudeongireul pa." *Dig a hole over there.*

The boy's lips, perhaps numb from the gag, trembled; without a word, nod, or even blinking, the branded man took the shovel and started to dig.

Beanpole, finished with his shit, undid the snap on his shoulder holster, cocked the hammer with a clink, and turned the muzzle toward both of their heads. There was no sound but the horrible dull clang of metal hitting against rocks; over an hour later, the hole still hadn't gotten much deeper. Beanpole yawned so widely that it showed in his Adam's apple, making his long chin even longer; rubbing his eyes with the hand holding his revolver, he gave an order.

"Gipi pa! Deo gipi!" *Dig deep! Deeper!*

Rain.

Woo-gun looked up at the sky . . . *splat* . . . forehead . . . *spli-splat* . . . lips . . . *spli-splat* . . . At first it fell in occasional drops on his face and ran down like sweat, but then it began to rain in earnest, falling hard enough that he had to look down to be able to breathe. The rain lashed and hissed, *jwaak jwak jwaak jwak jwaak jwak* . . .

The rain is dragging out my final morning.

The cops don't have umbrellas or raincoats.

We'll have to wait until the graves are dug deep enough.

Thirty minutes?

Maybe not that long.

Woo-gun took one breath and swallowed with the back of his throat.

But I'm still alive.

Think of something.

My soul is leaving me.

But I've got to think of something.

But there's no time.

No words.

Just the rain.

Ame.

Ame, ame   fure, fure
Kaa-san ga
Janome de   omukai
Ureshi na
Pitch, pitch   chap, chap
Run, run, run

"Geuman." *That's enough.*

The digging sounds stopped.

There was only the sound of the rain.

Woo-gun realized that he wasn't singing. After a few long, long seconds,

Woo-gun spread his fingers, aside from his thumbs with the wire wrapped around them, and clasped them in prayer. First Shorty's and then Beanpole's arms extended smoothly; they put their fingers on the triggers.

Bang!

Bang!

Blood and brain matter flew; the two tumbled forward, shovels still in their hands. Beanpole jumped into the hole, planted his foot on an arm, and pulled on the shovel as if trying to pull up a burdock root, but he could not steal from the dead what they had held at the last. "Je-egiral," Beanpole spat, having no choice but to crouch down by their heads, flowing with blood, to peel the shovels out of their hands finger by finger.

"Deureoga!" *Get in the hole!*

The man whose ears had been sliced off stood at the edge of the hole; Beanpole took the shovel in his hands like a baseball bat, then smashed the man in the back until he fell in.

Once all thirty of us had gotten in the hole, Shorty gripped the revolver with both hands and aimed at us, while Beanpole started throwing dirt in over us. Buried alive! They're trying to bury us alive! Both his lungs became as hot as if he had swallowed fire, and his heart ached, like it was being squeezed tightly. *Thu-thump! Thu-thump! Thu-thump! Thu-thump! Thu-thump! Thu-thump!* Anger blew through him like a gust, and his diaphragm began to cramp as if he were rolling around on the floor laughing and holding his stomach.

Long live the Democratic People's Republic of Korea!

It was like a dream where no matter how much you scream and scream, nothing comes out.

Long live the Democratic People's Republic of Korea!

The tall one threw soil at Woo-gun's face. There was dirt in his eyes and mouth. Woo-gun wiped at his eyes with his wrist, bit down on the rope, and stared up at the two men with his face covered in dirt and rain.

You bastards witnessed our deaths. Even if our deaths are reported you won't testify. And in a few years, you bastards will shut up too. But we witnessed you. And even if our mouths are closed by death, we will engrave our sixty eyes in your four eyes. When you hug your beloved wives, when you hold your darling children, our eyes, staring into yours right now, will dig into your wives' and children's eyes like fingers. Woo-gun put all the strength left in his body into his two thumbs. Ttudeuk! Eueuk! His whole body was filled with a glare like the August sun had exploded, and with his two hands now free, he raised them in triumph. **Long live the Democratic People's Republic of Korea!**

Feet like kicking heavy water at the bottom of the sea! Foot! Foot! Mouths, screaming, screaming, screaming, screaming! Mouths! Hands, looking for an exit! Hands! Hands! Hands! Heads everywhere! Hands! Eyes! Shoulders! Mouths! Noses! Ears! Feet! Faces! Noses! Eyes! Eyes! Hands! Heads! Eyes! Eyes! Mouth! Screaming with no breath left to scream! Scream! Heart pounding like a fist, *thu-thump! Thu-thump! Thu-thump! Thu-thump!* The grave was still moving. Beanpole and Shorty stamped on the ground as if actors in a stage show. His arms stuck out from the soil. His hands, their thumbs torn off from the second joint, grasped at the void; the rain washed off the blood, pouring it into the dirt. Beanpole dropped a large rock on his hands, then stamped on it. The last thing Woo-gun heard was the sound of his own skull collapsing . . . It's quiet . . . Am I saved? . . . Let me try to shake my head . . . I can't move it . . . My hands? . . . rock . . . paper . . . rock . . . paper . . . I can't move . . . am I dead . . . they buried us alive and killed us . . . But there shall be no eternal rest for us. Comrades! Awaken! Get up! **Let the ruling classes tremble at a Communistic revolution. The proletarians have nothing to lose but their chains. They have a world to win. Workers of the World, unite!**

TWENTY-EIGHT

Shuffle

| 셔플 | シャッフル |

Wheel of Fortune (X)

*Reversed—loss, unluckiness, unhappiness,
inability to escape one's destiny—*

The sun streaming in from the barred window briefly painted the prisoners' faces a familiar shade of madder red. The two men, arms around their knees, looked up at the small window near the ceiling as they spoke quietly, as if speaking to themselves.

"Two hours twenty-five minutes thirty-nine seconds . . . tournament record . . . Seo Yoon-bok . . . winner of the Boston Marathon."

"That was really something . . . the newspapers printed extras . . . it was like when Sohn Kee-chung won at the Berlin Olympics . . . was Seo's win three years ago now . . . I guess it must be, it's been five years since liberation . . . Aigu, time has really flown . . . it's going by too fast . . ."

"I suppose so much has happened . . . Lyuh Woon-hyung getting assassinated . . . your cousin going to Pyongyang with Kim Gu and Kim Kyu-sik . . . and then staying there . . ."

"Building the Democratic People's Republic of North Korea with Kim Il-sung, taking up the post of Minister for Censorship . . . you know, he told me, if you come to the North you could be a prefectural governor, hahaha . . . it'd be a miracle if this saved my life . . . four of my cousins have all . . ."

"Aigu, just because you're related to Kim Won-bong . . . Aigo, we're living in the end times . . ."

The two prisoners did not look at each other's faces. They wanted their faces to be illuminated by the evening sun, which would soon be lost, for just a little longer. The cry of a crow heading toward its roost echoed throughout the prison, but it did not reach their ears. Though both had been sitting in the same position for a long time, even the pain in their buttocks and lower backs was forgotten.

"Aigo, ireol suga . . . da teullyeosseo . . . da, aigo!" *What a mess . . . All of it—it's all fucked up. Everything.* The younger man shook his head, ran his tongue over his bloody gums, and spit out bright red phlegm.

"Ham Kee-yong, two hours thirty-two minutes thirty-nine seconds . . . Song Gil-yun, two hours thirty-five minutes fifty-eight seconds . . . Choi Yun-chil, two hours thirty-nine minutes forty-five seconds . . . they swept the top places at this year's Boston Marathon . . ."

"You won the five thousand meters at the Korean Olympics competition, didn't you?"

"Aigu, that was years ago now . . . running . . . what was the point of it . . ."

"Because you're a runner."

"I'm thirty-seven years old . . . my days as a track athlete are over . . . when the 1940 Tokyo Olympics were canceled, that's when my athletic life ended . . . although I guess my actual life's what's in danger now, ha." The older prisoner laughed without the slightest hint of emotion.

"What a twist of fate . . . you had the real ability to win a medal at the Olympics and yet . . ."

"A twist of fate . . . let's call it that . . . if I think back . . . No, I don't want to think back anymore . . ."

When the evening sun had disappeared, the inside of the prison was washed pale by the night, which had snuck in, and the faces of the two prisoners, marked on their eyes and cheeks from beatings, looked paler and shabbier.

"My friend Kim Wong-lyong made it to the London Olympics . . . him and his brother . . . Wong-lyong in the high jump, and his brother Wong-won in the triple jump . . . neither of them made it to the finals but still, their dream of being at the Olympics came true . . ." The older prisoner, now aware of his sharp coccyx, rubbed his tensed calves with both hands.

"It was right after the London Olympics, wasn't it . . . when Rhee Syngman became president of the Republic of Korea, and Kim Il-sung became leader of the Democratic People's Republic of Korea . . ."

"Yes . . . Kim Wong-lyong, when he came back from London, took me to Kim Gu's house, near Seodaemun in Seoul. . . ."

"Really?"

"Kim Wong-lyong is the oldest son of the yangban family that runs the mining industry in Haeju, Hwanghae Province, and Kim Gu is from Haeju, so they're sort of ancestral family friends. . . ."

"Did you get to talk to him one on one? What was he like?"

"How can a little guy like me judge what he was like? I was so nervous, I have no idea what I said to him, but I remember what he said very well."

"And what did he say?"

"If you need money, make money; if you need people, make people."

"Right."

"And as we were leaving, he said, jalharago . . ."

"'Do well . . .'"

"I only met him the once, but when I read the extra the day he was assassinated, my hands were shaking, I couldn't stop crying. . . ."

"Aigu, a man who risked his life for the anti-Japanese movement, getting killed by one of his own countrymen . . . Aigo, ireol suga!"

The older prisoner struck the mosquito that had landed on his arm with his palm and stood up, muttering in a dry voice the platform for the National Bodo League, the "re-education" program for suspected communist sympathizers set up by Rhee Syngman.

"We will give our full support to the Government of South Korea.

"We will fully oppose the North Korean puppet administration.

"We aim to eliminate and crush the communist ideology, which ignores human freedom and national character.

"We will strengthen our theoretical arguments to expose and crush the North-South Labor Party's policies.

"We will join forces with parties and organizations in the nationalist faction."

The older prisoner crouched down with a sigh.

The younger prisoner turned his face to the big moon outside the bars.

"I succumbed to the threats of the inspectors and added his name to the list of members of the Bodo League, was forced to advertise it as if it were an organization created by people who had changed their ideologies, was forced to speak at anti-communist talks, was rounded up in an exercise for the Winter Suppression Campaign, the government forces' operation to wipe out partisans in the winter of '49, and then after that was sent south with the People's Army, aigo . . . I heard one night he was put on a truck . . . when I was being interrogated yesterday, the guy said that the order given was to deal with dissident elements . . ."

"Dissident elements . . . deal with . . ." The older prisoner carefully rotated his ankles, one leg at a time, as he would were he getting ready to run.

"The only witnesses would be the executioners themselves, so it'll never be revealed who was killed and how. Those of us on the Bodo League lists get taken one day to a prison, factory, or warehouse, taken out by truck another day, and then we go missing forever . . . There's no coming back alive . . . we don't even get buried in a grave . . . according to the Bodo League bulletin, what's it called, *Patriot*, there's three hundred to five hundred thousand members. . . ."

"Aigu, are there that many in the Workers' Party of South Korea and the Democratic Patriotic Youth put together? They're taking away anyone who was even slightly involved in the union or farmers' movement . . . and those who were informed on, like me . . ."

"If all of them are 'dealt with,' the massacre'll outdo the waenom's attack on the March First Movement."

"Aigu, after thirty-five years we were finally liberated from the Japanese Empire, and not even five years later our own people are killing each other . . . haneuldo musimchi, aigo . . ."

"Why did your cousin go to the North?"

"I have no idea . . . or about my four cousins who were killed . . . or my uncle and aunt . . ."

"I wonder how they're doing now. I know they were kicked out of the house on Yeongnamnu and that they moved to a shack in Sanmun-dong. . . ."

"Aigu, the rumor is they're on starvation's doorstep. If anyone's seen going in or out someone will inform on them, so even relatives like us going to visit puts lives at risk. And yet they're going in the middle of the night or at dawn to take them wheat and rice."

"Aigu, do you think Kim Won-bong even knows what kind of trouble his family and relatives are in?"

"If he doesn't know I'm sure he can imagine . . . but that's how it is, this is war after all . . . I've never cursed or resented or mourned the fact that I'm related to Kim Won-bong. I mean, who could've imagined it? Five years after liberation and the north and south are divided. Why not Japan instead? Why didn't the United States, the Soviet Union, and the United Kingdom divide Japan? Shouldn't it have been? They're the ones that lost! Why, why did our country have to become a battlefield?"

"The Bodo League will be slaughtered wholesale. I mean, the guys who forced us to reject our ideology doubt our conversion. They must think that if the North's army comes south, then we'll join their forces. . . . How far has the North's army gotten, do you think?"

"They must be pretty close. Yesterday there was something obviously off about the guards' faces. It made me nervous . . . and it's so quiet."

". . . It is quiet . . . they just put down the barley rice for dinner, and they didn't even check on us, did they?"

"It's strange . . . the last twenty days or so, they haven't done inspections or patrols, have they?"

"It really is quiet . . . let's pick the lice off each other."

The younger prisoner laughed slightly.

"Hahaha, that's like your catchphrase."

The older prisoner stood up and suddenly did a headstand. "'Gotta get some exercise,' that's my other catchphrase."

"Hahaha."

"When I was hiding out in Japan, a woman from Osaka that I was seeing taught me her dialect. When I'm feeling down, those're the words that come to mind."

"Hahaha, I always heard, when Lee Woo-cheol runs, women run after him."

"Women don't run after me . . . they just wait . . . the difference is whether they're waiting for me ahead or back where I started . . . waiting . . . Aigu, all the blood's gone to my head."

"But your wife would run. I feel like she'd run and run and chase after you no matter how far you go."

"You think?"

"When your little girl was born, while you were locked up, my eomoni and wife helped her."

"Gomamne."

"We're neighbors, of course we'd help. But nowadays, you know, neighbors are informing on each other, killing each other . . . It makes me sad to think about it, but in a way, it was kind of more peaceful when the Japanese were here, when we were all united against the waenom . . . How old is your daughter now?"

"She's three, I reckon . . . my wife's almost thirty-two, so Shin-hwa's probably our last child."

"How many do you have altogether?"

"Two with my first wife . . . our oldest daughter, Mi-ok, well, Jeong-hee conspired to marry her off to a poor farming family in Jo-eum-ri, and our youngest, Shin-ja, got so sick of Jeong-hee's cruelty she ran off to live with some relatives in Busan . . . one child with the dancer from the OK Café . . . Shin-cheol, his mother came and took him away in secret one night four years ago . . . so now there's only the children that Jeong-hee and I had left . . . two boys and two girls . . . Shin-myeong . . . Shin-ho . . . Shin-hee . . . Shin-hwa . . . aigo, my arms hurt . . . used to be I could do fifty stretches while standing on my head . . ."

The older prisoner, still walking on his hands, came toward the younger prisoner, spread his legs wide, stepping over the hole of the privy, then slowly let down his legs and immediately began to do push-ups on the heavily splintered wooden floor.

"They've tortured you so much and yet you still exercise. Athletes really are something else . . . they've thrown a lot of athletes in here the last twenty days, you know . . . Kim Yoo-heon, the judo guy . . . Park Hong-shin, the soccer goalie . . . the boxer Kim Nam-yong . . ."

"Nam-yong couldn't stand the torture, when the interrogator stood up to take a piss, he stabbed himself in the belly with a pair of scissors. . . . Aigu, they said they took him to the hospital, but who knows if he's alive or dead now. . . ."

"Kim Nam-yong, wasn't he at the air defense lookout post with us?"

"Oh, yeah . . . I remember . . ."

"If you just worked the lookout post once a week, from eight in the morning to eight the next morning, you'd be considered a local conscript, exempt from army conscription. . . ."

"I never could fully believe that they'd exempt a healthy twenty-year-old like that. Just imagine, if we'd been assigned to the Chinese 13th Division or something, we would've wound up fighting against your cousin leading the Korean Volunteers in the fight against the Japanese. . . ."

"If the war had gone on a year longer, I know we'd have gotten draft notices. . . . We were supposed to take it in two-hour shifts, but you always let me sleep longer. Sometimes I'd wake up and realize I'd been sound asleep all night. And sometimes we'd stay up all night talking . . . I say talking, but it was mainly you listening to me talk. The ramblings of an immature boy rushing through the past and present, full of hopes for the future . . ."

"Oh yes, I remember. You were working at the Iwata Clinic, next to the Olympic. You said you didn't have the money to go to college, so you were going to take the licensing exam and become a doctor."

"Whenever I felt a little pessimistic about things, you'd tell a joke and made me laugh. And still, you make a joke and then you snort, oh, sorry, hahahaha."

"What's wrong with snorting, hahaha . . . no matter how long I looked through those binoculars, all I could see was the stars, never did spot a single

B-29 . . . I feel the same as you . . . it was peaceful then . . . we could talk about the future, at least . . . Now the only thing we can talk about is the present . . . not the future, much less the past . . . in those days everything was steady, clearly defined . . . now . . . everything's unstable . . . I don't know how anything's going to turn out. . . ." The older prisoner quit his exercises, pressed his kneecaps to his chest, and turned his sharp gaze to the moon.

"You and I, we're fated to look up at the night sky together . . . seven years ago in the lookout post . . . and now, even though we might be killed tomorrow . . ." The younger prisoner cast his heavy and sad eyes up at the moon, then chuckled quietly and shook his head.

"What're you thinking about?"

"Hahaha, it was funny, you know, the rice ball—hahahaha."

"Oh, the rice ball."

"Hahaha, when our wives bribed the guard so the things they sent us would actually get through, hahaha, and then when I was about to eat the rice ball that my wife sent me, hahahaha, they came through for inspection, ahahaha, and I hid it under my ass, and you shouted, aigo, anywhere but there!"

"If they'd found it, they would've given you a hell of a beating."

"Aigu, where better to hide something, and you went and opened the lid of the privy, ahahaha."

"It was wrapped in oil paper, it was fine."

"Hahaha, and then when you took the rice ball out of the privy, ahahaha."

"And I ate it."

"'Smells a bit,' you said, and started munching, ahahahaha."

"The other thing was pretty funny too. Remember, that young guy came in, right? He said he'd been transferred from the youth detention center in Changnyeong, but we realized he was a CIC or CIA spy, and we all gave each other a look. That was when we were with Go Man-seok from the Miryang Irrigation Association and Kim Yoo-heon, the judo-ka, I think? Was that after Kim Nam-yong stabbed himself with the scissors? . . . or was it before?"

"Before—Kim Nam-yong was there too. As soon as someone you don't know comes in you know right away they're a spy. On the first day they join in with whatever we're talking about, but the next day they always try to turn the conversation to politics. And then, sure enough, late at night on the second day, he asked, 'What d'you think'll happen if the People's Army attack?' Aigu, beoreoji gateun nom!"

"I said, well, obviously they'll kill us all."

"Because if you say the People's Army will save us, then you're as good as dead."

A black insect fell down from the ceiling and went under the lid of the privy.

"Aigu, ige mwokko! They stopped giving us DDT and look, the bedbugs are back in full force."

"It's 'cause they're not even letting our wives send us anything these days. Proof that the People's Army is getting closer. But you know I'm friends with the assistant head at the prison camp in Busan, and I think they've got a couple of things up their sleeves there."

"Well, that's no good now. The inspectors said that you and I were classed as A. B's and C's go to the camps, but A's get interrogated in the detention center and then shot dead. Aigu, I want a drink. I can't take waiting around to be killed sober."

Boom boom boom, the sound of artillery fire, and then the sound of a B-29 engine followed by a blast; the two prisoners instinctively looked at each other.

"Watda!"

"What's that smell?"

"Aigu, it's gasoline. They're pouring it around the detention center. They've got canisters of it in the interrogation room. They're going to throw hand grenades and destroy the place."

"So they're going to burn us alive."

Kim Seung-jae! Seung-jae!

"Someone's calling! He-ey! Help! Help!"

The sound of keys clinking against one another came closer, and the guard they had paid off opened the cell door.

"Get out quick! It's gonna blow! Daejeon has fallen. The People's Army came in like a damn swarm of grasshoppers, but the Americans are pouring some yellow powder from their B-29s, and they're dropping like bam-bam-bam, still holding their bayonets. It's dangerous out there. Go home!"

The two prisoners left the detention center and ran, barefoot.

"Where are you going?"

"Home."

"They'll arrest you."

"I'm not leaving Miryang. Even if tomorrow they convene the highest court-martial and execute me, I'm gonna spend tonight with my wife. Where are you going?"

"To Japan. If you see my wife, tell her that's where I went. Geureom."

"Josimhaeseo gasiso."

The two prisoners parted ways at Namcheong Bridge. The older prisoner slipped himself into the darkness. With each step a new explosion echoed, and from the darkness an even deeper darkness hovered into approach. A cold lump rose up in the back of his throat, a terror that threatened to swallow him completely. The prisoner exhaled all the air in his lungs with a trembling sigh, then started running. Domangchyeo! In-hale ex-hale Run! In-hale ex-hale to Japan in-hale ex-hale in-hale ex-hale to Japan!

SHUFFLE

The Tower (XVI)

Upright—calamity, destruction, ruin, misfortune,
sudden illness, danger—

It's almost dawn.

I think the rain's even stopped.

It started raining yesterday evening, seeming to grow harder with each passing second. The roof of the Nakano Factory is aluminum, so when it's pelting down, it sounds like someone's hitting a drum, *dum-dum-dum-dum-da-dum-dum-dum-da-dum-dum-dum*. Here, when I want to talk to someone about something, I have no choice but to whisper in their ear, but yesterday even if I'd put my mouth to their ear my voice wouldn't have carried.

It was late night. I don't know what time exactly. But I hadn't been asleep for long, so it must've been around midnight. The door to the factory opened with a squeak. A man with a gun came in. I don't know if he was a cop or CIC or what.

He yelled out names, but I couldn't hear for the sound of the rain. He stood us up in front of a wall, shone a flashlight in each of our faces, and shouted out each name as he went past us. Kang Man-jae! Here! Kim Kee-jeong! Here! He just shone the light in my face and then moved on to the older lady next to me: Park Nan-jong! Here! The people whose names he called were gagged with straw rope; then they put together their thumbs and bound them with wire. They marched more than a hundred people out in the rain and put them all in a big truck. They left behind six women and two men . . . just eight of us. I can't find my brother who was brought here with me. My eighth brother, Kim Deok-bong, he's six years older than me, which makes him twenty-three.

They're going to kill them. Maybe they're already killing them. Rumor has it they chain them together and bury them alive, or they make them dig a hole and then shoot them, but nobody really knows, except for the police, and you can't ask them.

Three of my brothers, Yong-bong, Bong-gi, and Gu-bong, all got taken away by the police one day, and they never came back. Someone told me they put you into three categories according to your charges: A, B, C. B's and C's might be taken to the Nakano Factory in Sanmun-dong or the camp in Gagok-dong, where they might be released, but the rumor is that A's are taken to the police station, tortured, and shot dead. The only one who successfully escaped is my brother Bong-cheol. Abeoji told me not to tell anyone, but he's hiding among the dockers at Busan Harbor.

I'm the youngest of eleven. The morning I was born there was a big fuss, everyone jostling to hold me. I grew up loved, protected, and cherished by my nine brothers. Our house, always so full of noise, is now just Eomoni and

Abeoji. Abeoji collapsed when my brothers were taken, and ever since then he's been bedridden. Eomoni is taking care of him, but they're running out of food. None of Kim Won-bong's family can get jobs, not even as toilet cleaners or porters, and even our relatives and friends, if they're seen going in and out of our house and someone informs on them, they'll be arrested, so they can't give my parents food regularly either. I'm worried about Abeoji. I see Eomoni's face every morning. The toilet is a temporary one, separated off with straw mats, and it's located outside. Of course, there's a policeman with a gun watching the door, but I look forward to going to the toilet in the morning because I can breathe in the morning air and I can see Eomoni's face. The fence surrounding the factory isn't very high. Family members that care about those of us locked up in the factory come to look over the fence, waiting for us to go to the toilet. When I go out, I don't wave, I don't smile, I just silently nod. Eomoni has come to check on us all this year, never missing a single day. She'll be there this morning too . . . but no matter how long I wait I can't see my brother anywhere . . .

One year and three months; 455 days, to be more precise. I was taken away two days after National Liberation Day, on August 15.

At that time, I kept a diary with a pencil my oldest brother gave me.

He's thirty years older than me; thirteen years before I was born, he went to Manchuria and didn't come back to Miryang, so the first time I set eyes on him was February 26, 1946.

For months, there'd been rumors that General Kim Won-bong would return triumphantly, leading the Korean National Revolutionary Army, and whenever Miryangers met in the street, they'd shout, "Long live Kim Won-bong!" All of Miryang was delighted . . . in those days . . . every single person . . .

The rumor that Kim Won-bong was coming home became reality when we heard that the people of Muan had rolled out the red carpet for him and the members of the Heroic Corps. All over town there was a lot of talk about moving our family to a magnificent mansion, and at the discretion of the mayor of Miryang, we were hurriedly moved into the Japanese-style house at the top of Yeongnamnu, where an ilbon saram named Kamikawa, who was the president of the Mujin Company, had lived before the liberation. The move happened hurriedly, but we just sat in a teahouse and drank ginger tea while we waited for all the moving and cleaning to be done. To the people of Miryang, Kim Won-bong was more than a hero—he was like a god.

We saw the sun rise without having slept a wink, got changed into our hanboks, and craned our necks: is he here yet, is he here yet? When Abeoji, unable to stand it anymore, ran outside, my eight brothers all ran out after him, and we stood at the top of the stone steps to Yeongnamnu. Every street was overflowing with Miryangers, all waving their hands in the air and shouting, "Long live General Kim Won-bong! Long live General Kim Won-bong!"

And there he was, my brother, wearing drab military clothes; he seemed less like my brother, Won-bong, than the famed General Kim Won-bong, and I thought I was going to faint standing upright, but his face under his round cap looked so much like mine that I was overwhelmed with the knowledge that he really was my brother, and my chest and the inner corners of my eyes became hot.

He put his hands together and apologized to Abeoji. "I've brought a lot of trouble upon you and though I'm the eldest son I did not protect the family. I'm sorry." Then he changed into the hanbok that Eomoni had sewn for him and the thirteen of us, Abeoji, Eomoni, Won-bong, Gyeong-bong, Chun-bong, Ik-bong, Yong-bong, Bong-cheol, Bong-gi, Deok-bong, Gu-bong, Bok-jam, and I all bowed in front of our ancestors' mortuary tablets.

It was the next morning. I was at the sink brushing my teeth, when I saw him coming up behind me in the mirror, so I blushed and took my toothbrush out of my mouth. He walked up beside me and smiled, and then he said, "Study hard and become somebody great," and gave me five dozen Tonbo HB pencils and an English dictionary. I took the gifts from his hands, and with my mouth still full of salt, I said, "Gomapseumnida."

He only stayed at home with us for one night, and I only spoke to him that one time. He moved into the headquarters of the Korean People's Liberation Party, not five minutes' walk from our house. I went with my brothers a few times to look, but there was always a sea of people, and it was not the kind of atmosphere where we, his family, could easily go in.

After that, he left Miryang and went to Busan, then Seoul, but in 1947 he was arrested on suspicion of leading a strike, and the police chief and county director even came to our house to ask us his whereabouts. We worried for his safety, after the assassination of Lyuh Woon-hyung, who founded the People's Republic of Korea and formed the Preparatory Committee for the National Construction of Korea, and who had done the same for our homeland as my brother.

And then, on April 9, 1948, my brother went with Kim Gu to Pyongyang to attend the North-South joint conference, and he stayed in the North; on September 9, 1948, he was appointed minister of state control for the Democratic People's Republic of Korea. He took with him only his wife and two sons; our family wasn't even informed that he was going to the North.

When the four left-wing partisans were arrested and prosecuted, our family was expelled from the house on Yeongnamnu; we moved into a shack in Sanmun-dong. My brother, who had returned home triumphantly and cast his dazzling light on our family, became the big, black shadow that engulfed us all.

My abeoji and eomoni and brothers all spoke little. In order to prolong the time dwindling by fear, I picked up one of the pencils my brother had given me and started writing in my diary, letter by letter, my vow. That I would become like my brother who had fought the Japanese Empire for our nation's liberation.

Three of my brothers had never read *Das Kapital* or *The Communist Manifesto* or *Socialism: Utopian and Scientific*, had never even been to a protest; they were slaughtered simply because they were Kim Won-bong's little brothers. Less than two years after that glorious day on February 26, the people who had thrown their hands in the air and chanted, "Long live General Kim Won-bong," were now capturing and killing us with those very same hands.

I was brought here with my brother Deok-bong. Abeoji and Eomoni pleaded with them, she's only seventeen, she's just a baby who doesn't know red from white, please let her go, but the policeman kicked them to the ground.

Nakano Factory is a textile factory built during the Japanese colonial era by an ilbon saram man named Nakano. All the sewing machines and looms are stacked in the corners. There's nothing more on the dirt floor than some straw mats; we have no mattresses or blankets. There's one window. One door. Cops with guns stand guard at the window and door twenty-four hours a day.

Aside from when we go to the toilet, we're confined inside the dark factory all the time, clothes and underwear the exact same as when we were arrested a year ago; they won't even let us wash ourselves. Morning, noon, and night we get one ball of barley rice each. I had a lot of blood coming out of me a few times, but I kept quiet because if I said something foolish they'd get rid of me. It wasn't my period; my period stopped the first month.

Miryang is a small city, so pretty much everyone knows everyone. The undercover agents or the CIC spies are always young men that nobody knows, so they're easy to tell apart.

Also they look at me and they ask, "Who's that girl?"

Someone says, "That's Kim Won-bong's little sister," and they agree, "Looks just like him. Two peas in a pod."

The men's and women's areas are separated by plywood, and if you try to climb over it or speak through it you'll get punished, but looking between the boards at my brother and seeing my brother looking back at me, that exchange of looks, gave us encouragement.

Oppa!

November 15, 1951. The day that became the date of my brother's death.

I don't have paper, but in my head I can pick up the pencil that my big brother gave me, and I can write as much as I like.

I don't cry. Crying won't bring my brothers back to life, and it won't get me out of here either. Crying doesn't change anything. I don't need emotions. They don't do anything for me. Words and my pride are the only things that keep me going.

Yesterday, I was allowed to live. Maybe they won't kill me. And if so, then I can live through anything. I'll live, and I'll get out of this factory, and I'll show them. I'll live, and I'll tell everyone what happened in this factory.

It's morning now.

From the window I can see a ginkgo tree.

This is the second autumn I've spent in the Nakano Factory.

The morning sun hits the ginkgo, and its leaves gleam like gold coins.

Banjjak banjjak. *Sparkle-sparkle.*

Pallang pallang. *Flutter-flutter.*

Cham ippeugunyo. *It's so beautiful.*
There's no sound.
Just the gleaming.
Inside me, my oldest brother's name still glimmers radiantly.
I'm the little sister of the freedom fighter Kim Won-bong.

SHUFFLE

Page of Wands

*Reversed—bad news, rumors, capriciousness,
secrets revealed—*

Across the bottom of the endless blue sky, scalelike clouds slowly drifted as if telling one another, follow me; red and yellow and purple leaves flutter-fluttered; in time with the leaves dancing as they fell, even the atmosphere flutter-fluttered . . . The women, baskets of laundry balanced on their heads, kicked at the hems of their chimas as they walked up the footpath between the rice fields.

Look, look   look at me
Like a flower that blooms midwinter   look at me

Ari, arirang   suri, surirang   arariga nanne
Coming over Arirang Pass

Having finally met him
I could not hear a word he said   I was so shy

Ari, arirang   suri, surirang   arariga nanne
Coming over Arirang Pass

Flutter-flutter, their chimas lapped forcefully against their plump legs, flutter-flutter . . . Their chimas went horizontal; the wind had stopped. The women, having tied up their hems with string and gone down to the riverside, stopped singing and looked at one another.

"It's bloodred."

"Aigo . . ."

"Last night, a big truck stopped here, you know."

"It wasn't ten or twenty shots . . . it was fifty . . . sixty . . ."

"No, it was over a hundred, *bang, bang, bang, bang, bang, bang, bang* . . . Aigu, I was so scared I couldn't sleep."

"It must've been over there."

"Nowhere else it could've been. That mountain's got that huge cliff, blocked off by giant rocks. . . . It was raining all night so it must've carried it all down."

"I bet they're not burying them well either. If they're not buried, then the crows and dogs will come and . . ."

"Andwae!"

"If you bury them, the police will come after you thinking you're one of them."

"We can't do anything but leave them there."

"Aigu, where are we supposed to do the washing?"

"I guess we'll have to do it in the well."

"I've got twelve people in my house, aigu, what do I do?"

"I guess it'll go back to how it was in two or three days."

"You really think all the blood will be washed away in a few days? It takes more than half an hour to drain the blood from a dog even if you hang it upside down. If it really was more than a hundred people . . ."

The six women's eyes meandered up the bloodred river and stopped at the rocks below the cliff.

"Crows."

"Aigu, it's black with them."

Lots of footprints remained on the muddy path up, rain collecting in puddles the shape of feet.

"Aigu . . ."

"Better stay away from there until the crows are gone."

"Not even then, andwae. We saw nothing, we know nothing. Isn't that right?"

"Aigo, ireol suga . . ."

The women untied the strings holding up the hems of their chimas and put their baskets back on their heads. The baskets lent their shadows to the women's faces, emotions disguised, and when one woman began to sing "Miryang Arirang" with her mouth closed, the group turned back the way they came, singing as they trudged as if they were a procession bearing a coffin to the graveyard.

I was mistaken   I was mistaken
I came here as a bride in a carriage   I was mistaken

Ari, arirang   suri, surirang   arariga nanne
Coming over Arirang Pass

The moment the wind lifted up the song from their lips, the souls of 134 people, whose blood poured into the river, whose flesh was being pecked at by birds, came out of their bodies and hatched into voices.

The bird crying in the pine trees   sounds so sad
Does it suffer   the curse of Arang?

Ari, arirang   suri, surirang   arariga nanne
Coming over Arirang Pass

The moon that falls on Yeongnamul   is clear but
The Namcheong River just   flows silently

Ari, arirang   suri, surirang   arariga nanne
Coming over Arirang Pass

In the brightly colored Arang shrine
Arang's spirit dwells

Ari, arirang   suri, surirang   arariga nanne
Coming over Arirang Pass

Their voices rose higher and higher, sucked into the depths of the smooth, blue sky, where none could catch them anymore.

SHUFFLE

Judgment (XX)

Reversed—weakness, indecision, delays, separation, solitude,
unable to change one's way of thinking or living—

In-hale ex-hale   in-hale ex-hale   in-hale ex-hale   in-hale ex-hale   what time is it?   in-hale ex-hale   my wristwatch's not ticking   actually it hasn't been   since yesterday   in-hale ex-hale   no   the day before   in-hale ex-hale   must not be wound   I forgot to   in-hale ex-hale   I didn't have time to worry about what time it was   looking at my watch now   in-hale ex-hale   I didn't really have the bandwidth for that either   wherever I look   in-hale ex-hale   there's no leeway   threatened by the cops   into joining the Bodo League   in-hale ex-hale   professing I'd changed   in-hale ex-hale   anti-Communist speech events   the Winter Suppression Campaign   in-hale ex-hale   in-hale ex-hale   the People's Army coming south from Cheonan to Daejeon   one month after I was thrown in the detention center   in-hale ex-hale   aigu   they poured out gasoline everywhere   in-hale ex-hale   and just before they were about to blow up the detention center with hand grenades   in-hale ex-hale   in-hale ex-hale   break out   escape   in-hale ex-hale   gonna wind my watch   in-hale ex-hale   aigu, andwae   what would I look at to tell what time to set it to?   in-hale ex-hale   the time doesn't matter   in-hale ex-hale   when I heard about the death of my brother in Busan   somehow I could see the rain falling as it crossed the Miryang River   in-hale ex-hale   in-hale

ex-hale   just sheets of rain   the bridge-less river   in-hale ex-hale   in-hale
ex-hale   when my brother was born   there was no bridge   when my brother
was born   in-hale ex-hale   I was twelve   in-hale ex-hale   before dawn I ran
to call my halme   she fed Eomoni raw eggs mixed with soy sauce   and put
my abeoji's paji jeogori over her big stomach and still   in-hale ex-hale   my
brother hadn't been born so   I ran to fetch Bu-san ajumma, who had had
seven babies   in-hale ex-hale   Bu-san ajumma jumped over Eomoni's belly
again and again but   my brother still wouldn't come out so   in-hale ex-
hale   in-hale ex-hale   so I ran   in-hale ex-hale   to the station to get the
ilbon saram midwife   in-hale ex-hale   my brother   my brother   my
brother   in-hale ex-hale   my brother was born   and the first time I held
him in my hands   I promised   that if anything happened to Eomoni and
Abeoji   I would protect him   I would feed him   in-hale ex-hale   I would
teach him   everything   in-hale ex-hale   in-hale ex-hale   not long after he
was born it started to rain   Eomoni fed him and sang a lullaby while it
rained   **sleep-a-bye baby   my precious child   gift from the angels   way
up on high   and when the dog barks   it's far from your room   in your
starlike eyes   a little bell of sleep rings**   in-hale ex-hale   in-hale ex-
hale   and when Abeoji died   in-hale ex-hale   in-hale ex-hale   I took my
sobbing brother out of the house   to the riverbed   in-hale ex-hale   I talked
to him, made him listen   ever since Eomoni told me she was pregnant   my
head was full of names for you   in-hale ex-hale   I couldn't imagine anything
other than having a little brother   a little brother   I just knew I would have
a little brother   and I wanted to give you a name right away   my   little
brother, mine and mine alone   in-hale ex-hale   I thought of names with the
word for "spring" in them   because there are flowers everywhere in the
spring   in-hale ex-hale   the grasses and trees are budding   boys and
girls   young and old   the elites and the untouchables   in-hale ex-
hale   Japanese or Korean   everyone feels like there's something to
celebrate   Chun-jae   Chun-ik   Chun-seon   Chun-ho   Chun-gi
Chun-il   Chun-haeng   Chun-su   Chun-gil   Chun-seok   in-hale ex-
hale   Chun-beom   Chun-yeong   Chun-tae   Chun-gu   Chun-
geun   Chun-un   Chun-sik   in-hale ex-hale   Chun-sik   in-hale
ex-hale   Lee Chun-sik!   sewn in the spring   in-hale ex-hale   puts out

shoots   and quickly grows   to become a big tree   in-hale ex-hale   I never
told Abeoji in the end   and he decided on Woo-gun   but   your big
brother   in-hale ex-hale   like the proud father of his first son   in-hale
ex-hale   thought of your name   in-hale ex-hale   Abeoji is dead   from now
on I'm your abeoji   in-hale ex-hale   in-hale ex-hale   by the time I finished
speaking he had stopped crying   was there   a bridge over the Miryang
River then?   no   back then   in-hale ex-hale   the pontoon bridge must've
still been there   August 9, 1938   the day that Sohn Kee-chung took the
gold in Berlin   in-hale ex-hale   there was a bridge there then   I remember
the special editions scattered all over the bridge   in-hale ex-hale   because
the next morning   is when my brother started running   in-hale ex-hale
in-hale ex-hale   I'd told him that if he overslept I'd leave him so   he
dashed out into the garden the moment the rooster crowed   in a cotton
shirt and paji   in-hale ex-hale   we did our warm-up in silence so as not to
wake anyone else in the house up   and then we ran on the pre-dawn
riverbank   in-hale ex-hale   in-hale ex-hale   you're going a little
bowlegged   that's right   straight   in a straight line   in-hale ex-hale   that's
it   heel down first   like you're rolling the sole of your foot   shifting your
balance   in-hale ex-hale   in-hale ex-hale   you're tensing your shoulders   if
you do it that much they'll go numb later   in-hale ex-hale   relax   let your
arms and legs be like a clock's pendulum   that's it   oh, now look   your hips
are swiveling side to side   you can feel it right   how much easier that
is   in-hale ex-hale   in-hale ex-hale   athletic shoes custom-made by Mr. Park
from the Western shoe store hanging in both my hands   in-hale ex-
hale   and the look on his face as I came through the garden   in-hale
ex-hale   "My shoes!"   in-hale ex-hale   the barley rice he'd just been eating
flying out of his mouth   getting right up from the breakfast table to put on
the shoes   in-hale ex-hale   running around the garden   "They're
amazing!   I feel like I could fly.   Hyung   gamsahamnida!"   he was eleven
then   or maybe it was just after he turned twelve   ai-igo   neomuhada!
sesaenge   maldo andwae!   in-hale ex-hale   in-hale ex-hale   the last time I
saw him was a long time ago   five years?   ani   when they imposed the draft
on Korea   and I ran away to Ilbon   that was 1943   in-hale ex-hale   seven

years without seeing him   we were running and I said   wanna go to
Japan   in-hale ex-hale   and he said   in-hale ex-hale   "I've got things   to
do here   in this country   in Korea"   in-hale ex-hale   like what   in-hale
ex-hale   "I can't tell you yet"   he said still running   "I have something to
ask you"   in-hale ex-hale   "Can I use the name Chun-sik as a pseudonym?"
a pseudonym?   "Why do you need one?"   in-hale ex-hale   "through the
family registration system we've been enslaved by the waenom   and now
thanks to them my name is Kunimoto Ukon   but as a way to show that in
my heart I don't have allegiance to them, I want to withdraw from the wae's
register   I can't use this name, Kunimoto Ukon, which is covered in shame"
in-hale ex-hale   "to continue my resistance   to oppose them   to be able to
fight I need a new name as my fortress   from now on I'll go by Lee Chun-
sik."   in-hale ex-hale   I stopped at the foot of Namcheong Bridge   we
didn't say goodbye   someday   in-hale ex-hale   when we're liberated from
Ilbon   in-hale ex-hale   I'll come home and we'll meet again   in-hale
ex-hale   he ran off   at some point he'd gotten much faster than me   in-hale
ex-hale   he ran off and never turned back   in-hale ex-hale   that was
it   and while I was hiding out in Japan   in-hale ex-hale   he transferred
from Choyang High in Busan to Gyeongnam High   in-hale ex-hale   in-
hale ex-hale   became the leader of the Democratic Patriotic Youth
League   in-hale ex-hale   surveilled by police   in-hale ex-hale   and couldn't
go back to Miryang again   aigu   my little brother   my beloved little
brother   shot in the leg while he was running on an athletics
track   aigu   ai-igu   wen-il-iya   in-hale ex-hale   there were almost a
hundred students on that track   but however much I went around
asking   in-hale ex-hale   I couldn't find a witness   not one   in-hale ex-
hale   not even one   in-hale ex-hale   in the dorms at Gyeongnam High, the
so-called Little Kremlin   in-hale ex-hale   the police swarmed in   some
went north   some joined the Bodo League and disappeared   in-hale
ex-hale   in-hale ex-hale   the Democratic Patriotic Youth League went
totally underground   where could I go to find my little brother's
comrades   in-hale ex-hale   any big action was likely to get you informed
on   in-hale ex-hale   in-hale ex-hale   I went to members of the track team's

houses in secret   in-hale ex-hale   they all said   "I don't know anything"
"I haven't heard anything"   but   one of them   in-hale ex-hale   prefaced
with "This is just a rumor so I don't know if it's true or not"   in-hale ex-
hale   in-hale ex-hale   "Lee Chun-sik was shot in the leg trying to climb the
wall   he was bleeding   as he ran through the baseball field   past the
pool   through the wheat field"   in-hale ex-hale   "he got to the top of the
hill   and passed out near the reservoir, is what I heard   they're saying he
died of blood loss at the hospital in Toseong-dong"   in-hale ex-hale   "but
actually they took him to Busan Prison   and interrogated him   no visitors
were allowed so nobody can confirm"   in-hale ex-hale   "the Democratic
Patriotic Youth guys   keep accusing the National Student Federation   'you
bastards informed on Lee Chun-sik and got him killed'"   in-hale ex-
hale   "everyone, even the students who have nothing to do with leftist
activism, was crying   everyone at Gyeongnam High loved him"   in-hale
ex-hale   "underclassmen like me, we all wanted to be him   the
upperclassmen all trusted him   the teachers were proud of him   he had
good grades and could really run fast   he wasn't just a handsome guy"
in-hale ex-hale   "there were a lot of fights between us and other
schools   and whenever he heard that someone from Gyeongnam was being
beaten up   he'd run straight there and finish the other guys off with a flying
kick"   in-hale ex-hale   in-hale ex-hale   "in short, he was our hero"   in-
hale ex-hale   "he meant so much to us   it's impossible to put into words"
in-hale ex-hale   I asked   in-hale ex-hale   where he was buried   in-hale
ex-hale   and the pole jumper from the track team   reminded me once again
before he answered   "I didn't see this myself so this is nothing more than
hearsay but"   in-hale ex-hale   "Dadaepo"   in-hale ex-hale   "some people
call it Sancheong too"   in-hale ex-hale   "He wasn't taken on his own   they
loaded him up in a big truck   with some people from the Bodo League"
in-hale ex-hale   "they killed them in the mountains   I heard they
might've been buried"   in-hale ex-hale   in-hale ex-hale   I ran   and
ran   in-hale ex-hale   over Mount Gudeok and Mount Siyak near
Dadaepo   in-hale ex-hale   I ran   but I never found him   in the villages at
the base of the mountains   in-hale ex-hale   I asked if anyone had seen a

truck carrying people   or heard gunshots but   in-hale ex-hale   nobody'd
seen anything   nobody'd heard anything   who'd done it   or who had
killed them   in-hale ex-hale   was he alive   was he dead   in-hale ex-
hale   should I look at the ground   or look into the distance   in-hale
ex-hale   no trace   no landmark   no signpost   in-hale ex-hale   nothing
eobbda   eobbda   eobbda!   I couldn't follow the path that my little brother
was dragged up   the path   there   in-hale ex-hale   at the reservoir where he
quit running and lost consciousness   in-hale ex-hale   in-hale ex-hale   is
where it comes to an end   I can only rely on rumors   in-hale ex-
hale   but   even those rumors came from the mouths of people gagged by
fear   in-hale ex-hale   the facts are only slightly blurred   but   whatever else
happens   in-hale ex-hale   I want to find my little brother's body   and bury
him in the soil of Miryang   in-hale ex-hale   in-hale ex-hale   no matter how
decayed   or worm-eaten he must be   by now   there must still be something
left of his self   even now   in-hale ex-hale   your big brother will be able to
tell you apart on sight   my right eye clouded with tears   and my left eye dry
with anger   but   if he's nothing but bones   in-hale ex-hale   aigu   if your
remains are all piled up like firewood   in-hale ex-hale   in-hale ex-hale
your big brother won't be able to tell who you are   in-hale ex-hale   Lee
Woo-gun!   Appear before me as a spirit!   Lee Woo-gun!   Run in front of
me!   Show me where you're buried!   in-hale ex-hale   in-hale ex-hale   Hey,
you!   If you don't answer does that mean you're alive?   in-hale ex-hale   in-
hale ex-hale   my only little brother   in-hale ex-hale   in-hale ex-hale   my
only hope   in-hale ex-hale   in-hale ex-hale   Lee Woo-gun!
Shit, I fell!   In-hale   ex-hale, Woo-cheol got back up. In-hale   ex-hale, it's
so dark, how long have I been running, I went into the mountains after
breakfast, in-hale   ex-hale   in-hale, I started running sometime after nine,
the sun has gone down so it must be about six so, hana   dul   set   net
daseot   yeoseot   ilgop   yeodeol   ahop   nine hours, aigu, no wonder my
legs are so tired, in-hale ... ex-hale ... in-hale ... ex-hale ... As he took deep
breaths and brought his breathing under control, the breathing of the
mountains of Sancheong got closer, *sol sol sarang sarang   sol sol sarang
sarang,* the wind slipped between countless leaves to bring the essence of

green itself, *sol sol sarang sarang   sol sol sarang sarang*, Woo-cheol's body, overwhelmed by grief and exhaustion, was swaddled to sleep with that grief and exhaustion, *sol sol sarang sarang   sol sol sarang sarang* . . . in-hale . . . ex-hale . . . in-hale . . . ex-hale . . .

Long live the Democratic People's Republic of Korea!

His heart was seized by the scream; Woo-cheol realized that he was moving as if trying to push off the soil himself. I see a shovel . . . two men . . . one tall, the other short . . . Aigu, there's dirt in my eyes, aigu, aya! Ayaaa, aiguuu . . . I'm dead, he thought, and in that instant a headache rang out like the morning bell. The pain told Woo-cheol that he was alive; he was overwhelmed by the reality that sleep had renewed.

They killed my little brother.

With his eyes still closed, Woo-cheol rubbed his head. Bone, he thought. A helmet made of bone, covered, a pain in my head gradually becoming worse . . . I heard my brother's voice in my dreams: "**Long live the Democratic People's Republic of Korea!**" In my dream I was my brother, covered with dirt while I was still alive—aigu, did they bury him alive? Is he buried on this mountain? Woo-cheol pulled his shirt out from his paji and slowly slipped his right hand under his shirt. Warm skin . . . moving stomach . . . chest moving with my heartbeat . . . I'm alive . . . I'm alive . . . and Woo-gun? . . . does that mean he isn't? The bullet missed, he played dead and waited for the men to leave, and then he ran . . .

Woo-gun is alive, Woo-gun couldn't have been killed, the thought is, no, of course they killed him, push aside the idea that there's no way he could've been captured and escaped, but the wish that he could still be alive clings to the edge of my consciousness like a smell that won't go away no matter how hard I try to push it away—Woo-cheol took his head in his hands and pressed in hard with his fingers. At the back of his eyelids a yellow circle with a black center burned into his retinas; he could see the jagged contours melting away into the sun. The sun's up. It's morning again. I don't want to open my eyes. But I have to, I have to find his body. He has no abeoji or eomoni or wife or children; I'm the only family he has. Aigu, Woo-gun, I'm going to find you. He opened his eyes; it was dawn. The sun blazed into his eyes, but he couldn't even tell where it was for the thick, gray clouds.

Woo-cheol stood up. As if it had been waiting for him to get up, the rain started to patter down, five minutes, ten minutes . . . Woo-cheol stood there in the rain. As he did the ground around him became muddy, dirt splashing into his athletic shoes; he was soaked up to his ankles. If I can't find his body now, then I'll never be able to push away the possibility that he survived, and I'll search for him until I die, and even if I did stop, I'd always be waiting for him to reappear.

Saa-saa-saa, the rain fell harder.

Saa-saa-saa, Woo-cheol's eyes were hit by the rain.

Saa-saa-saa, he looked down at himself to avoid the rain.

Saa-saa-saa, he screamed his brother's other name into the rain.

Lee Chun-sik.

When I was going around Busan asking about my brother, nobody knew the name Lee Woo-gun, but as soon as I said Lee Chun-sik, everybody knew who he was. Not just as a Democratic Patriotic Youth operative, but for his speed, for his ability to fight, he was renowned, as Lee Chun-sik. Aigu, the name I thought of when I was twelve, ai-igu, aigu!

Saa-saa-saa, Woo-cheol ran through the rain. Not the thirty-seven-year-old Lee Woo-cheol, but the twelve-year-old.

In-hale ex-hale in-hale ex-hale   I ran   faster than a horse   faster than the dawn   in-hale ex-hale   across the Dongcheon   running straight up Mount Chiltan   to call for my halme   in-hale ex-hale   my little brother's been born!   My little brother, he's here!   in-hale ex-hale   in-hale ex-hale   halme! Ireonaseyo!   I knocked on Halme's door   she came right out carrying a cloth bundle   and she said   in-hale ex-hale   "I just had a dream   a bright red crescent moon snuck into your parents' room"   in-hale ex-hale   "aigo   it was melting away like it was losing blood   I hope the baby's not born under a bad sign"   in-hale ex-hale   sansin halmae   sansin halmae   geujeo   musahi   taeeonageman   haejusiso   irae bimnida   in-hale ex-hale   in-hale ex-hale   in-hale ex-hale   in-hale ex-hale   in-hale ex-hale

SHUFFLE

The Hanged Man (XII)

Upright—punishment, pain, helplessness,
hardship, immobility—

It seemed impossible that it had ever rained. The February morning sun peeked its head out from between the clouds, and set the ice covering the Miryang River glimmering, as the Busan-bound local appeared from the base of Mount Chiltan, *chikchik pokpok, chikchik pokpok*, blowing its whistle as it crossed the railway bridge, and the cluster of swans swimming at Yongdu-mok craned their long necks up at the sky, *Caw! Caw! Ca-aw! Caw! Caw! Ca-aw!*

As she listened to the swans' song, Arang ran her hand along the stumps of the Japanese cherry trees planted by the ilbon saram to comfort their roots. I won't forget how you rained your white blossoms on my shrine every single spring, how you were felled the day the torii gates were destroyed and the shrine was burned, how your roots bear their han—hearing the *whoosh-whoosh* of the wind off the river coming up the stone steps, Arang took her hand off the cherry trees' stumps and stood up, then looked down at Nam-cheong Bridge from where the torii gates of the shrine once were. The heads of partisans had been skewered on the railing of the bridge. Hana, dul, set, net on wooden stakes, their rain-soaked forelocks still bloody, frozen like icicles, winter flies rubbing their hands on their wide-open eyeballs. All were men not yet twenty, not even some poor girls' husbands yet—some poor women's sons. And even if their four mothers held their sons' heads and cried out their names, they could not put them back with their bodies and bury them properly; all they could do was cry soundlessly in the rooms where they slept. Were they to lay bare their sadness as sadness, their anger as anger, they would be slaughtered as the family of a ppalgaengi.

Arang crossed the bridge, the strings of her white chima jeogori flutter-flutter-flutter-fluttering, and stopped in front of the partisans' heads, then extended her long, white neck and placed a kiss on each of their lips.

The first man cried tears of blood.

The second blinked, little maggots falling from his eyes.

The third posed a question with his eyes.

The fourth man spit out the lump in his throat in the form of a song.

From the top of Mount Odae to Jeju Island
Among the trees
Among the rocks
Among you and me
We are the battalion armed with blood protecting the freedom of our land
Sons of Joseon
We will crush the invading enemy
The People's bayonet

Arang joined the partisan's song, swaying her body like a willow tree, fulfilling the four heads with her eyes; then she embraced them, one by one, and ran her hands, as if summoning their severed shoulders, backs, arms, through the sky.

Friends, how wonderful it is
To cut the irons that bound our thirty million people
Bravely fallen revolutionary fighters!

With both her breasts Arang covered the outlet of his voice and hid the partisan's head in her thick black hair. As she did, the softest part of the skin beneath the chin of her long, white neck broke, and blood gushed forth like water from a spring at the bottom of a river.

The bird crying in the pine trees   sounds so sad
Does it suffer   the curse of Arang?

Ari, arirang   suri, surirang   arariga nanne
Coming over Arirang Pass

She stained the partisan's head bright red, like thighs damp with menstrual blood. Even when the Miryang River froze, when there was no warm breeze off the river, hers was the blood of a virgin that would continue to flow warmly for eternity.

The moon that falls on Yeongnamul   is clear but
The Namcheong River just   flows silently

Ari, arirang   suri, surirang   arariga nanne
Coming over Arirang Pass

A young girl with a bob, holding the hand of her younger sister, just a toddler, came across the bridge. Jeogeo mwoji? What's on those sticks . . . Heads? . . . of dolls? . . . No! People! They're real! Aigu, eotteoke haji? Severed heads! Eotteoke hani? Eotteoke halkka, should we turn back and run? But Omma sent us to buy rice, and if we go back without it you know she'll hit us, let's hurry past them, ppalli, ppalli! If Shin-hwa wasn't here I could close my eyes and run, but she's too slow, way too slow.

"Shin-hwa, ppalli jom georeola, ppalli." *Hurry up, walk a little faster.*

Why does bad stuff always have to happen to me? My appa wasn't around when I was born. Aside from my two brothers, there's my two sisters from my appa's previous wife and a brother from yet another woman. My omma was always beating them, kicking them, throwing things at them, or threatening them with a knife. As soon as Appa disappeared, Omma got really violent; then she married off Mi-ok, Shin-ja ran away, Shin-cheol got taken away by his real omma, and that left me, Shin-myeong, Shin-ho, and Shin-hwa.

When Appa disappeared a year ago, Omma explained it to us like this: your uncle was the handsomest man in Miryang and he was such a great runner he could've made it to the Olympics, but he was shot and killed at only twenty-three. And your appa didn't do a single thing wrong either, but some bad guys got him and threw him in a detention center. Right before they were going to burn the place down with gasoline, your oppa escaped, and now he's hiding in Ilbon. But as soon as he's proven innocent and his life's not in danger anymore, Oppa will come back. When people in town talk about us behind our backs, just keep calm, because your appa hasn't done anything wrong; I know that much at least, and I'm his wife—

But it's been a year now and Appa still hasn't come back, and in that time all sorts of bad stuff has happened, like how they killed hundreds of people at the Nakano Factory in Sanmun-dong and the barrack house in Gagok-dong . . . and those heads . . . hana, dul, set, net . . . aigu, there's four of them . . . what if Appa comes back to Miryang and they . . . aigu, museun mal-eul!

"Shin-hwa, ppalli, if you're any slower I'll leave you, hana, dul! Hana, dul! Hana, dul!"

There's so much bad stuff happening, it never stops. Like a stream of blood, trickling out *cheol-cheol-cheol-cheol* . . . when there's no more blood, then what? Will the bad stuff go away too? But if the wound doesn't scab over and heal, new blood will trickle, *cheol-cheol-cheol-cheol cheol-cheol-cheol-cheol* . . .

Tomorrow, I'm going to Busan. Today's my farewell to Miryang. But Omma told us we can't tell anyone, so I can't say goodbye to anyone, not even Hee-sun at the clothes store or Hyeon-joo at the home goods store. Omma said that if she opens a restaurant at Busan Harbor, then she can talk to people who've come back from Ilbon or who are going there, and once she gets enough money and information, then we can stow away to Ilbon too, but . . . aigu, what's going to happen to us? Will good stuff happen if we go to Ilbon? Why don't I feel like good things could happen? I'm so scared, I'm so worried. I feel like beyond those four heads could be more and more. More and more and more and more . . . But what if I don't feel anxious, what if I am the anxiety itself? Maybe I'm the bad thing . . .

Her little sister planted her feet and pointed at a severed head.

"Jeogeo mwoya?" *What is that?*

"Aigu, bomyeon an doenda." *No, don't look.*

The girl looked. Into the eyes of the man on the bridge. At a glance tremendous sorrow came rushing in, and the girl stood there, forgetting what she was looking at, what was looking at her. *Caw! Caw! Ca-aw!* A swan, she thought, as her heart began to pound, *thu-thump, thu-thump*, and her fear became frenzied like a cat put in a gunnysack; she put her little sister on her back and began to run.

In-hale   twice   ex-hale   twice   calm your breathing   in-hale ex-hale   and your body will naturally follow   that's what Appa told me   in-hale ex-hale   in-hale ex-hale   if something awful happens just run   when you run   you can get away from scary things   you can outrun sad stuff too   in-hale ex-hale   in-hale ex-hale   but   Appa!   Museopda!   Naeneun museopda!   in-hale ex-hale   in-hale ex-hale   in-hale ex-hale   in-hale ex-hale   in-hale ex-hale

SHUFFLE

Queen of Wands

Upright—good mother, good wife, hardworking, chaste—

My hands are so dry, well, of course if you shampoo and perm twenty people in a day your hands'll be dry, but this stiffness I feel, it's not your normal stiffness. My elbows, shoulders, and neck all pop and crackle like there's pebbles inside them, I mean, look, just raising my shoulders like that, you heard the cracking my bones made, right? When I'm shampooing you it'd help if you just tightened up your neck a little, my dear, think you could raise your head up a bit? You won't tell anyone, will you? No matter how much my arms hurt, I still have to hold your head in my left hand and wash your hair with my right.

But remembering hurts worse than the pain in my arms. I remember washing my little sisters' hair, you know. Shin-hee and Shin-hwa, me and my two older sisters raised them; they feel more like my daughters than my sisters. Their first smiles, the first times they rolled over in their sleep, the first time they sat up, the first time they crawled, their first steps, their first words—the one who was there, helping, encouraging them, praising them, that was me, not Omma, not Appa. Can you believe this? Shin-hee's first word wasn't *Omma* or *Appa*; it was *Unni*.

She just gave birth to them, you know; there's not a woman with prettier hands than her, so pale and smooth, because all the cooking, washing, looking after the babies, she made us do all that, while morning and night she groomed herself, so she could go out all day and walk around in her silk chima jeogori. She didn't have those babies because she wanted children, you know. She was my abeoji's mistress; she had all those kids because she was competing with his real wife, my eomoni.

Still, you know, she was better than my eomoni, who deserted us and ran off. Personally, no matter how much my husband betrayed me, I wouldn't run off and leave my kids. If you're leaving you take the kids with you, that'd be the normal thing to do, right? Your own flesh and blood, you know? Unni went to our eomoni's parents' house, up by the station, once, and she got our grandma to tell her that she'd remarried and was living in Changnyeong, and I think she even went to see her, but I don't want to see her face, I don't even want to hear what she has to say. Unni said she's got two sons and two daughters now and that she snuck out of the house to meet her in a field, where nobody would see them, but why the hell did my unni have to go through all that?! Why couldn't she let her own daughter, who had traveled over four hours to see her, into her own house?! Why couldn't she give her something to eat or tell her, "Come back anytime?"

"Shin-ja, your little sisters are here," said Mrs. Seo, the owner of Dongmyeonggwan beauty parlor, spitting the phlegm she'd just brought up into the washbasin.

"My little sisters?"

So I'm thinking this must be some kind of mistake, and I open the door and who do I see standing there but Shin-hee, with her little bob, holding Shin-hwa's hand!

"I'm sorry, would you please excuse me? My little sisters have come from Miryang."

Instead of saying anything, Mrs. Seo coughed and spit out phlegm again.

"Weniriya?" What's wrong? As soon as I asked, the two burst out into tears. I wanted to say something, but my chest and throat were full of tears too, and all I could do was hold Shin-hwa in my right arm and pull Shin-hee toward me by her shoulder.

"You did good finding me here, you know? Is it just the two of you? Where's Eomoni?" I stroked Shin-hee's hair gently.

"A customer heard you were working at a beauty parlor nearby . . . a year ago we moved to Busan and Eomoni's running a restaurant at the harbor . . . Shin-myeong and Shin-ho went to Ilbon a month ago . . . they went on a people-smuggling boat . . . they're waiting at a friend's place in Kokura . . . Unni, why don't you come to Ilbon with us? Come to Ilbon, because Appa's there, and then we can all live together!" Shin-hee clung to my thigh with both hands.

I couldn't do anything but keep my mouth shut. I thought if I tried to speak, I'd never stop crying, so the best I could do was occasionally nod. What should I do, what do I want to do? I had no idea what my own feelings were. If it was just my two little sisters, I'd go to Ilbon without a second thought, but with that woman—

I walked hand in hand with them to the street corner, then I stopped.

"Take care," I said. I squeezed Shin-hee's hand and untangled my fingers from hers.

"Unni! But you're coming to Ilbon with us!" Shin-hee stuck her hand out again.

Pinkie promise, cross my heart and hope to die, stick a needle in my eye, promise!

On today's menu I've got soondubu-jjigae, miyeokguk, galchi mujolim, mu namul, miyeok julgibokk'eum, and I should probably make some doenjang-jjigae and gulkkakttug'i, too, at least. In the steam rising from the pot, she smiled. To be exact, only her mouth formed a smile; the rest of her face did not move a twitch, and she made not a single sound. The only burble was from the galchi, mu, dubu, and jogae cooking in the pot.

She put some bright red beef on a cutting board and picked up a thick knife, cutting along the sinews to remove them, massaged in a sauce of soy sauce, grated garlic, and pepper and let it marinate, then minced some mushrooms she had rehydrated in water.

Aigu, I can't wait any longer, I'm getting on the boat tomorrow night, and by nighttime the day after tomorrow, I'll be in Ilbon, where he is! I don't know where exactly he is, but I know I'll be able to find him whatever happens. Doesn't matter how many years it's been, I'll put my nose to the ground like a dog, and I'll sniff him out, aigu, his smell! I'll never be able to forget it, my whole body smeared in his sweat, oh, I'm coming, oh yes, more, more, more, aigu!

She cut the tofu and pumpkin into the same size as the mushrooms, stuck her knife into the green and red peppers diagonally, stuck her finger into the holes and pulled out the seeds, then chopped the green onions.

I'm going to see him again! Aigu, nae sarang, nae nampyeon! When I finally see him, before he can even make a sound I'm going to jump and kiss him, undo the buttons on his shirt and pull his paji down, take his thing out, and, aigu, ppalli, ppalli, ppalli, anajwo!

She put the beef in the broth she'd made from dried sardines and dissolved in some doenjang, added the pumpkin and mushrooms, then put the tofu in, and while that cooked, she scooped a ladle-full of lye and poured that in; finally, she added the peppers, green onions, and some grated garlic and turned down the heat.

I'm not a nymphomaniac, it's not just my body that wants him, all of me wants all of him; that's how it's been since the first night. The first time we slept together he was married, but I knew one day I'd be his wife. Because I wanted him ten times, a hundred times, a thousand times more than she did.

She sliced the mu and diced it. **Ah-aigu, aigu, nae namja! I had two of his sons, two of his daughters, but he's worth more to me than all four of them together.** She tore the minari leaves off the stems, then slice-slice-sliced them up with mustard greens and scallions. **If God himself appeared right here in this kitchen and told me, I'll let you be with him in exchange for your children, then right now I'd push them all into the sea.** She chop-chop-chopped ginger and garlic, took the milky-white oysters she'd shelled in the palm of her

hand, **aigu, nae namja! Naneun eommago mwogo da piryoeopseo**, I'm not
a mother! **Naneun geu saramui yeojaya**, I'm his woman! He's my man, and
I'm his woman, that's why I had his children, as proof. She washed them in
salt water, then drained the water with a spoon, sprinkled red pepper flakes
over the mu, then mixed it up with a wooden spoon until the radish had
turned red, added the ginger, garlic, mustard leaves, scallions, and minari and
mixed it all together, then seasoned it with finely minced preserved shrimp
paste, sugar, and salt, mix, mix, mix, **seongneunda, seongneunda, ah-aigo,
aigu, mix me around with your fingers, ah-ah-aigo, more! With your
mouth, your tongue!** Gently, so as not to break the oysters, she mixed, seongneunda, seongneunda, seongneunda! Your parts and mine together, seongneunda, seongneunda, seongneunda!

Behind the US military market near the harbor in Busan was a street of
warehouses with thirty or so restaurants. The Olympic Restaurant was a small
shop with six stools lined up along a long, narrow counter. Shin-ja took the
cloth bundle from her back and set it on the counter, then stepped into the
kitchen. A large pot had been left on the stove. Shin-ja lifted the lid and peeked
inside. Some doenjang-jjigae no longer fit to feed anyone with a thin oil slick
on it and blobs of white beef fat floating in it here and there. Shin-ja felt the
blood rushing to her head and her face turning bright red. This was a brand-
new kind of anger to her, something akin to the urge to kill. An Jeong-hee!
She stole my eomoni from me, stole my father, stole my two little sisters. Aigu,
Shin-hee! Shin-hwa! I'll never see them again . . . They were taken far from
me; they'll go on with their lives and forget about me . . . I'm far from them;
I'll go on with my life and never forget them . . . Shin-ja cried into the pan,
unable to kneel down or leave, continually saying their names like a crab spitting out froth . . . Shin-hee . . . Shin-hwa . . . Shin-hee . . . Shin-hwa . . .

SHUFFLE

Knight of Wands

*Upright—departure, travel, adventure,
emigration, determination—*

Shin-hee!

Someone called my name; I opened my eyes.

A dream.

Unni.

Unni was crying.

I guess she might really be crying right now. Aigu, Unni. . . .

Yesterday morning, Omma told us, tonight we're getting on the boat, so I said I was going to go tell Unni, and Omma said, "Shin-ja can't come with us," and I said, "Ple-ease! I don't want to go without her!" I cried and begged, but she said, in Ilbon we're going to live just the six of us, Appa and Omma and Shin-myeong and Shin-ho and Shin-hee and Shin-hwa, and if you're going to cry like that I'll leave you here too, so if you think that's just a threat, then go ahead and cry, because your omma always keeps her word, and Omma's eyes were narrowed like a fox's, so I really tried to stop crying.

Unni.

When I called my unni Unni, Appa always told me off. Don't call each other Oppa and Unni, Hyung or Noona; if we don't call each other by our names at home, who will, because if a name isn't said, then it dies out . . .

But, you know, my big sisters will always be unni to me. I don't mind calling my oppas Shin-myeong or Shin-ho, but my two big sisters, I can't call them Mi-ok and Shin-ja, just like I can't call my omma and appa by their names. So whenever Appa is at home I always get their attention by saying, "Hey," or, "Sorry," to get around it.

Unni, I'm at sea right now. We're going to Ilbon, but I don't know if we're closer to Busan or Ilbon right now. What time is it? I wonder. We got on the

Jangsanbong around 9:00 p.m. They only told us to come to the wharf at night; they didn't give us an exact time, so we were there before 6:00 waiting. There were more than a hundred boats at the wharf, and we couldn't tell which one was the *Jangsanbong*, but around 8:00 p.m., the other eight people showed up.

It's a small fishing boat. If you saw it, Unni, I know you'd be shocked. It's so small. There's an engine room, and only one captain, and I guess normally about two people would be on board?

Unni, where do you think we're hiding? In the tank where they'd usually put the cod and flying fish. It's less than a quarter as big as the bath at Unha Public Bath, a little less deep than I am tall, and there's eleven of us hiding in here! Isn't that something?

Let me introduce you to the other people being smuggled on the *Jangsanbong*.

There's a girl with a ponytail who's in her twenties and her two teenage brothers, who both have short hair. The three of them are wearing matching white open-collar shirts and black trousers; they look like ilbon saram.

There's a lady with white hair done up with hairpins with her granddaughter, who is two or three years older than me; they're wearing dirty white cotton jeogoris and black chimas, and they look like they're from the country. What on earth were they thinking, because they'll really stand out if they go walking around Japan dressed like that.

There's a young woman with a newborn baby; she's wearing dark pink lipstick and has a perm, and her breasts, with the straps of her baby sling pushing down on them, are as big as watermelons. She's kind of pretty, but not as pretty as our omma.

The last one is a man wearing a threadbare navy-blue suit, with thick, black-rimmed glasses, and whenever I look at him he's wrinkling his eyebrows and he's smoking, so I'm trying to sit as far away from him as I can.

When we left Busan Harbor, the waves were high, and the youngest of the three siblings threw up so many times. Something that looked like white noodles started to come out, even though he said he hadn't eaten any noodles, and as he was wiping his mouth with the handkerchief that his big sister held out to him, the man in the suit shouted, those are ringworms he just vomited, aigo, it stinks in here, and started beating the wall, so I just swallowed down what had come up. I think I was able to manage it because my stomach was empty. There was so much doenjang-jjigae in the big pot at the Olympic and my stomach was rumbling, but Omma said, "It'll be hell if you get seasick, and anyway you won't die if you don't eat for a day," so she didn't let me eat dinner. We don't have canteens or any food either; all we have is toiletries and a change of clothes each, and some money that Eomoni sewed into her underwear.

I went up on deck and the sea was black; the sky and the sea were just as black as each other. Eomoni shouted at me from the tank: "Take care you don't fall in the sea, if you're going to pee, hold on to the handrail and take your panties down with one hand and don't let go of the rail even when you're peeing."

I said, "Gwaenchana, I just don't feel good so I wanted to get a little air," and then I sat down on the deck for a little while. The waves were just as high as before, so maybe we'll be able to sneak through easily. They told us we only pay if we get through successfully, but if a guard ship finds us and takes us back, I doubt the police would let us go without paying. Badaui sinisiyeo, please let us cross the sea safely. As I was praying toward the pitch-black waves, I remembered the tale of Shim-chong that you read to me over and over, Unni, and I felt like Sim-cheong and I got over my nausea.

"Unlucky Sim-cheong prayed to the heavens: I do not wish to die at all, but if it will release my blind father from his life of suffering, I will happily become a water spirit, so please make my abeoji able to see as soon as possible."

The engine noise stopped, and I woke up. I guess the fact that I woke up means that I had fallen asleep. I don't remember doing it, but I went back to the tank at some point. The sun was shining through the gaps in the boards. I didn't sleep well, so my eyes were dazzled and my mouth was dry and sticky.

The man in the suit who had been up on deck to smoke a cigarette said, that's the Saga coast. I needed to pee, so I got out of the tank, and everything was bright blue, and isn't it kind of strange that the bright blue sea and sky in the daytime was scarier than when it was all pitch-black at night? I spun around and couldn't see anything, so how did the man know it was the Saga coast? But if I asked the man, I knew he wouldn't give me a serious answer and he might get angry, so I didn't ask. The air we've all been breathing over and over again is warm, smelly, and heavy, and just breathing it makes you feel bad. So nobody's talking. And I feel seasick and tired and hungry and worried, so I don't want to talk, either. The big sister with her two little brothers, she said to Omma, "I just got my period, do you have anything?" and that was the first time I'd heard anyone speak for ages, but Omma just shook her head silently, eyes still closed.

The *Jangsanbong* stopped its engine around noon; they say that when it gets dark again they'll turn it back on and we'll go the rest of the way. I'm sure it's a tactic to not get found by the guard boats, but without the engine on, the shaking of the waves is at its worst. But sometime tonight we'll make it to Il-bon. If anything goes wrong, and we have to stay at sea another day, I just might start thinking about jumping into the sea.

The sun went down at sea.

The engine has stopped.

The captain opened the lid to the tank and explained that we had already arrived off the coast of Kyushu, but that it was too dangerous unless we waited until it was late at night; we will enter Moji Harbor after nine o'clock. The young mother carrying the baby huffed and puffed a little as she undid her baby's sling, opened the buttons on her floral-patterned blouse, and pulled her breast out. The sound of the baby suckling was loud, and for some reason, I started to wish I could have some milk too; I mean, after all, I'd had nothing to drink for a whole day but my own spit.

The man in the suit started murmuring to the woman. What does your husband do?

He's a detective in the Busan Police.

Oh, then why's the wife of a detective smuggling herself and her baby to Japan?

I was arrested because I was suspected of giving information to people on the left.

Aigu, how horrible, what will you do now?

I don't know yet.

You haven't decided?

No, not at all.

Do you have relatives there?

Not in Japan, no.

You're welcome to come to Osaka with me, you know.

The man in the suit put his hand on the woman's thigh and stole a glance at her breasts. Aigu, I couldn't take it; I closed my eyes. As soon as I did, I felt drowsy.

Dochakaetda naeryeo! *We're here, time to get out!*

The lid opened.

Rubbing my sleepy eyes, I climbed out on deck.

It was so dark I couldn't see a thing.

They hadn't put the lights on so we wouldn't be found, I guess.

We crossed the plank to the wharf and one by one came on land.

A Japanese fisherman lit the ground with a flashlight and guided us into the mountains. He led us to a spot, the only place where trees had been cut down and brush had been cleared, so it was probably used as a hideout for stowaways. Another flashlight approached, and it was his wife bringing us water, rice balls, and pickled radish. The fisherman asked the man in the suit for a cigarette. The two of them smoked side by side. The tips of their cigarettes burned redder with each puff, and their two faces hovered hazily in the air.

We all gave our money to the fisherman. It was dark, so I don't know how much the others gave him, but Omma gave him five thousand yen.

If you all go to town at once you'll attract attention, so I'll take you to the station one group at a time, but after that you're on your own, you know, I'll pray for your good luck, he said, stuffing the bundle of thousand-yen notes into his pocket.

We have to get on the train at Moji Station and go meet Shin-myeong and Shin-ho, who are in Kokura.

Then the five of us will go off in search of Appa.

Unni, I'm here, I'm in Japan now.

SHUFFLE

Queen of Cups

Upright—beautiful woman, good mother, beloved wife,
good household, consideration—

On today's menu I've got mince and tofu stew, seaweed soup, stewed beltfish and radish, radish namul, and seaweed stalk stir-fry, and I should probably make some miso nabe and oyster and radish kimchi too, at least.

In the steam rising from the pot, she contorted her defeated, exhausted, wounded face, but only her lips stayed a perfect straight line out of extraordinarily strong self-resolve. The only burble did not come from the beltfish, radish, tofu, and clams in the pot.

She put some bright red beef on a cutting board and picked up a thick knife, cutting along the grain in thin, thin slices, massaged in a sauce of soy sauce, grated garlic, and pepper and let it marinate, then minced some shiitake mushrooms she had rehydrated in water. **He's a liar. Every damn thing he said was a lie. He said he was Korean, but he never said a word about having a wife and kids back home. He said if we got married, then immigration would find out he was here illegally and they'd send him back, so I gave up on marrying him legally, but I still got my parents and relatives together and we had a ceremony at Kashima Jingu and even went to Atami on our honeymoon. Not long after, Shin'ichi was born, and he was so happy about the birth of his "first son" that I thought he'd jump for joy, so much so that I thought, you know, this is what they mean when they say "he's the apple of my eye," that's how much he loved him. Then he said, only children are so lonely so let's give him a little brother or sister, let's have a big family with lots of kids running around—the gall of the man!**

She cut the tofu and pumpkin into the same size as the mushrooms, stuck her knife into the green and red peppers diagonally, stuck her finger into the holes and pulled out the seeds, then chopped the green onions. **I never once** thought he'd cheat on me. He was my husband, and I was his wife, and I thought that's how it'd be forever, and that's what the kids thought too, until that day when it all ended. Then this bitch who suddenly knocked on the door comes bursting into my house, ranting something in Korean that I couldn't understand, and she slapped me. He didn't even try to protect me, his own wife. He just stood there, pale as a fucking ghost. Shin'ichi, who was only a year old, started crying. He wasn't the only one crying, because the two little bitches standing behind the bitch were at it too. The older one was about ten, and the younger one was five, maybe six . . . They were looking right at me and I gulped. Their eyes, noses, mouths . . . they looked just like him and Shin'ichi.

She put the beef in the broth she'd made from dried sardines and dissolved in some doenjang, added the pumpkin and mushrooms, then put the tofu in, and while that cooked, she scooped a ladle-full of lye and poured that in; finally, she added the peppers, green onions, and some grated garlic and turned up the heat. **The most unforgivable thing is that he gave all his kids names with** *shin*, **the word for "faith." Shin-myeong, Shin-ho, Shin-hee, Shin-hwa, Shin'ichi . . . With a name like that, no matter how his father betrays him, he'll go on be-lieving, he won't be afraid to trust, to follow through with something . . .**

She sliced the daikon and diced it, **that bitch just popped out four kids, doesn't make a peep for six years, and then she turns up a month ago and now,** she tore the seri leaves off their stems, then slice-slice-sliced them up with mustard greens and scallions, **here she is making me wash her brassiere and her knitted, yellowed panties, and you don't do a fucking thing, while she's off to the Suzuki Beauty Salon to get her hair permed and dyed chestnut brown,** she chop-chop-chopped ginger and garlic, took the milky-white oysters she'd shelled in the palm of her hand, **every day she's painting her fingernails and toenails a different color, perfume, new shoes, coats, suits, blouses, skirts, scarves . . . and they're all cashmere or silk imports! All the money he and I saved up toiling in a pachinko parlor, just to dress her up like a pea-cock, even though she's fifteen years older than me and has had four kids, she looks way younger than me and more with it!** She washed them in salt water, then drained the water with a spoon, sprinkled red pepper flakes over the daikon, then mixed it up with a wooden spoon until the radish had turned red.

Yesterday, when Shin'ichi came home from school, that woman and Shin-myeong, Shin-ho, Shin-hee, and Shin-hwa were eating watermelon, and when Shin'ichi asked if he could have some, that bitch told him that it was her watermelon, so when Shin'ichi came all the way to the pachinko parlor to tell me, crying, well, that's when I absolutely lost it and I told that man: I divide everything up equally for everyone, even watermelon, even if maybe one of the kids was especially good that day and ought to get more. At dinnertime, he tried to talk to her about it, I don't know how he tried to bring it up, because the two of them sat at their own table facing each other to eat. To eat the Korean food that I made, talking to each other in Korean, which I don't fucking understand, laughing with each other, while I was so rushed off my feet I couldn't hardly speak, and the kids were messing around and getting on my nerves, and that bitch laughs hysterically, well, I don't know Korean, but I sure got the gist of it, I could hear her laughing all the way in the kitchen . . . Shin'ichi ate at the same table with Shin-ho, Shin-myeong, Shin-hee, and Shin-hwa, but I always have my food in the kitchen, standing up, because I don't care for the stupidly hot kind of food they like to eat over there, so I just had some pickled radish and rice with green tea poured over it, added the ginger, garlic, mustard leaves, scallions, and minari and mixed it all together, then seasoned it with finely minced preserved shrimp paste, sugar, and salt, and mixed, mixed, and that bitch stayed up until the roosters crowed this morning walking around holding a knife in her hand. From the first floor to the second, from the second to the first, never saying a word . . . I hate those people; the slightest thing happens and they pull something on you. He's the same: when he gets angry, he grabs whatever he can lay his hands on and throws it; one time he even grabbed a hatchet from the storage room and chased Shin-hee around with it. When he gets into a fight with a drunk customer, sometimes he throws pachinko trays at their head . . . Maybe that's how they do things over there, but it's total insanity. Having two wives and five kids in a house this small . . . If it weren't for Shin'ichi, I'd have left him right away. But I've got to put up with it so Shin'ichi's not ostracized as an illegitimate child, so until he grows up and gets married, I'll have to be patient, gently, so as not to break the oysters, she mixed, mixed, mixed! Mixed, mixed, mixed!

SHUFFLE

The Fool

Upright—thoughtlessness, folly, whims, purposeless situation,
disordered personal life, wandering—

October 21, 1964: Two hours have passed since the start of the men's marathon at one p.m. It is now around three p.m. The athletes are finally returning to the stadium. Currently in the lead is Abebe Bikila, from Ethiopia. Runner number seventeen, Abebe has just entered the track from the south entrance. Wearing white shoes this time, Abebe, the hero of Ethiopia, runs. Applause erupts from the packed stands. He's running down the track, far ahead of all the other competitors, calmly, with his head slightly down. The barefoot champion of the last Olympics in Rome, running now for back-to-back Olympic gold. Wearing red shorts, a green shirt, and the honor of his homeland, Ethiopia. He's not slowing down at all. He's across the line. Abebe Bikila takes the gold. His time was two hours, twelve minutes, and eleven seconds, setting a new world record. Which is, of course, also a new Olympic record, a tremendous achievement. He truly is superhuman. Now, he's refusing the blanket offered to him by the staff; he's gone into the field instead. He's doing calisthenics, as if to say, I could keep going. And—well, the rest of the competitors haven't yet appeared.

Woo-cheol walked slowly around the floor of the Million Dollar, sometimes bending over and picking up balls that had rolled into the aisles with a magnetic rod. *Plink-plink, rumble rumble, bing-biing, plink-plink, rumble rumble,* with the advent of unmanned machines five years ago, there's no need to make Shin-myeong or Shin-ho run around behind them stuffing the balls in, and I don't have to shout, "Hurry up! Quit dawdling!" at them either. The big parlors in Tokyo, Nagoya, and Osaka have machines that can automatically refill the balls, with mechanical cups and traps. They say losers on average lose a day's wages, and if you win, thousands of balls come pouring out, so many they can't carry all the prizes, so the exchangers wandering around in front of the parlors with bundles give them a ten-yen discount on cash conversions, but this isn't Tokyo or Nagoya or Osaka; this is Edosaki, Ibaraki. If I wait six months, I can get secondhand machines for half the price. I refuse to buy the machines with cracks in the glass covered over with paper or the ones that are so rusted that no matter how hard you pull back the ball won't go, but the unreliable ones, where you have to hit it a few times for the ball to come down, our adjuster Yu can make those work like brand new. He can do any kind of machine: All Peephole ones, Dendenmushi, Big Chuckers, Comic Gates, Comic Centers, Jinmits, Rekonjister Mammoths . . .

> Finally, the second-place runner's come into sight. Japan's Kokichi Tsuburaya, wearing number seventy-seven. Applause and cheers coming from the stands again. The crowd has gotten to its feet, lots of Japanese flags waving now. Tsuburaya! Tsuburaya! If things stay as they are, he'll take the silver. Go, Tsuburaya! C'mon! He seems to be struggling. He's coming around the first corner into the straight. Just three hundred meters to the finish line, but Basil Heatley from England is coming up behind him, number eight. Tsuburaya doesn't look back. He's staggering a little. Just a little farther, c'mon, Tsuburaya! But Heatley is close behind. Watch out! C'mon, Tsuburaya! Coming around the third corner now, just two hundred meters to go. Heatley's speeding up! Closing the gap, from ten meters, five now, oh, he's passed Tsuburaya! Tsuburaya has been overtaken! But he's still in third place. C'mon, Tsubura-ya! Just a little farther to the finish. Just after Heatley, he reaches the finish line! Third place, bronze medal! This is the first time in the twenty-eight years since Berlin that Japan has won a medal in men's track and field! Two hours, sixteen minutes, and twenty-two seconds! Stupendous effort by Tsuburaya, the bronze medalist. He's taken the towel now and fallen on to the grass.

Woo-cheol called out to Yu, who was fiddling with the little nails on a machine with a notice reading CURRENTLY BROKEN, UNDER REPAIR.

"Hey, Yu, go put on a record for me."

"But, sir, the customers care about the Olympics; they'll leave."

"All that's left is the medal ceremony."

"Yes, sir."

"Don't you think you've been at that long enough?"

"I'll cut the spring, put an out-of-order sign on it, and swap it out. But, sir, Dove Hall's been paying out big all day; you can barely get past their parlor for the line of bicycles outside. Sir, when Dove's paying out, we've got to pay out bigger. It's a battle. If our customers are going around the neighborhood saying they won big, then people will ask what parlor, which machine, right? If you think of it as advertising, then it's cheap as it goes. Twenty cheapo machines, forty break-even, forty high-roller machines; if we don't do it this way, Dove'll crush us."

"Since even in this backwater shopping street there's a pachinko parlor right across the road. . . ."

"That's what they're saying at Dove too. After all, sir, you opened up after they did."

He sure is a smart guy and handsome too; he's got it all. And Shin-hee really likes him, so it's not that I don't understand why she might say he's the only one for her, but I said, he's a little older than Shin-hee and he left elementary school, so his reading and writing's not great, might there not be a better match for her? But to listen to Jeong-hee tell it, one of Shin-hee's classmates from high school was going to propose to her. She could never be happy being with a Japanese guy. And Yu's from South Gyeongsang, like me, and when I said that I'd send him to college if he married Shin-hee, then he said, in our language, ttanimeul haengbokage haejugennorago. *I promise I'll make her happy.* They'll be getting married next spring.

> The rest of the competitors are at the finish. Kilby from Britain; Sütő from Hungary; the American, Edelen; Vandendriessche from Belgium; and now, Japan's Kenji Kimihara. At two hours, nineteen minutes, and forty-nine seconds, Kimihara has taken eighth place.

"So Kimihara placed too?"

"Yeah."

"Then I'll put on a record now."

Woo-cheol saw Shin-hee standing on the floor. With every year she's more like Jeong-hee, and not just in looks; she has the same wild temper—once, when a customer tried to touch her butt she punched him so hard that his nose bled. And just like Jeong-hee wasn't meant to be a wife or mother, I doubt she's the type of woman who can settle down either.

> *He's a good man, the more you look at him*
> *And when I start drinking, he's the best in Japan*
> *Tokoton, Tokoton*
> *Darling, I love you, my lovely*
> *And flowers bloom at the Tokoton Bar*
> *He comes in ten days a week*
> *Tokoton, Tokoton*
> *Don't fall for him, I told myself*
> *But now here I am*
> *Tokoton, Tokoton*
> *And if he starts barhopping, it's proof that he's cheating*
> *C'mon, have a drink at the Tokoton Bar*
> *He comes in ten days a week*
> *Tokoton, Tokoton . . .*

"Yu, what the hell are you playing? Put on something faster; people won't bang through the balls to something this slow," Woo-cheol shouted, watching behind a customer's back as the silver ball ran around behind the glass, juddering over the four pins at the top, *clink-clink-clinking* as it squeezed through the cream-colored, red-bordered pinwheel, and hits off the "petals" around the traps.

> **Two hours, sixteen minutes, and twenty-two seconds . . . This is the first time in the twenty-eight years since Berlin that Japan has won a medal in men's track and field! Twenty-eight years ago . . . Berlin . . . Two hours, twenty-nine minutes, nineteen seconds . . .**

Woo-cheol rolled the name around in his mouth over and over, then with great effort, he said it aloud.
Sohn Kee-chung.

> **The crowd has taken to its feet, lots of Japanese flags waving now . . .**

Why doesn't this hurt me? . . . Any Korean would remember that moment at the finish line twenty-eight years ago . . . I no longer belong to my country . . . I don't belong anywhere in the world . . . the world isn't part of me . . . and I'm not part of it either . . . I don't even belong in myself . . . I'm being bounced off myself . . . *Plink-plink, rumble rumble, bing, rumble rumble* . . . I'm . . . where am I? Four thousand times I've started the day with—as you do when you run a store here—an imperial navy march, and I've ended it with "Auld Lang Syne," and next month I'll be fifty-two. Just another six hours until I play "Auld Lang Syne" again, but I can't finish myself. Am I the kind of man who's the main character in my own story?

How many years do I have to live with the feeling that I'm completely absent? Woo-cheol looked outside of the parlor. The reverse of the characters that Jeong-hee had written on posters to draw customers in caught his eye. **TREMENDOUS 100 PERCENT JACKPOTS.** Woo-cheol repeated words of condolence to himself. Eolmana aetonghasimnikka jinsimeuro aedoui tteuseul pyohamnida. I am very sorry for your loss, my deepest condolences. *Plink-plink, rumble-rumble, ping, rumble rumble rumble, plink-plink, rumble rumble, ping, rumble rumble rumble.*

SHUFFLE

The Moon (XVIII)

Reversed—perceiving deception and danger—

RHEE SYNGMAN ANNOUNCES RESIGNATION

After liberation I returned to this country and I have lived well in my beloved nation with my patriotic countrymen. I have no resentment over resigning; I have acted in line with the will of the people and I have carried out their desires, which was always my wish. According to reports, my nation and my fellow patriotic countrymen, with my beloved youths and students at their head, are demanding action from me, so I shall state a few things below, but I have only one wish: that my compatriots keep in mind the reality that the Communist Army is waiting vigilantly to invade our nation from the Thirty-Eighth Parallel, and that they must not be given the opportunity.

1. If it is what the people wish, I will resign as president.
2. It is said there were many irregularities in the March elections for president and vice president, so I have instructed the holding of a repeat election.
3. To eliminate some of the improprieties that occurred during the election, Chairman Lee Ki-poong will retire from public office.
4. As I have already agreed, if the people wish, I will amend the constitution to make the government one of cabinet responsibility.

Dong-A Ilbo, April 27, 1960

REPRESENTATIVES OF ALL POLITICAL PARTIES AND SOCIAL GROUPS!

Following the popular uprising in Masan in opposition to the fascist terrorism of American imperialism and Rhee Syngman's gang, the heroic struggle of the South Korean people is reaching new heights, from the riots in Seoul starting on April 19, spreading to Busan, Daegu, Incheon, Gwangju, Cheongju, Daejeon, Suwon, and more.

On the April 24 and 25, mass demonstrations and uprisings again spread through Seoul, Busan, Daegu, Jinju, Chuncheon, Daejeon, Masan, Cheongju, and elsewhere across South Korea.

Infuriated by the repression of American imperialism and Rhee Syngman's gang, who are brutally trying to suppress the legitimate resistance of the South Korean people with bloody bar-

barism, the citizens of Seoul have burned down Lee Ki-poong's mansion and destroyed all the puppet governing institutions.

By the April 26, there were crowds of more than 100,000 at these demonstrations, and the battle has intensified.

The crowd rushed like a surging wave to the Dongdaemun Police Station and other puppet police organizations, and they destroyed and burned them down.

The demonstrators surrounding Rhee Syngman's official residence broke through the lines of police and military police and forced their way in, arguing with Rhee and demanding his resignation.

Frightened and unable to oppose the pressure of the demonstrators, Rhee had to announce his resignation and declare that the election would be recalled.... The resistance of the South Korean people burns like a hand of fire that cannot be blocked by any violent suppression.

This heroic struggle of the South Korean people is an outburst of pent-up rage and resentment toward American imperialism and the Rhee Syngman gang, and it is a manifestation of their strong determination to live no longer under misrule.

This situation shows that the fervor of the struggle of the South Korean people, who seek a new politics, a new way of life, new leadership, principles, and freedom, can no longer be oppressed by any force... The "martial law" proclaimed by the Rhee Syngman gang, masterminded by the American imperialists, must be abolished immediately, and all schools should be reopened at once. Restrictions on movement and suppression of free speech must be lifted immediately.

Representatives of all parties and social groups!

We express our hope that all political parties, social organizations, and social-political activists who are concerned about the current situation in South Korea and the future and fate of our people will respond to our proposal... Regardless of the past, regardless of differences in political views or faith or property ownership, we must rise up without reserve for our country and our people. We cannot let the blood shed by the South Korean people go to waste, nor can we ignore their demands for which they are fighting to the death.

We must rise up as one in the sacred struggle for the peaceful reunification of our country and demand the immediate withdrawal of the American imperialist invaders from South Korea, who have plunged South Korea into a living hell of misery and suffering and who caused the miserable scenes of today.

Rodong Sinmun, *April 28, 1960*

It was the height of August. The blue sky squeezed the last light of the day from the sun sinking in the west and dyed the tops of the mountains red, but the cicadas did not seem to have noticed the sunset yet, crying out, *maeaemmaeaemmaeaem sseureuram sseureuram chireureureut chireureureut maeaemmaeaemmaeaem.* There was no wind. No people, either. She could see nothing moving except for one big, black kite, wings spread in the blue sky, and a truck driving up the gravel road between the mountains, scattering dust.

The truck was covered with a canopy, and its cargo could not be seen from the outside, but its canopy flipped up in time as the truck bumped over the rocks, and hana dul set net daseot yeoseot ilgop, she caught a glimpse of them: seven men and one woman.

"Aigu, the sun's about to set. Have to dig before it gets dark . . ." A woman, no longer so young, with a prominent forehead like a boulder, stuck her head out of the canopy.

"Huh? What'd you just say?" A man pulled at the fingers of the work glove on his right hand with his left, then wiped the sweat from his face with the balled-up glove.

"I said, we have to dig before it gets dark." She brushed her bangs, slicked with sweat, up off her forehead, and looked at the eight shovels lying at each of their feet.

"Why can't you just speak up?" The man pulled the glove from his left hand and grabbed the handle of a shovel with his sweat-dampened hands.

"Because I was talking to myself. Or do I have to talk to myself loud enough so you can hear too?"

It was the woman's cousin who broke the atmosphere, which was threatening to turn nasty.

"We can't go digging so often, because people'll catch on."

"But it'll be pitch black in two hours, and there's over a hundred . . ."

"Gwaenchana. The women in the village said that they weren't buried too deep, so we should be able to find them without much digging . . . There's a little roadside shrine. When I asked the ladies doing their washing what the little shrine was for, they said, 'It's because the bones keep washing down. Ten years ago, in the fall, they killed over a hundred ppalgaengi; the river turned red, and the crows picked at their corpses. As soon as we thought the river had gone back to normal, then the bones started to come. There were so many of them that we picked up the bones and built a shrine. Even nowadays, after a storm, they still come.'"

"You don't think they reported us to the police?"

"I thanked them for building the shrine and said, 'My cousin was also killed here,' and they got scared and said, 'If you get caught, don't tell them a thing about what you heard from us. Forget our faces . . .' Gwaenchana, we're fine . . ."

"Ah-aigu! That's no proof!"

"I showed you that clipping from the *Dong-A Ilbo*, didn't I? The dictatorship has fallen. The Democratic Party won the general election overwhelmingly. Times have changed. You can say what you want now; the politicians and students in Seoul are working together now, heading for unity. From hostility to dialogue. I'm sure in just a few years we'll achieve reunification and the honor of our slaughtered families will be restored."

"A lot of innocent people were murdered, and the families of those who were killed lived lives where they couldn't breathe freely, while listening to the laughter of the guilty who remain unpunished . . ."

"In this small town, victims and perpetrators live together, passing each other on the bridge. . . . But I've never thought about living anywhere else. Because we've done nothing wrong. My four brothers, who were killed for the simple reason that they had the same blood running through their veins as Kim Won-bong, and my abeoji, who died of grief, and me, locked up in the Nakano Factory for two years and then even after I was released went on to battle hunger with my eomoni—none of us did anything wrong.

"I don't go around telling people I'm Kim Won-bong's little sister, but if someone asks me I don't deny it. Of course, being related to him has caused me all kinds of hardships, but it's also thanks to him that I was able to endure those hardships. The pencils and English dictionary he gave me are treasures to me, and every morning I always say to his photo, annyeonghasimnikka?"

"You have a picture?"

"Just one; my abeoji hid it. It's a picture of the whole family, taken on February 26, 1946, the day when he returned home for the first time in thirty years. I was seventeen, he was forty-eight. I saw the picture the day I got out of the Nakano Factory. That day . . . aigu, there were less than ten of us left in the factory. The door opened, and I heard someone say, you can go home . . . I was the only one who could stand and walk; the rest were put on boards and carried off by their families. It was late afternoon, but the sun hurt my eyes so much I couldn't go outside. I'd been locked up in a dark factory for two years, after all. My eomoni, who had come to pick me up, waited with me for the sun to set before we went home. Abeoji, who was in his sickbed, called out and I cried. Ireukyeojwo, he beckoned, so Eomoni lent him her shoulder and he removed the boards in the storeroom and pulled out a photo. In the picture, my brother looks stronger and straighter than the ones I always see, and he's looking at me . . . Aigu, when the North and South are united, I'll be able to see him again."

"Is he alive?"

"Two or three years ago I heard he became the vice chairman of the standing committee of the Supreme People's Assembly and Medal of Labor merit, but there's a rumor that soon after he was dismissed and purged. If he's alive he'd be sixty-two . . ."

"He's alive. I can tell looking at the photo."

"I think he's alive too. Alive and coming back home. The men who went to the North, the ones who went to Ilbon too . . . Oh, I wonder whatever happened to him?"

"'Him'? Who do you mean?"

"Oh . . . you know . . . aigu, I can't think of his name . . . the marathon runner . . ."

"Lee Woo-cheol."

"That's it, Lee Woo-cheol!"

"I heard he escaped to Japan and he's been successful in the pachinko business, but I don't really know; it was just a rumor.

"Boy, how I'd like to talk to him. We talked so much, you know. I probably talked to him more than to my own wife. When I was twenty, at the air defense lookout post and we'd look up at the night sky and . . . and then when I was twenty-six, in the detention center . . . in the times when we thought we might be killed the next day . . ."

"I wonder if he's still running."

"He can't be, surely. I mean, he's eleven years older than me, and I'm forty-eight this year; aigu, he really could've won a medal at the Olympics, but what an unlucky guy. I don't know if I'm lucky or unlucky . . . I escaped when they poured gasoline around the detention center, just before they blew it up with hand grenades, but they got me again almost immediately and court-martialed me at the highest level. . . . Doesn't it make your hair stand on end? That's when I realized that it's not just a phrase—it really does happen. My wife went to my best friend, who was the deputy director of the Busan prison camp, and she begged for my life. So then they were going to take me to court for a normal trial, and my friend told the prosecutor that the army would vouch for my identity, so they released me the next day. If my wife and best friend hadn't helped me I know I would've been killed . . . just like your four brothers . . . we've found where Deok-bong was killed, but the rest who were taken to the police station, Yong-bong, Bong-gi, and Gu-bong, I don't think we'll ever find them as long as the bastards who killed them keep their mouths shut."

"I'll find them no matter how long it takes. . . . How much longer until we get there?"

"Maybe about half an hour."

Rubbing his hands together, the man listening to Kim Won-bong's sister and cousin speak tugged on the sides of his work gloves as he put them on, then immediately started rubbing his hands again.

"What do we do with the bodies?" he asked.

"Like we said at last night's meeting, we'll have to line them up near the pine trees at the athletics field and put them in coffins. Speaking of coffins . . ."

"There's five of them."

"You think that's enough?"

"Yeah, probably. They're scattered so much they're washing down into the river, after all."

"I guess we won't be able to tell whose bones are whose."

"We'll have a joint memorial service . . . they'll have to be cremated and buried together."

"I don't want to leave behind a single finger bone. . . . Aigu, even now I can remember that rainy night . . . the factory had a corrugated iron roof, and all night long it was hitting the roof like a buk, *dum-dum-dum-dum-dum-dum-dum-dum* . . . they stood us up against a wall and shone a flashlight in our faces, and as they called names they gagged those people, like, like this, and then they wound a wire around both their thumbs . . . I didn't hear my brother's name being called for the sound of the rain . . . Aigu, Oppa . . . Deok-bong . . . what kind of state are you in now . . . ?"

"Stop somewhere in the middle of the slope where it's easy to park. We won't be able to go any farther by truck. We'll have to walk up."

The engine stopped and the canopy opened. They got out at the spot where ten years ago, their abeojis and oppas and cousins and uncles had been forced to get out.

"We'll climb along the river, to over there, where the mountain drops off into a cliff . . . there's a hollow there, between big rocks where there's no escape," Kim Won-bong's cousin said, pointing up above the river.

"Aigu, sesange . . ." Another man, whose younger sister was killed, gulped, his Adam's apple rising and falling.

The mountain was bright red. Crows flew past like spears past the sun, which threatened to set at any moment, and as the words "the river turned red and the crows picked at their corpses" soaked into her skin with the setting sun, Kim Won-bong's youngest sister let out a moan and grasped her shovel with a sadness unthreatenable by anything.

The landscape had not changed in the slightest. The white steam of dinner being prepared rose languidly from the chimneys of the bark-roofed houses squatting in the valley. In this village in the last ten years two hundred people were born and three hundred died; many were involved in those lives, in those deaths, so being and not-being soon became a familiar part of life.

Only the 134 dead killed on November 15, 1951, remained new.

SHUFFLE

Ace of Wands

Upright—beginning, source, birth, marriage—

I had a baby . . . a girl, five pounds and three ounces . . . "had," it sounds like it's something that happened in the past . . . when I had her just thirty minutes ago . . . a very small baby girl . . . I'm a mother now . . . but I don't understand how . . . I was in labor for six and a half hours but the real feeling that I gave birth is nowhere in my body now . . . come to think of it I haven't heard her cry . . . her head came out, but her shoulders just wouldn't; I breathed out hard and summoned all the strength in my body between my legs . . . I gripped the handles on the delivery table . . . right shoulder . . . then left . . . they pulled her torso and legs out of me, slimily . . . but I haven't heard her cry . . . was she stillborn? . . . all the strength has left me . . . for months and months I waited . . . and she was born dead . . . "Congratulations, you have a healthy daughter," I heard the doctor say, and my consciousness slipped away . . . where is the baby . . . in an incubator . . . she was premature after all . . . the baby's in the incubator sleeping, don't worry, you did a great job, now have a little rest . . . she had the same kind of shoes as Fusako so that must've been the head nurse speaking . . . the baby I gave birth to . . . my baby . . . I haven't heard her cry, I haven't seen her face, I haven't even held her yet, my baby . . .

God, it's bright . . . it's morning . . . the weather's good . . . the curtains are open, I wonder who opened them, even though everyone's still asleep . . . but I'm glad I have a bed by a window . . . it really is such nice weather . . . when I went into labor it was drizzling . . . when I called the parlor and Yu came to get me it was starting to pour down, and no matter how fast the wipers went we couldn't see a thing . . . it was so scary . . . but I didn't say I was scared . . . I never tell him anything . . . and he silently gripped the steering wheel . . . the kind of man who says nothing to encourage or comfort his wife when she's in labor . . . rain . . . silence . . . when Kunio and I were silent it was a silence we shared, or it felt like we were up to our necks in the same water, and the longer the time we were silent went on for, I felt the closer we were, but when Yu and I are silent it separates us . . . each in our own silence . . . Dad opposed it, he said I could never be happy with an ilbon saram, but, Dad, now that I'm with Yu, a hanguk saram, I've never once felt happiness . . . we're both hanguk saram, we're both from South Gyeongsang, but I came here when I was five, and he came here when he was twenty, and we couldn't be more different . . . he's a decade older than me . . . Kunio was in my class at school, our birthdays were only three days apart . . . "were"—leave that in the past tense . . . he said he'd be disowned if we married, but he said we could elope and live in Tokyo . . . I couldn't disobey my father . . . I knew if I did he'd abandon me . . . is that a strange thing to think at twenty-one? But he abandoned me when I was three, you can't understand how I feel, not seeing my father for two whole years . . . so I did as my father said . . . I married Yu, the pachinko machine repairman, I had his child . . . a girl . . . my baby . . .

She came two weeks before her due date, so I have nothing ready, not my nightgown, toothbrush, toiletries, baby clothes, oh, not even my insurance card . . . what else . . . soap, of course, shampoo, and it depends on how long I'm in here for, but if I'm going to be in here a while, I'd like some books, oh, and some writing paper and envelopes and stamps too . . . I'll have a nap and once I'm feeling better, I'll write . . . excuse me, midwife, has Mr. Yu telephoned? . . . but isn't the husband usually waiting in the hallway? It's our first baby . . . he brought me to the hospital, did the paperwork, and went home, my god . . . he doesn't care about me in the slightest . . . he knows I went out with Kunio, and one time, in high school, he saw us talking on a park bench . . . he just got taken in by Dad's fine talk about sending him to college if he married me . . . but Dad didn't keep his promise . . . and Yu's resentful . . . I'm resentful . . . of my husband . . . the father of my daughter . . .

She was due on the seventh of July . . . the day of the Tanabata Festival, oh,

I wish she'd been born then . . . the cowherd and the weaver girl, married, were separated from each other on either side of the Milky Way by the wrathful Sky King, and only one time a year were they allowed to rendezvous . . . the night of the seventh day of the seventh month, in Japan the cowherd crosses the Milky Way and the weaver girl just waits for him, but in Korea, Eomoni told me that it's the weaver girl who crosses the bridge of wings that the magpies make to meet the cowherd . . . Eomoni . . . where are you now . . . you always disappear suddenly, and you don't come back for years . . . but she has her reasons . . . I wouldn't be able to put up with it for a day, no, not even a second . . . living with his ilbon saram lover and the son she had with your husband . . .

The nurses at the nurses' station are laughing . . . they must be looking at the babies' faces and laughing . . . see, they're doing it again . . . but it sounds so far away . . . I feel like I used to when Shin-ho would roll me up in a blanket and sit on me . . . oh, I don't feel good . . . the nausea's coming in waves almost . . . swelling . . . when it breaks, I'll vomit . . . oh, I'm going to throw up . . . I don't want to . . . I'm sick of it already . . . I've been throwing up for months already . . . why am I talking like this, just rattle-rattle-rattle-rattle-rattling away in my head . . . I'm so tired . . . and I'm so sleepy . . . I'm going to quit talking . . . I haven't slept a wink . . . time to sleep . . . it's not good for you if you don't . . . but when I'm not talking, I feel worried . . . so, so worried . . . anything . . . literally anything . . . I want someone to listen . . . someone . . . anyone . . .

The old man went into the hospital through the out-of-hours entrance. The outpatient reception would open at 8:00 a.m., and visiting hours were from 1:00 p.m. to 8:00 p.m., so nobody but hospital staff and patients were there, but the nurses he passed did not try to stop him, perhaps because he grimaced to look like a patient struggling with pain.

The old man took the elevator to the third floor, stopped in front of the nursery, and saw a little baby, sleeping in an incubator a short distance from the row of beds. He pressed his forehead to the glass and saw a pink band around the baby's right ankle.

LEE Shin-hee—6/22/68–6:18 a.m.

The bands were either pink or blue, so is that pink for girls and blue for boys?

The old man looked away from the baby and walked slowly down the hall of the obstetrics unit. Watanabe Akiko, Toda Kazuko, Suzuki Chiyoko, Someya Teiko, Kakura Sachiko, Kobayashi Yoshie, Sukegawa Atsuko, Satō Tetsuko, Ehata Seiko . . . He went on slowly, reading the names of the women written on the doors of the rooms, which housed four or eight women . . . He stopped at the door to room 312, where *Lee Shin-hee* was written, then hunched his already rounded back to look in at the faces of the sleeping women through the gaps in the blue curtains dividing the beds from one another.

The old man's daughter was in the bed by the window.

He got a stool, its green vinyl seat split and the foam sticking out, placed it near his daughter's shoulders, and sat down.

The old man crossed his arms and closed his eyes. As he was listening to the sparrows, kicking up a fuss in the cherry tree right underneath the window . . . the blue curtain started to billow . . . wind? The window's closed . . . is someone hiding in it? . . . the curtain curled back and a little girl with a bob . . . Mi-ok? Shin-ja? He reached out and pulled back the curtain, and the curtain changed into a blue chima . . . driven by an impatience that had no particular reason, he fumbled inside the chima and . . . nothing . . . nothing . . . there, he grabbed a kneecap, and just then the kneecap was pressed firmly up against the right side of his chest . . . two legs stretched out before his eyes, white like crescent moons . . . whose legs? Dark black pubic hair . . . the blue chima hung upside down from her navel, hiding her upper body . . . he grabbed the chima's hem and pulled it down, **andwaeyo, butagieyo, anything else you want, but not that, please, no** . . . my wife . . . my first wife . . . Chee In-hye . . . I undid the strings and her jeogori spilled open over her white breasts . . . I went to put my palms on her breasts and the strings of her pale blue jeogori fluttered . . . the blue chima swelled and tightened, swelled and tightened, binggeul binggeul, bingggeul bingggeul . . . and Kim Mi-yeong from the OK Café danced, one-two-three one-two-three one-two-three one-two-three. . . .

"Daddy."

The old man's eyes snapped open.

My daughter.

The hospital.

My daughter had a baby girl.

My lips won't move.

Nothing congratulatory is coming out.

I can't even give her a smile.

He tried to say her name, but instead he said Chee In-hye, Watanabe Akiko, Toda Kazuko, Kakura Sachiko, Sukegawa Atsuko, Satō Tetsuko, Ehata Seiko, Kim Mi-yeong, all these names of other women coming out one-two-three, one-two-three, one-two-three, one-two-three, one-two-three, one-two-three, one-two-three . . .

"It's a girl."

The old man realized he still had his hat on and took the flat cap off his head, but he could not remember the name of his daughter who was right in front of him.

"Dad, will you give me a name for her?"

The old man tilted his head back and slowly twisted it from side to side to loosen his neck.

"Miri."

The young mother let the name resonate in her head, then tried saying it.

"Miri . . . What characters would you use?"

"Beautiful land." The old man was careful not to let his unease come through in his voice.

"Oh . . . Miri . . . what a nice name."

"She has long fingers, she could be a pianist . . . but her face looks like she might cause her parents trouble." The old man pressed his index finger against his wrinkled lips; they were no longer numb.

"So you saw her?"

"I did."

"I haven't even seen her yet. How was she?"

"What do you mean, how was she?"

"What kind of face was she making?"

"Babies always look red and ugly, but she has pale, beautiful skin."

"Who does she look like?"

"Hmm . . . I couldn't say . . ."

"Where's Yu, I wonder?"

"Visiting time starts at one, right?"

"What time is it now?"

"Seven thirty."

"Oh, breakfast time."

"And Jeong-hee's not here at this important moment. She should be telling the midwife to feed you seaweed soup and white rice five times a day for the first week and not to let you have anything else . . . should I get Fusako to bring you food?"

"I'm fine, they feed you three times a day in here."

"No meat or fish."

He heard the sound of the trolley bringing around breakfast, so the old man looked away from his daughter, who had just become a mother, and stood up gingerly.

"Well, I'll see you . . ."

"Daddy."

"What?"

"Thank you."

The old man left room 312, back hunched just as it had been when he came in, and looked at the face of his granddaughter, who was moving her legs around in her incubator in the nursery. She still had nothing like an expression in her eyes or mouth, but her little hands seemed to hold all sorts of emotions. How many babies have I seen in my life now? Mi-ok, Shin-tae, Ja-ok, Shin-ja, Shin-myeong, Shin-cheol, Shin-ho, Shin-hee, Shin-hwa, Shin'ichi . . .

Woo-cheol   want to hold him?

May I?

Of course   you're his big brother   take his head in your right hand and support his body with your left   gently   gently now

The first baby I held was when I was eleven. My little brother. For the last two decades, I've avoided remembering my brother as a person who existed in this world. What he said, how he ran, even his name was something I shouldn't remember. If I remember, and I go into those memories, I'll get back to the day when I was told of his death. Every memory leads to that day, but that day is a dead end.

That night, unable to believe what had happened to my brother, with my fist shoved in my mouth to keep me from screaming, I awoke to the birds singing, and I was overwhelmed by the reality that this new day did not include my brother in it, that morning when I cursed the fact that I had woken up, that morning when I felt like I would never again wish someone a good morning—

When he left the hospital, a sunny, shadowless road stretched before him. A large cloud shaped like a ship overtook the old man's shadow. One by one, other clouds overtook the old man, heading into the western sky. They seemed not to be floating on the wind but instead to be moving forward with purpose and will. As if something brilliant awaited in the west . . . Miri . . . Miryang . . . the Miri Plains . . . Miri . . .

SHUFFLE

The World (XXI)

Reversed—inertia, setbacks, dissatisfaction,
endings without resolution—

"INDEPENDENCE"—ONE NORTH KOREA

Kim Il-Sung Thought for Young Boys and Girls

We go to a factory. The manager and chief engineer always say, "This was made with our nation's designs, our technology, and our materials."

We go to a department store. The guide tells us, "We do not sell any foreign products. Everything is domestically produced."

Most of the passenger vehicles driving around Pyongyang are Soviet-made Volgas. Occasionally I spot a Toyopet Crown or Nissan Cedric. When one reporter, Iwadare, makes a face that says, "But those are foreign-made," the guide tells us. "We make trucks, buses, and jeeps here. Soon we will make passenger cars."

There's more. When we visited Panmunjom at the Thirty-Eighth Parallel, the place where the Armistice Agreement was signed, in North Korean territory, has become a resting spot for visitors, and documents about the Korean War are displayed, but there is nothing about the People's Liberation Army of China, which also took part in the war. And in Pyongyang, at the Victorious Fatherland Liberation War Museum, they display documents that show the pattern of the Korean War, but there is nothing to do with the PLA here either. Looking at these two places would give you the impression that the Korean War was fought only by Koreans.

This emphasis on autonomy was clearly visible in the government's international connections. On the Month 7 and Month 8, a celebration of the twentieth anniversary of the founding of the country was held at the newly refurbished National Assembly Hall, and after a speech from Kim Il-sung, representatives of more than thirty governments and revolutionary organizations gave speeches; North Vietnam started, followed by the Soviet Union, the Viet Cong, Poland, Cuba, the Lao Patriotic Front, Mongolia, Bulgaria, the Japanese Communist Party, Hungary, and East Germany, in that order.

North Vietnam, the Viet Cong, Cuba, and the JCP are "independent" in the international communist movement, and I gathered that North Korea has a very friendly relationship with these independents. It struck me that China and Albania were nowhere to be seen among the delegates.

Why is it they emphasize self-reliance so much? It seems that this may be deeply rooted in the history of the Korean people. Despite their long history, the people of the Korean peninsula have constantly been invaded and threatened by the great powers that surround them. And in recent history, they were under Japanese colonial rule for thirty-six years. I was told ad nauseum about how dark life was for the Korean people under "Japanese imperialism."

And now, the reality is that the land and its people are separated along the Thirty-Eighth Parallel. It seems that this "we'll do it ourselves" idea of independence comes from these historical circumstances.

Political independence is impossible without economic independence. That's why North Korea is working on economic development to raise itself in the world. First, the exploitation of underground resources within their borders. And all the factories that we reporters saw were in full operation, their facilities being indeed expanded. They're also concentrating on training engineers. Compulsory education is for nine years (four years in "people's schools," five years in junior high schools), but the junior high schools also provide elementary technical education. At the junior high school, we reporters saw, there was lab equipment everywhere. Above this level are high schools and technical high schools; there are far more technical high schools.

The technical high schools are set up in factories in each region as well as on communal farms in rural villages. In factory areas, there are "factory universities." This is an arrangement that allows workers to learn the theory of communism and technology while working. I felt that this principle of "connecting education and production" was one followed throughout the educational system.

Then there's the "thought revolution." This is an attempt to transform the people into the Socialist Man, and it is done by teaching them the thoughts of Kim Il-sung.

Visit a people's school or a junior high school, and you'll find a "research room" for learning about the revolutionary activities of Kim Il-sung. Photographs and pictures explain the leader's background, his family lineage, his fifteen years as a partisan in the anti-Japanese struggle, and his activities since the founding of the nation. "Kim Il-sung Studies" is a required subject at both levels. These "research rooms" are also found in universities, factories, and rural communal farms. There is also one located in the Children's Palaces, the locations for children's extracurricular activities that are the pride of North Korea. At the Children's Palaces in Pyongyang and Kaesong, young boys and girls were studying fervently. We were told that study groups on Kim Il-sung Thought were also being held in workers' homes.

At night, we walked along the banks of the Taedong River in Pyongyang. Under the dim light of the streetlights along the river, young people were reading books. Some devote themselves to recitation. It felt as if the whole country was in a feverish rush to study, study, study.

The night I arrived in Khabarovsk having ended my three-week trip to North Korea, I saw a young woman in a miniskirt dancing with her lover to the rhythm of a band at a restaurant near the airport. That's when I realized that the women I'd seen on the streets of North Korea wore barely any makeup at all. I felt as if I had suddenly traveled to a different world.

Lee Woo-cheol stuck his scissors into the evening edition of the *Asahi Shimbun*. He just cut it out without reading it. He didn't intend to stick it in a scrapbook to cherish. Every word, every character, entered his eyes, but he did not wish to understand, imagine, agree, or oppose. He just didn't want to have an article about the twentieth-anniversary of the founding of North Korea on the same page as ones headlined *"1843 YEN HIGHEST CLOSING PRICE IN DOW HISTORY," "WATER SERVICE DISRUPTED, AS TOWN TOLD: 'FLOOD WARNING,'"* or *"STUDENT OCCUPATION IN DISSATISFACTION WITH CORRESPONDENCE EDUCATION."*

As Woo-cheol cut the piece from the paper he heard the telephone. *Ring-ring-ring ring-ring-ring ring-ring-ring ring-ring-ring...* Why isn't Fusako or Shin'ichi getting that? *Ring-ring-ring ring-ring-ring ring-ring-ring...* It stopped.

The breakfast that Fusako made has gone cold. There's a film on the rice porridge, and the applesauce has gone brown. I don't want to eat any of it, but I have to. Woo-cheol put the clipping in a drawer in the cupboard, then got down on his knees in front of the table slowly, put his hands to the tatami mat, and sank his hips into the cushion. Doing good, I think I finally got the hang of it, I haven't messed up once this week.

With extraordinary effort, Woo-cheol put half the porridge and five spoons worth of the applesauce away in his stomach, which was already two-thirds full. Fusako will sigh and say, what am I going to do with you if that's all you eat, but if I put any more of it in my mouth, I'll vomit... I can't... But maybe I'll try to eat one more spoonful. Woo-cheol put the applesauce in his mouth and closed his eyes. No matter how much he focused on his tongue, he couldn't taste it. Since the surgery last month, all food seemed to have lost its flavor.

Dr. Kikuchi says that I should try to chew each bite fifty times to take the strain off my stomach, that chewing well can also prevent diarrhea, but rice porridge and applesauce hardly need chewing at all, and the longer I chew for, the fuller I feel, making me lose the nerve to take another bite. A week ago, Fusako started to make the porridge thinner, but the lumps of rice stick in my throat. And when they do, I puff out my chest and breathe from the diaphragm like I was told to, and if I'm still having trouble after that, then all I can do is throw up. I hate vomiting. The sense of futility when I've spent half an hour chewing, afraid with each bite that I might throw it up, then swallow, finally, only for it all to come back up is far worse . . . I just want to get through today without vomiting.

Where's Fusako? Usually when I finish eating, she brings in a tray with hot water and my powdered medicine. Maybe she went to the store since I've barely eaten. I want to take my medicine. When I haven't had it I feel anxious. My left shoulder's starting to hurt, I've got chills all down my back, and I think I can feel the bile rising. Perhaps a good doctor sows seeds of anxiety in his patient's mind, and a good patient neither pulls up the sprouts that anxiety puts out nor gives it water or fertilizer to keep it from spreading. Right now, I'm a good patient. I tend that anxiousness; I follow orders. I avoid strongly stimulating foods, hot and cold foods, milk and dairy products high in fat, and I eat small meals about five times a day. But even after finishing a meal that follows all these orders, I can't let down my guard. Two or three uneventful hours later, it's already time for me to have to eat again; I come out in a cold sweat, dizzy, heart palpitating, stomach aching, and often diarrhea and nausea strike at the same time.

But one upside of this physical pain is that my mind is somewhat better off. I never have to doubt the existence of my body because it's always in some kind of pain. Before, I was always consumed, somewhere in the back of the back of my mind, by a sense of absence, and neither sleeping nor waking was easy. As soon as I'd manage to fall asleep, I'd be awake again, tracing my hands over my face and body over and over again to make sure that I was still there. I'd rather be woken up by nausea or diarrhea than shaken awake by existential anxiety.

Woo-cheol piled two cushions up and gently reclined his upper body onto them to keep the contents of his stomach from coming back up.

A square of the sky cut out by the window—the sky was a blue neither dark nor light nor high nor close.

Normal sky.

Normal life.

Soon to end.

I can't have much longer left.

Dr. Kikuchi and Fusako both talk the same talk about it being a gastric ulcer, but I've never heard of anyone having two-thirds of their stomach removed due to an ulcer. And people can tell when they're nearing death. The day before my surgery, Jeong-hee told me: madange nuni naerineun kkumeul kkwonneunde dangsini hok byeonge geollinge anilkka sipeoseo, *I had a dream that there was snow in the garden and I wondered if there was something wrong with you.* What kind of dream will I have before I die?

When Jeong-hee was here we'd put our pillows next to each other and talk in Korean, whatever we talked about, but I could see how sad and bored Fusako looked; since Jeong-hee left three days ago without a word, Fusako's been animatedly taking care of everything for me. Before we got together, she was a nurse after all, so I guess this is a pattern she fell into long ago.

Fusako doesn't have all the emotional ups and downs of a hanguk saram woman, but her inner strength's unmatched by anyone. Without a flicker of change to her facial expression, she can hold her own against anyone, even the customers who try to pick a fight saying that they put a ball in but nothing came out, the guys who come in with a lunchbox at opening and keep playing even as we're trying to close for the night, or the scoundrels who use magnets and wires to get the balls out.

And she's a hard worker. Even after closing time, she's there, counting up the takings, sweeping up, emptying the ashtrays, polishing the rails, cleaning the balls . . . Dirty balls get stuck halfway up the rail, so they need to be put in a jute bag every day and shaken back and forth, holding the ends of the sack. There's a lot of hard work to be done, but she works hard with the kids. I've heard people whisper that I'm so cheap I've got my wife, kids, and son-in-law running the Million Dollar, and I can't help but agree with Yu's opinion that profits would double if I hired five employees and built a parking lot, but, c'mon, at our level we're doing well enough running it the seven of us . . . stingy . . . cheapskate . . . well, they can say whatever they like . . . but money . . . do I want to earn more . . . what would I do with it . . . in Ilbon . . . I'll be selling pachinko balls at three yen a pop to ilbon saram . . . until I die . . . restocking the prizes . . . fifty bottles of shampoo . . . forty each of toothpaste and cream cleanser . . . thirty-five packs of Peace cigarettes . . . thirty packs each of Hilite and Hope . . . twenty-five packs of Bon curry . . . twenty packs of prawn crackers . . . fifteen packs of hard candies . . . ten of the chocolate drops . . .

SHUFFLE

The Chariot (*VII*)

*Reversed—Quarrel, dispute, difficult victory,
unrewarded victory, major obstacles ahead—*

Arang watched. As 134 people were punched, kicked, cut, gouged, stomped, dragged out, drenched, hung, forced to drink, scorched, had bones broken and were then imprisoned, gagged, had their thumbs bound with wire and were loaded into the back of a truck, plunged into a hollow off a cliff surrounded with big rocks and no escape, had guns aimed at their heads, disposed of with a *bang-bang-bang*, their eyeballs plucked out, flesh devoured, exposed down to the bone. **Arang watched.** As eight years ago they were finally found by their grieving families, put in coffins, placed in the furnace at a public crematorium, sprinkled with oil and set alight, crushed with a pestle, turned to dust in a mortar, put in a wooden box covered in cotton, wrapped in white cloth, cradled to the chests of their mourners wearing hemp mourning clothes with straw ropes tied around their stomachs and hemp veils on their heads, carried to the Kyo-dong jesasang halfway up the mountain, singing how can I, how can I, how can I on my own, the road to the next world is far but the mountain over there is Bukmansancheon, ehe eheyo eoriyeocha eheyo eheyo, as in front of the ceremonial table laden with rice, tangguk, watermelon, rice cakes, wine, and soy sauce they cried aigo, aigo, screaming names, shedding tears, he is not buried, he is not buried, he shall come back again, burial tools in their hands, chanting, we come into life empty-handed and we leave empty-handed, all in this world comes from nothing and returns to nothing, and when I too die, we shall share a grave, he is not buried, he is not buried, as they respectfully buried their dead.

Arang watched. As a policeman wearing a helmet and kneepads, carrying a shovel, climbed up to the place where those 134 were buried. And as he stood at the spot where their bodies were laid to rest and spat, "Ppalgaengi!" and thrust his shovel into the ground over and over, **Arang watched.**

Arang watched. As the policemen laughed distractedly, cigarettes in their mouths, undoing the knots of the white cloths with their dirty hands. **Arang watched.** As one of them opened the lid of a wooden box and threw the butt into the white powder of the mixed remains of 134 people, and said, "Ppalgaengi!" **Arang watched.** As the white police car drove toward the center of the city and handfuls of ashes grabbed from wooden boxes were scattered out the window, she watched.

Arang watched. As every rush of wind rose up and whoosh-whooshed down all the mountains; as the door of every house rattled, *whoosh-whoosh*; as ripples rose up across the river water, the lake water, *whoosh-whoosh*, well water, water in earthenware pots, all the water in town, turning it unreflective; *whoosh-whoosh, whoosh-whoosh*, rolling up every dead leaf and rushing up into the sky, ripping through thick clouds left and right, scattering them like a hen's feathers, coming to the last remaining cloud like a white pitfall in the sky and blowing right through it, *whoosh-whoosh*; as all the han of the living and the dead was enveloped in the light of the sun, Arang watched.

Arang listened. As the wind picked up every bone of the 134 people scattered across the city, turned into a gust, and blew down every road, *whoosh-whoosh whoosh-whoosh*, singing huskily with the millions of flakes of their remains, *whoosh-whoosh whoosh-whoosh* ...

Don't mourn the deaths of comrades
Who fell in battle with the enemy
Wrap their bodies in the red flag
The flag we swore to our death or victory
The voices of our comrades
Now reborn inside our hearts
Farewell, friends, on the path of enmity
Our blood shall seek revenge on your part
The bayonet of a comrade fallen in the White Terror
Sways in search of its villain
Let us destroy now and for all
The foes who sold off the freedom of our homeland
The people's battle song

What's that sound?
It's too weak to make out
It's bouncing and drifting   wandering here and there
Like as soon as the sound is made it wants to disappear
Like the sound of the wings of a honeybee trying but failing to sneak into a patch of violets swaying in the wind
Like a school bell announcing the start of class
What's that smell?
It's too weak to make out
It can't escape or seep through
Daffodils?
Salt?
A pine forest?
A waterfall?

Andwae   it's the breeze off the river
I'm on a sweetfish fishing boat going down the river
Aigu   what a good feeling
I'm lying facedown and something begins to buzz at the back of my
head   like thousands and thousands of starlings all returning at once to the
forest   I can't tell if it's getting closer   or farther away   I can't tell which
direction I'm hearing it from either   even though every sound has its
direction   humming voices   from everywhere   welling up   swelling
looking for an exit   voices without a body all at once   I don't know what
they're humming   with one voice   please let me hear you with one voice

Suddenly all the sound is silenced
Comrades!
Awaken!
Get up!
Lee Woo-cheol!
Pushed out of his sleeping body was the man whose name was called. Lee
Woo-cheol opened his eyes. He gently slipped out of the futon so as not to
wake his sleeping wife and reached for the athletic shoes at the bottom left of
the shoe rack. The last time he put them on was twenty years ago, when he ran
across the mountains of Sancheong looking for his brother's body. He slid his
feet into the shoes. He hadn't forgotten how to plant his heels and raise the
tips of his toes, straighten the twists where the laces crossed over each other,
pull the laces tight and double-knot them so they wouldn't come undone
while he was running.

He went out and for the first time he realized that it was still before dawn.
Woo-cheol walked quickly down the paved road, checking how his shoes were.
He turned down the alley and into total darkness, but as he listened to the sound
of the frost crushing beneath his feet and watched the white breath coming out
of his mouth, silhouettes of houses and telephone poles began to emerge tremulously, and by the time he reached the bank of the Tone River, it had gone light.

Lee Woo-cheol took one step into the new morning   in-hale ex-hale
in-hale ex-hale   in-hale ex-hale   into a silence that could not be filled with

any words   in-hale ex-hale   in-hale ex-hale   in-hale ex-hale   in-hale
ex-hale   in-hale ex-hale   in-hale ex-hale
in-hale ex-hale   in-hale ex-hale   in-hale ex-hale   in-hale ex-hale

JANUARY 15, 1971   SHIBUYA RESIDENTS OB ROAD RACE

5000 meters   Winner of the fifties age group   18m18s

in-hale ex-hale   in-hale ex-hale   in-hale ex-hale   in-hale ex-hale
in-hale ex-hale   in-hale ex-hale   in-hale ex-hale   in-hale ex-hale

APRIL 28, 1971   PRESIDENT PARK WINS THIRD TERM

The seventh presidential election in South Korea was held on April 27, with votes counted the same day; incumbent president Park Chung-hee claimed a resounding margin over Kim Dae-jung, leader of the largest opposition party, the New Democratic Party, securing a third term.

in-hale ex-hale   in-hale ex-hale   in-hale ex-hale   in-hale ex-hale
in-hale ex-hale   in-hale ex-hale   in-hale ex-hale   in-hale ex-hale

JUNE 3, 1971   "FIVE BANDITS" POETS ARRESTED UNDER ANTI-COMMUNIST LAW

On June 2, amid uproar Kim Ji-ha (real name Kim Yeong-il) and two others were arrested over the satirical poem "Five Bandits," depicting the disparities seen in South Korean life.

in-hale ex-hale   in-hale ex-hale   in-hale ex-hale   in-hale ex-hale
in-hale ex-hale   in-hale ex-hale   in-hale ex-hale   in-hale ex-hale

SEPTEMBER 12, 1971   SENIOR CITIZENS SPORTS COMPETITION

10,000 meters   Winner in the fifties age group   37m55s

in-hale ex-hale   in-hale ex-hale   in-hale ex-hale   in-hale ex-hale
in-hale ex-hale   in-hale ex-hale   in-hale ex-hale   in-hale ex-hale

OCTOBER 17, 1971   SILENCE SPREADS AMONG CITIZENS

South Korea's major universities, closed on October 15 due to security orders permitting military occupation and policing and an indefinite closure order, are as of October 16 under police surveillance and student demonstrations have disappeared altogether.

JULY 11, 1971   KANAGAWA MARATHON

10,000 meters   Third place in the fifties age group   37m29s

in-hale ex-hale   in-hale ex-hale   in-hale ex-hale   in-hale ex-hale
in-hale ex-hale   in-hale ex-hale   in-hale ex-hale   in-hale ex-hale

APRIL 2, 1972   SATIRICAL POEM OR SCAPEGOAT?

A long poem by Park Ji-ha, thirty-one, the poet famous for the satirical poem "Five Bandits" depicting the South Korean privileged elite as thieves, has again drawn the wrath of the government, and the April issue of the Catholic monthly magazine *Creation*, which published it, has been banned from sale.

in-hale ex-hale   in-hale ex-hale   in-hale ex-hale   in-hale ex-hale
in-hale ex-hale   in-hale ex-hale   in-hale ex-hale   in-hale ex-hale

APRIL 9, 1972   JAPAN SENIOR CITIZENS LONG-DISTANCE COMPETITION

10,000 meters   Winner in the fifties age group   37m6s

in-hale ex-hale   in-hale ex-hale   in-hale ex-hale   in-hale ex-hale
in-hale ex-hale   in-hale ex-hale   in-hale ex-hale   in-hale ex-hale

JULY 5, 1972   SOUTH AND NORTH KOREA
ISSUE JOINT STATEMENT

The South Korean and North Korean governments issued a joint statement on the peaceful reunification of North and South on July 4, after leaders from both sides visited the capitals of Seoul and Pyongyang from May to June to discuss the issue of reunification, revealing that they have agreed on seven items, representing a major opening in the gate to North-South unification after more than a quarter of a century's division.

in-hale ex-hale   in-hale ex-hale   in-hale ex-hale   in-hale ex-hale
in-hale ex-hale   in-hale ex-hale   in-hale ex-hale   in-hale ex-hale
in-hale ex-hale   in-hale ex-hale   in-hale ex-hale   in-hale ex-hale
in-hale ex-hale   in-hale ex-hale   in-hale ex-hale   in-hale ex-hale

AUGUST 24, 1972   MOUNT ROKKŌ MARATHON

5000 meters   Winner in the fifties age group   18m59s

OCTOBER 8, 1972   SENIOR CITIZEN SPORTS COMPETITION

10,000 meters   Second place in the fifties age group   38m4.4s

NOVEMBER 23, 1972   KANAGAWA MARATHON

10,000 meters   Second place in the fifty-to-sixty division   36m43s

DECEMBER 17, 1972   HACHIOJI SHORT MARATHON

10,000 meters   Winner in the sixties age group   37m36s

in-hale ex-hale   in-hale ex-hale   in-hale ex-hale   in-hale ex-hale
in-hale ex-hale   in-hale ex-hale   in-hale ex-hale   in-hale ex-hale

JANUARY 14, 1973   NEW YEAR'S TAMAGAWA ROAD RACE

10,000 meters   Winner in the sixties age group   38m49s

FEBRUARY 11, 1973   KATSUTA MARATHON

10,000 meters   Winner in the sixties age group   37m37s

FEBRUARY 18, 1973   OHME NEWS MARATHON

30 kilometers   Winner in the sixties age group   2h2m19s

in-hale ex-hale   in-hale ex-hale   in-hale ex-hale   in-hale ex-hale
in-hale ex-hale   in-hale ex-hale   in-hale ex-hale   in-hale ex-hale

JUNE 23, 1973   SOUTH KOREA ACCEPTS
RECOGNITION OF "TWO KOREAS"

South Korean president Park Chung-hee issued at 10:00 a.m. on June 23 a special statement on radio and television regarding basic foreign diplomatic policy centered on this fall's UN measures. The content revolved around seven items that the South Korean government will not oppose, including the attendance of both North and South Korea at international organizations, the membership of both North and South in the UN, and the status of both as UN observers, representing a significant change in attitude on the part of the South, which has long insisted on the exclusion of North Korea.

in-hale ex-hale   in-hale ex-hale   in-hale ex-hale   in-hale ex-hale
in-hale ex-hale   in-hale ex-hale   in-hale ex-hale   in-hale ex-hale
in-hale ex-hale   in-hale ex-hale   in-hale ex-hale   in-hale ex-hale
in-hale ex-hale   in-hale ex-hale   in-hale ex-hale   in-hale ex-hale

AUGUST 9, 1973   FORMER PRESIDENTIAL
CANDIDATE KIM DAE-JUNG ABDUCTED

Kim Dae-jung, forty-seven, former member of the New Democratic Party who ran against Park Chung-hee in the South Korean presidential election two years ago and was defeated by a small margin, was abducted on the afternoon of August 8 from a hotel in Tokyo by a group of five pistol-carrying men who appeared to be Korean, according to reports. The Tokyo Metropolitan Police and Kojimachi Police are treating it as an abduction; they are currently seeking Mr. Kim's whereabouts.

in-hale ex-hale   in-hale ex-hale   in-hale ex-hale   in-hale ex-hale
in-hale ex-hale   in-hale ex-hale   in-hale ex-hale   in-hale ex-hale
in-hale ex-hale   in-hale ex-hale   in-hale ex-hale   in-hale ex-hale
in-hale ex-hale   in-hale ex-hale   in-hale ex-hale   in-hale ex-hale

OCTOBER 4, 1973   ARTICLE ON DEMONSTRATIONS REMOVED

The *Dong-A Ilbo*, South Korea's main quality evening newspaper, today distributed and sold in Seoul an edition with twenty lines left blank on the front page. Immediately before printing, publication of the article was suspended by authorities; only that article was removed and in the late edition was replaced by another.

in-hale ex-hale   in-hale ex-hale   in-hale ex-hale   in-hale ex-hale
in-hale ex-hale   in-hale ex-hale   in-hale ex-hale   in-hale ex-hale

OCTOBER 8, 1973   WEST GERMAN INTERNATIONAL ALL AGES MARATHON

15 kilometers   Winner in sixties age group   57m59s

NOVEMBER 23, 1973   KANAGAWA MARATHON

10,000 meters   Winner in sixties age group   37m51s

in-hale ex-hale   in-hale ex-hale   in-hale ex-hale   in-hale ex-hale
in-hale ex-hale   in-hale ex-hale   in-hale ex-hale   in-hale ex-hale

JANUARY 9, 1974   SOUTH KOREAN PEOPLE SINK INTO SILENCE

Immediately after the emergency measures issued by President Park Chung-hee completely banning the movement for constitutional reform, evidence of a "chilling effect" has already begun to spread among the nation's people.

JANUARY 11, 1974   JAPANESE REPORTERS GIVEN WARNING

On the afternoon of the January 10, the South Korean government, which has suppressed the anti-government movement centered on the demand for constitutional reform through the invocation of presidential emergency orders, through its Ministry of Culture's Director of Overseas Affairs announced to Japanese correspondents stationed in Seoul that any statements in opposition to the Yushin Constitution will be punished by court-martial in accordance with the provisions of the emergency orders, offering what appeared to be a final warning.

in-hale ex-hale   in-hale ex-hale   in-hale ex-hale   in-hale ex-hale
in-hale ex-hale   in-hale ex-hale   in-hale ex-hale   in-hale ex-hale

JANUARY 13, 1974   NJSF NEW YEAR'S MARATHON

10,000 meters   Winner in sixties age group   40m36s

FEBRUARY 11, 1974   KATSUTA MARATHON

10,000 meters   Winner in sixties age group

FEBRUARY 17, 1974   OHME NEWS MARATHON

10,000 meters   Winner in sixties age group   38m39s

MARCH 24, 1974   SHINANO MAINICHI MARATHON

52.195 kilometers   3h6m33s

in-hale ex-hale   in-hale ex-hale   in-hale ex-hale   in-hale ex-hale
in-hale ex-hale   in-hale ex-hale   in-hale ex-hale   in-hale ex-hale
in-hale ex-hale   in-hale ex-hale   in-hale ex-hale   in-hale ex-hale
in-hale ex-hale   in-hale ex-hale   in-hale ex-hale   in-hale ex-hale

APRIL 4, 1974   SEOUL STUDENT MOVEMENT REIGNITES

Mass student demonstrations were held on April 3 across five Seoul campuses, including the Seoul Medical School, for the first time in three months. Nearly thirty student leaders were arrested in one day alone. That night, President Park Chung-hee issued emergency measures based on Article 53 of the Constitution, indicating that those belonging to the National Federation of Democratic Youth Students Union, which organized the anti-government protests, will be arrested without warrants and will be punished to the highest extent of the law, not excluding the death penalty.

in-hale ex-hale   in-hale ex-hale   in-hale ex-hale   in-hale ex-hale
in-hale ex-hale   in-hale ex-hale   in-hale ex-hale   in-hale ex-hale
in-hale ex-hale   in-hale ex-hale   in-hale ex-hale   in-hale ex-hale
in-hale ex-hale   in-hale ex-hale   in-hale ex-hale   in-hale ex-hale

AUGUST 11, 1974   SAN-BYAKU-SAI TRACK COMPETITION

14.1 kilometers   57m3s

DATE UNKNOWN, 1974
FRANCE OB WORLD ATHLETICS CHAMPIONSHIP SERIES

42.195 kilometers   3h0m18s

in-hale ex-hale   in-hale ex-hale   in-hale ex-hale   in-hale ex-hale
in-hale ex-hale   in-hale ex-hale   in-hale ex-hale   in-hale ex-hale

AUGUST 16, 1974   PRESIDENT PARK SHOT

South Korean president Park Chung-hee was shot by an audience member during his Liberation Day speech at the National Theater of Korea in Seoul on the morning of August 15. However, the shot missed—while the president was unharmed, one female student member of the chorus was hit by the stray bullet and died. The culprit was arrested immediately at the scene; it was later announced that he had a passport issued by Japanese authorities. The Seoul

Municipal Police immediately announced that the city was under martial law and that security would be strengthened throughout the metropolis.

OCTOBER 24, 1974   POLICE TAKE IN NEWS EXECS

South Korean security authorities, seeking to block anti-government influence in the media, called the president of *Hankook Ilbo* and the editorial director of *Dong-A Ilbo* to the Korean Central Intelligence Agency today for interrogation.

in-hale ex-hale   in-hale ex-hale   in-hale ex-hale   in-hale ex-hale
in-hale ex-hale   in-hale ex-hale   in-hale ex-hale   in-hale ex-hale
in-hale ex-hale   in-hale ex-hale   in-hale ex-hale   in-hale ex-hale
in-hale ex-hale   in-hale ex-hale   in-hale ex-hale   in-hale ex-hale

NOVEMBER 23, 1974   KANAGAWA MARATHON

10,000 meters   Winner in the sixties age group

in-hale ex-hale   in-hale ex-hale   in-hale ex-hale   in-hale ex-hale
in-hale ex-hale   in-hale ex-hale   in-hale ex-hale   in-hale ex-hale

DECEMBER 24, 1974
PAPER REFUSED BANK LOANS, ADS CANCELED

Reporters from the *Dong-A Ilbo*, one of South Korea's major newspapers, issued a "Declaration of Action for Free Speech" on October 12 and have since reported enthusiastically on the actions of anti-government movements, despite pressure from the authorities. However, the company has encountered the refusal of bank loans and the withdrawal of advertising contracts, and the reporters and management alike are facing arrests and attacks.

in-hale ex-hale   in-hale ex-hale   in-hale ex-hale   in-hale ex-hale
in-hale ex-hale   in-hale ex-hale   in-hale ex-hale   in-hale ex-hale

FEBRUARY 11, 1975   KATSUTA MARATHON

10,000 meters   Winner in the sixties age group

FEBRUARY 16, 1975   OHME NEWS MARATHON

10,000 meters   Winner in the sixties age group   39m18s

in-hale ex-hale   in-hale ex-hale   in-hale ex-hale   in-hale ex-hale
in-hale ex-hale   in-hale ex-hale   in-hale ex-hale   in-hale ex-hale

MARCH 25, 1975
ORDER ON DISSEMINATING FALSE INFORMATION ISSUED

South Korean president Park Chung-hee approved and put into force
a partial amendment to the criminal law that was forced through
an extraordinary National Assembly session. This change creates a
new crime of "endangering the security, interest, and dignity of Korean governmental bodies by distorting facts or disseminating false
information," whether domestically or overseas, punished by penal
servitude or imprisonment for not more than seven years.

APRIL 12, 1975   DISEMBOWELMENT AT DEMONSTRATION

At a demonstration of roughly three hundred students at the Faculty
of Agriculture of Seoul National University in Suwon City, Gyeong-
gi Province, April 11, around 11:00 a.m., one student, thought to be
in the fourth year of studies in the Animal Science Department, attempted suicide by disembowelment with a mountaineering knife
and was taken to the hospital in serious condition.

in-hale ex-hale   in-hale ex-hale   in-hale ex-hale   in-hale ex-hale
in-hale ex-hale   in-hale ex-hale   in-hale ex-hale   in-hale ex-hale
in-hale ex-hale   in-hale ex-hale   in-hale ex-hale   in-hale ex-hale
in-hale ex-hale   in-hale ex-hale   in-hale ex-hale   in-hale ex-hale

JUNE 8, 1975   NATIONAL OB ROAD RACE TOYAKO ONSEN

15 kilometers   Winner   58m39s

DATE UNKNOWN, 1975
BRITISH INTERNATIONAL ELDERLY RACE

25 kilometers   Third place in sixties age group   1h42m53s

in-hale ex-hale   in-hale ex-hale   in-hale ex-hale   in-hale ex-hale
in-hale ex-hale   in-hale ex-hale   in-hale ex-hale   in-hale ex-hale

SEPTEMBER 3, 1975
STUDENT DEFENSE CORPS ESTABLISHED

On the morning of September 2, inauguration ceremonies were held in South Korea for the establishment of the Student Defense Corps, and an estimated 1.5 million students from all ninety-eight universities and public and private high schools nationwide were inducted into the wartime-like system.

in-hale ex-hale   in-hale ex-hale   in-hale ex-hale   in-hale ex-hale
in-hale ex-hale   in-hale ex-hale   in-hale ex-hale   in-hale ex-hale

FEBRUARY 16, 1976   OHME MARATHON

10,000 meters   Second place in sixties age group   39m48s

in-hale ex-hale   in-hale ex-hale   in-hale ex-hale   in-hale ex-hale
in-hale ex-hale   in-hale ex-hale   in-hale ex-hale   in-hale ex-hale

MARCH 9, 1976   "WHIRLWIND" OF ARRESTS CONTINUES

The "whirlwind" of arrests by the Park administration, which has only gained force since the issuing of Emergency Decree No. 9, finally swept up former presidential candidate Kim Dae-jung and his wife on March 8, a decision signaling that anyone who opposes the emergency decree will feel the iron will of force crush them.

in-hale ex-hale   in-hale ex-hale   in-hale ex-hale   in-hale ex-hale
in-hale ex-hale   in-hale ex-hale   in-hale ex-hale   in-hale ex-hale

AUGUST 19, 1976   BRAWL ERUPTS AT PANMUNJOM

The United Nations Command announced on the afternoon of August 18 that two American soldiers were killed and nine US and South Korean soldiers were injured by Democratic People's Republic of Korea soldiers in the joint security area of Panmunjom, which serves as the point of contact between North and South Korea. This is the first time that a clash within the Joint Security Area has resulted in death.

in-hale ex-hale   in-hale ex-hale   in-hale ex-hale   in-hale ex-hale
in-hale ex-hale   in-hale ex-hale   in-hale ex-hale   in-hale ex-hale

SEPTEMBER 15, 1976
TURTLE MARATHON NATIONAL COMPETITION

25 kilometers   Winner in the sixties age group

in-hale ex-hale   in-hale ex-hale   in-hale ex-hale   in-hale ex-hale
in-hale ex-hale   in-hale ex-hale   in-hale ex-hale   in-hale ex-hale
in-hale ex-hale   in-hale ex-hale   in-hale ex-hale   in-hale ex-hale

DECEMBER 15, 1977
SOUTH KOREA ISSUES "RETALIATION LAW" FOR EXILES

South Korea's ruling party has announced plans for a bill setting out special measures for the forfeiture of property of those accused of "anti-state activities" in foreign countries; the bill is poised to be passed in the opening session of the National Assembly. The bill, announced on December 14, is strict, allowing for the forfeiture of property, as well as pensions and official decorations, through trial by absentia.

in-hale ex-hale   in-hale ex-hale   in-hale ex-hale   in-hale ex-hale
in-hale ex-hale   in-hale ex-hale   in-hale ex-hale   in-hale ex-hale

in-hale ex-hale   in-hale ex-hale   in-hale ex-hale   in-hale ex-hale
in-hale ex-hale   in-hale ex-hale   in-hale ex-hale   in-hale ex-hale

SHUFFLE

Death (XIII)

Upright—unwanted change, fruitless love, catastrophe,
breaking up, divorce, illness, disaster, death—

A long time ago . . . when I was five or six . . . I used to squat down here and build sandcastles. I'd pile up the sand and pack it together, and then I'd stick my hand in and slowly pull it out to make a hole. I guess they were more tunnels than castles . . . My friends from the neighborhood and I would compete against one another building moats too. We'd pack the sand up and build an embankment, then put water inside, and the one whose embankment collapsed first was the loser—a pretty simple game, but we were so happy when we won and so upset when we lost that, win or lose, we'd always shout, "All right, one more!" and we'd stay here, sitting on our haunches, until the sun set . . . A long time ago . . . A long, long time ago . . .

The whistle of the Busan-bound train interrupted Woo-cheol's train of thought. Today's the eleventh . . . not long left in the year . . . The nineteenth is my sixty-eighth birthday . . . Well, maybe I'll celebrate it sipping on some shochu as I sing to myself. Now that I think about it, this'll be the first birthday I've ever spent all on my own . . . Though it might be my very last . . .

When I hinted at going home, Fusako didn't even look up from the white shirt of mine she was ironing; all she said was "I see." And then not even a month later, she was the one who announced it was over between us. One morning, on a day off, while I was cutting clippings out of the morning newspaper as usual, Shin'ichi said, "Dad, I have something I want to tell you," and when the three of us gathered around the table, he said, "Mom doesn't want to be with you anymore." When I asked him which one of us he wanted to stay with, he said that he wanted to be with his mother, because she'd given birth to him, so I just said, "I understand," and got up. That was the last time I saw either of their faces.

You know, if you stay still somewhere like this too long, you'll freeze to death, so let's run, two laps around the embankment . . . Maybe just one lap today . . . There's a pain weighing on the center of my chest . . . Maybe I should go home and lie down instead . . . No, I'm gonna run, if I don't, then what's the point of me going home on my own . . .

Lee Woo-cheol stood up, took his hands out of his pockets, picked up a rock from the ground near his feet, and threw it into the river.

Well, that didn't reach the other side. All right, one more! A big splash. Aya! Holding his hand to his shoulder, Woo-cheol crouched down. My shoulder's what hurts the most . . . At the base of it there's a lump, the same size as a pachinko ball . . . I didn't tell Fusako, Shin'ichi, or my other children, but it's spreading . . . If I told them, they'd take me to the hospital and then the doctors would recommend surgery . . . And if I have surgery, then there's no way I'll be able to run . . . breathe in . . . out . . . in . . . Woo-cheol breathed deeply and stood up . . . out . . . no time . . . in . . . I only have time left to run . . . out . . . in. . . .

All right, one more! in-hale ex-hale I ran in-hale ex-hale I ran here in-hale ex-hale in-hale ex-hale I run in-hale ex-hale in-hale ex-hale in-hale ex-hale in-hale ex-hale it's almost kimchi-making season if I live till February next year in-hale ex-hale I can eat some good kimchi in-hale ex-hale can I wait that long in-hale ex-hale in-hale ex-hale if I do it'll be a miracle in-hale ex-hale in-hale ex-hale when I know I haven't got long left in-hale ex-hale should I call someone in-hale ex-hale in-hale ex-hale aniya I know I won't and even if I did I'd never say I'm about to die so please come in-hale ex-hale a telegram THIS IS DAD COME in-hale ex-hale aniya contacting them while I'm still alive in-hale ex-hale in-hale ex-hale when I'm dead I'm sure someone will contact them in-hale ex-hale who will come to my funeral in-hale ex-hale not Fusako Shin'ichi? in-hale ex-hale I don't know if he'll come or not in-hale ex-hale it would take a while for the

news to reach Jeong-hee   in-hale ex-hale   and Shin-myeong married an
ilbon saram and naturalized so   in-hale ex-hale   he won't come   and
Shin-ho   Shin-hee   Shin-hwa, all of them in Japan   in-hale ex-
hale   wouldn't be able to get here quickly   in this country I have   in-hale
ex-hale   Mi-ok   Shin-ja   Shin-cheol   in-hale ex-hale   I never did a thing
for the three of them as a father so   they probably don't want to see me   in-
hale ex-hale   even in death   in-hale ex-hale   In-hye   in-hale ex-hale   Mi-
yeong   in-hale ex-hale   I guess they've both remarried   in-hale
ex-hale   in-hale ex-hale   what a sad funeral that'll be   in-hale ex-hale   in-
hale ex-hale   but I never   in-hale ex-hale   chose my family   in-hale
ex-hale   I hated women   in-hale ex-hale   I never knew   what I was
doing   what I wanted to do   what I was trying to do   in-hale ex-hale   and
still I was   in-hale ex-hale   criticized for what I did   treated with suspicion
about what I wanted to do   always complaining about what they expected
me to try to do   in-hale ex-hale   always forcing me to live within a limited
circle   in-hale ex-hale   so I ran   in-hale ex-hale   but I couldn't be
alone   so I'd find a woman wherever I ran to and cling to her   in-hale
ex-hale   have another baby   in-hale ex-hale   make a family again   run
away again   in-hale ex-hale   in-hale ex-hale   of course I'll die alone   in-
hale ex-hale   but I'm not going to sit and wait for the moment to come   so I
run   in-hale ex-hale   toward death   in-hale ex-hale   in-hale ex-hale   right
through life   in-hale ex-hale   in-hale ex-hale   in-hale ex-hale   in-hale
ex-hale   in-hale ex-hale

Woo-cheol tried to shake his head. I can't move it . . . Is my head feeling
heavier? . . . heavier than a tray full of pachinko balls . . . but maybe it's my
pillow . . . it's too high . . . wish I'd brought the buckwheat pillow that Fusako
made for me . . . the underfloor heating's on too high . . . it's hard to breathe . . .
I need fresh air . . . fresh . . . air . . . himdeulda . . . in . . . out . . . Aya! It hurts
when I breathe . . . Gotta try not to breathe so much . . . in . . . out . . . the next
time I breathe in . . . and then out . . . I might not breathe in again . . .

Like a person unconsciously smiling as he looks at a baby's face, Woo-cheol
unconsciously began to cry. Then he became aware of the presence of another
him, looking down on him crying from the ceiling . . . So small . . . his body is

smaller even than my frame and empty . . . but . . . which of us is smaller . . . him or me . . . I don't know. . . . Pale lips hovering between me and myself . . . so far . . . even if I could reach out . . . I couldn't catch them . . . the lips are coming closer . . . overlapping with my own . . . water filling up in my mouth . . . Woo-cheol breathed in, greedily devouring the cold water and the lips, colder even than the water.

Pain is gone
Strength is gone
All my thoughts flickered
It's quiet
My god, it's so quiet
Has the world ended
The woman's lips opened
Lee Woo-cheol
Woo-cheol breathed out once to die
The end is still a way away
Still
A little more

I stood up from the kotatsu and went to the kitchen. Mama told us, "There's oxtail soup in the pot, and there's always rice, so eat around seven," but we had oxtail soup yesterday and the day before that and just the thought of it makes me belch. When it's just been made it's so good, it goes down like hot water, but after it's been cooking for a week, the tail bones fall apart and it gets really thick, and it makes me feel so sick I can't eat it. But I have to. It's eight thirty already. Papa brings home prizes from the pachinko parlor, so the drawers are full of cans and snacks. We got cans of peaches, mandarins, pineapple, and snacks, we got chocolate puffs, Bugles, cookies, prawn crackers, Chupa Chups, cheesy corn puffs, potato chips, chocolate bars . . . I picked out chocolate shortbread and a can of mandarin oranges. I like peaches too, but the mandarin syrup's obviously the best. If you pour some milk into it, it turns almost into yogurt and it tastes so good. But it's hard to open the can with the can opener, so I'm just gonna have shortbread and milk.

I ripped open the shortbread package and three of them shot out.

I got the milk out of the fridge and put it on top of the kotatsu. We drink straight from the carton, passing it around. My little brother shows us how he puffs out his cheeks and lets the milk warm up in his mouth and drinks it a little at a time, and then our baby brother tries to do the same thing, but it all shoots out everywhere. The kotatsu blanket is a real mess, covered in milk stains and cookie crumbs.

Take care of the house   eat dinner   have a bath   and then go to bed . . . Well, having a bath sucks, so I'm not doing that. And if I say we brushed our teeth my brothers will go along with it. Papa works in a pachinko parlor and Mama works in a cabaret, so they never get home before midnight. Sometimes it gets light outside and they're still not home yet. They don't get angry if we stay up till ten watching TV or fall asleep with candy in our mouths. I don't think Mama or Papa care very much about us.

I held an eraser against the space heater and played with it. I liked the smell of the rubber burning, and the burn marks it leaves on the heater are cool too.

My oldest little brother and sister were watching *The Best Ten*. My baby brother is asleep with just his head sticking out from under the kotatsu.

Suddenly, Halbi's face popped into my mind.

"Let's look at Mama and Papa's wedding photos," I said.

I pulled the thickest photo album off the bookshelf. It's too big to stand up on the shelf, so it has to lie on top of the other albums. It's not like the other normal ones covered in cellophane. The pictures are glued down on thick, yellowed paper, and there's Japanese paper between each page.

It's a special, precious thing that smells of leather and mildew.

Mama's wearing a jeogori with red, blue, yellow, white, and green–striped sleeves, and Papa's wearing a black triangle hood and some weird clothes that look like a dress. Halme's hair is dyed red, and she's wearing a light blue jeogori. Mama and Papa and Halme and Halbi are all Korean, which makes me Korean too.

Halbi's wearing a normal suit. He's drinking a beer and smiling and his face is bright red. When he smiles he lifts the right side of his mouth, so I try to smile the same way too. Whenever I meet people who know Halbi, they always tell me, "Gosh, you look just like your granddad, don't you; you're like his spitting image."

"I hope Halbi's doing OK."

My brother and sister don't say anything. On the TV, Toshi from the Tanokin Trio's singing: **"Your love woke me up like wham bam took it right out of me."** If I was looking at pictures of them, my siblings would be excited, but they seem bored of looking at this album full of pictures from before they were born. I'm not. When I look at pictures from when I was little, my memories are fuzzy or I can't remember anything and it makes me feel really weird. But I can't forget things in pictures that happened before I was born.

As far as I can remember, Halbi has come over to stay with us about ten times. And I remember how in the mornings, while it was still dark, he got changed into his workout clothes and went running. When he was young he was so fast he could've made it to the Olympics, everyone says. I think he's kind of a weird guy. He does things like one time he put a slug in his coffee and drank it and said it's good for you, and he chased around my baby brother, who's so shy he hides behind the curtains, shouting that he's gonna make him touch himself, and he doesn't touch the food that Mama makes, he just says, "The best food in Japan is Charamera Ramen," and then eats some instant ramen he makes for himself.

And then in the evening he always listens to the one record that Papa brought with him when he came to Japan. It's an old, black record, with a label that says "patriotic" on it. That's the only song that Halbi listens to. It starts off *Chikchik, pokpok.*

Chikchik   pokpok
Chikchik   pokpok   ttwii
Tteonanda tagwancheolli
Angaeseorin eung beolpaneul
Jeongeun deulgo motsalbaen
Ah, ibyeori jota
Dallyeola dallyeo   dallyeola dallyeo

haneureun cheonghwangjeoksaek   jeonyeok noeul tteodolgo
chachangeneun dambae yeongi
seorit seorit seorit seorit
pullinda   pullinda

He sings along with the record as it spins around and around, and before the song is even over he lifts up the needle and takes it back to the intro with the train whistle. He'll listen to it twenty or thirty times, so I've memorized it. If they played that song on one of those quiz shows where you have to guess the song from the intro, I'd buzz in right away. The title is "Ullineun Man-juseon."

Halbi is five foot nine, and that's taller than my dad, my teacher, or any other man that I've ever met. But his back is hunched and when he sits with his knees to his chest he looks very small and very sad.

I ran my finger over his face and the table from the wedding with its white tablecloth.

Brring brring brring rang the phone on top of the TV.

"Hello."

"Miri, is that you?"

"Yes."

"Where's your mom?"

"Work. Dad's not home either."

"All right, well, listen carefully. Your halbi has died."

My halme sounded far away, and I couldn't hear her clearly, maybe because she was calling from Korea. But I understood that Halbi was dead, less from her words than from the way her voice trembled.

I stood there gripping the black receiver. For some reason I imagined it was snowing on the other end of the line.

The fire in the heater burned red.

The photo album was still open, Halbi smiling forever.

TWENTY-NINE

Yeonghon Gyeolhonsig

| 영혼 결혼식 | 死後結婚式 |

Mid-August, high noon: from a dilapidated house at the base of Yeongnamnu where the cedar trees grow, the sound of the mudang's instruments, the buk, jing, jang-go, and kkwaenggwari, ring out across the Miryang River reaching the other bank.

Since the previous night, they have been holding a posthumous marriage ceremony, to release the binding han and sadness of men and women who died unmarried, bring them to their ancestral gods, and release them into a pure and free afterlife. The walls of the inside of the hovel are decorated with vibrant paintings of twelve shamanist spirits.

On the main altar, for Chilseongsin, Irwolsin, Sansindosa, Sambuljeseok, Daesinnopa, Yongwangjanggun, the spirits who love fruits, there are towers of apples, pears, persimmons, watermelons, oranges, grapefruits, bananas, chestnuts, jujubes, and tomatoes; and for Sansillyeong, Obangsinjang, Byeol-seongsin, Changbussi, Seongsumyeong, Choeyeong Janggun, the spirits who love meat, there are trays of grilled beef, fish, dried fish roe, jijim, mooncakes, steamed rice cakes, and more.

To the left sit, enshrined, a pair of large dolls, male and female, wearing wedding clothes.

The woman wears a chartreuse wonsam, with five-colored striped sleeves and long, white cuffs covering her hands; on her head sits a hwagwan decorated with imitation pearls, jade, gold, silver, coral, and other gems; shoes have been slipped on her white beoseon-clad feet; and her cheeks are reddened with circles of rouge.

The man wears a round-collared dallyeong robe, with a long belt tied over the chest and the back's embroidery of a flying crane, a black samo hat, and black, wooden shoes.

The eyebrows, eyes, noses, mouths, and hair of the dolls have been drawn on with brush and ink, and the lips have been colored in red delicately with the tip of a brush.

On the right side of the room sit the baksu, three musicians, and Yu Miri.

Three mudang sit in front of the altar. The middle-aged woman (Mudang 1), wearing a number of ceremonial clothes, is a gangsinmu, a mudang with experience of spiritual possession, while the fair-skinned young woman with long hair and the old woman with silver-rimmed glasses are gangsinja, initiate mudang.

BAKSU: *(banging the buk)* Mahabanyabaramildasimgyeong gwanjajaebosal haengsimbanyabaramilda. Miserable and fleeting, Yu Miri's grand-uncle, oh, unravel the han that burns in your family and enter the pure afterlife of the next world Wollijeondomongsang gugyongyolban samseje-buruibanyabaramilda. Lee Woo-gun, born April seventh in an eul year in South Gyeongsang Province, Miryang, Ne-il-dong, number seventy-five the sorrow of the han that permeates you is endless, and that han, which pierces through the earth to the heavens, may be grieved, but it cannot be undone namu amita bul, namu amita bul . . . the young girl who lived not even twenty years, who allowed herself to be swallowed by the sea, oh, young lady whose name we do not even know, you whose body rotted and became water, your flesh eaten by the fish, your white bones floating on the waves disappearing into the refuse of the sea, nam amita bul, nam amita bul . . . God of the seas, god of the earth, god of the water, god of fire, look upon their han and

lay it now to rest, mahabanyabaramildasimgyeong
gwanjajaebosal   haengsimbanyabaramilda...

He begins his refrain, with the mudang's wails intermingled, and the flames of the two candles that must stay lit all night flicker.

MUDANG 1: Hwoi, hwoi, come to us now from that world, to this world
without ties, this world with so much han, as you were born
to this world, oh, you who would bear no resentment had
you lived one hundred years, e-go, e-go, aigu, bulssanghaera,
our groom who died at twenty-three and, aigu, our bride
who died at just fifteen ... aigo, oh, you dead who have lost
your lives only to haunt this realm.

BAKSU: Guanseumbosal   namu amita bul...

MUDANG 2: Hwoi, hwoi, you dead, you honored dead, today, this very
day, your spirits, hwoi, hwoi, do not come here to hear sutras;
you come for your wedding.

MUDANG 1: Aigo, spirits, come celebrate your wedding. We have chosen
this day, this moon, this place for you. But you will leave
again. And the road you will leave down is one we all know.
And once you're gone and disappeared, the grass will
overgrow your path, flowers will grow rampant there, you
shall leave no footprints; there is no ferry to bring you back.
It is no road of meeting. There is nothing more sorrowful
than this. Aigu, aigu, you honored dead.

BAKSU: Namumahabanyabaramilda...

MUDANG 2: Aigu, aigu, you honored dead. Look at this girl who came
back here from a foreign land. Aigu, you dead, push away the
soil that covers your eyes and take a good look. Bring the
candle's flame closer and look closely. We who have called
you here today are not your enemies.

MUDANG 3: She is your brother's granddaughter. We call you here now.
Whatever form you took then, you may come back now

unnoticed, like smoke, like a silhouette, like a cloud, and leave before you're noticed.

MUDANG 2: You need no preparation. Just as you were born into this world with nothing but your body, come back today with only your spirit. We will see you in when you arrive; we will see you off when you leave.

BAKSU: Mahabanyabaramildasimgyeong gwanjajaebosal haengsim-banyabaramilda . . .

The baksu stands and goes out onto the veranda, then lifts the carcass of a pig from the new rush mat on which it rested onto his back and goes into the garden.

He spears the pig on a pitchfork and using a piece of ritual equipment and some salt he tries to make it stand, but no matter how many times he tries it will not stand.

MUDANG 1: Both are silent and the bride will not even reveal her name. And your grand-uncle perhaps cannot marry a woman whose name he doesn't know.

BAKSU: Wollijeondomongsang gugyeongnyeolban samsejeburuibanyabaramilda . . .

The mudang faces the altar and raises her hands toward the heavens; the sound of the jing and buk intensifies as she begins to rattle the bells around, *ttallang ttallang*.

She lowers both her arms, then raises her shoulders tremulously and begins to whirl around and around, binggeul binggeul.

She picks up the blue dragon sword and bends and jumps as if skipping rope, peoljjeok peoljjeok, as she spins around, binggeul binggeul.

Carrying a pitchfork on her right shoulder, she flutters her left hand up and down as she twirls, binggeul binggeul binggeul binggeul—then suddenly she stops and grabs the knife.

She repeats the gesture of cutting her arm with the knife, then presses the blade to her palm and cheek, sticking the tip of it into the softest part under her chin.

Then, again, binggeul binggeul peoljjeok peoljjeok binggeul binggeul peoljjeok peoljjeok—the sound of the jing grows even louder.

The mudang puts the knife in her mouth and pierces her cheek from the inside.

The youngest mudang takes Yu Miri's hand and pulls her to her feet, puts a white, cone-shaped gokkal veil on her head, dresses her in a long white jangsam with eight-foot-long sleeves, then ties a red sash embroidered with a large peony, above it seven stars, below it waves, with cranes, deer, and flowers to the left and right.

MUDANG 1: *(beckoning)* Hwoi! Hwoi! Iri oneora! Iri oneora!
BAKSU: Mahabanyabaramildasimgyeong gwanjajaebosal haengsim-banyabaramilda . . .

The mudang raises her hands to shoulder height, moving her wrists as she shuffles toward the altar, dancing around Yu Miri to invite her—

Yu Miri, imitating her, does the somaechum, domu, and hoemu. Then, suddenly, she leans back, pushing her chest toward the sky and falls to the ground, pounding her legs like a little girl whose toy has been taken away, then loses all the strength in her limbs and sprawls out, twisting her body to the left and right, puts a red chima over her head and begins to spin, binggeul binggeul binggeul binggeul—

YU MIRI: *(thumping down to the ground, flexing her nails against the floor, and spitting out words as if vomiting)* Aigo aigo aigo dapdapae aigo himdeureo who dressed me in this bridal gown who pulled my spirit from the bottom of the sea aigo!
MUDANG 1: Watda! Aigo, she is here.
BAKSU: Wollijeondomongsang gugyeongnyeolban samsejeburuibanyabaramilda . . .

MUDANG 2: *(tears spilling from her eyes)* I've cried enough for a river of tears, I've bled enough for a sea of blood, e-go e-go eh eh, aigo, oh oh . . .

BAKSU: Guanseeumbosal namuamitabul . . .

MUDANG 3: *(covering her face with her sleeves and sobbing)* Aigu, bulssanghaera . . . our poor bride . . . today is your wedding day . . .

BAKSU: Namu maha banya baramilta . . .

MUDANG 1: Why do you linger as a mulgwisin, a water ghost, instead of going to the pure land? Do you have no clothes and cannot go? Do you have no shoes and cannot go? Do you have no money? Do you have no love?

YU MIRI: I cannot marry anyone.

Yu Miri takes a folding fan decorated with the twelve spirits from the altar and holds it out in front of the mudang's face.

The mudang lays ten ten-thousand-won bills on top of the fan. Yu Miri snatches the money as if stealing it, crumples the bills one by one, and throws them in the mudang's face.

YU MIRI: Aiiiigooo if I had stayed in Miryang as a virgin I would've been one of the girls at the Arang Festival I would've had so many marriage proposals e-go eh eh he tricked me and took me away nobody knows he took me away I jumped into the sea and nobody knows that I jumped oh-iiii-oooooooh

MUDANG 1: Oh, daughter whose innocent body was defiled, whose soft heart was smashed. Oh, daughter who made her han an anchor and sank her soul into the sea. Your soul is pure, defiled by none. Wear these bridal clothes and go to the pure land.

The mudang puts her left hand on Yu Miri's shoulder and strokes her face with her left. Then she opens her mouth, closes it, opens, closes— She hits her own body with her fist as if to bring attention to something.

MUDANG 2: Osyeotseumnida! He's here, the groom is here!

BAKSU: Namugwanseeumbosal namuseogkamonibul . . .

MUDANG 3: The groom is gagged, we cannot hear him . . . There is dirt in his eyes, he cannot see . . .

MUDANG 2: Oh, our bride who drowned in the sea, our groom who was buried alive, I give my blood to both of you. I cleanse your defilements with blood.

The mudang, wearing only white socks, jumps out into the garden and grabs a combed rooster from the pair of chickens wrapped in red cloths lying on the daeryesang there.

The musicians, playing the buk, jing, jang-go, kkwaenggwari, and hand-bells, follow the mudang's movements. *Thump-thump-thump ding-ding-ding ra-ta-ta-tan ting-dum-ting-dum ra-ta-ta-tan . . .*

BAKSU: Mahabanyabaramildasimgyeong gwanjajaebosal haeng-simbanyabaramilda . . .

The mudang raises the white rooster in the sky, then takes it by its bound feet and beats the ground with it, beginning the daesalgeori.

Thud-thud thud-thud, the rooster tries to beat its wings and escape, but the mudang grabs it and slams it down.

There is the sound of flesh being crushed, of bones being broken.

The mudang sinks her teeth into the rooster's neck and, still holding it in her mouth, shakes her head, hitting it against the ground again.

She holds its wings down with her feet and decapitates it with the knife.

She bites into the throat, spouting blood, and slurps loudly.

Her teeth and tongue are bathed in blood; the area around her mouth turns bright red.

The mudang spits blood onto her palm and washes her face with it.

Blood coats her face, hair, arms, every finger, underneath her fingernails—
The headless rooster flaps its wings.

The mudang sinks her teeth into its body, some life still in it, then, gripping its lifeless head, she begins a shuffling dance.

BAKSU: wollijeondomongsang gugyeongnyeolban samsejeburui-
           banyabaramilda...

Without looking back, the mudang throws the rooster's head behind her.
Its beak points in the direction of the sea.

The mudang captures the twitching rooster from near her feet, spins it around above her head, binggeul binggeul, then slams it to the ground.

She picks up the head and again throws it behind her.

The beak points in the direction of land.

For an oracle inviting the soul of one who died at sea, if the beak points in the direction of the sea it is a failure; if it points toward land it has succeeded.

MUDANG 1: Our dead groom! Our dead bride! All your defilements have
           been removed.
MUDANG 3: Lee Woo-gun!

Yu Miri, who has been lying on the ground, slowly raises her head and looks around as if seeing the world for the first time.

YU MIRI: Lee Woo-gun   aigu, Lee Woo-gun   my first love
MUDANG 1: Our han cannot be cleaned away like a rooster's
           blood   the place where we were buried alive is   still
           red   not a blade of grass grows there   so red that birds
           in the sky avoid it   red!   We were innocent   and if we
           were guilty of anything   it was only fighting for our
           country   **don't mourn the deaths of comrades   who fell
           in battle with the enemy   wrap their bodies in the red
           flag**   red!   red!   red!   red!
YU MIRI: Aigu   sesange!

MUDANG I: Tell me your name   if I don't know your name   I cannot
           call to you   I know your face   you're the girl who was
           always playing jump rope by the river

YU MIRI: *(voice trembling)*   Aigu, you really remember me?

MUDANG I: you were always singing as I ran   **ame, ame   fure,**
           fure kaa-san ga janome de omukai ureshii
           na   pitch, pitch   chap, chap   run, run, run

YU MIRI:

Kakemasho   kaban   wo
Kaa-san no
Ato kara   yuko yuko
Kane   ga   naru
Pitch, pitch   chap, chap
Run, run, run

Ara ara   ano ko   wa
Yanagi   no   nekata   de
Naiteiru
Pitch, pitch   Chap, chap
Run, run, run

Kaa-san   boku no wo
Kashimasho ka
Kimi kimi   kono kasa   sashitamae
Pitch, pitch   chap, chap
Run, run, run

Boku nara   iin da
Kaasan no
Ooki na   janome   ni
Haitteku
Pitch, pitch   Chap, chap
Run run run

MUDANG 1: we only spoke once   near Samnamjin station
YU MIRI: aigu, that day   I got on a train   Mukden   Dalian
                  Wuhan   without telling my eomoni or hyung   aigu
                  wae geureon babojiseul haenneunji   why did I do such a
                  stupid thing
MUDANG 1: I was running   it was August   a bright, clear August
                  day   like today
YU MIRI: I said it's hot, isn't it
MUDANG 1: and I said it's going to be another hot one   jal gala!
YU MIRI: Annyeonghi gasiso!   That was all we said   ah   why was it
                  so hot that day   and so bright   I'll tell you my
                  name   only you   (*pressing her mouth to the mudang's ear*)
                  Kim Yeong-hee

Yu Miri puts the red chima over her head and spins around, binggeul binggeul, then faints.

BAKSU: Guanseumbosal   namuamitabul ...
MUDANG 1: (*speaking in her own voice for the first time*) If she'd been
                  brought up here, she'd have become a mudang.
MUDANG 2: (*in her own voice, as well, laughing*) Unni, she might've been
                  your protégé.

The baksu goes out onto the veranda, sharpens the knife, hits the pig's neck with it as if chopping down a tree, cutting into it little by little until the head falls off.

He divides the body into six parts: right front shank, left front shank, right belly, left belly, right hind, and left hind.

To the rhythm of the jing, the baksu dances with the pig's torso on his back, and after gesturing as if comforting a baby, he again performs the oracle of piercing the pig on the pitchfork.

It stands the first time. The consent of the gods has been obtained.

He hooks the shanks, belly, and hinds of the pig to the tips of the pitchfork, then stabs the pale, seemingly smiling pig's head on top.

He screws ten-thousand-won notes into its nose and mouth, stuffs its ears, immerses some in a vessel containing ceremonial liquor, then sticks them, dripping, to its back.

The wind blows, tearing the banknotes off.

The mudangs bend down and pick them up.

The one who had been filled with the spirit of Lee Woo-gun until minutes ago takes a mouthful of ceremonial liquor, then sprays it in Yu Miri's face.

Yu Miri opens her eyes, stands up, and goes out on the veranda.

She stands in front of the pig, its body splayed open like a filleted mackerel.

MUDANG 1: Right, now for the wedding.

On the eastern side of the daeryesang set up in at the south of the garden, the bridegroom's side, there is a flower vase filled with red beans up to the mouth, and on the western side, the bride's side, there is a vase filled halfway with sesame seeds; each vase had various plants in it: gardenia, spindle tree, bamboo.

The two yongtteok dragon cakes, made from long, thin rice cakes, have peeled chestnuts and jujubes for their heads, and jujubes drizzled with honey and sprinkled with sesame seeds, bundles of blue and red thread, two candlesticks, and bowls of rice have been arranged on the table.

The rooster, wrapped in a red cloth, not knowing that its time has come, clucks its head.

BAKSU: *(in the same tone as a holjaebi, the leader of proceedings of the jeonanrye)* Seodongbuseo.

The mudangs, like members of the bridal party, disappear and come out the corridor, their hands under the dolls' arms, walking down the white cotton cloth without the sound of footsteps; they set up the groom to the east and the bride to the west, facing each other across the daeryesang.

At the baksu's command, they imitate the washing of hands in the water bowl, the gyobaerye, the action of both kneeling at the same time to make their joint vow to share one hundred years together, and the hapgeullye, the drinking of rice wine from two cups made from the same gourd.

When the ceremony is over and they return inside the house, the mudangs carrying the dolls pass by Yu Miri and make her bow to them.

MUDANG 1: Thank you for choosing someone wonderful for me. We had short lives, so please live long enough for us both. We give you life, happiness, luck, and fortune too. We'll find you someone you can live with for eternity. We will block all exits for any evil that may happen to you. We'll open all the doors for any happiness that may come to you.

At the mudang's prompting, Yu Miri throws a particularly seed-filled jujube into the bride's underskirt and wishes for the good fortune of her descendants.

The mudang picks up the jujube and puts it in the bride's sleeve.

The mudangs carry the dolls into the bedroom.

There, the choryebang, the newlyweds' bed, has been prepared.

The mudangs take off the bride's crown and shoes and lay them to the left; then they take off the groom's hat and black wooden shoes and lay them to the right.

The wedding night has begun.

Yu Miri stands at the door and peeks into the room.

The baksu begins singing, and the other mudangs all join in.

All together:

Kwaejina chingching nane
Kwaejina chingching nane
Mister Star shining in the sky
Kwaejina chingching nane
Let's go, let's go, all of us, let's go

Kwaejina   chingching   nane
Across the river out to the white road
Kwaejina   chingching   nane
Many gravel paths by the river in this town
Kwaejina   chingching   nane
Many stories in each life
Kwaejina   chingching   nane
Put the loom up in the sky
Kwaejina   chingching   nane
Catch you a goldfish and make of it a shuttle
Kwaejina   chingching   nane
On the fifteenth of December
Kwaejina   chingching   nane
Chuseok in August is long gone
Kwaejina   chingching   nane
The date may pass but the sadness remains
Kwaejina   chingching   nane

The mudangs lift the dolls, which have signed the marriage certificate, and put them in a palanquin, filling the bride's sleeves with talismanic red papers.

MUDANG 1: Jal gasio budi, jal gasio! As we gather the water flowing from a thousand mountains, ten thousand mountains, to meet in one river, we do not pour in our sorrows. As we look out across the road to the other world, Unsangbanbong, cheongsanmangyeong, the roads of these piled up mountains, they look blurry from tears, ai ai ooh ohh, aigu, what a steep road, aigu, what a cold road, aigu, what a dark road, eee eee, however close the friend, however dear the eomoni, oh oh, the living cannot hold your hands, eh eh, they cannot. Annyeonghi gasio budi, annyeonghi jal gasio!

Two of the mudangs carry the palanquin into the river.
Once they are in up to their hips, they lower it into the river and let go.

The palanquin floats on the water and drifts away.
Yu Miri pours the ceremonial liquor into the river.
The road leading to the other world.
A road that never runs out of water.

MUDANG 1: Build a mansion in the pure land and live there for a
thousand years, ten thousand years. Share the same pillow
and the same dream. Let go and leave! Undo a thousand ties,
ten thousand ties, and leave!

Just as it was about to pass under Namcheong Bridge, the palanquin hit
the girder of the bridge.
The bride doll tilted and the red paper fell into the river.
The palanquin sank in the water.
Yu Miri watched.
As an arrow of light flew out of the water.
The light ran.
Dallyeotda!
The sound of breathing came closer.

In-hale ex-hale   in-hale ex-hale . . .

THIRTY

The End of August

| 8월의 저편 | 8月の果て |

In-hale ex-hale   in-hale ex-hale   in-hale ex-hale   running the August
riverside and   my eyes are blurred with sweat   in-hale ex-hale   if I don't
blink constantly I can't see but   in-hale ex-hale   I'm not sweating   in-hale
ex-hale   in-hale ex-hale   but I don't hear water   or cicada cries   is it really
August?   in-hale ex-hale   in-hale ex-hale   in-hale ex-hale   in-hale
ex-hale   nuni busida! I'm dazzled!   In-hale ex-hale   is it the river water?
in-hale ex-hale   aniya   it doesn't move that much   in-hale ex-hale   the
moonlight?   in-hale ex-hale   aniya   it's not that weak   like the sun
filtered through a magnifying glass?   aniya   in-hale ex-hale   it has no
focus   in-hale ex-hale   like the end of a cracked whip?   aniya   in-hale
ex-hale   it doesn't hurt   in-hale ex-hale   in-hale ex-hale   like a blade
cutting through a chicken's neck?   aniya   it's not that tense a light   in-hale
ex-hale   in-hale ex-hale   it's like the second your eyes open waking from a
dream   in-hale ex-hale   that kind of light   in-hale ex-hale   a second of
light   in-hale ex-hale   nuni busida!   It's so bright I can't see a thing   the
road   the houses   trees   people   in-hale ex-hale   the river   the
mountains   in-hale ex-hale   gone   all gone   in-hale ex-hale   gone
in-hale ex-hale   and all there is   is just the light   in-hale ex-hale   in-hale
ex-hale   in-hale ex-hale   what's going on?   I must've run pretty far and
yet   I'm not out of breath at all   look!   in-hale ex-hale   in-hale ex-hale

it's like when I run long distance slowly   in-hale ex-hale   I'll try going faster   in-hale ex-hale   faster!   in-hale ex-hale   is there something I want to say?   in-hale ex-hale   aniya   I've got nothing to say   in-hale ex-hale   I don't want to chase after words anymore   in-hale ex-hale   to catch up with words and overtake them   in-hale ex-hale   to get ahead of language   at a speed where words cannot follow me   in-hale ex-hale   shaking off every word there is   in-hale ex-hale   in-hale ex-hale   in a place far removed from language   in-hale ex-hale   I run   in-hale ex-hale   in-hale ex-hale   run! faster   faster, faster!   in-hale ex-hale   far away from myself   in-hale ex-hale   I won't turn back   in-hale ex-hale   whoever's there   whatever's there   in-hale ex-hale   I won't look back   and even if I did   in-hale ex-hale   I can't go back   aniya   I won't go back   so   in-hale ex-hale   in-hale ex-hale   I don't need a single landmark to make it back to myself   in-hale ex-hale   rankings   times   in-hale ex-hale   my name, even   in-hale ex-hale   in-hale ex-hale   just breathe out   just breathe in the wind   beyond your breath   in-hale ex-hale   beyond the wind   further and further beyond   in-hale ex-hale   in-hale ex-hale   to the second where life and death intersect   in-hale ex-hale   and beyond   in-hale ex-hale   in-hale ex-hale   in-hale ex-hale   in-hale ex-hale   in-hale ex-hale   in-hale ex-hale   in-hale ex-hale   in-hale ex-hale   in-hale ex-hale   in-hale ex-hale   in-hale ex-hale   in-hale ex-hale   in-hale ex-hale   in-hale ex-hale   in-hale ex-hale   in-hale ex-hale   in-hale ex-hale   in-hale ex-hale   in-hale ex-hale

Freedom!